PRAISE FOR THE

... From Publications and other Authors

"Gephardt excels at developing the canine characters. . . the XK9s prove irresistible."—*Kirkus Reviews*, on **What's Bred in the Bone**.

"Solid SF police drama . . . Gephardt engagingly conveys the four-footed perspective."—*Kirkus Reviews*, on *A Bone to Pick*.

"There were so many things to love about this book."—*Booker T's Farm*, on **What's Bred in the Bone**.

"There's laugh aloud humour and action-packed, spine-tingling suspense."—*Love2Read Reviewer*, on *A Bone to Pick*.

"Gephardt does a fantastic job of putting us inside of these animals' heads . . . She also has a great sense of humor, with some pages making me giggle as I read them.—*Dogpatch Press*, on **What's Bred in the Bone**.

"This novel is a dog-lover's dream!"—**Robin Wayne Bailey, author of the *Brothers of the Dragon* Series**, on **What's Bred in the Bone**.

... From Readers

"This whole series is on my instabuy list for life."—Amazon Review of *The Other Side of Fear*.

"This series continues to please me . . . this book was filled with adventure, fear and overcoming huge obstacles. I highly recommend." —Amazon Review of *A Bone to Pick*.

"I really enjoyed this book. . . Loved the dogs; their personalities really shine."—Goodreads Review of *The Other Side of Fear*.

"I did not expect it to be so good . . . A very good read. I look forward to the next installment."—Amazon Review of *What's Bred in the Bone*.

BONE OF CONTENTION

THIRD BOOK IN THE XK9 "BONES" TRILOGY

THE XK9S SAGA
BOOK 3

JAN S. GEPHARDT

For my intrepid housemates,
Pascal Gephardt and Tyrell E. Gephardt,
Beloved husband and son.
Your strength has empowered my journey through decades, challenges,
and oh, so many changes – and continues to this day.

CONTENTS

1. Shady and the Not-So-Diplomatic Appscaten   1
2. Charlie's Command Performance   8
3. The Murder Brothers   16
4. Doubts   25
5. Wina's Breakthrough   32
6. Where's a Way Forward?   39
7. An Elevator to Nowhere   48
8. Confronting History   58
9. "Oh, Crap" Moments   67
10. Questions on Questions   74
11. Tunnel Run   81
12. The Blue Building   88
13. Extraction   96
14. Setbacks   105
15. After-Action   112
16. An Offer   119
17. New Challenges   125
18. Pack is Family   131
19. Expanding Possibilities   137
20. A Manhunt and a Brokered Peace   145
21. Unsettling Developments   153
22. Charlie's New Assignment   161
23. Need to Know   168
24. Backstabbers and Boxes of Rats   175
25. Confrontation   184
26. Conversation   194
27. Fraught Train Ride   203
28. A Different World   211
29. Fish Tacos and Four Million Novi   218
30. Betrayal and Revenge   229
31. Treachery in the Black Void   236
32. This Whole "Celebrating a Holiday" Thing   247
33. Clear the Courtroom!   254
34. An Insider Tip   264
35. The Palmdale Club   273

36. A Beautiful New Year 282
37. Disrupting Things 293
38. Scary Things 300
39. A Place That's a Haven 311
40. The Early Crew 319
41. Three Guys on a Train 330
42. Echoes of Old Pain 340
43. New Challenges in the Hub 347
44. A Critical Analysis 358
45. Opening Moves 365
46. Stepping Out and Speaking Up 377
47. An Unexpected Connection 385
48. A Walk to the Park 395
49. Persons of Interest 401
50. Breaking News 411
51. Aftershocks 422
52. "One of Mika Zuni's LEOs" 430
53. Countdown to The Joint Session 438
54. The Combined Councils Joint Special Session 447
55. The Fredericks Formula 455
56. Unscrambling the Scramble 465
57. Topside Trauma 474
58. Moving Pieces 481
59. Crisis Management 489
60. On Behalf of All XK9s 499
61. Rana Station's Secret Weapon 510
62. Return to Gravity 523
63. Until All of My People are Taken Care Of 532
64. How Far We've Come 544
65. Rehoming 556
66. Free to Move Forward 567

An Image of Voices 583
Appendices 593
Who's Who and What's What 603
Acknowledgements 649
About the Author 653

CHAPTER 1
SHADY AND THE NOT-SO-DIPLOMATIC APPSCATEN

X K9 Shady Jacob-Belle couldn't see the entity on the bench in Glen Haven Park, but she could clearly smell it. Should she play coy, or go confront it?

Wait. You can't see it at all? Her human partner, Pamela Gómez, was seven kilometers away from Glen Haven Park, and she'd been focused on something else. But it was impossible to completely turn off their cybernetic brain link connection.

I didn't mean to disturb you. Shady had been running a protective perimeter around her mate, Rex, and his human partner, Charlie. Both of them were still on the "injured and recovering" roster at work after their adventures in space a couple of weeks ago.

Rex had emerged from several days of stabilization re-gen just before the Solstice celebration. But he had a lot of recovery—and eventually a new pair of lungs—still ahead of him. They'd come to the park today for some mild endurance testing, primarily for lung-damaged Rex. Charlie was in better shape, but an arm shield still protected his left arm.

She'd tagged along because it was a beautiful day, because she loved them, and because, well, due diligence. All weekend she'd fought a nagging sense that someone was watching her, but she hadn't managed to catch a scent or a glimpse of movement. Not until now, that is. Now she'd caught a whiff of a completely new smell.

Which had led her to this thing she couldn't see.

You didn't disturb me. I don't mind. This is very odd. Pam hesitated. *Do you have a sense of how big it is?*

Working on it. I love that you haven't questioned my sanity. Or my visual acuity. Shady gave the seemingly empty bench a long, hard sheepdog-stare.

Oh, please. She sensed Pam's impulse to roll her eyes. *After all this time, I know better. Scent factors do not lie.*

Shady cocked her head. She still could see nothing on the bench. Or was it . . . *under* the bench? Maybe if she got closer? She took a step toward it.

The entity's odor intensified and shifted into a nose-prickling, musky tone.

Shady caught a ripple of movement, something her predator's eyes had evolved to see. A slight bending of light, like a wrinkle, passed through the air near the ground. And was that a fleeting bit of shadow? This thing wasn't exactly breaking the law, but it was acting weird.

Her hackles prickled. Her gut hardened around a sudden knot of tension. What was this thing up to? Why hide, if its intent was benign? *Nothing suspicious has yet turned out to be benign. Why would this be different?* She uttered a low growl and broke into a trot.

The entity's scent intensified further. The ripple darted more swiftly. The shadow-patch flicked toward the nearest path.

That thing is pretty fast.

She sensed Pam's frown through the link. *Maybe you frightened it.*

Maybe it makes me suspicious. It's in stealth mode, and a long way

2

from the places Galactics usually stay. Time to end this. Shady leaped forward into a flat-out run. She didn't quite have Rex's six-meter stride, but few things on Rana Station could outrun an XK9 in hot pursuit. Shady cranked up the volume on her collar-mounted vocalizer. "Police! Stop where you are!"

The ripple and its fugitive shadow streaked away. Shady took a flight of stone steps in one bound. She lunged closer. Human pedestrians halted, confused. The entity blundered into the shins of a woman in a tennis outfit. She fell face first onto the grass with a shriek, then lay gasping. The entity arrowed away, a ripple in the light.

"Stop!" Shady tore past the woman. "Stop! Stop!"

The entity zipped up a meter-high secondary terrace to a flat place where several auto-nav cars stood idle. At the edge of Shady's vision, another auto-nav approached. The entity dodged between two of the dormant machines, then veered into a collision-path with the moving vehicle.

"Watch out!" she cried. "Car!" Auto-navs had sensors to keep them from hitting pedestrians. But would those sensors work with an invisible being?

The auto-nav's side door popped open. She glimpsed a dark blur leap inside, then the door slammed shut. *That thing has moves!* The auto-nav rolled away at a speed even Shady couldn't match.

Well, damn. She wasn't wearing her full duty-rig with all of its sensors, but her Cybernetically-Assisted Perception interface and its neural Heads Up Display remained always at her disposal. She pinged the auto-nav for its ID.

The words DIPLOMATIC VEHICLE flashed onto her HUD immediately. DO NOT PURSUE. FURTHER INFORMATION CLASSIFIED.

Heat surged through her on a wave of fury. She barked after the departing auto-nav. A futile gesture, but it vented a little of her frustration. *What the hell just happened?*

Pam's frustration echoed hers through the link. *Diplomatic?*

Oh! Wait! What ARE those things called? A new sense of frustration rolled through the link.

Shady flicked her ears, diverted. *Things?*

Beings. Some species of Galactic. We studied them in the Academy. What the heck were they called? They're six-legged oxygen-breathers — sometimes come through the spaceport, which is why we need to know about them. It's a being with really good camouflage. Changeable skin, like SCISCO's android has. Let me think.

Shady licked her lips then stress-yawned, her belly still tight. SCISCO was a recognized-sapient Farricainan cyberbeing. Ne also was a professor of explosives technology at Station Polytechnic, located in Orangeboro's Precinct Ten. Nir android focal object could change colors and patterns in any way the professor's mood dictated.

Meanwhile, here I stand, suddenly aware of yet another damned gap in my education! The XK9 Project had thought that dogs didn't need to know a great many important things about the wider Universe.

Pam closed the link as much as she could, but Shady had a sense of her partner yelling to her Amare. "Balchu! What's that species that can make itself invisible?"

Shady queried her CAP: *six-legged oxygen-breather that can make itself invisible.*

Appscaten! Pam cried, triumphant, at the same moment the word flashed onto Shady's HUD.

Okay. What's that? The HUD offered a deluge of information, which she stored for future reference with a sigh. *I should go check on the woman that not-so-diplomatic appscaten knocked onto her face.*

But by the time she returned to the scene of the knock-down, the woman had regained her feet. She smiled up at Charlie, whose right hand still steadied her elbow. Rex had joined his partner but stayed back. His breath wheezed through his injured lungs and his head hung low.

Well, of course she's smiling at Charlie. Through the link, Pam's laugh carried all the wry understanding of an ex-lover. *It's Charlie. Who wouldn't smile, if Charlie helped them up?*

Shady lolled her tongue with amusement. In her experience, most humans considered Charlie attractive. His charming smile and smooth, gracious manner calmed people. Made them feel that everything would be all right.

"See? Here she is." Charlie turned his smile from the woman toward Shady. "What did you find?"

"I think it was an appscaten." Shady snorted. "In full camouflage-mode."

The woman's mouth dropped open. "Really? An appscaten, in the flesh? I thought they only had those in realiciné thrillers!"

Shady swallowed a growl. "Oh, it was real, all right." Belatedly mindful of saying too much in front of a civilian, she added a silent text to Rex and Charlie. "And it really has diplomatic immunity, too." Then she shifted her focus to Pam. *How does this woman know about appscatens, but you didn't?*

Acidic disdain flooded the link. *I don't waste my time watching realiciné thrillers.*

"Oh, my God!" The woman clapped her hands to her mouth, eyes alight, then spread her arms wide. "I got knocked over by a real appscaten! D'you think it was a real appscaten *spy*?"

Shady laid back her ears but strove to keep her hackles down. *It certainly did seem to be spying on us.* She kept that thought and her growl within the link, however. Didn't want to frighten a civilian.

"This is so amazing!" The woman beamed at Shady. "First, I have XK9s talking to me, and now I learn I was knocked over by a real appscaten spy!"

I don't think you frightened her. Pam's amusement rippled through the link.

"Wait'll I tell my Ciné and Chardonnay Circle! Oh, my God! This is so thrilling!" Then her eyes widened and she stared up at Charlie again. "D'you think I'll need to give a statement? Like on *The Arm of the Law*?"

Shady cocked her head. *What is 'The Arm of the Law'?*

It's another stupid realiciné cop-show. I can't stand to watch it. The inaccuracies are just too nit-witted.

Nobody at home in Corona Tower watched it, either, as far as Shady knew. But Charlie nodded to the woman, focused on business. "A statement is probably not a bad idea. Let me give you the contact for Precinct Nine. Ask for Officers Seaton or Wells. Tell them Charlie sent you."

"You can't take it yourself . . . Charlie?" She batted her eyelashes at him and gave him a big-eyed, wishful expression.

Charlie solemnly shook his head. "Sorry, ma'am. I'm assigned to a different unit."

She gave him a sad nod, then froze. Her gaze flicked toward Charlie's arm shield, then back to his face. New awe filled her expression. "Oh, my God! I should've realized! You're *him*! You're the Hero of the *Asalatu*! The one who rescued Pack Leader Rex! Ohmigod-omigod-omiGOD! My name is Zona Dorsey, and I am so, *so* very honored to meet you! Can I get a selfie with you? Can I have your autograph?"

The warm bronze color of Charlie's face grayed. His brown eyes went a bit glassy.

At the other end of the link, Pam dissolved into laughter.

Rex thrust himself between the two humans. "So sorry! You must excuse my partner. We need to go home now. I am sure you understand."

"Oh, uh—" Zona stepped back reflexively.

"Rex, are you feeling unwell?" Shady also placed herself between the woman and Charlie. She called their auto-nav from its stall in the underground garage at Corona Tower.

"Yeah, sorry. Rex is still recovering." Charlie focused on his XK9 partner. He ran a hand across the shaggy black fur. "When he gets tired, well, we can't mess around. He's still healing."

"Oh." Zona gave Rex a worried glance. "Oh! Of course. I'm so sorry. It's an honor to meet you, Pack Leader!" She couldn't help but know the story, even though the public version wasn't complete. For nearly a week, the news cycle had contained little else.

Rex's dedicated pursuit of a suspect onto a spaceship that blew up a few minutes later made a dramatic story, just on its own. The fact that Charlie—already a decorated hero—had launched into immediate action to rescue his XK9 partner made the story even better.

"Such an honor! I hope you get well soon!" Zona respectfully backed off. "Thank you! Thank you, both—all of you, for your service!"

Charlie offered her a solemn nod, but Shady smelled the sludgy fug of unease in his scent. She'd seen him in this position before. Receiving thanks for his service or heroism always made him uncomfortable.

The espionage angle of the incident hadn't gone public. Very few people knew that Rex's unnamed suspect had been the Transmondian spymaster Jackson Wisniewski, who was now a Ranan captive in re-gen. Even fewer knew about the criminal Whisper Syndicate's involvement in the affair. Instead, the PR people had promoted the story of Charlie the Hero and his valorous "second act." Much to Charlie's chagrin.

"I have called the car." Shady made a show of giving Rex a worried sniff-over.

Her mate smelled as much irritated as exhausted. "Don't over-sell it," he texted silently to her HUD.

She gave his ear a playful nip, then nudged him toward the road. "Come with me. Our car should be here soon."

CHAPTER 2
CHARLIE'S COMMAND PERFORMANCE

OPD HQ, The XK9 Special Investigations Unit and assigned GR Chamber

"Come in and welcome." Charlie Morgan led his guests through the not-quite-finished new offices of the XK9 Special Investigations Unit. He stepped inside his and Rex's future workspace, then opened the brand-new entrance to what was now his personally-assigned Global Reconstruction Chamber.

His five visitors eyed the new area with open curiosity. They'd arrived as scheduled—even the two from Centerboro, the Ranan national capitol for the station's human population. Station Bureau of Investigation Director Adelaide Perri and Assistant Station Attorney General Lamont Niam must've started very early to make it here from Wheel Four by ten on a Monday morning.

"Thank you, Detective Morgan. I've been looking forward to this." Diminutive, dark-skinned Senior Special Agent Elaine Adeyeme led the way. She and her team had set up shop here in Orangeboro early last month within hours of the *Izgubil* incident, and she'd commissioned this GR. It wasn't finished yet, but she'd been eager to have it in a fairly advanced state to show their visitors today.

Elaine's boss Director Perri, a wiry older woman, followed her into the lower lighting of Chamber Three's interior. This was the first of several scheduled high-level strategy meetings in Orangeboro, so both wore formal SBI blue-black.

AAG Niam halted at the door and raised a dubious eyebrow. About Charlie's height, with silvered temples and the air of someone used to commanding the room, he gave Charlie a hard, appraising stare. "Since when are detectives also Global Reconstruction artists?"

Not an unexpected question, but it brought a wash of memories Charlie'd rather forget. He focused on the question, not his constricted gut. "I've, um, had an unusual career."

Behind Niam, Assistant Borough Attorney Regan Ireland frowned. "Morgan is a Class 1-A Certified GR Artist. In my office, we're delighted to have him available for GRs again."

Charlie gave her a small, grateful smile. The fashionably dressed ash-blonde prosecutor had been a fan of his work in the old days. Nice to know she remembered.

"He utilized his recovery period after the *Asalatu*, to qualify for the certification." Chief Klein brought up the rear of the little procession, also in formal regalia. He regarded Charlie with a broad, approving grin.

Niam gave Charlie a startled glance, then his eyes widened. "Oh. Right. Of course. The *Asalatu*." He offered a curt but respectful nod. "Thank you for your service, Detective Morgan."

Charlie returned the nod. He kept his face as bland and pleasant as he could, but all-too-familiar heartburn soured his stomach. *Trust Klein to play the "hero" card with Station officials.* "I live to serve."

"Come on in, Lamont." Perri beckoned from one of the charcoal-colored viewers' chairs. "Elaine says this'll put all your doubts to rest."

Charlie took the opportunity to lean closer to Elaine for a quiet word. "Where's Shiv?"

"He sends his regards, but an issue came up. He won't be able to join us." Charlie glimpsed her troubled expression despite the darkness in the room.

The depth of his disappointment startled him. Elaine's primary Lead Special Agent Shiva Shimon had contributed substantial investigative information for this GR. He'd been keen to see it, and Charlie'd been eager to show it off. "Nothing serious, I hope?"

Elaine released a quiet sigh. Her frown didn't ease. "Remains to be seen."

"Well, here's hoping things'll work out." *Damn.* Shiv had recently helped Charlie make a difficult medical choice about whether to accept augmentation treatments. Since then, the two men had begun a growing friendship. It extended beyond their work together, and also beyond Shiv's new personal connection to the XK9 Pack through his romantic relationship with Berwyn.

Charlie swallowed his dismay and retreated to his operator's rig. With a recently-developed extra twist to maneuver his arm shield into the narrow space, he settled himself at the controls.

His audience found seats in the cramped, semi-dark viewing gallery, bathed by the dim blue glow of the GR tank. Charlie released the tank from standby mode. Its glow intensified. The rest of the chamber fell into middle-darkness—except for a pulse of light from Niam's case pad. It illuminated his scowl for an instant before he grimaced and pocketed it.

Is he using that pad with his HUD? Good luck getting a signal in here. The chamber's confidentiality protocols required a physical connection to access the Station Net. Charlie blinked away afterimages. Eyes dazzled by Niam's device, he couldn't glean much about the others' body language.

Perri turned to Charlie, her face an indistinct shape in the darkness. "I apologize. I should have asked earlier. Where is Rex?"

"Down the hall at the Med Station. While we wait for his new lungs—the re-gen lab is still culturing them—we have to be careful. The finishers and painters are still working in here. The dust and fumes messed with his breathing more than he expected this morning." Rex had been adamant that he should come today, even though both Shady and Charlie warned about the air quality. Thank goodness the paramedics were based just down the hall.

"So, Rex hasn't been consulting with you on this?" He could now see well enough to make out Perri's startled expression.

"Not for most of it, no. I completed the bulk of this work while he was still hospitalized." Charlie's fingers rested on the controls. "I did use his audio, optics, and reports, though. Especially for the first part."

"These dogs truly can write reports? And they can talk with you? Like talking with another human?" Niam sounded more skeptical than Charlie'd expected.

"Didn't you see their presentation a few weeks ago?" Director Perri turned to him with a frown. "I thought the whole Station watched that or at least saw clips!"

Niam scowled back. "It looked—I don't know, staged. Rehearsed. How fluent are they in normal life?"

"I'll have to introduce you to Acting Pack Leader Shady Jacob-Belle." Elaine kept her voice even, but Charlie saw the fierce set of the small woman's shoulders. "I'm sure she'll quickly disabuse you of any notion that they can't speak well."

Charlie repressed a grin. Shady'd be delighted to school him, no doubt. Perhaps in several languages. He'd left Rex under Shady's supervision at the Med Station.

But at that thought his impulse to smile faded. Rex had vetoed all suggestions that he go to the Sandler Clinic, but Charlie hoped that once his respiratory distress eased he'd at least slide into the deep torpor of Healing Sleep. Healing Sleep could sometimes deliver miraculous recoveries, although it couldn't heal blown-out lungs from catastrophic decompression. Only a transplant could do that.

Niam's device pulsed with light again.

"Oh for pity's sake, Lamont! Put that damned thing away!" Perri glared at him.

Niam glared back, but pocketed it once more.

Chamber Three dimmed to deeper darkness. The GR tank filled with a static image from a surveillance recording, time-stamped 01:48 on November 6, Ranan Year 94—the day of the dock breach. The camera's view showed a tertiary warehouse corridor and a hatchway with location markings. Then the image faded behind a block of type.

"The following reconstruction shows the sequence of events that the evidence has shown led up to the breach that destroyed substantial portions of Orangeboro Docks two through twenty-five." Charlie's recorded voice-over spoke the words in the display. "The first indication that something was amiss came when a biological contaminant alarm sounded in Warehouse 226."

"Hold a moment." Niam scowled at Charlie, then shifted his focus to Elaine. "Why focus only on the dock breach? Wasn't this part of the plot to destroy the *Izgubil*? How were the brothers coordinating with the bombers?"

"We don't think they were." Elaine shook her head. "There's nothing to indicate they had any idea what was about to happen to their ship. If they'd known, why go back to it at all?"

"Are you saying the dock breach was somehow *unconnected* with the explosion?"

"Strange thought, right?" She gave him a wry grimace. "But there's only one point of crossover between the two crime sequences that we could find. We believe the dock breach affected the timing of the explosion."

"How?"

"The dock breach very likely surprised the bombers. We

think it may have forced them to initiate their detonation sequence earlier than they'd planned."

"Huh." Niam crossed his arms and returned his attention to the GR tank.

Charlie released the pause. His GR continued with an image of a naked young woman who appeared to be lying on her back, floating in the middle of the tank.

The sequence ran through the complainant's assorted injuries. Inset images of scans, autopsy photos, and physical items from Warehouse 226 illuminated points of evidence. Short, animated clips demonstrated how each injury probably had occurred. Charlie'd developed this sequence and reviewed it many times, but some of those recreations still made him wince.

According to Dr. Anika Chinbat the Medical Examiner, the young woman had died when she collided at high velocity with a warehouse bulkhead. The collision had crushed part of her skull and broken many other bones throughout her body. Charlie had reconstructed her shattered face and broken body to show how she would have appeared before her death in Warehouse 226. A subtext credited the forensic anthropology team from Monteverde University for their substantial reconstruction help.

Dr. Chinbat and consultants from the Crime Scene Unit had helped Charlie estimate the speed and force needed to create such injuries. No stumble, even if it happened while running, would be enough. She must have been violently shoved or thrown. He glanced away during that sequence. Several in his audience grunted with discomfort.

A new block of type appeared. Charlie's voice-over resumed: "The complainant's overall pattern of less recent injuries reveals evidence of a longer period of abuse. This supports the team's conclusion that she must have been a sex-slave held on the *Izgubil*. After the explosion, they recovered other bodies with parallel patterns of newer and older injuries. Also like them, she was recovered without clothing.

"Facts about her pursuers strengthen this link to the *Izgubil*.

START TEMPORARY INPUT, PENDING UPDATES. Suspects Rufus and Neil Dolan remained in re-gen at the time of this GR's creation. They could not answer questions. But in the vid that comes next, note their clothing. It shows that they wore the same style uniforms as other security personnel whose bodies we have recovered from the *Izgubil* wreckage, right down to the sheathed knives on their utility belts. END TEMPORARY INPUT."

The GR then rolled the surveillance vid of the brothers' escape through the same hatchway Charlie'd shown in the static image at the opening. The hatch slowly irised shut, but its safety overrides made it pause when Rufus and Neil plunged through to escape.

The two men were burly fellows, with distinctive tattoos of intertwining lines on their arms. New information flags noted that the tattoos identified them as members of a criminal gang from Uladh Nua called the Saoirse Front. Its members often worked for the Whisper Syndicate.

A new block of type appeared, again with Charlie's voice-over. "We discovered that nearly all of the dockside and ware-house security surveillance devices near the *Izgubil* had been tampered with. This evidence is documented in detail, in accompanying materials from the experts of SBI Special Investigations Team Alpha and the Wheel Two Port Authority's Forensics Unit. This GR will simply note that tampering with surveillance equipment is a common Whisper Syndicate tactic.

"The compromised devices were set to play back staggered, looped recordings of ordinary warehouse or dockside activity. Each loop is approximately 56 hours long. Under ordinary circumstances, no one would be the wiser. Continual digital review of such surveillance is cost prohibitive, especially for an area this big that rarely has security issues." He saw several in his audience nod. "They seem to have overlooked this camera and two others in very minor back-corridors. We're fortunate that this one gave us relevant material."

Now the GR showed a new clip. A small label flashed

"Morgan optics." In the video that followed, Rex thrust his muzzle near the now-closed hatchway to Warehouse 226. "Two men," his vocalizer voice reported. "We knew that. Brothers."

A label at upper left read, "DPO C. Morgan audio." Charlie's voice spoke from out of frame, the vid still directed at Rex. "Shared genetics make for similar scent profiles. DNA'll confirm. I've never seen him get it wrong."

"Lead DPO H. Fujimoto audio," a new label announced. "Brothers, eh? Might help narrow down an ID, especially with the tattoos."

"Wait," Niam said.

Charlie paused the playback.

"Each person's scent is *that* different?" Niam asked. "Just by smelling, can an XK9 truly say who it is? And even whether or not they're related?"

"Think of it like remembering a face, only considerably more definitive, and the person making the ID has a perfect memory," Charlie advised. "A face results from a person's genetic makeup, and so does their scent. That makes a positive scent-ID by a trained XK9 as good as a DNA match, in evidentiary terms."

"Huh." Niam returned his attention to the tank. Charlie released the pause.

In the recorded vid Rex said, "This way," and scratched at the handholds to turn. He bunched his haunches. Klein and Elaine drew in sharp, quiet breaths. Charlie grimaced. They both knew a good deal about microgravity, and both had spent enough time with XK9s to read that body language.

Charlie had cut the next bit. It wasn't part of the evidence, and frankly it was embarrassing. He'd forgotten how deep Rex's ignorance of microgravity had been that night, and how impetuous he'd been. No wonder Fujimoto had been leery. And no wonder Charlie'd gotten hurt. *If I hadn't been fighting off flashbacks . . . if I hadn't been so desperate to prove myself . . .* He released a small sigh. *Maybe I'd have had the sense to call a halt. Mm. Maybe.*

He chewed on his lip. The GR continued.

CHAPTER 3
THE MURDER BROTHERS

Charlie's Global Reconstruction Chamber

In Charlie's GR, a 3D map of the corridors around Warehouse 226 opened. His audience adjusted their positions in reaction. Niam, Perri, and Ireland all sat forward to examine the map. Elaine's hunched shoulders relaxed. Chief Klein glanced over his shoulder and nodded to Charlie with an approving smile.

Oof. He's seen the part I cut. Charlie nodded back.

Within the tank, pale blue-green wireframe lines stood out clearly on a darker background. A moving, hot-pink arrow extended through the map's framed-in passageways to an intersection. The location ID glowed.

Then the vid reopened. Detective Fujimoto held his badge up to a latch-pad reader. He, Rex, and vid-viewpoint Charlie now hovered by the emergency cutoff at the edge of the crime scene. "Override," Fujimoto ordered. "Extend crime scene to where XK9 Rex stops." The cutoff panel retracted.

Rex pulled himself through, claws scratching for traction on the handholds. In the vid his tether extended toward the viewer and wobbled with his clumsy progress. He proceeded along the corridor to an intersection with a larger passageway. "The brothers paused here." Rex sniffed along one side of the corridor. "They stayed for quite a while."

He moved over to a new spot and sniffed some more. "The older one held on here. See? There is blood from the girl they killed in Warehouse 226. There have been little cast-off droplets all along the way."

Charlie's optics zoomed in on a small rusty smear on the padded surface.

From Fujimoto's recording, Charlie'd found a clearer view of Rex as he sniffed along the cross-corridor's opening to the other side. "The younger brother held on here," Rex added. "Both emitted scent factors of fear and anger. I believe they stopped here to argue about something that frightened them."

The image paused for a new block of type and Charlie's voice-over. "START TEMPORARY INPUT, PENDING UPDATES. At the time this GR was made, investigators had been unable to question Rufus and Neil Dolan about what transpired here. We think it is possible that they had not intended to kill the young woman in Warehouse 226. They almost certainly had been sent to bring her back to the ship. Or perhaps they'd killed her in a fit of rage and now realized what they'd done.

"We speculate that this is where they discussed their situation and decided what to do next. The young woman would have been considered by the Syndicate to be a valuable piece of property, and the Syndicate is not gentle with operatives who make expensive mistakes. The Dolans were probably aware of their mortal danger. They also undoubtedly knew the Syndicate would hunt them down if they simply fled. Pending information from future interviews with the brothers, we think this is where they decided on a desperate plan to create a distraction that would make their trail harder to follow. END TEMPORARY INPUT."

The vid resumed. The view from Fujimoto's optics blurred

briefly. He'd moved closer to the corridor's metal framework. "No sensors or mics here, of course."

"Anything in the cross-corridor?" Charlie's voice asked.

With a gentle push, Rex floated past the opening. He stiffened. "Oh! Here the scent is much hotter! They were just here!" Another 3D map of the corridors opened within the tank. The hot-pink arrow reappeared. It extended through the passageways from the original cross-corridor to show the route Charlie, Rex, and Fujimoto had taken, following the brothers' scent, to Orangeboro Dock 18.

Charlie'd chosen not to include any vids from that transit. The raw inputs had been deeply uncomfortable to watch. Thank goodness none was needed to support the mission of the GR.

The next view showed the *Izgubil's* outer service hatch in the docking berth, based on a view from a surveillance camera. Charlie vaguely remembered this part. But in light of his injuries, most of his "recollections" from that night probably were impressions he'd later received from Rex through their brain link.

A line of text appeared near the bottom of their view: "Space Barque *Izgubil*, Orangeboro Docking Berth 18-C, approximately 02:22." Rufus Dolan's dark red hair and brown-shirted back sailed into the picture, floating in the dock's microgravity. He grabbed the handhold by the service-entry hatch. It irised open at his approach. All around him, a thin cloud of what appeared to be light blue mist floated from every piece of exposed skin.

The GR paused its action, freezing Rufus mid-move. Across the image words formed, again with Charlie's voice-over. "Since much of this reconstruction is based on scent evidence, the artist has added a new effect to show the scent-trace the Pack found. It looks like colored mist or dust. It is designed to show how shed skin cells fall and are distributed on surfaces. A person's scent is carried by the cells. XK9s guided and corrected these reconstructions. They are as accurate as it was humanly possible to make them." The words faded.

Rufus' hand landed on the hatch frame. Light blue "dust" drifted onto the metal frame housing like an outline around it. The man swung himself inside. He left behind a solid blue handprint with a dusty blue halo around it.

"The handprint is darker, because . . . ?" Niam half-turned to raise one eyebrow at him.

"Direct skin-contact dislodges a more concentrated layer of cells, and therefore a clearer scent." As Charlie spoke, the action in the GR paused itself. A line appeared, which led to an inset photo of the actual hatch frame as Rex's and several Packmates' wearable optics had captured it. A white hand-shape appeared, at exactly the place where Charlie had shown Rufus grabbing the frame. A list of five reference items appeared alongside, indicating the five independently-created XK9 crime scene reports that identified Rufus Dolan's handprint in this place.

"That's independent corroboration by five different XK9s," Elaine said.

"Huh." Niam slumped back in his chair and stared at the GR tank. The action resumed. Rufus disappeared inside the hatch. His younger brother Neil approached the opening next, exuding his own, yellow mist. He dived in headfirst behind his brother, hands reaching forward through the open hatch.

The view switched to a different vantage, this one inside the entry corridor. For the hardware part of the reconstruction, Charlie had relied upon his own and the Crime Scene Unit's vids, plus the manufacturer's schematics. The XK9s had entered under lower-light conditions, so their wearable optics' vids had been less helpful for the reconstruction of the corridor itself.

Nonetheless, the GR paused to compare each place that Neil or Rufus had made physical contact with a surface. Insets showed corresponding images captured by XK9s. The different colors of their "scent trails" overlapped in the GR but remained visually differentiated.

Niam watched in silence for several minutes, but then

seemed unable to resist another question. "How do the dogs keep the scents from getting all muddled up with each other?"

Charlie paused the GR again. "Can you see where the two scents overlap and where they are separate?"

"Well, obviously. That's not what I asked."

"We tried to give a sense of where the different scents are. Rex tells me that he can distinguish between scent traces as easily as you or I can see the difference between red and green. It's a particularly apt comparison, because we can't smell scent rafts, any more than XK9s can see either one of those colors."

Niam shot him a startled eyebrows-up. "They can't?"

"Blue, yellow, a little blue-violet, brown, and shades of gray. That's about it. Evolution gave them a vastly better capacity to see in low light than we have, but the tradeoff is that they can't see part of the visual spectrum that humans can. I chose the colors for the different scents in this GR carefully, because the dogs worked closely with me on them. I used colors they actually can see and differentiate. They were excited to be able to share something of what they experience."

"So . . . This truly represents how they smell a scene?"

"As much as possible, considering I can only take their word for what they smell. The XK9s helped make it as accurate a parallel as we could manage."

"Huh. Well, okay. Is there more?"

So much more. Charlie resumed the playback.

They watched in silence while Rufus and Neil made their way forward, closing and locking hatches behind them. Charlie had set it up so his viewers could see Neil move into a cross-section view of the escape pod area and start punching in delayed-launch codes. Once again, little flags popped up, in this case to identify what Neil was doing and cite evidence report numbers.

Director Perri sat forward. ABA Ireland's smile grew as the playback unfolded. Niam rose, then carefully navigated a few steps to one side. He watched the action from there for a moment, then returned to his seat with a respectful expression on his face. *Checking the 3D effect?* Warm satisfaction filled Charlie. He always made his GRs viewable from any angle, because people might view it from any of dozens of positions in a courtroom.

While Neil Dolan stayed busy in the pod bay, Rufus pushed past him into the cockpit itself. A cross-section of that area appeared, stacked in the GR tank above the view of the escape pod bay where Neil continued his efforts. This allowed viewers to see what each brother was doing, without making either image so small it would be hard to see details.

A new panel appeared, once again paired with Charlie's voice-over. "The investigation has so far failed to retrieve the *Izgubil's* 'Black Boxes.' They may have been destroyed in the ship's micro-deconstruction. It is possible that the Whisper Syndicate located them before the SDF could. In any case, the GR artist has not been able to use audio or biometrics for the next part of this reconstruction. What follows is an extrapolation based on data we *do* have. Investigators are still trying to identify the pilot."

The animation resumed. Once in the cockpit, Rufus pulled his knife and grabbed the female pilot from behind. Charlie'd represented her scent with a tint of blue-violet. He had chosen to show Rufus' and the pilot's mouths moving as if they were speaking, but he'd left the argument that must've ensued between them to the viewers' imagination. Those who could lip-read might make out "Pull out now!" from Rufus, "I'm locked in!" from the pilot, and "Breach it anyway!" from Rufus.

Contact scent on the pilot's body had enabled Charlie to show the choke hold Rufus had employed. The pilot's hands reached up to tug vainly at Rufus' arm. Rufus placed his knife against her carotid. The reconstruction mouthed the words "Breach it now! Right now!"

In response, her shaking hands flew over the controls. Charlie'd taken pains to ensure that he showed her handling the controls correctly to effect the maneuver. A GR artist never knew when someone on a jury might actually know how to do something shown in a reconstruction. Faking it in ignorance messed too much with the verisimilitude.

"Mm-*hmm.*" Charlie glanced over to see Chief Klein cross his arms with a nod and a satisfied smile. Well. Indeed, one *did* never know.

The GR cut away at this point, to show a spliced-in compilation of actual footage from the spacelane outside the dock. A label popped into view: "Compiled from surveillance vids." They watched the *Izgubil,* a center-core ship with two slowly rotating rounded holds, tear away from its berth. The breach deformed many sections of the Orangeboro docks in every direction.

This damaged or destroyed ships in adjacent docks and dragged the still-locked-on berthing cone with it. Even though he'd built the compilation himself and reviewed it a dozen times, the sheer force and violence of that dock breach still took Charlie's breath away. *I lived through that. Holy shit, how did any of us survive?*

The compiled surveillance-view showed the ship's movement into the spacelane as the vids had caught it during the actual event.

Back in the cockpit, Rufus kept the pilot under duress with his knife. He eyed the controls and readouts. Then a quick, sharp jerk of his blade across her throat released a huge, sudden cloud of bright-red blood droplets. They billowed into the cockpit and rapidly filled much of it.

Rufus pushed the pilot's still-flailing, jerking, half-decapitated body forward into her control panel. She fell against it then rebounded, tethered by her safety belt. Rufus grabbed a handhold to pivot. He propelled himself into the escape pod bay. The cross-section view of the cockpit closed and the pod bay section expanded to fill the GR tank.

By this time, Neil had finished with his launch codes and

climbed into one of the escape pods. He waited for his brother, elbows on the hatch frame. If anyone had been watching Neil's side of the action, they would have seen each motion he made, complete with information flags and evidence photos. But Charlie had discovered that every time he reviewed the full, finished reconstruction even he couldn't easily pull his gaze away from Rufus and his victim.

Rufus joined his brother in the last open escape pod. The two men ducked inside. The hatch slammed shut and sealed.

Then the view cut away once more, replaced by an image that filled the GR tank with a wide view of the *Izgubil*. The mangled remains of the berthing cone stayed locked onto it, trailing debris.

"Ah." Elaine chuckled softly. Charlie grinned. Yes, she'd seen this part before. A new label popped up: "Compiled from surveillance vids by GR Artist Ernest Porringer." Charlie'd decided to include a sequence that one of his former colleagues in Orangeboro's GR Unit had created several weeks ago. No need to duplicate Ernie's excellent work.

The ship appeared to drift across the tank, then one of its holds erupted into a bright flash. Millions of micro-decon-structed pieces tumbled away in all directions and the rest of the ship slewed off-course. Moments later the other hold erupted. The force of this blast slammed the ship into a different section of the dock. A barrage of escape pods launched from its bow, then another from its stern.

The debris field expanded. Escape pods shot away in all directions, but Charlie'd placed a pale yellow circle around one. Rufus and Neil had at first allowed their pod to move like all the others. It floated slowly out of sight, still circled in pale yellow, until it left the GR's view.

A new block of type popped up at the end, with one last voice-over from Charlie. "According to the Station Defense Force's follow-up investigation, this pod made its inconspicuous way out of the destruction on Wheel Two. It drifted slowly but with purpose to match velocities with Wheel Three and lock on to a maintenance portal." In an inset image, Charlie had rendered a combination of Wheel Three surveillance vids and his own reconstruction imagery. It showed the incoming pod as it approached and then docked to the portal like a mealybug on a plant stem.

"The pod remained there until it was discovered last week, still docked," the text and spoken part continued. "SBI Special Investigations Team Alpha and a cooperating Station Defense Force team recovered it. Forensic analysis yielded DNA from both Dolan brothers. They had already been located and taken into custody on Wheel Three at that point."

And please let me never have to render a GR of that scene. Charlie's stomach went queasy at the very thought.

The GR faded to black. The tank cleared to its default blue. Chamber Three's lights came up, and everyone in the viewing section released a collective sigh. But at first, no one said anything.

"Whew!" Elaine stood at last. She rolled her shoulders and stretched.

Beside her Perri lingered in her seat, a hand still over her mouth.

Chief Klein eyed Niam. The Assistant Attorney General also stood. But then he rubbed the back of his neck for several long moments and stared toward the tank, his gaze unfocused.

"Damn, Morgan." ABA Ireland turned to Charlie with a respectful nod. "I think that's your best one yet."

CHAPTER 4
DOUBTS

Civic Center Medical Station and "Pocket Garden"

Shady lifted her head and wagged her tail at the sound of a familiar gait. A moment later Chief Klein, all spiffed-up in his dress blues, stopped at the doorway to Rex's cubicle in the Civic Center's Medical Station. His scent wafted in with him.

She'd been dozing next to Rex's bed. Charlie's alert about her mate's respiratory problems had provided a reason for a short Emergency Family Leave—which still seemed an exotic, faraway concept. It was something the Transmondian XK9 Project on Chayko never would have countenanced, but it was a good thing she'd had that option today.

Rex had proved himself to be far from a model patient. Once the medical humans had somewhat eased his breathing distress this morning, he'd refused all appeals that he go to the Sandler Clinic. A specialized veterinary medical team could attend to him there, but no.

"XK9s are tough," he'd insisted. The vocalizer worked independently of his audibly-wheezing breaths—a mixed blessing when he was in this mood. "I shall be fine. Just let me rest a few minutes."

Charlie's high-ranking guests wouldn't wait. He'd been forced to leave. But there seemed to be absolutely nothing urgent going on in Central S-3-9, the war room for Elaine Adeyeme's *Izgubil* investigation. So Shady stayed, even after Dr. Sandler sent one of her techs over to monitor Rex's condition.

Sure, there were a lot of agents down there in the investigative center, staring at screens and running through Station Net-based leads. And sure, Shady could be doing some of that too, just as Pam was. But her efforts to help Ari Pryce, the vet tech, constrain her restive mate probably used the time better.

A while ago Rex had settled into Healing Sleep at last. *Thank goodness!* Despite a guilty sense that she was slacking off, she'd accepted Ari's advice and taken a nap of her own at that point. Day after day of worry over Rex had left her sleep-deprived.

Part of her still remained uncertain. Had the Ranans made a weird mistake when they gave Family Leave to dogs? Would she have to pay for it later? She'd spent most of her life subject to the inexorable demands of Dr. Ordovich and his trainers. They never made much allowance for either illness or injury, and certainly never for sleep-deprivation exhaustion from worrying over personal matters.

Oh, how I love Rana Station! She'd rested her chin on her forepaws and allowed herself to drift off.

But now here came her favorite police chief, bringing fresh motivation to wake up and make herself useful. She did feel better. "Hello, sir." She rose and met him at the door, tail high and set at full-fan.

Klein's broad grin and a sweet uprush of pleasure-scent rewarded her. He caressed her shoulders and neck with both hands. "How are you?" He glanced into the room. "How is Rex?"

"Rex is finally in Healing Sleep." She butted his chest with her head and basked in the delighted smell of him.

Pam's amusement echoed through the link. *You are such a suck-up.*

Hey, don't blame me. He started it. Shady lolled her tongue and snuggled closer for an ear-scratch.

Klein delivered it with gusto. "This never gets old, does it?"

"No. Never. A little to the left? Ah, yes. There you go." She sighed. "I probably should have let Dr. Sandler's tech watch over Rex, and returned to the war room by now, but I needed a nap."

"A nap is sometimes needed." He smiled. "It's just as well you stayed. There's someone I'd like you to meet before you go back to work."

A second man had halted outside in the hallway, well short of the door. The fearful wariness in his scent created a harsh contrast to Klein's pleasure and soured Shady's mood. She stepped outside and met his gaze. The door clicked shut behind her.

He leaped back a step. "*Crap*, that's a big dog!"

Klein turned to the other man. "In every way, and never to be underestimated." He performed introductions. The odd blend in the Chief's scent factors corroborated her evaluation that Klein felt both irritated by, and obligated to, this man. "Shady, AAG Niam has some questions that you're better-suited to answer than me."

Shady had long ago become inured to humans' rude way of staring directly at a dog, as Niam was doing now. She kept her ears up, although the beat of her tail slowed. "Good morning, AAG Niam. What questions shall I answer for you?"

Niam took a step backward but continued to stare. "That is damned uncanny."

Shady halted her tail. She narrowed her eyes but stifled a growl. "Questions? Hello?"

Niam's gaze shifted to Klein. "How does it do that?"

Okay, that's enough rudeness. Shady swept her ears back and growled. She allowed a flash of fang to show in case he'd missed the point.

Niam took another involuntary step back. The fear in his

scent factors ballooned to fill the immediate area with a sweaty, acrid stink. "Shit!"

"Address *her*. Directly." Klein's brows pinched above challenging dark eyes. "Ask any questions you may have. And please remember that XK9s are *people*."

"Um, well." Niam straightened. The scorched smell of defensive anger rose to displace his lingering fear-scent. "It—*she* should not forget who I am, either."

"I give respect as I receive it." Shady arched her neck with another low growl and let the hackles across her shoulders rise.

Niam retreated another step. He'd moved almost two meters down the hall by now.

You've come a long way since you got free of the XK9 Project, Pam advised through the link. *But don't forget Niam's the Assistant Attorney General for the Station's Criminal Division. He's likely going to handle some of our cases.*

You are an annoying wet blanket. I was starting to enjoy scaring him. Shady stress-yawned, letting all of her teeth show. Then she smoothed her hackles and lifted her ears. "Have we now performed enough dominance displays, AAG Niam? Would you prefer to do it some more? Or shall we try reasonable dialogue next?"

"Please," Klein muttered under his breath.

Niam gave a stiff nod, his expression wary, his body still poised for flight. He stayed in the hall. "I'm good with dialogue."

"Excellent."

"And while we're at it, how about if we clear out of the Med Station?" The Chief inclined his head toward the exit. "There's a pleasant little outdoor area nearby. We could speak more comfortably and privately."

Certainly 'privately' is advisable, Pam added through the link.

Shady knew the place Klein meant, so she trotted past the men toward it. Niam shrank back, then trailed behind Klein. A few steps down from the Med Station she made a left turn through a doorway and entered one of the many pocket gardens in the Civic Center complex.

Shady passed a wall where salad greens sprouted from tiered growing containers mounted one above the other from bottom to top. She, Klein, and Niam settled around a table in the open shade of a pergola where morning glories and cucumbers with tiny, just-forming fruits twined. The flowers' bright blue trumpets had already started to furl for the afternoon.

A service panel rose from the table's surface to offer refreshments. Klein and Niam ordered coffee. Shady asked for a bowl of water—a new item on these service panels' menus since last week.

"What did you think of Detective Morgan's GR this morning?" She cocked her head at Niam, who'd chosen a seat on the other side of the table, as far from her as he could get.

"It was quite, um, comprehensive. Convincing." Niam bit his lip.

"And the way it used scent evidence?"

"Rather—what one might call unique. It will be interesting to see how a jury reacts." The guarded, acidic edge to his scent told her he wasn't sure they'd react well.

"Are you convinced that scent evidence is valid, AAG Niam?"

Niam hunched his shoulders, then recovered himself and squared them. "The System Court recognized it as such, about a decade ago."

"But do you believe it? As a wise person recently pointed out to me, you are very likely going to argue—or at least oversee—some of our most important cases. One may intellectually understand that scent evidence is officially recognized. But genuinely believing it is more important."

"I'll admit, that GR made it easier to understand and believe in."

Shady let her tongue loll. "That is part of the reason we put so much effort into creating it."

"'We?'" Niam cocked an eyebrow.

"Our Pack. The XK9s and also the humans. Our whole Pack."

That skeptical eyebrow stayed up. "How can humans be in your Pack?"

A small robotic cart arrived bearing two mugs of hot coffee, a thermal carafe, and a bowl of fresh water. Klein gave it his thumbprint, then distributed the drinks. Everyone paused a moment for a sip. Or, in Shady's case, a nice long lap.

She licked her lips when she was finished and met Niam's gaze. "You asked how humans can be Packmates. It is quite simple. Each XK9 has a human partner. We have a cybernetic brain link that connects us and strengthens the bond of love that we formalized when we Chose them."

"You make it sound like becoming Significants." Niam gave her a quizzical frown.

"You're not far off," Klein said.

"Agreed." Shady lowered her chin in assent, human-style. "Both dogs and humans have long histories of inter-species rela-tionships, but Pack is a deeper thing than friendly acquaintance. Pack is family. And Pack necessarily includes our humans." She glanced at Klein and wagged her tail. "Extended Pack embraces many other esteemed beings as well."

The Chief grinned, then turned to Niam. "No, I don't have ear-scratching privileges with *all* of my officers. In case you wondered."

Judging from Niam's expression, he did not know how to respond to that.

"We all worked very hard on Charlie's GR." Shady dragged the conversation back to its original point. "We wanted to make sure it demonstrated both what happened, and how scentwork made that reconstruction possible."

"Well, you succeeded on both points. I've heard of other cases where scent evidence was introduced, but I've never seen or heard of a GR that demonstrated it."

"That is most likely because no GR artist ever asked any

XK9s about it before." Her hackles prickled. "When the Project was trying to pass us off as 'forensic equipment with a verbal interface,' they did not encourage any outsiders to interact with us."

"Part of the plot to conceal their sapience." Klein's brows pinched in a frown. "Ordovich did his best to make them believe that bad things would happen if they talked with outsiders—especially journalists."

"Mm. That fits. I didn't know what to expect, going in." Niam blew out a breath. "I paid attention to the forensic data cited. It's clear your crime scenes—especially that one inside the *Izgubil*—would have yielded far less information without the scent evidence. The idea to represent it as colored dust seemed strange at first, but it did make it easier to understand."

Her tail thumped the decking. "That was Charlie's idea. He is a very visual person. Humans can be useful in that way."

"'Useful?' Huh." Niam made a little grimace. "I hope Morgan's as good a detective as he is a GR artist. Otherwise, his talents are wasted in his primary line of work."

Klein smiled. "You'll get no complaints about his detective work from me."

Charlie might be an excellent human and all that, but the impression grew on Shady that her *own* excellent human was becoming increasingly pleased and excited about something. Echoes through the link suggested startled elation, concern, and maybe a little hunt-joy. *What is happening with you?*

I think we may have nailed her.

Who? Shady angled her ears back. *Who have we 'nailed'?*

Emer Bellamy.

Shady leaped to her feet. "Sir, could you please excuse me? We may have a major break in the *Izgubil* case."

CHAPTER 5
WINA'S BREAKTHROUGH

Civic Center Sub-Level 3, Corridor 9 SBI Investigative Center, AKA "S-3-9"

P am stood back, arms crossed, pleased about the new development. But she was content to stay apart from the tight cluster of agents gathered around Special Agent Wina Emshwiller's workstation.

SSA Adeyeme—Pam still found it strange to call her "Elaine" —had pride of place by Wina's left elbow. Director Perri peered over Elaine's shoulder. Once it was clear there'd been a break-through, both had hurried downstairs to get details.

Although Elaine stood and Wina sat, Elaine's head and shoulders came only a little higher. Several other agents gathered to angle in from the right and stare at Wina's screen.

Yeah, that was enough of a scrum. Pam didn't need to see the fine print on the spreadsheet.

"This is an incoming payment." Wina normally said little or spoke softly, but her voice held a note of triumph today. "It was made to Kieran O'Boyle's secret account on the *bancoscuro.*"

Oh, really. That alone was a breakthrough. The *bancoscuro* was a black-market exchange, allegedly based somewhere in the

Asteroids, and payments through it were notoriously hard to pin down. Pam and Shady had assisted with several lower-level bank employees' interviews lately, in which investigators asked about the *bancoscuro*.

The Special Agent leading that effort was SA Melynn Hunter, a pale woman of generous proportions with an even more generous amount of curly red hair. Melynn and her team wanted to know if there were links between any companies known to be associated with either the *Izgubil* or their primary suspect Emer Bellamy, and the *bancoscuro*.

That the payment had been made to Kieran O'Boyle was another breakthrough, and a major one for the case. A bit more than two weeks ago the Pack had definitively scent-linked him, along with seven other suspects, to gear that had been used to rig the *Izgubil* with explosives. Their evidence suggested O'Boyle was the team's leader.

Pam wasn't the only one on the investigative team itching to ask him questions. Unfortunately, the man himself seemed to have vanished. Rumors in the notorious Five-Ten sub-level, where he lived and normally operated, insisted he was dead. But scent evidence had given hope he might not be.

"The digital tags tell us the payment was made from Excelsior, LLC." Wina's voice quivered with excitement. Her tone dragged Pam's focus back to the present. "The money entered O'Boyle's account late in the day on November 6, 94. On November 7, O'Boyle disbursed money—the same amount to each of our current detainees. That is, Afiq Gonzalo, Elmo Smart, Wayne Purdy, and Atilla Usher, each got two hundred-fifty novi."

"Not damn much for a mass-murder charge and a Whisper target on their backs," Perri muttered.

"But not bad pay for one day of unskilled labor in the Five-Ten," Pam countered. Before she'd teamed up with Shady, she'd subbed on patrol in the notorious sub-level enough times to pick up a few things. "I've seen people killed over less than twenty novi down there."

Perri grimaced, but acknowledged her with a nod.

"O'Boyle's account says he also paid the same amounts to three other individuals," Wina continued. "It lists Bryan Kilgore, Fergus Allan, and Raghnall Wall." She pointed a skinny, pale finger at the display.

Ah. Pam and her colleagues knew those names, especially that last one. Usher and Purdy had willingly answered investigators' questions. Based on Usher's description, investigators tentatively identified their fifth, much more truculent and closed-mouthed detainee as Wall.

But Wina was still talking. "These payments add up to the *exact amount,* minus forty percent, of the total O'Boyle received from Excelsior!"

Elaine's eyes gleamed. "You found the payments to the installation crew."

"I found the payments to the installation crew!" Wina sounded as excited as the first kid to find the Prize Box at the annual Ag Fair Treasure Hunt. "Made with money from Excelsior. Which is part of Goromont Partners, which is owned by Shalidar, Inc., which is . . ." She hunched her shoulders. "Well, it goes seven more layers deep."

That tracks. Melynn and her team also had repeatedly asked about Shalidar and Goromont, as well as several other firms, during those bank employees' interviews.

"An important thing to understand is that all ten are shell corporations." Wina's voice grew scornful. "Not a single, flesh-and-blood employee. But they have an even more important thing in common." Wina turned to give Elaine a triumphant grin. "They all belong to Ashland Services."

"Ah." Elaine smiled. "And there it is."

Wow. The implications fell into place.

"Exactly!" Wina's voice went squeaky, but she rushed on. "As we have established, Ashland Services is a wholly-owned subsidiary of Moran Platinum. It's been managed for the past three years by Emer Bellamy!"

Elaine turned to Melynn, who stood near her elbow. "I think it's time for warrants."

"Writing 'em now, ma'am!" Melynn already had her case pad out. "Iruka, which judge should we take this to?"

"Qadhi, if we can catch up with her. She's not one to let the grass grow under her feet." Dark, slender OPD Detective Iruka Jones acted as Melynn's primary Orangeboro liaison. She also was a longtime friend of Pam's Amare Balchu. Normally Iruka worked Missing Persons, particularly when someone from the upper socio-economic levels was involved. Known around HQ as the "millionaire-whisperer," she'd been smoothing the way for the OPD with Orangeboro's wealthiest citizens for years.

"Forward me your report," Melynn told Wina. "That'll help me make a more convincing case!" She and Iruka headed for their dedicated work area.

Pam backed off, delighted by this breakthrough. Emer Bellamy was on their prime-suspect list because two different connections tied her to the case. Suspect or not, though, she was also rich and powerful.

Her father Hideki Bellamy Moran, secretly a sadistic pedophile, had died doing his worst in the the *Izgubil's* onboard brothel. A week ago at the reading of the will they'd learned that he'd left his massive business empire to Emer, who'd also been his junior partner for the last several years. That alone earned her a second look from the investigation.

But the thing that put her at the top of the suspect list was the other connection—to a man named Rory Fredericks. He'd been her Amare before he'd disappeared about a year and a half ago. A doctoral student in explosives technology, Rory had been perfecting the exact kind of cutting-edge explosives that had destroyed the *Izgubil*, before he vanished. It was a technique he'd pioneered, but he'd never had a chance to publish his work.

Rory's former faculty adviser at Station Polytechnic, Dr.

SCISCO-3750, had told the investigators that the explosives used on the ship followed Rory's prototype design, but they'd been significantly refined. Ne believed Rory himself must still be alive and in hiding, probably somewhere in the Asteroids.

Wherever he was, it must be at a facility where he could continue to develop his techniques. That ought to narrow it down—but unfortunately nowhere near enough. Space-based miners couldn't work without explosives. There were tech facilities on every other rock out there.

Iruka had worked the case back when Rory first disappeared. They'd done all they could, but they'd never found a trace of him, nor a hint of where he might have gone. After a while, the case went cold. Did Emer and her missing Amare secretly collaborate on the destruction of the ship as a way to kill her father and gain his fortune?

That had been a top hypothesis among the investigators until an unexpected Mahusayan connection emerged three weeks ago. Another ship, this one in Mahusayan space and seemingly unconnected to either Emer or Rory, exploded—rigged with Rory's signature formula.

There were other parallels, too, enough that both the Ranans and the Mahusayans had linked the two incidents. Those parallels had firmed up even more with the detonation of the small, Whisper-owned craft in which Rex had nearly died.

All these facts made it clear that there must be more wrinkles to this case, and other players in this plot, besides Emer and Rory. Rufus and Neil Dolan's apparently unrelated decision to force the *Izgubil* pilot to breach berth had muddied the waters even more. The investigation had found no reason to believe these two crimes were related, other than their timing. But it had taken them a lot of work to establish that.

Finding Emer's payment to Kieran represented a major break in the case. Before, they'd only had suspicions. Now she, too, was directly implicated.

I'm here, Shady said.

Pam turned toward the entrance. There was no missing her big, black sable XK9 partner. She met Shady's wise brown eyes across the breadth of the war room and felt steadier, more complete. *Good to see you. I guess Rex is in Healing Sleep, now?*

Shady wove between humans and workstations, headed Pam's way. *Charlie and I both begged him not to try to come today, but no XK9 wants to admit they're disabled.*

He is a rather hard-driving dog, but until he gets his new lungs, he surely must realize that pushing it is stupid. Pam frowned. *I didn't have him pegged as that heedless or prideful.*

It's neither heedlessness nor pride—more like ingrained mortal terror. Shady's ears swept back. *A puppy who wouldn't or couldn't do their work stood a good chance of being shot in the head, right there in front of the rest of us. Especially if Ordovich was on-site.*

A chill rocked through her, although she didn't doubt for an instant that the XK9s' creator, Dr. Gregory Ordovich, would be capable of such a thing. *Shot in the head? That's horrifying!*

Yes, but very motivating. Shady reached her, then stopped to lower her head with a growl. *None of us was lazy.* She pressed her body against Pam's lower torso—though not hard enough to shove her off her feet—and shuddered. *We wanted to please the humans. But a puppy who was hurt sometimes couldn't perform the required work.*

Pam stroked her partner's head with long, firm strokes. *That's monstrous.* She didn't have to bend far to kiss the top of that big, wide skull. *You know you don't have to worry about that here. You and Rex and the rest of the Pack surely must know we'd never do that!*

We do. Shady nuzzled her chest, then wrapped a big foreleg around her waist and pulled her close. *And I hope you never experience the kind of trauma you'd have to, to fully understand how grateful we are.* She held on for a long moment.

Pam returned the embrace fervently, her heart too full to speak.

Then Shady released her and took a couple of steps back. She glanced away. *But you remember that saying about old habits? When it's conditioned from birth, it's hard to shake. So, even when he's not conscious, Rex's lifelong experience fills him with anxiety over being injured.* Her hackles rippled in another shudder, then she shook herself. Dog hair flew every which way.

Pam brushed herself off, a mostly futile gesture. But she'd chosen her clothing to minimize the visibility of the inevitable dog hair. She slid a side-glance toward Elaine and Director Perri. At least she wasn't trying to appear professional in SBI blue-black. *That's a lot of stress-shed.*

I've been under some stress.

Pam gave her partner a considering gaze and tried to gauge the emotions that echoed from Shady's end of the link. *Do you need a moment?*

No. I've had several moments already. Instead, let us do some research. Do you know where Melynn and Iruka plan to serve their warrant?

CHAPTER 6
WHERE'S A WAY FORWARD?

S-3-9 SBI Investigative Center

S hady managed not to growl at Melynn. "What do you mean, Elle and I are not going with you?"

Beside her, russet-and-white Elle didn't completely silence her growl, but she lowered her gaze and turned her head to avoid giving their human leader a challenging stare.

"In general, it's better to avoid escalating a situation unless we have to." Melynn offered an apologetic expression.

"Believe it or not, showing up on someone's doorstep with an arrest warrant, a search warrant, and two enormous dogs who look like wolves as tall as Irish Wolfhounds—well, that just *might* seem kinda threatening to some people." Iruka's expression matched her tone. "Certainly it's more escalatory than two calm women at the door, even if we are wearing badges."

Shady snorted. "You might have a point." All the same, her hackles stayed up. "May we at least wait across the street, in case you need us?"

"We want to keep this as low-key as possible." Melynn frowned. "It would be best for all concerned if it's kept nice and quiet."

Like that will happen. Shady spoke through the link. *We're talking a mass-murderer, or at least an in-up-to-her-eyebrows co-conspirator. She's gonna be desperate.*

Probably. Pam blew out a breath.

After Melynn and Iruka left to serve their warrants, Shady, Pam, Elle, and Elle's partner, Misha, went to Anteroom Five to study a projected 3D plan of their destination that Misha had found. As they entered the room, a semi-transparent three-dimensional image of a multi-storied building rose from the middle of the tabletop.

Wait. I know that building! Pam stared at it.

Shady knew that building, too. It was the behemoth that obstructed most of the spinward view from Pam's balcony. *I thought that was a commercial building.*

Parts of it are. Pam's worry echoed through the link.

"There it is." Misha offered it with a sweeping gesture, then gave it a rueful grimace. "That's the Vinebrook. It's the Family compound of the foremost Founding Family in Orangeboro. That's where Melynn and Iruka are serving their warrants."

He let out a long breath and exuded musky scent factors of worry. "Elle and Shady, I think it's important for both of you to understand this. The Vinebrook is an important part of Orangeboro history. Not quite as important as the Civic Center, but it's a heritage location."

"Okay, explain." Shady snapped her ears flat. "What does this enormous—historic—pile of stone and concrete have to do with Emer?"

Misha grimaced. "She lives there."

Well, damn. So . . . you're neighbors? Shady lolled her tongue at Pam. *You really do live in a skeevy part of town, I guess.*

Nice. Real nice. Pam's mouth made a grim, straight line. Her scent factors smelled a lot like Misha's.

"Maeve and Basil still live there, too." Misha's voice echoed with awe and his scent factors shifted to cool, reverent notes.

"I'm sure that's why Melynn wants to keep this as low-key as possible."

"Maeve and Basil?" Elle cocked her head at him. "You surely cannot mean the Founders themselves?"

"Yes, actually. It's pretty amazing, but if their published biographies are accurate, both are 128 years old now. We must be as quiet and respectful as possible if we do go in. We don't want to trouble them. I'm told their health, especially Basil's, is rather fragile."

"Emer is their . . ." Pam frowned. Her unease echoed through the link and permeated her scent factors with an acrid undertone that set Shady's teeth on edge. "One of their nieces?"

"Oh, it's worse than that." Misha's face pinched and sharp notes of distress spiked in his personal scent-aura. "She's their great-granddaughter by direct matrilineal descent. Sorcha is her mother, eldest daughter of their eldest daughter Máiréad."

"And our arresting their great-granddaughter on suspicion of conspiracy to commit mass-murder will not trouble them?" Shady asked.

"No help for that, I fear." He shook his head with a scowl. "That'll have to be on Emer."

"But I guess keeping it quiet means no howling on the hunt. Right?" Elle bumped her partner's side.

"*Especially* no howling."

"You take out all the fun."

"Misha?" Shady studied the translucent image. "Why are some of the areas darkened?"

"Private areas. Not on public record anywhere."

Elle cocked her head. "Is Emer's apartment in one of those private areas?"

"Almost certainly."

"So, if we do have to go in and search for her, we'll be going in blind?" Pam scowled at the semi-transparent image.

"We shall still have our noses." Shady's heart lifted. "As long as there is a scent trail, we can follow it." She'd spent the last few weeks itching for a reason to hunt Emer Bellamy down. Now she actually might get a chance.

❖ ❖ ❖ ❖ ❖ ❖ ❖ ❖

9th Precinct, Port Hill Terrace Eight, Feliz Tower

G randma Hestia called rotate-for-break. *At last!* Hildie Gallagher dragged herself out from under the spidery robotic harvester she'd been trying to piece back together and laid her tools carefully into their slots in the well-worn caddy. "I got the actuator cranked in, but the dilator ring assembly's broken in a new place."

"How special." Anita-Maya bit her lip. "Well, I'll see what I can do. Clock's ticking!" Her cousin Cormac's wife was clever with persnickety robots. She could probably get the blasted thing working again faster than Hildie ever would.

"Good luck!" Hildie made a beeline for the nearest jackfruit tree and flopped down in the deepest patch of shade she could find. Throughout the near-decade of her work with the Orange-boro Emergency Rescue Team at the Hub, Hildie's off-time had rarely gone for farm work. Her Feliz Family's three hectares of intensively-farmed rice paddies offered endless work, but the Family respected her limited stints "dirtside." Those were desperately needed rest-and-recovery opportunities, and everyone knew it.

She'd forgotten how hard farm work could be, but last week everything had changed. Now she hung suspended in job-limbo on paid administrative leave, while the higher-ups debated her fate. Meanwhile, the harvester had broken down, exactly when a precision-timed super-crop needed bringing in. Here, at least, was something constructive to do.

Her cousin Lalu took the shady spot next to her. He grinned and handed her a bottle of water. "Heat getting to you?"

"Ugh!" Her parched throat and headache warned she'd overdone it. She downed several slow swallows. "We don't have these temperatures at the Hub. *Or* this humidity."

Lalu took a swig from his own water bottle. "You know, you're the one who usually warns *us* about dehydration and heat exhaustion. I expected you to pace yourself better."

"Doesn't count when it's me." She shook her head but didn't meet his gaze. "I'm in good physical condition. I should be able to push through."

"I thought it was your boyfriend who's supposed to be augmented, not you."

She wiped her face with her already soggy sweat rag. *Oh, yikes. That thing's gross.* She dropped it within reach, rather than put it back into her pocket. "Leave Charlie out of it."

"Oh, he's in it. Without him, you wouldn't be out of a job."

She scowled toward her feet. "LaRock is the reason I'm on administrative leave. Charlie . . . well, if he hadn't been the catalyst, it would've been something else. I don't regret my choice."

That was certainly true. Rex's life had been on the line. Nothing could have induced her to stand in Charlie's way. And Captain LaRochelle, AKA "LaRock," had been on her case practically from the day he arrived.

"Maybe not, but you hate hanging around here all day."

Got that right. "I shouldn't be the one on stand-down, LaRock should. I have work to do!"

"I'm gonna hope you're better at patching up people than you have been with that ring assembly."

She capped her water bottle and lay back on the orchard grass, enervated by more complex issues than the heat, although *yeah, I really did overdo it.* "The harvester needs a replacement ring assembly, not chewing gum and baling wire. I have topnotch supplies to work with in my med bay. And anatomy I actually understand."

"Oh, that ring assembly's pretty simple."

"Yeah. Pretty simply broken. In need of replacement." She closed her eyes, too sapped to find this nattering anything but exhausting. "It's even beyond duct tape. And that's my final diagnosis."

"Okay, Doc. And here's mine. We can patch up the harvester so it'll go a few more rounds, but you're on the brink of heat exhaustion. Go take a cool shower and a nap."

That sounded lovely. If she could muster the energy to get up. Her heat-dazed body didn't want to move, but that made her an easy target. The worries she'd tried to stave off with hard work swarmed her once again. What would she do if the Review Board decided against her?

Micrograv-based emergency medicine brought its own peculiar challenges. Her near-decade of hard-won specialized skills would go to waste on a dirtsider ambulance crew.

Her best friend Theresa insisted she should try again for med school, this time with a micrograv specialty. But Hildie's stomach did a nasty flipflop anytime she thought about that. She'd taken that horrible admission test once already: fresh out of Upper Levels, she'd felt ready to take on the universe.

As it turned out, not exactly.

She grimaced. Took another drink. She hated thinking about the fix she was in, but it wasn't going away. She didn't want to talk about it, either. What good would that do? Reopen the wound, that's all.

Ding! reverberated through her head. *Huh?* She activated her neural HUD.

"Capt. Consuelo Rodrigo, Monteverde Emergency Rescue Team," the ID said.

Hildie's pulse shot to full-gallop. She bolted upright and clicked the com. "Captain Rodrigo! This is Hildie Gallagher. Has something happened?" Her Orangeboro ERT crew was almost like family—*well, except for LaRock.* Her mind leaped to all the worst-case scenarios she'd witnessed over the years, and tried not to hyperventilate. *Is someone I know injured? Or worse? Has someone I love died?*

"Oh! No. God, no. Nothing bad has happened. Everything's

okay." Capt. Rodrigo sounded a bit rattled herself. "I'm really sorry. I didn't mean to alarm you."

Hildie took a moment to steady herself. "Um." She gulped. Her pulse thundered on. "When I saw the ID . . ." *Ugh. I really am a wreck.* Belatedly, she noticed Lalu's arm around her. His hand rubbed her shoulder in soothing strokes. Sudden tears threatened. *Crap!*

" . . . that maybe I could meet with you?" Rodrigo's words tumbled past her. "I was hoping you'd give me just a moment of your time."

Hildie blinked. Her lagging comprehension caught up with her. "Um, uh . . ." *Meet with me?* She blew out a breath and straightened. Lalu's arm lifted away, but he gave her a concerned stare. She focused on her call. "Um, I guess. When? Where?"

"I can be at Feliz Tower in about an hour, if you have time then."

I have nothing but time, except right now I reek. "An hour." *Can I be presentable in an hour?* "Okay, that . . ." She took in another steadying breath and struggled to center herself. "Um—may I ask what this is about?"

"I'd rather talk in person, if you don't mind."

❖ ❖ ❖ ❖ ❖ ❖ ❖ ❖

Civic Center Medical Station

D*ammit, dammit, dammit! I don't want to be stuck here. I'm missing out on everything!* Rex snapped his ears flat with a growl, then a coughing fit completely ruined the effect. He rode out long, painful spasms that nearly threw him off his med bed.

Dr. Sandler's vet tech Ari Pryce and a couple of the Med Station's paramedics leaped in to slap an oxygen cone over his nose and check his monitors. After a moment he had a sense of a new drug entering his system.

The spell passed. But his head spun, his chest ached, and fury radiated tight, hot anguish through him. *I hate this! I hate this so much!*

I feel you. I do. Charlie reached out through the link with a projection of love and reassurance. Rex always had a sense of his partner's general location when they were both conscious, even if separated. At a guess, Charlie was still in GR Chamber Three. *I wish I had something better to offer, but I'm afraid you're stuck for now. I'm sorry.*

Rex's gut tightened with rage. *I'm not an object of pity!*

Charlie's wry amusement echoed through the link. *Oh, how I remember THAT feeling. I know you won't believe me, but I truly don't pity you.*

Then what would you call it? Growling silently through the link avoided a coughing fit, but it wasn't nearly as satisfying as the real thing.

Heartfelt empathy. I remember how I felt when I woke up after the Asalatu accident. Suddenly I was already halfway to being twenty-three years old, and I didn't even remember turning twenty-two. I hurt everywhere, and I was too weak to feed myself. Believe me, I know how you feel.

I don't want understanding—I want relief!

Yup. Been there, too. It sucks.

Rex almost hazarded another actual growl. But if anyone could understand the claustrophobic, impotent fury of this weakened, breathless state, *yeah, Charlie probably does.* He'd been a hot-shot MERS-V driver. Handsome, athletic, top of his game, except for a demanding Amare. Then, in one crazy-short instant, shifting space wreckage half-crushed him.

I can't even pull off a damned growl without coughing. That makes me even more angry!

Totally normal to feel that way.

Charlie's maddening calm and tolerance tested every slender thread of Rex's patience.

Yup, I know that anger, too. You're just gonna have to deal with it. Have you decided to go to the Sandler Clinic yet?

I don't want to go to the Sandler Clinic.

You know that's where you belong. Maybe they can give you a better breathing treatment. One that'll last longer. Through the link he sensed that his partner stood up from the place he'd been sitting.

I don't want another breathing treatment. I don't want to NEED another breathing treatment. They're boring and they hurt.

No doubt. I'm coming back to the Med Station as soon as I can, to check you over in person. Got a number of functions to shut down before I can sign off here, though.

You can't make me go to the Sandler Clinic.

His partner clenched his jaws, drew in a deep breath—the rotten show-off!—then let it out to a count of ten. He closed the link as much as possible.

Rex almost snorted—caught himself in time. *Charlie's probably sick of my whining. Because I'M sure sick of it.* He didn't dare sigh or stress-yawn. Couldn't pace—legs might not support him. Merely sitting up made his head spin. *Dammit, dammit, dammit!*

CHAPTER 7
AN ELEVATOR TO NOWHERE

S-3-9 Investigative Center

U*h-oh*. One glimpse of Iruka and Melynn's body language said it all. Pam gave Shady a sidelong glance. *Seems like you'll get your wish.*

There could be no mistaking the eager hunt-joy in her XK9 partner's taut body and wagging tail. *At last!*

Elaine's Second Lead Special Agent Shawnee Kramer met the returning pair a few steps from the war-room's entrance. Elaine and Director Perri had left for the meetings upstairs a while ago, and Shawnee was Melynn's official supervisor. She nodded toward the side area where they'd viewed Misha's holographic Vinebrook model. "Anteroom Five."

Shady spun with a scramble of claws and bounded ahead, Elle on her heels. Pam and Misha grinned at each other, then trailed behind. Anteroom Five offered scant space for both XK9s, their partners, Melynn, Iruka, and Shawnee all piled in together. They bunched around the table with the humans elbow-to-elbow and gazed at Misha's 3D floorplan.

A moment later Shiv arrived. The big blond agent eased himself inside and quietly closed the door. Pam glanced at him, then did a double-take. *What's up with Shiv?* The normally-indefatigable fellow seemed uncharacteristically haggard. Concern stabbed through her. *Has something happened with Cinnamon's recovery? Is Berwyn okay?* No time to ask now, but if Pack was family, it also was an unparalleled gossip network. She'd learn soon enough if something was amiss in that quarter.

Oh, something is definitely wrong. Shady's hackles rippled. *But we don't have time to explore it now.*

"Well, we may not have located Emer yet, but the entire facility is now locked down." Melynn scowled at the translucent blue Vinebrook image. Ruddy patches stood out on the porcelain-pale skin of her face and neck. "We've lasered off Emer's quarters and posted UPOs at every entrance we could find. The Family is understandably upset, but so far they have cooperated with us."

"When you say 'every entrance we could find,' do you mean others might remain unsecured?" Shawnee eyed the map with a frown.

Melynn gave her boss a rueful grimace. "The possibility certainly exists. That place is enormous. We didn't have the personnel to do a thorough sweep, so we came back for the XK9 teams. They can cover more ground, faster and more accurately, than humans alone."

Shady and Elle growled their agreement, tails up and waving. Pam and Misha nodded.

Iruka met Melynn's gaze, then turned to the XK9 partners. "Be aware that even if you weren't born in a barn, you may feel as if you were, when we get inside the Vinebrook. To say it's opulent is playing it down. A lot."

"Actually, I was born in a barn." Shady's tail stopped waving. "It was called a whelping facility, but my mother said that was a fancy name for a barn. She hated that place."

Pam's arms prickled with sudden chill. *There it is again: the Project's systemic, pervasive abuse.*

"Me, too." Elle stress-yawned. "We all were."

"Oh, crap." Iruka stared at them. "I didn't mean—that's just an expression!"

"No offense taken." All the same, Shady flattened her ears. Her disgust echoed through the link. "We were considered livestock by the XK9 Project. Where else would livestock give birth?"

Steely determination tightened Pam's jaws and drew her brows into a knot. "Not on Rana Station, you won't."

"Got that right." Misha's chin jutted. Pam fancied even his mustache bristled with indignation. He stroked Elle's neck and she nuzzled his side.

We have a hunt to run! Shady uttered a quiet growl. *Let's not get distracted with dread of having puppies.*

The aversion in her partner's mental tone startled Pam, although she'd previously noticed that Shady tended to shy away from any thought of puppies. Pam gave her a closer examination. *You okay?*

Shady flicked her ears and pointedly focused on Misha's miniature Vinebrook model. "Exactly where does the warrant say we can go?"

"Our search warrant gives us access to the *entire* Vinebrook." Melynn's icy glare echoed in her voice. "The whole building 'or other associated environs, as necessary,' in order to secure relevant evidence and fulfill our arrest warrant. No restrictions."

Misha whistled. "That's a really broad mandate—especially considering *where* we're searching."

Iruka gave a curt nod. "We are to arrest Emer Bellamy on suspicion of conspiracy to commit mass murder. We are authorized to seize any and all relevant business and private records, or any other personal effects that may pertain to the case. No exceptions have been made for the ultra-private areas." Her dark brows pinched above her unusual, hazel-green eyes. "Mass murder. Our justice system takes that seriously. At least eighty-seven people dead on the *Izgubil* alone—that we've recovered.

Thirty-four more known to have been on the *Ministo Lulak*, if we link her to that."

"We need a plan." Shady eyed the schematic.

Melynn nodded. "That's why we came back. Let's talk."

❖ ❖ ❖ 🐾 ❖ ❖ ❖ ❖

OPD HQ and The Vinebrook

Within the hour, they'd developed their approach. Shady and Elle grudgingly waited by their OPD lockers, then accepted armor alongside their humans. Once back in Elaine's war room, Pam and Misha complained about the lack of head and neck protection for the dogs.

Hush. It's hot and confining enough already. Shady added a soft growl for emphasis.

Until you take a blowgun dart to the neck like Razor. Pam's upwelling worry echoed through the link. Its depth startled Shady, but she wasn't ready to give in. *It's not as if we're going to the Five-Ten.*

You don't know that. And even if we're not, I still hate that you're vulnerable. I don't want to think about you ending up like that.

Again, the depth of Pam's fear startled her. Shady snorted, but this time she acquiesced. Clearly, her partner wouldn't budge. Armored *and* shielded inside a police unit, they soon arrived at the real-life Vinebrook.

Shiv and his people reinforced the perimeter, waiting to see if they'd be needed inside. They tried to filter into the neighborhood quietly, but Shady could tell that somehow they didn't blend in.

They all look like cops because they all dress like cops. Pam's wry mental chuckle rippled through the link. *Dull, dark colors. Nothing flamboyant, because at heart, they're conservative souls. They just can't muster the upscale, stylish flair to look like everyone else on the street in this neighborhood.*

Shady decided not to puzzle over it. As far as she was concerned, everyone she saw was wearing gray-brown clothes in varying degrees of "baggy." *So, it is a human, visual thing. Got it.* She lolled her tongue, partly in amusement, but also to cool herself. That armor was damned hot.

Now that she stood outside the for-real Vinebrook, it appeared even bigger than she'd remembered from Pam's balcony view. From there it was several blocks away. No doubt it had lots of refined touches that someone born in a barn couldn't appreciate, but the sheer size of it made her heart sink. How many kilometers of hallway would she have to sniff, to run her quarry to ground?

They stopped outside the ornate, barred gate. Iruka scowled at it. "All right, you snooty metal trap, let us back in." She showed it her badge. Melynn did the same. Shady half-reared to show the badge on her armored chest to the reader. Pam fumbled for hers.

There was a long-ish pause. "Police persons Jones and Jacob-Belle, you may enter, if you insist. I suppose SBI Agent Hunter may as well enter, too." The gate's voice sounded like an aloof, rather bored upper-class man. "The other persons must stay outside."

"Damn it—" Pam freed her badge from where it had caught in her pocket, and showed it to the gate. "Here!"

Another pause. "Police person Gómez. Oh, very well. You too." The gate unlatched. It opened at a centimeter-by-centimeter crawl.

Misha and Elle showed their badges next.

"Oh, dear, more of you?" the gate's voice sounded, if anything, more aggrieved than ever. It continued its slow crawl open.

Melynn tapped her foot. "Is this the *program*, or is someone in the security station pranking us?"

"*Such* a bothersome, great crowd," the gate intoned mournfully. "Oh, very well: Police persons Flores and Finnian-Ella, you *also* may enter, if you *absolutely* insist."

The gate eventually opened enough for them to squeeze through. They didn't wait for it to extend to its full width but pushed forward. Once they'd passed inside, the gate snapped closed.

They tramped into a long, glass-walled corridor. Tactical boots rasped on polished marble floors. Shop displays featured elegant jewelry, gossamer clothing, and similar items.

"No price tags," Pam said. "I guess if you have to ask, right?"

"If you even have to *think* about asking, you don't want to know." Iruka led them through a carved archway into a central courtyard that seemed almost the size of Glen Haven Park. "And before you ask about shops in a Family compound, remember there are twenty-five floors and several hundred residents, not to mention at least that many employees."

Shady took in the colonnade and beyond it the courtyard. In every nook, she could glimpse white stone sculptures, vine-draped pergolas, trees, flowering plants, and various water features. Everything but the plants was white. *Hmm. Children's play equipment doesn't appear to be part of the décor here.*

You're right. Pam stood in the shadowed colonnade and blinked at the afternoon glare on all the white garden gee-gaws. *What made you think of that?*

I was comparing it to Corona. They have tables for Family dinners under the tree in the middle, and kids' play stuff all around the courtyard.

Pam's personal scent darkened with an oddly wistful sadness. *There was a small playground at school, but Mother never had much patience with toys.*

I'm sorry. Shady rubbed her head against Pam and savored the stroke of her partner's fingers along her neck. *Let us focus on other things.* She turned to Iruka. "Where is Emer's apartment?"

"This way." Melynn gestured to her left. "We marked it with

a beacon so we could find it again. This place is an enormous maze."

The Vinebrook's primary entrance was, as Shady had imagined, pretty well trampled over by several dozen people, many of whom were related to each other.

"Oh!" Elle stopped, nose up and working. Though by preference a ground-scent dog, she could work air-scents as well as any when she needed to. "I have found the trace of a daughter of Hideki. It is only a few minutes old."

Now Shady had it too: prickly annoyance and murky unease dominated in the woman's personal bouquet.

Elle led them into the courtyard. About ten meters in, they found a slender blonde young woman sitting on a bench gazing at a fountain. The woman glanced up at their approach, then froze with a gasp.

"Stop," Melynn advised their group in a quiet voice. "Let Misha and Elle engage her."

The woman scrambled to her feet. "Who are you?" She did not try to run away, but her scent and body language told Shady she wanted to.

Misha stepped forward. He introduced himself and Elle. "We have a warrant to detain Emer Bellamy."

The young woman frowned. "I already told one of your people I don't know where Emer is."

"Perhaps we should first establish your identity, ma'am. Are you Emer?"

The woman gave him an annoyed grimace. "No! I'm Orla." She hesitated, her frown deepening. "I suppose you want a thumbprint to prove that?"

Misha offered his case pad. "If you wouldn't mind."

Allegedly-Orla sighed, put her thumb to the pad, then gave a quiet groan when it also required a retina-scan. She bent to comply. The pad emitted a chime. "Congratulations, I'm now verified as being *me*." She gave him a resentful scowl. "Will there be anything else?"

"My colleagues and I have several questions," Misha kept his tone gentle, respectful. "Would you prefer to talk here, or in greater privacy at OPD Headquarters?"

Orla glared at him. "Gee, what a great range of choices."

Misha raised his brows at her, but she said nothing more.

Behind Shady, Melynn moved back down the path in the direction they'd come. "Need an escort to HQ for a witness." She kept her voice low. Neither Orla nor Misha seemed to hear, though Elle's ears twitched backward.

"You said you'd already spoken to one of our people." Misha kept his tone light and pleasant. "Where and when was that?"

Orla's scowl deepened. "Outside my sister's door, about five minutes ago. He said you have a warrant. Why do you want to arrest my sister?"

"This is in connection with the *Izgubil* investigation, ma'am."

"The *Iz*—are you saying she had something to do with that?"

"Do you recall her having said anything about that incident, ma'am?"

"About the—?" She stared at him. "You do realize our father died on the *Izgubil*, right? Of course we've talked about it!" She shook her head. Her scent suffused with anger, frustration, and deepening alarm. "My God. Maybe we should go to police headquarters. Do I need a lawyer?"

A text on Shady's HUD read, "UPO's coming. Clear the path."

Shady and Pam stepped onto a side path. Iruka joined them.

"You have not been charged with any crime." Misha stayed focused on Orla. "We simply need to ask some questions."

Orla's body tensed. "About my sister. Whom you want to arrest!"

"Everyone is presumed innocent until proven guilty." Misha gave her an apologetic head-shake. He kept his tone gentle, as if soothing a skittish puppy. "The more information we have, the better we can sort out the facts. You can help us, if you're willing."

Her defiant posture crumpled into fearful hunched shoulders and a troubled downward gaze. "This is a nightmare."

Elle moved back. A UPO walked up the path past Shady and offered Orla her extended hand. "Miss Bellamy? Would you please come with me? I can give you a ride to HQ."

Orla's face pinched with anxiety, but she stepped forward. The UPO walked with her toward the gate.

Melynn was back on the com. "Maybe have Wina or Gillie talk with her? Perfect. Yes, Petunia and Walter would be great for the XK9 team. Thanks." She glanced up. "*Now* to Emer's place!"

Near the elevators at the edge of a central atrium, Shady did a fast double-take. Here lay the recent scent trail of a different daughter of Hideki. She wrestled with the urge to give her "found the track" hunting bay, but Misha had said "no howling." She opted for her vocalizer instead. "I have the scent trail of a full sister to Orla, whom I suspect might be Emer. About an hour old. Running away from here. Strong fear-scent."

"Scent confirmed," Elle agreed.

"About the time of our first visit." Melynn met Shady's eyes with a frown. "Somehow, she knew."

"Corona Tower's gate announces visitors." Shady flicked her ears but stifled an impatient growl. "It's not as fancy as this place, so the one here probably does, too."

And I bet it probably sounds like the snootiest butler in the Universe. Pam's wry amusement echoed through their link.

I'm not gonna take that bet. Shady lolled her tongue. She followed Likely-Emer's spoor along the marble-floored hallway, down two flights of stairs into a service corridor, and finally to the doors of an apparent freight elevator. Had her quarry gone up or down? Shady sniffed the call buttons. "That is strange. She did not push either button."

Melynn caught up with them. "But the scent leads here? Was she with someone?"

Shady detailed the whole area around the elevator doors. Elle stood back to give her room. "No one is in exactly her time layer and no one ran with her. But the trail ends here. She came to this elevator and did not walk away from it."

"Maybe the elevator opened just as she arrived, and she didn't need to push a button." Pam pulled on a glove. "Let's call the car. She *must've* touched one of the buttons inside."

The elevator chimed like a carillon. The doors slid back. Pam held them open with her gloved hand so Shady could step halfway in. The floor of this elevator car had not been cleaned for about a day. Many individuals had used it in that time, but not one of them was the woman she'd been tracking.

CHAPTER 8
CONFRONTING HISTORY

The Vinebrook

No scent of her at all? Pam's breath shortened. She stared at Shady where she stood by the back-corridor Vinebrook freight elevator. *How is that possible?*

I am not sure. Shady backed out of the elevator and switched to using her vocalizer. "This is unexpected." She cocked her head at Melynn and the others. "Probably-Emer's trail leads right up to this elevator and does not lead away. Yet this car contains no trace of her scent."

"How could that happen?" Melynn frowned. "Did she somehow wipe away all her scent?"

Shady snapped her ears flat. "This elevator contains a day's worth of accumulated scent layers. It has not been wiped down. The woman we suspect is Emer simply has not been inside it."

"I must smell this for myself." Elle stepped forward, nose down. "Here is recent scent from a daughter of Hideki, not-Orla. The trail is very clear. It leads to this elevator." She checked all around the doorway. "There is no overlay, no departing trail. She came here." Elle stopped at the elevator's threshold, leaned in to sniff, then hesitated. She made another pass along the threshold and the crack between car and shaft, ears up. At last she raised her head to share an incredulous expression with Shady.

"Well?" Melynn asked.

Elle snorted. "Shady is right. The not-Orla daughter of Hideki did not enter this elevator car. There are scent layers, just as she said, but the Hideki-daughter-not-Orla left none of them. She did not step inside here at any time in the past 24 hours."

"Could the scent layers have been . . . " Melynn grimaced. "What am I saying? Nobody would even *think* to fake scent layers. Most definitely not in the space of an hour, while on the run."

"I do not know how it would be possible to fake them, in any case," Elle stress-yawned, ears back. "Scent deteriorates at a predictable rate. We could not estimate elapsed time, if that were not so."

"Ergo, Possibly-Emer did not get into this elevator car." Pam stared at it, not sure what to make of this.

"What did you smell at the edge?" Shady cocked her head at her russet-and-white Packmate.

Elle flicked her ears. "It was very faint. I thought I smelled a little hint of Emer in the crack. But it might be spillover from the hallway scent."

In the crack? Pam frowned. An image rose in her memory. Back when she walked a patrol beat at Grand Central Terminal, she'd observed many crowded morning commutes. "Could she have gotten into a *different* elevator car? You know, like those double- and triple-decker high-volume commuters they use for peak rush to and from the Hub?"

Misha's brows rose. "My sister takes one of those. It's such a long one-way trip they fill two cars, one on top of the other, for a single stop at our local terminal. That way, they can deliver twice as many people per trip."

"That would explain the scent trail anomaly." Melynn gazed into the elevator.

"And also the scent in the crack." Elle's tail and ears lifted. "There could be another car below this one."

"But this is just a freight elevator in a service—" The unfolding implications tightened Pam's chest and made her pulse pound faster. "Which means it's easily overlooked. Think about it. Emer has managed Ashland Services for what? Three years? It was a year and a half ago that her Amare Rory Fredericks disappeared. Do we really think the *Izgubil* is her first caper?"

"You're right. That's more the kind of thing you build up to." Misha's brows pinched in a fierce scowl. "A secret double car on an unwatched freight elevator in an overlooked service area? That could be a valuable asset for clandestine projects."

Pam's arm had begun to ache, still holding the elevator, but she hesitated to step inside and push any buttons. Didn't want to disturb evidence.

Lean on it with your back, Shady advised. *That won't destroy any evidence, because Probably-Emer never touched that part.*

Thanks. Pam shifted her position. *Oh, yeah. That's better.*

"For pity's sake, her great-grandparents are Founders!" Iruka shook her head. "It's not as if this Family is going to condone the kind of things we suspect she's been doing."

Melynn grimaced. "And yet, they condoned Hideki."

"Maybe they didn't know about Hideki." Iruka's face pinched with perplexity. "Or, if they knew, they didn't want to believe it. I've talked with a *lot* of Families recently who lost Family members on the *Izgubil*. They've been second-guessing themselves and agonizing over 'why didn't we realize?' Could even be an acknowledged vice, but 'we didn't think it had gotten this bad.' Founders' Families are just as prone to that as everyone else."

Ding-ding-ding-ding . . . The elevator set up a repetitive chime that might be melodious and pleasantly resonant, but it also somehow managed to make Pam's nerves crawl. "How long should I hold this door?" Her arm felt better, but doorstop-duty wouldn't win any prizes as a fascinating assignment.

"Just a bit longer, please." Melynn went into a middle-distance HUD-stare. "Yes, I need some techs who can deal with an elevator. We suspect there's a double car." She listened a moment, then focused once more on Pam. "The Fire Department is sending help." Her gaze returned to her HUD. "Ah, thanks. And I need UPOs to secure the elevator at this location."

Backup arrived within five minutes, in the form of three fire-fighters.

I guess firefighters get less friction from the snooty gate than police? Shady cocked her head.

They look pretty smooth to me. Pam gave up her post at the elevator door with a grin. Oh, my. Those firefighters were three very fine young men.

Shady lolled her tongue. *You do like shapely men, don't you? What would Balchu say?*

Pam's grin widened, but she didn't bother glancing away from this excellent front-row view. *If I didn't appreciate them, you both would worry something was wrong.*

Shady wagged her tail. *You have a point. We would.*

"Atrium. Let's regroup." Melynn inclined her head in the direction they'd come.

And not a moment too soon. Shady darted ahead.

Pam sprinted to catch up. The group soon returned to the grand atrium. Melynn lapsed into another HUD-stare, then spoke quietly on her com to what sounded like several different people in rapid succession.

The carillon peal of a different elevator's arrival behind her interrupted the string of calls. Everyone whirled toward it. Burnished brass inlaid doors slid open with a quiet *swoosh*. An extremely elderly couple stepped out into the polished marble hallway with stately care. They held hands to steady each other.

Woah! Is that really them? Pam hadn't expected to feel such a rush of awe. *That's Maeve and Basil! Themselves!* Almost reflexively, she placed her hand on her heart and lowered her head. "Prosper, Founders." The others did the same, except for Shady and Elle. The two dogs observed with heads cocked and ears up.

Do you understand the living Ranan heritage that's standing right here in front of us? Pam cocked an eyebrow at her partner.

I understand they're literally older than the dirt around here. Shady shot her a teasing tongue-loll and wagged her tail high.

Pam scowled at her. *Basil Bellamy Kimbrough and Maeve Kimbrough Bellamy are the last human Founder-couple on Rana of whom both are still alive. I'll have you know that's a big deal around here!*

I'm sorry. Yes, I do remember about the Fifty Founding Families and the Ki-ki-ki-ki Tiktitiki. Shady pulled in her tongue and dipped her head in acknowledgement.

That's more like it. It isn't very often you get to meet a living legend—much less a matched set. Pam forced herself to stop frowning. But seriously! The Fifty Founding Families had committed their entire, massive personal fortunes to help finance the construction of Rana Station almost a century ago. Along with more than a million smaller investors and the persecuted, fugitive Ki-ki-ki-ki Tiktitiki—a population of mutant ozzirikkians banished from their homeworld—they'd been able to establish Rana as a sovereign entity in the Chayko System. Without them, there wouldn't even *be* a Rana Station.

The two elders peered at Pam's group, then smiled.

"Oh, good," Maeve's voice quavered a little, but her bright blue eyes didn't appear to miss much. "We found some."

"Prosper, Officers." Basil offered a smile. "To whom do we have the pleasure of speaking?"

Melynn performed introductions. Pam had a sense of Shady flashing on Charlie's Great-Grandma Loretta.

Their skin has the same fragile, crepey texture. Same kind of thin white hair, too, and there's something about their scent that says "old." Shady eyed them dubiously. *They may be national heroes and living legends, but they're also Emer's great-grandparents. Did you notice how neatly they cut off the hunt by appearing at the moment they did?*

Pam scowled at her. *How duplicitous do they smell?*

Shady laid one ear back, but directed the other forward. Her nose worked the air currents. *No deceit in their scents. Not so far, anyway.*

Melynn called the XK9 pairs forward. Neither Maeve nor Basil seemed dismayed by the approach of two enormous, sapient, wolfish dogs in body armor. Maeve smiled and offered her fist for them to sniff.

Shady sniffed politely. *Gotta admit I can't detect the faintest whiff of an ulterior motive.*

Basil's hand shook slightly as he stroked Elle's neck, but Pam didn't think it was from fear. "So magnificent."

Charming. Shady wagged her tail. *But time is passing.*

"You need to know of a discovery by our head of security," Maeve said in her quavering voice. "Earlier today, our great-granddaughter took a secret elevator—one that is not supposed to exist—to a sub-level that *also* is not supposed to exist." Her wizened face hardened and her eyes acquired a dangerous sparkle. "It seems her father established a system of double elevators and secret exits in this building some time ago. We neither knew about them nor approved their construction."

Both of Shady's ears went up. *Woah. No love lost between her and Hideki. Maybe she did know what kind of man he was.*

Another elevator carillon sounded. A tall, grim-faced man in a plum-colored private security uniform stepped out.

"We recognize that some of you will need to go with Security Chief Garran, in pursuit of Emer." Maeve gestured toward the new arrival. "Other officers will need to gather more information from us. We have asked our Family and staff members to gather in the Crystal Salon, and to place themselves completely at the service of the OPD and the SBI. Please join us there, to question any of us who may be able to help you."

Do they know how their gate greets police officers? Shady shared a look with Pam.

Maybe not?

"Please also accept our deepest apologies," Basil added. "The very last thing we want for our dear Rana Station—our *dream,* our *shining hope*—" His face furrowed with worry and grief. "We cannot allow murderers to run free. Not even if they are our own flesh and blood."

The tall, grim-faced man in the plum-colored uniform strode over to the Founder couple. He offered a deep bow. A closer look made Pam adjust her estimate of his age upward. Fit and muscular he might be, but deep frown-lines carved his chestnut-brown face. His close-cropped hair had gone more white than gray.

I should think he'd bow and scrape. Shady curled her lip to show a flash of a fang.

Maeve turned to pat the man's hand, then returned her focus to Melynn. "Garran, here, will take you to the secret elevator, so that you may resume your search with better focus."

"Iruka, take the XK9 teams," Melynn said. "I'll coordinate things here and call in more interviewers from HQ. Good hunting and keep me posted."

Security Chief Garran led them back to the elevator Shady had found earlier. He nodded to the scenic firefighters and a pair of UPOs who'd apparently showed up after Pam's group left. They nodded back. "I see you've already found it. Let me simplify things." He pulled a remote-control pad from his jacket pocket with a scowl. "It took some—call it intense persuasion—to acquire this. We're holding its former possessor for your colleagues' questions." He squared his shoulders and drew in a sharp breath. "Allow the doors to close. The secret car is underneath this one."

Elle's tongue lolled long and her eyes sparkled. "So, that really was her I smelled. Probably upflow from when the car went down with her in it."

64

Once the doors had closed, Garran punched one of the buttons on the remote. The carillon sounded. The doors opened again, but this was not the same freight elevator car they'd seen earlier. These walls were a darker color and the floor had a different pattern.

"Yes!" Shady poked her nose inside the new elevator car, tail and ears up. "This smells right!"

Pam's heart leaped. *Now, maybe we—*

"Wait!" Iruka cried. "Where are the controls?"

Shady glanced upward. "Oh. Good call. None of the walls has a control panel." She backed away.

"Without the remote, it's a trap." Garran's face had gone stony.

Oh, he is supremely pissed off. Shady eyed him, then shot a sparkling glance Pam's way. *I'm surprised we can't see steam rising from his collar.*

The medium chestnut color of his face definitely had turned an alarming shade of brick red. He stepped into the elevator a bit the way Pam imagined one might step in front of a firing squad.

She couldn't hold back a small wince. *You think he's watching his career flash before his eyes?*

That would be my guess. Shady's tail waved high. Garran would get no sympathy from her.

"Let's see where this goes." Garran's voice sounded like rocks rubbing together. His eyes narrowed to glittering slits.

Pam, Shady, Iruka, Elle, and Misha stepped inside. They adjusted positions until all could fit into the tight space.

Garran punched a button on his remote. The doors closed near-soundlessly. For a giddy instant the car dropped. It stopped a few seconds later. But it took a moment for Pam to feel as if her stomach had unstuck from being squashed up against her heart and lungs and resumed its normal place.

"Oh, yes. That would cause upflow." Elle's tail whacked Pam's leg—and probably several others'—in the close quarters.

The doors slid back to reveal an underground parking facility. The sleek black-and-orange logo for Glide-Ride, one of the dozen or so private transport services that operated in Orange-boro, had been painted on the support columns. Limousines filled nearby slots.

Garran cursed.

Shady uttered a soft growl, but it was so low Pam barely heard it. *If he's a longtime retainer, this could've been done on his watch, and it smells like he never had a clue.* She switched to her vocalizer. "Close the doors. Go to another level."

Garran turned his scowl on her. "What?"

"Wrong level. No scent trail."

"Agreed," Elle said.

Garran gave the area outside the elevator one last, scandalized look, then punched another button on the remote.

Whoops! Did her feet leave the floor briefly?

The elevator car's plummet slowed, then stopped. The second level opened onto a short vestibule. Beyond it loomed a closed vault door big enough for even a man of Garran's height to walk straight in without ducking his head. If it had been open, that is. Which it was not.

Shady growled again. "Not here, either. Move on." Pam received a strong sense of Shady's impatience through the link.

Garran clenched his jaws and punched the next button.

The car dropped. When it stopped all the humans grabbed for the handrails to steady themselves.

"That's the last button." Garran's voice grated through clenched teeth.

The doors slid open.

CHAPTER 9
"OH, CRAP" MOMENTS

Civic Center Medical Station

Rex's HUD dinged. He startled out of a doze—but stopped a gasp before it was too late. His damaged lungs hadn't impaired his ability to smell. He could tell he was still at the Med Station, and Charlie was seated by his bed, without even looking. *I fell asleep?*

Yes. I hope it helped. Charlie's hand stroked him. *Your body is full of tension.* He kept up his slow, steady, soothing caresses.

That actually did feel good. Even in Rex's pissy, tensed-up mood, his muscles relaxed bit by bit.

Ding! The HUD again.

Rex winced. *Ugh. Who's calling me?*

It wasn't a call. It was a directive from Chief Klein: GO TO THE SANDLER CLINIC. THAT'S AN ORDER.

Rex opened one eye to glare at Charlie. *Did you put him up to this?*

Did I put who up to what? Charlie's brows rose. His scent factors held an odd mixture of surprise mixed with sardonic satisfaction.

I just got orders from the Chief to go to the Sandler Clinic.

Did you? Oh, good. He glanced up. "Ari? Chief's orders just came through. Let's pack him up and get moving."

"Finally!" Ari sounded exasperated. Their scent factors seconded that emotion.

Rex laid back his ears and showed his teeth. But with the oxygen cone over his nose, how much of his snarl could they see? *This is a conspiracy.*

Charlie grinned and ruffled the fur on his shoulder, then focused across him toward Ari. "How can I help?"

❖ ❖ ❖ ❖ ❖ ❖ ❖ ❖

The Vinebrook

Shady took one whiff and burst from the unauthorized elevator. *Yes!* The Almost-Certainly-Emer scent lay thick and fresh at her feet. The sweaty fear in the woman's personal bouquet had eased some, but harsh, sharp urgency and a musky smell of grim purpose had increased.

Tails high and noses down, she and Elle followed their subject's trail into a small, dimly lit half-circle room with three doors set into its walls. By now the odor-bearing skin cells had settled to the floor, but the path stood out to them as clearly as it would have for the humans if she'd spilled a paint trail. It led to one of the doors.

No surprise, the door was locked.

Garran's scent spiked with dangerous heat. He aimed a hard side-kick against a spot just below the latch.

Boom! The door bent but didn't give way.

Garran growled something inarticulate. Kicked it again, harder.

Both door and frame warped, but the latch still didn't give.

"*UuuunnGAH!*" Garran kicked it a third time. It banged open, smashed against a surface, then rebounded to bang on the

68

bent frame and drift ajar. Garran hammered it open again with one blow of his fist, then leaned against it, panting.

I think he needed that, Pam said through the link.

He does smell a bit less oppressed. Shady peered past him into a long corridor. It sloped slightly downward into darkness.

Garran straightened. He yanked his jacket back into place with a tug on its hem, drew in one more deep breath and blew it out. Then he stepped back.

Shady darted past him, focused on the scent. *Maybe we'll catch her after all.* Banks of lights flicked on for a distance of about five meters.

"Well, that makes it easier to see." Pam spoke aloud.

They neared the end of the lights. The next length snapped on. Shady led her little group forward. A third bank of lights flashed on, but Shady stopped. Her hackles prickled under her armor. *Oh, this is not good.* She stared into the darkness beyond this new section. Behind her little group, the section nearest the door flicked off.

From what Shady sensed through the link, Pam wasn't exactly surprised. *What do you think?*

I have a feeling I know where we're headed.

Yeah. A pit-of-the stomach kinda feeling, right? I think so, too. She felt Pam's frown but kept her focus on what lay ahead.

The stoutly braced, packed-regolith walls of the corridor stretched on ahead for many more meters. A long, straight, narrow path into pitch-darkness. Probably-Emer definitely had come this way, but a gut-deep wariness warned Shady they were headed into danger. She stopped. "Where are we?"

"What?" Iruka sounded impatient. But then, she couldn't see much from her position behind Misha. "We're in a tunnel you just found. What do you mean, 'where are we?'"

"How deep are we?" Shady had a sense they were pretty far down. The gravity seemed heavier here.

"That's hard to say." Iruka turned to Garran, who brought up the rear. "Do you have any idea?"

"My altimeter's not working." The security chief's voice grated harsh with anger. "Neither is my com. But I know Glide-Ride's garages are located from Sub-Four through -Six. Our first stop today looked like Six. I know it was *below* our lowest authorized level, which is Four. The other two stops are farther down, so I'd guess we're at about Sub-Level Nine here."

Iruka's frown deepened. "What are you thinking, Shady?"

Shady's hackles itched. "I am thinking we want a STAT element."

"I agree with her." Pam scowled. "I think we're headed for the Five-Ten."

The Five-Ten had been part of their first patrol assignment together, back when the OPD didn't have a clue how to optimize their XK9s' capabilities. It was the lowest sub-level in the Fifth Precinct: Level Ten, a literal underworld. Officially a storage area where no one lived, it actually had become a rather active off-the-books community, peopled by unregistered castoffs, runaways, and others smuggled onto the Station undetected. Not always fully criminal, but most definitely dangerous. Even for OPD officers.

Although they could've gotten a signal from any of the Enclaves in the Five-Ten itself, this tunnel was a dead zone. They had to retreat to the half-circle room before they could pick up the Station-net again. Garran scowled at his altimeter. "Crap, I was right. This is equivalent to Sub-Nine."

"It's a good thing you're already on good terms with the STAT Team," LSA Kramer—um, Shawnee said, once they'd been able to successfully place the call. "Wait where you are for further instructions."

It is nice, not having to explain the need for STAT. Shady let her tongue hang long. She'd feel a lot better going into the Five-Ten with a three-person element from Special Tools and Techniques as backup. Now the humans' insistence on body armor for dogs and humans alike seemed prescient.

The next voice on the com was Elaine's, a few moments later.

"Captain Hariri's sending an element from Red Team. Connect with them in the Glide-Ride garage on Level Six."

Back on Level Six, Iruka, Misha, and Pam rested on a bench by the driveway. Security Chief Garran stood nearby, arms crossed. He glared into the garage.

Shady's ears lifted. *What's that quiet, gritty sound?*

Sound? Pam blinked at her.

Oh. Shady lolled her tongue. *It's Garran's teeth grinding.* She contemplated the idle period that stretched until the STAT Team's arrival. "I guess it would not hurt to sniff around while we wait," she said through her vocalizer. *And where better to start than the pavement under my feet?*

"My thoughts exactly." Elle sniffed across the small, paved area to her left.

Shady explored to the wall on her right then quartered back toward the center. She and Elle moved outward from the doorway, seeking whatever scents they could find.

"Oh!" Elle stopped, her tail straight up. "Shady, please tell me I am not imagining things."

Shady arrived in two strides. "What have you found?"

"At the edge of this curb, down in the crack. What do you smell?"

Shady positioned her nose, then opened her mouth slightly. *I doubt I would have found this on my own, but she's right. The man we know as "Sir" from Kieran's Mystery Shed walked through here.* They'd associated this man's scent with the *Izgubil* explosives. *His trace here is faint, almost too old. But not quite.*

"Good work, Elle!" Pam's pleased approval surged through the link.

"Think I can pull a sample?" Misha already had the first glove half-on.

Elle laid her ears back. "It will not be a very good one. Perhaps with a drop of enhancer?"

Misha retrieved a small bottle from her panniers. "Same time period as the ones you found at the shed?"

"That is my guess. There is no explosive residue here that I could detect. But this sample is really crappy. Definitely the same man. That is about all I can say." Elle lifted her head to gaze toward the door they'd recently exited. She growled. "If he crossed the curb, do you think he went into or came out of the building?"

"Why else be here?" Shady sampled the scents between curb and doorway. *Nothing, nothing, nothing, nothing.* Of course, it was a really old scent. She kept sniffing. *Nothing, nothing, nothing . . . Wait. Was this—?* "Oh. Yes. Here is another little whiff of him." A scent-laced thread had caught on a nick in the door frame.

Pam captured it with tweezers, applied a spritz of enhancer, then bagged it. "Let's hope that gives it a chance to intensify."

Garran watched them, frowning. "A person of interest to you came into or left the building? Through this entrance?"

Iruka nodded. "Seems like he was here, whichever way he was headed. A man we really want to find. Would've been about eight weeks ago."

"There's *supposed* to be a log kept of all guests." Garran scowled downward, apparently trying to gather his thoughts. "We run vid-surveillance in public areas, but Miss Emer knows that. If she let him in and didn't want him seen . . . still, we should check it."

Hunt-joy welled up in Iruka's scent. "Even the most careful slip up sometimes. I'd certainly like to see what we can find."

"Sure. When we get back to my—" Garran stopped. His mouth sagged open with dawning horror. "Shit. About *eight weeks* ago?"

"Yes." Iruka stared at him. "What do you remember?"

"Hell, I think I *met* him. Emer brought a friend up to the Security office, start of November . . . just about eight weeks ago."

Shady's optics and audio pickups had been on since they'd entered the building. Now she made double-sure she pointed them at Garran.

Iruka's mouth fell open. "You *met* him?"

Garran ran a hand through his hair. "I . . . yeah, probably. I . . . Oh, fuck!"

"No, it's *good* that you met him. What do you remember?"

The tall security chief took several anguished paces away, then swung around to face them, emitting some of the strongest smoky, musky horror odor Shady'd ever smelled in a human. "Slender. A little taller than she is. Medium skin, straight dark brown hair, real dark eyes. She called him . . . um, Zan. That's it. Zan. His full name—well, almost certainly a false name, I guess —but it should be in the log."

He shook his head, face pinched. "She was showing off some of the new security features we'd just installed. He seemed interested. In a *professional* way, if you know what I mean. Asked intelligent, informed questions. Really seemed to know his security systems." His face crumpled with anguish. His scent factors collapsed into deep tones of humiliation and despair. "Stupid, *idiot* me! I figured he was in the business!"

Shady laid her ears back. *Oh, I'm pretty sure Garran got that part right. Just not the part about which side of the law this fellow's on.*

"Aw, *dammit!*" Garran groaned.

CHAPTER 10
QUESTIONS ON QUESTIONS

Feliz Tower

Hildie met Capt. Rodrigo at the Feliz Tower gate, surprised to see she'd worn her gold-braided, dark green uniform to this meeting. The sight of a solemn, uniformed officer on her doorstep made the still-damp hairs on the back of her neck stand up.

So, it's an official visit, even though no one's hurt or dead? She didn't know the woman well, because their paths rarely crossed. She knew all the front-line Monteverde crew, of course. But Rodrigo, like Capt. LaRochelle, almost never left her Borough's main Emergency Rescue Team base to go out on missions. *What could she want?*

"Thank you for seeing me." Rodrigo hesitated by the lines of shoes and house scuffs along either side of the entrance tunnel. She glanced at Hildie, who'd quickly showered and changed into a clean kurta, churidar, and her own pair of house-scuffs. Then she wordlessly bent to remove her shoes and slide into a pair of scuffs. She turned to Hildie and offered a polite bow. "Namaste."

Hildie smiled, bowed back. "Namaste. Please come in and be

welcome." She led the Captain to a table in the courtyard that was shaded by the nearer of two vine-covered pergolas. "May I offer refreshments?"

"Oh, I'm—" Rodrigo hesitated. From the expression on her face she'd been about to refuse, but now her brow puckered with worry. Concerned she might offend?

Hildie waited, curious how she'd decide. The refreshment offer had come as naturally as breathing, a habitual polite gesture. She hadn't meant to confront her guest with a hard decision.

"Um, sure. If it's no trouble?" Rodrigo bit her lip.

Hildie smiled. "We always keep a few things on hand for guests. I'll be right back." A trip to the fridge yielded options, but also allowed time to fret. *Why is she here? What does she want? Does she think I witnessed something?* Hildie filled a tray and hurried back to the courtyard.

Rodrigo studied the offering, then put one little brown kala jamun, and one diamond-shaped kucho nimki, on her plate. She took a sip of her drink and her eyes widened. "Oh, that's delicious!"

"Mango nectar. It's a favorite of mine. Glad you like it." *Can we get to the point, please?* Hildie munched a nimki—a dangerous move. After her flirtation with heat exhaustion in the paddies, the salty flavor with its smoky hint of black cumin tasted especially good. She crunched through three more before she could stop herself, then folded her hands in her lap and tried not to glance at them.

Both the jamun and the nimki disappeared from Rodrigo's plate. She took another swallow of mango nectar, then dabbed her lips with her napkin. "I'm . . . I must confess, I thought this would be easier to ask." She frowned, then smoothed her expression into neutrality. "Is there any chance you're . . . looking for a job?"

Hildie blinked at her. "I haven't received a verdict yet, but the Review Board is required to decide within threee months."

Although I might go insane if it takes three months to decide whether I'm banished from the ERT or not. She focused on Rodrigo's face. "What kind of job?"

The Captain's dark brown eyes met hers with a steady gaze. "I've heard a lot of good things about you, and your record is outstanding. A decade's experience as a micrograv paramedic—do you realize how rare that is? What's more, I think you're management material. I'm here because I've got a lieutenant's position that's opened up. It's on the night watch, but you'd have regular eight-hours, none of that twelve-hour nonsense."

She frowned. "That might work for dirtsiders, which is where LaRochelle got his start. But it's too damned long in micrograv. Too hard to keep your edge!"

"I've proved that often enough to scare myself from time to time." Hildie gave her a nod. *No more twelve-hours?* She couldn't deny that held a lot of appeal. So did a lieutenant's pay, especially with the differential for the strange schedule. *But full-time on the night watch? And more time spent on reports and meetings, but less hands-on work with patients? Do I really want that?*

"Please don't feel I'm asking for a decision right now. I expect you'll want to see what the Review Board decides, and I don't know if any other Borough has approached you yet, although that wouldn't surprise me. But when you think of it, there'd be little change in your commute."

That was true. All four of Wheel Two Boroughs' ERT bases had been built right next to each other. They formed a complete ring around the cylindrical Hub.

"You already know many of us, especially on the front line," Rodrigo continued. "My crews have a lot of respect for you. I think you'd find a warm welcome, and you'd have—I promise—a Captain who appreciates your value."

A Captain who appreciates me? Her throat tightened and tears threatened. *Crap.* She swallowed hard. "It's definitely an interesting offer."

Rodrigo nodded, stood. 'Excellent. All I ask is that you consider it. And—whatever you decide—good luck, Sergeant."

"Thanks." There were a lot of drawbacks, but the offer held more appeal than she wanted to admit.

Her purpose accomplished, Captain Rodrigo didn't linger.

Hildie stared after her. *Away! She can take me away from all the bad parts. The grinding twelve-hours, the always-uncertain schedule, the continual demands, the constant cloud of disapproval— I could be done with all of that!*

She pressed her fist to her mouth and bowed her head. Her eyes flooded, then overflowed in bitter streams. *I've been minimizing the hell out of it, haven't I? How can I go back, with LaRock there? How can I even think about it?* She shivered.

She turned to go into the tunnel, then stopped. Walked back to the still-open gate and the looping white path that led down the Tower's approach. *But—I love my job. I've loved it for almost a decade. It's always felt so 'right.' So true and real.* She'd taken great joy in the sense that this was where she wanted to be, the work she wanted to do. That certainty had become a central truth in her life. When everything else got confusing, that was the one sure thing that didn't change, the one thing she could count on.

Until now.

How can I feel this way? She shook her head. *But again, how can I not? My job has just purely sucked for months.* She ran her hand over her face.

Could I really do that? Work for Monteverde, not Orangeboro? She stared out across the wide, terraced valley without seeing it. *Work with a whole new crew? On a weird-ass schedule that puts me out of sync with . . . well, everybody?* She bit her lip. *Get real. That mostly means out-of-sync with Charlie. Everyone else is used to not knowing when I'll be called next.*

The XK9 Special Investigations Unit worked the day watch. *We've just gotten back together. Would this ruin it?*

After a while she wandered back into the courtyard. Back to the table under the pergola with its abandoned chairs and plates, its uneaten snacks, and Rodrigo's half-finished glass. *Other Boroughs might also contact me?* That thought made her head hurt, but it also straightened her spine and lifted her chin. *Maybe Theresa was right.*

Her friend's fierce expression that night rose in her memory. LaRock had screamed at her that she was fired and to get off his deck. She'd left in a haze of worry—about Charlie, about Rex, and about her job. It was Theresa who'd pulled her back from the abyss later that night. She'd fed her and calmed her down.

Rodrigo's words, "A decade's experience as a micrograv paramedic—do you realize how rare that is?" echoed things Theresa had said that night.

Hildie grimaced. *Theresa's usually right. She's brilliant, and she sees things I sometimes miss. But where does that logic chain lead me?* She sat down with a thump, demolished the rest of the jamuns, then polished off the nimkis with barely a thought. Too busy trying *not* to reach the obvious conclusion: *If Theresa's so brilliant and wise, maybe I should genuinely consider the other thing she said.*

Hildie hadn't told anyone about that, not even Charlie.

She drained her glass, then at last allowed herself to ask. *What if she's right? Should I—could I—do I dare—try again for med school?*

❖ ❖ ❖ ❖ ❖ ❖ ❖ ❖

The Vinebrook

"Damn, damn, damn."

Pam stared at Vinebrook Security Chief Garran. "What's wrong?"

"Miss Emer acted so *proud*. Like she couldn't wait to show him off!"

"What?" Iruka stared at him, fists clenched. "Show Zan off?"

Garran scrubbed his face with both hands then looked up with a haunted expression. "Aw, hell. The guy I'm thinking about? I was pleased for her. First time I'd seen her act so happy with a man since Rory Fredricks disappeared."

"Wait. So you knew Rory Fredericks, and you're sure this Zan guy wasn't him?" Iruka quirked a brow at him in the glare of the Glide-Ride garage's overhead lights.

Pam drew in a quiet breath. She could guess the next part. *Aw, crap.*

"Oh, he's definitely not Rory." Garran's mouth made a wry twist. "Rory was tall, pale, kinda pudgy, brown hair, freckles. Not exactly . . ." He hunched his shoulders. "Rory . . . well, he wasn't a real good match for her."

"I worked that case." Iruka nodded. "They did seem an unusual pair."

Dammit! Well, it's progress to know more. But Zan is definitely not Rory Fredericks? Rats!

Shady swiveled an ear in her direction. *How much did you have on 'Sir' being Rory?*

Ten novi. Pam grimaced. *I was so sure!* This mystery man, "Zan," was the main guy whose scent had been all over the explosives in Kieran O'Boyle's secret shed—the explosives later used to destroy the *Izgubil*. He was an even bigger suspect than Emer.

"Don't get me wrong." Garran shook his head. "Rory was smart and all, but he just wasn't in Miss Emer's league." The big man shook his head. "All the guy knew was chemistry and physics and blowing things up. He'd talk your leg off about the damnedest shit, but half the time I don't think he was speaking Standard, at all."

"No, he was speaking 'technology.'" Elle's mate Tuxedo was the Pack's most enthusiastic explosives wonk. He'd been known to lapse into "not Standard" tech-speak, himself.

"So, then, tell me about Zan." Iruka offered Garran an encouraging smile. "How was he different? This is valuable information."

Garran's expression turned rueful. "I remember I really *liked* him. He and Miss Emer seemed so sweet on each other. I thought they were cute. Real well-matched. Some judge of character I turned out to be!"

I'll say, well matched. Just the sweetest little pair of mass-murdering lovebirds you could imagine. Shady growled.

"Well matched?" Iruka's brows went up. "Like maybe they're from the same kind of social background?"

Garran nodded, shoulders slumped. "If he wasn't born to it, he's learned real well somewhere. Articulate, confident. Knows what spoon to use, what to wear for dinner versus tea, all of that."

Not born in a barn, then, I guess. Shady showed a flash of teeth.

No, probably not. Pam released a soft sigh. *I wouldn't know any of those things.*

"This is all very helpful," Iruka focused on Garran with evident rapt interest. "Did he or Emer mention where he came from?"

"No." Garran frowned. "He speaks like a cultured man, but there's something about the way he says his 'w's and 'th's that's kinda different."

Shady's head and ears came up. "Mahusayan, perhaps?"

Garran blinked at her. "Well . . . maybe, yeah. Could be. But wherever he's from, he's at least as smooth as Hideki was, back when he first turned up to court Miss Sorcha." He hesitated. "Actually, this Zan fellow reminded me a lot of Hideki when he was that age."

Pam exchanged a sour glance with Shady. *Oh, that can't be good.*

CHAPTER 11
TUNNEL RUN

A Tunnel Under The Vinebrook

S hady's spirit lifted. She and Elle wagged their tails at the first whiff of the Red Team trio. This was the STAT element who'd helped Rex arrest Dr. Ordovich a few weeks ago. They and the rest of the STAT Team also had joined the Pack in the Five-Ten more recently to round up some of Kieran O'Boyle's explosives-installation crew.

Now Sgt. Valda Aylward, accompanied by Kwan Chukwu and Marceline Koening, decked out in full tactical gear, tramped across the Glide-Ride garage to join them. They'd brought SA Frankie Freas with them.

Pam grinned. *In just his normal SBI garb, Frankie seems seriously underdressed for the occasion.*

Shady lolled her tongue.

Iruka introduced everyone, then turned to Garran. "Special Agent Freas is your ride to HQ."

The big man gave her an apprehensive stare. "Am I under arrest?"

"No, but we have a lot more questions."

He nodded, shoulders stooped.

81

"We'll need the log and surveillance vids you mentioned, too. You and SA Freas should secure them before you go."

Freas and Garran took Shady's group to the half-circle room, then rode the elevator up.

The trio from STAT Red had Master Mix portions for the XK9s, plus ration bars for the humans. Pam and Misha retrieved their collapsible food and water bowls from their panniers.

Shady and Elle snapped up their food eagerly, but Iruka eyed her ration bar with a notable lack of enthusiasm. "Oh, yum. My favorite."

Sgt. Aylward shook her head. "Bad idea to run an operation on an empty stomach—you'll need the energy."

"Do you prefer peanut butter?" Marcy asked. "I'll trade."

"Thanks. I like those marginally better."

Marcy handed it over with a grin, then bent to give Shady and Elle ambidextrous ear-scratches. Pam, Iruka, and Misha worried their way through the tough, chewy bars for several minutes.

"Ready for another hunt?" Kwan asked Shady.

"We have already been on this hunt for some time. Welcome aboard."

"Lead on, then, girlfriend." He patted her shoulder. "Let's finish this."

Shady again took point. On a hunt, XK9s always took the lead. As Acting Pack Leader Shady's role included calling tactical moves, although Iruka made the final decisions. Elle followed Shady, trailed by the humans.

Lights in five-meter sections once again flashed on as they progressed, then shut off when the last in line passed their motion triggers. The all-OPD group settled into an easy, distance-eating jog, but the packed-regolith walls stretched ahead into darkness for a long time.

Shady half-closed her eyes, focused on the scent. In this part of the long corridor-tunnel, Probably-Emer had stopped running. Here, she'd moved forward with sure, purposeful strides. The anger in her residual scent grew stronger by the meter, and her fear diminished. *Why is she angry?*

Because she's been made—and forced to run. Pam's fierce hunt-joy put a wag in Shady's tail.

Hunt-joy swelled within her. *There could be other factors, too. But why the relative fearlessness now? Does she believe no one would follow her here?*

How likely is it that pursuers without XK9 noses could have found that hidden elevator, much less this tunnel? By the time she made it this far, she must think she'd left any pursuit stymied and far behind.

True. Shady enjoyed a moment of pride in her and Elle's accomplishments, but that didn't stop her push forward. *For pity's sake, how much farther?*

Pam's pace faltered for a couple of strides. *I just realized the vents in the ceiling have cobwebs on them. This structure seems well made and meant to last. But how old is it?*

Didn't Maeve say Hideki had this built? That means Hideki did business in the Five-Ten, maybe for years. And if UPO Anthony is right about who rules the Five-Ten, that pretty much has to mean he was coordinating in some way with the Whisper Syndicate.

It also could explain how he ended up on the Izgubil, if he worked with them.

Shady snorted, but never slowed her pace. *Consider how far into the rest of Alliance Space his investments reached. If he was dealing under the table he'd need an underworld outlet. That could mean Turlach O'Boyle and Ostra Import-Export. Maybe that's how Emer met Kieran.*

Pam gave a soft chuckle. *That's a lot of "maybes," but Emer and Kieran seem to live in such different worlds. It might just answer how they found each other.*

What are the odds that the fathers introduced the younger generation to each other, in that case? Shady's fierce amusement spurred her forward. *That would be something. They sealed their own fates.*

Hideki's fate is sealed, anyway. Pam kept her pace even despite the slight irregularities underfoot.

Lynne and Henry say it's all over the Five-Ten that Whisper's soured on Turlach. If he's been their man all these years it would have to be over something big. Veteran Five-Ten UPOs Lynn Anthony and her partner Henry Sevencrows had recently reported that the elder O'Boyle had suffered a bad beating not long after Kieran disappeared. *Since no one messes with Turlach because Whisper supposedly has his back, who else would dare?*

But who knows how accurate the rumor mill in the Five-Ten is? Through the link Pam's impatience with the spotty intel crackled with irritation. *I mean, the rumors all say Kieran's dead, but Rex found his living scent on our hunt.*

Shady's ears went up. *Ah. At last!* A door took shape in the gloom beyond their current lighted corridor section.

Locked, like the one they'd found earlier.

Tall, burly Kwan Chukwu stepped up while the rest of the group caught their breath. "I'll handle this."

Shady stayed well back to give him room for a kick, but he bent to pull an implement from his belt-pouch. The door swung open near-silently. "There you go." He stepped back.

Well, the unit does have "Special Tools" right there in the name. She lolled her tongue and met Pam's laughing eyes.

The shadows grew distinctly lighter up ahead. The murmur of movement and whiffs of fried food came through more strongly with every step. The final section did not light up. *A measure to keep it from being discovered by Five-Tenners?*

Shady stepped forward. A rough cloth drape that smelled of Almost-Certainly-Emer and a woven bamboo panel blocked the terminal opening. She eased past the drape and placed her nose by the edge of the panel.

What's out there? Pam asked.

She sorted through the mélange. *Rats. Dust. Mildew. There's got to be a composter nearby, because I also smell garbage.*

Yeah, that's the Five-Ten all right.

Good thing HUD-beeps can't be heard outside of the recipient's skull. Shady texted news of their Five-Ten arrival to the others, then studied the smells that drifted past her nose.

No presence nearby. No respiration or heartbeats, except for the ones in her group. She pushed her nose past the panel, centimeter by centimeter.

Behind her, the team stood still and silent.

"I love working with competent pros," she texted to her group. "I've practiced with Transmondian teams who couldn't be this quiet if their lives depended on it."

Silent pleasure came back to her through the link from Pam. *Where have we arrived? Can you tell?*

Shady poked her whole head out. Compost bins stood at ragged intervals on both sides of a narrow, regolith-gravel passageway. Tall storage units with solid, windowless walls rose to the shadowed, cobwebby ceiling. Lights shone from a couple of shorter residence buildings. *Congratulations. We've found an alley.*

I'm shocked. Shocked, I tell you.

I know. Right? As far as Shady could tell, the Five-Ten was almost all alleys. Even what passed for streets here were narrow two-lanes at their biggest, except for an occasional plaza. No whiff of a bogey—or, really, of anybody—on the downdraft.

This place seemed quiet and isolated, but *seeming* and *being* were often deceptive in the Five-Ten. She stepped clear of the bamboo panel and in her head a countdown began. *How long till we're intercepted by a Whisper-affiliated goon squad?*

Give it no more than twenty minutes, Pam answered.

Elle emerged into the alley behind her, then Pam and Misha.

Murky light had settled over the Enclave. Shady sampled the air currents, hackles prickling. "I'm pretty sure this isn't Toro Enclave," she texted to the group. Toro was the one she knew best, of the six enclaves.

Argent. Or maybe Twardy. Shady sensed Pam's frown through the link without needing to glance back at her. *If we're where I think, Toro is left from here, the full width of this enclave away.*

The rest of the team emerged one by one, with only the smallest swishes of fabric or grate of footsteps on gravel. Nice work, especially in tactical boots. They trailed her.

"Probably-Emer went down the alley to our right," Shady texted the group, then followed the scent trail.

I think you can ditch the "probably," Pam said through the link. *Who else would it be?*

Ninety-nine-point nine percent likelihood is probability, not certainty. You know what they say about getting ahead of the evidence.

Smartass.

Ha. Shady lowered her nose to the scent layer. Emer had gone the length of the alley then squeezed down a passageway between storage buildings that was so narrow Shady's panniers scraped on both sides. From there she'd climbed a fire escape.

Shady jumped to its lower rungs and pulled herself the rest of the way up with a helpful push from Pam. The structure rattled under her weight, then made soft clangs and pings as she followed Emer's trail along it. Her hackles prickled with a sense of someone watching, but no one in the neighborhood raised an audible alarm. The team walked below. Elle ranged ahead.

Shady stayed on Emer's track. It left the fire escape, led along a balcony to . . . Shady jumped to an adjoining flat roof. *Yes! Here it is.* She followed Emer's scent to the roof's edge and peeked over.

All clear in her landing zone—but that gravel didn't give much. She straightened, shook, then cast about until she reacquired Emer's track on the porch steps.

A meter or so away, her Packmate Elle's purposeful movements telegraphed that she also had acquired a scent. Elle stopped, tail up. "This is interesting," she texted to the group. "I have Kieran O'Boyle! He is very much *not* dead. He met Emer here about an hour ago."

What? Kieran? But now Shady smelled him, too.

Wow! Pam's excitement pulsed through the link to match

Shady's own and filled the air with the sharp, invigorating smell of excitement.

"Take the lead," Shady texted back to Elle. They followed, trailing Emer Bellamy and now also Kieran O'Boyle. Fear, sweat, stress, and illness permeated O'Boyle's scent. *Did Kieran have the same feeling of being watched that I have?*

Maybe, Pam said. *If he's smart, he'll be worried.*

Their two subjects' spoor lay fresh and clear along the way, not quite hot but very recent. *Maybe we'll capture both!*

What a great find that would be. Hunt-joy surged from Pam's end of the link.

The trail led them partway down their current alley, then into a passage so narrow Shady feared her panniers really wouldn't fit this time. She dragged them through, but it took effort and likely left scrapes on both sides. Tall, burly Kwan in his tactical gear had even more of a struggle. From the amused annoyance in his squadmates' scents when they had to push him through one extra-tight spot, he'd endure some ribbing once it was safe to talk.

At the end of the approximately two-meter-long squeeze-through, Elle stopped. Her tail went straight up. "Oh! Hello."

CHAPTER 12
THE BLUE BUILDING

The Five-Ten, Twardy Enclave

D*on't know who Elle's talking to,* Shady told Pam through the link. *I can't catch a scent.* Up ahead in this narrow little Five-Ten alley, her Packmate had encountered someone. Now the two XK9s, their partners, Iruka, and their STAT element companions must halt. The air currents—such as they were in this tight space—told Shady nothing. Her back crawled under the gaze of imagined watchers.

Elle opened her audio and optics to the rest of the squad. Three women had pressed themselves against the far wall of a small open space. They clutched baskets of half-peeled fruits and vegetables, and they appeared terrified.

"It cannot be a dog. So huge," one woman whispered to her companions in Oroplanian Urdu.

"Did it speak Standard?" A second woman spoke the same language as the first. It wasn't exactly the dialect Shady spoke, but she had no trouble understanding them.

"Anybody else here speak Oroplanian Urdu?" Shady texted to the rest of the squad. "If not, I can talk to them."

Oroplanian Urdu? Again? Pam asked through the link. *Can this be a coincidence?* It was the second time on this case that they'd encountered this language variant, unusual on Rana Station.

"Give Shady a chance to talk with them," Iruka's voice on the com whispered.

"Elle, back up out of sight," Shady texted. "We do not wish to frighten them."

Everyone in their group retreated a few steps.

"Did it run away?" the first woman asked. "Where did it go?"

"Are you sure it was not a dog in the shadows that just seemed big?" the third asked. "Maybe the voice was a trick of the echoes here."

"No. It was huge, huge! And I swear it was a dog!"

"Now, Elle, repeat after me. Assalam-o-alaikum." Shady used her vocalizer so her Packmate could hear the pronunciation and correctly say "hello."

The women gasped, but still did not flee.

With Shady's coaching, Elle stumbled through more phrases. "Do not be afraid. Your eyes did not play a trick. I am a very big dog, but not a mean dog. My friends and I mean you no harm."

"Dogs don't talk," the first woman answered. "Who are you?"

"What did she say?" Elle asked. "Shady, this isn't working. What should I do?"

"Let me answer." Shady cranked up her vocalizer, despite worries about calling attention to her small group. "My name is Shady Jacob-Belle. I do not wish to alarm you, but you should know that I also am a very large dog. I am a police XK9, like my friend you saw a moment ago."

"I heard about how the police have these huge new dogs," one woman said. "Abdual was telling me. They are very smart, he says. Smart as people."

"Please convey our thanks to Abdual. We hope more and more Ranans will understand that we are as smart as people.

May we come out of this . . ." *What's the right word?* "This little path? It is too narrow. Not comfortable."

"Come slowly."

"You can go forward now, Elle." Shady nudged her Pack-mate's armored haunches. "Do not show your teeth or make eye contact. I need to get up there."

Elle pulled herself out of the opening. The women gasped.

Shady pushed past Elle, urgent to *move.* But these women might know something important. "Assalam-o-alaikum. I am Shady. This is Elle."

The women drew in sharp breaths and shrank back. They stared at her, clutching their baskets and each other, but curiosity battled with fear in their scents.

"Can we go now? What's taking so long?" Sgt. Aylward stood with the other humans farther back down the passage.

"She's establishing trust," Pam replied in a soft voice. "If we don't frighten them, perhaps they'll share information."

"How many others are with you?" the tallest of the three women asked Shady.

"Six humans are with us." Shady kept her ears up, though her feet itched to move. "We are all police officers. We are searching for a blonde woman about your height. She came through here not long ago, guided by a man who has not recently bathed."

"Oh." The tall woman made a derisive noise in her throat. "You seek the Arrogant One, and also the one who fancied himself a shrewd dealer and now is on the run, yes?"

"You know them."

"They do not bother to know us." She frowned, then pointed with her left hand toward another passageway. "They are in their hiding place over there, that they think is so secret. Like rats in a burrow. Under the dirty blue building across the next alley."

"Under the building?"

"Yes. They think we do not see them. They made a door in

the side alley. In the ground. Very sneaky, yes?" She kicked a small puff of dust in the same direction she'd pointed. "Be careful. They have EStees."

Shady dipped her head low, in the women's direction. "Shukriya. Thank you. We honor your gift of knowledge." She turned in the direction the woman had pointed, then texted to the rest of her group. "She says Kieran and Emer are armed with EStees. They're hiding in a secret underground room, accessible through a trapdoor across the next alley. Please show them respect when you come through their space."

Elle turned and followed her. Pam emerged next. She nodded to the women then scrambled to catch up with the XK9s. *Great. A basement. That's no better than an attic.* Both were dangerous places to corner an armed suspect.

"Good job, Shady." Iruka spoke quietly on the com. Officer after officer emerged from the narrow passage, nodded or touched their helmet, then turned down the new path. Thank goodness, this one was wider than that last narrow squeeze-through.

The tall woman had steered them true. Emer and Kieran's trail led to the next alley, across it, and then into another side-passage next to a dingy blue-gray building. About halfway down its side wall, Shady found the trapdoor. Its surface had been made to appear like the rest of the dusty ground, but it was clear to smell that Emer and Kieran had entered here. If a person's nose was as dull as a human's, the entrance would not have been easy to spot.

She curbed her urge to start digging. "How should we get them out?"

"Secure the perimeter." Sgt. Aylward used a firm but quiet tone. "Shady, Elle, can you find any other trapdoors? There's probably a back way out."

Elle and Shady each took one side and sniffed along the base of the building. They found several vents, nothing more. Shady's feet itched to run. *It's only a matter of time till we're noticed.*

We probably already have been, Pam answered. *Whisper enforcers might arrive any moment.*

Kwan followed Elle, while Marcy trailed Shady around the outside of the blue building. The STAT officers placed pickup mics at each vent. Maybe Kieran and Emer would say incriminating things, or let something slip that could aid in their extraction. The STAT people also sent in tiny cameras that buzzed so softly it was hard even for Shady to hear them. These were much tinier than the ones the Transmondians had sent into Corona Tower a few weeks ago.

"Found another trapdoor," Elle reported. "Just to leeward, by the base of a storage building. It has not recently been used."

"On it." Sgt. Aylward moved into position to cover it.

An OPD patrol unit pulled up at the mouth of the alley. At first Shady thought it might be their friends Lynne Anthony and Henry Sevencrows, but this was another pair. They checked in with Iruka's group, promised to swing by regularly, and also vowed to speed back ASAP if things went bad.

"Getting anything?" Iruka asked Marcy.

Shady could hear a muffled female voice. It sounded angry. She moved closer to the vent.

"—stink like days and days of built-up shit! You're disgusting. When was the last time you took a bath?"

"*You* try hiding out from Whisper and the OPD for two fucking months in a basement with no plumbing, and see how good *you* smell!" a man yelled back.

Shady lolled her tongue and texted a transcript of this exchange to the others. "He has a point," she added.

Marcy gave her an exasperated grimace. "Why did we just drop mics, if you can hear them that well?" she whispered.

Shady flicked her ears and texted her reply. "We did not know I would be able to hear them so well."

Probably-Kieran was yelling again. Shady bent closer. "—didn't know till an hour ago that Your Ladyship was going to blow her cover and have to run! Excuse me if I risked my life getting you under cover, instead of taking a lavender milk bath!"

Shady texted this transcript, too. She noticed Elle did the same, confirming hers. *Excellent.*

"Fuck you, Kieran. It wasn't that dangerous—and no one saw us. Calm down."

Well, there's your ID confirmation that the man is Kieran, Pam said through the link.

"You don't *know* that no one saw us. You don't know anything! My God! Do you realize what Whisper will do to us?"

"Whisper won't fucking touch us. My Zannie will come and save us. I sent him the code, and he has a plan."

"Wake up, Buttercup! Your precious 'Zannie' is on the far side of the Asteroid Belt by now, if he knows what's good for him—and even that won't be far enough if Whisper ever figures out who screwed them over!"

"No! He promised! And he loves me. He'd never abandon me!"

"He loves your money, you pathetic whore. Now that he's gotten his revenge, you'll find that's all he really loves."

Sgt. Aylward stood like a shadow by the trap door. She motioned to Marcy. "Cover the other exit," she instructed in a quiet voice. "Send Iruka here."

Marcy wasted no time and made almost no sound.

"It's a bad idea to hang out here too long." Aylward said when Iruka had drawn close enough to hear her. "This neighborhood isn't real sweet on the OPD."

Iruka nodded but frowned. "I'm worried about the rumor of those two EStees. Do your cameras show that they have them? Are they in reach?"

"I've got two human-shaped heat signatures, but my gnats haven't picked up visuals yet. Still working on that."

Shady'd been paying too much attention to Iruka and Sgt. Aylward. *Oops, I lost track of what Emer and Kieran were saying.*

Elle's got it, Pam reassured her. *Plus we have recordings from the mics.*

In that case, I need to talk to our incident commanders. Shady slipped through the shadows to join Aylward and Iruka. "I should remind you that there are two of them, and you have two XK9s," she said. "Send us in. Our fur and our armor will make it difficult for an EStee to do us any harm."

Pam slid in next to her. "Shady is right. They can end this now, while our subjects are distracted by their argument."

"Got a visual," Kwan's voice came through their HUDs. "Don't see any EStees. She's in a skinny little dress and sandals. He's . . . heh! No wonder she's mad. He's stripped down to his skin, leaning back in a chair with his arms crossed. He just belched at her. Pretty impressive belch. Oh, yeah, she's going ballistic. If you want them distracted, now's your moment."

"Marcy, shape charge on your trapdoor," Aylward ordered. "Elle, Shady, pick your target and prepare to rush them."

"I shall take Kieran. For Rex and Charlie," Shady texted to the team.

"And I shall gladly go for Emer," Elle added.

Marcy placed a tiny shape-charge on the trapdoor's lock, then scuttled backward around the corner into the alley.

Boom! The trapdoor blew open.

Emer and Kieran screamed.

Shady and Elle leaped down into the hideout.

Emer staggered backward. She smacked into a dirt wall.

Kieran's chair fell over. He landed on his back.

Shady reached him in one stride, then snarled in his face.

He spread his hands wide in surrender.

Marcy and Kwan thundered down the steps, EStees drawn. "OPD! Hands where we can see them!"

"Oh, thank goodness!" Emer straightened from a defensive cower and lifted her hands in apparent supplication. "Officers! This man tried to kidnap me!"

"Oh, thank God!" Kieran whimpered, still lying on his back, arms splayed. Tears streamed down his dirty, haggard face. "Thank God! *Thank God* you're not Whisper!"

CHAPTER 13
EXTRACTION

The Five-Ten

Kieran didn't resist when Pam zipped on cuffs. *Yikes! Emer sure got one thing right.* Even without clothing to accumulate extra grime, sweat, and other excretions, Kieran reeked.

His filthy, emaciated body trembled. Tears streamed down his gaunt face and trickled through his scraggly beard. "I just—I give up. Take me." His voice broke in a sob. "I give up. I give up."

Against her better instincts, Pam gave his shoulder a gentle pat. "Calm down, man. You're all right. We're not monsters."

His shaggy, greasy mop of hair flopped up and down in an emphatic nod. "I know. I know. Thank God!"

Emer, on the other hand, tried to yank away from Misha's handcuffs. "What the fuck! You idiot! I'm the *victim*, here! What do you think you're doing?"

"Emer Bellamy, you are under arrest on suspicion of conspiracy to commit mass-murder." Misha pinned her arms behind her back and tightened the cuffs.

"The *hell* you say! This is outrageous! Do you know who I *am*?"

Misha's face remained stony. "You have the right—"

"I'll have your *badge,* you asshole! I'm a taxpayer! You fucking *work for me!* Get me my lawyer!"

"Found two EStees." Marcy snapped some pics, then pulled on gloves and bagged them.

"Prisoner transport en route," Sgt. Aylward spoke quietly from the trapdoor above. "ETA ten minutes. Local UPOs are here for security support."

"Keep our prisoners in the basement till the transport's here," Iruka ordered. "I'm not chancing a damned blowgun!"

With a swish and a scrape, a couple of pop-up canopies unfurled above the entrance trap door. Pam smiled. *That'll help give us visual cover.*

"Ready when transport comes," Kwan reported.

Was he carrying those things in his pack? Pam cocked her eyebrow at Shady. *No wonder he barely fit through those narrow places!*

That would explain it. Shady wagged her tail. Her pleasure over the successful hunt radiated through the link to Pam.

"Prepare to board," Aylward directed. Then a few minutes later, "Okay. Come on up."

Misha and Elle took Emer up. Pam and Shady followed with Kieran. The view-shielding pop-ups covered most of the distance from the trapdoor to what passed for a street running alongside the dirty blue building. She'd expected a PTV, but their transport arrived in the form of four police units.

Their operators had triggered the cars' smart paint to hide normally-visible ID numbers and other markings. Visually, who could say which was which? The sleek indigo vehicles with their dark-tinted windows would be impossible to see into without specialized equipment. *Does Whisper have that kind of equipment here in this Enclave, ready to deploy? I don't know enough to guess.*

Me neither, Shady said. *Mike Santiago might know, if he was here to ask.*

I bet he could make a better guess than we can. Santiago, the

Senior Special Agent in charge of Special Investigations Team Alpha, was the Station's foremost law enforcement expert on the Whisper Syndicate—and incidentally also Elaine's Significant. Perhaps he was helping coordinate their extraction to HQ.

One by one, the OPD vehicles pulled up to the canopy-tunnel's mouth to open a side door. Misha forcibly propelled Emer toward the first one. Elle ran containment on the other side. Pam wouldn't swear Emer's feet touched the ground even once. Elle dived into the back. Misha thrust Emer in next to the XK9 and strapped on their safety harnesses at top speed. The door slammed shut. Misha leaped into the front. The car moved away as his door closed.

Pam and Shady followed on their heels with Kieran. Unlike Emer, he staggered and stumbled along with them, weak but willing. They followed the same order: XK9 and detainee in the back—strap in—human partner up front. The car pulled away while Pam was still buckling herself in.

How severe is the threat assessment? She checked her inputs but found nothing. Then she focused beyond her HUD and noticed their escort was Henry Sevencrows.

"Woah, Henry." Pam flashed him a grin. "You won the Smell-o-Rama Jackpot."

"Hi, Pam. Hi, Shady. Hi, Kieran." Sevencrows glanced back to give them all a quick nod. Henry and Kieran had a long history. "Glad to see you're not dead, man." He returned his attention to their surroundings.

"Me, too." Kieran sighed. "Sorry about the stench."

"I've smelled worse." Henry dismissed it with a shrug. He stayed focused on anything moving outside the car. "Remember, I work here!"

"I have smelled much worse," Shady agreed. "Indeed, I have eaten things that smelled worse."

Pam's jaw dropped. "Are you nuts? Why?"

"Well, she's a dog, for one." Henry grinned, but kept a steady lookout.

"When we were four, we did a unit of open-bushland search and evasion drills." Shady's tail thumped the seat. "They sent us to Farm Eight in the central Sylvanian uplands for the course. There was a Chaykoan lifeform there, the Five-Lined Firetail. They were everywhere. Little darting, buzzing things. They lived in the rocks. They emitted a stinky gas when you bit into them that was pretty raunchy, but their poop had an even more piquant tang. Better yet, it made us fart for three days."

"Okay, I'll—um—*bite*." Henry continued to scan their surroundings, but a smile flickered on his lips. "How were three days of Firetail-poop farts a good thing?"

"We hated the handlers there. They were demanding, they kicked us, and they never fed us enough." Shady uttered a soft growl. "We knew they hated our farts, so we'd make a game of running the rocks. We'd snap up Firetails and any poop we could find. Then we'd do all we could to hold it in, till we were in a small, enclosed space with one of the handlers. Their reactions were deeply satisfying."

"I can't imagine why they kicked you," Kieran murmured.

Shady's ears snapped flat. "They started it."

"Moral to that story? Never piss off an XK9." Pam stared at her. "I had no idea you could be so vindictive."

Shady lolled her tongue. "You still have no idea."

"Somehow, I feel less self-conscious," Kieran said.

Henry shoved the manual override on and yanked the car sideways. It plunged forward with a squeal of tires. Their course veered onto the narrow verge by the road and sideswiped a storage building.

Something slammed hard into their side, just in front of Pam's door. Enveloping padding wrapped her before she could even gasp but Shady yelped.

The car stopped. Pam's pulse hammered in her ears. *Shit! What—* Her narrow view suggested the car was pinned against the building.

Shady's terror through the link fueled her own. *Out! Fight! Run!*

But Pam could barely move, and neither could her partner. *Whisper. It must be Whisper.*

And I'm helpless! Shady half-growled, half-roared. She twisted ferociously against the restraints. *Must get free!*

Stop! Keep your head. Pam fought her own panic. *We're not helpless! Henry's not out of tricks yet!*

She sensed more than saw Henry twist the car's control yoke, then push it upward.

Tricks? What tricks? Shady's terrified confusion threatened to shred Pam's own control.

Boom! The car's front end shot upward. Metal shrieked against metal. Then the front fell back down hard. Landed on top of something. It rocked back and forth, then lurched forward.

The sudden forward-surge pressed Pam back into her seat. Next moment, her harness and the padding around her kept her from smashing into the dashboard when the car jolted to a halt.

Shady yelped again. *The hell? What's happening?*

Pam struggled to breathe, to think straight. *I know what this is. Hang on.* She couldn't see much, but she'd watched demos of this tech. *Damn, I hope this works!*

The car lurched forward again, this time with a loud *bang* of metal punching through metal, then a long, harsh *scre-e-ech* of the sharp ratchet-blade tearing free.

Yes! This is what it's built to do!

Built to—

Just hang on.

Another lurch forward. *Bang!* The ratchet-blade slammed home again. Whatever they were clawing their way over or out of, it would never be the same. *Scre-e-ech—Bang! Scre-e-ech—Bang!* Lurch by lurch, the car hauled itself free of whatever obstacle had been meant to pin it.

The weapons mounted inside the unit's roof thundered a staccato burst.

What was that? Shady's panting breaths rasped.

Defenses auto-target anything that approaches.

Defenses? Active weapons? Smooth. So we really aren't helpless.

Helpless? Oh, no. Not at all.

Another burst of fire from the roof, then the car rolled forward on what felt more like a level road.

The protective padding retracted from around Pam.

She twisted to see what was going on. Glimpsed a line of smoking holes stitched along a wall and across a wet, red splash that could only be blood. She couldn't see who had left it.

Henry punched the unit forward. Made an abrupt pivot into an alley. They covered a block before Pam could finish a breath. Sped through a small, thank-goodness-empty plaza, then plunged into another, even narrower alley.

Pam hung on and clenched her teeth.

They clipped a composter that had been placed too far out from the wall—a problem Pam knew was endemic in the Five-Ten's alleys. The composter spun into the center of the alley behind them. It strewed garbage in a wide arc before it came to rest against a neighbor's back door.

"That bastard gets a ticket," Henry muttered through his teeth. They screeched around another turn, then slowed at last. After another block Henry re-engaged the auto-nav and let out a long, slow breath. Then he turned to them. "Everybody okay?"

Pam rubbed her neck. "What hit us? It happened so fast!"

"Small cargo transport."

"Shit, man. That was some amazing driving!" Kieran gaped at him.

Pam hadn't yet learned to drive one of these vehicles, although she'd signed up for the course. All Five-Ten regulars probably were *required* to take it, though. Good thing Henry'd been an apt pupil.

"I do not think Rex's auto-nav does that," Shady said.

"Henry, are *you* okay?" Pam eyed him.

"We made it away from the ambush. I'll be good when we're out of here." His jaws clenched.

❖ ❖ ❖ ❖ ❖ ❖ ❖ ❖

S hady's breath and pulse took a while to ease, especially considering all the sudden chatter on the command channel. Their narrow escape hadn't been the only one. The other cars—including the two decoys carrying Iruka and the Red Team element—also had evaded interception attempts of various kinds. Chief Klein had scrambled the rest of STAT and every available officer for the mop-up.

She sampled Kieran's scent factors again. Beyond the grime and sweat, she smelled dusty-smoky fatigue, but also rancid illness. Aching low tones of sadness vied with raw, dark, persistent fear. He sagged against his seat and let out a long breath once they pulled into the vehicle transport elevator and the door closed.

"How do you feel?" She cocked her head at him, ears up.

His eyes had drifted closed, but now he glanced up at her. "My life is crap." He sighed. "I guess it always has been. But I'm still glad we didn't die back there."

"Henry is a good driver."

"Just a bit." Kieran shook his head. A brief, rueful smile curved his lips. "Got a damn fine toy, too. I had no idea these babies could do anything like that."

"Neither did I, but I gather my partner did."

"D'you guys think you can actually keep me safe from Whisper?" A faint flicker of fresh, clear hope sparked in his scent.

"Damn sure trying." Henry glanced back at him. "We're your best hope, I'd say."

"Fuck-tonne better than that worthless Zander Hoback." The sharp stink of resentment rose in his scent, tinged with hot, acrid hate.

We have a name!

Or at least an alias, Pam agreed through the link.

Shady dipped her head in a human-style nod. "How long did he let you rot in that basement?"

"Shit." Kieran scowled. "Felt like forever. Prob'ly *woulda been* forever. I was so damn stupid. I fucking *believed* him. I mean, I actually thought maybe there was a chance, you know? What a putz!"

"A chance?"

He blew out a derisive breath and shook his head. "Wishful thinking."

The elevator halted and the doors rolled open on a beautiful Ranan afternoon. Kieran crossed his arms and glared through the window. Shady doubted he was admiring, or even noticing, the sunny, verdant landscape. He said nothing more.

They made the short trip to HQ in minutes. While they rode Shady texted Melynn, Shawnee, and Elaine. "Kieran blames his current situation on someone named 'Zander Hoback.'"

The sally port enveloped them in shadow. They pulled up at Detention Intake. Pam bailed out, then opened Kieran's door and reached to unbuckle him.

"Wait." He held up a hand. "D'you think I could have a—like a cover or something? There's a lot of people here."

Henry released Shady's restraint harness, then pulled a blanket out from under his seat.

Kieran didn't smell as if he meant to try anything, but Shady circled the car to stand beside Pam. Just in case he got any ideas.

They wrapped him in Henry's blanket and turned to find a security detail had arrived to surround them.

Shady glanced back at the car. It appeared almost as sleek and flawless as it had when Henry'd pulled up to receive them outside the dirty blue building in the Five-Ten. A couple of last dimples and wrinkles smoothed flat as she watched.

Wow. You'd never know it saw any action.

Now I want to learn to operate one of those things even more! She caught a ripple of Pam's fierce eagerness, but then her partner's input through the link shifted to surprise. *Woah. ALL the brass showed up for this one!*

A couple of long strides brought Shady inside on her group's heels, to find Elaine, Director Perri, and Chief Klein focused solely on them. Apparently Henry's car had gotten here first.

Maybe Kieran recognized Klein, or perhaps he realized what the emblems on their uniforms signified. Whatever clued him in, he clutched his blanket tighter around his naked self and straightened to face them.

"I'll tell you anything I can." He searched their faces, shoulders squared but body not quite steady. That little tendril of hope-scent returned, brightened, strengthened. "Keep me safe from Whisper, I'll tell you everything I know. And I know a helluva lot!"

CHAPTER 14
SETBACKS

S-3-9 Investigative Center

S hady had hoped to sit in with Pam on Kieran's interview.
LSA Kramer shook her head. "You and Pam saw more than enough action in the Five-Ten. You need at least a high-level scan. Sevencrows has already gone in for his."

Shady glanced down but couldn't quite stifle a soft growl. She clenched her jaws to keep from snarling.

Through the link Shady got a clear sense that Pam's neck ached but her partner seemed no more ready than she was to back off. "You'll need an XK9 team for Kieran. I think we established a rapport in the—"

"Not right now. I hate to say it, but O'Boyle's probably gonna need more than just a simple scan. Making sure he's stabilized has to come first."

Shady's hackles rose, but she kept her head bowed and her snarl sheathed. "Isn't it best to interrogate as soon as possible?"

"Can't have a willing witness croak on us in the middle of an interview." Kramer frowned. "I'm sure you noticed he's ill."

She's right, dammit. Pam turned toward the door, still reluctant but now resigned. *Ranan law has strict rules about detainee* treatment. *I don't know what your Transmondian trainers taught you, but our legal code spells it out.*

Her hackles rippled. *This still feels like needlessly coddling the prisoner.* She followed her partner into the more bureaucratic part of the Civic Center complex.

That's your Transmondian training talking for sure.

Shady halted in the Med Station's doorway. *Wow, this is like stepping back in time.* This being Rana, no daystar's apparent transit occurred, so not even the quality of the light had changed from this morning. Even though so many other things had happened since then.

Is Rex still here? She lifted her nose but found no fresh scent. No furry black lump in the back area. No current scent of Ari Pryce, either, although Charlie had come back to the Med Station a few hours ago.

Pam stopped at the receptionist's desk. "Where's Rex?"

The receptionist glanced up, then turned toward Shady. "Sandler Clinic. They got their orders a while ago." He paused, blinked, then focused on Shady again. "Just got new orders for you, too. Sandler wants to do your after-action scan there. Can you get there on your own, or should I call a car for you?"

"I can go on my own. Thanks." The short walk would do her good.

Pam's worry surged through the link. *Keep an eye out. Whisper may not be happy with ANY of us right now.*

Of course. Though I hope the OPD has given them enough to think about in the Five-Ten for the moment.

Maybe.

A med-station staffer with a case pad and a serious expression approached Pam. "Detective Gómez? Come with me." Pam followed him through a nearby doorway.

Shady left via the Atrium, with its waterfall and green wall of growing things. Scents and sounds from Central Plaza burst upon her full-force when she stepped through the outer doors.

She leaped the central stairs and flowed into an easy lope at the bottom.

Ah, yes. Movement feels good. She stretched her legs and let the rhythm soothe her. The pavement, the soil, each part of every tree and plant contained its own small universe of distinctive odors—and that was before one considered the scattered, individual humans she swept past. But a feeling of being watched prickled her back. She moved faster, senses alert. Nothing she could pinpoint seemed amiss . . .

Wait. Again?

She halted, her body tense. Double-checked the air current then caught a brief burst of movement at the edge of her vision. Her belly hardened. She swung toward the movement and growled. *Oh, you think so, do you?*

Pam's surprise echoed through the link. *The same appscaten?*

The very same. Shady sprang after it, following the ribbon of its scent in the air. *I'm not letting it get away this time!* She halted at the corner by a glass-walled shop. Sorted through the scents that flowed past on the breeze. But the wily appscaten hadn't lingered upwind of her for long.

After the Glen Haven Park encounter, she'd researched appscatens. They had four strong but slender legs, which explained this one's speed the other day. She'd glimpsed its movement somewhere close to the place she now stood. Airborne scents had moved on, but . . . She lowered her head, intent on the scent layer just above the pavement.

Have to rely on scent, 'cuz there's no way it's not in stealth mode. The creature's photosensitive skin reportedly could change colors and patterns with breathtaking ease. She could personally attest that this individual used this trait quite capably for camouflage.

Where did you go, you damned bug? She'd learned that appscaten bodies had three segments, not unlike an insect on Earth—if an insect could grow to be the size of a greyhound.

Unlike insects, however, appscatens weren't invertebrates. They could and did grow that big.

She lost the faint scent, quartered left, then reacquired it. Couldn't see any sign of it now, but she doubted it was far away. *I bet you can see me, even if I can't see you.*

An appscaten would be incredibly difficult to sneak up on. The most descriptive article had said they had six eyes. Two commanded the view from the upper thorax above where the arms attached. Two more covered the vantage from the sides of the creature's domed, triangular head. Unfairly enough, they also had two on the back of their thorax. In pictures their eyes looked like large, shiny black buttons, but when in camouflage mode they closed their eyes to nearly-imperceptible slits.

She quartered right . . . *Ah. There you are, you slippery little git.*

The damned thing's birdlike feet wouldn't make much contact with the ground. And although they had skin, appscatens didn't shed as many skin cells as humans or ozzirikkians. This made it hideously difficult to track, especially on the hard, scent-muddled pavement of the public street. She grumbled and sniffed and lucky-guessed her way along its faint trail toward a nearby stone building.

No appscaten would be a creature to attack lightly, from what she'd read. In addition to the eyes, their head also included a mouth with sharp, pincerlike tusks. Two slender arms, edged with serrated spines, each ended in six, claw-tipped digits. Subcutaneous bony plates armored the horizontal main body. *I bet one of those bone-plates would make a great chew toy.*

Shady! What are you thinking? Pam demanded through the link. *Appscatens are fellow sapient beings!*

Oh, it's just an angry fantasy.

And stop thinking of them as "thing" and "it." They're a person.

An extremely annoying person. A person I want to pin down and question.

What there was of the scent trail ended at the stone building's wall. She stared upward, ears back and teeth half-bared. Her research had said that appscatens could climb, but not how well they could scale a sheer stone wall. *I'm betting those claws and grippy-toes make it*—She growled. *Sorry. Make them—a real good climber.*

Probably, Pam agreed. *And thank you.*

Shady studied a shadow under a balcony three levels up. Was it darker than it should be?

She eyed that shadow for several seconds with the patience of a hunter. No helpful downdraft swept by, only an unwelcome cross-breeze. The suspicious, oddly bulky shadow stayed perfectly still. *Oh, you're a crafty devil, aren't you? What do you want with me?*

"Um, Detective? Is everything okay?" A UPO approached her. "Something I need to address?"

Shady glanced toward her, then refocused on the balcony.

Aw, dammit! That balcony shadow had lost its indistinct lumpiness and gone two shades lighter.

She snorted but saw no point in displacing anger onto a would-be helpful colleague. "No. Thank you. It is gone now." She licked her lips and shot one last baleful glare at the balcony. *Someday soon, Appscaten! You and I are going to have our talk. And you'll have some serious explaining to do!*

"Well, you'd begun to draw a crowd," the UPO said. "I thought I should ask."

Huh? Shady blinked. Several dozen civilians had gathered. They were all staring at her, their scent factors unsettled. *Oh.*

Remember you're in public, you're enormous, and XK9s still aren't an everyday sight around here. Worry tinged Pam's reaction through the link.

Gut tight and pulse pounding, Shady made eye contact with several of the civilians who smelled the most unsettled. *How I wish you or Rex were here!*

Say something. Reassure them, Pam prompted.

"Thank you, Officer. No problem, it turns out." She glanced toward the crowd again and increased her vocalizer's volume.

"It is my job to keep Orangeboro safe. I smelled a possible person of interest, but they are gone now. There is no threat."

Relief washed through the civilians' scents. Several of them smiled.

"Wow. That's good to know." One of the foremost "worriers" nodded to her, echoed by others. "Thank you!"

Shady wagged her tail. "You are most welcome."

The crowd dissipated. With a nod to Shady, the UPO resumed her beat.

Shady's pulse gradually settled back down to a more normal rate.

Her HUD dinged: Monica, Dr. Sandler's receptionist. "Are you all right? We expected to see you by now."

Shady let out a gusty sigh. "Hit a small snag," she texted back. "On my way now." She turned once again toward the clinic.

❖ ❖ ❖ ❖ ❖ ❖ ❖ ❖

Central Plaza District, The Sandler Clinic

Charlie pushed up from one of Dr. Sandler's waiting room chairs. This was the third one he'd tried. None seemed to fit right. He paced the length of the small room and back. Couldn't shake the image of the techs as they'd wheeled Rex's med-bed away. So very *little* filtered in through the link to him!

Yeesh. Think of something else!

Is Razor's physical therapy over yet? He checked the time. *Hmm. Don't want to interrupt him and Liz in the middle of a nap.* They usually took a rest period after a session. Razor's partner, Liz, often had to help hold him up or steady him for his exercises— and Razor was as big as Rex. Liz was tough, but she'd be exhausted by the end of a workout like that. Having done more than his share of PT, Charlie understood Razor's need as well.

Should I check on Berwyn and Cinnamon again? There'd been a hand-written DO NOT DISTURB sign on their door when he'd checked earlier. *Maybe they're up for a visit now. But better text first.*

His text bounced back with an automated reply. "I'm sorry. I'm not accepting calls right now. Please try again later."

Yikes, did Cinnamon take a turn for the worse? He bit his lip. *Best not jump to pessimistic conclusions. They could be napping, too, and simply don't want a caller.*

Which leaves me . . . exactly where I was before.

He thumped down into a different chair. *No, dammit, they're all too small, too hard . . .* He drummed his fingers on its arm. He'd sent a text to Shady with his and Rex's new location. And one to Hildie, ditto. Then later another one to the Family. *What else is there to do?*

Dr. Sandler stepped into the doorway.

Charlie leaped to his feet.

"Well, we have him stabilized. He's now in Healing Sleep." She walked over to Charlie, her face somber, and gestured back to his seat. "Let's talk."

Uh-oh. Charlie's stomach went leaden. He groped with numb fingers for the chair behind him and sat. "Okay."

"Rex's lungs have sustained substantial additional damage from the irritants he inhaled this morning. This will make it harder to keep him breathing and functional until his new lungs are ready for transplant." Her brow furrowed. "I need to wait for the results of another test, which will take at least an hour. If it comes back with the readings I think it will, I then may be able to explore a new option for him."

"A new option?" He sat forward, inclined toward her.

"I don't want to give you premature hope." She grimaced. "It's entirely possible we may have to put him on a ventilator in a medical coma for the next three weeks, just to keep him alive long enough for the transplant."

CHAPTER 15
AFTER-ACTION

Civic Center Medical Station and S-3-9 Investigative Center

The med techs spent about an hour on deep-muscle treatments for Pam's whiplashed neck and back, then applied pain-patches and handed her some extras to use as needed.

P.A. Fadhili took over her case once the scans were finished. She gave her a stern frown before she left. "No more suspect take-downs, or tangling with any more murderous criminals today. Got it?"

"Got it. Formwork, here I come."

"Don't forget those pain patches can cause drowsiness in some people!" Fadhili called after her.

Of course they do. Intent clusters of cops gathered in some of the branching hallways on her way to the SIT Delta war room. She dodged a speed-walker with a grim expression, too focused on his HUD to notice her. How bad *were* things in the Five-Ten? Everyone she encountered appeared to be busy.

"Two STAT elements are engaged in a pitched battle with about fifteen EStee- and blowgun-armed toughs," Iruka confirmed, once Pam reached the war room. "Last word says they've about got that locked down. Three probable Saoirse Front members captured, so far. They're not talking, of course. But those tattoos are distinctive."

Pam settled in with her formwork in the privacy cubicle next to Anteroom Five, and . . . startled up out of a doze sometime later. *Oh, for pity's sake. Did I finish this report or just fall asleep on it?* Her neck had stiffened up again. *Fadhili sure got the "drowsiness" part right.*

She straightened, stretched. The pain patches had gone cool. *Do I dare apply more?* Not much privacy to take off her shirt here. And did she really want new ones that would knock her out again? She stood, frowning. *Maybe a cup of coffee?*

Melynn passed her cubicle, then backed up. "Good morning, Sunshine."

"Ugh. How long was I asleep?"

Melynn waved a dismissive hand. "Those pain patches always wipe me out, too. I hope you're feeling better."

"Not much, but thanks. Do I have keyboard impressions on my face?"

The red-haired Special Agent laughed. "A few. That position can't have helped your neck. Maybe you ought to take Health Leave and have your Amare apply new patches once he gets you home."

"Oh, that's tempting." Pam rubbed her sore neck. It didn't help. "How's Henry? And how's Kieran?"

"Henry went home, like you should." Melynn scowled. "Kieran's dehydrated, exhausted, malnourished—all of that. He's in the Secured Wing at Orangeboro Med under 24/7/382 protection. We're all salivating to get at him, but the doctors say tomorrow."

"Damn." She'd been hoping they'd slap in an IV and send him back.

"They're guessing he's been in hiding and eating almost nothing since the *Izgubil* exploded, maybe even from the moment they rigged the damn ship. A good two months of hiding out and semi-starving. On top of a lifetime eating the normal 'Five-Ten diet,' which for most people is insecure at best."

Pam frowned. "If the Council would admit that people actually *do* live there, it would—"

"Yeah, good luck with that argument." Melynn's mass of tight red curls swept back and forth with her head-shake.

"How'll they explain the pitched battle with STAT today?"

"Oh, they'll manage somehow. They always do."

"Mm-hmm." *And we can't question anything about it, because police officers aren't supposed to get "political."* She didn't have to say that to Melynn. Special Agents weren't supposed to get "political" either. Pam clenched her teeth, chest tight, then consciously relaxed her jaws. "Something is going to have to give eventually."

"One would think." Melynn grimaced. "Not holding my breath. And speaking of breathing, what's going on with Rex? Is Shady with him?"

Pam sketched a picture of Rex's respiratory relapse and subsequent removal to the Sandler Clinic. Before she'd said much she felt Shady's attention through the link, but her partner didn't correct her. Must have it fairly straight, in that case. "Balchu and I were planning to swing by for a visit at the clinic tonight, even before Shady went there for her scan."

"Just make sure you also rest. I'll clock you out starting now, but I want you and Shady here when we finally *do* get a crack at Kieran tomorrow!" She continued on her previous course.

Pam called Balchu to see if he could get away early.

He arrived at her cubicle within minutes, ready to go. As ever, her first glimpse of him brought Pam a warm rush of pleasure. He offered a smile and a handclasp. She replied with her own smile and a quick kiss—but that required tipping her head. She winced, then rubbed her sore neck with a grimace.

"Okay, that's not good." He frowned and ran a finger across the patch on her neck. "This one's gone cold."

"Melynn told me to take Health Leave for the rest of the day."

"Do it." He gave her a teasing grin. "That way I can take Family Leave and make sure your new one is positioned right."

"Not to mention it means you get off early, too."

"Irrelevant. When my queen is in need, I'm there."

"I do still need to stop by the Sandler Clinic. Shady's there with—" Her com beeped. She blinked into her HUD. "Chief *Klein* calling?" She clicked it on. "Hello, sir. This is Detective Gómez."

"Please come up to my office, Detective. Is Shady with you?"

"She's at the Sandler Clinic with Rex."

"Ah. Makes sense. However, there's a matter we need to discuss."

Her throat went dry. *Uh-oh. Have I screwed something up?* "I'll be right there."

❖ ❖ ❖ ❖ ❖ ❖ ❖ ❖

Feliz Tower

Hildie reached up into a long stretch with both arms on an inhale. She held the stretch, lengthened it, then slowly lowered her arms and bent forward with a long, full exhale. *Oh, yeah, this morning's gonna haunt me for a while.* She straightened, then searched with her fingertips under the still-damp ends of her meter-long hair for the worst of the aches in her lower back.

She'd *thought* she was in better shape than this. A chunky or unfit paramedic was more liability than asset in the rigors of micrograv. *Clearly, farming uses different muscles.* With a groan, she reached for a jar of Grandma Hestia's favorite analgesic cream.

Yeesh, what a day. First her heat exhaustion in the paddies, then Capt. Rodrigo's visit! She'd tried to follow Lalu's suggestions of a shower and a nap. But although fatigue weighed her down the best she'd managed was a short, fitful doze.

Too many questions kept cycling through her head: *What shall I do? I mean, I'll wait for the Review Board, of course . . . Dammit! Or should I wait? I don't want to wait! Ugh! Should I at least buy the study guide for the Med School test? Should I actually say yes to Rodrigo? I need to talk to Theresa. I need to talk to Charlie. I probably should talk to Grandma Hestia. I . . . can't make up my mind. What should I do?*

She'd set out food for her cat this morning, but Kali had turned up her nose at the offering. Probably miffed by her mistress's restlessness and irregular new schedule. It still sat in her bowl, uneaten and crusty. *Probably poison by now.* Hildie took the dish to the kitchen and dumped it into the compost receptacle for protein-based waste. *There. One decision made: I won't poison my cat.*

She returned to her room to find Kali in a hunched, tense coil of black, orange, and white fur on top of the chifforobe. The little calico glared at her with resentful blue eyes.

Some companion animal you are. Hildie half-threw herself into the upholstered chair in the "reading corner" of her room. She'd been following a fantasy adventure series that had kept her engaged for years, and the latest book had just come out. *Maybe Dagmar and her dragon can get my mind off my troubles for a while.*

She read the first few lines, then frowned and chewed her lip. *Could I even function on Graveyard Watch? Every day, always Graveyard? Yikes. Maybe the Med School Exam would be easier . . . shorter pain, anyway. But how much humiliation? Oh, I wish the darn Board would just decide already!*

She stiffened, her throat tight. *Crap, I did it again. Maybe a short relaxation meditation.* She hadn't made it through the last one. *Another try at one couldn't hurt, right?*

Her com trilled with Charlie's personal chime.

Oh! Her heart gave a joyful leap. "Hi!" A rush of energy hastened her pulse and lightened her chest. It *was* about time for the end of his shortened workday. "How was Rex's first day back?"

"Would you be willing to meet me at the Sandler Clinic?" Charlie's tone stayed carefully neutral, but a chill of alarm shortened her breath.

"Of course. How bad is he?" Too late, she noticed an earlier text from him. When had that come in?

"His first day back didn't go well. Are you at Feliz? I can send Rex and Shady's car."

"I am. Will you stay there with him tonight?"

Quiet sigh through the com. "I don't *think* it's that serious. But if it's not too much trouble, I'd like to see you."

The subtle strain in his voice told Hildie he was worried. And he only resorted to that understated tone when he yearned for her to do something, but didn't want to seem pushy. "Should I pack an overnight bag?"

"Would you mind?"

"I'm already packing. I'll be ready for the car."

"Thanks." He probably didn't mean for her to hear quite that much relief in his voice. "Love you. See you soon."

Kali leaped down from her perch with a thump. She gave Hildie one more reproachful stare, then stalked away, tail lashing.

Her Imperial Exaltedness is not amused. She's recognized the signs I'm leaving again. Hildie grimaced. "Oh, girl, I'm sorry."

Kali removed herself. Even if she heard the apology and understood the human words, they were Officially Not Speaking.

Too bad for Kali, this was the new pattern she and Charlie had recently settled into. Once he got off work she wanted to spend time with him anytime she could. She threw a few last necessities into her overnight bag.

Then she sent an explanatory text to Abi and Smita, her younger brother and his Significant. Technically, this apartment was hers and Abi's, but functionally the place belonged to Abi and Smita. When she'd been working crazy back-to-back twelve-hours in micrograv, it hadn't mattered if all her stuff consolidated down from half the unit into this one small bedroom.

But Abi and Smita had been Domestic Partners for almost three years. They'd recently started talking about a future that included children. *They need their own place.* Hildie held out big hopes for her relationship with Charlie, but it hadn't even been two months yet. *Surely that's too early to make plans?*

He'd expressed similar feelings—and worries. They'd agreed not to rush things. All the same, more than once when she was with him at Corona Tower he'd said, "This place just seems more *right* when you're here." Charlie's apartment already had accumulated a fair amount of "Hildie stuff." Otherwise she would've had to pack more.

But if she ever did move into Corona for keeps, what would Kali make of Rex and Shady?

A *ding* on her com announced that the car had arrived.

She hurried down the steps.

CHAPTER 16
AN OFFER

OPD HQ, Chief Klein's Office

"Come. Sit." Klein gestured toward a chair that faced his desk, then settled into his own chair on the opposite side. He quirked an eyebrow at Pam. "Have you checked in on the construction work for the XK9 Special Investigations Unit?"

Especially after Rex's misadventure there this morning, she and Balchu had been curious, even though it was supposed to be off-limits as long as it remained a work zone.

"We tried to stay out of the workers' way, but we do like how it seems to be developing." Pam eyed the Chief. He didn't *look* angry. She cleared her throat. "We could tell you worked with Rex on the planning. And I know Charlie's glad for the Chamber Three access."

"That GR of his is outstanding, by the way." Klein's smile stretched wide and genuinely warm. "I hope the rest of the dogs and humans will find that suite a congenial place to work, too."

Emboldened, Pam smiled back. Her pulse steadied. "I think we'll do fine."

"Needs a logistics coordinator, though. Normally, I'd pull

seasoned personnel from other units to fill the top slots in a new one."

Her breath caught, but she held back from wild speculations. "Isn't that what Detectives Penny and Fujimoto are supposed to do?"

Klein's smile went rueful. "They're tasked to mentor a unit full of rookie detectives. I expect they'll stay plenty busy with that. No, I'm talking about someone to manage logistics and day-to-day matters." He again focused pointedly on Pam. "I figure one sergeant on the Day-Watch should cover it."

Pam's heart rate shot up. A little more than a year ago she and Balchu had both passed the sergeant-qualification course. "Sir, are you offering *me* the sergeant position?"

"You did take the course and pass with good marks." The Chief inclined his head toward her. "Granted, that was a while ago, but I assumed you'd still be interested. Are you?"

Is he kidding? Her breath came short, but she managed to croak out, "Yes!" *Yeesh, was my voice squeaky enough?* She cleared her throat, strove for a more sober tone. "Um, yes, sir. I definitely would still be interested."

Your voice was fine, Shady reassured through the link, although even XK9 ears couldn't have heard her all the way from the Sandler Clinic. Pam envisioned a laughing tongue-loll and tail-wag. *Congratulations.*

Klein didn't seem worried about any squeakiness either. He grinned with evident delight. "Excellent. Based on the logistics work you've already done on the *Izgubil* investigation, I expect you'll handle the job well. And I'm grateful I don't have to train someone about XK9s from scratch. Unfortunately, we can't wait until official promotions in April—I need you now. I'd like to make it official tomorrow morning."

❖ ❖ ❖ ❖ ❖ ❖ ❖ ❖

Civic Center Rotunda, OPD HQ, and Central Plaza

"**O**utstanding!" Balchu wrapped his arm around Pam's shoulders once she'd returned to the central rotunda and explained Klein's question. She could discern no jealousy in his broad grin. "You'll be great! When should we be there? Can families come?"

"Um, the Chief said 6:55 for a quickie ceremony." She frowned. "I didn't ask about families, but I want you there."

"Families are usually welcome for stuff like this." Balchu grinned. "I hope I get to do your pinning?"

"Klein asked if I wanted Mother to do that. Can you imagine?" She shook her head. Her mind balked at forming a picture of it. *MY mother, participating in an official police function?* Her mother's intense loathing of the police had been one of Pam's initial motivations to apply to the Academy—to piss her off. "Absolutely, you may do my pinning."

Balchu's grin stretched even wider. "I bet my parents will come if they can get free. Would you mind?"

Before she'd met Balchu's parents, Pam wouldn't have believed any parent would actually go to that much trouble on her behalf. But Tuya and Feyodor had far, far different attitudes about family than her own mother. It was entirely possible they'd actually show up. Surprised pleasure warmed her. "That . . . actually, that would be nice."

Balchu pulled out his case pad and started texting, right there in the rotunda. "Okay with you if I ask Nani and Rose?"

"I guess, sure. Why not?" Pam watched him, her throat tight. *SERGEANT Gómez. I'm actually gonna be . . . oh, my God. What will Liz say, if I'm now her boss?*

Are you serious? Shady's tone came through the link loaded with amusement. *Pack is Family. When Rex and I became Command Staff they didn't disown us.*

But it's kind of a police tradition, at least among humans. Pam grimaced. She'd seen it happen. *You gain a higher rank and you're no longer "one of us."*

Weren't you coming over here tonight to check on Berwyn and Cinnamon, and to look in on Liz and Razor? Ask them for yourself.

I was coming to check on you, but point taken. Pam drew in a breath and straightened. *Pack-as-Family might even outweigh tradition.* Anyway, she could hope. She didn't need to wonder what Tuya and Feyodor would think. Or even Sarnai—"Nani"—and her Amare Rose. Balchu's family would want to celebrate. If they could manage it, some of them might even *be there* tomorrow at 06:55, despite the short notice and the ungodly hour. They were so . . . *supportive.*

But thinking of them brought her to the dreaded question: *Should I contact Mother?*

Shady, always in touch through the link, didn't respond to that thought.

Pam crossed her arms, a gesture that kind of turned into a self-hug before she could stop it. Earlier in the year she hadn't mentioned her candidate status in the XK9 program to Mother before she left for Planet Chayko. Granted, there'd been a very short lag between the announcement of candidates and their departure.

But she'd figured Mother wouldn't care anyway. Or worse: Mother would likely lecture her on how all police were bastards. Or maybe deliver a diatribe on how police dogs were vicious tools of oppression. Or how only a fool would go to strange planets, or get her hopes up about anything.

Whatever. Pam hadn't wanted to hear it.

But on the night of her return to Rana Station she, Shady, and Balchu had barely stepped inside their too-small apartment before a message arrived from Mother: *You might have let me know.*

That evening had already delivered an emotional overload. Shuttle-lagged and still only half-acclimatized to 1-G, she'd staggered onto the Presentation Ceremony stage. When Chief Klein introduced her and Shady to all of Orangeboro along with the other new XK9 teams, she hoped she'd managed to look presentable.

After that, out of the spotlight behind the stage, Balchu's formal Amare proposal gave her another head-spinning moment. In retrospect, she realized he'd been building up to it all through his campaign to redeem himself, but in that moment it caught her off-guard. She'd said "yes" before she could second-guess herself.

But Shady wasn't happy about it. All the way home that night, Pam had walked a thin margin to keep peace between Shady and Balchu.

Maybe the accumulation of all those shocks made *"You might have let me know"* hang over her even more oppressively than it should have—but at the time it felt like a cloud of shame.

She was a terrible daughter.

Against her better judgment, she'd called.

Mother—being Mother—had given her a royal chewing out for being an inattentive shit, then hung up on her.

Pam had let out a little moan. Both Balchu and Shady had started to demand why she'd even bothered to . . . but then they stopped and simultaneously moved in with hugs, snuggles, and commiseration. Their first moment of agreement had been in support of Pam after Mother'd laid another cheap, crappy, downer-move on her.

Pam pulled her mind away from *then. Be here now,* she chided herself. *After that shabby treatment last time, it would serve Mother right if I never called her again.*

Can't argue with that, Shady agreed.

A call—or, really, any contact was just asking to get kicked in the teeth. Pam rubbed a hand across her face with a silent groan. Well, if Mother could send a text, so could she.

"I'm being promoted to Sergeant. Now you know," she texted, then hit *send* before she could second-guess herself.

Balchu glanced up from his case pad with a joyful laugh. "This is wonderful! Mom and Dad have both said they can come! Even Nani . . ." He stopped, gave her a closer examination. "What?"

Her mouth went dry and her vision swam. She half-waved the case pad with a grimace. "I told Mother."

"Ah." He wrapped her in a hug.

She leaned into his embrace, grateful to her core that he understood. *I found a really good guy.*

A guy who's learned a helluva lot since that night when he didn't attend the watch party, Shady put in. *I'll admit he surprised me.*

"Let's go see Shady." Balchu gave her arm a gentle tug. They threaded through OPD HQ's corridors, then out through the glassed-in Atrium to the front steps. The fragrant air of Central Plaza's orange grove engulfed them in rising mist. By now they'd reached the normal end of their watch.

She half-expected that Mother might never acknowledge her message. But they hadn't left Central Plaza before Pam's HUD buzzed with an incoming text from her.

Pam steeled herself. *Would it hurt you to say something nice, for once?* She bit her lip and opened it.

"Oh, that's brilliant," Mother wrote. "Now everyone will hate you."

Pam released a soft sigh. *Yeah, thanks for that.*

CHAPTER 17
NEW CHALLENGES

Central Plaza and the Sandler Clinic

P am didn't feel like talking for the rest of the block after she received Mother's message. But then she drew in a deep breath. She squeezed Balchu's hand and focused on Shady. *How are things on your end?*

Dr. Sandler's still evaluating Rex. He's now in Healing Sleep. Hildie arrived a little while ago. She, Charlie, and I just got to Razor's room. We're planning to wait here.

Pam passed all of this on to Balchu.

"They still don't have a plan for Rex?"

Pam gave him a worried frown. "I don't think so."

"Here's hoping they come up with something soon." They walked in silence for almost another block before he spoke again. "You've had a pretty busy day, so I almost hate to bring this up. But have you heard the news from Transmondia?"

Pam rubbed her forehead. *"Now* what?"

"Well, you knew they dissolved the government at the end of last week, right?"

She frowned. "They kicked out their Prime Minister or something like that, didn't they?"

"Yeah. Well, they held a High Council vote today and guess who's running things now?"

During her stay there, Pam had eventually given up trying to understand the Transmondians' dozen-or-so small parties with their shifting coalitions. It was hard enough just keeping up with the four on Rana. But she knew the worst possible outcome. Several of the Popular Growth Forum's top leaders had invested heavily in the XK9 Project. "Please tell me it's *not* the PGF."

"Got it in one." Balchu grimaced. "They teamed up with a couple of others to form a slim majority."

More power for the PGF meant nothing but trouble for the Pack. "That can't be good."

"I wouldn't expect so, no."

Uh-oh. And now we have another new problem, Shady said through the link. *It involves Berwyn and Cinnamon. When you get here, come straight to Razor's room.*

"And to think I was happy about my promotion. Briefly." Pam blew out a breath and conveyed Shady's latest update. Balchu squeezed her hand in solidarity. *We're almost here,* she told Shady through the link. She and her Amare soon walked up the steps to Sandler Clinic's new security door.

"Hi, Pam, hi, Balchu." UPO Ax Gerwitz greeted them from the reception desk. It appeared Sandler's receptionist Monica had already left for the day, but Ax often covered security during Swing Watch for the two—now three—recovering XK9s here. "Dr. Sandler is examining Rex now. Shady, Charlie, and Hildie are with Razor and—" He broke off with an embarrassed expression on his round, usually-cheerful face. "Well, I guess you know where Shady is."

"We stay in touch." Pam smiled. "How about the rest of our resident Packmates?"

"Liz is probably about to wrap up Razor's post-workout massage. I expect they'll be happy to see you in Razor's room. But Cinnie's in Healing Sleep." He gave them a worried glance. "And Berwyn isn't accepting visitors."

Pam frowned. "What's up with Berwyn? Is he all right?"

"No." Ax's lips pressed together in a flat line. "He hasn't been all right since he and Shiv broke up."

"They *what?*" Pam stared at him. She and Balchu had just been here yesterday, and everything had seemed fine in that quarter. "When did that happen?"

"Late last night, according to the techs on Graveyard. They were still together when I left at midnight, but the techs said Shiv seemed upset when he left, not long after that. Berwyn reportedly hasn't managed a smile since then."

Pam bit her lip. "I noticed today that Shiv looked as if he hadn't slept well, but I didn't have a chance to talk with him."

"I think Dr. Sandler is pretty disgusted with the two of them. Berwyn's state of mind isn't helping Cinnie at all." Ax grimaced. "Sorry, but that's all I know."

"I'm grateful for the heads-up." Ax's "cop-grapevine" intel briefings were always informative. *Mm, speaking of which,* if she wanted all of OPD to know about her promotion, telling Ax should get that information well on its way. *On the other hand, if I sit on this, he may be less forthcoming next time.*

Ax's round face split with a delighted smile when she told him. "Congratulations, Sarge! Maybe your news will get Berwyn's mind off his broken heart for a moment."

"I wouldn't count on it." Balchu grimaced. "Berwyn seemed pretty invested in that relationship." He glanced at Pam. "And a broken heart can be all-consuming."

Ax gave him a rueful grimace. "Let's hope his resolves as positively as yours did."

❖ ❖ ❖ ❖ ❖ ❖ ❖ ❖

Shady pushed open the door to Cinnamon's darkened room. Her Packmate lay still, barely seeming to breathe, deep in Healing Sleep. But even from across the room, Cinnamon did not smell right. Shady padded to the med-bed and gave her a thorough sniff-over. *Oh, this is worse than I expected. Even in Healing Sleep, she feels a level of pain.*

Ax said she wasn't doing well. Pam's tone through the link echoed Shady's worry. Pam and Balchu had joined Charlie, Hildie, Liz, and Razor in Razor's room. Although Razor had improved enough that Liz now often went home at the end of each evening rather than stay here, she remained on Emergency Family Leave. She still spent much of each day here with her XK9 partner, but she had gradually started learning to also take better care of herself.

Dr. Sandler still had not emerged with a verdict on Rex. That worried and distracted Shady enough that she hadn't been able to settle into the conversation. She couldn't just sit and wait, not even when surrounded by Packmates. With Rex out of action, she was the acting Pack Leader. And it was time to take stock of both Cinnamon's physical condition and Berwyn's mental state. She uttered a long, low growl upon finding that the former was precarious.

Then she swung her head toward the privacy-curtained partner's sleeping nook. She studied the scent factors emanating from the large-ish center of heat back there that was Berwyn. He was awake, but hadn't spoken. She snapped her ears flat. "You and I need to talk."

"I don't want to talk to anyone right now." The throat-catching scents of anguish and heavy melancholy that emanated from behind the curtain made this no surprise. He smelled like himself, but she'd never encountered such depression in his scent factors before.

Humans. What're you gonna do? Shady swallowed another growl. "Tough. You have sulked in there since last night, and meanwhile Cinnamon is failing." It was unfair to say that, but perhaps anger would penetrate some of his depression.

"I'm not sulking. I'm—"

She let the silence hang and opened the link wider to Pam.

"I don't know . . . how *not* to feel this way." His voice went soft, almost a broken whisper. "It's like I'm drowning, and I can't see a way out."

"Tell me what happened."

"That's just it. I don't really know what happened. One minute things seemed fine, and then it was like something inside of him just *broke*. He froze. Stared off into the middle-distance. At first I thought he'd received a disturbing com-call, but then he kind of shuddered. He stared down at the floor for maybe a minute, and I realized he was doing some kind of patterned breathing. His whole body was trembling. I'd never seen him like that. He was kinda starting to scare me, but then he glanced up at me with those piercing baby-blues of his."

Berwyn's scent swirled with anguish. "He stared straight at me, cold and hard, and he said, 'I'm sorry. We have to break this off. I clearly have a lot more crap to work through.'" Berwyn shifted behind the curtain, released a long, heavy breath. "And then he just stood up and left."

Shit. Clearly, Shady needed to confront Shiv next. But for right now, she pushed past the curtains. Berwyn hunched on his cot with his arms wrapped around his updrawn knees. She hopped up onto the cot next to him, even though there wasn't actually room for her. The cot shook under the weight of both of them. She couldn't give Berwyn a human-style hug, but she knew who could. And nothing would help Cinnamon more right now than for her partner's mood to improve.

She placed one foreleg across his back and snuggled close. "You need your Pack."

He shook his head. "What can I say to them?"

"They are your Pack. You do not need to say anything. Not unless you want to." She returned to the floor, then turned to him. "Come. This place is depressing."

He hesitated.

She replied with a low growl.

He straightened from his fetal curl, but stayed on the cot.

She placed her jaws around his forearm. Kept her mouth soft, but with enough teeth to get his attention. "Come."

"You wouldn't—"

"Do not test me." She gave him a stern sheepdog-stare.

He sighed, but stood and let her lead him by the arm to Razor's room.

There Pam and Liz immediately wrapped him in a silent hug. Charlie put his arm across Berwyn's shoulders. Shady and Razor leaned in to warm any part of him that they could reach. And while he didn't exactly hug *Berwyn*, Balchu hugged Pam and leaned in to touch Berwyn's arm. Hildie watched with a worried expression.

CHAPTER 18
PACK IS FAMILY

The Sandler Clinic

Until this moment, with one arm linked in Liz's and the other wrapped around Berwyn, Pam hadn't been on the *giving* end of a situation like this. Last time the Pack had responded to a similar moment, *she'd* been the brokenhearted one at the center. Her Pack had surrounded her, accepted her, and given her new courage after that wrenching break with Balchu on Choosing Night. She met Shady's eyes and smiled. *So —this is how it feels.*

Pack is love. Shady wagged her tail and nuzzled closer.

They held it for a while, until Shady and, a second later, Razor, backed off a pace, ears and tails up and tongues long. Pam gathered through the link that this was a response to a shift in Berwyn's scent. The humans backed off too at this cue. Pam couldn't smell the change, but the mood in the room lightened.

"Berwyn, may I fix you some tea?" Liz asked. "We'll listen if you want to talk and understand if you don't."

Berwyn sat down on the suite's small couch with a sigh. "Tea . . . actually might be good."

"I like the lemon balm blend I'm going to fix. It's good for calming and relaxing." Liz reached the suite's kitchenette in a couple of steps. "Charlie, you probably need some, too. Anybody else?"

"Would you mind making me a cup?" Hildie asked.

When she and Balchu had first arrived, Pam thought the young woman seemed oddly familiar, then realized who she was. She'd "seen" Hildie through the link many times, and on the vids of the "graduation night" when Pack received their Class B micrograv certifications. Beyond basic introductions, however, they hadn't been able to talk much before Berwyn arrived.

"I didn't mean to intrude on a Pack moment." Hildie's gaze darted toward Berwyn. "I just wanted to be with Charlie while we wait for a verdict on Rex."

Berwyn's brows went up. "Is Rex okay?"

"No." Charlie's shoulders sagged. "He should never have gone anywhere near GR Chamber Three and the new office space today. Not with all the airborne particulates from the construction. But I couldn't convince him not to come."

"He is a very large and stubborn dog." Shady gave Charlie a commiserating expression. "I could not stop him either." She shifted her focus to Berwyn. "Rex is finally here, under proper care, and in Healing Sleep. But he has resisted it all day, and he has been extremely obnoxious the whole time. Dr. Sandler is doing another analysis on him, but I hope she keeps him in Healing Sleep for a while."

"I'm kind of embarrassed to admit I hope so too." Charlie grimaced. "Sharing a brain link with him in between his short naps hasn't been pleasant."

"What is keeping Dr. Sandler? I thought she would be back by now." Shady's worry over this delay came through the link loud and clear to Pam.

Hildie's gaze stayed on Charlie. "You seem a bit happier than you did when I first arrived, though."

"Well, you're here. And Shady was correct—as usual. Being with Packmates helps."

"She used that line on you, too?" Berwyn managed a small smile. "Be damned if she isn't right, though."

"And speaking of being among Packmates—" Shady's tail rose in a high wag. "Pam has been sitting on massive news that affects the Pack."

Everyone turned toward at her.

Oh, thanks. Pam gulped and straightened. She cleared her throat. "Um, the Chief offered me a promotion this afternoon." She hunched her shoulders, which made her sore neck and back twinge. "You see, Balchu and I both took the sergeant's course about a year ago—"

"Woah!" Liz straightened from her tea-making with a huge, dawning smile. "Does this mean you'll be *Sergeant* Gómez? Of the new XK9 unit?"

"Um, yeah. Don't hate me, okay?"

"Are you kidding?" Liz laughed. "This is gonna be amazing! Congratulations!"

"Same here—Congratulations!" Berwyn's smile seemed wider and warmer this time. "A sergeant who *understands*— that'll be a massive help."

"You always did have a great head for logistics and the big picture." Charlie offered a warm nod of approval. "I think you'll do well."

"Speaking as one sergeant to another—well done." Hildie smiled. "I was worried at first that my crew might be jealous, but it all worked out just fine. I bet you'll find that's true for you, too."

"Wow, thanks." Pam's chest expanded with warmth. "I'd forgotten you're a sergeant, too. Any advice to a newbie?"

Hildie's smile widened into a grin. "Let's stay in touch. I'm glad to help if I can."

"This isn't exactly a normal toasting beverage, but I'd say the moment calls for one." Liz handed out mugs of tea. "Sorry I can't offer much of anything else. Crispy pita chips and a little hummus, anyone?"

"Just because we all descended on you at once that doesn't mean you're obligated to feed us." Pam shook her head. She focused on Berwyn. "But I do wonder about you. When was the last time you ate real food?"

He avoided eye contact and stared at his tea. "I haven't been real hungry."

"Uh-huh." Her gaze met Liz's.

Liz grinned. "Order out from LEO's?"

"I'll go pick it up," Balchu offered.

"We'll definitely stick around to offer a toast." Charlie wrapped his arm around Hildie. "To the new sergeant!" They both raised their tea mugs to her, then took simultaneous, incongruously-dainty sips of the steaming brew.

Berwyn tried to follow suit then gasped. "Oh, that burns all the way down!"

"I *said* it wasn't a toasting beverage." Liz offered him an apologetic grimace. "Sorry I don't have anything better."

"Congratulations!" That was a new voice. Pam spun. Dr. Sandler stood in the still-open doorway. "I hate to pull you away from a party, Shady and Charlie, but I've completed my analysis and placed some calls. Now we need to talk about what's next for Rex."

Charlie nodded but still seemed worried. "Clarity would be good."

"What are your thoughts?" Shady's ears swept up and forward. Pam understood and shared the soaring hope she sensed from her partner through the link.

"First of all, I want to keep him here for a while. And I may have a solution that will help to stabilize him without putting him on a ventilator till we can finish growing his lungs."

Charlie's eyebrows rose. "A solution? Something we haven't already done?"

"I have an ozzirikkian colleague who's involved in a therapeutic development study. Ti is in late-stage cross-species clinical trials of a new temporary treatment for lung trauma."

"Oh! I think I've read about that one." Hildie brightened. "They pioneered it on Koanna and now they're coordinating with the SDF on clinical trials with humans and ozzirikkians. This is the one that utilizes nanotech, right? For lung-trauma patients on space voyages?"

"Exactly." Dr. Sandler's smile brightened. "Yes. It's designed for use on ships in space—for lung trauma patients who have to be stabilized for a longer time than is optimal. Sometimes they might be months from any port with a decent hospital. My friend thought a one-off auxiliary study on an XK9 might offer preliminary insights for yet another species—and also get the Pack Leader back on his feet more solidly until we can finish growing his new lungs for him."

Charlie turned to Hildie. "You know about this?"

"Oh, yes." Hildie's back straightened. "A little, anyway. We were hoping these studies might eventually offer insights for emergency practice. There's also the probability that we might have to deal with incoming patients who've had the procedure out in space, if it catches on." Her eyes sparkled with new interest.

Pam glanced at Shady. *She's been on stand-down for a week, right? Think she's hungry to get back out there?*

Oh, you know she is. Shady lolled her tongue. *For her, this shop-talk is like light and water to a wilted plant. I'm grateful to bring her expertise onboard. She can help us make better judgments about Rex's treatment.*

"Let's go down to my office." Sandler regarded Hildie with a delighted grin. "I can show you the proposal in more depth."

Hildie turned to Charlie, then turned toward Shady as well. "You guys okay with me doing that?"

"Yes!" Shady's tail ratcheted up to double-time.

"If you wouldn't mind." Charlie's face relaxed with relief.

The three of them followed in Sandler's wake.

Pam turned back toward the others in the room and met Balchu's pensive expression. "What?"

Her Amare chuckled. "So that's Hildie, eh? Seems to me that Charlie has a 'type.'"

Liz laughed outright. "You know, I think you're right!"

Even Berwyn grinned. "The man definitely has a point."

Pam scowled at them. "What are you talking about, a 'type'?"

Balchu took her gently into his arms, his face alight with mirth. "Fit, gorgeous, highly professional ladies—*sergeant* material—with warm brown skin and long, dark hair. Not that I have any quarrels with that. I'm kinda partial to that type, myself."

Pam bit her lip. "I . . ." She laughed, considering it. "You're probably onto something, there, Detective. Except, based on what Shady's told me, I've begun to suspect that Hildie's not just 'his type.' For Charlie, she's the *prototype*. They were best friends on the ERT before the *Asalatu*."

"Oh, that explains so much." Liz grinned at Berwyn. "Don't you think?"

He nodded, then sighed. "Nice to see some people's love lives actually work out, after all."

"Well, eventually. So far." Pam frowned. "But the *Asalatu* was years ago. Here's hoping it doesn't take you that long! Shall we talk about what we all want for dinner?"

CHAPTER 19
EXPANDING POSSIBILITIES

The Sandler Clinic

Hildie took a deep breath. *Let me not make a fool of myself in the first sentence!* But her pulse beat high and curiosity tugged. "Am I correct that they're using a new type of dendrimer-based genetic amendment? With—I think it's a liposomal delivery agent, right? To release the regenerative pharmacon more exactly where it belongs?"

"Why, yes!" Dr. Sandler's eyebrows shot up. "That's exactly right. How do you know about it?"

Shady cocked her head, ears up. Charlie gave her a curious glance, but neither spoke.

"From the *Journal of Microgravity Therapeutics.*" Hildie cringed inwardly. *Will she think I'm silly?* "My friend and I try to keep up with the literature, and it's given us interesting glimpses into the science. But we're never sure if we've interpreted it right."

She and Theresa often spent as much time researching terms and comparing information from educational materials as they did reading any given study in that quarterly journal. Some of their colleagues—okay, most of their colleagues—thought it was a waste of time and maybe a bit pretentious. Her belly tightened, but she needed to ask. "As I understand it, nanomedicine isn't as dependent on gravity as most treatments because of its quantum nature. Is that a reasonable assumption?"

"That's partly correct." Sandler led the way down a short, narrow hallway. Hildie followed her closely while Shady and Charlie trailed behind. "Gravity does have an effect, because it influences the structures being acted upon. That said, according to Kirritokti, my colleague, nanomedicine keeps proving itself more and more useful in micrograv." She opened the door at the end. "Of course, in Rex's case that won't be a factor."

"But this particular technique is building on accepted science, and it's *applicable* to a micrograv setting. Right?" Hildie hoped she'd drawn the right inferences from the study's abstract and introduction. Was her fluttery stomach a sign of eagerness to learn, or fear she'd presumed too much? *Eh, it's both.*

"Yes, certainly." If Sandler was humoring her, she hid it well. The small, curly-haired woman seemed as eager to talk about it as Hildie. "The Koannan technique has become the standard of lung trauma care, in-species, over the last three of our decades. But expanding it to therapeutics for other Galactics has required a whole range of accommodations."

"That makes sense. We have a somewhat different protocol for each species, no matter how common the injury." No human or ozzie brain could hold all those facts, so at work on the ERT they had standards of emergency medicine for two dozen species loaded into their CAPs. She could access them via her HUD at need. *And a good thing, too.*

Dr. Sandler stepped inside her office and pulled up three screens. "Take a look at these tables." She scrolled to find similar tables on each one. "Here they compare three sequences of regenerative conjugate dosages using this technique and show the uptake percentages."

Hildie's core warmed, and she couldn't resist a smile. *I under-stand all of that! I really AM making sense of those published studies. Oh, this is fascinating!*

"There's a cumulative resistance that builds up in each—but it develops at different rates across a rather narrow range for each species. A lot depends on the particular drug and delivery vector, but can you see the variations by species?"

"Yes." Hildie found the parallels easy to identify. "How do you think XK9s will compare?"

"We do know that XK9 physiological responses compare more closely to human than ozzirikkian results."

"Because both have Terrestrial origins?"

"We think so."

"How closely?" She gazed at the human chart on the left. "What range of variation do you anticipate with XK9s?"

"It's hard to say. In truth, it's not possible to say much about XK9s too broadly. Even if you count the entire population, they're such a small sample that large-scale studies are impossible. Individuals vary a lot. But we'd like to start establishing some hard data with Rex's case. Based on other dosage reactions, we think we can get close to an efficacious therapeutic balance fairly quickly. But we don't *know*."

"Not until you've tested it. Got it."

"Rex did himself a huge disservice this morning. Without this option, we'd probably have to put him on a ventilator within the next week or so, and keep him sedated till his lungs are ready. But his misfortune gives us an opportunity to test this new technology—and *maybe* help him breathe much better." Sandler turned to Charlie and Shady, who'd trailed them to the office. "If you'll agree to try it."

Shady pinned Hildie with a sheepdog-stare, studied her for a moment. "You think we should, do you not?"

Yes, absolutely. Hildie gave her a worried grimace. "It's not my place to decide, but yes, I do."

"We're grateful for your advice." Charlie eyed Sandler's charts and hunched his shoulders. "I'm having a bit of *déjà vu* in reverse, I think. Rex can't weigh in on this decision while he's in Healing Sleep. That means our guessing game tonight parallels my Family's dilemma over me, after the *Asalatu* accident. I was on life support. They couldn't ask my opinion before they chose the re-gen regimen. It worked out mostly okay, but I can't help wondering what unforeseen side effects we'd be signing him up for—no matter what we choose."

Sandler nodded. "Understand, please, that there *will* be side effects whatever you choose. Two or three weeks in a medical coma on a ventilator will add a lot of bad ones."

"Yes, if we can avoid that—" Hildie grimaced. *Where to begin, on those?*

"As his mate, I say we go for the nanotech." Shady gave a short, human-style nod. "You and Hildie both smell as if you earnestly believe this could work. Rex will not tolerate being an invalid. Today proved that, without question. If we can spare him the aggravation and get him back into the action sooner, we should."

"As his partner, I agree with his mate." Charlie smiled. "Let's give him a chance to breathe better, sooner."

Hildie's abdomen relaxed.

"So it appears that our Rex is headed into The Learned Kirri-tokti's clinical trial. Good!" Dr. Sandler appeared as relieved as Hildie felt.

❖ ❖   ❖ ❖   ❖ ❖   ❖ ❖

Once they'd finally made it official, Charlie was ready to go home. He wanted to eat something, relax, and curl up with Hildie for the night.

Shady, however, clearly wanted to join the party in Razor's room. She cantered down the hall ahead of him and Hildie, tail high and ears up.

Hildie smiled up at him. "Let's go make an appearance. We can quietly duck out in a bit."

"You don't mind?"

"It's been a wild day for both of us." She slid an arm around him.

"Is it any wonder I love you?"

They arrived to find that the party had expanded and spilled out through Razor's "back door" into the Clinic's exercise yard. Dr. Sandler's rooms were XK9-sized, but not for *that* many XK9s. Connie and snow-white Crystal had come with Georgia. They'd responded to a text that Razor originally had sent to Elle and Tux.

Charlie'd heard that Connie, Crystal, and Georgia had become roommates now that Tux lived with Elle, Misha, and Misha's Significant Hallie in Glorioso Tower. The Glorioso contingent also had arrived, led by the other pair of declared XK9 Amares, Tux and Elle. They'd come well-supplied with pizzas, soft drinks, and bottles of Misha's Family's "Orangeboro Glory" Amber Ale. Misha knew to hand Charlie a cold one. He offered another to Hildie. She accepted with a smile. The drinks came in handy for another toast to Pam's new status.

Moments later half-brother XK9s Scout and Victor loped in, tails up and tongues lolling. The XK9 "com tree" had been busy. Their humans Nicole and Eduardo followed. A few minutes after that Petunia and Walter arrived. Eventually Charlie managed to introduce Hildie to everyone. He noticed that Berwyn seemed to have perked up considerably.

At the center of it all stood Pam, eyes bright and cheeks flushed, with a pleased, somewhat overwhelmed expression on her face. She'd rarely seemed so beautiful and joyous. Charlie smiled, warmed through. It was good to see her this way. He remembered how much like an outsider she'd often felt, even when they were together on Chayko. *Outsider no longer, Sergeant. Way to go!*

Hildie squeezed his hand. "Should I be jealous?"

"Of Pam? No." He met her teasing gaze. "I was just thinking how she's changed since back when we all first arrived on Chayko. I think she's in a much better situation now."

"With Balchu?"

"Balchu definitely stepped up. But I mean just generally. The Pack has been good for her. Shady's been extremely good for her. And I think she'll be a good sergeant for us. That said, at the end of the day it's you I prefer to go home with."

"Glad we're still agreed on that point. Ready to bug out yet?"

He blew out a breath. "I was ready to bug out once we settled Rex. At least now you've met the Pack. Both the dogs and the humans."

"A lively bunch." She grinned. "They seem really nice."

"They are. And in a very real way, the dogs are right. Pack *is* a kind of family. We're especially proving that to Pam and Berwyn tonight."

❖ ❖　❖ ❖　❖ ❖　❖ ❖

OPD HQ, Meeting Room Two

It wasn't over by seven, but Pam didn't notice. Nobody else seemed to care, either. The morning quickly turned surreal.

Everyone assembled in HQ's Meeting Room Two, the big one that had just been renovated last month. At least, she'd *thought* everyone was there. She'd expected Chief Klein, the active-duty XK9 pairs, Charlie, Shady, and Balchu.

No surprise, Rex wasn't there. Shady had said he'd regret missing it when he woke up and discovered it was over but no one wanted to wait for his recovery.

Hildie's presence did come as a surprise. She was the first of many. "Everyone" kept expanding.

The doors opened for Feyodor and Tuya, as well as Sarnai, Rose and a couple of strangers who'd joined them. Balchu's family hurried over to Pam and Balchu with huge grins on their faces.

"Oh, *congratulations*, Sweetheart!" Tuya cried. "You look beautiful in your dress blues. I'm so *proud* of you!" She pulled

Pam into an enthusiastic hug that Pam found herself returning with more fervor than she'd expected. Her chest swelled with aching, warm joy. Her throat went tight and her vision swam, but she'd be *damned* if she allowed herself to cry!

"Now, now, give her some air," Feyodor urged. "Hugs can come later. We're holding up the ceremony."

Tuya stepped back. "We brought some extended family, too —" She turned partway toward the strangers, but there was Capt. Danvir, ready to guide them to a good viewing-spot. "Okay, you can meet them later!"

But they weren't the last arrivals. Here came both SBI Command Staffs. First Elaine, with Shiv and Shawnee, then Mike with his two LSAs Dominic and Sara. Most of the rest of Special Investigation Teams Delta and Alpha followed them in. The still-active members of the OPD task force Klein had assigned to assist Elaine in the *Izgubil* investigation trooped in behind them.

The doors opened yet again for—*Oh, my.* Pam's breath caught. Here came Razor, wobbling in on unsteady legs. Liz supported him on one side and Berwyn supported him on the other. Even more startling, Tim, Terry, and Ben clustered around Berwyn. Her old friends the Four Amigos had reunited once more. *Good for them. Berwyn probably appreciates their support.* They nodded to her with waves and huge grins, then took places along the walls.

Next, Afua, Etsu, and Shuri hastened to take places next to the Amigos. Her friends and former podmates from the first month of XK9 training wore patrol uniforms that suggested they were either just coming off watch or just going on.

Pam's mind reeled. Where had all these people come from? *How'd they all—at this ungodly hour—why would they even—*

Because they're your friends. They care about you. They want to celebrate with you. Shady's tail fanned high and happy.

You told them, didn't you?

They appreciated the intel.

Pam's head spun. She had grown up lonely, never making or

expecting to have friends. Yet here was this enormous room, full of people she knew. People who'd come here for *her*. This was even more amazing than last night's party at the Clinic. For a moment her breath wouldn't come. How could this be real?

Then Chief Klein stepped forward to speak the words of the ceremony.

He led her in the oath, an echo of her original swearing in as an officer. Thank goodness *he* remembered all the words! She repeated them through numb lips. Her pulse thundered in her ears.

Balchu pinned on her new insignia. She recognized that he was doing his best to keep a solemn expression. But once she was pinned, he gave her a huge hug before he stepped back. The room erupted into applause.

CHAPTER 20
A MANHUNT AND A BROKERED PEACE

Meeting Room Two and S-3-9

Shady stepped forward to congratulate Pam as soon as Balchu let go, but then she backed off so the others could crowd in, including Balchu's family and the couple Tuya had tried to introduce earlier.

"Pam, this is my blood brother, Chase, and his wife, Anya," Feyodor said.

"We've been so eager to meet Balchu's Amare!" Chase stepped forward to take her hand. "He's a nephew to me, and we're delighted to have this chance to meet and congratulate you."

"How very nice of you." Pam used her professional persona, but Shady sensed and smelled her bewilderment. *Who are they? Why are they here?*

Shady noted strong speculation in Balchu's stance and scent. *Ask your Amare, but don't be surprised if he can't answer definitively. Something is up, but he's still putting it together.*

Then Pam's former podmates, Afua, Etsu, and Shuri surrounded her with a group hug. The Amigos crowded in right behind them. Shady lolled her tongue and moved farther out of the way. Her friendless-no-longer partner needed to feel this moment completely.

And meanwhile, Shady had a man to hunt down.

A man who'd suddenly disappeared from the room. *Oh, you think you can somehow just fade out of the meeting and that'll be the end of it?* She laid back her ears with a barely sheathed snarl. *Think again, Shiv.*

It didn't take much of a scent-tracking dog—or for that matter much of a detective—to follow him to the war room. He had a little office next to Elaine's. Shady pushed inside before he could close the door behind himself. "We need to talk."

He gave a guilty start, then retreated behind his workstation. "I don't want to talk about it." Upstairs in Meeting Room Two, his gaze hadn't left Berwyn. His scent factors had stayed in the aching low tones of pure grief then, but now, they ratcheted into sharp high notes of pain and embarrassment.

"That is too bad." Shady followed him, hackles prickling. "When you mess with Berwyn, you mess with Cinnamon's healing. And both of those things mean you are messing with my Pack."

"I—" He gave her a despairing grimace. "I should never have tried this. I'm—I'm a bad bet. I knew I'd screw it up. Berwyn's better off not getting involved with me."

Shady penned him into his boxed-in back corner with her large, bristling body and pinned him with her sheepdog stare. "Too late. Berwyn is involved. I was there at the Solstice. I know how both of you acted and smelled—how you've related to each other ever since. What happened?"

Caught in the space behind his workstation, he couldn't escape. She didn't relish going a round with an augmented, trained fighter, but she'd won her last matchup with one, and Shiv knew it. She also could smell his reluctance to fight with her, as well as how much he hated this whole situation.

He glanced away. "Call it a flashback. I guess that's sort of what it was. An emotional flashback, if that's possible."

"It is, trust me." She'd had enough of them to know. "What did you feel?"

"I had . . ." He blew out a long, weary breath. "I had an Amare. We'd had some . . . um, call them disagreements. I thought we'd worked through them."

"Apparently not?"

"I'm poison. My job—all the travel—the weird hours." His expression turned rueful, maybe even haunted.

"Did your Amare know about your SBI career, going in?"

"He wanted me to quit. Wanted to take me on tour with him. Wanted me to *be there* for him."

She swallowed a growl. "But he knew about your career from the start?"

"I tried to accommodate him. I took a leave of absence. I went on his tour with him. But I felt so—" He grimaced, clenched his fists. Prickly, stifling mid-tones of exasperation and discouragement suffused his scent profile.

"Frustrated?" she offered. She lifted her ears and smoothed her hackles.

"Irrelevant. Frivolous. *Useless.*" His mouth made a wry twist. "Like all I was allowed to be was just—just *eye candy.*" Now the sharp, edgy reek of humiliation blended into his scent. "I'd been in charge of entire investigative task forces. Suddenly all I was supposed to do was fetch drinks, look good, and give him back rubs. I couldn't hack it. I loved him, but I just—I *couldn't.* I guess I just couldn't love him enough."

"Wait a minute." She didn't bother to silence the growl this time. "He tried to change your entire nature and reason for being, but somehow you are the toxic one?"

"It's this job. I loved it more than I loved him."

"Mm-hmm. And how much did he love you?"

Shiv shook his head. "You don't understand. He had so much he wanted to give me."

"Let me guess. Luxury. Fame. Money. Who was this guy?"

"He flies racing yachts on the championship circuit, so,

yeah." Shiv's shoulders slumped. "Fame, money. Any luxury I could even dream about."

"But not the autonomy to choose your own career."

"Now you sound like E." He scowled at her.

She snapped her ears flat and let her hackles rise fully. "Elaine is a smart woman. She also is in a high-risk business. Yet somehow Mike does not demand that she ditch her career so she can wait on him."

He avoided her gaze. "Mike and E. are a special case. They both understand this work."

"So does Berwyn."

"Until I screw up. Until I walk back into danger."

"Isn't yacht-racing dangerous?"

"Yes. Very. But one high-risk vocation per household is enough." He glared at her. "No, don't bring up Mike and E. again—they're different. I don't know how they do it."

"Then I shall bring up Pam and Balchu, instead. Do you seriously believe that any time Pam and I go into the Five-Ten Balchu does not fear the worst? Do you imagine that Pam is totally calm any time Balchu goes after smugglers?" She growled again. "For that matter, how about Rex and me? Do you think for one instant that I have never wondered whether Rex will live long enough to grow old?"

"That's different. You're both in the business. You knew the risks going in."

"You and Berwyn are both in this law enforcement business, too. And if you were already an SBI agent when you and Nitwit-Face became Amares, he knew the risks, too."

"Intellectually, he knew. But not from the gut. When I came home on a health leave after I took a knife to the shoulder, Denny was almost beside himself."

"In other words, Denny is not as brave as Pam." She curled her lip and ran a background search through her CAP for *top-ranked space yacht racer Denny.*

Shiv winced. "I didn't mean to mention his name. And he's plenty brave."

Her CAP returned a two-month-old news item at the top of a long list: DENIS LAGRANDE WINS CHAYKO SYSTEM CHAMPIONSHIP FOR THIRD STRAIGHT YEAR. She snorted. "Brave is as brave does. If you do not want me to mention Denis LaGrande by name, I shall continue to call him Nitwit-Face. And he may be brave in a space yacht, but he is a coward in love."

Shiv stared at her. "*That quickly*, you ran a search?"

"Would you not have done the same?"

He glanced away again. "Later, probably. I can't use the CAP that fast."

"Neither can Pam, or any other human I know."

"Another point for XK9 sapience." He sighed. "I suppose Berwyn hates me now."

"Berwyn is devastated. He does not understand what happened. He thinks maybe he did something wrong."

"No! He's wonderful. *I'm* the screw-up!"

"Nitwit-Face LaGrande is the screw-up. You will not be, if you are brave enough to tell Berwyn what your flashback was about."

"Would he even talk to me, at this point?" Now jittery, sharp pain blended into the resurging, deeper ache of grief-scent.

"I may have to enlist some help from Packmates to hold off the Amigos, but I think Berwyn would talk with you."

❖ ❖ ❖ ❖ ❖ ❖ ❖ ❖

Meeting Room Two

P am released a happy sigh and waved a gloved hand to Shuri, Afua, and Etsu. They all had patrols to get to, so they couldn't linger. Most of the other non-Pack members had already left to go about their day, as well as proto-Packmate Hildie. Charlie'd escorted her out but promised to be back shortly. The Chief had asked the rest of the Pack to hang around for a quick meeting on a new development that had emerged overnight.

Pam shared one last hug with Tuya, another with Sarnai, and a third with Rose, while Chase and Anya watched with smiles. An enveloping bear hug from Feyodor finished the familial goodbyes before she and Balchu stood arm-in-arm and waved to them as they left.

The family. Her throat tightened. *MY family. They seem to have claimed me.* She shot a grateful glance toward Balchu. He stood next to her, resplendent in his own dress blues, and that man looked *fine.*

The big double doors closed behind the family—then opened again.

Pam's breath caught. There stood Shady. *With Shiv.* She'd gathered a muddy sense of their confrontation through the link, but no details of what they'd said. *Nice work!*

It's a start, anyway. But her partner had focused on Berwyn. In a synchronized move that could not have been accidental, Tux, Elle, and Scout positioned themselves between the Amigos and Berwyn. Razor and Liz exchanged a glance, then she stayed close to him as he made his way a few unsteady steps so that Berwyn stood alone.

The room fell silent. Pam's pulse jumped to a faster tempo.

Shiv approached Berwyn but stopped a few paces away. Shady shadowed the agent's advance into the room. She stopped a half-meter behind and to his left.

Berwyn held his ground, his face masklike.

"I—I'm sorry I hurt you." Shiv's voice was so quiet Pam almost couldn't hear. "I honestly didn't intend that."

Berwyn gave him a skeptical eyebrow-cock.

"Stupid, I know. How else could you feel, considering—considering what I did." He glanced down, shoulders hunched, then up to stare at Berwyn with a worried expression. "You deserve better. I want to explain, if you'll listen."

"I'll listen." Berwyn's chin lifted, his expression wary.

"Is there someplace a little more private?"

Berwyn glanced at the people around them, both humans and XK9s. "*Here* is good. I'm with my Pack."

"With your Pack." Shiv grimaced, then nodded. "I get it. I do. It's a better support system than I'd realized."

Yes, it is. The thought warmed Pam, just as it surely must be strengthening Berwyn in this moment.

"They have my back." Berwyn gave his erstwhile lover a challenging stare, fists clenched. "Do you?"

Shiv swallowed. "I'd like to earn that honor again."

"So, explain what happened."

The big blond agent glanced toward Shady. "Your acting Pack Leader assures me that emotional flashbacks are a thing that can happen." He swallowed. "I, um, well, I believe I had one last night. Somehow, suddenly I was reliving a very bad moment from a previous relationship. It—it made me think I'd never be able to love anyone again, without—without having more of those flashbacks." He glanced away, then met Berwyn's gaze once more. "I figured you didn't need some flaky, dysfunctional, emotional wreck messing up your life."

"Too late." Berwyn's mouth made a wry twist, but his eyes warmed.

"So it seems." Shiv rubbed the back of his neck and stared at the floor. "I, um, figured that out, too. With a little help. Again, too late."

"Maybe not too late." Berwyn's frown softened. "But you've got to stop trying to avoid dealing with it."

Pam had never seen the normally unflappable Shiv appear so off-balance. He lowered his hand but endured a little shudder and sent a despairing gaze Berwyn's way. "I've been trying to get past it for years."

"There is no getting *past*. No getting *around*, either."

"Have to go *through?*" Shiv grimaced. "That's—I guess that's pretty clear at this point. But maybe with some mediation?"

"You want to bring in a Listener?"

"Do you mind?" Shiv hunched his shoulders again. "I think maybe I have a lot more baggage than I realized."

"That's probably a good idea." Berwyn took a step toward him. "Maybe I can help you unpack it?"

"I really could use your help." Shiv closed most of the remaining distance between them. He half-reached out but stopped short. "If you wouldn't mind?"

Berwyn smiled. "I could do that." He offered his hand.

Pam held her breath.

Shiv hesitated, his face full of half-disbelieving hope. Then he stepped forward to clasp Berwyn's offered hand.

CHAPTER 21

UNSETTLING DEVELOPMENTS

OPD HQ Atrium and Grand Central Terminal

Hildie and Charlie reached the glass-walled Atrium at the OPD entrance. She hesitated. *How I wish we didn't have to—*

She felt the gentle tug on her elbow she'd hoped for, turned quickly, and pulled him into her embrace.

He lingered long enough for a good, solid kiss, then pulled back with a rueful expression. "Gotta go."

"I know. Me, too." She gazed after him. He retreated into the nether reaches of the OPD where she'd needed special, limited-time permission to go. Had to get back for the Chief's announcement, whatever that was about.

And she had a breakfast date with Theresa. Her HUD buzzed with an incoming text: *Ah, speaking of whom . . .* "Five minutes to touchdown. You there yet?"

Grand Central Terminal lay less than 200 meters from the OPD steps. "On my way," she texted back and pushed through the big glass doors.

If she and the elevator car were racing, Hildie won. Theresa'd said A-12, so she made a short search, then watched the readout above the door as her friend's car slowed toward the end of its 15-kilometer transit from the station's Hub.

Huh, that's funny. She'd answered Theresa's text but a light still blinked at the bottom of her readout. *Did I miss a message?* It was probably Abi or Smita, wanting to know—

Shit. Her pulse thundered and everything around her seemed to go dark. "Treva LaRochelle," the ID said. *LaRock's personal account?* She struggled to force air into her lungs. *He's not supposed to contact me.*

"Hey, girl, you gonna just leave me hangin'?" Theresa wove through the crowd, then stopped. "Uh-oh. What happened?"

Hildie retrieved her case pad from her pocket and opened it to "Messages Waiting." She handed it to Theresa. "I'm not sure when it arrived. I just noticed it."

Theresa's face hardened. "Send it to your lawyer. Don't open it."

"That's what I planned. I couldn't believe it, though. What possessed him?" She forwarded the unexpected message to Endesha Odi with a note: "Have not opened this but couldn't just delete it and pretend it didn't happen. Advice?" She glanced up from her case pad. "There. I guess now let's have breakfast?"

Theresa smiled. "I'm ready for pancakes from Grand Central Breakfast upstairs." They stepped onto an escalator.

Before they'd reached the top, Hildie's HUD beeped with a text from her attorney. "Woah. That was fast. Odi just replied."

"What did she say?"

Hildie opened it and read aloud. "Good call, not to open *or* delete it. We need to talk. When can you come by my office?"

❖ ❖ ❖ ❖ ❖ ❖ ❖ ❖

Meeting Room Two

S hady took a patch of floor in the front row to the left of Pam's chair in Meeting Room Two. Balchu sat on Pam's right. Other Packmates, including Liz, Razor, and Berwyn . . . and here came Charlie. They all found places to sit near the podium where the Chief stood.

The last of Pam's well-wishers who weren't both Packmates and OPD officers left to get on with their day, except for Elaine and Shiv. Elaine stood by the Chief's side, arms crossed. Shiv waited for a nod from Berwyn, then took a seat beside him. *Good. We'll get him roped into the Pack soon, if all goes well.*

Shady turned her attention to Chief Klein.

He and Elaine glanced at each other, then he focused on his audience. "We've received troubling news this morning. It hasn't been officially announced yet, but Ranan news agencies will soon be reporting that the Transmondians have initiated an embargo on Ranan wine, beer, and spirits."

Startled, angry scent reactions came from several directions at once. Shady glanced over her shoulder. Charlie, Misha, Berwyn, and Walter all had straightened with outraged expressions.

Corona makes wine, doesn't it? She could feel Pam's frown without even checking. *And that was Glorioso Ale we were drinking last night. I know Walter's Lang Family grows hops for its main cash crop, and Berwyn's Pabiyan Family owns a distillery, along with its carnerie and dairy.*

So they're not just embargoing Rana in general? Shady cocked her head at Pam. *They're striking at XK9 Families?*

Pam blew out an unsettled breath. *Sure seems that way.*

Chief Klein nodded to his listeners, his expression grim. "You're not wrong to believe those commodities were targeted specifically. The Transmondians have told our government that to get the embargo lifted, we must return the Pack to the XK9 Project."

Now everyone's scent factors spiked with alarm.

But the Chief lifted his hands in a soothing gesture. "We said 'no.' In very strong terms."

"Even the Premier?" Charlie asked.

Klein's expression went rueful. "Both Vice-Premiers made strong statements. That blocks her from acting otherwise, although she may publish a dissent. Mayor Idris has officially declared that Orangeboro would not allow its XK9s, whom we now consider citizens, to be deported. To her credit, Council Chair Chan, in her official Orangeboro role, backed her up on that."

What? That's a surprise. Pam gave Shady an astonished eyebrows-up. Beatriz Chan was far from a notable XK9-booster. Only a few weeks ago, she'd tried to get the Council to deny XK9 recognition as sapient beings.

"Sir, do we know why she did that?" Shady wished she could talk about this with Rex.

Klein grimaced. "Her true reason is anybody's guess. But when I asked, she first said that this is clearly what her constituent Borough has decided, and as our representative she has a duty to represent us."

Yeah, right. Such a patriot, that one. Shady smelled the sludgy dubiousness shared by everyone in the room.

"Then she told me that she does not appreciate being played, as Premier Iskander and Ambassador Nunzio tried to do on the night of the presentation."

Ah. That makes a bit more sense. Pam's frown did not ease, however.

"So far, and I hope for the duration, you have allies throughout Station government." Klein sounded and smelled to Shady as if he wished he felt more sure of that. "And of course, before anybody can drag you back to Transmondia, they'll have to get past the OPD."

Okay, on that part he's definitely certain. Shady's wasn't the only tail thumping the floor.

"They'll also have to get past the SBI," Elaine added. "Not to mention SDF Intelligence. Director Perri and Commodore Cornwell both made a point of issuing strong statements."

Oh, that is interesting. Shady lolled her tongue. *Cornwell is standing up for us?* Rex didn't trust "spooks," as he called them, and personally disliked Cornwell. She hadn't been too favorably impressed by him, herself. *But we'll take the support, for sure!*

"You are as safe as we can make you. Rana Station vigorously asserts your right to stay here," Klein continued. "But we're convinced this embargo is only the beginning of an escalation that could get ugly. Transmondian trade embargoes tend to expand, for one thing. I imagine the humans among you may recall three years ago when they embargoed Pinakamaroan silver."

Shady could sense her partner's grim nod, but she herself had no idea what he meant. She accessed the Station Net, but before she could run a search, Klein spoke again.

"That embargo jammed up pretty much all Pinakamaroan trade. That's because the Transmondians claimed they 'had to' check every container in every Pinakamaroan cargo ship to make sure they weren't transporting 'contraband.' And they did this at every spaceport and transfer station they control, which in this system means most of them. Pinakamaroan trade ground to a halt."

Shady's imagination leaped ahead, to a near-total blockade of Ranan exports. *What would the Station do if that happened? How could we survive?*

I don't know. The depth of Pam's worry terrified Shady.

"With no jump point in their region, the Pinakamaroans had to give in to the Transmondians' demand for 'favored access' and below-market silver prices, or face economic ruin." Klein scowled. "Lucky for Rana, we're practically parked on the Chaykoan Jump Point's doorstep. They'd have to commit an act of war to bar us. All the same, this situation is shaping up to be a bad one, and likely to get worse."

"What can we do, sir?" Berwyn asked. "What can we ask our Families to do?"

"It's time to bring into play any influence any of us or our

Families have. Let Councilwoman Chan and Mayor Idris know how much you appreciate their support. Ask your family members to help spread the word about how smart XK9s are, and how much they want you to stay here and remain safe."

❖❖ ❖❖ ❖❖ ❖❖

Urban Orangeboro, Harris & Odi Law Firm

*D*o I really want to know? Hildie accepted a quick hug from Theresa. Then her friend settled into a chair in the richly-appointed waiting room of the Harris and Odi Law Firm.

"Ms. Odi will see you now." A slender receptionist in a silk dress led Hildie down a thick-carpeted hallway to one of the offices.

Her Family-funded attorney Endesha Odi was too young to be the named-partner Odi. Most likely a daughter, granddaughter, or other near kin. Certainly she had the self-possessed presence of a woman certain of her power and position. Always well-dressed, today she wore a tailored charcoal pantsuit and a tightly-wrapped, rust-colored hijab that framed her serious ebony face.

"Might want to sit down for this." She offered Hildie a wry smile and gestured to one of the chairs in front of her desk. Somchai Saidi, from the Safety Services Employees' Union, had risen to greet Hildie with a nod. He sat back down in the chair next to hers.

The receptionist offered tea or coffee. Hildie declined. She'd already consumed enough coffee at breakfast to make her fingertips tingle. Once that was settled, Endesha gave her a grim frown. "Well, we had a strong case already. Now we have an even better one."

Hildie drew in a sharp breath. "What did he send me?"

"A dick pic." Endesha grimaced. "Sent at 04:27 this morning with the message, 'Can't stop thinking of you. Can we talk?'"

"Drunk again," Saidi muttered.

A small wave of cold dizziness swept through Hildie. "How could he be that stupid? Are we—are we sure it's from him?"

Endesha's lips tightened into a mirthless line. "I suppose we could ask for a forensic physical examination to establish a positive ID on the photo."

What a special job for some poor forensic scientist. Hildie's train of thought derailed there for a moment. "Um, I was thinking more of an electronic trail."

"Oh, it appears to be from his actual account. I had that checked first thing." Endesha turned to Saidi. "There's a history of excessive drinking?"

"A recent one." He scowled and ran a hand across his mouth. His eyes twitched back and forth, a "tell" that he was reading from his HUD. "Two drunk-and-disorderly misdemeanors. One filed by a tavern in Central Fifth District, and the other . . . here it is. In Ruby Prism of the Orangeboro Entertainment District. He's now banished from both establishments."

"*How* recent?"

"Last couple of weeks. Both happened after the day he tried to fire our client. Plus, he's got repeated failures to show up for mandated counseling sessions since then."

They're talking about LaRock doing all that? Hildie struggled to imagine this. The man had always acted odd around her, but this seemed out of character, even for him. *Whatever's wrong with him, he's self-destructing without any help from us.* Her team had filed a harassment complaint. And they were prepared to countersue for wrongful termination if the Department upheld LaRochelle's order. Was that enough to spark this reaction? Or was there more to it? *Not my problem, thank goodness.*

"I'll file this as an evidentiary addendum to our harassment complaint." Endesha quirked an eyebrow at Hildie. "Unless you want that forensic ID confirmation?"

"I suppose it doesn't matter whose dick it was." She wrinkled her nose. "Pale skin?"

"Yes."

An involuntary shudder quivered through her. *Probably his, then.* "File it."

CHAPTER 22
CHARLIE'S NEW ASSIGNMENT

OPD HQ and S-3-9

Charlie headed for Elaine's S-3-9 investigative center as she'd requested, after Klein's bombshell briefing about the embargo ended. He'd lingered a few moments to speculate about *how hard will this hit us,* and compare thoughts with Packmates. But that was just collective stewing. *Not much to do but get back to work.*

He left Meeting Room Two in a haze of free-floating anxiety. Corona's wine sales made up roughly twenty to thirty percent of their overall income, depending on the size and quality of the crop. They sold most of their small-batch artisanal wine on Station, so exports weren't as big a deal as they might be to Glorioso—and definitely would be to the industrial-sized Pabiyan Distillery. But anything that hurt the Ranan economy would cripple sales of luxury products.

He halted in the hallway behind Liz, Berwyn, Shiv, and Razor.

The big, black-and-tan XK9 had stopped. He wavered on his feet, then abruptly sat down.

A chill prickled the back of Charlie's neck. "Is Razor okay?"

"No." Liz's face pinched with worry. "He's been up too long, and this news is hard to take."

He shot a glance at Shiv, caught him glancing his way, and nodded.

"Liz, stay with him and calm him." Shiv turned to Berwyn. "Can you find some kind of cart or dolly we could lift him onto?"

"You bet." Berwyn jogged away in the direction of Civic Center Maintenance.

"He's awfully heavy." Liz's worried expression didn't ease.

"I am sorry to be such a bother." Razor's ears clamped against his skull. He panted so fast Charlie worried he might hyperventilate.

"It's all right." Charlie stroked the XK9's shoulder. He caught himself projecting strength into the link, even though Razor couldn't receive it. "Everybody has moments when they need help from friends. Don't worry. Shiv and I can lift a lot more weight than you might think."

It wasn't common knowledge that both of them had undergone physical augmentation treatments. Charlie'd taken that option only a few weeks ago, but the treatments had speeded and enhanced his healing after significant dock breach injuries. They'd already made him physically stronger than he'd ever been in his life. Shiv had received his treatments nine years ago, after even more catastrophic injuries from being shoved off a primary terrace by a fugitive criminal.

Berwyn returned triumphant, pushing a furniture dolly. Shiv and Charlie scooped Razor up with ease and laid him gently onto its carpeted surface.

"Charlie, your arm—" Liz eyed his arm shield.

"It's fine. I'm good." Charlie shrugged off her concern. Shiv had more than lifted his share of the weight, which allowed Charlie to help while favoring his still-healing left arm. "I hope you have a ride back?"

"We do." Berwyn propelled the dolly.

Charlie and Shiv escorted him, Liz, and Razor to the sally port, where an auto-nav from the clinic awaited. He and Shiv once again gently lifted Razor, this time from the ad hoc "gurney" onto a cushion that awaited him in the car. There'd be plenty of help and equipment at the other end of their short journey, however, and duty called. They waved them away, then turned again toward S-3-9.

Shiv said nothing more. Charlie couldn't guess what his companion might be thinking. They walked shoulder-to-shoulder back through the Civic Center in silence. At the elevator Shiv turned to him.

"Has E. talked to you about the GRs she wants?"

"More GRs? Well, why not?" Charlie smiled. "As long as Rex is undergoing treatment and I'm on short workdays, it'll be a chance to brush up on my proficiency."

"That's one way to look at it." Shiv grunted. "Try to hold that thought." He went into a HUD-stare. "Yes? We're at the elevators. No, I don't think so."

The doors slid open. They stepped inside, but apparently Shiv's com call hadn't ended.

Now what's up? Charlie tried halfheartedly not to eavesdrop, although Shiv's replies of "Hmm," "Probably," and "Stick that to the wall and come back to it later," were less than enlightening. He stared toward the elevator car's ceiling and chewed on his lower lip. *What kind of GR does Elaine want me to make?*

In the war room there seemed to be a lot of people up and moving around. Several of the agents within view appeared to be closing down their workstations and gathering bits of gear as if preparing to depart. *Mike's people.* The SIT Delta agents remained focused on tasks. *Where is SIT Alpha going?*

"Dom, hold a moment." Shiv strode off toward Mike's primary LSA, Dominic Wei.

Okay, then. Charlie wound his way through the war room and attempted to avoid blocking anyone's path. Elaine, Shiv, Shawnee, and Mike all had small offices along the same back corridor as the Morgue Annex, on the war room's far side. Once he reached it, he rapped on the frame of Elaine's closed office door to alert her he'd arrived.

"One moment." Her voice came through the door muffled.

A man's voice, also from inside, said something Charlie couldn't distinguish. Sounded like Mike Santiago's voice.

Charlie retreated several steps to allow them some privacy. His new vantage allowed him to keep Elaine's office in view, yet also observe action in the war room.

Sarabande Cutler, Mike's second LSA, paused near Charlie with a nod and a smile. She'd helped him get his arm shield into a transit hammock on the Trans-Hub train a couple of weeks ago and had seemed disposed to be friendly ever since.

Charlie smiled back. "Are you guys headed somewhere?"

"Centerboro." Her brows pinched. "They've found several pipe bombs and other explosive devices near legislators' homes and offices recently."

"Why call Alpha? Isn't there a whole unit devoted to explosives that's *headquartered* in Centerboro?" It was, after all, the Station's national capital for humans, and home of the primary HQ for the "human side" of the SBI. The ozzirikkian capitol in Zhokikim Timi on Wheel Five hosted parallel offices for ozzirikkian Ranans.

"Some bigwig got the notion that Whisper's behind the bombs." Her frown deepened. "We've told them it's not the Syndicate's M.O.—too open and obvious. But when the Powers that Be demand our presence . . ."

"Got it. Well, safe travels."

Elaine's door opened. Mike stepped outside but held Elaine's hand a moment longer. He grimaced, gave her hand one last squeeze, then turned to stride away.

She gazed after her Significant for a moment and blew out a long breath. Then she squared her shoulders and turned to summon Charlie.

He followed her into her office.

"Pull up a chair. First of all, that GR you showed us yesterday was superb. Director Perri keeps mentioning it. Did I know you were that good, and wasn't the GR fascinating, and you know— that sort of thing. I'm certain she'd be campaigning hard to recruit you for the SBI's Global Reconstruction Department, if you weren't already a Reserve Agent and Rex's partner."

"I'm glad she's pleased." Charlie met Elaine's smile with one of his own. *Here's hoping Assistant Prosecutor Niam was equally convinced.*

"Now, then. I am told you're a specialist in GR blood spatter depictions. Is that correct?"

Where'd she hear that? "It's true I've done a fair amount of GR 'bloodwork.'" He did rather pride himself on his spatter depictions, although it wasn't exactly something a man could brag about to his Family.

"Good. I have five crime scenes I'd like for you to run through your GR process. If possible, I'd like for you to enhance the visibility of the blood in them."

Charlie frowned. "I won't misrepresent a scene."

"No, that's not what I'm asking. They're plenty gory on their own. But what we've got are vids and stills from after the fact, not recreations of the process. We have spotty data on some, although for one we have scent evidence and contemporaneous audio. I'd like at least a short representation—based on the existing evidence—of how the sequence was likely to have unfolded in each."

"Scent evidence? Contemp—" His gut tightened. *"Plenty gory on their own," she'd said. Oh, crap. She's talking about the Dolan scene in the Sionainn.*

"Yes. We were extremely fortunate to have access to Elle and Petunia's services in Howardsboro. They created excellent reports that should aid you with one of the reconstructions. And multiple wearable sensors picked up audio, so we now have a sense of the pacing."

Oh, yeah, it's the Dolan scene. Damn, damn, damn. Should've guessed, from Shiv's reaction. He tried keep his response out of his expression but had a sense that he'd failed. "You have five scenes like *that* one?" He repressed a shudder.

She gave him a rueful grimace. "We have twenty-four. The five I want from you are all Ranan cases, however. Most of the others were committed in Uladh Nua. Three were in Transmondia."

Holy shit. "How long has this been going on?"

"The oldest cases are from Uladh Nua. They date back as far as 42 years ago. Since Knife Woman might—by a long stretch—be in her early thirties, we're sure she didn't commit all of them."

"Why has the wider law enforcement community never heard about them?"

"Some of the Chaykoan cases were briefly sensational locally, but for various reasons, the police didn't release the details of most." She curled her lip. "And all of the Ranan cases happened in the lower levels—places like the Sionainn and the Five-Ten."

"Let me guess. There was no need to 'cause a public panic.'"

"Why, Charlie, however did you know that?" She gave a brief, mirthless laugh. "We believe the five Ranan cases represent the work of two different executioners. Forensic scientists had already speculated that one was a woman. The other is taller, demonstrably stronger, and probably had some training in surgical techniques. Likely male, although that's a hypothetical at this point because we haven't isolated a definitive DNA sample."

He nodded. "That'll mean using a generic figure for those reconstructions. I'll be interested to read all of the analyses. Are the ones committed by the possibly male unsub as high a priority as Knife Woman's? Presumably this is for her case?"

"Ultimately, three are for her case, but we won't need those for a while. She won't be able to stand trial till sometime after she comes out of re-gen. The other two actually are more important. We need those fairly soon, to make the point that there's at least one Whisper Syndicate executioner still at large on the Station."

Understanding dawned. "Emer Bellamy doesn't believe she's in danger if we release her, and we need to convince her that she is?"

Elaine beamed at him. "God, I love working with bright people!"

CHAPTER 23
NEED TO KNOW

S-3-9 Investigative Center

"A word, Acting Pack Leader?" Shady glanced around, ears up. She and Pam had arrived in the war room to find it in a state of upheaval. Since then, she'd been sniffing out more information about Alpha's impending relocation, but she hadn't expected a direct interaction with LSA Dominic Wei. Mike's second-in-command had never made any effort to speak with her before. "Yes?"

Wei offered a brief, insincere smile. His scent factors muddled sludgy unease with a nose-prickling edge of irritation. "Mike says we need some XK9 Reserve Agents, and I'm to ask you which ones we can have."

"I shall need a few more specifics, before I can answer that." Shady made an effort to keep her ears up and her hackles down. She could guess what errands LSA Wei might have in mind. But she didn't like his demeanor, and after Klein's briefing this morning, she'd settled into a foul mood. "When do you need them, for what purpose, and has Chief Klein authorized their deployment?"

"Um. Yes, the deployment's authorized. We need them today,

and probably longer. And, we need them because . . ." He grimaced. "I can't tell you why."

"Well, that was easy. You may not have any of them." She turned away. *I do not need this added aggravation.*

"No! Mike says we need them."

She gave him an unamused stare and sensed Pam's uptick of worry through the link. "Perhaps Mike should come talk to me, then. He might make more sense."

"It's need-to-know only." He clenched his fists. "I don't think you have clearance."

She showed a flash of teeth. "As their commanding officer, I need to know. Presumably they will learn the nature of their mission soon enough, which implies that XK9s do have clearance. Would you send any of *your* agents to an unknown location, for an unknown purpose, for an unspecified amount of time? Just because a disrespectful OPD commander demanded it?"

"You're not Rex, so I . . ." He hesitated. "Sorry. I didn't mean to come off as disrespectful. Actually, we need to take them to Centerboro. We'll almost certainly ask them to check for explosives, and we'll probably need them to follow scent trails."

"So this is about the Centerboro pipe bombs that supposedly are the work of the Whisper Syndicate?"

His mouth fell open. "How do you—" He shook his head, then blew out an impatient breath. "Yes."

"Apparently not all of your agents got the memo that it was need-to-know only." She swept her ears back and reviewed current XK9 assignments. Razor, Cinnamon and Rex were on health leave. Victor and Eduardo were working on Lew Penny's murder case, consulting with Petunia and Walter today. Scout and Crystal had deployed with Nicole, Connie, and the STAT Team to help keep a lid on things in the Five-Ten.

But Tux and Georgia had recently rotated off of a study with SCISCO and some of nir colleagues. Meanwhile, Elle and Misha were currently helping with SBI formwork, on standby to assist with interviews of Emer Bellamy. There could be a remote possibility that the heiress might be inspired to say something to them other than "Lawyers."

But not so far. To date, Emer only seemed willing to throw more and more attorneys at the delay in setting her bond. She would face mortal danger if she set foot outside of OPD detention, and everyone Shady knew considered her an extreme flight risk, but she so far had not been deterred.

"Take Tux and Elle." Shady hated to send them to another Wheel. But the two mates would take care of each other and their specialties matched Wei's assignment perfectly. "How long will you be gone?"

"I wish I knew. Maybe two or three days."

Great. That runs into Calendar New Year, which the humans, at least, will hate. She stress-yawned. "Let us go round up the troops and break the news."

❖ ❖   ❖ ❖   ❖ ❖   ❖ ❖

S-3-9 Investigative Center and OPD Interview Suite M

P am left it to Shady and Dominic Wei to catch up with Tux, Elle, and their humans. *I wish them safety and success! And, um, 'have a beautiful New Year'?*

Yeah, right. Shady focused elsewhere.

Balchu had moved ahead of her once they'd arrived in the war room, but now he returned with an odd little smile on his face.

She lifted her eyebrows. "What?"

"I just got a call from Uncle Chase."

'Uncle' Chase? "Who—" The name rang vague bells. *Oh, there was something about a 'blood brother.'* She frowned. "Wait, the guy with your dad this morning?"

"He invited us to lunch at his place today."

"Today? Well, that's lovely, but I'm not sure I'll have time.

We're supposed to interview Kieran any time now, and interviews can take a while."

"I told him that, but he said please come if possible. Ideally, around 12:30. I, . . ." He gave her a quizzical glance. "If it's what I think it is, it might be kind of important."

Something about his tone made her examine him harder. Her chest went tight. *I don't have time for this!* Worries about the embargo, a threat of pipe bombs in Centerboro, the need to prepare her mind for the interview—!

She squeezed her eyes shut. Scrubbed her face with both hands. Then she drew a deep breath and let it out slowly. *Let all the stress go with it. Center. Be here now.* She straightened and refocused on Balchu. "I don't need more puzzles, love, and I don't need another distraction. I'm maxed out already. So be straight with me. What do you mean, 'this might be important'?"

He took her by both shoulders and gazed at her with a serious expression for a moment, then bowed his head and stepped back. "You're right. This is a bad time. You need to get your mind straight for Kieran. Look, if you finish in time and want to get away for lunch, we can talk more on our way there."

Mysteries upon mysteries. "Okay, that sounds fair. And lunch away from my desk might be nice."

"Let me know when you're out—whenever that is. Don't stress over lunch. I'll explain to Chase if we can't." He gave her a quick kiss.

Pam's HUD dinged: Melynn. "We have a go-ahead from the doctors. They're bringing Kieran to Interview M."

Pam and Shady hurried upstairs, but stopped short when they saw the gathering outside Detention Suite M. She pressed her lips together and shared a glance with Shady. *I suppose I should've expected a crowd for this.*

Yeah, probably. But I didn't, either. Too distracted. Shady stress-yawned.

Pam realized she was clenching her teeth and consciously relaxed her jaws. *Gotta refocus. Again.* She waved a silent "Hello" to UPO Lynne Anthony, who stood on the far side of the group, and offered a silent nod to ABA Regan Ireland.

"Congratulations, Sergeant." Ireland smiled at her.

Pam stammered out thanks and tried to hide her astonishment. She'd encountered the tall, glamorous attorney only a handful of times before, and wouldn't have guessed the woman had even noticed her.

"Nothing!" Sound Tech Samuels called from inside Observation M. "Now try."

"Testing, testing, testing." Melynn's voice came from inside Interview M.

Not transmitting, Shady reported.

"Nothing!" Samuels yelled. "Hold on."

Pam sidled over to stand next to Lynne, a muscular middle-aged officer who'd spent her career patrolling the Five-Ten. Pam knew Lynne, and her partner Henry Sevencrows, fairly well after several years on the Fifth Precinct beat. Lynne also had joined the Command Staff as a "local expert" during their push to round up Kieran's crew a few weeks ago. *Probably here to consult again.*

Shady wagged her greeting.

Lynne grinned at them. "Congrats from me, too, Sergeant. Is that why you're all dressed up?"

"No time to change, after the quickie ceremony upstairs." She lowered her voice. "How's Henry?"

His senior partner grimaced. "More shaken than he wants to admit. Still on indefinite Health Leave."

"He was so brilliant, yesterday." Pam hoped her respect showed on her face. "Absolutely rock-solid, and he got us out of a terrible jam."

"Okay—*now!*" Samuels bellowed.

Pam and Lynne stepped back a little farther.

"That was his fifth close call in the last month and a half. He's been the target of three blowgun darts." Lynne's face pinched with worry. "Fortunately, the one armed with poison completely missed him and we got a good DNA match from aspirates on it. But the other two had razor tips, and one of them didn't completely miss."

"Are they only shooting at *him*?"

"Oh, they shoot at both of us, but I'm shorter. Less of a target." She shook her head. "And then there was the domestic assault case who tried to deliver a beatdown on him last week. I was busy with the female. She wanted to pile on, too, so I had my hands full. One of those times I wished I had so much as an ozzie half-limb, you know? Better yet, three or four good hands."

"Oh, yeah. Been there." Pam had been outweighed and overtopped by more than one uncooperative detainee. And at times she would've loved to have an extra hand or even an ozzie-type stub. Ranan ozzirikkians' ancestors had evolved in a remote part of their native planet, a disfavored "mutant" group. They often had only four full limbs, rather than the normal six. Even if they did grow a middle pair, it often didn't develop completely.

"Anyway, time I got to my EStee, both Henry and his detainee were pretty bloodied-up. Now this attack, on top of it all? I can see why the guy needs a break from work."

"I'm sorry he's had such a rough time. It's my general impression that you and he treat the Five-Tenners fairly, and at least some of the people down there respect you."

Lynne shrugged. "As fairly as the Council allows. Anyway, we're police and they're mostly unauthorized. That tends to limit the warm fuzzy feelings."

"Yes!" Samuels cried. "Got it!"

Melynn emerged from Interview M. "Thank goodness! We really need high-security-*everything* for this subject." She surveyed the assembly in the hallway. "Thank you for coming, ABA Ireland. Will you and Lynne fit in there okay?"

"We'll be fine. Only a *little* bit cozy." Ireland gave a rueful chuckle and stepped inside.

Shady poked her head through Interview M's open doorway. "We shall be 'cozy' in here, too."

Melynn, Pam and Shady took a moment to examine the setup. The little room appeared like most others in the Detention area: a metal table bolted to the floor and a few chairs. The room's large array of devices for both audio and visual data collection stayed hidden in the walls and ceiling.

"They're on their way." Melynn led them back into the hall and closed the door. "Oh, my. Just got another notice. Kieran's coming with an entourage. In addition to his security detail—who *will* wait outside—there's an attending nurse. *And* he's got a lawyer."

"A lawyer?" Pam drew in a quick breath. Foreboding sent an extra little shiver through her belly. "So—is he going to talk or not?"

Melynn bit her lower lip. "He's promised he will. But how much is a promise worth, when the person who makes it is a mass murderer?"

CHAPTER 24
BACKSTABBERS AND BOXES OF RATS

OPD Interview Suite M

S hady lifted her ears. An inner door rumbled open: sounded about the right distance away to be on the back wall of Interview M. She heard shuffling footsteps and low voices inside. *He's here.* She tested the air currents by the closed door and caught a whiff of Kieran, redolent with hospital odors. *Yup, he's in there.* Two other humans had come in with him from the Detention side.

"I'm told they're inside now." Melynn nodded to Pam. "Good to know the soundproofing is effective."

Shady let her tongue loll.

Smartass. Just 'cuz you have dog ears. The corner of Pam's mouth twitched with a suppressed smile.

"Okay. Ireland says go on in." Melynn waved Shady forward.

Kieran sat in a wheelchair, attended by a burly nurse from Detention's Infirmary. Kieran seemed paler and more scrawny in his clean hospital gown and bed jacket.

Another man took a seat next to him—Ansar Hadi, Assistant Borough Public Defender. Shady'd encountered him on two other cases.

Once everyone was in place, Melynn introduced herself, Pam, and Shady. She issued the standard arrest warning about how anything he said could be held against him and closed with the regulation notice that the interview was being recorded. "For the record, please state your names."

Kieran straightened in his wheelchair. His scent filled with an uprush of sweaty fear. "Kieran O'Boyle." Then he turned to Hadi.

The attorney introduced both himself and the attending nurse, whose name was Brutus. "My client has agreed to enter a plea of 'guilty' to the charge of aiding and abetting mass murder, conspiracy, and also to a list of other charges detailed in the documentation I'm submitting . . . now." He hesitated, then nodded.

Shady guessed that meant he'd forwarded the plea documents to ABA Ireland and she'd acknowledged receipt. She couldn't have read them yet, however.

"My client further agrees to cooperate fully with the investigation, in return for the reassurance that he will be held in protective custody for the rest of his natural life."

That's one you don't hear too often. Pam shot a quick, ironic glance toward Shady. *A defendant to asks to be "reassured" of life-long imprisonment?*

A plea like that would be an instant death sentence in Transmondia. Shady still wasn't convinced Rana's prohibition against death sentences was a good idea.

Ranans don't believe in throwing people away. Her partner's brows pinched briefly, then smoothed to neutrality again.

"And, further," Hadi continued, "that he shall be secured and defended by the Orangeboro Public Safety Department from any and all bodily or mortal threats, either from the Whisper Syndicate, or from any and all other enemies."

There it is. A grin tugged at Pam's lips. *By "lifelong," he's hoping that means a longer life. Not to mention health care, a roof over his head, a decent bed, and three squares a day. None of those are guaranteed when you live in the Five-Ten.*

It says something, when prison is the better alternative. Shady stifled a growl. *A Ranan prison is most certainly better than torture like the Murder Brothers suffered.*

The Whisper assassin Rex called "Knife Woman" had mutilated and eviscerated the so-called "Murder Brothers" alive, two weeks ago. She'd hastily slit their throats before she fled from Shady's oncoming mate. But Neil and Rufus Dolan hadn't had time to bleed out before the Howardsboro paramedics could stabilize them. That might not have been much of a favor, considering the extent of their injuries.

"Knife Woman" herself was also now in custody—currently in re-gen, after her fight with Rex. A quicksilver prickle of worry rippled Shady's hackles. *What "other" enemies might he mean?*

Emer's boyfriend "Zannie," maybe? Pam quirked an eyebrow.

They waited for a few minutes in silence, then Melynn spoke. "I have just been assured by Assistant Borough Attorney Ireland that those terms are acceptable to the Prosecutor's Office."

Okay, that explains the lag, Pam said through the link. *ABA Ireland must've reviewed Hadi's packet of plea offers and consulted with her boss.*

Yeah, that was my guess.

Melynn turned to their subject. "Kieran, let's start with your opening statement. Please describe your part in the plan to attack the space barque *Izgubil.*"

Kieran's eyes widened and his jittery, frightened scent factors intensified. He gave Hadi a worried eyebrows-up, but the attorney nodded.

Their subject drew in a deep breath. "Um, okay. Well. Um, Zander Hoback gave me the plan. I gathered a team. Zan ran 'em through the drill a couple of times and we, um, we followed the plan." He gave them a tight little twitchy smile. "That's kinda the nutshell." He rubbed his left arm with his right hand. "Um, yep. That was . . . what we did." The bitter reek of shame rose in his scent, along with an odd mix of high-key hope and sweat-drenched terror.

Melynn elevated her eyebrows.

Kieran squirmed in his chair. Ran a hand through his newly-short, clean hair. "And then, well, Emer paid me the next day. You prob'ly want to know that, too, don't you?" His thin, dry laugh sounded more nervous than amused. "I, well, I took my cut and then I—um, I paid the guys." He hunched his shoulders in a way that gave Shady the impression he thought they might criticize this. "I mean, you don't stiff those Saoirse blades. They'll fuck you up bad."

That confirms at least one thing. Shady didn't wag her tail or shoot a side-eye toward her partner but satisfaction warmed her. All of Kieran's crew, scent-ID'd as part of the installation team, had since been captured. Distinctive, Celtic-knot tattoos had marked three of them as probable Saoirse Front members but to a man they'd refused even to give their names.

Melynn waited, eyebrows still up.

Kieran ran a hand over his face, then wiped it on the sleeve of his bed jacket. "And, um, Thumper's my man. He's not much of a friend, but he's what I've got. So I had to pay him, don'cha see."

Thumper. That's Elmo Smart's street name. Rex had told her that. Rex and Elmo had their own history, which had played a part in Kieran's undoing.

Thank you! I didn't want to break into his opening statement. Pam typed a note on her case pad and sent it to Melynn, who replied with the faintest of nods.

Kieran bit his lip again and ran his hands along his upper arms a few times.

Assistant PD Hadi turned to Kieran, offered an encouraging nod.

"I mean, you know, after all that, well, it didn't seem fair to stiff Till. He's not all there but he swung that applicator all day long like a real champ. And I couldn't pay him without payin' Feek and Wayne, 'cuz then they'd know . . ." Kieran blew out his breath. "So, yeah. Maybe I'm a putz, but I did pay 'em what I promised. All of 'em, and all I promised. Sorry."

Somehow he seems to think we'd be disappointed in him for paying his men? Shady didn't cock her head physically because she didn't want to convey puzzlement to Kieran, although with all the silent body language already being directed at him, maybe that wouldn't matter?

I wonder if that's him responding to how Turlach would react. That little furrow reappeared between Pam's eyebrows. Kieran's father Turlach O'Boyle was Whisper's man bought and sold, as far as the OPD knew. On Whisper's behalf, he had come to effectively rule Toro and several other Enclaves in the Five-Ten out of his storefront, Ostra Import-Export Emporium.

Normally untouchable behind a wall of Whisper muscle, Turlach recently had received a serious beating. He'd refused to talk about it when Henry asked—"just to poke the bear," as Henry put it. But that beating had come not long after the *Izgubil* met its fate.

Kieran laced and unlaced his fingers in his lap. His sour, sweaty scent factors filled the little room. "And, um, you probably want more details, don't you?" His mouth made a thin, unhappy line and he seemed to shrink down into the wheelchair. "I don't know what else to say, so . . . ask?"

Sour impatience mingled with bright, vigorous high notes of relief and excitement in Melynn's scent factors. "All right. You've given us some places to start. Let's go back to Zander Hoback. Who is he?"

Kieran's mouth twisted with disgust. "Now *that* guy's a class-A douchebag. Got a silver tongue and a helluva nerve. Emer thinks he walks on water, but if he does, it's 'cause oil and water don't mix. What a greasy slimebag!"

Yes, but how do you really feel, Kieran? Shady lolled her tongue below the edge of the table.

Pam kept her face still, but her scent filled with peppery exasperation. *Did you notice how specifics-free that description was? How did that advance our knowledge?*

"How did you meet him?" Melynn asked.

"He started coming into Ostra with his boss. I figured at first he was just Ferro's flunky. Never said much, always held back, but his eyes never stopped moving. I used to watch him. You could look at him and tell somebody was home upstairs, know what I mean?"

Melynn nodded. "And this is which Ferro, that he worked for?"

"Shit, I hope there's only one!" A shudder rippled through Kieran's thin body. "I'm talkin' 'bout Allard. Ol' Hatchet-Face, the Whisper honcho, you know? Same guy as went to space dust with that cursed ship."

"So . . . this Zander Hoback. You say he *worked* for Allard Ferro?"

"Yeah, ain't that a kick? A Whisper guy knocked off his boss *and* the biggest cash cow the Syndicate had. Fucker's got conchos, you know? What a backstabbing shit-turd. Shoulda known he'd do me that way, too, but like I said that guy can spin out a great story!"

"Kieran, let's talk a bit more about how you and Zander Hoback decided to attack the *Izgubil*." Melynn kept her face calm and neutral, but her itchy, skeptical scent told Shady she thought he was stalling.

Shady wasn't so sure. Kieran's scent factors told a complicated story of fear, caution, and rage—but also frustration. What fueled any of them, she could only guess. She noted only her empirical observations in her interview log. Perhaps others' insights could yield patterns she didn't perceive.

"*We* didn't decide to attack the ship." Kieran's mouth made a rueful twist. "Zan had it all worked out. He told me—told all of us—what we were going to do."

"What made you go along with him?"

"Oh, don't get me wrong. I loved the idea. I *wanted* to hurt Whisper. I hate them. I especially hated *that ship*." The virulent stench of resentment and rage in his scent left Shady in no doubt that Kieran had relished—still did relish—a chance to strike out with murderous force against the Whisper Syndicate.

"What is it about *that ship* that made you hate it?"

Kieran's face pinched with pain. He bowed his head. "Cheree." His voice went lower and softer. "Turd sold them Cheree."

"Okay, I need some context, please. What does that mean? Is 'Turd' a name?"

"Yeah. It's what I call the old man when he can't hear me."

"To clarify, 'Turd' is your father Turlach?"

"Yeah. My own special pet name." He grimaced.

"And he sold someone? Named Cheree? To the Whisper Syndicate?"

A shudder rippled through Kieran's scrawny frame. He seemed to scrunch in on himself, head bowed. His voice dwindled to a mumble. "*Told* her we couldn't let him see her. Did everything I could think of. Took her clear up to Duro, but it didn't matter."

Shady could follow scent, but human maps were visual abstractions that often left her more confused than enlightened. *Duro is an enclave?*

Farthest one from Toro in the Five-Ten, Pam explained through the link. *Clearly not far enough.*

"She was new—come down in one of the boxes with a new load of rats, and he didn't glimpse her 'cuz she had a hood on," Kieran continued.

'Rats.' Shady knew that slang. It meant 'warehouse rats,' people who'd jumped ship or been ejected from ships at port. Unauthorized and unidentified, they somehow arrived in the

Five-Ten in startling numbers without crossing the Port Authority's sensors. Once there, they became exploitable, desperate vics for the lords of the Five-Ten to prey upon.

"She didn't understand. Didn't want to hide all the time." Kieran's face spasmed with grief. "Damn, damn, *damn* fuckin' old ghoul! In my sleep I sometimes still hear her screamin'."

"You thought that's what he'd do?"

His scent filled with the reek of anguished resentment. "Fuck, yeah. I *knew* it. I just—I couldn't tie her up. She had such soft, tender skin. Ropes bruise, you know, and I just—just couldn't bear to do it. Prettiest little thing I ever saw. So sweet—I never wanted to hurt her. Not *ever*. *God*, I wished she'd believe me!" His voice broke.

By now he'd bent nearly double in his chair. He breathed long, labored breaths. His scent had filled with the aching lowtones of anguish. Shady cocked her head, ears up. His whole body shook. No, he wasn't quite crying. But holding back from it brought a new uprush of pain-scent's deep rawness and the smoky, sour smell of fatigue. Those gradually blotted out everything else.

Shady noted all these things in her interview log. *What's this about "boxes" loaded with rats?*

Good question, but let's give him a moment. Pam kept an eye on him.

Kieran's nurse Brutus punched something into his case pad and shot a frown toward Hadi.

The attorney's brows rose, then he turned to Melynn. "I'm advised that my client's vital signs indicate he needs a break. We may be able to continue after he's had a chance to rest."

Melynn frowned, but nodded.

Wait! We're stopping? Just like that? Shady stared at Pam.

Yeah, we are. Have to, dammit. Both scent and echoes through the link said Pam hated to stop as much as she did. *You'll please note that Brutus works for us, not for Kieran's defense team. And Kieran may be a mass-murdering lowlife who was willing to consider tying up his girlfriend against her will, but he's already confessed and he's cooperating.* Pam's face went rueful. *Gotta admit sometimes I'd like to shake him and scream GET TO THE POINT! But ultimately, we don't want to kill either him or his will to talk before we can wring him dry.*

Shady swallowed a growl. *I suppose killing him WOULD be counterproductive.*

CHAPTER 25
CONFRONTATION

S-3-9 Investigative Center and Greater Urban Orangeboro

B alchu intercepted Pam at the entrance of the war room, eyebrows up and scent factors full of questions. Shady gave a quiet snort and left Pam to explain that this might—or might not—be a long break.

SIT Alpha had bugged out. Already their scents had settled and cooled, along with those of Elle, Tux, Georgia, and Misha. Just a few muted voices broke an unaccustomed quiet in here. She could walk the room's length without bumping into anyone or waiting for someone to pass. Unsettled, she turned three times and lay down on the dog-hair-covered pad in their usual corner cubicle next to Pam's preferred workstation. *Might as well write reports till we hear if we're going back in.*

The smells of Kieran's grief and fatigue lingered in her nose and mingled with her own worries. Transmondia's embargo loomed like a specter in the background. *Why does Rex have to be in nanite re-gen? He's the genius politician—I don't know what to do!* Rex's health brought its own load of care to pile on top of her. Dr. Sandler had said when the readings came back in the right ranges, the treatment could finish. Sometime tomorrow, maybe, but maybe the next day. *It's all a big experiment. Will it even work?* Hildie had thought it would. That brought her a little hope. *But will XK9s still be free by the time the treatment ends and he wakes up?*

Yes, they will. Pam slid into the workstation's ergonomic human-style chair. It adjusted to her shape with a quiet whir. *Believe it. The Chief promised.*

Shady stress-yawned. *I love him for that, but the Chief is only one human. If we are to depend on the good will of politicians such as Beatriz Chan and Premier Iskander—who both outrank the Chief—how firm can his promise be?*

You're borrowing trouble. Try to think of something else.

As if there's anything more important.

Focus on your formwork.

Shady licked her lips. *I can try, anyway.* Her HUD dinged: a message from Balchu to both her and Pam. The headline made her breath catch: "EMBARGO SHUTS DOWN WAYLAND TRANSIT IN SOLARA CITY."

Balchu had added his own comment: "It begins."

Shady's stomach went cold. She sensed a similar reaction through the link and shared a worried glance with Pam. *Now what?*

Pam grimaced. *I guess we'll see.*

I don't want to wait and see. Like an unbreakable, invisible net that kept shrinking in on her, fear for the Pack's future made her breath come short and hard.

We'll get through it. Pam's worried expression and the doubts that echoed through the link and in her scent said her partner wasn't quite as sure as she wanted to be.

This room is stifling. Shady leaped to her feet, hackles up. The cubicle was too small. She couldn't breathe.

Shady! Steady up! Think. Pam reached out for her.

Shady backed away, bristling. *I can't breathe! I don't know what to think!* Panic strangled her.

Shady, seriously! Stop a minute. Slow down. Think!

Think about what? She must walk—must move—must run!

She whirled and trotted away toward the exit. *Hunkering down and waiting is for prey. I am NOT PREY!*

Wait! Where are you going?

I need to clear my head. She hoped Pam got the unspoken fact that she needed no company at this moment.

In her wake she sensed Pam's worried sigh. *Don't bite anybody, okay?*

Shady growled. *Depends on how much they mess with me.* She had no patience—not even for her partner's alarm and dismay.

The trapped feeling didn't ease outside the cubicle. Her throat closed and her pulse shot up. Even if it was less full of people than normal, she couldn't pace in the war room. Not enough open floor space. She wove between workstations, then burst out into the subterranean hallway, but—too narrow!

Part of her knew she was overreacting. The rest of her didn't care. She bounded to the stairs. Leaped upward from landing to landing until she reached Ground Level. Weird, but the exertion helped her breathe.

She darted and dodged through the halls—didn't knock anybody over, although she startled a few people. At the sally port she paused only long enough for the badge-reader to release the gate.

Freed of that human warren at last, she set off at a hard run across Central Plaza. In next to no time, she'd left the relatively open expanse of the Plaza behind.

Urban congestion closed in around her. But the pedestrians she encountered took one glance and fled. She paid them as little heed as she had to Pam's alarm or the people in the hallways at OPD HQ, but the continued course corrections grew ever more annoying.

She needed to get out of this place. Turned her path toward the terraces of Starboard Hill. There should be a park along here . . . at the first pedestrian switchback, she headed upward. The zigzag route presented a gentler grade than a hard, straight-uphill climb.

But switchbacks built for humans were almost as tedious as the stairs she'd avoided by leaping from landing to landing. She eyed the distance from the gently angled path beneath her paws to the one above that continued upward in the other direction. Her tongue slid out with a surge of fierce challenge. *Yeah, I can take that.* She set her feet, tensed her haunches, then sprang up to the level above.

Yes! Did it! She sprinted up the path a couple of long strides, then half-spun and launched herself to the next level up. After a couple more of those her tongue hung long and her pace at last slowed, but she'd mastered her terror and fury. *Now maybe I can start to think straight.*

She moved from the switchbacks onto a "scenic overlook" turnout as soon as the chance arose. She'd encountered a few people on the switchbacks but saw no one on this turnout.

Still panting, she trotted across its level surface to the security-barricaded edge. The ubiquity of Listeners probably explained why Safety Services reports didn't log many suicide attempts at places such as this.

It wasn't like back in Transmondia, where any high place might invite despairing jumpers. All the same, the Orangeboro officials weren't taking any chances, either of suicides or accidental falls by thrill-seekers who disregarded the rules. There were several levels of barricades, and there'd be netting below the last one, though she couldn't see it from here. Her friends on the STAT Team got a "net job" occasionally.

She stared out across the Sirius Valley. *"Scenic," huh? Whatever.* Visuals were never particularly her thing. Not like a great smell or an exhilarating flavor. The turnout had been built halfway between Terraces Five and Six, so the view wasn't as wide as the one from Corona Tower's roof. But it did cover more distance than most urban-core dwellers could glimpse. *Scenic enough for a human, I guess.*

She paced back and forth along the edge and tried to focus her mind away from trivialities. She knew Pam feared trade would back up as a result of the embargo, and economic stress might make Ranans turn on the Pack. She could understand that money was a lot more important to humans than it had been so far to her. Of course, she and all of her kind had been enslaved for money. She probably should give it more attention.

Dammit. Rex is so much better at human politics than me! She bristled and paced and growled. Pressure weighed her down. *I'm the acting Pack Leader. The fate of the Pack—maybe all XK9s— could ride on my decisions. It just isn't—*

A new scent slid past on the light breeze. Her head snapped up. *What? Again?* She turned toward the smell with a snarl. "All right, Appscaten. Let us get this straight right now. I am seriously *not* in the mood to be spied on today!"

The appscaten didn't move or speak. Or become visible, the stinking coward.

Oh, you are so asking to be mauled! Shady growled from the depths of her fury. "If you can understand me, then damn it— decloak, or change to your normal color, or whatever it is you do! I want to see who I am talking to!"

The source of the scent still did not move. The only sounds came from across the valley or somewhere below, borne on the breeze. To all appearances, Shady stood alone on the "scenic overlook," snarling at thin air.

"Promise you won't—won't chase me? If I do?" The voice sounded kind of tight and frightened.

Her hackles prickled and bristled. She clamped her ears against her lowered head and neck, and couldn't quite manage to sheath her snarl. *That damned thing has reason to be frightened.* "If you stay right there and reveal yourself, there will be no reason for me to chase you."

"Okay, but I'll warn you—I—um, I have to be naked to pull off a good camo."

She snorted. "I am not wearing anything either, except for my fur and police harness." The harness with the fully activated sensor rig, but why mention that minor detail?

The appscaten made a crackling noise something like a human wadding up a piece of paper. Appscaten laughter? Terror? *Do appscatens feel such emotions?* Somehow it didn't sound menacing. "You have a point." All at once an extremely odd-looking being stood about three meters away from her.

She blinked, not quite sure she understood what her eyes were telling her. "May I approach and smell you?"

Purple, blue, and several tones of gray and grayish-brown that a human or another appscaten might see as colors washed over the creature's skin. It—they—emitted a rapidly shifting succession of odd, sharp, acidic scents. The shiny black eyes on the "shoulders" of the thorax blinked, then the two eyes on either side of the creature's triangular, pale-domed head, a ripple of movements.

Two forelimbs extended from the shoulders on each side of the thorax. Although they were edged with rigid, spiky structures that appeared capable of creating fearsome wounds, the appscaten drew them close to its thorax. A defensive gesture? "Thank you for asking, but that thought terrifies me."

"I asked because it will reassure me. Then I shall attempt to be less terrifying."

The appscaten rocked backward on its mid- and hind legs but did not run. Its back blurred with a brief vibration. Purple and white streaks rippled over the skin between the thorax eyes. "I will allow it. Please do not chew on my back plates."

"I have no such intention."

"But you did, during our last encounter. You said so, to your partner."

She had lifted her ears, but now she snapped them flat once more. "I was angry with you. And what I said to my partner was supposed to be private."

"Sorry."

"How did you even hear it? We were talking in our link!"

"I'm sorry. I do not know. I felt it in my thorax, like a faint sonic whisper."

Okay, that's concerning. But she made an effort to lift her ears again. Took a step forward.

The appscaten held their ground, although the purple-and-white streaks rippled faster. Their scents oscillated in parallel with the colors. "I—actually—am not supposed to make direct contact with you."

"Oh, merely to spy on me?" Shady managed to half-swallow her growl.

"To observe. Unobtrusively, we had hoped. We underestimated your sense of smell, I fear."

"Who are 'we'?"

"I apologize, but I should not say." Now the appscaten's back vibrated even faster and their thorax pulsed with ripple after ripple, again echoed in their scent factors. The bilateral toes at the ends of its—their—forelimbs clasped together in spasms, rather like a human wringing their hands. "But please understand that we do not mean you ill."

"Right." She gave the creature an angry, dubious glare. "Like the Transmondians did not mean me ill, when they filled my home with surveillance devices?"

"No. Not like that. We genuinely do not mean you any harm."

She suppressed another urge to snort and stepped closer. Once her nose had come within a few centimeters of the creature's color-oscillating skin she realized it, too, was vibrating. The micro-spasms enhanced the ripple effect. She took a few moments to sniff the creature over.

She found this individual's vocalizer strapped in a notch between head and thorax. *So that's where they put it.* It was well hidden. She worked her way to the back plates, which vibrated in a different way from the thorax skin. These vibrations sped up as she approached. "What makes you vibrate?"

"It is an involuntary reaction of a system in my body that somewhat compares to your neural system. My people's bodies react this way when we are frightened or upset. Our natural reflexes make us "go background" whenever we feel this way. That is, the emotion triggers the camouflage effect. I am making a very hard effort to keep from going background right now."

She stepped a few paces back.

The appscaten's vibrations slowed some.

"I think perhaps a human would say that I had violated your personal space with my sniff-over. If I step back until you feel comfortable, will you stop vibrating?"

"Possibly. Of course, as long as I am neither "background" nor clothed, I shall continue to feel uncomfortable."

Where would an appscaten feel the need to be covered by clothing? It seemed a somewhat personal question, so she didn't ask. The poor thing—being—person—seemed ready to shake itself—themselves—to pieces already. She took another step away. The vibrations slowed slightly. But at this rate she'd back right over the edge of the scenic overlook before the creature stopped vibrating. "If I say you may go background, will you stay and talk with me?"

The appscaten's eyes did that sequential blinking thing for three rapid cycles before it—they—lowered those spiky forelimbs and answered. "What do you want to talk about?"

"If you are supposed to observe me, I presume that means you have questions. How about if you simply ask them?"

"Not all can be asked or answered with words."

"Fair enough, but 'not all' means 'some.' Let us start with one of those."

"And if I were to stay and ask you questions, you will not mind if I go background?"

"I will understand why. Then I will not be as angry as I was before."

"Fair enough, but 'not as angry' means still somewhat angry."

Shady lolled her tongue at that. "Okay, stick around and talk. Let us test it."

The appscaten blinked out of sight, except for a subtle distortion around where she now knew their edges were, and four hard-to-see lines that could be slitted eyes. It—they—did not run away. "Are you angry now?"

She wagged her tail, ears up. "No. I am still curious, but not angry. Thank you."

"You are welcome."

"Are you still vibrating?"

"Yes. But not nearly as much. You appear uncannily much like a vorriten, only with fur. That is an ancestral predator. We seem to have an instinctive fear-reaction when we see one, even though we are now civilized beings."

"I also resemble an ancestral predator of humans, but most of them seem to have gotten used to dogs over time. Instead, our two species developed a strategic alliance."

That crackling-paper sound came again. "Perhaps humans are wiser than we thought."

"Who said it was the humans' idea?" She flicked her ears. "Some humans are wise. Some are very foolish, and sometimes they are evil. Sometimes they gather into groups that seem to grow more foolish or evil, the bigger the group becomes."

"Sadly, that also can sometimes be true of appscatens."

"I do not think we have yet answered any of your questions that can be asked in words."

"We will not be able to cover all of them in one conversation."

"Try me with one, anyway."

"Why were you running up the switchbacks like that? It was very hard to do."

She swallowed a growl. "You were following me."

"I was trying—at least to keep you in view. I am getting too old for this kind of thing."

This sounded so much like something Ted would say, she lolled her tongue. "For an elderly creature you seem to have some pretty decent moves left in you. I must say that auto-nav escape in the park on Sunday was pretty smooth."

"I'm not sure I'd say *elderly*. But—" The creature emitted a crisp, somewhat sweet scent. "You thought my escape was smooth? Truly?"

She wagged her tail. "Truly. I was irritated, but also impressed."

That paper-crackling sound returned. "Nice to know I've still got it."

CHAPTER 26
CONVERSATION

Level Five Scenic Overlook Just off a Pedestrian Switchback

S hady cocked her head and eyed the deceptively empty-seeming space a few meters away on the scenic turnout's gravel. "I figured you probably went to appscaten spy school and learned all kinds of fancy athletic moves there."

"No, I never went to any such school. I will say it again. I am an *observer*."

"Right. As if that makes a lot of difference to me when I realize I am being watched. Whatever you call it, it bothers me."

"I do sincerely apologize for that. But today I think—it seemed to me that you only noticed me when we arrived here. Why did you climb the switchbacks the hard way?"

Shady lowered her head, ears back. She glanced away from the place where she could smell the appscaten. "I was upset. When dogs are upset we must move. Sometimes we pace. Sometimes we run up switchbacks the hard but fast way."

"Why were you upset, if I may ask?"

Shady's chest constricted and her breath came harder. She paced a few steps, turned, then paced back. Made herself stop.

Sat, but started panting very fast. *Should I answer this appscaten's question?*

Are you inclined to? She pictured Pam giving her a startled stare.

I don't know. I'm kind of surprised to say I am. She was back on her feet and pacing before she could stop herself. She glanced in the appscaten's direction. "I do not know you. Why should I tell you any such thing?"

"There is no reason why you should," the creature agreed. "I am curious, that is all. It would aid my observation if I could add your reasoning as a field note."

Shady snorted. "I will readily admit there was very little reasoning behind my unusual approach to the switchbacks. And what do you mean by 'field note'? Are you some kind of naturalist? Here to observe the XK9 in its natural environment?"

"I am not a naturalist, although I will confess that I am what you probably would call an academic. I normally spend most of my time conducting educational activities and doing research."

An irritable prickle rippled through Shady's hackles. "You have taken some care to define what you are not. Not a spy. Not a naturalist. Is this a game we are to play indefinitely? How about if you simply come out with it? You undoubtedly know that I am Shady Jacob-Belle, and that I am an Orangeboro Police detective, so in that way you have the advantage on me. I do not even know your name."

She had a sense that it—they—were doing that eye-blink sequence thing again, although probably not, since she didn't see any eyes suddenly opening and closing in midair. "Fair point. Very well, my actual name is—" the appscaten made a rattly-whooshing noise of the sort a bamboo wind chime might make if it could sneeze.

Shady blinked. *I'd love to see what vibrates and where, when this creature makes that noise.* "Pardon, but how am I to create that sound?"

"Don't worry about it. Speakers of Standard call me Kurtzu."

"Just Kurtzu?"

"Ra-Sven-shumma Kurtzu. But Kurtzu is my given name in Standard."

"Pleased to finally meet you, Kurtzu." She moved closer, sat, and extended a paw. "Do appscatens shake, um, appendages?"

"When on Rana we do. And you may call it my 'hand' in Standard." It—*they*—shifted their bird-claw hand and spiky forearm out of "background" and shook Shady's paw with a firm but not uncomfortable bilateral grip.

"What are your pronouns, please?"

Kurtzu let go. Their arm and hand faded to background. "You may use 'he, him, his' for me."

Shady cocked her head again. "Do appscatens have genders like earth creatures?"

"Somewhat like, I suppose. During our mating cycle appscatens phase into one of two breeding genders. When speaking Standard, the language uses gendered pronouns, so we normally take the pronoun that more closely approximates our breeding-gender configuration."

"So . . . you are an 'outie,' not an 'innie'?"

"Something like that." Kurtzu made the crumpling paper sound again.

"What does that sound signify?"

"I suppose you could call it curiosity, amusement, or perhaps astonishment." The sound came again.

"Are you enjoying this conversation?"

"I should remain objective, but I must admit . . . yes."

"Me, too. But I would enjoy it even more if you told me what your job is."

"I should not . . ."

"I told you mine."

"Oh, very well. The word in Standard is 'xenosociologist.' I study the cultures and behavior of species other than my own."

Shady's ears went straight up. "In other words—you are a

scholar of how and why various groups of individuals act as they do?"

"I, er, yes. In my normal job I am a teacher and researcher."

"What we would call a professor. Like SCISCO and the other professors at Station Polytechnic, or the learned masters among the ozzirikkians? Except in your own field?"

"Why, yes. Quite right. Very good."

"And you, as a xenosociologist, can understand and perhaps even predict how large groups of individuals might act or react?"

Kurtzu did not immediately respond. His scent shifted through a variety of modes in much the same way the colors had oscillated across his thorax when she could see him. She struggled to guess what the scents might mean. At last, he asked, "Do you wish to ask me about a large group of individuals?"

"The Transmondians have imposed an embargo."

Kurtzu's scent shifted again. It oscillated into a deeper range of harshly acidic, throat-catching odors. " Yes. They have."

"They levied it against Ranan beer, wine, and spirits, which particularly hurts the XK9-sponsoring Families of Corona, Glorioso, Pabiyan, and Lang. But my partner Pam, Chief Klein, and others believe they will use it to slow down all Ranan trade. The price for lifting the embargo is giving us—my Pack—back to them."

She was up and pacing again before she could stop herself. "The Transmondians want to kill us or scramble our minds before the Observation Commission's delegation arrives. If they have their way, the Commission will never know that we were sapient because none of us will be left for them to evaluate."

"It is clear you are upset all over again." Kurtzu's scent shifted again and again until she wasn't sure *what* she was smelling—but it wasn't pleasant.

"I think I would be vibrating very fast if I was an appscaten." She stress-yawned and resumed pacing. "My mate Rex is our Pack Leader. He understands far more about human politics than I do. I am only the Acting Pack Leader, while he undergoes a treatment for his broken lungs."

Her throat had gone dry from panting. She couldn't stand still. "I am pretty good with predicting what individual humans will do. But Rex is the politician. I do not know what to expect from larger groups such as political factions. I do not know enough to make a plan to protect my Pack. This terrifies me."

She halted, chilled anew. *Why am I saying all of this to some random appscaten I don't even know? I should be smarter! More suspicious than this!* But Kurtzu had revealed himself, even though he was clearly terrified of her. He had allowed her a sniff-over, had admitted he was frightened. In the face of such courage and honesty it was hard to remain suspicious.

"You are right to worry about the Transmondians," Kurtzu said.

Her pulse pounded hard in her neck and ears and belly. "I also worry about some of the Ranans." Shady eyed the spot where she could smell that Kurtzu still stood. Was it her imagination, or could she kind of *almost* see him? "Premier Iskander in particular worries me. She wants to work with the Transmondians and to completely deny that XK9s are sapient. That is what she has wanted from the very beginning. She came to Orangeboro—but then did not stay to watch our presentation. Her only purpose was to bully Chief Klein into repudiating us and make the Borough Council rescind its vote. When she failed in those things, she left."

"For a being who claims not to understand politics, that is a rather astute analysis."

Shady shook her head. "That is Rex's analysis. I was angry and confused, but I only understood after he explained."

"And the question you wished to ask me is—?"

"Will Premier Iskander succeed this time? Will she and her faction convince the other Ranan legislators to return us to the Transmondians if we cost them too much money?"

"I would observe that these are still rather astute questions from a being whose sapience has been questioned."

Yes, she was almost certain she could see him a little bit, now. "Again, I am working from others' wisdom. My partner worried about these questions, and now I do too."

"Do you believe the ozzirikkians and the Farricainan cyberbeings would agree to return you to Transmondia? Do you believe the humans of Orangeboro would?"

A little of her tension eased. "SCISCO would fight it. I do not know nir siblings, but a whole host of them spoke on our behalf from near space to the Borough Council before they voted."

"And the humans of Orangeboro?"

"Chief Klein and the OPD would fight to keep us. Not only did he say so, but they already stood up to Admiral Virendra and the SDF when they came to collect us." She hesitated. "I do not think Elaine Adeyeme would agree to give us up, either. I smell her as a human of character and integrity, much like Chief Klein." She flicked her ears. "In addition, much of her evidence depends on our analyses."

"Excellent. And the Orangeboro Council?" Kurtzu's body appeared even more solid now.

"Well, the Orangeboro Council did affirm our sapience already."

"Based on what you know of individual humans, do you believe the Council members would eagerly change their votes and say 'No, sorry, we were wrong before'?"

"No." Shady's ears swept back. "No human likes to say 'sorry, I was wrong' about anything."

"That also is my assessment." Kurtzu's triangular head canted to one side, rather like an XK9 cocking his head. "Did you know that long ago the Amethyrians demanded that the human Founders of Rana return their ozzirikkian co-Founders for elimination, or prepare for a war against them? At the time there were fewer than two million humans on Rana and the Station was not yet finished."

Shady eyed Kurtzu. He now appeared almost as solid as the gravel into which his birdlike toes dug their claws. She studied his scent. It smelled somewhat like cool, frosty air. She doubted that was a scent factor associated with deception. "No. I did not know that."

"To their credit, the humans said 'no,' even though the Amethyrian assault force outnumbered and outgunned them overwhelmingly."

"How is it that Rana Station survived and we still have ozzirikkians?" It was a piece of Ranan history Shady had never learned—if true.

It's true, Pam said through the link. *I haven't heard it framed exactly that way before.*

"That was the point at which the Alliance was finally able to step in and send the Amethyrians back home," Kurtzu said.

Shady snapped her ears flat. "What do you mean, 'finally able'? Were they not able all along?"

"Alliance law forbids interfering with in-species disputes. Only when the Amethyrians threatened the humans did it become an inter-species matter."

"So, they were sitting there watching? And they were willing to allow the Amethyrians to commit genocide on our ozzirikkians—but do nothing to stop them?"

"Regrettable as it is, in-species genocide is not a matter with which Alliance Law allows interference." Kurtzu dipped his head, glanced away briefly. "Otherwise, Alliance forces would be intervening everywhere, all the time. The Alliance has great resources, might, and influence—but even we have limits."

Oh, that is interesting. "Do I take it, then, that you speak for the Alliance? Is that in an official capacity of any sort?" *Like, for instance, as a member of the Observation Commission?* She tried to close the link and think that thought as quietly as possible.

Kurtzu went background immediately. He emitted a scorched-edged acidic smell Shady had by now pegged as a fear-scent, but this time it alternated with some other nose-burning emotional scent. "Forgive me. I misspoke. Appscatens, like humans, ozzirikkians, and cyberbeings, are Alliance citizens. Alliance history is the history of all of us."

Good try at a save, but I'm not buying it. No sense in antagonizing him, though. "Okay, it is your turn to ask me a question now."

"I have a great many." He hesitated again. His scent went through another of those odd oscillations.

Could appscatens, unlike dogs or humans, only feel one emotion at a time? Did their scents come in waves because when their emotions became complicated, they phased quickly from one to the next in a repeating pattern? *Fascinating.*

"Perhaps my most urgent question is . . . you have repeatedly perceived me despite my backgrounding, and it bothers you a lot when you notice that I am observing you unannounced."

Got that right. "Yes it does."

"I completely understand why you might feel upset, since it is clear you have powerful enemies. But I cannot do my work—which is to observe your natural behavior—if my presence is *affecting* your behavior. Is there any way I can respect your wishes and yet also make the observations I've been tasked to make?" His scent factors gradually smoothed out and expanded into something that smelled a bit like wet rocks.

"Is there a reason why we cannot simply meet and talk periodically? That way I can answer your questions in more detail. I also will not feel threatened or angry. You shall get the information you need. And perhaps you can help me understand how to interpret and predict human politics. We can teach each other what we need to know."

"A—a standing appointment? Oh, dear. I might need special permission for that."

Do "puppy eyes" work on appscatens? She gave it her best try. "Surely you can learn a lot about my species by talking with one of us."

"Well, that's true."

"So, you shall ask permission? Because you cannot observe from afar?"

"For a special situation, that might be possible."

"Thank you. Would you care to meet somewhere in particular? Any time of day that works best?"

"I . . . I'll have to get back to you on that one."

Shady forwarded her contact info. "I must return to headquarters now, but thank you for your counsel and your willingness to speak with me. I shall look forward to seeing you—literally—again soon."

CHAPTER 27
FRAUGHT TRAIN RIDE

Portside Level Five Leeward Commuter Train

P am took a seat by a window on the starboard side of the train. "Okay, explain this again, because when you said 'go to lunch at Chase's place,' I thought . . . well, never mind. Where are we going?"

"Becenti Tower, Seventh Precinct." Balchu took her hand. "Uncle Chase and Aunt Anya live there."

"Wait! A *Family Tower?*" Pam half-rose from her seat, but the doors had closed. Too late to run. *I don't know anything about how to behave at a formal Family luncheon!* She swallowed hard. "Are you sure I look okay?"

Through the link she received an impression of a lolling tongue from Shady. Her partner hadn't been included in the lunch invitation, so she'd stayed at HQ to finish the formwork she'd abandoned earlier. *If Corona's any guide, you're better than good.*

Balchu chuckled, unaware of their link-based exchange. "We'll be over-dressed, but they'll understand."

It's not like I have anything else that could live up to Chartered

Family standards. It had been a busy day between her promotion, news of the embargo, Kieran's interview, and Shady's adventure with Kurtzu. She'd never managed to change out of her dress blues. She grimaced at her Amare. "Here's hoping."

The train glided away from the platform.

Amusement sparkled through the link. *You'll be fine.* Now she could almost feel the thumping tail.

"You'll be fine." Balchu grinned at her and squeezed her hand.

Her stomach clenched, but she blew out a long breath and tried to think calm thoughts. "How come I'm only just now learning where we're going?" *When it's too late to back out?*

So it'll be too late to back out. Shady's mental voice brimmed with amusement.

"Well, full disclosure: I really wanted you to come, and I figured if I said too much, you'd find an excuse to stay at HQ." Balchu eyed her. "Forgive me?"

"Maybe." She hunched her shoulders. "I might, if you fill me in on some things. First, your 'Uncle' Chase . . . isn't actually related to Feyodor. Did I get that right?"

"By physical lineage, no. They would tell us that they're 'twin sons of different mothers,' but in fact they've been friends since birth. And they've been through a lot together, since then. 'Blood brothers,' in every sense."

"And you call him 'Uncle,' because of that?"

"Nani and I call him 'Uncle' and Anya 'Aunt,' because that's what they've been to us all our lives. It's how we grew up thinking about them."

"How does that . . . feel?" Pam eyed him with curiosity. "Older relatives who aren't parents? What's that like? Where do they fit into a child's life?"

He studied her face for a few moments. "Did you ever have a teacher who just really liked you and believed in you?"

"Like a mentor?" She smiled. "Ms. Platt, my P. H. & L.

teacher in Mid-Levels." Physical Health and Lifestyle had been one of her favorite classes all through school. "She wanted to recruit me onto her Junior Quiddo team. Mother wouldn't hear of it, of course. But Ms. Platz always tried to encourage me when I was in her class, even after that. I figured that might mean she actually did like me, and wasn't just being nice because I had good aim and quick reflexes."

"How could she not like you? I bet you were smart and cute, even then."

"Mm. Well, I was kinda moody in Mid-Levels." She stared out the window but couldn't focus. "I guess, who wasn't moody in Mid-Levels? But Ms. Platt wasn't like a relative. I took her classes for three years, and I only saw her at school. Never encountered her again after that. It was always just Mother and me, really." She released a small sigh. "Well, from the time I was four, anyway."

He paused longer than she expected. Long enough to make her glance round at him with one brow up.

"I know that in my head, but it just hit me again." He offered a rueful half-smile. "I'm sorry you never had an aunt or uncle. It might've made things easier for you."

"Mother would've found a reason to push them away." Pam shook her head. "Never mind. Instead, tell me why your father and Chase are 'blood brothers.'"

"Oh, the details of that will take far too long to tell. I could never cram it all in before we get to Vista Heights Station."

The train had already slowed for its first Precinct Six stop. They waited till the hubbub of departures and onboarding had finished and the platform slid away behind them.

"Have you ever heard of a place in Transmondia called Northwest Butterknowle?" Balchu asked. "It's pretty remote."

Pam blinked at him. All the Northwest Butterknowle jokes she'd heard during her training with the XK9 Project in Transmondia came back to her in a rush. "As in the place that's so backward they don't have roads? And it's so far up in the mountains even compasses don't work there? *That* Northwest Butterknowle?"

"They have roads." Balchu gave her somewhat hurt expression.

Pam couldn't suppress a chuckle. "But it actually exists? I thought it was some kind of mythical place. At Puppy Farm One, if they told us to walk out to Training Field F, the farthest one from campus, the staff rolled their eyes and called it Northwest Butterknowle!'"

That's the only way I ever heard people talk about it, Shady agreed through the link.

"Well, surprise. It actually is a place." He sounded more than a little miffed. "Granted, it's pretty small. And it's more than half the continent away from Solara City. And yes, it is up in the mountains. But Dad and Chase really were born there. They almost share the exact same birthday."

"Northwest Butterknowle must be bigger than I thought. What are the odds of that?"

"Well, um, special circumstances, in this case. They were born exactly nine Earth-Standardized months after the Blizzard that Blocked the Pass." He frowned. "No, don't stare at me funny. It's a real event. It was a bad storm. Real people died in it. Dad and Chase say that before they left, the folks were still having a Big Blizzard Remembrance Day every year."

"Blizzard. That's snow, right?" She'd seen some, during XK9 training. Weird stuff. And colder than she'd thought possible.

"Dad says they told him it piled up to nine or ten meters high along the Pass—which is a *road,* please note."

"Noted." *Although nine or ten meters of snow boggles my mind.* She bit her lip. "And when the blizzard blocks the road and traps you in Northwest Butterknowle, how *do* you while away the time?"

"Exactly. Everybody called them the Blizzard Boys."

The train was already slowing for the second of its two stops in Sixth Precinct. "You'd better cut to the Feyodor-and-Chase, love, but I think I get the point. Why did they leave?"

"As Dad would say, why wouldn't they? It actually is pretty small. And there was adventure to be had on the Norchellic Frontier—which they figured was just down the hill. Turns out it was several mountain ranges east, and *then* down the hill."

"Wasn't there a war going on?"

Balchu's face sobered. "I'm not sure how fully they understood about that, when they left. As Uncle Chase says, they were 'seventeen-year-old boys, with all the wisdom that implies.'"

The train stopped. A new outrush and inflow ensued. But once the noise had settled somewhat and the train gathered speed, Balchu didn't immediately pick up his tale. Instead, he rubbed the back of his neck and studied her.

She met his gaze. "What aren't you telling me?"

He glanced away. "Oh, there's loads more stories. We don't have time for a tenth of them."

"That's not what I mean. From your expression, you're trying to decide if you should tell me something else. It's probably about Chartered Families, and you probably think I won't like it. What is it?"

He gave her a small, worried smile, then glanced away again, head bent and brow puckered. He drew in a deep breath and let it out slowly.

"Becenti . . ." He stopped. "I think I know what Mom and Dad's 'big secret' is."

A chill went up her spine. She didn't have to ask what he meant by that.

A few weeks ago, Tuya, Feyodor, Sarnai, and Rose had met them at LEO's Grill. The stated reason was to introduce Balchu's sister and her Amare to Pam and Shady. It had been a nice visit, but they'd all picked up a distinct feeling that Feyodor was excited and eager to tell them something that Tuya didn't want him to talk about "yet." Balchu had dodged her attempts to speculate about it since then, but that hadn't stopped Pam and

Shady. Ever since then they'd been speculating, at times rather wildly, over what Feyodor's secret might be.

At the other end of the link, Shady focused her full attention on Pam.

"And it has to do with Becenti?" Her pulse sped up and her throat went tight. "The secret?"

The train passed the "WELCOME TO SEVENTH PRECINCT" sign.

"I think so." He shifted in his seat and avoided eye contact. "You see, Becenti is what they call a 'fading' Family. That means it's getting smaller, not larger. I know Chase and Anya have been worried about it for several years. Three younger Family members in our generation have recently 'married out.' It's a problem."

Her pulse kicked up another notch. *Oh, let me be wrong about this.* What little Pam knew about Chartered Families had been filtered through Mother's jaundiced viewpoint or observed from a distance. As far as she was concerned, they lived in a whole separate world—one she was happy not to share.

I don't think you're wrong, but let him tell you, Shady advised.

Shit, shit, shit. She drew in a breath. "Why is 'marrying out' a problem? Aren't people free to marry as they like?"

"Of course, they are." He glanced at her then away again. "But when a Family takes out a fifty-year mortgage on a Tower and accepts the civic and tax responsibilities of a Charter, they have to maintain a reasonable likelihood that the Family will remain solid and solvent for several generations."

Gran Annie and Aunt Hannah have been giving Rex and me 'Charter lessons' recently. There are a lot of responsibilities that come along with the financial advantages. If too few people tried to carry that load it would get burdensome really fast, Shady said through the link.

The quiver in Pam's gut amplified her growing unease. "So, Becenti has too few people? Is there a minimum number for a Charter?"

"As I understand it, the minimum number depends on the size of the property, the age of the mortgage, and the type of crops they grow." Balchu rubbed the back of his neck again. "The Family's number of minor children also counts somehow. Number of adults in community service counts, too. Not sure about that formula."

Both young children and workers in public service bring substantial tax breaks, Shady said. *I know this because the Borough Clerk wasn't sure an XK9 counted as equal to a human when it came to the subsidy for a Family member in service work. After Annie and Hannah got their teeth into that argument, however, the Clerk had an epiphany. He decided that, of course, XK9s who are sworn officers and paid like detectives should get a detective's bonus. And, beyond that, it stands to reason that a Pack Leader and an Assistant Pack Leader should receive leadership surcharges on top of the bonus.*

The train began its slowdown on approach to Vista Heights Station.

"Is Shady talking to you?" Balchu asked. "You have that expression on your face. She's been listening in, hasn't she?"

"Of course, she has." Pam managed a small smile. "She says there are big tax breaks for little kids and Family members in public service work. She and Rex are part of Corona Charter now. Apparently, their humans have been explaining how things work. And I guess that explains how they can recruit people from rich Families. People like Charlie, Misha, and Hildie—even though they pay normal-people wages. I've always wondered."

"Me, too." Balchu gave a slow nod. "That . . . actually could have a big bearing on how someone with Family responsibilities might justify going into a lower-paying field. Interesting." He gave Pam a speculative glance. "I wonder how much a Detective Level One and a Detective Sergeant are worth, in Family subsidies? If my guess is right, you and I might turn out to be valuable assets."

Her gut tightened. *I don't want to be a valuable asset!* But she kept that thought confined to the link.

Oh, of course you do. Shady snorted. *You take pride in your work and in being valuable to the Department. We all do!*

But I mean—all of a sudden, I feel like a commodity. Her cheeks burned.

The train glided into Vista Heights Station and slid to a smooth stop.

CHAPTER 28
A DIFFERENT WORLD

Precinct Seven, Level Five, Vista Heights Neighborhood and Becenti Tower

B alchu stood as soon as the train fully halted. He held out his hand to Pam. "We'd better move. Stops don't last long."

She took his hand and reluctantly followed.

People eyed their dress blues, stepped aside, and nodded respectfully. A clear path opened for them.

Whuh? Pam mustered enough awareness to smile at all the deferential people around her. She strove to keep both her wits and her footing. *What is up with these folks? I never saw any such attitudes from the crowds at Grand Central.*

Balchu responded to their fellow passengers' reactions with polished grace. He didn't seem surprised.

The people at Grand Central see cops in dress blues all the time, Shady answered, although from HQ her only view was what Pam shared through the link. *There's always some kind of government thing going on in the Civic Center. They're used to it. I guess Vista Heights doesn't get a lot of dignitaries.*

'Dignitaries'—if you mean us—is ludicrous. But you might have a

point about our outfits. She and Balchu smiled and nodded their way across the platform, up a long escalator and out of the station to a broad, split sidewalk. Half angled to their left, half to their right. She eyed the fork, clueless. "Now where?"

"This way." He took the right fork toward the spinward part of Precinct Seven. "It's an easy stroll." The sidewalk paralleled Rim Five Road at a half-meter remove to the left from vehicular traffic. Their route followed a gradual outward bow in the land-form. A grassy berm rose between the right-hand side of the road and the hundred-meter plunge at the edge of Terrace Five on its far side.

Pam gazed past the well-maintained bamboo pole fence that hugged the sidewalk's edge on their left. Her steps faltered to a stop. Uniformly-spaced rows of broad-leafed green plants stretched a hundred meters back to the primary terrace wall. Built up against the terrace's cliff-face stood a tall, multi-story residence tower with white walls. Her stomach went cold as a stone. *This is a totally foreign world.*

"Are you okay?"

Pam blinked, turned to Balchu. "I'm, um, fine. It's all just so . . . *green.*"

He laughed. "Market Garden isn't exactly all pavement and steel."

"No." She offered a wan smile. "Not like in Solara City, for sure. Some streets there don't even have so much as a planter box." She shook her head, then stared again at the white tower with the orderly rows of whatever-they-were growing at its feet. "This is a verdant fantasy, compared to Sixth Level."

He squeezed her hand. "Don't let it shake you. Folks here are just plain, ordinary people. Friendly. Hardworking. They're good neighbors, good friends."

Even to someone like me, who doesn't know which spoon to use, or what to wear for dinner versus tea?

You don't have to know that at Corona. Probably not here, either. A soft growl resonated through the link. *Don't make it harder than it has to be.*

She drew in a breath and turned away from the white tower. *One step after another. Just walk.* She stared at the sidewalk. "To be in a Family, don't people need to be related to each other?"

"Not necessarily. There actually are three ways for a Chartered Family to grow. Have more kids, of course. 'Marry in' more people." He glanced back at her, brows up.

She lengthened her strides to catch up. "And the third?"

"It's the place where Chase has always wanted us to come in —A merger."

A chill raced up Pam's back. "That's why we're here, isn't it? They want to look us over? See if we're good enough?"

"No!" The heat in his voice startled her. She lifted her gaze to face his scowl. "We'd have been full-on Family for my whole lifetime, if Chase'd had his way. I think I know who held us at arms' length all those years, and why that might have changed now. But 'are we good enough' has *never* been the question. We wouldn't be here if they didn't already know that we are and want us!"

"Are you sure they'll think that—about *me*?" She stumbled to a halt. Her vision swam with hot tears. She'd grown up in a small rear-entrance apartment behind a dingy little retail storage facility, the Thriff-Tee Safe-Tee Store on Sub-Level Six of Precinct Five. A place people weren't even supposed to live, for pity's sake! Her chest and throat ached with dread of humiliation. "I'm—I feel like an impostor here. Like they'll see right through me, dress blues or not."

"Pammie. Listen to me." He'd stopped when she did. Now he gently coaxed her into his arms. Then he touched his forehead to hers and simply held her until she stopped shaking.

"I still feel . . ."

"They will see what *I* see. No, don't twist away, listen to me. They'll see a beautiful." He kissed her on the forehead. "Brilliant." Another kiss, this one to the tip of her nose. "Accomplished." A third kiss, and this one lingered on her lips. "*Wonderful* person. I don't care where you grew up, and neither will guys who grew up in Northwest Butterknowle. Trust me, Pam. I mean this. You are so incredibly far beyond being merely 'good enough,' I can't even express it."

Her face was probably all blotchy, and for sure her nose must be red. She glanced up at him through wet lashes and gulped. "You spin a pretty good tale there, Nowicki. You've almost got me convinced."

"Good." He pulled her hard against his chest one more time, pins and buttons and all, then slowly released her, his gaze intent. "You gonna be okay?"

She blew out a breath. Gave him a watery smile. "Fake it till I make it, right?"

He smiled. "No faking needed, in my opinion. Own it. C'mon. Let's go have lunch."

They walked past tower after tower. All seemed to have about a hundred meters of frontage, but the towers she glimpsed from across growing crops or above the branches of orchards came in varied heights. They also displayed a variety of colors: pale yellow, dark orange, candy pink. From each level on every tower, balconies jutted out, draped with vines. She couldn't identify any of the plants.

"Here's Becenti." Balchu extended his arm. Another bamboo pole fence enclosed the property, which appeared to extend all the way from Rim Five Road to the base of Terrace Six. Raised beds, jammed with masses of plants she couldn't name, lined a short gravel driveway on both sides. At the end of it stood a rectangular green residence tower. There appeared to be three apartment levels above the ground floor, from what she could see through the nearest leafy growths. It appeared each level had its own vine-draped balcony. The plants visible above the top of the outer wall probably indicated a rooftop garden.

She'd once gone to Corona Tower to pick up Shady after a night with Rex. Corona would dwarf this place, but Becenti seemed plenty big to Pam. And a whole lot more prosperous than the Thriff-Tee Safe-Tee Store.

Keep 'faking it.' You're doing great. Shady projected strength and confidence to her through the link.

Balchu clasped her hand and led her forward. "Entrance is over here."

She trailed him through an entrance gate into a rectangular courtyard. Three tiers of interior balconies rose above them. Pam tried to visualize just how much added floor space the balanced interior and exterior balconies must give.

"Ah! Excellent! You're here!" Pam spun to see big, broad-shouldered Chase stride toward them, arms stretched wide. "Balchu! Come introduce the rest of us to your lovely Amare!"

Balchu grinned. "Hey, Uncle Chase! Thanks for the invitation! I've been eager to bring her here."

"Welcome to Becenti Tower." Chase beamed at her and led them over to a group by a table under a tall tree in the courtyard's center. "You've met my wife, Anya."

Pam nodded. "Nice to see you again. It was very kind of you to come to my promotion this morning."

"We were excited to come." Anya smiled and clasped Pam's hand. "We've been looking forward to meeting you for so long! Let me introduce you to the rest of the Family! This is our son Miguel, and his wife Soledad."

A couple who appeared to be a few years older than Pam and Balchu stepped forward with smiles to shake hands.

Next came Anita, Conchita, Amiri . . . and a whole bunch of others. Balchu greeted each with smiling familiarity. For Pam they quickly melded into a confusing sea of faces. But everyone seemed welcoming until a tall older woman appeared on the second balcony up.

"*Police?*" she cried. "Chase! What have you done? How could you invite *police officers* here? No! This is not acceptable! Get them *out of here* right now!"

Everyone in the courtyard fell silent.

Pam went cold, her fingers abruptly numb. The woman's rejection was exactly what Mother had always warned her to expect. *She thinks I'm unworthy. Low-class. Unsuitable.* She gripped Balchu's hand hard. Her pulse hammered in her ears.

Woah! Through the link, she felt every fiber of Shady's attention snap alert. *Who is this woman, and what does she have to hide?*

No clue. Both for Shady's sake and for her own, she focused on the old lady. Her hair, almost white, frizzed around her head like an aureole. The deep lines in her brown face clenched in a fierce scowl and her sharp black eyes sparkled with suspicion. *If you were here, you'd be reading her scent factors. I really wish I could smell them for you!*

You and me both!

Chase turned to scowl up at the woman, a fist on each hip. "That is more than enough, Grandma Raya! We already explained this situation to you. We even took a Family vote. You had an opportunity to tell us about your objections then—and you wouldn't explain them! Now they are my honored guests— mine and Anya's! Balchu is practically a son to me. I will not send them away!"

The others also frowned and nodded their agreement with Chase.

I have got to meet this woman! Shady's yearning to be there in person echoed through the link. *You didn't think you'd be merging into a mystery, did you?*

I'm not merging into anything! At least not yet.

"They will bring shame to this Family!" Raya shook her head fiercely. "We will rue—"

"Mother!" A man of about Chase's age rushed out onto Raya's balcony. "Stop this! The only one bringing shame on the Family right now is you! Hush that hollering, and come inside!" He propelled her through the nearest doorway out of sight.

Chase turned back to Pam and Balchu, his face pinched with unhappiness. "I am so sorry! I don't know what set her off. She's been so distraught—and frankly paranoid—ever since Grandpa

Onyx died. She won't talk to Listeners—won't even talk to us. Please, Pam, don't let her turn you away from us. We've been so eager to meet you, ever since you returned from Chayko! We wanted your first impressions to be good ones!"

Amusement sparkled through the link from Shady. *Oh, yeah, they have totally got a merger in mind.* This analysis seemed to give her partner a lot of satisfaction.

I guess we'll see. Yeesh. Whose side are you on, anyway?

Yours. Always.

"Come on over here and let's chat a little, while we wait for Feyodor, Tuya, and your sisters." Anya smiled at Pam. "Congratulations on your promotion. It was nice to meet Shady this morning. She's quite amazing. I can only imagine how interesting your work with the XE9s must be!"

You have no idea. Pam allowed Anya to draw her over to the table at the foot of the tree. Several of the others had already started bringing out food. "She was happy to meet you, too."

"We'll have to invite her along next time."

Oh, yes! The sooner, the better! She caught a sense of Shady's tail fanning at top speed.

Pam smiled. "I'm sure she'd like that."

CHAPTER 29
FISH TACOS AND FOUR MILLION NOVI

OPD Global Reconstruction Unit

For once, Charlie harbored no urge to complain about his mandatory shortened workday. His tight abdominal muscles eased only fractionally as he ran through GR Chamber Three's shutdown routine.

Elaine had predicted these first four execution GRs could only show fairly short extrapolations, and she'd called that right. *But oh, man! Those were enough.*

He'd worked from Medical Examiners' reports and observable evidence documented after the sites were discovered, but that was all the information available. There'd been no witness statements. None of the security surveillance imagery usually available for GRs. Stills or vids of scenes, yes. But no "before" images for three of the four complainants. And, *thank God*, there was no audio for the four cases he'd worked on today. He wouldn't be so lucky with tomorrow's GR—but he'd save worrying about that for then.

Surfaces. Focus on rendering the surface details. He'd dragged that old GR artists' adage back into his mind about every minute, it seemed. Not that it helped much. He'd let the auto-build render the ickiest parts, but then came the finishing, which was most of the work. *Get clinical. Distance yourself emotionally, as much as you can.* He grimaced. Another piece of sage but useless advice.

Individually, each of these four was a fairly short job. But when the *surfaces* he rendered were trembling, living muscles being sliced open, or disemboweled torsos with the guts spilling out . . .

He'd halted frequently. Taken lots and lots of long, deep breaths. He'd kept his breakfast down, but it had been a near thing several times.

Autopsies established a probable order for the knife-cuts on these four, although the extent of the mutilations on one of the vics had made that especially difficult to establish. Certain body parts had been cut off and removed from each of the scenes—perhaps as trophies? Or maybe as proof of completion?

Through them all, he'd tried to focus only on how the liquid of a certain viscosity would have been flung off, or where the highlights would shine on slippery, organic wetness. But no amount of clinical mental distance from *those* surface details could make him unsee them.

Charlie shuddered. *If these GRs don't convince Emer Bellamy that a Whisper execution is a horrific way to die, nothing will.*

The image generator purred through its final backup and shutdown, then went silent. The lights in Chamber Three cycled up from darkness to neutral-running mode. Charlie clambered out of his rig, taking care to extricate his arm shield so it wouldn't catch on the metal frame. He stretched. Breathed through a few more of the structured patterns that were supposed to calm him.

No matter how he yearned to think about something else, today's reconstructions kept dragging him back. Yes, the third and fourth scenes he'd worked today probably were Knife

Woman's work. And those might need touching up if the Dolan scene revealed that he'd missed a nuance.

But he could say "done and good riddance" to the two from the unsub he'd privately nicknamed The Grim Scalpel. That guy —he felt certain this executioner was a man—most definitely had been through medical training at some point. *No, not just medical. Surgical.* Charlie would bet on it. The cuts were too certain, too precise. No hesitation marks at all. Whoever he was, he knew what he was doing, and he knew human anatomy inside out. Next to him, Knife Woman was an untrained, amateur butcher.

He stopped at the new door. It led out to his future office. But the nascent XK9 Unit's home base would still be a hard-hat area for another few days. *I don't need that much of an obstacle course tonight.* He reversed directions and slipped out the back way, using what had formerly been the front entrance. Trips through the Orangeboro GR Unit were considerably more congenial now that his old nemesis Missy Cranston was no longer running things over here.

Ernie Porringer and the newly-elevated Acting GR Unit Supervisor Jenny Evans stood in the hallway. They halted their quiet conversation and glanced up with smiles at his approach.

"Hi, Charlie. How's it . . . going?" Jenny's smile faded after a closer examination. "Oh, man. You okay?"

He blew out a breath. "I'm, um, actually headed for Dr. Mariel's."

"Bad one?" Jenny's eyes softened with worry. She and Ernie knew better than his other colleagues about the toll a bad scene could take on an artist.

Charlie grimaced. "Four of them."

"Damn, man. For the SBI?" Ernie asked.

"Yeah. One more tomorrow and I'm done, though."

"Surface details," Ernie said.

"Not helping." Charlie shook his head. "Not on *these* surfaces."

"Oh, that *is* bad. Hang in there." Ernie patted Charlie's shoulder.

"Ask Doc for a hypno-sleep session," Jenny suggested. "That usually helps, even if nothing else does."

He nodded. "Here's hoping."

Ernie glanced at Jenny. "I bet what you just told me would perk him up."

Jenny smiled. "It might, at that."

Charlie quirked an eyebrow, more than ready for something new to think about. "What's up?"

"Word is out that Secretary Pandra was worried enough about your assault charge against Missy to actually review the vids and audio your rig recorded."

He blinked. "You're kidding."

"Yeah, who expected that?" Ernie chuckled. "I mean, due diligence when it means accountability for his sister?"

"My source says he about hit the roof once he got a load of her in action." Jenny's eyes sparkled with fierce pleasure. "Couldn't have been timed better. That was right after OPD's PR department started filling the Station's news feeds with the story about you, back in 'hero-mode,' saving Rex at the Hub."

His gut tightened. "Oh?"

"Yeah—and there she is on full aud-vid, trying to scratch your eyes out." Ernie grinned. "*Not* a good look."

"Anyway, long story short, the Family's attorneys negotiated a plea deal." Jenny blew out an exasperated sigh. "Well, of course they did. But she's gonna hate it, even if it could've been worse. Under the plea agreement, she quietly retires. Never speaks out publicly about this or any other Safety Services Department incident, especially nothing involving you."

Some of the tightness in his gut eased. *That would be nice.*

"Oh, but there's more." A vengeful grin spread over Ernie's face. Charlie might've been Missy's favorite target, but Jenny and Ernie had suffered their share of abuse, too.

"You'll love this part." Jenny's expression matched Ernie's.

"She also must undergo a full psychological evaluation. *And* she has to *follow* any treatment recommendations. *Plus,* she serves ten years under house arrest in lieu of prison."

His gut unclenched a bit more. "Oh, she'll hate every minute of that!" *Ernie was right.* He could actually smile. *But I still better go check in with Doc.*

❖ ❖ ❖ ❖ ❖ ❖ ❖ ❖

S-3-9 Investigative Center

"**B**alchu and I decided to grab some street tacos. Want to join us?" Pam pushed back from the workstation and lifted her arms in a full-body stretch. Kieran hadn't been cleared for a second interview, so most of her day after lunch had gone to reports and studying up on the requisition forms sergeants were supposed to file for their units. They were more varied and extensive than she'd imagined possible.

Nearby, Shady did her own series of full-body stretches before she answered. "Charlie called a little while ago and asked for a ride home."

Charlie's still here? Pam frowned and switched to the link for a personnel matter. *He's seriously past his mandated cutoff.*

Shady switched to the link, too. *Apparently he's had a bad day. Elaine had him working on a number of really troubling, grisly GRs. After he finished, he spent an hour with Dr. Mariel, then another at the gym. He's now physically exhausted, but still upset.*

Her pulse picked up. Charlie might not be her lover anymore, but he was a friend, a Packmate, and part of the unit the Chief had just made her responsibility. She hadn't seen his personnel file yet, but she knew him well enough to guess he might have a history of depression. *I think you'd definitely better take him home. And I should touch base with Elaine about those GRs.*

Thank you. See you tomorrow, in that case. Shady gently head-butted her and rubbed her face across Pam's torso a couple of times, a move she called "scent-loading." A quick flick of her tongue touched Pam's cheek, then her partner was off to rescue Charlie.

"Short delay," she texted to Balchu, then strode over to the back-hallway offices of the SBI leaders. Elaine's door stood ajar, the light on inside. Pam rapped on the frame and peeked in.

The SSA had been frowning into a HUD stare, but at Pam's knock she blinked and refocused. "Hello, Sergeant. I was just about to call you. Dr. Mariel logged a Staff Well-Being flag on Charlie a few minutes ago."

Pam let her brows rise. "Because of the GRs?" *Now I definitely need to check his file.*

Elaine let out a soft grunt. "You think? I just got schooled a little while ago by Regan Ireland on how immersive the process of building a GR truly is. I'd been told they have an 'auto-build' function in those rigs, and I guess I overestimated what it can do. She commed me, worried, after we received one notice after another from him that he'd finished—all told, *four* of them today. Didn't think he'd turn them around so fast."

"Charlie is nothing if not conscientious." She offered Elaine a wry grimace. "He's not notable for sparing himself, either. One moment—let me ask Shady—she switched to the link. *Charlie's not planning to do the fifth GR tomorrow, is he?*

He's trying real hard to psych himself up for it. Says he needs to get them done before Rex is out of re-gen.

Ah. Thanks. Pam grimaced. "Shady says he's trying to finish them all before Rex comes out of re-gen."

"Oh, crap. Of course." Elaine sat back in her seat and with an expression of dismay. "Like when Rex did that horrible interview for the SDF. He waited till Charlie was safely in re-gen, so his healing wouldn't be complicated by it. Dammit! I didn't even think about that."

"I really don't believe Charlie should do another GR tomorrow."

"No shit." She blew out a breath. "I'd simply tell him to stop, but I'd like to give him a face-saving alternative, because an SWB isn't . . . *hmm*. He said something a few weeks ago . . ." She went back into a HUD stare.

Her eyes tracked rapidly back and forth, then her frown shifted into a smile. "Ah! Found it, and it's an excellent idea." She refocused on Pam. "You have Kieran in the morning tomorrow, but we've now learned about how long he's likely to last. Is Shady busy in the afternoon?"

❖ ❖ ❖ ❖ ❖ ❖ ❖ ❖

Precinct Five, Market Garden Neighborhood, Pam and Balchu's Apartment

Pam flopped down on the Central Plaza public bench next to where Balchu sat with a mostly-finished plate of street tacos. "Thanks for waiting."

He wiped his mouth and grinned. "I was hungry, and you didn't say how long you'd be." He picked up his last one.

"Fair enough. What's good?"

"Get the fish. Best ever!" He finished his taco and licked his fingers. "In fact, I'll come with you. I worked up quite an appetite this afternoon."

She laughed. "Doing what?"

He hesitated, gave her a somewhat worried sidelong glance. "I spent a lot of it on the com with Uncle Chase and Uncle Luis, actually."

They got in line, but Pam had lost her appetite with his mention of the two Becenti Family members. At Balchu's urging they ordered a to-go bag. Neither said anything more till they'd received their food.

"Mind if we head home?" Balchu asked. "I'm not sure we should have the conversation I want in public."

"That works for me." The foreboding flutter in her stomach eased some when they left Central Plaza.

Their little flat in the Market Garden District lay only a few blocks away. Pam caught herself noticing all the myriad patches of green as they walked. Berry bushes, vegetables, flowers, and herbs filled the planter-boxes that edged the sidewalks.

Unlike the plants she'd seen in Precinct Seven, she actually recognized most of these. People's window-boxes overflowed with fruiting tomato or squash vines. "Vertical gardens" had been set up on almost every block, built with rows of soil-filled trays on frameworks against the walls. Most had been planted with leafy salad greens.

Except for the personal window-boxes, it was all publicly-available food, tended by street maintenance bots. She knew many neighbors who'd make the better part of a meal from what they could pick and carry home. No hoarding or resales allowed: civic services monitored the security feeds, and apparent violations sparked quick follow-up. But it was always there for personal and family use by the residents.

As long as everyone followed the rules, there was food for all. She wasn't the only one who occasionally might've gone hungry without them. "You're right. It's definitely not all steel and concrete around here."

"Just sayin.'" Balchu plucked a curly-edged lettuce leaf in passing and popped it into his mouth. "Can't get fresher than that."

They climbed the metal steps to their place over the Ultra-Fast Tempura shop. They'd lived above it for a couple of years but never patronized the joint: got enough of their rancid oil just from smelling it. *I will not miss that.*

Shady's alert attention focused on her immediately. *You're thinking about moving to Becenti?*

Definitely not yet! I need to know about Balchu's conversation with Chase and Luis, for starters.

Elaine just called us and told Charlie she's postponing that last GR for now. She wants me to come to HQ in the morning for Kieran's interview, then go back home to pick up Charlie. We're going to Monteverde in the afternoon.

Monteverde? Why?

I'll explain later. Have your dinner and your conversation. I'll butt out.

No you won't. Pam chuckled. *You'll listen in.*

Well, yeah. But I won't interrupt.

Right.

Balchu finished wiping the top of their battered coffee table. He set the taco bag on it, then turned to their tiny kitchen for plates and napkins. Pam shed her dress blues and her bra *at last*, washed up, and sank with a sigh onto the sofa. Once he'd shucked out of his own dress blues, Balchu joined her.

"Oh, yeah. Lots better than the middle of Central Plaza." Balchu leaned back and stretched out his long bare legs with a sigh. He snagged another taco.

"The call with Chase and Luis?" She raised her brows and bit into her own taco. *Oh! He was not wrong. This is wonderful.* Suddenly she had an appetite again. *Needs beer, though.*

"Uncle Luis was elected Head of Household after Grandpa Onyx died." Balchu paused to finish his mouthful.

Pam returned from the kitchen and handed him one of the— well, technically it was a bottle of ale. Orangeboro Glory, to be exact. She settled in next to him and snuggled up. "Elected Head of Household, and?"

Balchu frowned. "And he got his first glance at their finances. The *real* books."

His first? Shady asked. *Corona shares a monthly financial report with all adults in the Family.*

Pam rested her chin on Balchu's shoulder. "Shouldn't Family members be kept more aware than that?"

His frown didn't ease. "Apparently Onyx and Raya shared reports, but what Luis found in the Family's trust account doesn't match the reports. He's pretty freaked out about it."

Well, that explains a lot. Cold certainty pooled in her belly. "How much is missing?"

"Four million."

"Damn!" Pam stared at him. *That's more money than—holy shit!* "Is there anything left?"

"Only about two and a half." He gave her a troubled frown.

"Two and a half novi?" Her mouth dropped open.

"No! Not quite that bad." One corner of his mouth quirked up. "Two and a half million. We're not ruined yet."

She gulped. Pulled her wits together and activated her cop-mind. "So, where'd it go? Gambling? Were they scammed?"

"Luis thinks 'scammed' is more likely."

"Either way, that's a job for your unit. *Not* Gorman, please." She scowled. She'd met Alf Gorman back when he was a Detective Level Three, before he made sergeant. She'd never seen any reason to revise her opinion after a terrible first impression.

I've never seen a reason to, either. Shady's low growl echoed through the link.

"Right there with you." Balchu said. "I've asked Lt. Shevchenko to put Akkari Matika on it. I can be the Family go-between, but of course I have to stay hands-off the investigation itself."

Pam nodded. "So . . . is Becenti bankrupt?"

"No. It's not as solvent as Chase thought when he invited us in, but it's not broke yet." He pursed his lips, glanced sideways at her. "If it was down below ore, we might be in trouble. Too hard to service the debt on the tower. But we'll be okay with two and a half. It can be built up again, and there's a chance we might be able claw back some of the four mil, if we can nail the scammer."

"It all sounds like frightening amounts of money to me." Pam shivered. "I have no idea what most Chartered Families own. What's 'average'? What's 'enough'?"

Corona's Family trust is worth fifty-four million. It's all tied up in investments, of course. She received an impression of Shady giving herself a whole-body shake, then circling a couple of times before she lay down in her bed. *That might not be typical, but who knows?*

Pam gulped. Fifty-four million novi presented as hard an idea to wrap her mind around as nine or ten meters of snow. *I don't think that helped me.*

Money is just a concept. Does that help?

No. Stop 'helping.'

CHAPTER 30
BETRAYAL AND REVENGE

OPD Interview Suite M

S hady couldn't quite stifle a soft whimper of eagerness, couldn't quite still her feet in the hallway outside Interview M.

"He just came in." Melynn lifted her gaze from her case pad. "As . . . hmm. I guess Shady has already figured that out." She hesitated—must be getting a transmission Shady wasn't receiving. "Okay, got a go-light. In!"

Kieran remained wheelchair-bound. Public defender Hadi and Brutus the nurse took the same positions as yesterday, but without the IV pole. An additional day-cycle of food, rest, and appropriate hydration had perked up their subject considerably. He sat straighter, smelled less ill. And he actually smiled to see them.

Oh that is so strange. Pam exchanged a quick, worried glance with Shady. *I've never seen a subject smile in a situation like this before.*

Melynn ran through the obligatory notices and warnings, listed everyone's names for the official recordings, then asked, "Kieran, would you like to make any opening statements?"

Kieran's smile widened. "Have you ever tasted honey? It's the most amazing stuff! They gave it to me for breakfast today and I just want to say *wow*! The food here is amazing!"

Melynn stared at him for a beat. Her scent factors ballooned with sharp, high notes of surprise. "Um, duly noted. I actually meant a statement about the case."

"Oh, I know. But it's just—I never tasted anything like that before. So, thanks! Um, about the case." His expression shifted to pinched discomfort and the bright joy in his scent leached away, replaced by the musty off-notes of unease. "I, um, I don't know what to tell you. But ask and I'll answer. You guys gave me honey, so . . . I'll do my best."

Be nice if that worked on all murder conspirators. Shady cut her eyes toward her partner.

Pam's scent suggested she was struggling to keep her expression solemn. But Kieran couldn't see it if Shady dipped her nose below table-level and lolled her tongue.

"Okay then, let's talk about Zander Hoback." Melynn inclined her head toward Kieran. "You said he worked for Allard Ferro, of the Whisper Syndicate. Exactly when and how did you meet him?"

"Oh, man. I'd have to say that was about three years ago." Kieran's gaze drifted a bit to the side. His expression shifted to the subtly haunted appearance it had habitually developed in their previous interview each time he accessed personal memories.

"Turd used me as his flunky back then. Kept me at Ostra, waiting by his elbow all day. It was boring as fuck, but especially after the thing with Cheree, he always wanted to keep an eye on me. Ten years, he kept me on the hook. Didn't trust me to do shit on my own for fear I'd stab 'im in the back. And it's not like I didn't want to." He grimaced. "One day Ferro comes in and *his* flunky is this new guy, Zan. Said the old one died."

"Now, as I recall 'Turd' is your father Turlach," Melynn said.

Kieran's brow pinched. "Don't remind me."

"And the 'old flunky' was who, again?"

"Oh. Name of Gordy. Never got a last name on that one. I first saw him around 85, 86, sometime in there."

"So, this Gordy came in with Ferro, since about eight years ago?" Melynn raised her eyebrows.

"Yeah."

"And Zan was the replacement after Gordy died, about 91?"

"'Bout then, or 90, maybe."

"How long had Allard Ferro been coming to Ostra?"

"I don't remember a time he *wasn't*."

"Ferro came there to do what?"

"Turd took all his orders from Ferro. When they needed him to shake somebody down, see. Or whenever they had a shipment coming through."

"'They' means . . ."

"The Syndicate."

"And the shipments consisted of what?"

Kieran grimaced. "It varied. Sometimes girls. Sometimes little kids. Three to five, usually. Sometimes they sent six or seven at a time. We'd hold 'em in a storage building with good sound-proofing anytime Ferro brought 'em in." He shuddered. "I hated those runs. But we never dared ask questions."

Shady kept her snarl sheathed. *I want to know where those buildings are!*

"Lotta times, though, it was just stuff they had us store for them," Kieran brightened a little. "I'd take Gordy—or later Zan —to wherever they needed to either take the stuff or get it from. Boxes, barrels, crates of shit. Usually I never saw what was in 'em." His mouth made a rueful twist. "I never wanted to know, you know? Bad as it was with the girls and the little kids, who the fuck knew what was in the boxes? Sometimes they reeked pretty bad."

Shady growled, but only through the link. *I'd like to take a whiff of a few of those boxes. Bet I could tell you what was in there.*

I bet you could, too. Pam kept her face neutral. *I wonder if they used the same storage buildings for both their slaves and their "stuff."*

And where they are in the Five-Ten. Shady nodded.

"We're going to need directions to those buildings," Melynn said.

"Oh, they were different each time. Turd had about three or four dozen we might use at any given time, and he traded them out alla time. I don't think any of 'em actually belonged to either him or Whisper. We had to keep changing them, because the locals would see. And some of those people didn't mind talking to cops, you know?"

"How did Turd gain access?"

Kieran shook his head. "Beats me. I know he was paying a lot of the storage company guys, so probably that way. But he never let me in on that side of the business. The one time I tried, couple of them Saoirse blades caught me. Fucked me up pretty bad."

"Did anything change when Zan started coming in?" Melynn asked.

"Yeah." Kieran offered a rueful smile. "Zan was a lot more fun than Gordy. He'd tell wacko stories and say rude things about the bosses when they couldn't hear. He an' me, we kinda saw eye-to-eye on some things. But he was a backstabbing shit from the git-go, you know? Said he spaced ol' Gordy cuz he wanted his job, and I believed him. He'd get this cold, mean expression and say he had to look out for himself, cuz nobody else was gonna."

"And you liked that?"

Kieran made a face and shuddered. "Not that. No, that gives me the creeps. But he didn't show himself that way alla time. Mostly it was wild stories and cheap shots at the old guys. I liked those. Made me feel good. But Zan's a goer and a doer like I never could be." He shook his head and grimaced. "He was always working an angle."

Shady alerted on an uptick in their subject's scent of the raw, grinding smell that signaled inflammation. *He's starting to get tired. Some part of him has started hurting, but I can't quite pinpoint where.*

"Figured I oughta do that, too, you know, do more like he did." Kieran lifted his head and squared his shoulders. "He'd say how he stole money on the side and was putting away a stash. Always working things like that. I knew he had big ambitions, even back then, and I was right."

"Why do you say that?"

"Well, after Zan got blooded in the Syndicate, he started running his own things." Kieran shifted in his wheelchair, then reached around to knead his lower back with his knuckles.

There it is. Around the kidneys. That's where it aches. Shady noted this in her log.

"Ferro had to get another flunky, and I told Turd I wasn't gonna be *his* flunky anymore, neither," Kieran continued. "He tried to whup on me like always, but that time I whupped him." He gave Melynn a grim, bitter smile. "Whupped him real good. I was that sick of him, you know? So he put me on running a crew in the storage stacks, and after that I didn't have to see his ugly face as much."

"But you continued to see Zan?"

"Yeah. Sometimes he'd bring shit down, like Ferro. Stuff for us to store—but he never brought no kids or girls. He always kept saying how I should get blooded, too, so they'd trust me more, but I dunno." He grimaced and shifted in his wheelchair again.

"You 'don't know' what?" Melynn's eyebrows rose.

"I guess I'm not smart enough, not—well, I don't like the hands-on killin', you know? It's just I'm too soft-headed." His fingers worried the edge of his bedjacket until a tremor started in one hand and he let go of the cloth. "Can't look 'em in the eye and kill 'em, somehow."

Oh, but remotely by the dozens is okay? Shady swallowed a growl.

Pam bit her lip. *So it would seem.*

"When did he approach you about the *Izgubil*?"

"Oh, I think he had me pegged for helping him a long time before he asked me to do anything." Kieran slumped in his wheelchair. "He'd come by my place of an evening, bring me beer and food. He's the first one ever give me pizza. We don't get those in the Five-Ten."

Shady dipped her nose beneath the table-edge and lolled her tongue again. *Clearly, the way to Kieran's heart is through his stomach.*

Mm. Pam kept her apparent focus on Kieran and her face straight. *Next interview, maybe we should bring pizza.*

"Would you say he'd been planning this move for some time?" Melynn asked.

"Thinking back, I don't think he was ever *not* planning it. Stories he'd tell, you know? They were lotta times about somebody doing him bad, and how he'd get back at 'em and they'd never be able to touch him."

Kieran stared for a moment into the middle distance. The haunted expression came over his face again. "That was the key for him, see. Really gave him a kick, makin' it so they couldn't touch him. When he was younger, people done him bad a lot. After he grew up he put his head to doing them all back that ever done him." He shivered. "That's why I made a promise to myself that I was never gonna do him bad."

"If that's the case—why are you talking to us today?"

Kieran's scent went instantly white-hot, shot through with resentful reek. "Almost two months of starvin' in a fuckin' damn *basement*, that's why!" His brows lowered into a thunderous scowl, and his whole body shook.

With anger? With illness? Shady studied his scent, but the harsh reek of fury blotted out the rest.

"I did exactly what he asked me to, and I never, *ever* broke faith!" His jaw jutted. His eyes narrowed to slits. He vibrated with anger. "But then what? Nary a word. Hell, I expected Whisper's goddam butchers every minute—for near-on two fuckin' damn months! And I like to starved to death, in with it!"

Is that anger? Pam asked *Or is he shaking with exhaustion?*

It smells like . . . Shady dug into the scents she was receiving. *Both. But exhaustion is gaining on him.*

"*That's* what turned me on him, the stinking bastard!" Kieran scowled at Melynn. "That's why I'm spillin' my guts right now. An' *that's* why I'll tell you every damn little thing I know! After all I done for him, he done me *anyways!*"

His gaze went distant. It shifted away from Melynn and into a malevolent glare toward something only he appeared to see. "So, okay, Zan, you asshole! This is *your* code. And this is *me*, doin' you *back!*"

CHAPTER 31
TREACHERY IN THE
BLACK VOID

Corona Tower, and Rim Eight Road Leeward to Monteverde Borough

Charlie had already forwarded the coordinates to Vuzvishen Tower. When Shady's auto-nav arrived from HQ, it only needed to pause in Corona's driveway long enough for him to climb in.

He placed his hospitality gifts of a cut-flower bouquet and a small box of seasonal crescent cookies in pockets on the forward console, then settled against the seat cushions for the twenty-minute drive into their next-door Borough of Monteverde.

The car backed out and proceeded leeward on Rim Eight Road.

Shady eyed the offerings. "Police calls do not usually involve bringing gifts."

"They do when the visit is to the Family of a friend, and they're doing me a favor." He smiled. "Georgia set it all up by com from Centerboro this morning. She suggested something like these might help ingratiate us."

"Serafina fixed you up with the gifts? Is one of them supposed to be from me?"

"Aunt Serafina does good work, but not this time. Uncle Dolph made the cookies this morning—they're part of a bigger batch for tonight's dessert, but he said we could spare these for a good cause. I went down to our cutting garden and chose the flowers myself. As to which is from you? Take your pick."

"I have a section on the upper left side of my panniers that should accommodate the vase. Did Georgia say anything about their progress in Centerboro?"

Need to be careful, here. He'd read some things into Georgia's tone that might or might not be accurate, considering how off-balance he'd felt today. "I'm under the impression that she couldn't say all she would've liked about the case, even on a police com. Only that they'd 'found some things,' and Misha's worried they won't get home for the New Year."

"Is she sorry to miss the chance to go on this visit with us?"

"Her words? 'Better you than me.'"

Shady's ears angled toward him. "What does that mean?"

"When I asked her, she said basically, 'Don't get me wrong. They're dear people, and I do love them. I know they love me. But it's much easier to love them when they're in Monteverde and I'm not.' So, no regrets for her. I don't think missing the New Year 'at home' in Monteverde will bother her."

"Interesting. Now I am looking forward to this trip even more."

"Mm." He shifted his weight. They lapsed into silence, each with their own thoughts. He'd suggested this interview himself, but that had been weeks ago. *Why are we doing this now?*

"What is wrong?" Shady cocked her head at him.

He ran a hand over his mouth, grimaced. "Why *this* assignment? Why *now*? Why'd she take me off the final execution GR?" He'd been too exhausted and depressed to think about it last night, but that question had nagged all morning.

"Did you yourself not suggest this interview and request leave to conduct it?"

"Well, yes. But that was weeks ago." His life in the past

decade seemed to be divided into discrete segments of *before* or *after* some particular traumatic event. *Before or after* the *Asalatu*. *Before or after* the dock breach. This particular question had arisen *before* the Dart exploded—yet another chasm ripped in his timeline.

Here on this side of it—*after* the Dart—he'd had to dig up his personal notes to reconstruct his own thinking. He'd hatched the idea on his first day with the joint OPD/SBI *Izgubil* Task Force, after his latest medical leave. He'd been reviewing shipping manifests that day, trying to figure out why someone thought the *Ministo Lulak* and all the souls on board had to die.

He was faced with a notorious lack of reliable, consistent information from the Asteroids. They were a patchwork of independent outfits, pirate operations, and scattered sections of the Belt in space claimed by nearby sovereign Stations. Rana, Mahusay, Singkori, and Primero Stations all "owned" pieces of the Belt, but no one had created a comprehensive database for all. He'd soon run out of documented sources and was grasping at straws when he remembered Georgia's grandfather.

But a different question niggled at him now. "Did Doc file an SWB on me?" A Staff Well-Being flag on one's file wasn't supposed to be a bad thing, but it wasn't exactly a badge of distinction, either.

"What makes you ask that?" Nothing about Shady's attitude or regard changed.

She has a great cop face. I wonder what I'd sense if we were connected through a link? He eased out a sigh and turned away. "It wouldn't be the first time."

"Last night, it did not seem to me that you were eager to finish that last GR." The emotionless vocalizer-voice made her reactions even harder to read.

"'Not eager' has nothing to do with it."

Her hackles rippled, and that sheepdog-stare made his innards squirm. "I cannot answer for Elaine. For myself, I should prefer to talk about this afternoon's interview. We now have somewhat less than half an hour, according to my auto-nav's timer. Why are we traveling to a neighboring Borough to speak with Georgia's grandfather? Is this for the *Izgubil* case?"

She's right. Time to focus on the work at hand. He activated his files and pulled up an odd snippet of bad poetry that had caught his eye. The saboteurs of the *Ministo Lulak* had sent it a few minutes before detonation. The Ministobrila representative stationed in the Port Authority Traffic Control Center at Mahusay Station was reportedly still puzzling over it when the ship lit up.

"Let's start with this. Have you seen it?" The case book had preserved a copy in the original Mahusayan, alongside a translation into Standard. He forwarded both versions to Shady, then explained the situation, the recipient, and the timing. "Those who received it could do nothing but wonder *What the—?* before the ship came into range of Traffic Control's scanners. It was destroyed while it remained too far away for them to rescue anyone."

She went into a HUD-stare. "I was briefed on it."

Charlie had taken classes in Mahusayan during Upper-Levels, but unlike Shady, he'd never even achieved conversational fluency. He'd taken a glance at the Mahusayan again this morning, but then gratefully returned to the translation. It said:

S hame to the Pilot for a reckless course.
       Overreaching ambition makes fools.
How many lives destroyed? Now payment comes.

"T hat is not a bad translation." Shady flicked her ears. "The version in Standard does not capture the implication of invoking a curse in the two Mahusayan words rendered here as 'payment,' and the translator chose 'reckless,' where I would have used 'irresponsible.' But it captures the intent." She met his gaze. "I would also note that it is almost the exact same phrasing used in the message Commodore Montreaux received, just before Wisniewski's Dart was destroyed."

Charlie blinked. "I remember she read it to me, and I realized I had to get into a MERS-V *right then*. If Chief Klein and Hildie hadn't let me go out, we couldn't have reached the Dart's passengers in time. The regular ERT would've lost precious seconds searching for them, but my link with Rex saved several lives that day. The wording was close enough that I recognized what it must be, but I don't know if it's exact."

"I stand by 'exact.'" She forwarded a text:

S hame to the Colonel for a reckless course.
    Overreaching ambition makes fools.
How many lives destroyed? Now payment comes.

T he bottom of his stomach dropped into an abyss. The bolt of helpless terror he'd felt in that moment came back with a dizzying rush. "I, um—I guess we can assume they chose 'reckless' because it scanned better? And that the Mahusayan curse was intended once again?"

"Those are safe assumptions, I think. We know who the 'Colonel' in the second warning is. Do you believe Georgia's grandfather can tell you who the 'Pilot' is?"

"We'd be extremely lucky if so, but maybe. Or at least get us closer to figuring it out. I've been reading what your reports in the case book say about Kieran's interviews. I have the impression that Kieran's in his mid-30s. Does that seem close?"

"His Citizenship record says he was born in 58, so he's 36."

Charlie nodded. "And from what we've gathered, it appears that Zander Hoback is about his same age. Assuming Zander is the mastermind he seems to be for this operation, did something catastrophic happen to him or his family when he was younger?

Maybe something that placed him in Whisper's hands? Or is that a dead end?"

"There is little point in second-guessing. It is not a bad hypothesis." She lolled her tongue. "We shall soon know if Mamoor can help us."

"There's got to be *some* kind of Mahusayan connection." He scowled out the window without seeing much. "A connection that somehow ties him to either Ministobrila, the mining collective, or the Taios Collective that owned and crewed the ship. And definitely there's a connection to the 'Pilot,' whoever that is."

"You think Mamoor will know?"

"I hope. Georgia said her grandfather only fully retired from consulting in the Asteroids about six years ago. I thought he might have heard about a catastrophe, if any such thing has happened in the last few decades. Or maybe he knows who the 'Pilot' might be."

Shady's ears swept back, then forward, then back in the way of a dog encountering something unknown. "Security Chief Garran said Hoback knew high-class manners. Also, he has a faint accent that I guessed might be Mahusayan, based on Garran's description. And from what Kieran says, Zander Hoback's life revolves around somebody 'doing him bad,' and then 'he'd get back at them and they'd never be able to touch him.' That is a direct quote."

"That might explain the cryptic poetry. Kind of a 'neener-neener-up-yours-sucker' sendoff. It also explains the timing."

"Indeed. It would appear that for him, revenge is a dish best served cold—and just out of reach for recourse." She growled. "You are correct. Somehow, the 'Pilot' is the key. Figure out who that is, and I bet it explains the *Ministo Lulak*."

❖ ❖ ❖ ❖ ❖ ❖ ❖ ❖

Monteverde Borough, Vuzvishen Tower

A t *last!* Shady tried to keep her tail from thumping the ground too enthusiastically—not that the humans seemed to be paying her much heed. Charlie, Mamoor, and the other humans *finally* had emptied their teacups. The ritual of tea and polite conversation had grated on her patience for nearly half an hour. Through the link, Pam kept counseling patience. And although Shady increasingly wanted to pant and pace, Charlie seemed at ease.

But now Georgia's grandfather nodded to her colleague. "I believe you are having questions for me?"

Ketevan and Olena, Georgia's great-aunt and grandmother, respectively, stood. Ketevan gathered the tea things. Olena deftly removed the cookie plate, which bore the last handful of Charlie's uncle Dolph's crescent cookies.

Radivan, the other elder gentleman who'd joined them at the table in Vuzvishen Tower's courtyard, just missed grabbing one more. "Don't be stingy!"

But Olena carried them away, chin high. "You already had three! I'm saving these for *actual* New Year's Eve tomorrow! *Dolph Sanger's* cookies must be savored, not gobbled!"

"She is eating them when ball is dropping on show." Mamoor chuckled. "My wife is being only *slightly* more in love with me than with Dolph Sanger, I think."

Charlie grinned. "He'll be pleased to know he has such an ardent fan."

Mother never let me watch any realiciné growing up. Pam's amusement sparkled through the link. *But I saw a couple of Sanger's dramas after I graduated from the Police Academy. I always thought he was handsome for an older guy. I knew he was from Orangeboro, but I never connected him to Corona.*

I shall see if any cookies are still available to bring to you tomorrow.

Mamoor inclined his head toward Charlie. "On duty, you are? No vodka for telling of tales?"

"Sorry, no vodka, thanks. Tea is my limit on duty. But don't let me stop you."

"Is not for drinking in front of guest having none. You asking now what?"

"First, I'd like to share a small, cryptic clue, and see what you make of it." Charlie's eyes twitched toward Mamoor in a gesture that told Shady he'd shared a document.

Georgia's "apodeddi" went into a brief HUD stare then his grizzled eyebrows rose. "Quite the malediction this is. It coming with what more?"

"It arrived at Mahusay Station Traffic Control, a few minutes before the *Ministo Lulak* was 'micro-deconstructed' within sensor-range, but just out of reach for rescues."

Mamoor leaned back in his chair but his bright black eyes studied Charlie. "*Ministo*? Being on board was perhaps person by name Kalan Ministo?"

Shady sat up straighter and angled her ears more directly toward Mamoor.

Charlie stiffened. "Yes, there was."

Mamoor's eyes went hard and his scent factors seethed with distaste. He gave a curt nod. "Good. I am being sorry for rest of crew lost, but *zat* bastard—no."

Wow. Paydirt already. Shady didn't try to restrain her thumping tail now.

"Why do you call him a bastard?"

Mamoor launched into a litany of underhanded dealings. It seemed that Kalan Ministo had long been infamous among Mahusayan asteroid miners as a double-dealing cheat. He would trade on his home Collective's fame and local power. But then, if complications arose or accidents happened, he all too often would stiff his contractors and tell them to sue him if they didn't like it. The nickname "Pilot" was one he'd given himself, hoping it would catch on.

"You know of course how is with nicknames one is giving to oneself." Mamoor's bushy left brow arched upward while his mouth made a wry twist. "We only calling him 'pilot' when mocking behind back."

"So, you think he was the target."

"No doubting. Not with poem."

Charlie nodded. "I mean, the general reputation is bad enough, it seems. But is there any specific incident of 'over-reaching ambition' that might apply?"

"Oh. Beyond counting." Mamoor's hand gave a dismissive wave. "But if I picking one only? Tonquin Base. That is total bad deal."

"Okay. Tell me about Tonquin Base, please."

"Is asteroid name official"—he spoke the words for "1224239" in Mahusayan—"Ogun. I read it on enough maps, reports, I remember. Story always coming back to mind when I read."

Charlie nodded. "A mining base?"

"Longtime, large, mine for ridkoz— how you say? Rare earths. Also all platinums and as well nickel. Of quality high, first two centuries. But mining out last ore about year . . . Is maybe 68, 69 Ranan." He shrugged. "Zis happens. Mine till asteroid gone. Move next in group. All under Ministobrila Collective lease in Ogun Group asteroids. Deal is lease to Tonquin, protect from pirates, split proceeds. Is frequent arrangement."

"And normally moving is not a problem? There are other asteroids in the group?"

"Is big effort, moving. Expensive. For Tonquin, moving triple rotation habitation pods, excavators, haulers, mass drivers tracks, most of 250 people, one-quarter being children. Expensive moving, protecting, but after set up is ready operation. Go straight back working."

Shady tried to imagine this, but she didn't know enough about mining.

"Mm." Charlie frowned. "So, what happened?"

"Kalan agree move, pay, protect. They beginning move. Pods detach, equipment packing, removing from remnant. Last step bring remnant with, to finish last extraction. All move another in

Ogun Group, I forgetting number. Is going as planned. Base administrator messaging Ministobrila all is well. Six months, maybe year, then back at work in new place." He frowned. "But then Iron Hand is making Kalan big offer. He not resisting. Taking money for own wealth, not collective. For pulling security detail."

"Iron Hand is a pirate group?" Charlie's slight frown and deadpan expression did not match his hot, outraged scent factors.

What a bastard! Shady's hackles spiked. She snapped her ears back and snarled. "How could he do that and stay in the Ministobrila Collective's good graces?"

"Kalan is claiming they surprise with forces greater, unexpected, very savage. Kill some security, pulling rest back and paying to shut mouths. Collective choosing believe him. Not much else to doing, after attack all finished, they think. But not everyone is shutting mouth after decades going by. Talk spreads."

"What happened to Tonquin?" Shady asked.

"Administrator Hoback is sending frantic messages to Ministobrila, but Tonquin people all strung out in fifteen ships. Is no defending without Kalan. Is bloodbath."

Administrator Hoback? Her ears went straight up. She sensed Pam's full attention through the link.

"Administrator Hoback?" Charlie asked. "He or she was the leader of Tonquin Base?"

"Was old, well respected independent mining family." Mamoor nodded. "John Hoback Fourth was good leader. Honest, people say. Mining expert, studied Mahusay Technology Institute and Rana Station Polytechnic. Good manager, knowing logistics, running base—but not fighting. Not equipped. They carrying mass driver parts, loaders, other things they need for new Tonquin. Not weapons."

"He didn't happen to have a family, did he?" Charlie leaned in toward Mamoor. "This administrator?"

"Oh, yes. Wife, two sons, a daughter. All dead or taken, like everyone. Investigation finding bodies in space later, also wrecks of two ships from the fifteen. Pirates spacing old people, lower-level workers, all who resist. Taking top specialists, young women, children. Making specialists do work in their mines, or sell to other outfits. Selling young women, little kids to Whisper, Dushlan, maybe one other new group forming at Singkori Station. Taking equipment for own mining or to selling cheap."

Of course they did. It's what pirates do. Pam's shudder echoed through the link.

"What happened to Administrator Hoback himself?" Shady cocked her head at Mamoor.

"Killed. They finding his body on bridge of wrecked flagship."

"But no sign of the children." *Just to be clear.*

Mamoor shook his head. "No children. Attack was happening closest to Ranan space. They selling to Whisper, probably."

CHAPTER 32

THIS WHOLE "CELEBRATING A HOLIDAY" THING

Back in Orangeboro, Precinct Ten Agricultural District

S hady wrapped up her report about the time her car crossed the border back into Orangeboro. She wouldn't have noticed that they had, but Charlie said the fencing by the Rim-Runner tracks changed in color from green to orange at the border.

She glanced out the window. To her the fencing all seemed about the same brownish-gray color as before. "I shall have to take your word for that."

"I promise." He grinned. "Thought you might like to know we're back in Orangeboro."

"A little more than halfway home. I wonder if Dr. Sandler will call tonight." The doctor had said that, depending on the readings she got, Rex might be brought out of his nanite re-gen tonight. Or it might not happen till sometime tomorrow.

"The uncertainty is a bit unsettling, isn't it?" Charlie grimaced, then resumed his HUD stare.

I guess he's not done with his report, yet.

You XK9s are faster with HUD-work than most of us humans. She sensed a touch of envy through the link from Pam. *Gotta say, that was a really fruitful interview. I wonder if you didn't learn more from "Apodeddi" Mamoor than we did from Kieran today.*

We did learn a lot. I'm pleased. She stared at the passing landscape of high-yield growing environments, called "Hi-Ys" for short. The ones across the valley resembled shelves stacked with giant glowing boxes on the "stairsteps" of terraces. *But Kieran's not finished. I think we can learn more from him.*

Agreed, Pam said. *I have a feeling he knows more than he thinks he does, if we just keep him talking.*

Exactly. Mamoor had no idea what we were seeking. Kieran doesn't either. We just have to keep digging. They'd entered a district where intricate complexes of shining metal cylinder-and-pipe structures interspersed with the Hi-Ys. Those were meat- or dairy-production facilities, according to the signs posted on or near them. "This is most definitely different from 'agricultural districts' in Transmondia." She used her vocalizer to include Charlie.

"Too true." He gave a wry grunt and refocused on her. "We can't afford to waste anywhere near as much space as they do on Chayko. History says there was a time when our ag districts seemed a lot more like our residential areas do now. But these days, the population's way too big. We can't grow enough for everybody without those high-yield facilities."

"Are we in any danger of running short?"

Through the link, she sensed Pam's sigh. *Maybe of Master Mix.*

"No worries, at least not yet." Charlie eyed the passing view. "We still have plenty, and enough for export. Although of course, there are 'purists' who won't knowingly eat anything from the 'Hi-Ys' . . ." He shook his head. "It helps keep a lot of our smaller farmers in business, so I guess there's a place for everything."

"I guess." Another cylinders-and-pipes facility came into view. "Oh! There is Pabiyan Distillery!" Its distinctive star-and-bottle design spread across nearly the whole side of one big cylinder, clearly visible across the valley from Rim Eight Road. Lights along the tops and sides of the structures glowed as local Station time drew toward evening.

"I suppose it's a good thing liquor and spirits aren't the only things they distill there," Charlie said. "Maybe the embargo won't harm them as much as those Popular Growth Forum ghouls in Solara City are hoping."

I wish, Pam agreed through the link.

"That would be nice." But the reminder of the embargo soured her gut and made her hackles prickle.

Next moment, the com beeped: Dr. Sandler for both her and Charlie.

"Good news," Sandler said. "The Learned Kirritokti likes Rex's readings. Ki says we can transition him out of re-gen tonight. He will not be conscious until after we give him a cycle of Healing Sleep, so you can probably skip coming in tonight and just plan on taking some Family leave tomorrow."

Shady met Charlie's eyes. "I want to give him a good sniff-over tonight. Would that be possible?"

"Certainly, if you truly want to do that. It is within your rights. When can we expect you?"

Don't blame you. Pam hesitated, then added reluctantly, *Do you want me to meet you there?*

Go home with Balchu and eat your supper. I'll see you tomorrow.

Thanks.

"We're halfway through Tenth Precinct headed spinward," Charlie said to Dr. Sandler. "Figure about half an hour."

"In that case you may have to wait a little while till he's fully stabilized. We'll be ready for you with updates."

Once the vet had clicked off, Shady met Charlie's eyes. "Thank you."

He offered a wry grin. "It might sound silly, but I just want to run my fingers through his fur and feel him breathing."

"It is no sillier than my sniff-over. Being there in person will change nothing for Rex. But I shall sleep better."

"Me, too." He hesitated. "I wonder if Hildie's still shopping in town. There's a little boutique in the Gaudí District that she and several of her cousins love."

"Shopping?"

"Finishing up some New Year shopping."

"I see. Would she like to meet us?"

A rush of warm pleasure suffused his scent. "Let me call and find out." He went into another HUD stare, and soon was speaking with Hildie.

Shady programmed their new Sandler Clinic destination into the auto-nav, then gazed out the window and tried to focus on something besides the warm, one-sided love-talk Charlie soon slid into. She snorted. *I feel like a voyeur. Why aren't they Amares yet? They're clearly crazy about each other.*

People do things in their own time. Pam chuckled. *Can I help distract you somehow?*

Maybe. What is "New Year shopping?"

A lot of people give each other special gifts at the New Year. The Christians probably make the biggest deal over gifts at this time of the year, but they do it a few days after Solstice on their own holiday.

Like Mike and Elaine. They'd been elated to get away for a couple of days—also to Monteverde—for an event called a "Christmas Mass" and a celebration at home, actually *on the day* of the holiday, with their Family at Providence-Brightstar Tower.

Yes. She had a sense of Pam's parallel thoughts about the two senior SBI agents. *But most of us Ranans celebrate with gifts and parties for the New Year, even if we don't have a particular religion.* Her eager anticipation bubbled through the link. *I usually have to work, but once I get off-duty, it's my favorite holiday.*

Why?

Mother never celebrated anything, but at school we always had music and small gifts from the teachers at a party before the New Year break, and Balchu has gotten me into the habit of spending special time together celebrating the holiday whenever we can coordinate our sched-ules. It won't be a problem this year, which will be nice. I understand why Mike and Elaine were excited about being able to be there "on the actual day."

This whole "celebrating a holiday" thing mostly mystifies me. The XK9 Project staff observed holidays on Chayko, too, but that only meant irritation and inconvenience for us.

How so?

Because for a day or two each holiday there'd be a skeleton staff at Project facilities. She stifled a growl. *They were supposed to cover at least the bare minimum of maintenance activities. And I have to say that sometimes they did a decent job.*

Only "sometimes"?

Which kennel worker pulled holiday duty made a lot of difference. Most of the time, we never got to leave our run enclosures. They'd feed us late and forget about sanitary cleanup. We learned all kinds of ways to open gates and raid pantries, but those usually only worked once. Next time they'd take counter-measures. All too often, we'd be trapped in a run for two days with a diminishing water supply and no food.

Eww. Yeah, with a past like that I can understand how you'd feel. But I bet you're in for a whole new holiday experience this year. There's no way Corona Family will do that.

I suppose not. So I guess we'll see. She glanced over toward Charlie.

He'd leaned back in his seat with a wide grin. "Oh, and by the way, you have a diehard fan in Monteverde."

She cocked her head. *I do not think he's talking to Hildie now.*

"Olena Ismeryatochno Volkov," Charlie said. "She's my colleague Georgia's grandmother. Her husband was my interview subject."

Maybe his uncle? Pam hazarded.

Charlie grinned, oblivious to their link-based exchange. "Oh, yes. He predicted she'd hoard the last of your cookies to eat while watching your show. He said she never misses it." He listened a moment, then laughed. "Agreed. Anyway, since it's your dinner rotation, I wanted to let you know we'll probably be real late."

Gotta be Uncle Dolph, Shady agreed.

"Oh—and if we don't get there before you have to go to bed, break a leg in Centerboro!" His face relaxed into an expression of joy and affection. "You, too! Good night." He lowered his chin with a sigh and lingering smile on his lips, then glanced over toward Shady.

She lolled her tongue. "It appears we may have several friends and Family spending the holiday in Centerboro this year."

❖ ❖ ❖ ❖ ❖ ❖ ❖ ❖

The Sandler Clinic

S hady is here. Charlie is here. I can breathe. Rex yawned, so it must be a dream. He hadn't been able to—

You can yawn now, Charlie said through the link. *You gonna wake up pretty soon?*

Maybe. This was really vivid for a dream. The bed beneath his body didn't feel quite like home. *Sandler Clinic? Re-gen? Uh-oh.* It did feel rather much like coming out of re-gen, but different this time, somehow.

To confirm, yes. You are coming out of re-gen. It is now the morning of New Year's Eve. We, um, had to make some fast decisions, since your new lungs still aren't completely grown yet.

Shady's urgent nose detailed his face and neck. "He is not quite out of it yet."

Oh, I definitely feel 'out of it.' I have missed things again. Rex blinked, found Charlie's face, caught a glimpse of Shady's shoulders. She'd started sniffing along his forelegs and belly. *Oh. Got it. She means out of re-gen. Damn, I'm slow. What happened?*

You insisted on going into an area full of volatiles and did an awful lot of damage to what's left of your lungs. Charlie's expression went half-rueful, half worried. *You are large and bull-headed. I couldn't stop you.*

Ah. Memories filtered gradually back in. *Crap.*

That was my thought.

"Is he making any sense in the link, yet?" Shady's face swung into view.

"Beginning to." Charlie's mouth twitched with a suppressed grin. "Give him a few more minutes." His hand stroked Rex's neck. "Welcome back, Big Guy."

Shady didn't have to say anything. She climbed onto his bed, snuggled up next to him so she could rest her face against his neck, then expelled an enormous sigh. "It is good to have you awake and better."

"Good to be better." Rex's eyes drifted closed. *Good to breathe. How did that happen?* But he couldn't stay awake long enough to understand Charlie's answer.

CHAPTER 33
CLEAR THE COURTROOM!

The Sandler Clinic, S-3-9 Investigative Center, and a Civic Center Courtroom

Time pressed on Shady. It was past time to go to work. Although Family Leave said she didn't have to go, how could she abandon the Pack? Her pulse sped up, but then her gut tightened along with her resolve. *I'm responsible. I can only do my best and hope it's enough.* She flattened her ears and re-examined her mate.

Rex remained groggy, but he was breathing much better, thanks to the experimental nanite treatment. The main difference from last night was that he was—sort of—conscious now. Charlie sat by the big black dog's bed in the little Clinic room. One hand rested on Rex's shoulder. Charlie inclined his head toward Rex with a small smile. *Talking through the link. That's a place I can't go.* She licked her lips and stress-yawned. *Every once in a while I envy Charlie.*

Mm. I get it. Pam's wry amusement came through the link. *Occasionally I do, too, because he lives with you. But I must admit— even if Balchu and I do move to Becenti—you're probably better off at Corona.*

Shady's ears went up. *You're willing to admit you're thinking about it?*

I guess I am. Apparently Becenti really does want us to merge. And the rest of our family really wants to do it. Shady caught a sense of Pam's uncertainty, her tight chest and self-doubt. *In every logical review of the idea that I try to do—all the "pro and con" lists—It makes perfect sense for us to join Becenti Charter. So—what's my problem?*

You've internalized too many of your mother's ideas. To me, that's your sticking point. Shady lolled her tongue. *I probably should ask if you noticed that you referred to Balchu's parents, sister, and her Amare, as well as yourself and Balchu as "our family" just now.*

I did? Um. Pam hesitated. *I, um. I guess I did, didn't I? I don't know what to say to that.*

How do you feel about them? Are they becoming your Pack?

A complicated twist of fear and affection came through the link. *They—I—well—I kind of liked it when Tuya hugged me and told me she was proud. I really feel honored and amazed by that. By—by all of it. I mean, all four of them came to my thing on Tuesday at the crack of dawn. Who does that? And they—*Shady had a sense of her partner blinking faster to fight tears. *They really do seem to like me. And I—that feels good.*

Scent factors do not lie. They definitely like you. And they are good people. They will be good Packmates for you.

Now she received a sense of dawning amazement, as well as a thawing of fearful hope. *That's quite an endorsement.*

Are you free to talk with Balchu about this now?

Pam hesitated. *Maybe.*

I think you should, if you haven't already.

I'll—um. I'll think about it.

Shady had a sense she'd pushed her partner about as far as she could for now. *Okay, reframe. How's it going at HQ?*

Detention's medical team says Kieran had a rough night. He's developed a virus that most people are vaccinated against before they turn five. Yes, there was definitely relief in her partner's response.

But Pam's grimace also communicated clearly through the link. *He's vaccinated now, so maybe that'll help shorten the duration. Yeesh.*

You keep saying Rana doesn't throw people away, but I don't think the Five-Ten got that memo.

Pam's wordless reply felt something like a growl. *Anyway, I think Sgt. Koro and I can finish the last of my orientation this morning. You can stay at the Clinic as long as you need to.*

Shady replied with her own growl. *I am the Acting Pack Leader. I need to assess the situation.* The weight of that responsibility lay like a boulder in her gut and made her hackles prickle. She glanced over her shoulder. Now Charlie and Sandler's vet tech Ari Pryce were deep in conversation. *Charlie already told me he'll see Rex gets home once he's released, and that he'll stay with him today.*

They're letting him go home?

Dr. Sandler says his test results so far indicate that once the sedatives all wear off he should feel almost like his old self. That nanite intervention won't be as good as new lungs, but it should definitely help him function much better till they're ready to do the transplant.

Here's hoping.

Go talk to Balchu. I'm not doing much good here, so I think I'll head over to HQ once I get an update on plans for Rex.

See you soon, in that case.

Shady left Charlie in charge of transporting Rex home. She'd barely put her nose and one forepaw into the war room, however, before Elaine called to her.

"Oh, Shady! I'm glad you came in, and I'm happy to hear Rex is doing better!"

"Thanks. What do you need me to do?"

"Can you attend a bond hearing this morning?" Elaine's brows pinched. "Normally, I'd want Elle there, but she's still in Centerboro. I hoped, even though Pam's busy, you'd make time. ABA Ireland and I both want an XK9's evaluation of how this works out. Emer will face charges in Orangeboro first, so the legal proceedings must be held here. And they start with her bond hearing in about twenty minutes."

"I guess, why not?" She flicked her ears. "How did she manage a court date on New Year's Eve? I thought this was the start of a rather significant holiday on Rana."

"Oh, it is." The tiny Senior Special Agent could pull off quite a fearsome scowl. "But Emer is a prominent member of this Borough's foremost Founding Family. I'm certain that was a factor, along with the argument that such a prominent citizen should not be incarcerated on a major holiday without a conviction."

Mm. She's not incorrect to think this whole situation is all kinds of wrong.

Hush! Pam's irritation echoed through the link. All too predictably, she'd skipped Shady's advice to talk with Balchu. Now she was trying to follow Sgt. Koro's latest input.

Sorry. Shady clamped down on the link as much as she could and focused on Elaine.

"This hearing was pulled together at the last moment, so we are . . . mm. Less prepared than would be optimal." The SSA massaged her temples and grimaced. "There is a possibility you might be called to testify."

Okay, that makes it more interesting. And how very special for ABA Ireland. She tried not to share this reflection with Pam. "Why is Borough Attorney Masato not arguing this case, if Emer is so important?"

"Adlai Masato is . . ." Elaine half-lifted her hands, then sighed and shook her head.

Shady wagged her tail. "Yes, that also was Rex's opinion of him."

Upstairs in the Civic Center, she found a spot in the area behind the prosecutor's table on the left-hand side of the courtroom. Onlookers and journalists filled the rest of the seats. Shady recognized Orla Bellamy among them. Emer's sister sat in the area directly behind the defense team's table on the right-hand side of the courtroom. A middle-aged woman dressed in black sat with her. The latter's scent profile identified her as Emer and Orla's mother, Sorcha Moran Bellamy.

ABA Ireland took her place at the left-hand table as prosecutor, accompanied by an assistant. Iruka and Melynn took seats next to Shady.

The defense attorney, a tall, solemn man in a well-tailored suit, took his place at the table on the right. If Pam were here, she'd probably come up with an irreverent nickname for him. "Stuffed Suit," maybe. Or, considering his sober, lined face, perhaps "Pruneface." Yeah, that fit better. Shady licked her lips and wished her partner was here but tried not to let her thoughts leak too badly through the link.

The secured elevator from the detention level rumbled open. Three officers escorted Emer Bellamy to her seat at the defense's table.

This afternoon Emer wore a bunchy prison jumpsuit, with her long blonde hair tied back in a simple ponytail. The first time they'd seen her in this getup, Pam had told Shady the jumpsuit's orange color made the woman look a bit like a pumpkin. Looked yellowish-gray to Shady, but then so did pumpkins.

Emer kept her eyes downcast, lips pressed together in a mirthless line. Although she might appear submissive, rage surged through her scent factors. No shackles or cuffs bound her slender wrists or ankles, but she smelled like bottled-up fury.

Shady created a new memo and logged this observation, then shared it with Ireland and Elaine.

"All rise," the bailiff said.

The Honorable Rachard Faysal arrived wearing a long black robe and a somber expression. Everyone sat down on cue. Shady studied the judge, a round man with a bland round face and absolutely calm, neutral scent factors. If he was perturbed about working on New Year's Eve, he did not show it on any level.

If only she could use her link to ask Pam what she knew about him! But echoes from that quarter warned that her partner had enough to think about already. She settled for a quick

Station-Net search, but it yielded only official biographies. No juicy background gossip to explain how Faysal had drawn the short straw. *Dammit.* She swallowed a growl and focused on Ireland's opening statements.

The Assistant Prosecutor laid out the charges against the heiress. She expressed concern that Emer Bellamy was a significant flight risk, since she'd been apprehended in the act of attempting to leave the Borough.

"But our most compelling reason for requesting denial of a bond is the serious danger to the defendant's life, should she venture beyond these secured premises," she concluded. "The *Izgubil* was the property of the Whisper Syndicate. The combined forces of the OPD and the SBI had considerable difficulty extricating Ms. Bellamy and her co-defendant Mr. O'Boyle alive from the sub-level commonly called the 'Five-Ten.' It is therefore reasonable to assume that the Syndicate has no intention of waiting for a Ranan court of law. Their remedy for losses, even those of a considerably lesser magnitude than the *Izgubil*'s value, is an extraordinarily gruesome form of execution by torture."

Pruneface sounded as disdainful as he smelled when his turn came to speak. He used exactly the sort of multisyllabic lawyer-speak Shady'd anticipated, to cast contemptuous doubt on "any evidence that might remotely link my client to this crime." He also discounted the flight risk she represented and said her presence in "a storage area" could be explained by her legitimate business interests. "As to any claim of danger to her person," he concluded, "we seriously question what possible threat could be presented by storage silos and unarmed private security personnel."

What possible—! Shady's pulse thundered through her body. A roar of protest rose from her core, but she clamped down on it as hard as she could. *Can't growl. Can't pace.* Her hackles must be puffed out to the max, but she lowered her head and stress-yawned half-a-dozen times to keep from snarling at him.

"We are prepared to demonstrate through firsthand witness

statements and GR evidence *exactly* the sort of threat Ms. Bellamy faces," ABA Ireland countered.

The Honorable Faysal drew in a short breath and banged his gavel. Now his scent factors suffused with a dark, acidic blend of fear and anger. "Clear the courtroom. Principals and witnesses only."

Should she leave? Shady glanced toward Elaine, then settled back down at her gesture. *Potential witness. Got it.* She tried not to share this thought too clearly with Pam but sensed her partner's worried interest.

There followed a short, tense conference between Emer's attorney and ABA Ireland. Then suddenly all of the humans were focused on Shady.

Ireland eyed Pruneface coldly. "The prosecution calls Acting XK9 Pack Leader Shady Jacob-Belle as a witness."

Yikes. Shady stood.

"Wait. A *dog*?" She'd only thought Pruneface sounded disdainful before. Now his tone utterly dripped with disparagement.

"A sworn officer, and a citizen of Orangeboro," Ireland countered. "XK9 scent evidence has been affirmed as admissible evidence in Chayko System courts of law for more than a decade. We already have ample precedent here in the courts of Orangeboro. And thanks to her vocalizer, Assistant Pack Leader Jacob-Belle can testify for herself."

One of the court officers hurried to remove the human-appropriate chair from the witness stand. Shady stepped up to its former position. The railing between her and the rest of the courtroom topped out at her mid-chest level.

The bailiff met Shady's gaze. "Do you affirm that the testimony you are about to give in this hearing is the truth, the whole truth, and nothing but the truth?"

Shady broadened her stance and returned the bailiff's eye-contact. "On my honor as a Ranan citizen and sworn officer of the Orangeboro Police Department, I do so affirm."

It was the standard affirmation human officers used, but until five weeks ago XK9s couldn't claim citizenship. This was the first time she'd used the full affirmation as a Ranan citizen in addition to her "sworn officer" status. A tingling sensation swept across her. Her chest expanded and her pulse steadied. *Yes. I am a citizen. I am your official equal, Pruneface!*

"Please describe your experiences while you and your fellow officers were transporting Mr. O'Boyle and Ms. Bellamy from the place where your team apprehended them to the Detention Suite at the Orangeboro Police Department Headquarters," ABA Ireland said.

Shady's jitters eased. She'd rehearsed the protocols for giving witness statements since she was three. This situation called for a long-familiar mental state. Centered there, she delivered a factual narrative of the events she'd experienced in clear, unequivocal statements of fact.

The dawning consternation in Pruneface's scent gradually shifted into deepening dismay as she spoke. But he rose when it came time for cross-examination and did his best to shake her certainty.

Shady replied with her unwavering sheepdog-stare and countered every question. Her confidence came from knowing she had a highly superior autobiographical memory, and she damn well *did* remember what happened.

Don't get too cocky, Pam warned.

I thought you were busy. Hush!

Pruneface eventually shook his head and turned away. "No further questions."

Once Shady could step down, Ireland entered into evidence Prosecution Exhibits One and Two, "a pair of Global Reconstructions relevant to our argument that Ms. Bellamy faces extreme mortal danger, should she be released." Ireland turned a pointed look toward Emer and Pruneface. "They depict forensic evidence from recent past murders by a Whisper Syndicate executioner who at this time still remains at large and active on Rana Station.

We fear she would become his next assignment, should she be released on the requested bond."

She added that the GR artist who'd created them was currently on leave, so they would be presented by a member of the Orangeboro Global Reconstruction Unit named Ernest Porringer. "The scene depicted in Exhibit One was discovered in a storage silo on Fifth Precinct Sub-Level Eight in Greensboro, Wheel One." Ireland focused on the judge. "The crime scene shown in Exhibit Two was found in a storeroom in Sixth Precinct Sub-Level Four in Centerboro on Wheel Four. This unsub's work displays distinctive signature features, so we can link them with a good amount of confidence." She turned to glance at Emer and Pruneface again, then returned to meet the judge's gaze. "The range of locations demonstrates that he seems able to move throughout the Station undetected."

The Honorable Faysal's body language and scent exuded reluctance, but he accepted the GRs. The courtroom darkened. Its built-in GR tank at first glowed blue, then resolved into a vision of grisly horror.

Shit. Shady quelled an urge to back away, even though it was only a visual display that she saw in gray and brown tones. Thank goodness it smelled like any other GR tank: just hot wires, metal, and polymers. *I would not want to smell that scene, although I know Elle and Petunia have already processed a similar one.*

Bad?

Oh, yeah. Shady eyed the image of a suspended, bloody meat-bag that in the original scene would have been a naked human corpse, but she tried to share only a glimpse of it with Pam through the link. *No wonder Charlie was depressed that night! He rendered four scenes like this in a single day.* She flicked her ears and stress-yawned, then refocused. *However, speaking of smelling things . . .* She turned from the GR to the defense table.

Pruneface had abruptly collapsed onto a chair. He stared at the GR with a slack-jawed horror that reeked in his scent factors with raw, visceral revulsion.

Emer sat as if frozen with her shoulders back, chin up, and eyes narrowed. A throat-catching blend of sharp, icy terror and chilling, harsh calculation filled her scent.

Charlie's GR methodically highlighted item after item in the scene. For each, it zoomed in close to offer a short, graphic animation of how the knife-cuts most likely had been made and how they would have affected the anatomical structures of skin, soft tissues, organs, and bones Little flags with evidence-code identifications lit up, one by one. Some offered inset crime scene photo comparisons. Each stayed bright long enough to be read through twice before it faded out and the next one lit up.

No one spoke for a long moment after Exhibit One came to its gory conclusion and the GR tank went blue, but Shady clearly smelled the fear and repugnance in nearly every human's response.

"That's enough. Don't bother with the second one." Emer's scent had sharpened into darker, colder tones. She gave Ireland a hard, icy glare. "I retract my bond request."

CHAPTER 34
AN INSIDER TIP

Corona Tower

Rex sighed, an ability he'd taken for granted until recently. *It certainly seems that Shady has been busy.* He lay on his bed with his back against Charlie, who'd stretched out next to him in Shady's usual place. He'd finally been able to stay awake long enough for Charlie to fill him in on some recent events.

He now knew about the Transmondian embargo, Shady's exploits in the Five-Ten, and that both Emer Bellamy and Kieran O'Boyle were in custody. They'd touched briefly on Shady's encounters with the appscaten Kurtzu, things Kieran O'Boyle had told the investigation so far, and the fruitful trip to Monteverde.

Charlie ran his hand along Rex's side, then leaned toward him and set up a delicious ear-rub rhythm. *Resuming one's life after re-gen can be kinda overwhelming, even when your partner hasn't been making Universe-level history while you were out of it—which I promise, I haven't.*

Having another multi-day gap in my memory bothers me. Rex pushed past the smothered frustration of having missed impor-tant things. *I'm never supposed to forget anything!* It rankled even more because it wasn't the first time in recent weeks. He'd also gone through an abrupt stint of re-gen after Wisniewski's Dart exploded. That treatment had kept him alive after being spaced, but it left another hole in his memory.

It's a bizarre kind of time-warp sensation, Charlie agreed.

He growled, but it didn't ease the hot, tight, frantic fear those memory-gaps inspired. His consensus position as Pack Leader increased the pressure. *If I miss things, it could be fatal for the Pack.*

We've managed to stave off disaster so far. And realistically, you can't remember what you weren't awake to experience. Charlie's fingers found all the right spots. *It's uncomfortable, definitely. I feel you.*

In more ways than one. Rex relaxed into the ear-rub and leaned against his human. He closed his eyes. *Probably better for my peace of mind if I just try to live in this moment, for now.*

Good plan. Charlie's ear-massage continued.

But all at once there was a third presence in the link. Rex sensed Charlie's visceral astonishment, then his hot, defensive reaction. *Who—*

Hello, SCISCO. Rex lifted his head and rolled onto his belly. His ears went up, but his back also prickled with rising hackles. He'd grown to like the cyberbeing professor, but nir mode of contact today chilled him. Ne had only done this once before, and the reason had been a looming crisis. *What has happened?*

He felt Charlie pull back some from the link, uncertain but willing to follow Rex's lead.

I wish I could allow you to recover in peace, SCISCO said. *But I fear you must prepare for a new challenge. XK9s are being betrayed right now in Centerboro.*

Centerboro: the human political capitol of Rana Station. Rex's heart clenched. He didn't doubt that SCISCO spoke from certain knowledge. Officially, ne worked as a professor of explosives technology at Station Polytechnic University. But ne also seemed to know far more than an ordinary human professor about developments in the Chayko System . . . at approximately the moment they happened.

Premier Iskander's faction in the Commonwealth Party includes Commercial Councilmember Nesbit Zeman and two of his allies in the Legislative Council, SCISCO said. *Those three persons are preparing a resolution. They plan to introduce it when the Combined Councils convene in a Special Session to discuss the Transmondian embargo next week.* Ne hesitated. *Do you know about the embargo?*

Charlie just told me. Rex stifled another growl, chilled anew by this threat to the Pack and his ineffectiveness against it.

Good. If passed, the resolution would suspend all declarations of XK9 sapience until the conclusion of the Observation Commission's evaluation, whenever that may be. And in the meantime, it requires full cooperation with the Transmondians. That, of course would be calamitous for the Pack.

So—if I may break in—this doesn't have anything to do with the XK9s currently in Centerboro? Charlie asked.

The—? Rex turned to stare at his partner.

No, rest easy about that, SCISCO answered. *Tux and Elle are safe. However, they have frequently been frustrated by Ranan Executive Security's unwillingness to believe their information. That has fostered doubt in some members of Centerboro PD, as well.*

The RES serves Iskander before all others, Charlie said. *And CPD has no experience with XK9s.*

They also resent the SBI, SCISCO agreed. *Both Director Perri and AAG Niam have had to weigh in repeatedly, to remove impediments placed by those agencies.*

Impressions through the link inclined Rex to think something about this surprised his partner. Charlie's scent warmed and a little smile curved his lips. *I'm heartened to learn that Niam has stood up for them.*

SCISCO's tone lightened. *Your GR made quite an impression on him, Detective. So did meeting Shady.*

Questions multiplied upon questions for Rex. *Do we know if the Observation Commission actually has decided to come to the*

Chayko System? He set aside Charlie and Shady's speculations about Ra-Sven-shumma Kurtzu's mission for the moment.

Yes. They must, Charlie said. *They became obligated to do so the moment the Orangeboro Council acknowledged XK9s as sapient beings and made you citizens. The Commission has no choice but to send an investigative delegation.*

They may already be here, SCISCO added. *They prefer to conduct the first part of their observations unannounced.*

Indeed? Charlie's tone shifted to speculation. Rex felt his thoughts also flick to Shady's new friend Kurtzu.

SCISCO's link-presence emanated a zest of curiosity.

That makes good sense, to send them in quietly. Charlie's pensive nod mirrored impressions through the link as his thoughts leaped to possibilities. *If anyone is trying to conceal falsehoods, that's a good way to catch them.*

Rex snapped his ears flat. His pulse thumped harder. *But if this is a known practice, why would Iskander risk it? Aren't there penalties for attempted coverups and countermoves, if the OC rules in our favor?*

It is not a known practice, SCISCO replied. *I have reasons for knowing about it that need not concern us at the moment. Iskander's faction almost certainly doesn't understand their risk, or they wouldn't try it. But this is exactly the kind of behavior the OC wants to catch. Now, then. What were you not saying to each other about an appscaten?*

Between the two of them, they explained what they knew.

SCISCO's amusement sparkled through the link. *The OC hasn't investigated a scent-primary species in more than two centuries of your years. Clearly, they are out of practice!*

So, you think Kurtzu is from the OC?

I think Shady's guess is a very good one. SCISCO's amusement lingered, but Rex had a sense that nir resolve had hardened. *I shall have to investigate this Professor Ra-Sven-shumma Kurtzu further. But first you should meet with Chief Klein.*

I'm on health leave at the moment. Rex stress-yawned. *Does Klein know about this proposed resolution?*

I believe he and his friend Sacha Guzmán are discussing it right now. You should be party to the conversation, if possible. How fragile is your health? It is hard for me to gauge such things in corporeal beings.

He's on doctor's orders—and Shady's—to stay home and rest, Charlie said. *He needs to follow their directive.*

This is unfortunate. I shall speak again with the Chief. I believe he has plans to confer with you, but he may hesitate because of your health.

Charlie chuckled. *Also because the last two times he checked in, Rex was asleep.*

I have been asleep more than I want, today. To his disgust, Rex yawned. Then he snorted, hackles prickling. *I shall attempt to stay awake for a while longer.*

Another bubbly swirl of amusement came through the link from SCISCO. *I shall suggest that the Chief should try again sooner rather than later.*

❖ ❖ ❖ ❖ ❖ ❖ ❖ ❖

Chief Klein's Office

"Thank you, Acting Pack Leader, Sergeant. Please take a seat." Klein gestured to the chair and dog bed in front of his desk.

Pam did her best to still her worries. She clutched her case pad and sat. *Second call to the Chief's office in a week.*

The last time worked out pretty well. Relax. Shady took the extra-large dog bed Klein had installed for Rex.

"I'm glad I could catch you at a moment when you were available." Klein nodded to each, then centered on Shady. "I understand the judge ruled to keep Emer Bellamy in custody."

Shady snapped her ears flat. Pam tasted her dissatisfaction through the link. "He cleared the courtroom of all but principals, attorneys, and witnesses, and sealed the record. After I described our extraction from the Five-Ten and we watched the first of Charlie's GRs, Emer herself called a halt. She withdrew her bond petition and agreed to stay put."

"Good. About Emer, anyway." The Chief drew in a long breath and straightened. He turned to Pam. "How are things going with Sgt. Koro? Has she gotten you up to speed?"

"I think she's stuffed my head about as full as possible for now. She did say I can call her whenever I need help."

The Chief nodded. "That's excellent. The next week or so is going to be pretty disrupted for all of us, so I hope you're prepared."

"Me too, sir." Pam kept her face calm, but her gut clenched. *NOW what?*

"Disrupted?" Shady cocked her head, ears up. "What has happened?"

"We've gotten a disturbing report from Centerboro."

Shady snapped her ears flat. Her hackles puffed out. "What is the Premier up to, this time?"

"Not Iskander herself. Not this time." Klein grimaced. "No, it's a group of her allies in the Commercial and Residential Councils. I've received an insider tip from a knowledgeable source that ComCouncil Member Nesbit Zeman and two of his colleagues in the ResCouncil plan to introduce a resolution that threatens the Pack."

Pam's pulse sped up. "Do you know what their resolution says?"

"I'm told it would suspend all declarations of XK9 sapience until the conclusion of the Observation Commission's evaluation, whenever that may be. And in the meantime, it requires full cooperation with the Transmondians."

Pam's gut went cold.

"No!" Shady leaped up. Her fear reverberated through the link. "That would mean returning us to the Project. We cannot allow that!"

"Absolutely not. We. Will. Not. Do. That. Understand me."
Klein rose, leaned forward, and met her eyes. "They take you
over my dead body."

Shady paced in place, panting hard. "I do thank you. I know
you mean it. But there must be a better way."

"One would hope." He blew out another breath. "At any
rate, we now have a new primary objective. Defeating this resolution must be our foremost focus until the threat is dealt with.
Zeman and his colleagues plan to introduce their resolution
when the Combined Councils convene in a Special Session to
discuss the embargo next week. We have only a short time to
convince the Combined Councils to reject it."

"Next week?" Shady launched herself into agitated pacing
around the room. "Where do we even begin?"

"And sir—what can we do?" Pam gave him a worried frown.
"We are police officers. We are not supposed to get 'political.'
What is it *legal* for us to do?"

"We are not supposed to get 'political' about matters of
public policy. We are not supposed to take sides in public
debates—but there's one exception. That's when we ourselves
are the subject of those public debates." Klein's face went cold
and grim. "There's a long history of precedent in that particular
instance. Police agencies most certainly have both a right and an
obligation to argue against a proposed course of action when it
might harm the effectiveness of the force."

"The XK9s are only one unit, and a very new one at that."
Pam's throat went dry. "Couldn't they argue—with some justifi-
cation—that we managed to be effective, even before we got
them?"

"They could argue that, and undoubtedly they will try." The
Chief's scowl deepened. "To that claim, I can reply that the XK9s
already have boosted our effectiveness in measurable ways. This
means that removing them would measurably harm it. Officer
survival and well-being also are most definitely important to our

effectiveness. So is corps morale. But those are supporting arguments. We have an even better tactic."

Pam bit her lip, chest tight. "Wouldn't anything else be 'too political'?"

"Nothing is 'too political' for the civilians who are our allies." Klein offered a wry smile. "Think about it. The Orangeboro Council has voted to affirm that XK9s are sapient beings. Our officials have instituted policies throughout the Borough to ensure that you are treated as such. We have many allies here in Orangeboro. Some of our most influential Families have accepted XK9s into their Charters."

"Such as Corona?" Shady stopped pacing. "My new appscaten friend Kurtzu pointed out to me just the other day that humans dislike saying 'sorry, we were wrong.' This, he suggested, would make the Orangeboro Council reluctant to disavow us." She lifted her ears with some effort.

The Chief responded with the first genuine smile she'd seen on his face since he'd greeted them. "I was quite encouraged to learn of your new friend. And I think he is right about the Council."

"He also suggested that neither the ozzirikkians nor the Farricainan cyberbeings of Rana would be likely to support anything that threatened the well-being of a minority population."

"I agree. So you see that our first important task is to gather our allies and explain the situation." He hesitated. "Sorry, that is our *second* important task. First, we must alert the Pack, including our officers in Centerboro and our convalescent Pack members Rex, Razor, and—if she can withstand the stress of it—Cinnamon."

He shifted his focus to Pam. "Sergeant, we need to set up a meeting. I want all active-duty Pack in Orangeboro, both XK9s and humans, to gather in Meeting Room Two, and I'll invite Elaine to sit in, as well as anyone else she chooses from her team."

An icy chill fell over her. *Oh, shit. This is my part. I'd better do it right!* "When shall I tell them to assemble?" She met his eyes and kept her voice steady. Through the link she felt Shady's sturdy confidence in her.

"This afternoon, but we'll need to do some setup first. We already have a secured link to the Sandler Clinic. I want another one to SBI HQ in Centerboro for our officers there, Director Perri, and others she may choose to include. We'll need a third secured link to Corona Tower, because now that he's awake our Pack Leader needs to be a part of this."

"Okay. How can I make that happen?" She gulped but kept her chin up, centered on the goal. *I'll be intimidated later.*

You've got this, Shady said through the link.

"Archy can guide you." The Chief hesitated, brow puckered. "There's an additional link we might be able to coordinate, and on that note there's one more thing, Sergeant. I need to send you this."

Pam's HUD dinged: somebody's contact info.

"Don't give this to anyone else. The content warnings will say that, too, but I want to emphasize it."

"Whose info is it?"

"Vincent Bellini's." Klein pinned her with his worried gaze. "He's Sacha's personal secretary. You'll probably be talking with him a lot."

The Vice-Premier's personal secretary? Pam swallowed hard. She pushed back against new dizziness and her speeding pulse. "I'll guard it with my life, sir."

CHAPTER 35
THE PALMDALE CLUB

Corona Tower

I n the end, Charlie decided to bring one of the lounges into his living room from the balcony outside his bedroom. Rex could use that during Chief Klein's meeting this afternoon and save Charlie the effort of moving that enormous orthopedic bed out and then back again. He made sure his three little house-keeping bots were set to detail it thoroughly. Corona's outdoor and indoor areas communicated in many ways, but the nightly mist meant dust and tree detritus did accumulate far more thickly on the outdoor things.

While the bots were occupied with the lounge, he considered next moves. Klein had encouraged him to invite several of the Family's senior members to the second of today's meetings. But all he had in his living room was one elderly brown hand-me-down couch from household storage. The prospect of bringing people in for meetings at his place stirred up an unaccustomed eagerness. There'd been a time when he *enjoyed* playing host. That . . . Hmm. *Maybe it's time to get back into the habit. But Hildie's right. This place needs an overhaul!*

In the depths of his five dark years of depression, redecorating—even simple housekeeping, simply hadn't occurred to him. Now he itched to spruce the place up. But work on the case, non-negotiable naps when his energy ran out, and the physical therapy needed for healing all took time. Add in his time spent with Hildie, and he hadn't carved out an opportunity.

All the same, people would need more places to sit. Today.

He unstacked six of his ten chairs from the "dining annex" on the wider section of his interior balcony. As he worked, an itchy sense of being on the cusp of another massive change dried his mouth and jangled his nerves. *Rex's Pack Leader status is dragging him into politics, and farther from policing. Is that my future, too?*

He refocused on the chairs. They'd sat stacked up next to their matching, folded table in the back corner of his empty, leaf-strewn interior balcony for years. He hadn't touched them since Felicia left. Hadn't even thought to direct the bots to keep them clean. Now he pulled apart elaborate draperies of dusty cobwebs bedecked with old leaves and insect carcasses and set them in a ragged crescent outside his living room entrance.

Politics. He grimaced. He'd just begun to settle into his work as a detective—and he *liked* it. Loved the renewed chance to do part-time GR work, too. His chest tightened. *The "hero" role, the public persona—the farther Rex goes into politics, the more I'll have to play that part.*

Uncle Hector and Pat Cornwell, the young SBI signals tech who also happened to be SDF Commodore Farooq Cornwell's nephew, emerged from the elevator and stopped.

"It's been a while, hasn't it?" Hector gave the cobwebby chairs a startled stare.

"Since, um . . ." Charlie had to stop and think. His gut plunged. "Wow. Since the playoffs in 89, I guess." *I wasted so much time!*

Pat's eyes widened. "I graduated from Upper Levels that trimester!"

Well, that's depressing. Am I old already? Charlie offered a smile and a shrug. "It's been a strange half-decade." *Oh, man, 'half decade' sounds even worse!*

Uncle Hector gave him a knowing look and grinned. "C'mon, Pat. Let's get going on that security upgrade."

Charlie stared at the cobwebby chairs, then drew in a breath, straightened, and went to check on the bots down the balcony. They were only maybe halfway through the work on his lounge. *How dusty could it possibly . . . um. Well.* He blinked a couple of times then shook off a brief pang of chagrin. *Need to borrow some more bots if I want clean places for everyone to sit at the meeting.*

Are you all right? Rex asked through the link from his bedroom.

I'm, um. He stopped to recenter. Took a steadying breath. *I'm fine. Need more bots. Too late to buy more today, though.* He pulled out his case pad and texted Fee. She was home with Hakan on the next level down, although Manny had left a while ago for the restaurant. She'd probably lend him some of hers.

❖ ❖ ❖ ❖ ❖ ❖ ❖ ❖

Feliz Tower

"**N**ot till *after* Big New Year?" Hildie sat, her knees abruptly watery. *Another month till a verdict? Another month in job-limbo?*

"There's a backlog, and all the holiday breaks are making it worse," Endesha Odi explained on the com.

Hildie blew out a breath and slumped against the back of the reading chair in her Feliz Tower bedroom. "I see. I think."

"Cheer up. They originally wanted to schedule it in March." Odi offered a grin via the HUD-view.

"Oh. Well." Hildie blinked, her chest still tight. "Then I guess end of January is, um . . . soon? In relative terms. In that case, good job getting them to move it up."

Her attorney's smile vanished. "Here's hoping the earlier date allows them to square away the harassment question."

A cold pit opened in Hildie's stomach. "D'you think that'll be a problem?"

"If it is, you may be on the wait-list even longer than March. But we most definitely need to nail that part down first."

"Yeah. Definitely." She gripped the chair's upholstered arms with numb fingers.

"But now you have a hearing date you can put on your calendar."

She nodded. "That I do. Thank you."

Long after her attorney had ended the call, Hildie sat in her chair. She couldn't think. Wasn't sure what she felt. After a while, Kali hopped into her lap and curled up. She started kneading with her forepaws, her purr like a small motor. The cat's vibrating warmth against Hildie's tummy felt good, but those needle-claws dug deep.

The small, sharp, persistent pains brought her out of her daze. "Yikes! Looks as if no one's trimmed your daggers for a while." She gently adjusted Kali's position, grabbed the clippers she kept on the side table, and focused on carefully trimming them one by one.

Kali eyed her but allowed it. Her purr faltered, but it resumed once Hildie had finished.

Hildie stroked the cat's lush, soft fur. Some of her tension leached away. Maybe there'd be enough distractions over the next few weeks to keep her from getting too frantic.

Tonight was "Calendar New Year," the official gateway to the widely-celebrated "Big New Year" holidays just after the middle of the month. Tonight, the whole Station would officially ring in Ranan Year 95. And for once, tonight, she wouldn't spend the whole time treating light-show-induced seizures, plus an assortment of drug-overdose toxicities. Calendar New Year was always a busy night for paramedics.

So strange to realize it won't be, for me, tonight. Charlie'd invited her to join his Family's celebration, then stay to greet New Year's Day and feast on his cousin Manny's cinnamon rolls for breakfast. If Calendar New Year was a pivot toward the future, she couldn't think of a way she'd rather celebrate it. *It'll be a glorious night.*

She caught her breath, dizzied all at once by a sense of stepping through a doorway that was irrevocably closing behind her. *So many possibilities! This month to come—how much will my world change before it's over?* Her chest tightened and her pulse ratcheted up. *Oh, my.*

She should get up pretty soon. She needed to pack her overnight bag and change her clothes. But not just yet. A heart-squeezing lightheadedness gripped her, left her in an odd between state of both terrified and exhilarated. *Mmm. Might hold off standing up, just at the moment.*

Besides, that "heavy" 4-kg. cat was pinning her down.

❖ ❖ ❖ ❖ ❖ ❖ ❖ ❖

Corona Tower

Rex awoke to people's voices. Sounded like Charlie, speaking in a low voice with Hector and . . . Pat Cornwell? *Dammit, I fell asleep again. What time is it?*

I was about to come get you. I brought in one of the lounges, so you'd have something softer to lie on than the floor.

Rex lifted his head and flicked his ears. *What about the sofa?*

Reserved for Gran Annie and Aunt Hannah.

Oh. How many people are we hosting?

Just you and me for the first call, but we'll have a larger group in a while. You probably need to check for a message from Chief Klein.

The bottom-level readout on his HUD blinked. He scanned Klein's text quickly, then dismounted from his bed leg-by-leg. He paused to let his head stop spinning, and then he walked almost steadily down the hall to the living room. Charlie had positioned the lounge next to the hall entry arch, so his path was as short as possible. Rex lay down on it gratefully, tongue hanging long. *My stamina sucks.*

Dr. Sandler says it'll get better. Just keep working on it. Charlie stepped back from examining a small black boxlike object mounted on the wall. It glinted with optics and flickering indicator-lights.

That is new. It was mounted next to a blank expanse of newly-repainted wall. A large, 3D-vision wall screen had previously hung there, although it had shorted out and stopped working before Rex arrived on Rana. A few weeks ago, Transmondian listening devices hiding behind it had exploded and shattered it, so now it was gone. *What is that box-thing?*

It's a high-security-encrypted input-output device for vid feeds. Your HUD is your receiver.

That explains why I thought I heard Hector and Pat.

Yes. Charlie smiled. *We're state-of-the-art now, thanks to the OPD, SBI, Hectorvault Security Systems, and SDF intelligence.*

Rex's hackles prickled. *SDF Intelligence? I trust your uncle Hector—but Pat's uncle Rooq? Not so much.* Station Defense Force Commodore Farooq Cornwell was the Ranans' head spook, and spooks were a class of humans Rex had learned to despise.

As Pat explained it, Transmondian Intelligence wants you XK9s real bad. That gives Station Intelligence leverage on them. And they'll gladly take every leverage opportunity they can find.

But how much of a microscope does that aim at me?

I don't think we had much choice, but that's one big reason why the rig's out here, not in your bedroom. Charlie's parallel misgivings echoed through the link.

In my bedroom? Hell, no. Thank you. Good call!

Rex's com beeped again. Chief Klein's face appeared on his HUD. Capt. Archy Danvir and Press Liaison Joslyn Stark flanked him. What Rex could see of the area behind them appeared to be the wall that framed the dais in Meeting Room Two. "Hello! How are you, Rex?"

"Much better than I might have been, thanks." Rex's tail thumped the lounge. "Is there any chance we shall speak with your friend on this fancy new rig?" Rex had met Klein's long-time friend, Sacha Guzmán, last month. He was currently one of Rana's two Vice-Premiers, but he and Klein had met as children in their local Orangeboro neighborhood school. They'd remained good friends throughout their respective, eventful careers. The connection had proved helpful to the Pack several times so far.

"Sacha sends his greetings and best wishes for your recovery. It is probable that we'll talk with him personally during the next meeting, when we bring in the Families and other allies. But he tells me this countermove from the so-called 'Palmdale Club' was exactly the sort of thing he'd expected."

"Palmdale Club?" Charlie had parked himself on a dining room chair next to Rex's lounge.

Rex's ears swept back. "Palmdale?" That name rang an unpleasant bell. His hackles prickled.

"You know the name?" Klein's brows shot upward.

"I know there is a Palmdale District in Solara City," Rex answered. "According to a kennel worker at the XK9 Project named Clyde, it is where all the rich bastards live. That is all I know, except that in general Transmondian bastards are very bad people."

"Too true." The Chief nodded. "And, good catch. Yes, that's where the name originated, and it is indeed home to some extremely rich and powerful Transmondian bastards. The Palmdale Club is a sub-group within the Ranan Commonwealth Party. They want much closer ties with the Transmondian Government than Rana has now."

Charlie scowled. "Next best thing to traitors, I'd call that."

"You're not necessarily wrong." Klein probably smelled as worried as he appeared, but even state-of-the-art human-made coms didn't provide an adequate interface to know for sure. Then the Chief paused, gazed at something beyond the pickup camera focused on his face, and smiled. "Are we all here?"

Several more images popped up on Rex's HUD. He saw Tux, Elle, Connie, Misha, Director Perri, and a few other humans in a small meeting room. Through the link from Charlie, he learned that one of the men was Assistant Attorney General Lamont Niam.

A broader image opened next, to show the audience area of Meeting Room Two. It was filled with all of the active-duty Pack members still in Orangeboro, both dogs and humans, along with Detectives Lou Penny and Helmer Fujimoto. Rex also spotted Assistant Borough Attorney Regan Ireland.

On another channel view, Elaine, Shiv, and Shawnee sat scrunched together in what was probably Elaine's office.

One more opened, this one from Berwyn and Cinnamon's room at the Sandler Clinic. It showed the room's two main occupants plus Liz and Razor. Rex noted that Cinnamon's ears were up, her eyes bright and focused. Razor lay alongside her, and somewhat propped her up.

"Excellent. Thank you for joining us," Klein said. "It's important that everyone in the Pack and our most trusted law enforcement colleagues hear this all at once. A common ally, who must remain anonymous but whose knowledge is reliable, has alerted us to a new threat. If we can head it off before it reaches the Combined Councils, that would be best.

"First, I want the Pack, in particular, to understand that under absolutely no circumstances will the OPD surrender any XK9, or allow any XK9 to be surrendered, to the Transmondian Government." Klein's stone-hard face and cold glare left no doubt that he meant exactly that.

"Agreed!" Elaine nodded her head for sharp emphasis. "SIT Delta stands with the OPD."

"And the rest of the SBI," Perri put in.

"And the Borough Prosecutor's Office," Ireland said.

"And the Station Department of Justice," Niam said.

Rex let out a breath he hadn't realized he was holding. *This is the kind of backing we hoped for.*

The Pack has more friends than you might think. Charlie smiled at him.

"Now for the bad news," Klein continued. "A group of Council members who call themselves The Palmdale Club has developed a proposal which they plan to submit for a vote during the Special Session." He explained the gist of the proposal. "It is absolutely essential that this resolution not be accepted by the Combined Councils. Our job is to make sure all of our ResCouncil and ComCouncil Members receive enough information about XK9s to choose wisely and well."

"How do we propose to do that?" Berwyn asked.

"That's where it gets tricky," Klein's expression went rueful. "As police officers and government officials, we ourselves cannot by law engage in any kind of political lobbying or advocacy. We can provide information, but that's all. We must rely on our civilian Families, friends, and allies to lobby for us."

"Are we allowed to at least *ask them* to do that?" Berwyn asked.

"Absolutely, yes. I wanted to be able to answer questions the Pack may have before we go any farther. But you should know that Sergeant Gómez, Captain Danvir, and Ms. Stark have been extremely busy this afternoon. They've set up a broader series of meetings with many of your Families' leaders and our Borough Representatives. They'll be coming online to join this conference in about twenty minutes. In the meantime, we're here to collect and respond to as many of your questions as possible."

CHAPTER 36
A BEAUTIFUL NEW YEAR

Corona Tower and Feliz Tower

I n light of all the mind-bending developments of the afternoon, it hardly seemed possible to Charlie that the holiday could go on as usual. He finally forced himself stop, go take a shower, and put on new clothes. But during much of that process he couldn't pull his thoughts from recent events.

Klein and SCISCO's revelations of the Palmdale plot were heart-pounding enough. But the Pack meeting, and even more, the expanded meeting after that, had provided a number of amazing moments. This afternoon the entire Orangeboro Council, the borough's three National Combined Council Members, the Mayor, and her full Cabinet had affirmed their support for the Pack.

Residential Council Members Reika Bannerman and Sebastian Zupan both had appeared wearing their official Council Braids, to make their affirmation a matter of official record.

Charlie wasn't the only one in his living room who noticed that Orangeboro's sole Commercial Council Member, Tyra Herzog, did not wear hers. Although she nodded agreement with the affirmations of support, she hadn't done so *officially*.

He'd shared a chill of unease through the link with Rex over that. But Herzog had joined in the affirmation, and she was supposed to speak for Orangeboro. He hoped that meant she'd make her support official when it counted in the Combined Councils.

After that, XK9 Family after XK9 Family had pledged to act as advocates. That included a new one: Becenti Family was still only potential-Pack, but they clearly had been impressed by Shady and Pam. The Pack even received support from Monteverde-based Vuzvishen Family, on behalf of Georgia, and Providence-Brightstar Family, on behalf of Mike and Elaine. Learning that the famous artist Rafe Santiago was actually Mike's *brother* had given Charlie a small, private star-struck moment.

At Gran Annie's insistence, Charlie'd called Hildie before the second meeting and invited Feliz Family to join the massive conference-call. Her parents and Grandma Hestia had been in virtual attendance with her when not only Sacha Guzmán, but also the ozzirikkian Vice-Premier Kizzitikti Zhokittik came on. The two Vice-Premiers explained how important it would be to go to Centerboro in an organized lobbying group.

A plan had emerged through the afternoon. Led by Families, XK9 supporters would bring their Pack members with them to Centerboro, starting this weekend. XK9s and Families alike would try to meet as many ResCouncil and ComCouncil members, and answer as many of their questions, as possible.

"Yes, you'll have to talk to journalists, too," Joslyn Stark warned the Pack. "Tell them the truth. Answer their questions. The people who taught you never to talk to journalists are the ones who don't want people to realize you're sapient."

So many logistics. So many preparations, and only one day before we leave on Saturday. Charlie's world had subtly shifted and broadened today. His mind tugged him toward his hopes and concerns about a future with Hildie—*No, better not rush things there. Can't afford to mess that up!*

The shower helped him do a mental reset. Absorbed in the somewhat mindless task of dressing, the flow of his thoughts at last shifted toward New Year's Eve with Hildie. Some of the tension in his gut and shoulders eased.

A year ago, I would never have imagined . . . hmm. Never could've dreamed so very many things that now are realities. He'd been on patrol duty last New Year's Eve. An eventful but bruising start to the year, for sure. He hoped to have a lot more fun this evening.

Last week he had decided against borrowing Shady and Rex's car to pick up Hildie tonight. After one glorious day of riding the switchbacks in a Citron Flash, the XK9s had returned to using the boxy, beige, OPD-issued vehicle Chief Klein had placed at their disposal for security purposes. The immediate threat from the Transmondians might be over, but the Chief worried, all the same.

Rex and Shady wouldn't begrudge Charlie's borrowing it, but he wanted something more special for Hildie tonight. Something prettier, and with fewer layers of dog hair. Following what had begun to shape up as Family tradition, he'd managed to reserve the last Citron Flash still available for tonight.

He descended the steps into the garage and found the sleek, electric-yellow auto-nav waiting. Its near door opened when he approached.

"Good evening, Charlie," a woman's sultry voice greeted him.

Smooth. That biometric-recognition pseudo gets better all the time. "Hello, Carmella. Adjust vocal sexiness way down."

"As you wish." The car's automated voice didn't go blandly neutral, but now it sounded less like it was trying to seduce him.

"Good." *That's more appropriate for picking up my girlfriend.* He smiled and inserted himself. "Carmella" glided more than rolled up the driveway, its next destination already pre-loaded.

Charlie leaned back into the seat's supple upholstery and

used his CAP to trigger a lumbar massage. *Oh, yeah. That feels wonderful.*

Times like this, it was good to be part of a Chartered Family. He could thank his parents and Aunt Hannah for the "frequent renter" listing on Corona Family's account with Town Cars On Call. That, plus the fact that this was a short-duration rental early in the evening, had given him the access tonight. Even so, on his detective's pay alone, this model would've stayed out of reach. Back when he'd been with Felicia, that would've been the end of the story. But Gran Annie hadn't even hesitated when he told her why he wanted a little extra.

"An investment in the future, I see." His grandmother smiled, her eyes lively. She'd issued a special dispensation from the Family Trust's liquid account without further discussion. "Have a beautiful New Year."

He certainly hoped the traditional Ranan greeting would be more than mere words tonight. After Hildie's disappointment over her hearing date, and in light of the threat to the Pack, Charlie hoped the car would give them both something to smile about.

Feliz Family had granted him access to the garage instead of making him park by the road: he appeared to have risen in their regard. No need to hike the white gravel path that zig-zagged its way up from the rim road through the rice terraces to the entrance tonight. Or, on second thought, were they simply saving Hildie the trek down to the car?

The Flash had barely turned onto the driveway before a crowd of kids and more than a few Feliz Family adults emerged to stare at it.

Then Hildie stepped from the garage's entrance, and Charlie lost focus on everyone else.

He hadn't seen this dress before. It clung and flowed and teased and sparkled in extremely artful ways. For their last big events, Hildie had worn an elegant saree. Tonight's dress employed the same red and gold colors, but for a considerably different effect.

She eyed the car, laughing. It rolled to a smooth halt and opened its doors.

"You have arrived—" the automated voice began.

"Park," Charlie ordered.

"Parking," the car replied.

He stepped out, offered a little bow. "Namaste. Gotta say, all of a sudden *my* New Year turned a lot more beautiful!"

❖ ❖ ❖ ❖ ❖ ❖ ❖ ❖

Corona Tower

S hady nuzzled Rex's ear. "I might have begun to understand why humans like these things called 'holidays.'"

He responded with a tongue-loll and a return nuzzle. "It is more fun when they invite us to the party."

They lay side-by-side in Corona's courtyard near the Memory Garden's roses and water feature. Replete with holiday goodies and worn out from giving doggie-back rides to the under-six crowd, Shady was content to rest. So far, she'd rate tonight as vastly superior to sitting in a cold, dark kennel, wondering if the humans would remember to feed her.

"Okay, it's time to get ready!" Charlie's cousin Quinn called out. "C'mon, kids! It's almost Two-Thirds New Year!"

Huh? Shady and Rex exchanged puzzled head-cocks.

The adults of Corona Family gathered with their children in the dining area under the big oak tree. Everyone found a chair. Curious, Shady and Rex joined them.

What is Two-Thirds New Year? Shady asked Pam through the link. Her partner and Balchu had declined an invitation to go to Becenti Tower's celebration tonight. Instead they'd opted for a quiet New Year at home.

No clue, Pam replied.

Shady widened the link so Pam could sense more of what she saw. Rana Station's precision-timed twilight slowly shaded toward darkness. The strings of tiny lights strung around the courtyard sparkled ever more brightly in the deepening shadows and rising mist. Corona's children gathered around Head of Household Gran Annie.

"So, what's tonight?" she asked them.

"New Year!" several answered.

"And what do we do on the New Year?"

"Eat cookies!"

"Stay up late!"

"Get doggie-back rides!" cried Lacey, Charlie's younger niece.

"Doggie-back," her little cousin Hakan echoed.

"You guys get doggie-back rides all the time," almost-nine-year-old Grant scoffed.

"*Like* doggie-back!" Hakan insisted.

He's not wrong. Shady wagged her tail. *He never seems to get enough rides.*

You and Rex are very tolerant. Impressions through the link told her Pam was smiling.

It's fun for us, too. Shady couldn't explain it, but she got a rush of pleasure each time she made a human child laugh with her antics. The occasional backaches were worth it. *Here's hoping I'll still be on Rana next year to give more rides.*

You will be! Let's not worry about that on the holiday. Pam's misgivings echoed through the link. *I want to focus on hope tonight. Besides, we gave you our word we wouldn't let them take you.*

I know you'll try. She stress-yawned and made an effort to reframe. Then she opened the link as widely as possible, so Pam could see and hear all that she could.

Annie and the household's children talked for a while more about their New Year traditions, then she asked them to offer ideas about things they'd like to do in the future.

Answers ranged from Hakan's unsurprising "More doggie-back!" to Grant's rather startling "I want a patent on something I invent."

That one hangs out with his great uncle Hector a lot.

I'd hate to think what Mother would've said to me if I'd popped off with something like that. Unhappiness echoed from Pam's end of the link.

"Now that you have some ideas for the future, who can tell me the difference between Calendar New Year and Big New Year?" Annie asked.

"That's easy," Leeli answered. "Calendar New Year is tonight, and it's only one night. "Big New Year lasts a *week!*"

"And when is Big New Year?" Annie leaned forward and nodded to her.

"I think—is it three weeks from now?" Leeli hesitated.

Annie smiled. "Can anybody help her?"

"Yes, Leeli, three weeks," Grant didn't *quite* roll his eyes. Quinn, his father, caught his gaze and frowned. Grant heaved a dramatic sigh, but then he gave his younger cousin what appeared to be and—mostly—smelled like a genuine smile. "That was good remembering."

Do you know what that's all about? Shady asked Pam. *What's 'Big New Year'?*

"C'mon, Grant, help me pass out the drinks." Quinn beckoned his son toward the kitchen.

Like much of Rana, Corona Family must celebrate Lunar New Year, Pam said.

Another Earth holiday? Like Solstice?

Her partner laughed. *Pretty much. Rana doesn't have a moon, any more than it has solstices, but that doesn't matter. Somebody figures out an official date somehow. The point is that every once in a while people just need to kick back and have fun.*

I guess you didn't have "Two-Thirds New Year" when you were a kid?

The impressions through the link from Pam shifted to an

ache of melancholy that made Shady regret she'd asked. *Mother didn't believe in holidays. Or in anything special for kids.*

"Mama, just about time," Charlie's mother Mimi prompted.

"So it is." Annie lifted a case pad from her lap and set it up on the table so everyone could see. When large glowing numerals on it flashed "10," she led the Family in a countdown. Several of the bright-eyed younger ones had to follow their parents' lead to get the numbers right. Then they lifted glasses of what smelled like sparkling apple or grape juice and cried "Happy New Year!" at the stroke of 20:00.

After that, they cheered, threw confetti in the air, and blew little off-key horns that hurt Shady's ears. She and Rex barked to add to the din, since maximum noise-making appeared to be the objective. Everyone laughed and clapped and hugged each other. Then the parents took their kids upstairs to their various bedrooms. Time for bed!

I wish them luck. Shady eyed their departing forms. *I bet it'll be a while before some of those little ones get calmed down.*

Pam didn't answer.

Shady sifted through the impressions she was receiving. Grief mingled with soul-deep yearning.

Better give her a moment. Shady projected all the love she could.

❖ ❖ ❖ ❖ ❖ ❖ ❖ ❖

Hildie relaxed against Charlie's strong, firm body and took another sip of her wine. Contentment warmed her. Tonight she meant to shove all worries aside and enjoy the moment.

They had joined one of Charlie's cousins, a couple of cousins-in-law, his sister, and his brother-in-law in a cozy circle around a domelike radiant space-heater in Corona's courtyard. The portable heater, a golden-orange orb that softly pulsed inside an intricate, deep-red latticework cage, functioned well. At this hour, the mist had risen enough to give the evening a chilly edge, but the heater—and Charlie's embrace—held it off.

The kids had long since celebrated "Two-Thirds New Year" and gone to bed. Their parents had rejoined the party, some with nursery monitors in their pockets.

"People say that what you're doing when the year changes gives a foretaste of what the coming year will bring." Charlie's sister Caro grinned at her companions. "So, here's the question: What were you doing last New Year's Eve? Did it offer any omens for the year?"

Her husband, Andy, kissed her cheek, then leaned back in his seat with a smile. "I was right here with you, playing this same game, last year. And here I am again. So I guess I got a pretty decent omen."

"Last year was my first in a long time when I wasn't working on New Year's Eve." Fee cradled her wineglass in both hands. "It was my first year with Hakan. Always before, I worked because I knew Manny would have to. Last year we were still on Parental Leave, but the restaurant was short-staffed, so Manny went in. I thought I'd be lonely, but Caro, you and Andy—" she nodded toward them. "And Quinn—you and Gloria—" Now she turned her warm smile toward them. "You made me feel like such a *total* part of the Family! I was exhausted and depressed, and you just really circled me with love." She placed a hand on her heart and blinked back tears. "Was it an omen? Well, that sense of being *one of us* hasn't faded since then."

Hildie bit her lip and blinked away a tear of her own.

"Well, that kind of covers it for us, too, then." Gloria's smile matched Fee's. Quinn nodded his agreement. "We've kept tabs on you since then, because you've had to do so much whenever Manny's away."

"You know he hates the need to be away," Charlie put in.

Hildie glanced toward her lover. Of all his cousins, Manny was Charlie's nearest age-mate. The two had grown up close as brothers. And although they'd followed different careers, neither could count on being home for all the special days.

"I know." Fee nodded. "We talked about it even before we became Amares. My job at the Port Authority can make for long hours. And a sous-chef is *always* busy—especially on holidays, when others want to celebrate. We decided we didn't care, we loved each other anyway."

They sat for a while in a warm, satisfied glow, but then Caro turned to Charlie. "How about you? I know you worked patrol last year, but you came home early with a bunch of bruises, and you wouldn't talk about it."

"Mm." His puckered brow and wry mouth-set told Hildie he still didn't want to talk about it. "Remember when I needed to testify in that corruption case after I got back from Chayko? Well, New Year's Eve was when the case blew open."

"You were in a fight?"

"Yeah."

Hildie gave him a rueful smile, then stiffened as memories filled in. *Woah.* The docks had gone alive that night with talk about a patrol cop who'd taken on his dirty partner in a spectacular brawl on the Spiral. It had broken open a child-trafficking ring in the Prisms of the low-G Entertainment District. The Port Authority had locked down an interstellar transport called the *Dodavira* that night—part of the fallout from the case. That action had added even more to the buzz. *Was Charlie the patrol cop at the center of things?*

He sighed. "I was under a scanner when everybody started yelling 'Happy New Year,' so I guess that *was* kind of an omen." He glanced at his arm shield. "That was also the night I decided to apply for the XK9 program."

If Rex and Shady were here, they'd be ears-up and tails wagging at this comment. Hildie had no trouble picturing them, but they'd retired to their bedroom after the kids had Two-Thirds New Year. Charlie wasn't the only one still healing: Rex had been dragging his tail and yawning a lot by then, even though Shady had given all the doggie-back rides.

"Sounds portentous to me—I'm convinced." Andy grinned at him, then kissed Caro again. "I think you're onto something, sweetheart."

Caro chuckled and turned to Hildie. "How about you? Any omens to share?"

"I was working a twelve-hour that night." She grimaced. *One of the first, but certainly not the last.* "I guess that *was* unfortunately an omen. I didn't join the countdown to 'Happy New Year,' because I was helping a patient vomit safely in microgravity."

Charlie's arm tightened briefly around her. "Ah, yes—the glamorous life of a Medicine Goddess."

She laughed, then shook her head. "And yet, I miss it." *Well, some of it.*

"Is Theresa working tonight?" His concerned gaze studied her.

"Yeah. And Eli. The rest of the team, too—it's all hands on deck for New Year's Eve, and we were understaffed already. Without Oz or me, I'm sure they won't have any downtime at all."

"Strength to them." Charlie raised his glass. The others joined the collective wish, or prayer, or thought, or whatever it was.

Here's hoping it somehow helps, because Safety Services won't let ME do anything of the sort. Hildie drew in a breath and straightened. "So, how about you, Caro? Did what you were doing offer any portents?"

"Ha! Full circle. As Andy said, I was right here doing this, but with slightly fewer people. History *does* repeat, but this year it got better."

"Unfortunately, our glasses aren't self-refilling and my snack bowl is empty." Gloria stood. "Who's ready for a refill-run?"

CHAPTER 37
DISRUPTING THINGS

Corona Tower

Colored lights erupted across the arched ceiling of Wheel Two's sky windows. An echoing boom sounded, then more in thunderous volley after thunderous volley. Charlie hugged Hildie and stared upward at the show. He sensed Rex's half-rouse, but then his partner slipped into a deeper Healing Sleep. *Yes: Sleep. Rest. Keep healing.*

Nearby, Fee's nursery monitor went off: Hakan was awake and crying. She whirled, sprinted for the steps. Caro pulled out her own nursery monitor, but it carried only Sophie's voice: "It's okay, Lacey. You're all right. Go back to sleep. It's just the big people's New Year. It's noisy but you're okay."

Charlie chortled, caught by surprise when an old memory resurfaced. "Holy crap, Caro—she sounds just like you!" He shot his elder sister a laughing glance.

"Really?" Andy's brows went up.

"Oh, yeah—dead serious, even when I swore I wasn't afraid. We were maybe—what? Three and seven?"

Caro's jaw dropped, then she recovered. "Something like that. Wow, I'm surprised you remembered."

"You were my beacon." Charlie grinned. "Just sayin'—the apple doesn't fall too far."

Andy pulled her close. "Happy New Year, darling. You're Mother of the Year already."

Charlie refocused on Hildie and met her laughing eyes. "What? I'll bet you did the same for Abi."

"I keep forgetting you're the 'baby' of your generation." She shook her head, still smiling. "And definitely quite the *bae* now."

There was only one possible reply to that, but it involved using his mouth for something besides talking.

Once the light show ended, the party broke up.

Someone flicked off the space heater. The courtyard's colorful lights dimmed. Ranan Calendar Year 95 had arrived, for well or for ill. *Time for bed.*

He and Hildie took the stairs. They also took their time. He eyed her in the dim light. She took each riser with easy grace, matching him stride for stride. A soft smile played on her lips, but she didn't meet his gaze. *What's she thinking? Dare I ask?*

It had been a lovely night. Hildie's presence made it *right* in ways he couldn't begin to express. *She completes me* seemed such a trite, easy phrase. But how else to say it? No one he'd ever met made him feel like this.

She glanced up at him, cocked her head almost like an XK9 with a question. Her smile widened. "What?"

"I just—I can't express how much I love you right now." *Oh, crap, too much?* "Not that I want to rush you, or put undue pressure . . ."

She shook her head. "Relax, Morgan. I like it."

He gave her a worried grimace. "I just—I don't want to get this wrong."

"Your instincts are pretty good."

"You *did* bring your overnight bag?" *Crap and double-crap. Damfool thing to say—I helped stow it.*

"As I recall, you *did* invite me to stay over."

He couldn't repress his smile. "Please consider yourself *permanently* invited to stay over!"

She halted, gave him eyebrows-up. "Um, 'permanently'?"

"Oh, crap, I did it again. I—Hils, I—" He sighed. "It's late, I've had a fair amount to drink, and um—I guess all my polite filters are down more than I thought."

"Does that mean you're saying what you really think?" She placed an unsteady hand on the banister, set one foot on the next step, but then stopped.

He hesitated. Let out a long breath. "We agreed to take our time. To let things develop without rushing. I'm trying to respect that."

"My question stands, Morgan." She turned to face him full-on. "How do you *really* feel?"

Shit-shit-shit, what should I say? He gave her an apologetic grimace. *Okay, what the hell. Why not the truth?* "I hate being away from you. This place feels desolate when you're not here. I wasted five years flailing around when we could have—"

He hunched his shoulders, but then consciously relaxed them. His pulse thudded hard in his throat and ears. "Any doubts I may have had are gone. But I know you may not be in the same place. And I want *you* to feel like it's right, before—*if* we move on to any new phase in the relationship."

"What if we've already given it enough time?" Her eyes challenged him. "What if a further delay is stupid? I mean, I'm five years down that road, too. And it seems to me that things have *developed*, even while we've been trying to put on the brakes and be prudent."

Charlie didn't move, just stared at her with dawning wonder. An icy chasm of terror opened in his gut, but he couldn't stay silent. "Are you—?"

"Am I serious? Yes." She lifted her chin. "Do I feel like we're rushing too fast? No."

Charlie gulped. His pulse raced. "In that case, I guess there's only one question left. Will you marry me?"

She froze, her eyes huge, but she didn't turn away. "Yes."

* * * * * * * *

Hildie melted into Charlie's hug, her head spinning. She met his kiss, strove to prolong it—but after a while he relaxed his grip some. She gazed up at this compelling, beautiful man who'd just transformed her life.

"You know, um . . ." She grimaced. "They probably won't let us skip all the Amare, Significant, and Betrothed stuff. I mean, I don't think we're allowed to go straight to—I'm not sure Orangeboro would let us do that."

"I'm no lawyer, but I don't think so, either. For the record, that's where I'd like to see this relationship go, but—" He studied her face. "Yeah, we probably should do the in-between stuff first, don't you think?"

She nodded and resumed her climb up the stairs. "Agreed. But I'm glad to get it out in the open. I've been secretly thinking it for—well, for a while." *Since way before I was ready to admit it, that's for sure!*

They arrived at the fifth level, stepped off the stairs, and walked out onto the balcony near Charlie's—um, near *their* bedroom's courtyard-facing French doors. "*My* inner balcony. *My* bedroom." She spoke in a quiet voice. Tried to feel that it was real, but she couldn't quite get all the way there yet. *Oh, yeah, that's officially a mind-bender.*

He pulled her into another hug. "So, you're okay with moving here?"

"I doubt you and Rex and Shady and Kali and I would be too comfortable squeezing ourselves into my tiny little bedroom at ho—at, um, at Feliz."

Feliz as—as "not home." So utterly strange to consider that!

"You okay?"

"Disoriented. But yeah. Definitely okay." She bit her lip. "Still adjusting."

His expression went rueful. "I can only imagine." He took a step toward the bedroom door, then glanced back when she didn't follow.

Hildie bent to slip off her shoes. "I'd like to establish a place for shoes that's out of the mist. They'll get too wet, otherwise."

He hesitated. "Makes sense. Um, probably not under the lounges, then." He bent to remove his own shoes.

Not under the lounges. Good thought. The lounges' pads already had been taken inside, most likely by the housekeeping robots. The openwork grids that remained would dry quickly once the mist receded, but they'd provide lousy shelter for shoes.

She picked up her pair. "We can store them in the closet for the short term." *I'm already changing things. Disrupting things. Is that bad?*

He smiled. "I have some ideas, actually. Let's discuss them later."

"I guess all of a sudden there's a lot to discuss." She followed him inside, her head abuzz with new imperatives.

"It would all be a lot easier if we didn't need to leave for Centerboro on Saturday." He hesitated. "Well, Rex and I do. I don't know if you—"

"I'm your Amare. I'd say that going to Centerboro with you and Rex is where I belong."

"You've been my Amare for about a minute. That doesn't mean I can take you or your schedule for granted." He tugged her gently closer and gave her another one of those patented, mind-blowing kisses. "I'm delighted you want to come. I wanted you to come with me, if possible, even before our decision tonight."

"'If possible.'" She frowned. "That's a good point. I *think* I'm free to travel anywhere I wish on Rana, as long as I don't miss the hearing. But I probably should ask Endesha."

"Probably." He hesitated. "I'd also rather our new status be official before we leave, but how could we possibly fit in a dinner for our parents?"

"If I know our parents, they'll make time whenever we ask. The harder question is *where?* We'd be trying to book a dining room on very short notice—on *New Year's Day,* for pity's sake!"

He pulled out his case pad, poised an outstretched index finger, then stopped with a grimace. "This is stupid. I already know what I'll find if I check any of the fancy restaurants that would usually be a good 'parent dinner' place."

She grimaced. *For New Year's Day, they're already booked. With long waiting lists.* "Oh, Charlie." She met his worried gaze. "Saturday!"

"Yeah, our timing does truly suck."

"What'll we do?"

"First of all, let's not panic. We'll figure something out."

"Right." She caught her breath at a wild thought. Corlee Wirth's Cock & Bull Pub was a down-at-the heels dive on Sixth Precinct Level Three, but it had been her "comfort place" for several years. She and her best friend Theresa even had their names on a little plaque that Corlee had installed behind the salt and pepper at one of the booths in back. After the incident with Wisniewski's Dart, she'd introduced Charlie to the pub and its regulars.

Hildie gulped. "I bet Corlee would give us a back corner. There's even a booth with my name on it."

He chuckled. *"Literally* on it. Wow. That would be cozy."

A sudden image of Mom, Dad, Mimi, Ted, Charlie *and* her, all trying to squeeze into that little four-person booth at the Cock & Bull gave her a chest-spasm. *Dad might laugh—no, he would laugh. No doubt about that. Mom? Not so much.* Her mouth went dry. *And what would Ted and Mimi think?*

"I wonder if we could make it work, though." Charlie's expression turned pensive.

She blinked at him. "Seriously?"

"Think about it. It's kind of become 'our place' in the last two weeks. And it was *your* place even longer. Where could we possibly go that would be more perfectly 'us'?"

True, Corlee and the regulars had welcomed Charlie into their circle without hesitation. Hildie and he had shared many meals, and many more drinks, at the Cock & Bull in the two weeks since then.

But. Cold grew in the pit of her stomach. "The Cock & Bull is definitely *not* the kind of place Mom would . . ."

His jaw tightened. "There's ideal, and then there's possible. We'll be 'official' at the end of it, wherever we do it."

"We will. You're right." And after all, it wasn't as if they were asking for permission from their parents. The dinner was a traditional courtesy, one it was clear that Charlie also wanted to observe. Preferably before the Centerboro trip.

She pulled out her own case pad and typed, "Corlee, when you get this, please call me? Charlie and I have a huge, massive favor we need to ask about tomorrow—well, technically now I guess it's tonight."

CHAPTER 38
SCARY THINGS

Corona Tower

R ex startled awake. The last shreds of his dream melted away into the shadows of his predawn bedroom. He sniffed the air. *Nothing burning. Okay.* His tense gut eased. *It's okay. It was that dream again.*

Shady's nose touched him. "Are you all right now?"

"I am." He nuzzled her ruff, leaned his forehead against her. "I was tossing around in the Dart with Wisniewski again. Why does that one keep coming back?" He'd had it a few times between his stints in re-gen, and this made twice, now, since he'd gotten home.

"*Post-traumatic* is the term people use, and it is for good reason." Shady snapped her ears flat. "It means the experience was terrifying—which, of course it was. How could it not be? Your brain is still processing it." She nudged him to lie back.

He rolled over and exposed his belly to her. The long, calming strokes of her tongue relaxed him caress by caress. He reviewed his memories, both of the dream and of the incident that had inspired it. Neither memory was pleasant to revisit, but certainty and personal experience drove him to a deeper examination. *An insight is lurking in there somewhere.*

A little over two weeks ago, in Rana Station's Hub, he'd caught the scent of Col. Jackson Wisniewski. The Transmondian spymaster had been a longtime sponsor of the XK9 Project. Rex knew him, and his detestable stench, all too well. But Wisniewski's main job wasn't torturing dogs. It was overseeing Transmondia's espionage against Rana Station.

Presented with a hot scent trail, that day Rex had chased the slippery spy onto a small, fast space yacht docked inside the Wheel Two Station Defense Force Base. Outrageous enough that a Transmondian spy's yacht was docked *inside* the SDF Base. Worse yet, it later turned out that the vessel belonged to the Whisper Syndicate. Wisniewski had conspired not only with the now-disgraced traitor SDF Admiral Nolan Virendra, but they both also had colluded with Whisper.

Exactly what contraband and how many spies had entered the Station through that covert entry point? How much had come through into the Station, and for how long? He'd like to clench his jaws much tighter around those issues—but later. For now, he'd leave those questions to Mike Santiago, Rana's foremost law enforcement expert on the Whisper Syndicate. Mike, Ranan Military Intelligence agents, and the Port Authority's investigators were said to be competent humans. They probably could handle it without his supervision, at least until the Palmdale Club had been dealt with.

The Transmondian "Acquisitionists" in Wizniewski's arm of the Intelligence Service appeared to have found common cause with the ambitious Virendra. They were part of a faction of the Popular Growth Forum who wanted a greater role for military leaders in their own government. Virendra must've seen them as kindred souls. But the connection between the Whisper Syndicate and Transmondian intelligence had blindsided everyone, even Mike Santiago.

On top of everything else, it now seemed clear that both

Whisper and Wisniewski had attracted the newly-identified Zander Hoback's vengeful wrath. That Whisper remained a target was no surprise after the *Izgubil*. But the cryptic message SDF Base Commodore had received just before the Dart incident made it clear Wisniewski himself also was a target.

Ranan law enforcement had no repair records for the Dart-Class space yacht Wisniewski was using. Thus, they couldn't know when it might have been rigged or where Hoback might have recruited a new crew of riggers. Had O'Boyle and his team rigged other Whisper ships before the *Izgubil*? How many ships were rigged that way? Certainty filled him. *Not all of the team had participated in other rigging jobs, or surely the guileless Atilla Usher and Wayne Purdy would have mentioned it.* "Shady, has Kieran said anything about rigging other ships?"

She glanced up, flicked her ears. "No. And in spite of his best efforts to be as vicious as his father, he seems ashamed to have been involved in all those deaths on the *Izgubil*. However, I should ask Melynn if she's planning to question him about other ships."

"Charlie seems sure that the Listeners on the Detention staff eventually will get our Saoirse-Front detainees to talk. I would not put it past any of *them* to have been involved with rigging several ships."

Shady's scent factors echoed the uncertainty he himself felt that those "Saoirse blades" would ever say a thing. "Pam has predicted that, too. I do not know how they plan to manage it."

"Charlie says the approach is based on human psychology. Also that is not coercive, and involves no torture. Not a quick process, but, as he put it, 'inexorable.' As far as I can tell, Ranan law forbids any harsh treatment of prisoners, although I cannot imagine how that would work. I guess we shall see."

"Eventually. Maybe. Why do you ask?"

"The Dart-Class yacht belonged to Whisper, and it was rigged to explo—um, micro-deconstruct. I wondered if that particular one was targeted because of Wisniewski, or if there are other ships in Whisper's fleet out there, quietly waiting for an opportune moment to be destroyed."

Her hackles puffed out and her scent factors darkened with revulsion. "Great questions." Her tongue flicked up to touch her nose, a self-reassuring gesture. Her eyes went into a middle-distance HUD-stare.

Well, no time like the present to ask a question, I guess. Happy New Year, Melynn. He returned to his analysis. How did the dream compare to his memories of the event? He concentrated on holding both dream and memory in his mind, impression by impression. During the event itself he'd been focused rather exclusively on Wisniewski's trank pistol, which he could smell was loaded with deadly neurotoxin darts.

The weapon had been knocked from the spymaster's hand in a tumble across the deck. Wisneiwski'd been making strong efforts to regain it, even as the ship's tight maneuvers tossed both of them around like rag dolls. Rex had been just as concerned with trying to keep it out of his reach. *And* with finding and getting into an escape pod. Through the link, Charlie'd been frantically urging him to enter a pod as soon as possible . . . *Oh. Of course. After the neurotoxin, I ignored ALL of the smells.*

But the dream had not. On rare occasions Rex had dreamed of touching something or being touched, and had a sensation of actually being touched. Often at that point he'd awaken, and try to determine what, outside of the dream, had touched him. Sometimes it was easy to guess, but sometimes he couldn't plausibly conclude that anything had. Same with smell. Sometimes there was an odor component to his dreams, sometimes not. He didn't have conscious memories of smelling the burning nanotimers during the event, but this dream had become so vivid it woke him up. *Because of the smell. I had to immediately check if something was burning, didn't I?*

Next logical question: did I actually smell something I wasn't aware of at the time? Or am I supplying a burning smell from my imagination? He stepped through the actual memory again, this time more slowly. He focused on the smells.

Wisniewski's personal profile. His sweaty fear, his dark, raw fury. Old scent profiles of others who'd passed through the ship earlier. Most prominent among those was the man Wisniewski called Fowler. Fowler had been the partner of Knife Woman, the as-yet-unidentified Whisper executioner who'd attacked the Dolan brothers.

Rex had chased both Fowler and Knife Woman in Howardsboro the day before. Then he'd inadvertently killed Fowler in an access tunnel to the SDF Base's dock. Rex shuddered. Gave himself a moment to reset. *Not ready to deal with that yet.* He swallowed, stress-yawned. *Back inside the Dart. Was anything burning?*

He strove to clear his mind and simply observe without analysis. During the actual event he'd been all urgent action. Now he worked through the memory slowly, methodically. Sifted through impressions one by one. *Wisniewski's personal scent. Fowler's. The trank gun's polymers and metal, the cabin's metal decking. Fowler's blood, still misting off of Rex's body. Nothing burning.*

He could not have smelled his harness's maneuvering jets. Even though he and others commonly used the phrase "burning jets" as a description for moving independently in micrograv, that was a misnomer. His micrograv harness used nitrogen-gas jets, not any type of burning fuel, to maneuver. Nitrogen was ubiquitous in the atmosphere of Heritage Earth, and the theory went that dogs had never evolved scent receptors for it because there was no survival need for them. Whatever the reason, it was one of the very few gases no XK9 could detect by smell.

Within seconds of entering the cabin, Rex had closed his jaws on Wisniewski's wrist—the one attached to the hand that gripped the trank pistol. His teeth had clamped down on steel-tough augmented bones and immediately there'd been more blood. *Wisniewski's blood, hot, fresh, and metallic, filled his mouth and nose.* More distantly, he still smelled the congealing older remains of Fowler's blood.

He and Wisniewski collided with the cabin's back wall. *What did I smell then? Blood, Wisniewski's fear and anger. The metal surface. Nothing burning.*

Wisniewski had screamed at the pilot to launch. After that Rex and the Transmondian had become projectiles—his harness jets hadn't been up to the challenge of countering those G-forces. If both had not possessed super-tough bones and fortified organs they might've been smashed to mush. As it was, it hurt like hell, dizzied him, disoriented him. He pushed all that aside. Inventoried scents again. *Blood. Scent profiles. Metal decking. Oh.*

There it is. Just a hint, a small whiff. Easy to miss.

He and Wisniewski smashed into another wall. He struggled to separate from remembered pain, focused only on the scent. *Okay!* Now he had the scent for sure. Rex doubled down on his analysis, because "burning" was never only one smell. The smell of any given combustion depended on the substances that were burning. *This smell? Hmm.* He sifted through his impressions. *Maybe a touch of sulfur, kind of a hot-wires smell, with a complex of subtle undertones. Consistent with the explosives they'd found in the wreckage of the* Izgubil. *One component of those explosives—not the full profile.*

The burning I smelled is Rory Fredericks's fuses, after they started burning. His gut tightened and his feet tingled, an echo of panic. *Is this how it smells, right before you die?*

"Rex, stop!" Shady muzzle-grabbed him, her mouth soft but insistent. "Breathe longer, slower breaths! I do not know what to do if you hyperventilate."

"Ah." He pulled free as she released him. Took an even, cautious breath, held it, then let it out slowly. Repeated that cycle several times until his world steadied.

"Another dream?" Her worry-scent edged into a sharp, raw blend. He could see well enough in this middle-darkness to observe her tense, upright ears, the little pucker between her furry brows.

"No, I was awake. Examining my memory. I did not

consciously mark it at the time, but the nightmare helped me realize that on Wisniewski's Dart I smelled Rory's fuses burning. I now have identified and noted what that smells like. I would know it, if I ever smelled it again."

"No wonder you seemed about to hyperventilate." Her jaws gaped in a stress-yawn and her feet twitched as if she wanted to pace. "Let us earnestly hope you never do!"

He swept his ears back and angled his nose downward. "I wish I could somehow transfer it to a scent card so I could share it."

"So the rest of the Pack could . . . do what?" Her snarl glinted. "Know enough to panic, just before they get blown up?"

He growled but kept it to a low rumble. "That assumes there is no way to stop it, once it has started. But Fredericks built in a delay between ignition and detonation. Perhaps there is a way to interrupt the countdown. Wouldn't that seem a reasonable safety measure? To have a way to stop it, at need?"

"Tux or Crystal might hazard a guess, but I imagine that is a question for Dr. SCISCO."

"You are right." *Does SCISCO sleep?* He'd communicated with nem often enough through the brain link to have a sense of how to make contact.

Oh, hello, Rex! Nir pleasure swept through the link. *I thought corporeal beings were customarily asleep at this hour, but it is delightful to hear from you. I hope your New Year was beautiful.*

It was, thanks. I hope yours was, too.

Every time-increment that passes when I am free is a beautiful interval. To what do I owe the pleasure of this contact?

I have managed to identify a scent-profile for Rory Fredericks's nanotimer-activated fuses, once they have started to burn.

Nir surprise reverberated in the link. *How?*

He explained about his nightmare, the nature of his highly accurate autobiographical memory, and his process for isolating the profile.

I can sense that was an upsetting process. I also have a sense that you wish to ask a question.

Once it has started burning, is there a way to stop it?

Ah. I can imagine you would like to know of one, should you ever smell it again. Yes?

Most definitely yes.

I cannot immediately answer, sorry to say. When I am working with a student, I prefer to push them to explore safety questions of this type as part of their developmental process. Far more students survive to graduate when we insist upon that, I have found.

Did Rory develop a way?

He may have, but not to my certain knowledge. I had posed the question to him. Developing an answer was part of the work he had not yet completed when he disappeared.

But—you do know of a way, I hope?

I had some ideas that might work, but remember: this is a new technology. I wanted him *to explore it. If I solved all of my advanced students' problems for them ahead of time, they would not learn as much. Tux, Georgia, Crystal, Connie, several of my graduate students, and I definitely should run some experiments, however.*

After our Centerboro trip, my specialist Packmates could join you in that work.

I look forward to it.

❖ ❖ ❖ ❖ ❖ ❖ ❖ ❖

Pam and Balchu's Market Garden Apartment and Becenti Tower

"I told you I can't go!" Pam's stomach clenched in a tight knot. She stared at Balchu, head pounding. *What is he thinking?* "And you can't wear that!"

"Oh, that's where you're wrong." He laughed and shook his head. "This is exactly what to wear. When they say 'informal' they really mean it. If anything, it's a contest to see who can show up in the shabbiest rags."

This went against everything she'd ever seen or heard about Chartered Families. It simply made no sense.

Balchu aped a fashion turn in his baggy old threadbare workout clothes. "I'll get extra style-points for the holes in the knees."

"You'll get kicked off the train!"

"You know they can't do that."

The equity codes on public transit were pretty strict. "Well, maybe not, but they'll want to."

"If they try, I'll flash my badge and write them a ticket. Then we'll see who's good with public shaming."

He'd be justified in doing so, true. She bit her lips, realized she was literally wringing her hands, and made herself stop. "You *swear* you're not spoofing me?" Terror of humiliation brought tears to her eyes. *Damn it!*

Balchu strode to her, took her in his arms. He cupped her face with one hand and gently wiped away her tears. "Pammie, understand this. I know how out-of-your-depth you feel about this whole Chartered Family thing. But you can trust me on this. It's not some cruel practical joke at your expense. It really is their New Year's Day tradition. Becenti Family has done this for all the years I can remember."

She shook her head, still disbelieving. "Why?"

"Because people can get so caught up in work and pressures and demands placed on us, we forget how to relax. We forget how to have fun and just be comfortable with each other. New Year's Day breakfast is kind of a 'reset' for Becenti Family. A break, you know? To remember we're all just people. We don't have to be 'on' all the time."

What does that even look like? She could think of nothing to say.

"We usually make waffles and pancakes. Some sweet break-fast wine or spiked coffee might be involved, but it's not required. If you want to tell jokes or tall tales, great. If not, no problem. Sometimes there's a card game, sometimes a jigsaw puzzle. But everything is optional. You can just sit back and watch, if you want."

"And everyone . . . wears old clothes?"

"Yeah. Because the old, worn-out clothes are the most comfortable."

"That can be true." *At least, in the right setting.*

"C'mon. Let me dress you so you'll fit right in."

The train crew let them on and didn't say a word about their saggy, faded, holey workout garb. Balchu had guided her to dress in an ancient gray sweatshirt jacket from her Police Academy days. The zipper no longer worked and both sleeves sported holes in the elbows. Her black leggings had a hole in one knee and a permanent layer of Shady's shed hair. The ragged green tank she wore over her faded old sports bra had somehow caught a splash of bleach earlier in its career.

Some of their fellow passengers gave them a side-eye but kept mum. Balchu leaned back, put his hands behind his head, and grinned. He'd told her to "own it," and that did seem to be working for him.

"Remember how they all treated us like dignitaries the other day?"

"A far cry from now."

"But you held your head high, kept your back straight, and greeted everyone with poise and grace. Do that again."

Still doubtful, she tried to follow his lead. Somehow, when she walked with a confident, upright bearing she did feel a bit less ridiculous. All the same, on the walk from the station to Becenti, she imagined neighbors hiding behind their vine "curtains," staring and gossiping.

But then Anya met them at the gate with a massive grin. She wore a faded, once-red t-shirt with chopped-off sleeves and purple yoga pants that might have been new as recently as a decade ago. She gave a cry of delight and enveloped them in a hug. "You came! I'm so glad! Welcome back, and Happy New Year!"

Turned out Balchu'd been right after all.

CHAPTER 39
A PLACE THAT'S A HAVEN

Fifth Precinct Level Three, Cock & Bull Pub

Charlie'd already been nervous. But his gut twisted even tighter into nauseated knots the moment Pari and Dara stepped out of their sleek luxury auto-nav wearing formal evening attire. They stared at the less-than-posh exterior of the Cock & Bull Pub.

"Hi, Mom. Dad." Hildie strode forward to greet them with a frown. "Didn't you remember I said this is not a formal place?"

Pari shot a worried glance at Dara. But Hildie's mother raised her eyebrows and wrapped her silken pallu a little more tightly around herself. Her chin rose, a mannerism that reminded Charlie of her daughter. "This is an important occasion, Hilde-gaard. One dresses to honor the *event*."

"Mmm." Hildie herself had worn Charlie's favorite pale-cream wrap with the low neckline and the little red flowers on it. She placed her hands on her hips and gave her mother a wry, disapproving look. "Okay, be that way. Ted and Mimi are less than a minute away, so let's wait for them."

Dara's silver-rose saree was beautiful, Charlie'd have to give it that. But it seemed wildly out of place on the pub's gravel entry-path in the deepening dusk, illuminated by garish, glowing beer signs. Dara regarded the signs with a faintly appalled expression. "Are you sure this place was the best you could do?"

"This is my favorite eatery on the whole entire Wheel, Mom. And Corlee made the back dining room available on less than a day's notice—*tonight*, of all nights!"

A shining Citron Flash pulled up near them. *How'd Papa manage that? Yikes!* Charlie's gut notched another twist tighter.

Mama extricated herself from the low-slung auto-nav with a laugh. "Oh, I'm gonna have to take more Yoga classes if you mean to keep renting this thing!" She wore a nice, presentable red dress. *Thank goodness!* It more nearly paralleled the dressy-casual styles he and Hildie had chosen.

Papa emerged from the other side. He grinned at Mama. "Get your classes lined up, because I'm spoiled!" He turned to Pari and Dara and his smile never wavered. "Hello! Good to see you again." He extended a hand to Pari.

Hildie's father returned the handshake with a grin. "Good to see you, too, Ted."

Dara offered Mama a much warmer smile than she'd given her daughter. "Hello, Mimi. I must confess there have been times I feared we'd never see this night."

"It's pretty special." Mama nodded and smoothed down her dress.

Charlie rubbed his damp palms along the lower edge of his jacket as surreptitiously as he could and took a deep breath. "Shall we go in?"

Papa gestured toward the door. "Lead on."

Hildie walked up the ramp first. Charlie held the door until the rest of their party stepped inside. *That's odd.* Only a few patrons seemed to have come tonight. Charlie saw no more than a handful of people. Some were individuals he recognized by sight, though not by name. He didn't know the others. Normally this place would be packed—especially on a holiday. And normally there'd be a lot of familiar faces among them. *What's up with that?*

Dara stopped a few steps inside the door. "My. This place certainly is . . . rustic." She twitched the shimmering folds of her saree away before it could brush the edge of a well-scrubbed but use-scarred table edge.

"It's quaint. Cheerful." Her father smiled at Hildie, but from his expression he was trying to convince himself. It *was* kind of a down-at-the-heels-seeming place, with an interior that probably had appeared a lot more fresh and stylish three decades ago.

"It's been my haven for a long time." Hildie remained outwardly serene, although he knew she must be quaking inside. "I think it's the best possible place for this dinner. Wait till you taste Corlee's cooking!"

"I'm sure it'll be as exquisite as the décor," Dara muttered.

"It'll be fine." Papa nodded to Charlie. "When you find a place that's a haven—well, that's special. Surface details mean less than love."

"And 'available tonight with next to no notice' is nothing to pooh-pooh," Mama added. "We didn't have a lot of lead time."

"Agreed." Charlie gave his mother a rueful smile. "We both wanted to have this dinner here from the beginning, but we did our our due diligence. We checked several places in the River Park Arts District. I was actually surprised a couple of them found openings for us as soon as next week, but we didn't want to make everyone wait till after the Centerboro trip."

"We appreciate that." His mother gave him a wide, happy smile. "We've already been waiting long enough!"

Corlee emerged from the back room and gave them all a huge grin. "Welcome! Come on back. We tried to fix it up real special!" Like her pub, she probably had seen better days, but Charlie had taken a liking to her from the start. With her large, sturdy frame and capable, well-worn hands, she might not be elegant, but she was always *comforting*. Little wonder the crews of the high-stress Emergency Rescue Team came here to relax.

Charlie, Hildie, and their parents followed the pub's barkeep-owner into what normally was the Game Room. Charlie and Hildie stopped with a gasp inside the door. Corlee and her rag-tag staff, at least half of whom were recovering addicts from the Health Department's Rehab Program, had transformed the place.

A large round light fixture hung from one of the ceiling beams in the center of the room. Normally it illuminated the pool table, but now it hung over a big round dining table draped in a white cloth and set for six. Someone had strung many colorful streamers, each with one end attached to the light and the other to one of several ceiling beams near the room's edges. Balloons and paper flowers clustered artfully at both ends of each streamer. On the back wall hung a handmade banner on a bed sheet, bright with marker-ink and sparkling with glued-on mineral glitter. It read, "Congratulations, Hildie and Charlie!"

"What do you think?" Corlee asked. "Is it okay?"

Hildie's eyes swam with happy tears. Charlie wasn't sure she could smile any more broadly. "It's *beautiful!*"

He probably had a big sappy grin, too. "You guys outdid yourselves. This place looks amazing."

"Oh, I'm so glad! I was afraid it wouldn't be fancy enough."

"It's perfect," Hildie said. "Mom, Dad, Mimi, Ted, why don't you sit down?"

"Right! I'll get the bubbly!" Corlee darted out.

Mama chuckled and took a seat. "I can see why you like this place." Papa settled with apparent contentment next to her.

Charlie's gut finally relaxed a little. He glanced at Hildie, but her focus remained on her parents.

Dara eyed her chair as if worried it might soil her saree, but Pari held it for her till she sat, then took the place next to her.

Charlie and Hildie remained standing. Corlee hurried back in, followed by a couple of her servers. They quickly distributed glasses for sparkling wine. Charlie gave his a second glance. It glinted with crystalline fire under the light. Corlee popped the cork, then poured a measure into each glass with the ease of long practice.

Once everyone had their drink, Charlie took Hildie's hand. "I'm sure you're not going to be terribly surprised by the news we wanted to share tonight. We had every intention of going slowly and making sure we knew each others' minds before we took any drastic steps. But, well—" He turned to Hildie.

"We both decided that five years are long enough to wait." She offered them a fierce grin, as if daring them to contradict her. "So when Charlie asked me to be his Amare, I knew there was only one answer I wanted to give. I said *yes!*"

"Congratulations!" Ted lifted his glass to them. "Welcome to the Family, Hildie!"

The others joined the toast. Pari and Dara directed their welcomes to Charlie. Then they all tucked into a dinner that turned out to be wildly eclectic and decidedly multicultural— but delicious. Pari and Papa relaxed into a conversation that Charlie couldn't hear, but it made both men smile. Even Dara gradually seemed to lose some of her high-strung tension.

Through the link Charlie sensed that Rex had arrived in the other room. He received an impression of a growing crowd before his partner clamped down harder on his access. *I thought it was too quiet out there earlier.*

Rex responded with amusement but nothing more.

Dessert was chocolate lava cake and fresh strawberries with whipped cream. Charlie smiled. That was Hildie's absolute favorite. Clearly Corlee knew it, too. Afterward, everyone sighed and sat back. Both Papa and Pari unbuttoned their jackets. The conversation came to a satiated lull.

Then Dara straightened and opened her little clutch purse. "I think it's time for Grandma Hestia's gift. She thought you might not have had time to get any yet, and she wanted you to have these if you like them."

Charlie gave Hildie a puzzled glance but his new Amare sat taut and upright, eyes wide and mouth open in surprise.

Dara offered Charlie a small black-velvet box. "Why don't you open it, and Hildie can explain what they are."

He opened the little box to reveal two golden ring sets, one sized larger and more tailored, the other smaller and more intricate. Their distinctly old-fashioned design struck him as beautiful in a simple, elegant way. The emeralds and rubies that adorned them blazed with superb color and had been cut to perfection. The Amare ring he'd bought for Felicia—the one with the diamond that had cost more than two months' pay—would've seemed cheap and tasteless next to these.

Hildie's cheeks had gone dusky rose. Her eyes shone with unshed tears. "Is Grandma *sure* about this?"

"How many granddaughters who've finally found their true love does she have?" Dara smiled. "That's a direct quote, by the way."

Hildie glanced up to meet Charlie's gaze with wide, awestruck eyes. "These were my great-grandparents' rings. Grandma's parents. Great-Grandpapa Arksa Chakraborti ran a successful asteroid-mining operation that allowed him to buy in for the Founding of Rana Station. This gold came from the very first asteroid he developed. He had the ring sets made by a well-regarded jeweler in Oroplania to celebrate his relationship with Great-Grandmama Hildegaard Gallagher."

Charlie's breath caught. "Your namesake." His skin tingled. "Wow. I, um," he swallowed. "I sure hope you like them, because I think they're amazing."

She reached out and plucked the little box from Charlie's grasp. "Let's see how well they fit." She lifted the larger Amare ring. "Could you give me a hand, here? Preferably the left one?"

He obliged. She slid it on, bent to kiss his hand along with the ring, then lifted her chin with a mischievous grin. "You're a marked man, now, Morgan!"

"Works for me. My turn." Hers was a little looser on her finger than his had been on his hand, but he hoped not dangerously so. "Back at you, Gallagher. Claimed and tagged."

"Do you have a good, secure pocket for that box?"

He eyed the other rings and offered up an ardent wish that their plans would work out and eventually he'd wear all of the larger set. Then he snapped the box shut and slipped it into an inside jacket pocket. "Right here, next to my heart."

"Oh, you do that romantic shit very well." Her hazel eyes sparkled.

He cupped her beloved face with his newly-beringed hand, then enjoyed a long, heartfelt kiss. "Wait till we get home," he whispered.

"That's so beautiful I might cry," Papa said.

"I'll get you a hankie." Mama dug into her bag.

"Happier, my dear?" Pari asked Dara.

She sighed. "It'll do. This place isn't the Vista From Twenty-Five, but we'd probably have had to wait eighteen months to do this there."

"She *does* remember we're a cop and a paramedic, right?" Charlie muttered to Hildie, still holding her close. The Vista from Twenty-Five was a rotating restaurant atop one of the tallest buildings in the urban heart of Orangeboro, and the most prestigious venue in town. But Dara was right about the probable wait. And six hundred novi a plate did *not* fit into his and Hildie's combined budget.

Hildie replied with a small grimace. "I'm not exactly the high-maintenance 'fairy princess'-style daughter she always dreamed of, but I guess she'll just have to deal."

"Medicine goddess trumps fairy princess any day, in my book." Charlie snuck in one more kiss, then turned to their parents. "May I take it we have your blessing?"

"Figured that out, did you?" Papa laughed and nodded to Pari. "Always knew that boy was bright."

Corlee poked her head through the doorway. "How's it going in here?"

"Oh, Corlee this was so wonderful!" Hildie half-danced over

to the door to show off her ring. Charlie followed. Their parents trailed behind them.

"They're beautiful. But I think you better come on out and show the rest of us." She stepped back and opened the door wide.

The previously-empty main room of the Cock & Bull Pub was now filled to maximum capacity—maybe a bit beyond— with pub regulars and friends. Rex and Shady sat, tongues lolling long, next to Theresa. Hildie's best friend literally vibrated with excitement. She bounced from foot to foot, backed by her boyfriend Kodi. Hildie's longtime paramedic partner Eli stood nearby. So did Caro, Andy, Abi and Smita.

They were far from the only friends present. Oz and his wife, ERT pilot Veda, even the drivers from the *Triumph*—as well as Eddie Chism from the STAT Team and his wife, Gwen. Brock and Aleya from Blue Team, too. All of the able-bodied Pack-mates, both XK9s and humans, along with their sweethearts, had joined the party—even Tux, Elle, Georgia, and Misha, newly returned from Centerboro just in time to go back. And so had Berwyn and Shiv. Plus Misha's Significant, Hallie, and many of Charlie and Hildie's assorted cousins.

Rex stood. "Congratulations!" He turned to Hildie. "And welcome, this time even *more* officially, to the Pack!"

CHAPTER 40
THE EARLY CREW

Orangeboro Grand Central Terminal, Safety Services Express to the Hub, and Wheel Two Topside Terminal

S hady exited her auto-nav at Orangeboro Grand Central in predawn darkness and thick mist, but stopped outside the building, ears up. *Wow, I've never seen this place so empty and quiet.* Behind her the car quietly closed its door and departed for Corona.

Crap, you're already there? Through the link she sensed Pam still struggling through a groggy morning haze.

You went into the wrong line of work for a night owl.

On the other end of the link Pam yawned. *Be there as soon as I can.*

Tell Balchu I believe in him. He'd recently confided to Shady that part of his life's mission apparently was to get Pam coffeed up and out the door each morning. She lolled her tongue and stepped into the doors' reaction zone. They swept open for her.

Grand Central wasn't exactly dead-empty, but most of the humans she encountered moved as if they were approximately as wide awake as Pam. Or, for that matter, Rex and Charlie this morning. Rex needed to check in at the Sandler Clinic for one last blood draw and respiration check before Dr. Sandler cleared him for the trip. When Shady'd left Corona today, the only one of her housemates up yet was Hildie. Charlie's new Amare had been head-down in a box of clothes hastily hauled over from Feliz Tower yesterday, still packing for Centerboro.

The sharp, warm aroma of brewing coffee echoed the smells she remembered from Corona. Here at Grand Central, tendrils of the distinctive scent permeated the big building. It lanced fresh and clear across a muddle of older, ingrained odors from machinery, dust, the residual essence of stressed humans, and several dozen other sources.

She crossed Georgia's trail, still airborne and intermingled with sugared coffee, then followed her into the Hub-Bound waiting area. "Good morning."

Her Packmate greeted her with smiling blue eyes over her mug. She took a long, slow sip, then leaned back against the padded seat. "I hope you had a beautiful New Year."

"It was eventful, as you know."

"There wasn't much chance to talk at the pub last night, but I owe Charlie's uncle a massive 'thank you!'"

"Oh?" Shady cocked her head.

"I'm not sure Baba Olena's feet have touched the ground since the ball-drop." She laughed. "She insisted on replaying that clip on the com for me when I called."

"Clip?" Shady's tail fanned. "What did Dolph do? I went to bed at Two-Thirds New Year and haven't heard a thing about it."

"Ah. Well, at several points in the broadcast they always read a random selection of greetings from people in the audience to friends or family who may be listening." She shrugged. "Because of Baba Olena, we never missed it when I was a girl—I haven't kept up with it since. But clearly, they still do that."

"I think there is a group from our Family that always tunes in, too, but I figured it was from loyalty to Dolph."

"To be fair, he's an excellent entertainer. Doesn't dance like he used to, but his comic timing is excellent." Georgia's grin stretched wide. "Anyway, Tato and Mama tell me he waited till the end of the last batch of well-wishes. Then he looked directly into the camera and said, 'I have one more greeting. This one's for sweet Olena in Monteverde. I'm so happy you enjoyed my cookies. Have a beautiful New Year.'"

"Oh, my."

"Exactly." The warmth in her laugh and her scent factors expanded, fragrant with pleasure and affection. "I'm not sure Apodeddi is still her Number One, after that."

"Oh, Mamoor will win her back. Your grandfather is charming."

"That he is. And he, at least, believes in me." A strain of sludgy, prickly-acid ruefulness blended into her scent. "I just wish the rest of the Family would accept my choices."

"Oh, you mean, 'That Georgie. We worry so much. When will she find safer work'?" Shady angled her ears back. "We heard variations on that theme a lot during tea. I now understand your comment about loving them better when you are in a different borough."

Georgia blew out an exasperated breath and focused on her coffee. "Did they try to get you to talk me out of my life choices?"

"Charlie and I told them you are amazing at your work, and we would never try to dissuade such an outstanding expert."

"Wow. Well, thanks for that vote of confidence." She glanced at Shady with a sad little smile. "I'm truly gratified you believe in me. But I fear nothing will convince them. Why can't they understand I don't *want* a 'safe' job—and all so I can have *babies*, of all things!"

"I do not know." Shady stress-yawned. *I don't particularly want puppies, either—but I don't think I have much of a choice,* she added through the link.

Pam's worry echoed back to her. *Let's cross that bridge when we come to it. First, we need to make sure the Pack is safe.*

You're correct about that. Shady's ears went up. *Also, you are much closer.*

Yeah, we're in sight of the Grand Central entrance. I see the group from Glorioso, too. They just got out of an auto-nav.

Everyone converged on the elevator within the next few minutes. Between all the humans' luggage and gear bags, it was just as well they had the Safety Services Express car to themselves. For Shady it wasn't an issue: all of her gear, plus some of Pam's, was already secured in her utility panniers' pockets.

Once they and all their effects were secured and the elevator was boosting for the Hub, Misha and his Significant, Hallie, exchanged a look and clasped hands. Their scent factors shifted from brisk, businesslike, bright warm midtones into sharper, excited, and nervous notes.

Tux and Elle lolled their tongues and wagged their tails.

"Go ahead," Elle urged her partner. "Tell them."

"Um," Misha cleared his throat. The skin over his cheekbones darkened. "Well, I guess maybe Charlie and Hildie inspired us, and, um, we'd been thinking about it for a while, so . . ."

"Last night we submitted the first of our Betrothal form-work." Hallie's eyes sparkled and her scent filled with sweet, high-toned joy.

"Woah! Really? Congratulations!" Georgia cried. "Hallie, you should know that Misha's been chewing on that idea, the whole time we were in Centerboro."

"Oh, he has, has he?" Hallie turned to him with a laugh. "And you said you were playing it close to the vest!"

"I didn't talk about it *that* much." He turned to Georgia and lifted his eyebrows. "Did I?"

She just laughed.

Shady, Pam and Balchu added their congratulations.

Your turn to go next. Shady slid her eyes toward Pam.

We have nothing to announce yet. Her partner frowned.

But didn't you say "yes" to Becenti on New Year's Day?

We're still . . . clearing up details.

But you're doing it? You didn't get cold feet?

Oh, my feet are like ice, but we did say 'yes.' Including . . . including me. She gave a little head-shake and reached over to grasp Balchu's hand.

He gave her a smile. "Yes?"

"Nothing. Just 'love you.'"

"Love you, too." He kissed her then returned his focus to whatever Hallie was saying.

Oh. Right. The Family's reactions. That's what Hallie's talking about. Apparently Glorioso Family approved of Misha and Hallie's decision. Shady thumped her tail. *I bet Balchu's parents and sisters are just as excited over your news.*

Pam bit her lip. *Oh, they are. But I don't want to think about it right now. Not till we're back from Centerboro and we know for sure that nobody's plotting to deport you for economic reasons!*

Agreed. That was the whole point of this trip, after all. She gave Pam another sidelong glance. *When do you plan to move in?*

Pam scrubbed her face with her hands. *After we get back from Centerboro! At some point.* She hunched her shoulders then took another breath and lowered them. *Chase and Anya have invited us to come out next week, assuming we're back. But we've got to go, be successful, and come back first.*

Could I come with you? To Becenti? I'd love to go sniff the place over. Not to mention the people. It was more pleasant to talk about Pam joining Becenti than to think about the Palmdale Club's plot, or all the enemies they might have on the Combined Councils. Her hackles rippled.

It's not more pleasant for me. Pam scowled at her, then sighed. *But sure. I'd like to bring you. And maybe when you come you can offer me some guidance. About all of it.*

Oh, and speaking of guidance, there IS a Listener working with all of you, isn't there?

There are four, all told. Pam grimaced. *One of them is specifically working with me.*

Good! That was what I thought I'd gotten from the impressions.

Yep, I'm a head-case all on my own. Balchu will attend most of the sessions with me, but I'm under no illusions—Sheila's mainly there to keep me from climbing out onto a ledge.

Your Listener's name is Sheila? Shady kept her tone light, but the fact that she was talking with a Listener at all showed how much she had outgrown her mother's pernicious influence.

She seems nice. Pam nodded. *And talking with her . . . Well, so far, so good. I think maybe it's helping. I was a bit relieved to learn there's another for the rest of Balchu's relatives, even though they've been de facto members of Becenti for a long time. I guess there are adjustments for all of us.*

How about Raya? Did she come around yet?

I'm not sure. I know the current Becenti group has a Listener holding sessions with them, too. That's to help ease the tensions of adding us. And Anya says there's a fourth one in the mix, trying to work with Raya. I'm not sure how well that's going, even though her secret's out about being scammed, now.

Do all merging Families get this kind of support?

That's my impression, yes. Pam's welter of clashing reactions and emotions over this welled up through the link.

Merging Families is a big deal.

Bigger than I realized, that's for sure. Pam's scent factors filled with tight, hot odors that spoke to Shady of a struggle to stay calm while overwhelmed. She gulped a deep breath and let it out in quiet, measured puffs. *Orangeboro has mandated this level of support for any merging Family. Sharing living space and a Family Trust Fund with others, even if they're not total strangers . . . it's a lot. And—truth, here—I probably would have gone catatonic if they'd hit me with all of it at once.*

Shady nodded, human-style. There'd been a dedicated Listener assigned to Corona before Rex and Charlie even got back from Chayko, and she knew there also had been one assigned to consult when she and Rex became Amares, although they hadn't felt much need to talk with him. *Hmm. Wonder if Charlie and Hildie get one, now that they've announced their new status?* It probably wouldn't hurt, come to think of it.

The elevator slowed.

New urgency surged within her. There was little point in stewing over the latest threats, both to the Pack and to all XK9s everywhere, while riding in the elevator where she couldn't do anything about it. But in a few more minutes, she and the others could shift to a new leg of the journey. Her thoughts leaped ahead. What would they find in Centerboro?

Humans and XK9s pushed free of the elevator into Topside Terminal's cool, echoing spaces once the doors opened, then took a Safety Services shuttle to the Port Authority Base. There they donned their micrograv harnesses under the watchful eye of the property supervisor working the end of this watch.

Neither Balchu nor Hallie had a Class B microgravity certification, so they weren't issued harnesses. Instead, they rode in front of the luggage on a micrograv sled electronically tethered to Misha's harness.

Harnesses and sled freed them from the tubes and poles to which most lowly Class-A certs were restricted. Forepaws worked even less well in those spaces than human hands. Buoyant joy and warm gratitude lifted Shady's mood. A whole team of experts at Station Polytechnic and Learned Masters from Wheel Five's Institutes of Ascended Contemplation had devoted themselves to designing the XK9s' microgravity harnesses. With her Class B certification, she could go anywhere a human or ozzirikkian could in microgravity, given parallel equipment and security clearance.

Time to catch a loop train. These short-haul workhorses of the Trans-Hub System carried most of the traffic between Wheel terminals. This one's loop took it from Wheel One to Wheel Four and back, with ten-minute stops at each Wheel Terminal, so passengers could get on or off. The trip to the Hub on the hyperbarically-equalizing Safety Services Express elevator had taken the usual thirty minutes. Transits from one Wheel to the next also took approximately half an hour each.

Shady growled softly, then swallowed hard against the need to *go faster*. She estimated their trip from Grand Central Terminal in Orangeboro on Wheel Two to Grand Central in Centerboro on Wheel Four would take a little more than two hours. They'd awakened before dawn but wouldn't arrive till mid-morning. *Ugh! I want to be there NOW.*

I feel you, partner. Shady didn't have to look to sense Pam's frown. *I want to be there now, too. There's still so much to do!*

You seem less daunted by the work now than you were yesterday.

Oh, I'm daunted as hell. Pam's scent shifted into sharper stress-notes. *But I have a list, now. And I know how to do the things on that list. I'll get overwhelmed again later, I'm sure.*

You underrate yourself.

Mm. Pam's frown deepened. *We'll see.*

They arrived just as the train pulled away. Shady snorted. *Dammit! Add another ten minutes!*

"That happened the last time, too." Tux laid back his ears. "I believe the elevators must be just off-sync with the trains."

"They wouldn't be, if we hadn't had to stop and get our gear." Georgia shook her head. "And then, last time, it turned out we didn't even *need* the gear. We stayed in 1-G the whole time."

That wouldn't be the case this time. They were scheduled to address the Combined Councils on Tuesday. Rana Station was a rarity in the Alliance: a sovereign state with two major species jointly ruling it who did not share a mutually comfortable gravitation. Humans were less uncomfortable in ozzirikkians' native gravity than the reverse, but both were equally at ease—or unease—in microgravity. So the Combined Councils Chamber was located in the Hub, exactly halfway between ozzirikkian Wheel Five and human Wheel Four.

Shady swallowed again and licked her lips. It wouldn't do

any good to hyperventilate *now* over a presentation to the Combined Councils that was the better part of four days away.

"What is Centerboro like, these days?" Balchu gripped a handhold and turned carefully toward Georgia and Misha, a wise precaution, considering Newton's laws in microgravity. "I haven't been there since the class trip in Upper Levels."

"Me neither," Pam agreed.

"It seems more congested now. Everyone moves even faster than I remembered." Misha shook his head with a rueful expression. "We didn't get a lot of time to sight-see. Some of the bombs we found had been placed at memorials, but that's hardly the same thing."

"Not even close." Elle's hackles rippled and her ears snapped flat. Hallie bit her lip and snuggled closer to Misha.

"We found several near offices, too." Georgia frowned. "It was the weirdest thing, though. They all appeared to be professional work. Some of them were fully armed and could have exploded to create considerable damage. But most of them would never have gone off."

"What?" Pam lifted one brow. "Why not?"

"It was different things with each of the duds we found. It wasn't wired quite right. Or it had a wire loose. Or maybe one bad solder, in spite of the fact that the others were perfect. A variety of other things. Different flaws, and several different kinds of devices."

"They had different appearances, payloads, and mechanisms, but they all had the same two subjects' scents on them." Tux flicked his ears. "No fingerprints, barely enough DNA to yield an iffy partial match. Very faint scents, but consistent."

"Could you draw preliminary conclusions?" Pam asked.

"Whoever made them did not want us to connect all of the devices to one source. They also meant to scare us, but in most cases not to actually blow things up." Elle showed her teeth, but kept her muzzle pointed downward. Shady agreed with the precaution, even though there weren't many people around at 06:30. No sense giving anyone a needless scare.

Shady cocked her head. "Did you recognize the scent profiles?"

"Unfortunately, no." Another flash of Elle's teeth. "But I would recognize them if I smelled them again."

"That's why Mike insisted on bringing you, I'm sure." Pam's pleasure surged through the link. "Partial touch-DNA isn't conclusive. A scent profile is."

"True." Elle's tail fanned. She fired jets to counter the wag and stay in place.

Five newcomers arrived from one of the Class A tubes. They stared at the XK9s and lingered near the gate, apparently bound for the same train. They stayed at least a meter away, but close enough to kill any discussion of the case.

Silence descended on Shady's group.

What was that about a class trip? Shady cocked her head at Pam and went back to the link.

Sometime during our final year of Upper Levels, all Ranan students take a two-day field trip to Centerboro with their civics classes. Savage pleasure echoed through the link from Pam. *Mother swore all year that she'd forbid it, but everything was paid for by the school, and the trip was required if we wanted to graduate. Which I most definitely did. Anyway, the officials would have asked a whole slew of questions she didn't want to answer, if I didn't go. So she had to allow it, after all.*

You enjoyed it.

The trip itself was even more fun than foiling Mother's plan, and that's saying something. I still didn't have any friends, but it was the first time I'd ever spent a night away from home. I got a full-sized single-person bed! I could eat whatever took my fancy on the menus. I never wanted to go back home.

How much longer after that before you went to the Academy?

Two months, fifteen days, 14 hours, and 23 minutes from the time I got home. Pam grinned. *Not that I was counting, or anything.*

Lights abruptly flashed to life on the arrivals-and-departures board: TRAIN INBOUND. It started a countdown.

At last. Shady eyed the five Class-As and moved closer to the gate so she'd go in first. They held back, apparently unwilling to contest this order of things.

The train slid into the terminal tube, nearly silent, and halted. Its hatches irised open, but no one emerged. Shady ignored the automated voice that warned her to "mind the gap" and leaped forward.

Halfway into the vestibule, however, a newly-familiar scent caught her by surprise. She halted, every fiber of her body alert. "Elle! Come here! Do you smell this?"

Elle pushed forward then halted. "Woah!" She met Shady's eyes, then sent a text to every officer in their party: "Zander Hoback entered this car about five hours ago."

CHAPTER 41
THREE GUYS ON A TRAIN

Three Guys on a Train

T he stationmaster grabbed a handrail to anchor himself. He gave Pam a pained, pleading expression. "It's been a really long night. Are you *sure*?"

Pam hooked a foot under a stability bar, crossed her arms, and gave him her best deadpan cop-face. "Scent factors do not lie, not even in microgravity. Neither do XK9s. Pull that car and the baggage unit into a siding and hold the crew. We need to take statements."

Time pressure thundered to the beat of her pulse, but her course was clear. *Dammit!* She'd already fired off notices to Elaine, Melynn, Chief Klein, and the Crime Scene Unit. Search warrants for the train cars and security vids should arrive shortly. Meanwhile, she could interview probable witnesses.

"The baggage unit? We'll have to unload—"

"You'll do no such thing. That's a potential crime scene."

He stared at her. "*Crime*—what the hell? People need their luggage!"

"Are all the bags properly tagged?"

He grimaced. "They're *supposed* to be."

"Then people will get their luggage. *After* we're done inspecting, and not a moment sooner."

The stationmaster glared at her. She glared back until he glanced away and sighed. "Yes, Officer."

"That's Detective Sergeant. No, don't turn away, yet. I also need the security vids, ASAP. And that record better be intact!"

"Yes, *Detective Sergeant*. Whatever the hell. Excuse me." He shifted his attention. "Yeah, we gotta pull it into the siding. Baggage, too. *Yes*. And the crew has to stay. Yes, I *know*. But the lady—" he glanced over his shoulder—"the *Detective Sergeant* says they need to give statements." He hesitated. "Of course, all of you. The *police* don't care who's waiting for you in Howardsboro!"

We can't afford to worry about inconveniences we cause. This is important! Pam bottled her anger and shoved it deep. Making a three-person crew who'd been working all night stay over for an indefinite time longer wasn't at the top of her list of "things to do for fun," either. But a hot lead on their prime suspect's recent movements wasn't something she could overlook. "We'll need three rooms where we can question them."

The stationmaster's face scrunched with frustration. He heaved a dramatic sigh, then went into a frowning HUD stare. "Um, nursing lounge, break room and . . . aw, hell, logistics booth, I guess. It's kinda tight, but it'll have to do."

An area plan popped up on Pam's HUD with the designated volumes marked. "We'll make it work. Thanks." She pulsed jets out of the stationmaster's office. Three scowling people crowded forward.

"I get fined if my babysitter has to wait for me!" one man yelled.

"My Significant's waiting to take me home. Mona's gonna be *that* mad if I make her late to work!" another cried.

"This screws up my on-time record!" The woman in the group clenched her fists by her sides. "This is *not fair!*"

"Then you'll cooperate fully, and we'll take as little of your time as possible." Pam beckoned to Balchu and Shady. "Leave the car and the baggage unit to Tux, Elle, and their partners. We need to interview these people."

She called the other two XK9 teams on a group com-call to explain. Elle and Misha sealed the passenger car and oversaw its move. Tux and Georgia did the same for the baggage unit.

A pair of workers wearing the high-visibility garb of the terminal's tech crew began the uncoupling process. A shuttle engine backed into position in a nearby siding tube. Before they finished, the search warrants arrived.

The Class-As and Hallie stayed well out of the way, but they watched the whole proceeding with evident interest.

Pam assigned the angry woman to Balchu. He could calm agitated people—especially women of about that age—better than anyone she knew, maybe including Charlie. Shady could take the man with the babysitter. Pam beckoned to the guy with the Significant. "Come with me, please. And understand that full cooperation takes less time than stonewalling us."

"Can I call Mona?" her interviewee asked.

"No. We prefer that you not speak with anyone till you've given your statement. The replacement crew will have to explain your delay." She led him to the logistics booth and made sure her wearable optics and audio rig were recording properly. Then she issued the requisite warning that the interview would be recorded but held in strict confidentiality. She introduced herself and asked him to give his name.

"Malik Jepson." He glared at her.

"Thank you, Mr. Jepson. "Did you notice anything unusual about the passengers who were in your car during the loop run that included the period from around 01:30 to approximately 02:30?" Shady, Elle, and Tux each had estimated that approximate time window in their preliminary evaluations.

He frowned. "We don't get a lot of passengers on graveyard unless it's a holiday. If you'd asked me about New Year's Eve,

well, that night the train was pretty full. Tonight, not so much."
He let out a long sigh. "Lemme think. At 01:30, we'd have been
here. Wheel Two. That was right before the end of our first loop
—we originate from Wheel Three. And if they stayed till 02:30, it
means they got off at Wheel Four."

Her HUD beeped, inaudible to her interviewee. A message
from Elle: "Hoback was with two other men. They occupied the
far side of the car from the platform, near the back. Entered and
exited where Shady first entered, even though it's supposed to
be entrance-only. Hoback's scent suggests he was ill or injured.
Petunia or Victor could probably tell you which, but they're not
here yet. And his companions have augmentations. I don't
recognize either scent profile."

Meanwhile, Jepson bit his lip. He stared upward and off to
one side with a little frown. "I'm tryin' to picture who was on it
then. There was a lady with a cat in a carrying case, and let me
tell you, that cat was *not* happy. It growled and yowled and—I
never knew those damn things could make that much racket.
Before we got to Wheel Three one of the big guys at the back of
the car got out of his sling, made his way forward, and told her
she'd better make it shut up or he would. I woulda told him to
can his threats, but she went down to the opposite end of the car
and tried to make it hush. Then she got off at Wheel Three."

"Tell me about the big guys at the back."

"That was a strange trio." He frowned. "They didn't hardly
talk at all. It was like the little guy in the middle was sick and the
two big guys were mad at him. I figure maybe he went on a
bender for New Year's and did something to piss off his pals."

"What made you think he was sick?"

"He hung there in his sling between the big guys kinda
curled in on himself, like his stomach hurt. I was half worried
he'd upchuck, and that's a real biohazard in micrograv. But he
didn't. Thank goodness! We'd'a been sidelined real quick if that
happened, and deep-cleanin' puke is the worst!"

"Did his companions seem worried about that, or about him?"

"No, they were real short with him. Like I said, I figured he'd done something that pissed them off but good."

"Can you describe them?"

Jepson's frown deepened. "The big guys were big. The middle guy was little."

How helpful. She kept her neutral cop-face in place. "What color was the little guy's hair?"

"I dunno. Brown? Yeah, kinda brown. Main thing to me, he looked sorta green around the gills, if you know what I mean."

"Gills?" Pam blinked at him and scrambled to think what kind of Galactic had gills but could breathe this atmosphere. "He wasn't a human?"

"Oh, sorry! No! That's just a stupid old expression. No, he was a human. Sorry. I meant he seemed sick to his stomach."

"Oh. Okay." *Whew!* "Thanks for clearing that up. Other than 'big,' was there anything else you can remember about the big guys? Any interesting tattoos, any unusual jewelry or facial hair? How about the guy who threatened the cat lady?"

"No tattoos, no jewelry at all." Jepson chewed on his upper lip and scowled.

Probably rules out Saoirse, then. The unease in her gut intensified. If these guys were augmented, they were probably from Transmondian Intelligence. *Was Hoback their accomplice? Or their captive?* She tried to shield her speculations from Shady through the link and focused on Jepson.

"Buzz-cut hair on botha them. The big guys." From Jepson's expression, he hadn't taken much of a liking to them. "Hard to say what color, but dark. Not blond, gray, or red, you know? Like ex-military types. Big muscles, like they lift weights in sub-levels alla time."

"Pale skin? Dark?"

"Paler than the little guy."

"Both of them?"

"Yeah. An' the guy that threatened the cat lady—he had real light-colored eyes. Kinda uncanny-lookin', you know?"

"Light gray or blue?"

"Yeah, something in that line."

"Let's talk more about the little guy. You said he has brown hair. How long was it? How about skin color? Eyes? Around what height?"

"His skin's about your color, maybe a little more sallow. His hair's kinda shaggy. Floppy-floaty, you know, like he hadn't had a haircut in a while. And kinda greasy. He stared at his stomach a lot, kept his head tucked, you know, and sorta hunched. Hard to say how tall, or anything about eye color except dark."

She asked more questions and circled back through his account several times, but it grew ever clearer that she'd tapped the extent of Jepson's memory. As far as he remembered, there'd only been those four humans and a loud cat in a carrying case during that part of the train's run. She forwarded her work contact info to him in case he remembered anything else, then sent him home to Mona.

❖ ❖ ❖ ❖ ❖ ❖ ❖ ❖

Orangeboro Safety Services Express to the Hub

Rex held still so Charlie could buckle him, in but he wanted to bark and run. Maybe he'd want to do flips once they hit microgravity. He could breathe! Not quite as easily and thoughtlessly as before, but better! Having Ari Pryce traveling in his party did ease his mind, but still. At this moment he felt ready to take on all the challenges Centerboro could throw at him.

He felt good. Much better than he had since the decompression event. *Despite* yesterday's drama. This was no doubt thanks to multiple nights' Healing Sleep, on top of his nanotech treatment. Dr. Sandler hadn't hesitated to clear him for travel.

Ari had taken a seat on Rex's right and strapped their med-bag in beside them.

Rex let his tongue hang long with pleasure. The elevator hadn't yet reached low gravity, where a tongue-loll would feel strange. He spoke aloud so all his companions could hear. "The last time I took this elevator to the Hub, I was headed for Howardsboro with Shiv, Berwyn, Cinnamon, and Dominic Wei."

"And we know how that turned out." Ari scowled.

"Here's hoping this trip sees way less bloodshed." Charlie took the fold-down seat between Rex and Hildie, and strapped himself in. He shot a quick glance at Rex. *Though it's anybody's guess what we'll find in Centerboro—or at the Hub, for that matter.*

Through the link, Rex sensed his partner's thoughts darting back to Shady's astonishing discovery on the train. He growled softly. *Save it for when we get there.*

Hard not to speculate. Charlie shook his head. *I know it's not good to leap ahead of the evidence.*

Scout and Victor should arrive at the Hub soon, if they're not already there. I'm particularly interested in what Victor finds. All the reports pointed to Zander Hoback having some kind of health issue. Was he ill or injured? Drugged? Discerning such things was Victor's specialty. *We'll have more reports once they've had a chance to analyze the scent evidence.* Neither spoke aloud, because their companions weren't privy to the case.

Agreed. Charlie turned to Hildie. Rex knew she often disliked it when the two partners used their link to speak privately, even if only for a minute or two. Charlie's scent-shift to a more concil-iatory blend confirmed he was thinking about that, too. He smiled at her. "The last time *I* took this elevator, I wore a much heavier arm shield. One of Mike's agents had to help me buckle in when we were in micrograv. I hope this arm shield is easier to manage."

"The last time *I* took an elevator to the Hub, I was going to work." Hildie sighed. "Back when I still had a job."

"You *might* still have one." Charlie quirked a brow at her.

"If I can stand to work with LaRock again?" She grimaced and looked away. A rueful, acidic prickle mingled with nose-itching low tones of dread in her scent factors.

Rex leaned forward to meet her gaze. "Do you genuinely want to go back if LaRock is there?" She didn't exactly smell eager to leap back into her old job.

"That's the problem. I don't."

"Can't say I blame you." Charlie placed his hand over hers. His new Amare ring sparkled under the strip of small, bright lights that circled the elevator car's ceiling. Rex had *mostly* forgiven them for making the decision to become Amares while he was asleep. After all, he and Shady had done the same exact thing to Charlie a few weeks earlier, while Charlie was in re-gen. Being on the receiving end wasn't nearly as much fun.

"You know I'll support whatever option you choose." Charlie leaned toward her, his face and scent dark with concern. "Gotta say I've been trying unsuccessfully to imagine what options you're considering. I figured you'd tell me when you're ready, but—any hints?"

"Yeah, we definitely need to talk." She eyed Ari.

"I can put in noise-cancelling earbuds while I listen to my novel." Ari smiled at her. "I'm just here to help if Rex has a problem. I don't want to pry."

She offered an apologetic smile. "Do you mind? With everything going on, we haven't had much time to talk."

Ari fished the earbuds out of a pocket, inserted them carefully, then nodded. "Alert me if you need me!" Their voice boomed louder, now. "Can't hear a thing but the narrator!" They leaned back in their seat, stretched out their legs, and closed their eyes.

"Okay, then." She glanced at Rex.

He snorted. "Do not expect me to do anything of that sort. I want to hear every word, and I intend to express my opinions. You may be Charlie's Amare now, but you are part of my Pack, not to mention part of my household. Your plans directly affect me."

"Fair enough." Her eyes darted sideways to focus again on Charlie. "He'd listen through the link anyway, wouldn't he?"

"Not a chance in Hell he wouldn't."

She laughed. "Anyway, Rex, you're right. This will concern you, too. I assume that any decision I make influences the whole household now, doesn't it?" She blinked as if startled, then bit her lip and glanced at Charlie. "Budgets are another thing I guess we'd better discuss."

"Let's talk about your options first."

A com-call interrupted. Rex blinked. *From Shady?* "This is Rex." He widened his link with Charlie.

"Are you cleared for the trip?"

"We are on our way up." He glanced at Charlie and Hildie. They returned curious looks.

"Pam just made it to the Wheel Four Hub Terminal with Balchu. They will be in Centerboro soon. Scout and Victor just arrived here."

"Good."

"Tux found some fairly faint explosive scents. But he could not find anything more than that in the baggage unit. When Crystal comes through, we shall need her to confirm or alert us to anything we missed."

"That seems reasonable." Rex nodded, although Shady wouldn't be able to see the gesture.

"Things are going well enough here, but Pam is going to need me in Centerboro. Melynn is on her way up, but she just departed. When you get here, I want to hand things over to you, if you are up for it."

"I shall take care of it." Rex wagged his tail.

"Thank you! I shall look forward to seeing you!" Shady rang off.

"Well, that's interesting." Charlie nodded to Rex, then reached over to tap Ari's arm.

They pulled out one earbud, elevated their eyebrows.

Charlie explained the new situation to Ari and Hildie.

Ari nodded. "Thanks." They replaced the earbud and closed their eyes again.

Rex checked the time then made eye contact with Hildie. "We still have a good 20 minutes. Please continue with the options you are considering."

CHAPTER 42
ECHOES OF OLD PAIN

Safety Services Express to the Hub

R ex waited, ears up. Judging from scent factors, his query about her options made Hildie uncomfortable, while Charlie shared his curiosity. Rex tried to push aside his impatience and wait as impassively as Ari, who sat on the far side of him, oblivious thanks to their earbuds.

Hildie grimaced, clenched the edge of the fold-down elevator seat, and drew in a deep breath. "I guess I'd better start with a visitor I had a few days ago." She told them about Captain Rodrigo's visit, and the offer of a lieutenant's position on the Graveyard Watch for Monteverde's ERT.

"Wow. A lieutenant." Charlie squeezed her hand. "You'd be great at it, you know."

"But—graveyard?" She frowned and turned away. "The differential for night work would be good, I suppose. It would be so strange to wear Monteverde colors."

"Well, you don't have to decide yet. Any other options?"

She bit her lip. "I don't think I'd like being a downside paramedic."

"It would be a criminal waste of your micrograv skills." Charlie frowned.

"Yeah." She shot him a shy glance. "That too, I guess. I was thinking how clumsy I'd feel."

"I suppose there might be some of that. Not that I'm having much luck imagining you as clumsy." He regarded her with a warm, admiring expression echoed in his scent factors.

Her scent factors, on the other hand, told Rex she wasn't being completely open yet. She'd been considering another option . . . at least one. He cocked his head at her. "Yes, yes. What else?"

She frowned at him. "What do you mean?"

"If you were speaking to Charlie, I should expect you to tell him to 'spill it.' What else are you considering?"

"Scent gave me away?" Now her scent suffused with jittery, acidic guilt.

Rex just stared at her.

Her gaze flinched away from him. Silence stretched, then she sighed. "Theresa thinks I should try again for medical school."

"Woah!" Charlie gave her a surprised eyebrows-up. "All through both times I've known you, this is the first time I ever remember you mentioning it. What do you mean, 'again'? Did you try once before?"

She nodded. Her scent went all muddy-prickly-rueful. "Right out of Upper Levels. I'd wanted to be a physician my whole childhood, so it seemed like the logical next step. If I could pass, I'd enter an accelerated program. I'd always aced my tests, especially during the final two years. Often, I barely needed to study."

"You underestimated how hard it would be?" Charlie quirked an eyebrow.

"Oh, yeah. Big-time." She scrubbed her face with both hands, then gave her head a vigorous shake. "I totally *bombed* it. It was really ugly."

Charlie opened his mouth to say something, but his smoky-musky scent factors signaled his uncertainty. *Should I push this?*

It needs further discussion. Rex stifled a growl. *I know how bad it can feel to normally get top marks, expect to do well on a test, and then blow it.* "So? You tried again, right?"

She shook her head but kept her face turned away. Sharp high-notes of embarrassment and sludgy shame filled her scent. "No. Once was enough."

Dr. Ordovich never would have let me avoid re-taking a test—but I never wanted to shrink from a challenge. He snapped his ears flat. "You did not even try?"

Now she scowled over her shoulder at him. "I blew it. I mean, I didn't even come close. I couldn't do the math, didn't—well, never mind. Clearly, I wasn't as smart as I thought!"

"Clearly, you were still a child." Now he growled aloud, focused on Hildie, and pushed past Charlie's rising consternation. "You reacted with childish emotions, not your intelligence."

Hildie seemed to shrink in on herself. Her scent filled with harsh, hot humiliation.

"Rex!" Charlie's anger surged through the link and filled his scent. "That is *enough.*"

All down his back and across his withers, his hackles prickled and rose. He clamped his ears to his skull and turned his glare on Charlie. "When someone makes a foolish choice—"

"Her choice is *hers.*" Charlie glared back. "When we come right down to it, *her* choice is the only one that matters. She has the right to decide however she likes."

Rex drew in a breath—but there would be no winning this argument. Charlie was defending his mate. Hildie had curled into a ball of misery and scrunched her eyes shut. Frustration tightened his chest. He snorted and turned away.

They rode on toward the Hub in silence.

❖ ❖　❖ ❖　❖ ❖　❖ ❖

Hildie turned in her seat, so she didn't have to face any of them—especially not Rex. But his words reverberated through her mind. *A child . . . childish emotions . . . a foolish choice . . . *. She scowled, heart pounding hard. *Foolish? What is wrong with that dog? Can't he see I blew it? I needed to find a new direction?*

She tried to hold onto that, but it slipped away like water through her fingers. She glanced at him. Hackles up and teeth half-bared, he and Charlie stared each other down. He appeared even more enormous than usual, and utterly terrifying, although her new Amare didn't seem the least bit fearful—just royally pissed off.

Yikes. She flinched away and averted her eyes, but the hurt redoubled. *What makes Rex so damned sure it was a foolish choice? The nerve of that dog! What does HE know about . . .* She halted the thought. Where *was* Rex coming from, on this?

She reviewed all she'd learned about him from Charlie. Rex's "creator" Dr. Ordovich had considered him to be the perfect dog. And seriously—Rex did seem to be pretty darn superlative. But what a set of expectations to meet! How much intense pressure had he felt to perform?

He'd probably—no, he'd *undoubtedly*—faced hard tests, too.

She took another surreptitious glance at the huge black XK9. *Had* there been hard tests for him? Or was he so superb he'd sailed through every one? It would be easy to assume so.

But would it be accurate? Charlie had told her Ordovich gave Rex frequent beatings throughout his puppyhood. That didn't sound as if he'd sailed through everything with ease.

What do I make of that? Am I really, truly the thin-skinned little diva it seems clear Rex thinks I am? Her hands clenched the arms of her seat. *Dammit!* She shouldn't feel this ashamed for making a decision she'd had every right to make!

Except.

Except her Family hadn't been happy with it either, back then. They didn't rag on her about it—well, not as much as they might have. But she could tell they were disappointed. Grandma

Hestia most of all. That had hurt even more than failing—but not enough to make her willing to go through that ordeal again.

She drew in a long, deep, cleansing breath, then blew it out all at once. Didn't help much. The leaden weight in her gut persisted, even as the gravity diminished.

❖ ❖ ❖ ❖ ❖ ❖ ❖ ❖

Throat tight with frustration and gut uneasy, Charlie clenched his teeth. He knew Rex in this mood. That dog might stop vocalizing his objections, but he wouldn't stop thinking they were justified.

What could Charlie say to Hildie, in any case? He'd defended her—and what he'd said was true. It was her decision. Problem was, he agreed with Rex. He'd thought he knew her well, but this didn't seem right. This didn't sound like his intrepid Medicine Goddess—not even a little. She'd always seemed so sure, so clear-eyed and strong.

Now her hands clenched the edge of her fold-down seat in a death-grip, her whole body hunched and tense. She'd turned her face away, so he could only guess at her expression. Not for the first time, he wished he could analyze scent factors, because he had no idea what she must be thinking or feeling right now— other than *really bad.*

Deeply unhappy. Humiliated. Fundamentally shaken. Rex met his gaze and lowered his hackles. *I have a sense that no one has ever reacted in quite such a forcefully negative way to her face. I did not mean to deepen her pain. As her reaction continues, I'm gaining a better sense of it. I think this is an old trauma that wounded her more profoundly than I first thought.*

Charlie nodded. *And there's a whole lot more to it than 'I took the test and flunked badly.'*

Definitely. Failing the test doesn't smell like the main thing she's reacting to.

It helps at least to know that. Charlie chewed on his upper lip and debated whether he should touch her.

She's all bound up in a ball of misery behind a wall of defensiveness. I am not sure how to guide you.

Charlie placed his fingers gently on her arm. She snatched it away, still avoiding his gaze. *Um, okay. I guess touching was the wrong move.*

Apparently. Rex let out a big sigh then stress-yawned. *Probably best to give her some space to work it out.*

Like I had much option, but yeah.

They lapsed into silence. The elevator car climbed. Gravity noticeably lessened.

Hildie's hands clenched and unclenched on the arms of her seat. He recognized the patterned breathing she used. A common one for stress-relief, it didn't appear to be helping much.

Rex gave a little growl and refocused. Soon Charlie could sense that he'd immersed himself in the report Shady had forwarded.

Yeah, best not to disturb him, either. He needs to get up to speed.

The familiar, unwelcome flutter of low-G anxiety gradually set in. The floaty-stomach nausea strengthened. His subliminal tremor deepened in synchrony—no matter how hard Charlie tried to think happier thoughts. Time for his own patterned breathing routine. He'd endured this transition into micrograv unusually often in recent weeks. Although his post-traumatic reactions had lessened somewhat on the recent trips, they still showed up each time.

He couldn't control this stubborn, unwelcome artifact of his near-death in the *Asalatu* disaster. He certainly hadn't figured out how to end the reactions altogether, but at least he no longer feared they would destroy him. They'd abate when he returned to one-G. Meanwhile—all through the next few hours until gravity returned on the descent to Centerboro—he'd simply have to endure them and stumble through as best he could.

He rubbed his face and let out a shaky sigh, then started a new breathing pattern.

Rex shifted position and rested his chin on Charlie's lap—well, actually, at this point, Rex's chin floated slightly above his lap. But solid love and concern came through the link. It steadied him.

Thank you.

Hildie's warm hand closed on his.

He met her gaze.

"I may be angry with your partner right now, but that doesn't change how much I love you." She nestled closer against him. "You shouldn't have to ride out stress reactions alone between feuding housemates."

"We can at least agree on that." Rex's tongue stroked Charlie's cheek. *You also probably should see Shady's full report. Maybe that will offer a distraction.* He forwarded it.

Maybe. Thanks. Charlie hoped both could understand how much their support helped. Even though his hands still shook.

CHAPTER 43
NEW CHALLENGES IN THE HUB

Wheel Two Topside Terminal

R ex jetted on ahead once Charlie'd helped him into his micrograv harness. He left his human partner with Hildie, Ari, and their luggage in a nearby public waiting area. Hildie was perfectly capable of handling things and helping Ari on her own, but Rex had a sense that his partner wanted to linger with her. Perhaps he meant to speak with her more, once Rex was out of earshot.

Good luck with that. He tried not to share the thought, then shifted his focus to what lay ahead of him. A long, cylindrical train passenger car and a shorter baggage-carrier unit awaited in a side tube behind a laser-defined perimeter. Uniformed Port Authority officers hovered at each end of the cordoned-off section of cars.

Shady emerged from behind the baggage unit and jetted over to him. They'd parted only a few hours ago, but they took a moment to greet each other in a joyous, simultaneous midair loop. Micrograv harnesses allowed a unique sort of greeting-dance and sniff-over that was too much fun to skip.

Shady broke off before Rex was ready. "I need to get downside to Pam. It is a relief to be able to hand this scene over. Melynn is probably twenty minutes out, but the sooner I get to Centerboro the better."

He fell in beside her, aligned to her attitude and vector. "I read the report you sent."

"Then you are mostly up-to-date. Victor, Scout, and their humans are still double-teaming in the passenger car. Crystal and Connie are reviewing Tux and Georgia's work in the baggage unit and consulting with their housemate Arden. Since she is on the STAT Team and also an explosives expert, I let her in."

"I would have done the same." A new item appeared on his HUD: a roster of all officers currently on the scene.

"CSU did a preliminary scan, but they'll go in for a more detailed review after the Pack is finished."

"Am I the last XK9 to arrive in the Hub?"

"Petunia and Walter are with the Lang Family delegation. They were delayed at Grand Central, but I am not sure why. I do not think they have left yet."

The signs near the main train tube started flashing.

"I must go." Shady glanced toward the signs.

"With no human? How will you get into your transit hammock? Should I send Hildie with you?"

"I feel certain Hildie would rather travel with Charlie. Besides, I am an autonomous Ranan citizen. I should be able to travel independently." Doubt lingered in her scent factors, but her determination overmatched it.

He knew better than to protest. Apparently she had a plan for dealing with the transit hammocks, although he couldn't imagine how. "Good luck with that."

The train glided to a smooth halt. The hatches irised open.

He checked to make sure the audio and optics on his rig were on.

She met his eyes. "The scene is now officially under your supervision, Pack Leader."

"I accept the scene's supervision, Assistant Pack Leader." His HUD blinked. The transfer had been logged.

She gave him one last nuzzle then jetted away. Several humans debarked at the far end. Shady swooped inside through one of the nearer hatches.

Rex paused to watch. After a while the hatches closed and the train pulled out. *Okay, then.* His autonomous Ranan citizen mate was on her way.

❖ ❖ ❖ ❖ ❖ ❖ ❖ ❖

Trans-Hub Loop Train from Wheel Two

Shady entered the train's passenger compartment on a burst of jets, then braked. *Oh. So that's what he meant by a transit-hammock.*

The words made a lot more sense now that she could see the net bags attached all around the cylindrical car's inner bulkhead at evenly-spaced intervals. Most were occupied. By humans who'd pulled themselves inside with . . . *uh-oh.*

With their hands. As in, those wonderful human appendages with the opposable thumbs that Dr. Ordovich had not seen fit to give to XK9s. Since the Station Polytechnic team of roboticists and prosthetics engineers had not yet worked out the bugs in their designs, XK9s still didn't have any thumbs.

Not yet, anyway. Dammit. Now she wished she'd looked just a *bit* farther inside before she caught that whiff of Zander Hoback in the vestibule of the first car she'd entered. Beyond the vestibule this morning, she actually had never been on any Trans-Hub train before.

That's why I asked you to wait till you could ride with Charlie, Hildie, and Ari. Pam's mental voice through the link emanated worry. *Can you get off again?*

The hatches all irised shut. The Trans-Hub train pulled away from the platform. The transit hammocks all tilted toward

Shady's end of the car. She drifted backward until she bumped against the end wall. *Um, no. I don't think so.*

Oh. Well, you ought to have an interesting ride. I'm sorry, but you're on your own. I can't physically get to you from here, and I really have a lot to do.

Focus on your work. I am an autonomous Ranan citizen. I should be able to figure it out.

But bumping gently against the back wall had already begun to irritate her. The car's momentum settled into a steady pace and carried her along inside. She fired jets to move to the open middle area around which the transit hammocks floated.

"Oh, my goodness! What are you doing there?" One of the car's attendants jetted toward her, then braked about a meter away. "How did you get in here?"

"I came in through that hatchway." Shady inclined her head toward it and fired jets to keep herself from going into a spin. She adjusted her position to align with the woman who'd confronted her.

"Where is your handler?"

Shady laid her ears back but kept her snarl sheathed. "My *partner* went on ahead of me to Centerboro two hours ago. I do not have a 'handler,' because I am an autonomous Ranan citizen in my own right."

"Oh. Oh, dear." The woman eyed her with a worried expression then glanced over her shoulder as if someone behind her might offer help. "How do you expect to ride in here?"

"As comfortably as any other passenger—would be my *preference.*" Her hackles prickled all along her back. "I believe it is your job to make sure that I do." The woman's uniform clearly marked her as a train attendant. Shady'd spent nearly an hour interviewing a man in a matching outfit already today.

"Oh, dear. Um." Now the woman was actually wringing her hands. She glanced backward again. No help seemed to be approaching from that direction.

"Let us think this through." Shady stress-yawned.

The attendant gave a little squeak and jetted backward. Then she continued to retreat in the direction she had come.

Crap. Wrong thing to do. Shady suppressed another yawn and followed her. "You can help me if you will just stop and listen."

"Don't hurt me!"

"I do not intend to hurt you." She continued her gradual progress toward the other end of the car in the woman's wake. "I am XK9 Shady Jacob-Belle. It is my job to protect people, not hurt them." *Unless they ask for it by, say, running away.* She stifled a growl. "Would you please stop and help me?"

"No! Don't hurt me!" The attendant jetted away.

Shady fired braking jets and halted near a large, empty transit hammock. "One-star review for you, I guess." She took a moment to smooth her hackles then glanced around. All the humans in the car stared back at her from their hammocks.

She flicked her ears and sniffed for a whiff of commiseration or empathy. Found several. *Okay, then. Plan B it is.* "Is there anyone here with an opposable thumb or two, who would care to help an XK9 into a transit hammock?"

"I could reach it from this side." A man in a warehouse company jumpsuit reached out to grab the large, empty hammock on one side. He nodded to a woman in a welder's outfit on the other side of it. "You there—yes, you. Could you grab the net so we can pull it open for her?"

"Oh . . . kay." The welder grabbed another part of the netting and pulled. "Like this?"

"Wait. I can get this side." Another man, this one in business attire, leaned out to pull it in a third direction. Between them they created a triangular opening.

"Thank you. That is perfect!" Shady pulsed jets to insert herself and pivot inside. She halted with her head protruding from the hammock. "Release it now?"

Her three benefactors let go. The hammock enveloped her. She cut her jets and came to rest inside. "Rana Stationers are the best people in the Universe. Thank you!"

"You're welcome. So, XK9 Shady. Where to?" Warehouse Guy grinned at her.

She wagged her tail, then fired jets to keep from swinging into Welding Woman. "Centerboro. How about you?"

❖❖ ❖❖ ❖❖ ❖❖

Wheel Two Topside Terminal

C harlie did his best to ignore the impending dread that clawed at his composure. He paused a moment to center himself as best he could, then took Hildie's hand. "It shouldn't be too long. Melynn is already on her way."

"We'll be just fine." She smiled and hooked herself to a stability anchor in the Wheel Two Departures waiting area. Because space was normally tight in the Hub, her anchor had been placed so close to Ari's that they practically brushed elbows.

Not that it seemed to bother Ari. They'd already settled in again with their novel.

"I can follow Ari's lead—I'm about halfway through the latest 'Dagmar' book. And I, um—I guess I have a few things to think about, if I can't stay focused on the novel." She gave his hand a gentle squeeze. To his disgust, he couldn't quite still the tremor in it. She frowned. "Are you okay?"

"If I can stay busy, it's better." He inclined his body to give her a kiss. "I'll keep you posted."

"Go. Distract yourself. I'm good."

"Always better than good. No matter what." He turned toward the lasered-off crime scene area, grateful that he'd once again been granted a micrograv harness, even though he still hadn't had a chance to renew his Class-B.

Rex had shared Shady's report with him, so he'd already gathered a sense of what he was heading into. Probably wouldn't need a GR of this scene, but a visual scan couldn't hurt.

Connie, Eduardo, and Nicole would cover scent-card work with their XK9s. Rex, as supervisor, most likely wouldn't need Charlie for that, but it was never a bad idea to be available. Just in case.

He badged his way past the Port Authority's perimeter and moved toward his sense of Rex's location.

"Hey, Charlie! I figured if Rex was here you must be, too." A CSU tech approached with a friendly smile . . . and a completely shaved head.

Charlie blinked. It took him a moment to recognize his oddly-transformed friend. "Russell?"

"Ha! Got you, didn't I?" That laugh, and the wide grin that came with it—*those* he recognized. Russell Tyjani had been a Tier One partner-candidate and one of Charlie's podmates in Solara City, back before Rex and the rest of the Pack Chose their partners.

"Wow. Yes, you did." Charlie shaded his eyes. "I think I might need eye protection, man! What's with the—?" He gestured toward Russell's head.

Russell's grin never faded. "Oh, a few things. My old lady and me, we split up after the Chayko trip. Then I made Head Tech, and I wanted to do something new. No worries about bonnets or hair nets if you don't have any hair, so it's faster suiting up."

"I guess it would be. I'm sorry to hear about your relationship, though." As he recalled, Russell had been kind of irritable when it came to talking about his "old lady," back in Solara City.

"Oh, don't be. That trip, the month apart—it finished a long process for us. It was time, you know?" He shook his head, still smiling. "So— you've had an eventful life, lately, from what I've heard on the news." He inclined his head toward the arm shield, then his gaze fixed on Charlie's left hand. "And you have an Amare, now, too? When did *that* happen?"

"Um, officially—last night."

"Wow. Congratulations!" But his smile quickly turned worried. "Did you have to leave her behind already?"

"No, we're headed for Centerboro together. Although it seems the XK9s who went over first have discovered an unexpected detour for us."

"Seems like a lot of XK9 teams are headed for Centerboro." His raised brows—he did still have eyebrows—made it clear that was a question. The OPD and SBI had focused on the embargo in their public statements and downplayed sending XK9s to Centerboro. They'd been more specific with Families and Borough officials about the troublesome Palmdale Club proposal, but Charlie knew Klein was trying to avoid the appearance of police directly lobbying the Combined Councils.

"A lot of us are traveling with representatives for our Families."

"I hear they sent Tux, Elle, and their partners over there earlier." Russell's brows pinched, speculation in his eyes. "And yet they were heading back again today?"

The cop grapevine strikes again. "That was for a different case. They came home for the New Year." Charlie hesitated—but Russell was OPD, and he'd gotten a better chance than most to learn firsthand that XK9s were no ordinary dogs. "On top of the embargo, the Transmondians have allies in the Combined Councils. They're spreading disinformation about XK9s, so our Families figured we should come along with them. That way, they can arrange to give Councilmembers a chance to meet some actual XK9s. They can decide for themselves if they think they're sapient."

"Good luck with that." Russell scowled. "We need to do something, that's for sure. My Family trades in robotic components, but suddenly, *somehow,* we can't get anything shipped in-system. Thank goodness we still have access to the jump point."

"You said it. Meanwhile, Orangeboro is standing firm so far. Returning the XK9s is not negotiable."

"Damn straight!" Russell's jaw jutted and his dark eyes sparked with anger. "Transmondians already call too many shots in this system. They think they can bully smaller sovereignties into doing whatever they want. Seems to me it's about time someone stood up to them!"

"Here's hoping. How's CSU doing with this crime scene?"

"Such as it is?" His face shifted to an expression of perplexity. "Seems like it wouldn't have been pegged as much of a scene at all without the scent evidence. We did some global laser-imaging from each passenger-car entrance and some through the far-side windows, but we're still waiting for the XK9s to finish before we really get in there."

Charlie nodded. "There's always the chance you'll find something helpful."

Russell's gaze shifted toward something behind Charlie's right shoulder. He heard the quiet hiss of maneuvering jets and turned to see Crystal, Connie, and their raven-haired housemate Arden on approach.

"I believe we are the last of the explosives specialists to examine the baggage unit?" Crystal cocked her head at Russell and Charlie.

Russell nodded. "Unless Rex wants to review it, yes."

"As I understand things, the only other Pack members still on their way up are Petunia and Walter," Charlie added. "I believe they need to double-check a scent Elle discovered in the passenger car."

"Here's what we found." Connie handed Russell an evidence bag full of individually-bagged, labeled scent cards and sealed touch-DNA tubules. Tamper-evident red-and-yellow evidence sealers secured each.

Hmm. Charlie eyed the full bag. *Either they found a tonne of good evidence, or it's all partials and iffy samples, so they took as many as possible for coverage.*

"There are forty-seven scent cards and nineteen touch-DNA tests," Crystal added. "We'll upload our reports shortly."

Russell noted this on his case pad. He, Connie, and Crystal formalized the chain of custody with a round of thumb- or nose-prints and retinal scans. "Anything else?" At the XK9 team's head-shakes, he grinned, nodded his "chrome dome" to them all, then jetted away to secure the new evidence.

Crystal nose-bumped Charlie's arm. "May I assume you are seeking Rex? He is surveying the passenger car."

"Without me?"

Crystal let her tongue slide out. "Scout, Nicole, Victor, and Eduardo are the ones working with scent cards."

"He is supposed to conserve his strength. Anything you can share about the baggage unit?"

The three housemates shared a frown. "We didn't find much explosive," Connie said.

"We wouldn't have found *any* without Cryssie." Arden reached out to stroke the white XK9's shoulder fur with a smile.

"The residue we did find seemed to be secondary transfer," Crystal added. "Picked up by accident on something—a sleeve or a glove, maybe, that brushed against residue. Then, whatever that was, it later brushed against several surfaces in here. Very faint trace is the result, but it was there. Also two scent profiles we do not recognize, although both are augmented."

"That should radically narrow the field of possibilities. Can we definitively compare them to the men who accompanied Hoback?" A deep, cold pit formed in Charlie's gut. *Augmented. Does that mean Transmondian Intelligence?* The last bruises from his encounter with an augmented TIS agent in Howardsboro had only recently faded. "Any idea what it all means?"

"Shady, Elle, and Tux confirmed that the explosives-handlers whose scent was in the baggage car are definitely the same men who rode with Hoback. But those augmentations are deeply concerning," Connie said.

"And what little explosives residue we did find is fresh." Crystal's ears snapped flat. *"This morning fresh."*

"It's likely the men handled the explosive materials early today and took precautions that were almost completely successful at removing all traces." Connie's worried blue eyes met his.

"Are any of the secondary traces consistent with Rory Fredericks' formula?" Charlie glanced in the direction Russell had gone.

"All of them." Crystal lifted her ears. "It is rarely that clear-cut, especially with such a terribly faint trace, but these? They all have characteristics that are consistent with the materials used to deconstruct the *Izgubil,* the *Ministo Lulak,* and Wisniewski's Dart."

Hairs rose on the back of Charlie's neck. "Can you draw any conclusions from that?"

"Again, too early. We need to compare notes with Tux and Georgia." A subtle shudder ran through Connie's slender frame. "But I have a feeling it means nothing good."

CHAPTER 44
A CRITICAL ANALYSIS

Safety Services Express to Centerboro

R ex stress-yawned. He yearned for a series of whole-body stretches, but the safety harness must stay on for another ten minutes. Charlie shouldn't remove it until the hyperbarically-equalizing Emergency Services Express elevator came to a halt inside Centerboro's Grand Central Terminal. *Will this trip ever end?*

All things eventually do. Charlie, strapped in beside him, reached over to give him a chest-rub. "All things considered," he added aloud, "I'm grateful for the Express."

"Got that right!" Hildie, strapped in on the other side of Charlie, gave him a worried glance. "How are you and Rex holding up?"

"We're getting closer to 1-G, so I'm happier." Charlie's tone mirrored the sludgy ruefulness in his scent. The anxiety component in his bouquet had diminished, but dusty-smoky notes of exhaustion continued to mount.

"A good thing, true." Her brows pinched. "But I meant how's your energy level? Any pain? And don't try to tell me you're not tired because I won't believe you." She leaned out as far as the harness allowed, to include Rex in her concerned gaze. "You, too, Rex. If it hadn't been floating in micrograv, I'd swear your tail was dragging."

Rex stress-yawned again. "I could use a nap." His energy and enthusiasm from the start of the trip had faded far too quickly. Such a relief to turn the Hub scene over to Melynn after his 20-minute stopgap coverage! Simply operating in micrograv was exhausting enough. But the implications of what they'd found there weighed him down even more.

Victor had determined that Zander Hoback almost certainly had received at least one beating—he'd found scents of residual blood and inflammation strongly suggesting that. But Hoback also was chemically restrained with a dose of a common muscle relaxant while on the train. Victor and Scout, as well as Shady, Elle, Tux, Crystal, and Rex himself all agreed that the men with him were augmented and had left scent-factor residues suggesting grim intent.

Transmondian Intelligence agents holding Hoback under duress? Hard to avoid that hypothesis. And they also had some of Rory Fredericks' signature explosives materials. His hackles prickled anew at this reflection. *The SBI is on top of that now. I'm glad to let them—*

His HUD dinged: Director Perri.

"This is Rex." His gut had only started to relax. All at once it tensed up again.

"You're ten minutes out, right?"

He checked the readout, heart sinking. "It just clicked over to nine."

"Excellent. I have one of Santiago's agents waiting to meet you. I want you to join us in a meeting at SBI HQ. We need a first-person report on what you've so far learned from the Hub Terminal scene."

"Roger that." His hackles prickled. "May I ask—"

"Santiago's agent will explain. Perri out."

"Change of plans?" Charlie gave him eyebrows-up. Hildie echoed the expression.

Rex nose-bumped Ari's arm. They looked up, then removed one of their earplugs.

"That was Director Perri." Rex explained the change of plans.

Charlie turned to Hildie with a concerned expression. "Do you want to go on to the hotel alone?"

"No, I'll wait. Ari will need to stay close, for Rex's sake. I plan to hang around and keep an eye on *you*."

Ari nodded their agreement.

"Whatever you'd prefer." Charlie gave her an apologetic grimace. "Rex and I need to discuss some details of the case that we can't share just yet. We'll need to speak through the link."

"Thank you for explaining." She stretched up to kiss him.

His hand lingered on her cheek. "I wish I could tell you more. Thanks." Then he shifted his focus to Rex. *Needing a first-person report implies there'll be a Q and A. Did she say who we're meeting?*

❖ ❖ ❖ ❖ ❖ ❖ ❖ ❖

Centerboro, SBI HQ, Director Perri's Meeting Room

Charlie paused by the meeting room door in Director Perri's executive suite, but Sara Cutler shook her head and gestured him forward. "I'm to wait out here. You and Rex are on your own." She stepped back, then retreated to sit with Ari and Hildie.

"Come in," Perri said through the com.

Charlie pushed the door open and held it for Rex. Exhausted he might be, but the big black XK9 strode into the room with ears up and neck arched, Pack Leader to his toenails.

"Welcome." Director Perri stood with a gesture toward the low, round platform that stood at the opposite end of the elliptical table. Mike Santiago occupied the chair to the left of the platform.

Through the link Charlie sensed Rex's instant animosity toward the man on Santiago's right, whom he recognized as Commodore Cornwell of SDF Military Intelligence. But the Pack Leader's outward body language appeared unchanged. He hopped up onto the platform and sat, his gaze focused on Perri.

Charlie placed his hand on the empty chair to Rex's right and gave Perri a questioning eyebrows-up. At her nod, he sat—then realized the man on *his* right was Assistant Attorney General Lamont Niam. *Interesting gathering.*

You think? Rex's focus on Perri didn't waver.

The SBI Director performed quick introductions. She identified both Rex and Charlie as Reserve Agents, but prefixed Rex's title with "Pack Leader." Two pairs of uniformed women occupied the chairs that flanked her. She identified the ones in the black Ranan Executive Security uniforms on her right as RES Chief Wilmott and Deputy Chief Reinhold. The other two, in the tan garb of the Centerboro PD, turned out to be Chief Nakoa and Counter-Terrorism Coordinator Hami.

"We've been reviewing the reports from the Hub terminal," Perri said. "Our guests from the RES and CPD have questions about the scent evidence." She inclined her head toward RES Chief Wilmott.

Wilmott frowned and focused on Charlie. "Exactly how much credence are we to place on 'secondary trace transfer' that exists in such a miniscule amount that our normal instruments won't even register it?"

"The scent is faint, but relatively fresh," Rex replied. "And it is complete enough that we can match it to the unique blend used to destroy the *Izgubil,* the *Ministo Lulak,* and Jackson Wisniewski's craft."

Wilmott's eyes widened when Rex spoke for himself. She stared at him. "So you say. Why should I believe you?"

Rex flicked his ears. "Decades of tested and cross-tested XK9 accuracy, verified by independent research. The fact that XK9-sourced scent evidence is admissible in every System court.

What further evidence do you require? I shall offer it, if it is physically possible."

"I'm frankly dubious about the broad assumptions you made, when drawn from such a small quantity."

"They are not assumptions." Rex snapped his ears flat, then lifted them again. "This is the unanimous, independent analysis of two other forensic olfaction specialists as well as myself. All of us are trained, tested, and certified in explosives detection."

"As you might recall, I have already pointed all of that out." Cornwell folded his arms and glared at her.

"As have I," Niam put in. "I also took some time to be convinced, but I've now seen enough to be confident of XK9 scentwork."

"You say our analysis includes 'broad assumptions,' but that is inaccurate in another way." Hackles rose across Rex's shoulders. "They are in no way 'broad.' The specific chemical compounds we detected in these samples are fully detailed in our report. We compared them, point-by-point, to the samples taken from the wreckage of those vessels. If you have read the report in any depth, you also will have noted the comparisons with other formulas used in commonly used explosives. Those comparisons give the basis for our analysis that the blend we detected matches the Fredericks formula."

"How can dogs be specialists?" Wilmott shook her head. "I find this whole assertion implausible."

Hami, the CPD Counter-Terrorism Coordinator, inclined her head, her expression grim. "That report was written by a specialist, no question. The comparisons are sound."

"Would *you* reconfigure *your* overall security assessment based on it, Etta?" Wilmott's lips flattened to a thin, dubious line.

"I'm afraid I'm going to have to." Etta Hami's expression didn't lighten. "We've already had more than our share of bomb scares around here lately. And those are just with devices using the more common gamut of explosives. Without instruments attuned to that unique formula, we'll inevitably miss things. And I can't afford to miss!"

"How much can *you* afford to miss, Ilma?" Cornwell, the spymaster, cocked an eyebrow at Wilmott.

"Fuck you, Rooq." She scowled at him then turned her glare back toward Rex. "Who *really* wrote that report?"

"Tuxedo Moondog-Carrie is the primary author of record for that section," Rex replied. "And I must say it definitely reads like Tux's work."

"The *dog* writes its reports in the style of peer-reviewed journal articles?" She gave him an incredulous stare. Charlie figured her scent factors must be off the chart in the disbelief range.

Rex lolled his tongue. "He is currently working on a series of journal articles with Dr. SCISCO 3750, so that seems likely."

Chief Wilmott's jaw dropped. "The cyberbeing professor? Are you joking? Can that even be true?"

"Really?" Coordinator Hami leaned forward, eyes alight. "Are these about the Fredericks formula? When are they coming out?"

"Etta! You can't possibly give credence to this!"

Hami scowled at her. "You haven't worked with XK9 Tuxedo. I have. He's really good. I was dubious at first, too, but now I'm convinced."

"Could we please stipulate at this point that we're mostly in agreement that we should take the explosives alert seriously, and move on the augmented scent profiles?" Cornwell asked. "I have some urgent questions about those."

I'll bet he does. Charlie bit his lip.

I did not expect him to back us up. Rex's suspicion of the man he called "Rana's chief spook" did not feel as if it had abated.

"I'm still not convinced." Wilmott traded glares with Cornwell.

"But will you *ever* be?" Cornwell asked her.

"I am," Hami said.

"I came here to vouch for the XK9s," AAG Niam said. "Nothing I've heard today changes my mind."

"I've seen too much to doubt." Charlie didn't imagine his voice counted for much in this crowd, but he'd be damned if he just sat there like a lump.

"Me, too," Santiago added.

"And I've sponsored this briefing to alert our sister agencies," Perri said, once it was clear neither Deputy Chief Reinhold nor CPD Chief Nakoa planned to weigh in. "You have your majority of attendees, Rooq. Let's move on, because we don't have time to waste. Ask your questions."

Cornwell turned to Rex. "What's your assessment of the unsubs who accompanied Hoback? TIS?"

Rex laid back his ears. Hackles rose all along his back. "I can think of no plausible alternative. Not Saoirse, because they have no tattoos, according to our witnesses. Moreover, I do not recall an instance in which Whisper has augmented its toughs. But the Transmondian Intelligence Service routinely does."

"And they now have your mass-murdering mastermind Zander Hoback? Alive, under duress, and in their custody?"

"That is our likeliest analysis of the scent evidence."

"And they also possess some of his signature explosives."

"That is our . . ." Rex's hackles had by now fully bristled out. "Yes. We are convinced that they do."

"So, then." Cornwell met Rex's gaze, challenging him. "They have their captive expert and they have some of his explosives. What are they planning to blow up?"

CHAPTER 45
OPENING MOVES

Centerboro, State Pavilion Hotel Board Room

P am took a moment simply to breathe, then keyed her com. "How's it going?" There was only so much she could directly monitor, perched on a large rolling chair in the Fourth Level Board Room of Centerboro's State Pavilion Hotel.

"Rex, Charlie, and Hildie just arrived, along with Ari." Balchu covered a position in the lobby to monitor arrivals. "The Corona group is getting the room above ours. More good news: the hotel's software patch to accept nose prints seems to be working now."

"This hotel has been very accommodating. The nose print update went faster than I expected." A small knot of stress released in Pam's gut. "And the room above ours was Shady's choice. For once, tonight, she won't be far away."

Her partner had arrived a few hours ago, after what she'd described as an "interesting" train transit, and immediately asked to be put to work. Pam had sent her to one of the smaller meeting rooms down the hall, where a volunteer corps of experienced professionals had set up an impromptu dog-grooming salon. Shady was helping coordinate and make calls from there.

Liz had worked with some of the Orangeboro groomers to coordinate that dog-grooming effort. Razor was forced by his health to stay home, but Berwyn had volunteered to stay behind. That way, he could assist as Razor's "spotter" during physical therapy and also stay close to his own XK9 partner Cinnamon. Liz would go back tonight, once she felt certain the groomers had it covered and she'd given a couple of interviews in the early evening.

Pam massaged her temples. She'd known this trip would be challenging, but she'd had little clue about how *incredibly much* detail must be covered. She'd thought with Families taking the lead on Council Member contacts she'd have somewhat less to do. But now she must coordinate between at least eight Family leaders as well as her XK9s' schedules.

She had primary contacts already in Centerboro for Corona, Glorioso, Pabiyan, and Lang—all of whom she'd expected. Their representatives had been party to the second, broader com-conference meeting on New Year's Eve. But Vuzvishen's Apodeddi Mamoor also had arrived this morning to represent his Family. *That was a fun reunion to watch. Georgia was both astonished and delighted.*

Tux is excited to talk with him some more, Shady replied from the grooming room. *They've had little chance to talk in any detail yet, but he and Georgie plan to meet her grandfather for lunch.*

That may be their best chance for an uninterrupted talk anytime soon. The schedule is filling up, and the explosives experts are in considerable demand for consultations with law enforcement, too. The implications of their discoveries this morning left a persistent heavy coldness in her gut. *The TIS didn't drag Hoback and his explosives to Centerboro for nothing. What do they plan to blow up here? Do they only have a little material, or was it a lot, and just well-packaged?*

Well-packaged, for sure, Shady replied. *None of our experts has a sense of how much they've acquired. Tux thinks there's got to be a connection with the dummy bombs he and Elle found.*

A new chill shuddered through Pam's gut. *Those bombs were all over Centerboro. If they're connected . . . does that mean they're going to attack us everywhere? Or were the dummy bombs just misdirection?*

Oh, it seems rather clear they were meant for misdirection. Through the link she received a sense of Shady's hackles prickling. *But if the Transmondians were truly behind those dummy bombs, how can we convince the RES? They seem dead-set that the Whisper Syndicate is to blame for them.*

Well, for one thing, Iskander won't want to hear of any other hypothesis. Pam scowled. *It was the Premier's fault this Palmdale group even got a toehold. She thinks good relations with the Transmondians are good for trade, and nothing else matters.*

Good for trade, right up till they can just take over all the way? Shady's growl carried enough resonance, she might not have kept it in the link. *Of course, I'm predisposed the other way. I am quite willing to suspect the Transmondians of anything, no matter how bad.*

And neither viewpoint is objective enough to do a clear-headed analysis. Nor is any of it getting my work done! She turned back to her scheduling problems. She hadn't expected that any other Families' representatives would be interested, but already several had contacted her.

Mike and Elaine's Providence-Brightstar Family was sending their Head of Household Salvador Santiago, who was —if she'd gotten that right—Mike's father, along with Dawn Adeyeme, Elaine's mother, and Mike's younger brother Rafe. They were supposed to arrive in about an hour, but thank goodness she could leave that coordination effort to Mike and Elaine.

She'd already met Chief Klein's formidable aunt-in-law Kianga Odigo, Head of Amadi Family. But the most astonishing contact for Pam was the message from Chase that he and Anya would arrive later this afternoon on behalf of Becenti.

All the complexities made her head spin. What a relief to

have both Shady and Balchu covering their ends of the operation! *What would I have done without them?*

"I think we have five more incoming parties, then we're all here for today's batch," Balchu reported from the Lobby.

Five more, and it's already afternoon. How are we going to do it all?

"One last XK9 team inbound and almost here," Balchu added. "Apparently one of the Lang Family group had a medical emergency at Grand Central Station. Walter's great-aunt. She's now at Orangeboro Med and stabilized. Pretty good prognosis at this point, but she gave everyone a scare. The rest of the group, including Walter and Petunia, should arrive within the next hour."

No one in the Pack had given any interviews yet. She'd heard that Corona Family's Hannah Chahine and Pabiyan Family's Aurelia Glenn—who she'd learned was Berwyn's mother— already were coordinating directly with Sacha Guzmán's secretary Vincent Bellini. *Fine with me. That makes them Bellini's scheduling headache.*

Pam had helped set up half a dozen interviews for late afternoon, mostly for Shady, Victor, and Elle. Those were all with members of the Capitol Press Corps and a few legislative aides, based on Vincent's guidance. No interviews with actual members of the Legislature, yet: most of them wouldn't arrive in town till tomorrow. She ran her hand over her face and stared at her screens. *Yeesh. This is all so sudden and rushed.*

Well, yeah. Pam had a sense of Shady's lip curling and a prickle of rising hackles. *Everything's been thrown into a stew by the embargo and the Commonwealth Party's intransigence. And our little discovery at the Hub didn't exactly help us get a jump on the scheduling.*

Got that right. The Legislature normally didn't meet this soon after the New Year holiday. But Legislature leadership had decided they needed this special session to deal with the fast-metastasizing trade crisis. If Pam had hackles, hers probably would be up and prickling right along with Shady's.

The embargo targeted a small sector. But, as everyone had predicted, over the course of the past few days, it had progressively snarled more and more shipments of *anything* that moved between Rana Station and Transmondia's several dozen spaceports.

The Transmondians had declared they must "take steps to insure that no contraband would be smuggled in." As a result, nearly all Ranan businesses, from manufacturing to the tourist trade, had been impacted. It was a well-practiced scenario in the Transmondian playbook of unfair trade practices. *Can't really blame the Ranan Commercial Council for demanding a Special Session.*

Just as the Transmondians wanted. More prickling hackles and irritation emanated through the link. *And for all the wrong reasons.*

That's why we're here. Pam stared at the screens of schedules she'd pulled up on the boardroom table. They'd grown too big and complex for her to juggle them all on her HUD. She'd reached the point where she now needed three screens, just to keep her headache at arm's length. *I don't think they'll get the Orangeboro Council to rescind its recognition. So that's something.*

And it's not as if rescinding the Council's recognition now would stop the Observation Commission. I think that ship has already left port and landed here. Literally.

And thank goodness for it! Pam tried a few chair stretches. They didn't help. Monday's whiplash injury had left her vulnerable to pain in her head, neck, and upper back. She had a few pain patches left but hesitated to risk the drowsiness that came with the relief.

Ordovich's program isn't large, as government programs go, Shady mused through the link. *But it's been a pet project—no pun intended, because we are NOT pets—of several prominent government officials. Including military leaders.*

And the Transmondian Intelligence Service. Can't forget the TIS.

Pam stepped away from the screens. She stretched her arms high above her head and rubbed her neck.

Oh, believe me. I'm not about to forget the TIS. Especially not after what we found on the train.

We've already had this conversation, unless you have something new to add. She walked out the to the atrium-side balcony that also served as a hallway. It overlooked the hotel's open central area. From the fourth level above ground, Pam had a sweeping overview of the lower-level walkways.

Nothing new, no. Just worries. I know Rex wanted to give us an up-to-the-minute debrief for all Pack members before tonight's press conference. If Perri ever gets done with him, that is.

Pam nodded, even though Shady couldn't see her. *I really want to know more, including anything CSU found after we left.*

"News feeds are saying five more Transmondian destroyers arrived at the edge of the international boundary this morning," Balchu reported on the com. "They're as close to the Jump Point as possible without crossing the line."

Pam rubbed her temples, but her headache throbbed all the harder. The Transmondians had been bringing in one or two warships every day or so since the embargo began. "How many are we up to, at this point?"

"I don't know." Balchu sounded about as unhappy about this as she felt. They shared a moment of discouraged silence. Then Balchu caught his breath. "Ah! In other news, Rex and his party just headed upstairs."

Did you catch that? Pam asked through the link. *Rex is going to his room.*

Is he still in the lobby? On my way down!

Soon enough, she spotted movement on the far side of the atrium. Rex, Charlie, and Hildie reached the elevators. No surprise the guy with the augmentations and the good pair of lungs had wrangled most of the luggage, even if he was still wearing an arm shield. The elevator doors opened. They stepped in. Shortly after that, she spotted them on the Level Three walkway along the open atrium. Shady met them there, tail fanning with a delight that also surged through the link.

They walked to the room above the one on Second where she and Balchu had already dumped their luggage. Hildie palmed the door and pushed it open. She stepped inside, rolled her suitcase out of the way, then held the door for Rex, Charlie, and Shady.

Pam watched them and smiled. It was a promising sign that Rex didn't need a cannula and oxygen feed, despite his exertions in the Hub. The door closed behind the three new arrivals from Corona Tower.

How much longer does Charlie have to wear that arm shield? Pam asked.

He can start taking it off for short periods next week, if Dr. Zuni gives the okay.

She nodded. *I bet that'll be a relief.*

Shady's focus had already shifted away from Charlie.

Give them all my best wishes. Pam turned back to her scheduling screens with a sigh. She stood and stared at them for a while, but she'd about hit the end of her resources. Mindful of her partner's preoccupation with Rex, she settled for muttering to herself. "Sure would help if I knew some of the people we're meeting. Maybe then I'd have a better idea of who to send where." She scrubbed her face.

Her com rang: no ID. Maybe another one of Guzmán's aides? Several of them had called today, in addition to Vincent. "Sergeant Gómez." Still felt strange to answer that way, but at least she'd stopped stumbling on "Sergeant" after about the fifty-eighth time.

"Hello, Sergeant. My sibling Dr. SCISCO 3750 asked me to contact you and offer you my help. My name is QUAERO 3426."

Pam's mouth dropped open. She'd forgotten there were other Farricainan cyberbeings on Rana. Now her reeling brain recalled there actually were seven others besides SCISCO, including two who'd located their source nodes here in Centerboro. She groped for her chair. "Um, hello. I'm honored to greet you, and I really want to thank you for calling. What—what sort of help did you plan to offer?" Her cop-brain immediately leaped to another question: *What do you want?*

"I know literally everyone in Centerboro, right down to the minor-but-important details." QUAERO spoke in a light, offhand tone, but Pam's breath caught at the implications of that statement from being with capabilities that likely paralleled SCISCO's. "I'd be happy to advise you in regard to your question, if you wish. I presume that might be helpful?"

"My, um, my question?" Pam frowned, but a shiver of anticipation gave her the answer before QUAERO did.

"It's true you didn't state it as a question, but more as a wish. You said you'd like to know some of these people. As it happens, I know all of them."

❖ ❖ ❖ ❖ ❖ ❖ ❖ ❖

State Pavilion Hotel Public Areas

Hildie closed the hotel room door quietly and stepped out onto the walkway that overlooked the atrium. Rex had fallen asleep almost the moment the door closed behind Shady a while ago. Since then Charlie had dozed off three or four times, then startled awake, while trying to review his schedule.

"Give it up, already, Morgan! Rest!" she'd admonished him. "You and Rex both need to dazzle them tonight at the press conference. I'll step out for a while. Please—take a nap! Let me know when you're awake again."

"What will you do?"

"Explore. See if I can help out somewhere. Stay out of here so it's quiet and you can *sleep*." Her mission thus outlined, she'd stopped to brush her hair and tie it up again before leaving. Charlie had already joined Rex in slumberland before she made it outside.

She smiled and stepped over to the railing. The atrium soared many stories above her, topped with an oval skylight that echoed the building's shape. Down on Ground Level a tree grew at each end and shaded those areas. But in the central part directly below her, bright light from above illuminated everything.

Both people and objects were far enough away to seem like dolls and doll furniture. She easily identified the reception area, plus other spaces that appeared to be a restaurant, perhaps a lounge-type area, and over there by the left-hand tree—was that a teahouse setup? *Hmm. Interesting.*

She probably should volunteer to help Pam or the Pack . . . but how? With what? The trip here had left her feeling tired, too, and thoroughly depressed. She didn't want a nap but didn't feel particularly energetic for volunteering. *What I really need is a little "alone time" to sort out my thoughts.* Certainly no alcohol would be a good idea in this mood, but maybe a soothing cup of tea?

She took the nearest stairs, both for the exercise and for a better chance to view more of the action at ground level while she walked down.

"The Arts of Tea," proclaimed a sign by a line of tall green bamboo stalks that leafed out more fully above her head. She walked in, and the echoing activity of the wider area muted. *Huh. Must be the effect of the bamboo. That bodes well.* A half-dozen small alcoves invited entry, but few people stirred inside the teahouse.

A willowy young woman with blonde and fuschia hair in long braids and a pink kimono-style jacket greeted her. "Welcome. Do you have a preferred tradition?"

"I—" Hildie blinked. "I just came here for a quiet cup of something herbal and a little solitude."

The pink woman smiled. "Long trip?"

"Wheel Two, with a sidecar of drama."

Blonde and fuschia braids shifted in echo of her nod. "I've got you covered. Care for a scone?"

"I shouldn't . . ." But it had been a long time since she'd had a scone.

"After that trip, you've probably *earned* a scone. Come." She guided the way to an empty alcove filled with comfy chairs, plants, and small tables. A water feature burbled down one wall. The pink woman pulled a screen up from the tabletop and pointed to suggestions.

Hildie relaxed into the cushions and let out a long breath, once Pink Woman departed with her order. She closed her eyes and visualized the tension draining out of her body, a little more fully with each breath. Steadied after a while, she opened her eyes and discovered her tea, a little timer, and a small blueberry scone on the table beside her. She chuckled. *Points to Pink Woman. She read the room.*

That scone did tempt her. She took a tentative nibble. *Oh, nice.* The timer gave a quiet chime. Hildie lifted the infuser from her cup and set it in the shallow bowl that Pink Woman had provided for it.

Sip, nibble, sip, nibble . . . Her headache receded. All the yammering worries did, too. *Rex and I will work out our differences. I don't have to decide about med school right now. By the end of January I'll have a ruling—it won't actually be forever.* She savored the moment, eyes closed.

"That smile on your face says you're thinking sexy thoughts," a gravelly male voice said, from far too close by.

Hildie gasped, startled out of her reverie. Hot tea splashed her hand. She stared up at a man who leered at her from less than a meter's distance. *Damn it! I let my guard down!*

At least ten years older than Hildie and a good ten centimeters taller, the man wore expensive business attire and smelled faintly of whiskey.

She glared at him. "Your psychic powers are for shit. Go away!"

He thrust out a fleshy lower lip in an unattractive pout and leaned forward to loom over her. "Oh, don't be like that, pretty lady. I'm just offering pleasantries."

Like hell you are. He'd neatly trapped her between the table, the comfy chair, and a large potted plant that blocked her on the right. Should she shove the table at him? Chuck the last of her tea at his head? Self-defense moves flashed through her mind: *Instep! Groin! Nose!*

A low, guttural growl from a clearly-nonhuman throat froze both of them. "You will step away from my Packmate. Right. Now." The order rapped out in a somewhat-tinny, monotone female voice.

Fleshy-Lips broke to Hildie's left with a strangled cry. He whirled to face the new arrival, then staggered backward. Bumped into a nearby chair and clung to it, eyes huge.

Like all of the Pack, this golden dog was massive—especially now, all spiky with her hackles up. Her snarl tracked Fleshy-Lips' movements, and those teeth looked effing *enormous.*

"You heard what my Packmate said to you," Petunia told him. "Go away!"

Fleshy-Lips bolted, frantic.

Hildie and her XK9 defender watched him go, then Petunia swung her big, broad head back toward Hildie. Her ears went up and her hackles smoothed. "Are you all right?"

"Yes. Thank you." Hildie let out a shaky breath. "It's been a while since I practiced my self-defense moves. I appreciate the intervention."

Petunia let her tongue loll. "That actually was fun. And a great stress-reliever. I have been itching to growl at someone—someone who deserved it, that is—for most of the day. We spent more than two hours at the hospital. Then we had all that time traveling from Orangeboro, being stared at the whole way. And we all had to match our pace to that of Walter's Granny Ifiok."

"Oh, my. Well, I'm kinda sorry to offer an opportunity, and I was definitely sorry to hear about Walter's great-auntie. But I'm grateful you stepped in. How did you happen to be here?"

The shaggy blonde tail waved high, but skillfully missed hitting anything. "Granny Ifiok must have her tea."

CHAPTER 46
STEPPING OUT AND SPEAKING UP

State Pavilion Hotel Ballroom A

This isn't so bad. With Charlie at his side, Rex paused by the steps to the dais the hotel staff had erected in Ballroom A. He surveyed the assembled crowd. He'd spoken from a stage to an audience of humans once before. It had worked out okay. He could do it again.

Charlie's warm confidence radiated through the link. *So, I don't have to be your emotional-support human this time?*

Rex glanced over and slightly up to glimpse his partner's grin, but he'd known it would be there. *I don't need the support as direly this time, but I'm glad you're there.*

The last time he'd held a press conference—a month or so ago in Orangeboro—Rex had been beyond nervous, but Charlie's sturdy confidence and strength steadied him. He later realized that keeping him strong and steady had utterly exhausted Charlie, who'd only recently emerged from re-gen at the time. But his partner had come through for him—and not for the last time since then.

"Okay, go!" Joslyn Stark's familiar, com-linked voice spoke in his ear. Chief Klein's Press Liaison was another trusted ally. Her presence here also helped him relax some.

"Esteemed guests, please welcome Pack Leader Rex Dieter-Nell!" Chief Klein's voice boomed in the speakers.

Rex leaped up to the dais, paused for an instant to center himself, then strode to the middle of the stage area. A spotlight flooded him with brightness, dazzled his eyes. His head spun until his breath came back but the seating chart on his HUD stayed visible. He slightly widened his four-square stance for stability and waited, tail waving, for the applause to subside.

"Good evening, and thank you for coming. My Pack and I welcome this opportunity to talk with you and answer your questions." Scent factors welled up to him from his audience: bright surprise, warm pleasure, and sparkling excitement, yes. But also sludgy doubt, sharp suspicion, and the reek of skepticism. He recognized some of the personal scent bouquets from last time, but not all.

"We have come here to support our Families' advocacy for us. They have brought us to Centerboro in response to a proposed resolution which the Combined Councils are set to consider during the upcoming Special Session. Reference CCSR 6, for the text of the proposal." It had officially been filed today, so they could talk about it *at last*. Joslyn had set things up so she could distribute the proposal's text to each attendee on this cue.

Gasps and murmurs echoed through the room from beyond the spotlight's glare. Scents roiled with redoubled surprise. In some profiles it mixed with an odd, worrisome edge of chilly fear. Swarms of tiny cameras hovered and buzzed. Their miniature lenses glittered with reflected light from the follow-spot.

"This proposal directly threatens the Pack's safety and survival." Rex had regained enough of his vision and bearings to make out the marks on the dais that Joslyn had promised would be there. "Our Families and we are deeply worried about any plan that would send us back to Transmondia."

He stepped forward to the downstage-center mark directly in

front of him and paused, ears up. If only he could see better, to make more direct eye-contact! He let his gaze sweep what he could see of the room and focused on scents he recognized from last time. He offered a small nod to each one that smelled even slightly sympathetic.

"The proposal would suspend all declarations of XK9 sapience until the conclusion of the Observation Commission's evaluation—whenever that may be." It took little effort to let his hackles rise on that line. "And in the meantime, it requires full cooperation with the Transmondians."

He snapped his ears flat and shuddered. "We know all too well what that means. Full cooperation with the Transmondians would force us to return to Solara City against our will. There, our former enslavers from the XK9 Project might compel us to undergo brain surgeries that are not medically necessary. That was the original plan, at least allegedly. But it seems equally likely, based on the recent fates of several other Generation 48 XK9s, that they might simply kill us."

More concerned or openly upset murmurs spread through the crowd.

He lowered his head, hackles still up, ears still back, and paced to the downstage-right mark. "Either way, we would be placed at the mercy of humans who have never in our lives shown us mercy." He paced to the downstage left mark. "They would show us even less regard this time, because it has become clear they seek to destroy all evidence of XK9 sapience."

He returned to the downstage-center mark. "Understand that our Families have pledged to do all in their power to keep us on Rana. They already have lawsuits ready to file, as a first step. Nor would we XK9s go willingly, although enough determined humans could physically compel us. We are lifelong witnesses to the fact that the XK9 Project is extremely adept at deploying stun-bolts, prods, nets, whips, and cages."

Revulsion filled many of his viewers' scents. Not all, but he'd expected that. He moved back to downstage right. "Moreover, they and their Transmondian Intelligence Service allies have shown they will not hesitate to use deadly neurotoxin darts. Indeed, they already have used them against us here. On Rana Station."

Hot, startled scent factors rose to him from several parts of the audience. *Good. Joslyn predicted that would spark some outrage.*

It certainly sparks outrage in me. Charlie quickly clamped his end of the link tighter.

Rex kept his focus. "They injured our Packmate XK9 Razor Liam-Blanca so gravely with one of those darts that he is still in rehab. He could not join us on this trip. We fear he may never fully regain all of his capabilities." That wasn't an exaggeration, dammit. Dr. Sandler had stopped talking about a complete recovery lately and shifted to accommodations.

He moved back to downstage right, closer to Charlie. "Another Transmondian agent fired a dart armed with that same neurotoxin at my partner, OPD Detective and SBI Reserve Agent Charles Morgan. I am intensely grateful to say that the agent missed." He nodded toward his partner.

Charlie, resplendent in his dress-blues and Medal of Valor, walked up the steps and stopped at the stage right mark on the dais. Another spotlight illuminated him, still in his arm shield. He nodded to Rex and took up a parade rest stance.

"Our Families and our other allies will fight any and all efforts to send us back to Transmondia. We XK9s of the Pack will resist with every last erg of strength. I have been assured that no human officer of the Orangeboro Police Department would support such a forced removal. Nor would any agent of the Station Bureau of Investigation. Both of those agencies have declared their firm belief in our sapience. They have pledged to defend us, even if it requires disobedience to a Station-level official's order."

He paused to let that sink in and returned to downstage center. "We hope the Ranan people would refuse to accept any effort to override a Borough's constitutional authority. We

Ranans know it is unconstitutional to rescind a recognition of citizenship that a Borough Council has officially made to acknowledge and protect a minority population." Scent factors told him that point had stirred the response he'd hoped. Few in this crowd failed to understand the implications.

He pointed his nose at a cluster of scent factors that emanated from people who were reacting as he wanted. "We hope our fellow Ranans would not support any action as extreme as combat against our law enforcement agencies. We fear that either action might trigger a cascade of extremely unwelcome outcomes. Not only for the Pack, but also for our entire Station."

He once again swept the ballroom with his gaze and briefly paused at each sympathetic scent. "We have come here to urge the Combined Councils to reject this proposal. We are willing to talk with anyone who wishes to question the idea that we are sapient. Meet with us. Let us answer your questions. Or speak with our beloved human partners and the Families who know us best. They have brought us here to offer testimony, and to support their petition to kill this proposal. We are here to give whatever evidence you require."

The room lightened and the spotlight on Rex dimmed enough to allow him a better view.

Shady mounted the dais from the stage left side. Pam climbed the stairs behind her, all shiny with her sergeant's insignia and a loop of braided aiguillette from her left shoulder epaulette. Shady took her place beside Rex. Charlie and Pam crossed to stand behind their respective XK9s.

Tux, Elle, and Scout bounded onto the stage right side of the dais, while Victor, Crystal, and Petunia leaped onto the stage left side. Their partners followed up the steps, solemn in their dress blues. The Pack, dogs and humans, formed two ranks to face their audience. Chief Klein announced their names as each took their place. He stepped onto the dais last and strode over to take a position between Rex and Shady.

"Now," Joslyn cued Rex.

Rex's tail was already wagging. "The Pack owes particular thanks to Chief Kwame Odigo Klein of the Orangeboro Police Department. When he realized our true nature, he made the courageous decision to refuse to be our owner. Instead, he has become our honored commanding officer."

A new round of applause followed this announcement. Were these journalists as clear-eyed and courageous as the Chief? *Time to find out.* "We will now open the floor for your questions. We are prepared to answer them here in this formal setting, or more informally in smaller groups. We have access to both this and the adjoining ballroom space for the evening, if you wish to speak with us individually. We also have aides standing by to create a request list for one-on-one interviews."

Several dozen hands rose immediately, with cries of "Pack Leader!" "Here!" "Rex!" "Pick me!"

Rex chose a man on the front row. His HUD chart said he was Robert Walters, a well-regarded veteran correspondent from a respected agency. His nose told him the man had been in Orangeboro for the other press conference and was inclined to favor the XK9s' cause. "Yes, Robert?"

A smile tugged at the man's mouth, but he didn't let it take over. *Striving to stay neutral.* "How did you learn of this proposed resolution?"

Rex let his tongue loll. "It is a matter of public record when a resolution proposal is advanced. But the Pack and our Families also have numerous allies. The initial heads-up came from one of them."

"That 'ally' wouldn't have been Vice Premier Guzmán, would it?"

"Not in this case, no. However, Vice Premier Guzmán and his staff have been quite helpful. He is, after all, an Orangeboro native, and he is protective of Boroughs' rights."

"And also a good friend of your Chief's."

"We are most grateful to the Vice Premier." Rex cocked his head. "Did you have another question?"

More urgent hands waved at him. More people called out, "Pack Leader!" or "Rex!"

He focused on a woman two rows back. "Helen?"

"What makes you say the XK9 Project might subject you to brain surgery?"

"That is the supposed reason why they issued their 'product recall' several weeks ago—the one Orangeboro refused to comply with. The Project said that a chip in our brain links had gone bad. It needed to be removed and replaced, they told us, or it would kill us."

He glanced at his Packmates, who stood with ears up and eyes bright. "If their horrific predictions had played out, by this time some of us should be dead. We had reason to suspect from the beginning that it was a false ploy, but it troubled us. Therefore, we obtained a warrant to have our chips examined locally by a top-level expert in cybernetics whom we trusted to be fair. Dr. David Santos of Station Polytechnic University performed the scans and found the chips to be in perfect working order."

"Why do you believe the Project wants to kill or injure you?" Edie-Rachelle Morrow asked from another part of the front row. She worked for a different news organization than Robert but had similar standing.

"Because they already have done so." Rex's hackles had smoothed when he spoke of Dr. Dave, but now they rose again. "They killed perfectly well-functioning, adult, *trained* XK9s who were working at an agency in Oroplania. I believe you were present last time in Orangeboro, when we howled an elegy for them." The Pack had received several startling offers of recording contracts after that.

Morrow nodded. "I remember it well."

"I would be astonished to learn that they have not killed or attempted to kill other XK9s within their reach. I fear most for the XK9s they still claim to 'own,' including the helpless dams and puppies at their puppy-farm facilities."

She and others stared at him, eyes wide and scents roiling with revulsion. Several people exclaimed with revulsion or dismay.

"Are you saying the Project would kill *puppies*?" a man on the second row asked. Byron Thornton, according to the HUD chart. He, too, had been at the press conference in Orangeboro.

Rex snorted. "Killing puppies is nothing to them, Byron." His lips curled in a snarl. "They do it routinely, starting with a culling at birth in the presence of the puppies' mothers. I doubt any adult XK9 anywhere has not survived a culling event. They probably also have witnessed at least one execution of a puppy in training."

"How many have you personally witnessed?" Thornton's face and scent broadcast both horror and fascination.

"Three early puppy cullings and five executions." Rex shuddered again and glanced down before his gaze returned to the journalist. "Dr. Ordovich, Dr. Imre, or the head dog-wrangler whom we knew as Pee-Wee Pederson either ordered them or personally carried them out. I do not enjoy recalling them."

The evening rolled on endlessly after that. Rex and his Pack answered every question, although they seemed endless. But Rex couldn't shake his pit-of-the-stomach unease, especially in light of Thornton's line of questioning. *How will the Pack's enemies respond to this? How many grown dogs and puppies have my words just endangered?*

CHAPTER 47
AN UNEXPECTED CONNECTION

State Pavilion Ballroom A

W *hat a day!* Pam rubbed her throbbing neck, yawned, then moved to the next several tables in the now-silent Ballroom A. She retracted a few more table screens into their compact "travel" configuration, then gathered them up to put on the OPD Media Office's cart.

"Sergeant, *enough.* You can stop for the night." Joslyn Stark placed a hand on her arm. "Seriously. Pace yourself. I've got this."

"You've done so much for us—"

"When did you last eat something?"

Pam hesitated. "Balchu has brought me a couple of sandwiches. And Hildie sent me a wonderful carafe of tea and some really tasty blueberry scones. I owe her a massive favor, for sure. That was . . . um, a while ago, though."

Joslyn grasped her shoulders, turned her to face the exit, then walked her toward it. "You need another meal. And maybe a stiff drink. And to go to bed."

Shady, Elle, and Petunia came through the doorway. "Oh,

good, you captured her." Ears up, Shady wagged her tail. "Thank you, Joslyn."

"I'll now remand her into your custody, if you'll make sure she's well cared for." Joslyn grinned at them.

"That is our mission," Petunia replied.

"Balchu and a room service dinner are waiting in your room. Come." Shady's firm intent came strong and clear through the link. *Resistance is futile. Better get with the program.*

Yes, Assistant Pack Leader. Pam yawned again. *That does sound heavenly.* She crossed the lobby toward the elevators, herded by three very large "sheepdogs."

A few meters away, a man stopped to glare at them.

"What is his problem?" Elle asked.

But Petunia snarled at him. "I am watching you. Leave my Packmates alone!"

Woah. Did those two tangle today?

She'd asked Shady, but her new friend QUAERO answered through a text on her HUD. "Yes. And you might be interested to know that man is Residential Council Member Quentin Berik. He is a member of the Palmdale Club."

Pam drew in a sharp breath. "That guy's in the Palmdale Club. ResCouncil Member Berik. Quentin Berik."

"What, for real? Fleshy-Lips is a Palmdale creep?" Petunia's ears bounced.

Pam grimaced. "Calling him a 'creep' is probably—"

"He is an active threat to my life, the lives of my dearest friends, and my kind in general." Petunia snorted, ears back and hackles puffed out. "Saying 'creep' was me restraining myself." She eyed Berik with more hatred than Pam had seen an XK9 exhibit since Dr. Ordovich's perp-walk to Detention.

Shady and Elle echoed her body language and her glare. The rage that blasted through the link from Shady left Pam shaken. "I was going to say 'not helpful,' but point taken." They walked several more steps toward the elevator. "Um, 'Fleshy Lips'?"

"He also is a creep for another reason." Petunia growled. "Let me tell you about our encounter earlier today."

❖ ❖ ❖ ❖ ❖ ❖ ❖ ❖

State Pavilion Lobby and Beyond

S hady found the scent again quite easily. It had only recently settled to the floor. She turned back to Rex with a tight throat and a chill of foreboding. "Promise me you will not do anything rash."

Her mate clamped his ears to his skull. "Rash? No. But I want to be able to recognize scent of an enemy."

A fair request. I'd rather know, too. All the same, the seething rage in Rex's scent worried her. "Here." She lowered her nose to the strongest nearby patch. It would have yielded an excellent scent-card sample, were Quentin Berik a suspect or the focus of a police pursuit. *Maybe at some point he will be.* She allowed herself a moment to relish that thought. No need to worry about upsetting Pam with such reflections. Balchu had insisted on applying pain patches in the two worst spots. Her partner would be deeply asleep for some time to come.

Rex lowered his nose to the short, dense nap of the Ground Level Lobby's carpeting. He studied the scent for several long seconds. At last, he lifted his head. "Thank you."

"You are welcome. Will you come to bed, now?"

He replied with a soft growl. "Where was he going?"

She answered with a growl of her own. "Probably to bed. Where you and I should go. We have a busy day tomorrow."

"Quite true. But indulge me for a moment." He lowered his nose and followed the scent across the lobby.

Like I could stop you. Shady snorted but followed him.

The scent trail led them to the outer doors, but then Rex halted. His head went up and his ears swept back. He uttered another soft growl.

"What is it?" Shady cocked her head.

Rex's hackles puffed out. Peppery impatience filled his scent. "Charlie is worried about our leaving the hotel. He says it is a strange city to us, and there might be danger."

Shady lolled her tongue. "We are rather large, generally capable dogs. Has he looked at us lately?"

"He is worried about snipers, or something. I do not believe that Transmondian agents will be watching for us here or expecting us to leave the hotel tonight." Rex pushed past the doors. "I told him the trail probably ends at the pull-up for auto-navs and to stop worrying."

"'Stop worrying' never seems to work with Pam when she is in the mood to worry." Shady followed him outside. "I am just as happy she is sound asleep right now."

Rex sniffed his way down the steps, then to the right along the sidewalk. "Apparently he did not leave via auto-nav from here." He followed the man's scent along a sidewalk that paralleled the driveway. Once it met the street that ran past the hotel, the trail led them to the right again.

They continued a few more steps, then Rex lifted his head with yet another growl. "Charlie has asked us to wait. He is getting dressed. I told him we are free Ranan citizens and we can go wherever we like, but he insists he must come with us."

"He might be helpful for opening doors."

Rex snorted. The irritation in his scent redoubled. "He will not be helpful in this mood." He lowered his head to the pavement and continued down the sidewalk at a trot.

Shady blinked, but then hurried to catch up. "You will not wait?"

"He can find me." He set a brisk pace down the sidewalk.

About halfway to the corner, a distant cry halted Shady. "Rex, seriously—stop! Charlie is nearly here!"

Rex laid back his ears but halted. "He just made a good point through the link. We may draw unwanted attention if he has to run after us."

Charlie's speed-walking was conspicuous enough. Shady wagged her tail at his approach. He hurried to join them.

"Thank you for waiting!" Charlie's burst of speed had left him breathless.

Rex growled but averted his eyes. "You know we are perfectly capable—"

"There are 'human things' you may not completely understand."

"Hmm, maybe." Rex resumed following the scent trail. His puffy hackles and peppery scent told Shady he wasn't convinced.

They arrived at a bar about a block and a half from their hotel. The sign by the entrance said "Closed," but several humans lingered inside. Rex moved toward the door. "There is no outward path. He must be in there!"

"Wait." Charlie frowned. "Let me try something, before you barge in." He went into a brief HUD stare, then took a deep breath and centered himself. "Wait here, please." He pushed open the door.

"What was on his HUD?" Shady texted Rex.

Her mate lolled his tongue. "He checked to see what Berik looks like."

"We're closed." The guy who spoke sounded distracted.

"Am I too late?" Charlie asked. "Did I miss him?"

Shady cocked her head and glanced at Rex.

"Miss who?" asked the man who'd said they were closed.

"Quentin! Was he here? Did I miss him?"

"Quentin *who?*" The person's voice shifted lower, his tone suspicious.

"Berik. You know, the Council Member?" Charlie sounded confused. "I'm sure this is the place."

Rex clamped his ears against his skull. "How can Berik not be in there?"

Inside, Charlie was saying thanks and never mind. His footsteps turned toward the door, then stopped. Shady heard a low voice, quite near the door. A woman?

"Thanks." Charlie used a similarly low voice. A moment later he pushed outside and urged Shady and Rex back. When they'd retreated several paces along the sidewalk, he glanced over his shoulder. "One of the waitstaff caught me at the door. She said Berik left through the back with 'Ash' and 'Nez.' I slipped her a twenty-piece."

Shady gave the man an appreciative look. *Well, what d'you know? "Human things" really are a thing.*

"Thank you." Rex wagged his tail. "'Through the back'? Is there an alley?"

Charlie nodded. "Nearly always, in a business district. Fewer traffic snarls during deliveries if they bring it in the back. I'm guessing 'Nez' might mean Nesbit Zeman. *Now* can we go to bed?"

Shady ran a quick review of Council Members' names. She'd memorized them from reviewing Pam's lists. "And 'Ash' will be Ashton Cole."

"Oh. You probably are right." Rex had read Pam's lists, too.

"Who?" Charlie asked.

"Ashton Cole. Residential Council from New Hibernia Borough, Wheel One. Commonwealth Party," Shady replied. "He is on one of Pam's lists."

"And Nesbit Zeman is the Palmdale Club's leader." Rex's growl underscored the suspicion in his scent. "I wonder where they went after they left." He eyed the premises, then his nose swung toward a gap between the restaurant and the next building on the left. He hurried over. It was barely wide enough for single file.

Shady followed her mate. "Only one way to find out, I guess."

"I'm not going to be able to stop you, am I?" Charlie followed, but the musty off-tones in his scent made his reluctance clear.

They emerged into an alley lined with recycling receptacles. Rex halted. "Hello. This is interesting."

"What?" Charlie still smelled like he didn't want to be here.

But Shady quickly discovered what Rex had found. "I thought they would separate, but they did not." The scents of Berik and two others had turned left. They'd all taken the same path toward the far end of the alley.

❖ ❖ ❖ ❖ ❖ ❖ ❖ ❖

An Alley Behind the Bar

Rex's memory flashed briefly on the Five-Ten—but no. This alley really wasn't the same kind of place. Yes, it was dark. But that was because it was night, not the eternal gloom of the dangerous Orangeboro lower level. And even though this alley was lined with an assortment of recycling and composting bins, it smelled way cleaner than the Five-Ten.

Also, although tall buildings' walls lined both sides, these were not blank storage silos or ramshackle, moldering habitations where the poorest and least-legal denizens of Orangeboro hung out. These were the backs of tall, well-kept hotels and office blocks, arranged in straight, orderly rows on either side of a comparatively wide driveway. This alley appeared as broad and open as the largest thoroughfare through the Five-Ten. Larger, actually.

"The alley parallels the street." Charlie stopped, went back into a HUD stare. Rex received a dim sense of a map-grid. "Looks as if your subjects are headed farther away from the hotel. This alley opens onto Third Street on that end."

"It actually is helpful to have you along." Shady nodded, tail up, then looked to Rex. "Assuming we are going to keep following the Palmdale men, I mean."

Rex flicked his ears. Anger and a bottled-up inner pressure to *move—go—learn* puffed up his hackles and prickled down his back. The more he could learn about these men, who might *all* be Palmdale co-conspirators, the better. "Why would we not?"

"Because you are angry, and we are moving farther and farther from our friends and allies. Because we are in a strange city where we do not know the local environment. And because we are out of our jurisdiction." She growled. "Those were just the first reasons I thought of. Also, it is late. We have a long day planned for tomorrow. And we—"

"Enough! You are making it hard to think."

"She makes good points." Charlie nodded to her and spoke aloud. "I'll make another: we are skating very close to police harassment by following them."

"Is that what your bout of play-acting in the bar was all about?" Rex regarded him, ears back.

"I was attempting to give you plausible deniability, but answer your question." Charlie smelled as doubtful about this enterprise as Shady did. "Also, think ahead. If we *should* find something actionable, what then? If you were doing something illegal when you found it—such as stalking Berik, Zeman, and Cole without probable cause—that's an illegal search. What part of the 'fruit of the poisoned tree' concept don't you get?"

Rex hesitated. He paced back and forth a couple of times. *Dammit.* He'd been pushing that worry aside through this whole adventure. "It is a public street."

"Alley." Shady showed him a flash of teeth. "We are skulking down an alley."

"It is a public alley." He flicked his ears. "We have as much right to be here as they did. In any case, *they* are the ones who are skulking. Do you not smell it in their scent factors? They are up to something."

"Keep telling yourself that." Shady snorted and gave herself a full body shake so vigorous it made her ears flap audibly. Even in the dim alley light, he saw stress-shed hairs fly. Once she'd finished, she gave him a fretful lip curl. "I think this is a bad idea."

"Okay, then answer me this. Why did they come this way, and not out the front door of the bar?"

"A short cut?" Shady cocked her head at Charlie. "You are correct that their scent is full of anxiety and deceptiveness."

"That, and a measure of edginess. It makes me think they were trying to be secretive. Sneaking along alleys is what conspirators do. I do not think they want to be seen." Rex checked above, then around their location. "There is no surveillance here. Where are they going, to worry about being seen or recorded as having passed through?"

Charlie blew out a breath. "That's a fair question. It makes my cop-instincts sit up and take notice—but kindly note that Shady's right. We are *not* in our jurisdiction."

"We are SBI Reserve Agents. Does that not make all of Rana Station our jurisdiction?"

Charlie grimaced. "What SBI case are we pursuing, albeit without a warrant?"

My existential dread does not give probable cause? He sent one last heartfelt plea through the link.

Not in any court of law I know about. The link made it clear that Charlie really did understand. He regretted that it was true. *Your anger made you reckless.*

Rex turned away. *Double, triple dammit.* "You are right." He heaved an exasperated sigh. "We should not track them."

"Thank you!" Shady gave a little shiver. Sweet, high, warm notes of relief blossomed in her scent.

"So, then." Charlie eyed him. "Can we go home now?"

Rex did a quick, full-body analysis. He did not feel sleepy, or even tired. Wound-up and restless, yes. Still worried and angry. Plus now frustrated. He wanted to run and howl, not go home to bed. "If I cannot track the Palmdale men, I cannot. But I am not ready to turn in. Could we maybe just go for a walk, instead?"

Charlie and Shady both gave him suspicious eyebrows-up.

"A walk." Charlie's mouth made a grim, unamused line. "In the middle of the night."

"Humans and dogs take walks all the time, night or day. It is relaxing. And a popular bonding ritual." Rex lolled his tongue and wagged his tail. Should he try puppy-eyes?

Charlie didn't lose the skeptical expression or smell. He crossed his arms. "A bonding ritual."

"Yes. You and I have not taken a walk—just for the heck of it —in a long time. And I am still restless and worried. It would help me relax."

"I could walk some." The muddy clashing mid-tones of dubiousness lingered in Shady's scent, but they shifted subtly lighter. "Maybe we could have a bit of a run, if we can find a park?"

Perhaps a *hint* of puppy-eyes wouldn't hurt. "Is there a park on Third Street?"

CHAPTER 48
A WALK TO THE PARK

Alley and Third Street

Charlie's eyebrows went up again, clearly visible despite the gloom of the ill-lit alley and the rising mist. Then they lowered into a frown. His renewed suspicion of Rex's motives rolled in through the link in thick waves and resounded through his scent factors. "Why Third Street?"

"Did you see any parks between here and the hotel?" Rex cocked his head at his partner and met Charlie's stern gaze. "Because I did not."

Shady held her peace, but Rex smelled her unease. He stood close enough to feel the tension in her body.

Charlie uncrossed arms. "No. There were none."

"So, please. Open your HUD map and see if there are any parks nearby."

"On *Third* Street?" Dark, itchy suspicion surged in his scent.

"Third Street is the next street over from where we found no parks. But it does not have to be on Third. Anywhere nearby is okay."

"A park. Got it." Charlie went into a HUD-stare, still frowning.

Rex quietly texted Tux and Elle. "Shady and I are having a walk with Charlie. He is searching for a park where we can run off some nervous frustration. Would you like to join us?"

"Are you inviting the whole Pack?" Tux texted back.

"Since you were just here, I thought you might know places in Centerboro, if Charlie can't find one."

"A run in the park would be nice," Elle texted. "Where are you? Can we just follow your scent?"

"We made a little alley detour. Don't bother with that. Go to the right from the hotel entrance, then down to Third Street. When you get to the corner, text me if you cannot see me partway down Third on your right."

"Roger that," Elle texted.

Rex and Shady sat while Charlie studied his HUD map.

Finally, his gaze shifted to focus on them. "We actually do need to go down Third. Looks as if there's a park a few blocks away. We need to continue to the end of the alley, turn right on Third, then go left on Alvarez Boulevard. It's called Alvarez Park and it's almost a full hectare in size."

"I have invited Tux and Elle to join us," Rex said. "They know Centerboro somewhat, and I thought they might help us find the park."

Charlie grimaced. "Didn't trust my map skills?"

"As it happens, they are restless, too."

They proceeded down the alley. Rex tried not to focus on the scents of the Palmdale Three. All the same, their trail grew fresher as Rex and his two companions proceeded toward Third Street. He didn't even have to sniff the ground. They were catching up so quickly now that the scent cones had barely started to collapse. The anxiety and stress in the trio's scent factors tugged at his curiosity. "What has upset them? They don't know we're anywhere nearby, so it can't be us."

"I'd guess our presence here in Centerboro shook them up." Charlie gave Rex a worried frown. "I thought you weren't going to track them."

"We are literally wading through their fresh scent." Rex snorted. "You cannot see it, but I am walking through a fog of it."

"True," Shady added. "It is all around us."

"Oh." Charlie angled his head toward them. "I guess that *would* be kind of hard to ignore."

"Indeed. And since it's here, literally at the tip of my nose, I have to wonder. Did they not think we would respond to their resolution?"

"I imagine they didn't think the Pack would learn about it." Aching, mid-tone scent factors signaled Charlie's worry. "They probably also wouldn't have imagined we'd come in such a large, unified group."

"And they do not know where the tip-off came from. How could they?" Shady asked.

"That would definitely worry me, if I were making secret, evil schemes." Charlie gave a low chuckle. "Maybe they'll have a few bad nights' sleep because we're here."

Rex, Charlie and Shady reached the end of the alley. It opened onto a street with several traffic lanes. Rex sifted through the scents on the breeze. "So this is Third Street."

"Let's wait here for Elle and Tux." Charlie crossed his arms and leaned on the building wall beside the alley's mouth. "The fewer large dogs wandering alone in the night, the better. Are they bringing Georgie and Misha?"

"They did not say, but based on the way you insisted on joining us, I would not be surprised." Rex lolled his tongue. No sign of them yet, however. He scanned their surroundings.

This late, he hadn't expected many people would be out. By far the most recent scents here were the three still-airborne scent-raft trails of the Palmdale men, damp-sharpened in the misty air.

❖ ❖ ❖ ❖ ❖ ❖ ❖ ❖

Third Street and Alvarez Boulevard

S ounds reached Shady. Quiet panting and the faint thuds of at least one—no, two—no, *four* Packmates' hurried footfalls approached. She turned to gaze up Third Street in time to see Tux and Elle power around the corner. Their partners appeared before they'd made it halfway down the block to Shady, Rex, and Charlie's alley. Their ears lifted and their tails sped up. Georgia and Misha jogged down the empty street behind them.

Shady hurried to meet them with Rex on her heels. They conducted a quick greeting-dance of wagging and sniffing, then turned back toward Charlie once the humans had caught up. He met them on the sidewalk for a much less exuberant human greeting ritual.

"Are you guys headed for Alvarez Park?" Misha asked. "Hallie found it on a map while I got the dogs harnessed up."

"Got it in one." Charlie grinned. "Hallie wasn't up for a jog in the night?"

"No more than it appears Hildie was." Misha laughed. "What do you bet me they get together for some girl-talk while we're gone?"

"I wouldn't put it past them." The fragrant affection in both men's scent factors swelled. They turned down Third Street toward Alvarez. The Palmdale plotters had gone this way, too, but perhaps that didn't need mentioning.

Elle sent her a text. "I smell a fresh trail from old 'Fleshy-Lips.' Is that a coincidence?"

"Not entirely, but we are NOT following him now," Shady texted back. "No police harassment tonight. Even if we do happen to be raging with curiosity."

"Got it."

Meanwhile, Georgia shook her head. "Connie and Arden would probably have come, but Crystal just groaned and rolled over when we invited her along."

"To be fair, she did more than her share of interviews tonight." Tux's tail wagged in broad sweeps. He focused on his partner. "Who knew she enjoyed playing to crowds? Or that she is not shy about singing?"

"That one has the heart of an entertainer," Rex said. "It was good to see her enjoying herself. Tux, I am surprised she did not talk you into singing with her."

"I did one duet with her. Once." Tux growled. "Because you made me."

"How could we have known? Who could guess how any of us would react to a spotlight and people's attention?" Elle's hackles rippled. "I might have guessed that you would be a good orator, Rex. You always were persuasive. But Dr. Ordovich never would have allowed any of us to do such things."

Shady snorted. "That is certainly true."

They reached the intersection with Alvarez Boulevard. Shady noted, but did not mention, that the Palmdale trio had crossed the street here. "Where next, Charlie?"

"Cross the street, then go left. Alvarez Park is two blocks down."

No traffic. Shady and her XK9 Packmates loped across, leaving the humans to keep up or trail behind as they preferred. *They know where we're headed.* But on the far side of the street, Shady pulled up short. "Our Palmdale trio also turned left."

"Irrelevant," Rex replied. "We are not following them, we are going to the park. I, for one, am looking forward to a bit of a romp." All the same, his tongue hung rather long and the hot smell of inflammation had ticked up in his scent.

"Charlie cannot smell where their trail goes," Elle added.

"True." Shady led the way to their left. Half a block down, the Palmdale trio's scent turned right up a flight of steps to the entrance of an apartment. *Do all three live there?* Curiosity burned, but she continued past, headed for the park. Rex hesitated, then followed her.

"Wait! Stop!" Hunt-joy swelled in Elle's scent.

Tux leaped to her side. "Oh! Yes! We must call Mike Santiago!"

"What? Why?" Charlie halted just short of Tux and Elle.

But Georgia was already pulling scent cards out of Tux's pannier and Misha had gone into a HUD-stare. "Sorry to bother you, sir, but we have a fresh scent trail for Nervous Guy."

Shady cocked her head at Elle, while Tux and Georgia pulled scent-samples in the dim light. "Who is Nervous Guy?"

"We found his scent in a contemporaneous layer with that of the bombers on Wednesday." Elle's tail wagged double-time. "He is a person of extreme interest in the pipe bombs case!"

CHAPTER 49
PERSONS OF INTEREST

An Apartment Building on Alvarez Blvd.

"Oh, that is interesting." Shady shifted her gaze back and forth between Elle and Tux. Their scents bubbled with sharp, harsh urgency. "So, you have probable cause to believe this man was working with the bombers?" His trace had settled onto the entry walk and the steps leading up to the apartment building's entrance, but it remained strong with recency.

"The would-be bombers. Remember, most of their devices were defective." Tux's tail ratcheted up to a faster tempo. "That is how we were able to learn so much. If they had exploded, the scents would have been destroyed."

"These are the devices you were telling us about at Topside Terminal, back in the Wheel Two Hub."

"Yes. The ones we believe were made to look like different bombers' work."

"And thus a multi-faceted threat." Elle added.

"Their devices were defective—and you think that's on purpose?" Charlie's frown and the musky doubtfulness in his scent factors told her he wasn't entirely sure this made sense.

"You were not with us when they brought us up to speed in the Hub," Shady replied.

"We believe they were defective to give the wrong idea about their origin, as misdirection." Elle nodded to Charlie. "But the people who made them do not seem to have wanted to actually blow things up."

"Perhaps they wanted investigators to suspect Whisper, or other unnamed terrorists," Tux added. "And maybe to congratulate themselves for finding the devices 'in time.' That's what the RES people were doing until we scent-linked them. Then Georgia and Joe Raach from the SBI Explosives Lab pointed out that they would not have gone off in any case. RES Director Wilmott minced no words about how much she disliked that analysis, but CPD Counter-Terrorism Coordinator Hami endorsed it."

Charlie pursed his lips. "As I remember it, Mike's team was called in because someone thought the Whisper Syndicate was behind the bombings."

"That is correct." Elle's tail stopped moving. "The RES and Centerboro PD both were pushing that narrative rather hard when we first arrived."

"Did either of them object when Mike showed up with XK9s?" Charlie lifted one eyebrow.

"Hami seemed startled but happy to see us." Elle snapped her ears flat. "Wilmott and the RES agents objected, for all the usual reasons people cite before they work with us."

A sour surge of understanding weighted Shady's gut. *I know that stupid routine too well.*

Misha came out of his HUD stare. "Mike and several of his people are on their way here. He is alerting Coordinator Hami and getting a warrant to pursue the scent of our person of interest."

"Excellent! That ought to help uncover some things." Rex's ears swept upward. "We should examine the grounds." He eyed the building. "There undoubtedly is a back door, maybe others. Not to mention fire escapes." Rex's hackles rippled.

Charlie gazed upward. "It gets worse. There are skybridges from the top floor to the buildings on either side." He shook his head. "Maps. I need different maps. And a floorplan, if possible. Hang on." He went into a HUD stare. Georgia and Misha took a few more scent samples.

"While you are at it, capture these three." Rex pointed them out. "My purpose is to note who has recently entered this building and may still be inside. This is Quentin Berik's scent."

"Oh, really?" Georgia's brows rose. "The one that harassed Hildie?"

Charlie stiffened. "He *what?*"

"Oops." Georgia's scent shot through with acidic chagrin. "I guess maybe she meant to tell you later?"

"Petunia made short work of that incident and sent him packing," Elle said. "It was only later that Pam's new friend alerted us to who he is."

"In what way did he harass Hildie?" Charlie's face had gone stony. There was a new, dangerous tinge to his scent that Shady did not remember having smelled before.

"Petunia told us she caught him looming over her at the teahouse in the lobby. He was trying to flirt with her, but Petunia could see and smell that she felt threatened. So, she growled at him and told him to go away. It appeared to scare the crap out of him. She said his reaction was most satisfying."

Charlie's scent and expression continued to smolder. He clenched his fists, then took a long, slow breath. "I'll have to thank Petunia. And Berik better watch himself."

Shady pulled in her tongue and took a moment to evaluate what she sensed from Charlie. *It probably is a very good thing that Berik is only here as a drift of scent rafts at the moment.*

"We should do a perimeter sweep of the building," Rex said. "Let us gather as much legally available information for Mike and his people as possible."

"Good idea." Shady activated her harness's onboard sensors and logged in with a basic report of location and situation. An apartment building with public access areas along the front and sides would not be off-limits to a perimeter survey. She trotted along the base of the building itself with Rex. The humans' walkway lay perhaps a meter out, parallel to the building's outer walls.

"The RES never wanted us involved. They would not listen to us." Elle sprinted ahead to the area below the first fire escape. "They never did move away from the idea that the bombs—including the inoperable bombs—could be from any other source but Whisper." She stopped speaking to focus, then lifted her head. "This exit is clear. No one has come down this fire escape in—oh, probably months."

Shady had pushed ahead of Rex to the second fire escape while Elle worked the the first. "No one has used this one in months, either."

"RES Chief Wilmott all but ordered us to follow the 'Whisper did it' narrative." Misha's frown had become a pensive scowl. "We continued to find no evidence to support that. But we left it on the table because we found it difficult to lock in on *any* particular hypothesis."

"We certainly did not find the 'Whisper hypothesis' as self-evident as she seemed to." Elle leapfrogged Shady to the corner of the building. She peered around it, then disappeared toward the back.

Tux and Georgia had not yet emerged around the corner from the front of the building. *Are they following, or clearing the other side?* No one had an Admin Channel on this hunt, so Shady couldn't be sure. Trusting them to take care of themselves, she followed Elle.

A small auto-nav parking area and a rear drive formed a half-circle arc that led from an alley that paralleled the street to the rear doorway, then back to the alley. Elle focused on the base of the nearest rear-side fire escape.

"The ones who gain most from a wrong assumption that the bombers were Whisper-sourced would potentially be the Transmondians, the Palmdale conspirators, or a third party," Charlie mused.

"I would wonder more about Hoback if we did not believe he has been captured by the Transmondians," Rex walked by Charlie's side, tail drooping and tongue hanging long. "Also, Elle! Am I correct in my impression that the explosives were not the Fredericks blend?"

"You are correct. They were not," Elle replied. "I keep thinking about the people who happen to be in the same building with the bomber."

"That does not mean they are associated," Charlie said.

"It does not mean they are not," Elle replied. She sniffed around below the second rear fire escape.

Moving the conversation to texts would allow Shady to push ahead, potentially out of earshot. She headed for the rear exit and texted all of her Packmates. "Could we XK9s please text?"

"Good idea," Rex texted back.

"Georgie says to tell you she's waiting in front for Santiago and Hami," Tux texted. "Both have warrants, and both are bringing more people. Hami will cover the skywalks to adjacent buildings but wants one of us to join each of her skywalk groups once they arrive. She also has UPOs moving in now to cover the garage exits ASAP. Note also that Baker-side fire escape One is clear. Moving to Baker Two."

Elle's head lifted from beneath the second rear—"Charlie"-side—fire escape. "Both Delta-side fire escapes are clear. So is Charlie Three."

Shady sniffed along the back sidewalk that led to the rear exit, detected a pair of older profiles, then leaped across to the other side. "So, Tux, how often does a professionally-built bomb fail to detonate?" she texted to the group.

"It can happen, but not as many times in a row as the ones we were checking this week. Baker Two is clear."

"Charlie Two is clear," Elle texted.

"What places or monuments did they—not—blow up?" Rex asked.

Shady finished her survey of the rear exit. "Back door was last used roughly two hours ago, by two unknowns. Inbound scent-trace. One of them—suggestively—is augmented, but he is not one of Hoback's captors. I leaped the sidewalk to keep it unmarked. Moving to Charlie One," she texted the group. "Elle, check if either of those two are known profiles, please."

"On it."

"The places where we found duds? Along the foundation of the Capitol, for one," Tux texted to the whole group. "We also found them by the office building of the Commonwealth Party."

"Founders' Fountain," Elle added. "The Helen Rana Memorial."

Rex, his partner, and Misha at last emerged around the corner into the shadows in the building's back area.

"Before we got there, the CPD had found both live and dud devices at the residences of several ComCouncil and ResCouncil legislators," Tux added. "I should also note that no place in any of the ozzirikkian Wheels was targeted, either by fakes or real bombs."

"So we're talking all humans." Shady snorted. "That tracks."

"We have another hit!" Elle texted to everyone. "Soldering-Smoke Woman! That's another would-be-bomber suspect, for Rex, Charlie, and Shady's information. She walked in through the rear entrance in the same time layer as the man with augmentations."

A tingling bubble of elation and a heady hit of hunt-joy surged through Shady. She savored them while she sniffed around the base the final fire escape.

"Gee, what if they'd placed a bomb at the Popular Democracy Party's Headquarters?" Charlie grimaced. "Think that one would've blown up?"

Rex texted Shady alone. "Sacha Guzmán is PDP, in case you needed that explanation."

"Oh. Thank you. Ranan politics are almost as confusing as Transmondian politics."

Misha gave a short, mirthless laugh. "They didn't dare. Too easy to get caught on that level of surveillance coverage."

"Too tempting to actually detonate it, perhaps." Charlie shook his head, scent factors disgusted. "They didn't want human blood on their hands. However, I imagine XK9 blood would be okay by them."

"You have drawn a conclusion?" Shady cocked her head at him. *Not that I haven't, of course.*

"Let's just say I have a working hypothesis. We won't know if it's right till we test it."

❖ ❖ ❖ ❖ ❖ ❖ ❖ ❖

Around the Apartment Building

After SIT Delta and the Centerboro PD Counterterrorism Squad arrived, events moved quickly. Rex gladly accepted Command Channel access. A surge of new, warm delight blossomed within him. For the moment, it pushed back against the growing weight of his fatigue.

He'd already had a full night with the press conference's stress. Then he'd covered several blocks and sniffed out all these exciting new possibilities. Now he was content to cover the apartment building's rear exit with Charlie. Let his Packmates and the other humans do the more vigorous legwork.

Neither he nor Charlie needed to say anything. They simply moved into position on each side corner at the back of the building. No one would scramble down any side or rear fire escape or bolt out through the rear exit unseen.

CPD police units arrived with lights but no sirens and

blocked the two garage openings. Strobing streaks of light washed nearby building walls.

Shady had joined Mike's group—Sara Cutler, plus his and Charlie's friends Beck Crombie and Jack Evanovich—inside the building. Moments later her text reported what the Corona group had suspected from the start. "Yes! Our Palmdale conspirators and the bombers all entered the same unit. Rear center, Level Three. We have them!"

Rear center. That could mean us. Rex's gut tightened and his breath came shorter. He shifted his primary focus to the back door but kept the Baker-side fire escapes in view.

"Portside skybridge covered," Tux reported, echoed a nanosecond later by Etta Hami's voice on the com. "None of our subjects have come this way."

"Starboard skybridge is locked down," Elle and another CPD officer reported on separate channels a moment later. Rex lolled his tongue and exchanged a glance with Charlie. "No suspects came this way, either," Elle added.

Thunderous knocks reverberated through both Mike and Shady's pickup mics.

"SBI! Open the door!" Mike bellowed.

Rex panted, on edge. He strove to listen for any slightest sound over the thunder of his pulse. Charlie drew his EStee. Its brief, faint flicker signaled that the bio-lock had recognized him. It powered up with a barely-perceptible whine.

"Open the door! SBI!" Mike repeated.

Rex scanned for any new scent, any hint of movement.

Boom! The distinctive sound of a hand-swung ram rattled through his com. *So much for the door. Probably proud-of-his-muscles Beck on the ram.* He lolled his tongue and sharpened his focus.

Probably. Charlie grinned. He took up a shooter's stance and gripped his EStee, but kept the muzzle down.

A burly form burst through the window by the center-rear fire escape. Glass and the smell of blood blew out into the air. *Augmented and angry,* Rex warned.

On it.

The agent didn't bother with the fire escape's steps. He swung down, grabbed the handrail to launch himself outward, then landed, rolled, and sprinted forward faster than any human Rex had ever seen.

Charlie bolted the man, a solid center-mass hit.

The agent dropped like a felled tree. He slid forward on his face and came to rest almost at Charlie's feet.

❖ ❖ ❖ ❖ ❖ ❖ ❖ ❖

C harlie let out a long, shaky breath, but this was no time to relax. He kept his EStee in one hand, trained on the fallen agent's head. Groped for zip-cuffs with the other but came up empty. *Damn. I'm in civvies. No zip-cuffs!*

"Suspect down! Rear exit! Need zip-cuffs ASAP!" Rex called through the com.

Their captive groaned and stirred.

Rex landed next to him and roared a growl into his ear. "Lie still!"

The man stiffened, then subtly gathered himself.

Not even a little. Charlie bolted him again, this time at the base of his skull. That had proved effective a couple of weeks ago in Howardsboro. The agent went limp again. *That should do it for now, I hope. Really don't want to shoot him again.*

If he weren't augmented, two bolts could be fatal. Rex's ears bounced up, then flattened again. *He does not smell as if he's dying.*

Good. 'Cuz we have questions. Charlie bent and found a strong, steady pulse. *No, probably not gonna die on us for a while yet.* Relief doubled down on his accumulated exhaustion and adrenaline-crash. It made him light-headed for an instant, but he kept his feet.

You all right? Rex cocked his head.

Ready for this night to end pretty soon.

No shit. Me, too. His tongue hung long.

Three CPD officers raced around the building's corners, one from Baker-side, two from Delta. They hesitated, holstered their EStees, then moved forward. "Nice work." The officer in the lead extended a zip-cuff.

Charlie accepted it and holstered his own EStee. "This is an augmented Transmondian agent. I'll need two more for his wrists, plus triple-cuffs on his ankles."

She hesitated. "Are you sure?"

"Just trust us and give him the zip-cuffs," Rex growled. "We have dealt with the TIS in the past. Augmented people smell different, and they are unbelievably fast and strong."

"TIS, huh? That's not good." She handed over the extra zip-cuffs, then moved to the agent's feet. Once the man was secured, they rolled him to his side so he could breathe better.

Charlie ran a hand over his face. "How's it going with the rest of the team? I kinda zeroed in there for a while."

The CPD officer grinned. "We've scored quite a jackpot tonight. Coordinator Hami is beyond pleased. Your XK9s make an incredible difference."

CHAPTER 50
BREAKING NEWS

State Pavilion, Pam and Balchu's Room

P am startled awake. She hadn't felt a wet dog-nose poked into her cheek in weeks, but—*Shady?* She rolled over, straight into a dog-breathy tongue-lick. Excitement reverberated through the link.

I can't wait any longer for you to wake up! I have so much news! Her partner pranced from paw to paw, panting and emanating delight.

"Okay, Shady, she's awake. Give her a little space, now." Balchu laughed and raised a mug of steaming coffee into Pam's view. "It's ready when you are." He set the mug on her night-stand and urged Shady over to the other side of their hotel room. "You know Pam. She's not one to wake up fast."

Urgh. Got that right. Pam struggled through brain-fog, rubbed her eyes. The curtains were still drawn, but light glowed around the edges. *What time is it?* Her eyes might be bleary, but the HUD showed 07:00 clearly. *What happened to my alarm?* She'd set it for six.

I disabled it. Shady stayed by the window, but Pam had no trouble perceiving her continued delight through the link. *You needed your sleep, and we've had a new development that supersedes the meetings we'd previously set up for this morning. Rex and Charlie are about to start a press conference with Mike, Director Perri, and Director Hami. Hildie, Joslyn Stark, and your friend QUAERO have rescheduled the early interviews till an hour or so after it ends.*

Pam shoved herself partially-upright against the pillows. She groped for her mug and her bearings, but her mind reeled. *So many questions!* "Okay, tell me."

Shady and Balchu both spoke at once, then he fell silent and let Shady talk. She told the story of Rex's determined quest, Charlie's intervention, and then their alternate plan to go to the park with Elle and Tux.

"And you're telling me this because—?"

"Because it gets better. Be patient! On the way to Alvarez Park Elle made an amazing discovery! We had crossed the trail of one of their bombing suspects from earlier in the week."

"Oh." Pam sucked in more coffee. Her mind grew less foggy as Shady described the hunt they'd mounted with Mike, agents from SIT Alpha and Coordinator Hami's people.

"In the end we bagged two of the bombers from earlier in the week." Shady's tail wagged nonstop. "Plus, Charlie took down an augmented Transmondian with a great shot to the center of his chest. They got him triple-zipped before he woke up. Of course, he clammed up immediately, but he is almost certainly a TIS agent."

Pam bit her lip. *Is that really good news?*

"Better yet, we caught three Council Members holed up with them!" Shady's entire body wriggled. "One is that creep, Quentin Berik. Best of all, another one is Nesbit Zeman himself!"

Pam lifted a hand. "Wait. *What?*" XK9s didn't lie. And Shady clearly believed this—but it didn't make sense. She shifted her focus to Balchu. "How is that possible?"

He shook his head. "It's totally stupid. Didn't he trust his aides? Why meet with the Transmondian and the bombers *now,* of all times? How could he risk exposing himself and his co-conspirators like that?" He shrugged. "But it's true."

"We captured him and two Palmdale co-conspirators with a TIS agent and two bombers." Shady bounded across the small room and back. "He is totally discredited! How can anyone believe him now?"

"What has Premier Iskander said?" Pam set her mug aside. She gave her face a vigorous rub and threw off her covers.

"The Premier's office has issued a brief statement calling for a complete investigation," Balchu answered. "Zeman's office pushed back with some cockamamie story about conducting a 'sting' operation against the Transmondians when an opportunity presented itself. Berik and Cole, the two ResCouncil Members, have accused the SBI of framing them for political purposes."

"And of course, the Transmondian Embassy denies their government had anything to do with any of this." Shady bristled, ears clamped flat against her skull. "They say the man we're calling an agent has never worked for them and they have no idea who he is."

"Okay, *that* I believe—that they'd deny everything." Pam gulped the rest of her coffee, then held the mug out to Balchu for a refill. "Did QUAERO know about this?"

"Ne says ne tried, but nir anonymous warnings to the RES and CPD went unheeded," Balchu said. "You were the first person who was truly receptive to nem, and ne still had to be careful. Ne said cyberbeing citizens who live among corporeals are strictly forbidden from interfering in corporeal beings' politics unless it directly affects them or the well-being of their source nodes. Even then, they are to stop at the least intrusive measures possible."

"I guess that explains some of nir caginess. But—forbidden by whom?" Pam realized barely in time that the new coffee was really hot. She changed what would've been a big gulp to a more cautious sip.

"Ne will not say." Shady shook her head. "I am not sure I understand, but that is what ne said."

"Maybe it is a stipulation of the Alliance," Balchu suggested.

Pam considered her contacts with QUAERO. "Perhaps, considering what I've glimpsed and inferred about nir capabilities, it is the cyberbeings' own code. To keep us from fearing them."

"That might be true." Balchu gave her a worried look. "Anyway, the press conference is about to go live onto the news feeds. Care to watch it from here? Or shall we hurry downstairs to see it happen in realtime?"

❖ ❖ ❖ ❖ ❖ ❖ ❖ ❖

State Pavilion Ballroom A

Hildie took a seat next to Chief Klein's staff publicist, Joslyn Stark, in Ballroom A, but her focus stayed on Charlie. By some miracle, he was on the dais and looking fine in his dress blues, but getting him this far had been a struggle. Just waking him up had been hard enough.

Dr. Sandler had authorized a stim for Rex, but no such luck for Charlie. "Sorry, I can't advise a stimulant at all," Dr. Zuni had told her, after congratulating her on her new status. "I'm not willing to chance any such thing till after he's out of that arm shield and we've got him on a maintenance regimen. I especially don't want to trigger any unexpected imbalances or sensitivities when he's in the public eye."

She most definitely did *not* want to risk another "sensitivity" reaction. Not after Charlie's response to an earlier dosage misstep. It had sent him into terrifying rages with little warning and caused a short-term rift in their relationship. *But without a stim, how long before he needs to rest again?*

With Hallie's company and comfort, she'd followed the action vicariously last night. Piecing together their men's terse, infrequent and often-cryptic updates had told them some important parts of the story. She'd worried early in the evening when Charlie insisted on taking his EStee. But Hallie said Misha had his, too, and it was better to have them if they needed them. In the end, she was grateful he had it. *Lesson learned: trust your cop's instincts.*

She released a long, worried breath. *This is my life now.* Hallie's practiced calm and sturdy confidence—and a couple of companionable glasses of wine—had most definitely helped last night. *Will I come to be like Hallie? Pragmatic, even when he might be in trouble?* In the light of morning, Hildie admitted the evening's adventures had been interesting, though also nerve-wracking. And they had worn both Rex and Charlie out.

Pam, clutching a mug of coffee and accompanied by Shady and Balchu, had arrived in Ballroom A just about the time Coordinator Hami showed up. Most of the Pack had already arrived by then, and the rest came soon after, followed by Mike and Elaine.

According to a text from Shady, Pam was disgusted to have slept through all the excitement. Hildie smiled. *Yeah, in her place I probably would have been, too.* Now the XK9 Unit's new sergeant took a last gulp of coffee and handed her mug to Balchu. She walked with Coordinator Hami to where Rex, Chief Klein, Mike, and Director Perri stood. They began a low-voiced conversation.

I wonder when they'll begin. It's past the announced time. Hildie glanced around. Ballroom A was filling rapidly. One whole side had been taken over by the press. Reporters did quiet sound checks. Camera operators adjusted lights and positioned their swarms of tiny cameras. They buzzed and swooped and jockeyed for the best angles on the still-unoccupied podium at the front-center of the dais.

She recognized several Heads of Families in the audience, including Charlie's grandmother. His aunt Hannah and Berwyn's mother Aurelia from Pabiyan Family joined Rex and

Charlie's group by the steps to the dais. *It's going to be a while longer, at this rate.*

To distract herself, she checked her news feeds again. *Wow that's encouraging.* Many Ranans all over the station had taken to the streets this morning. There'd been a small protest in Orangeboro's Central Plaza after the Pack left for Centerboro yester—was it only yesterday? *Yikes.*

That first protest had been pro-trade and against sapience-recognition for the XK9s, but OPD sources—what Charlie called the "cop grapevine"—reported it never amounted to more than a dozen people. Some officers who'd worked security at the scene said they'd overheard comments that made them suspect those "protesters" might even have been paid to go there.

Once the news feeds picked it up, however, there'd been a much larger counter-protest. Initially it was led by, of all things, a "Ciné and Chardonnay" club from Ninth Precinct.

Oh, my. She bit her lip, briefly distracted. *When you get the Ciné and Chardonnay circles out to counter-protest, you really have hit a nerve.* Most such groups that she'd ever encountered tended to be long on gossip and wine, but not all that politically aware. *I guess the XK9s have changed that? At least for now, maybe.* She frowned. *Ninth Precinct? Is that a coincidence?* Something made her doubt it.

In any case, the counter-protest had grown and grown until most Central Plaza traffic halted. Several businesses opened their doors so employees who wanted to could join in. According to the latest updates, quite a few XK9 supporters—and a growing number of anti-Transmondia demonstrators—were back this morning, with all their Families and friends.

And this time, not only in Orangeboro.

Probably because of the protests, she, Joslyn, and even QUAERO had fielded dozens of new requests for XK9 interviews today. Both from the press and from legislators.

She'd managed to build in a short break for Rex and Charlie after this news conference—maybe she could at least feed them breakfast and pump a little more coffee into Charlie. But, of course, the Pack Leader and his human partner were in the most demand of all.

At last! Perri, Klein, Rex and Charlie, accompanied by Hannah and Aurelia, mounted the three steps to the dais and took seats around the central podium. Mike and Shady followed, a half-step ahead of Elle, Misha, Tux, and Georgia. Once they were seated, Aurelia Glenn stepped to the podium.

❖ ❖ ❖ ❖ ❖ ❖ ❖ ❖

Thank goodness he and Charlie could sit through most of this press conference! Rex glanced at his human. Hildie had let them sleep as long as she'd dared, but it hadn't been long enough. Charlie put on a creditable outward show, but the raw heat of inflammation and heavy ache of fatigue filled his scent.

Rex's lung-nanites undoubtedly were hard at work. But taking the stairs, rather than leaping up as he had last night, still left him breathless. He rested his chin on Charlie's lap.

Aurelia had moved to the podium. "Welcome! Thank you for coming. We recognize that this change of plans was sudden, and we appreciate your flexibility."

A round of applause interrupted her. She smiled and waited it out.

"As you'll soon learn from SBI Director Perri, there's a law enforcement update to share," she continued once the clapping subsided. "It is likely we would not have received this break in the case if some of the XK9s we're sponsoring this weekend hadn't decided to take a walk with their humans. They planned to work off some excess energy with an evening excursion to Alvarez Park." Her smile widened. "But they did far more than that. Now here's Director Perri to tell you the rest."

Perri introduced the XK9s and partners who'd been involved in last night's action. At Joslyn's cues he, Charlie, and the others stood. Perri sketched in the action: crossing a suspect's trail, the report to the SBI, the quickly-procured warrant. She described how the XK9s and Coordinator Hami's task group had surrounded the building to cut off all exits, and the subsequent surprise raid on the apartment.

"Thanks to our XK9 Reserve Agents and their partners, we now have captured two suspects scent-linked to the case of the pipe bombs laid at monuments and government offices. We also apprehended several other persons of interest," she said.

More applause. Rex generally loved being at the center of admiration. And this applause did make him feel happy. *But could we please sit down pretty soon?*

I feel you. Charlie's mouth twitched.

"Sit down before you fall over," Joslyn's voice in his earpiece advised.

Good enough! He and Charlie gratefully reclaimed their seats.

"Three of last night's detainees have been questioned and provisionally released. Three are still in custody," Perri continued.

I hate that the three Council Members plotting against us will still be out there at large and free to do as they like. Too bad she can't say their names. His hackles prickled. *Seems like a rigged game, to me.*

Politics. I think one of the rules is to try and rig the game, Charlie said through the link.

Rex allowed himself a soft growl, then once again rested his chin on Charlie's lap. His partner's hand stroked his neck and ears. He closed his eyes. Perri's voice continued . . .

I am truly sorry, Rex, but I have terrible news.

He startled awake at SCISCO's words, gut chilled.

There's been a most troubling development in Transmondia. I am informing Kwame of this at the moment, too—just as QUAERO is alerting Laidie Perri and Pam. Puppy Farm One came under attack this morning.

Rex went cold all over. Unreality spun his head. *Puppy— Puppy Farm—How? Why?*

All the humans ne had just named suddenly emitted much greater stress-scents. Perri stopped whatever she'd been saying. "One moment. I'm receiving an update on another matter."

Now everyone stared at Director Perri. She, Charlie, and Chief Klein smelled of harsh, acrid astonishment and the scorch of angry outrage.

Rex struggled to think straight. *This can't be right. But if SCISCO said it . . .* He ran patterned breathing and slowly steadied.

"What's happening?" Joslyn asked through the com.

"Let me tell them," Rex's resolve hardened. He dragged himself to his feet.

Perri turned. "Once again, please welcome Pack Leader Rex Dieter-Nell. With his partner, Reserve Agent Morgan."

Rex's nerves sparked through his hackles, his skin alive with tension. He made an effort to lift his ears and refrain from snarling at his audience as he stalked forward and connected his vocalizer to the public address system. It connected with a soft *pop*.

"We have just received extremely troubling news of a developing situation in Transmondia. This information comes from a highly trustworthy source, although I am not at liberty to identify them."

It apparently started about 05:00 local time, SCISCO said through the link. *Transmondian Special Forces have bombed and partially destroyed Puppy Farm One.*

Rex gasped and licked his lips, his mind reeling. He searched for a focal point in that sea of human faces, gut heavy as a stone. Charlie quietly went down on one knee next to him so their faces were almost on the same level. Strong love and support poured through the link. Charlie's steady hands stroked his shoulders and back.

He couldn't see Shady or his Pack, although he smelled their worry and curiosity from the stage behind him. He spotted Hildie in the crowd, her expression full of loving concern. *You are not alone,* Charlie said through the link. *We love you.*

Rex lifted his head and licked his lips again to steady himself. "This morning at dawn Transmondian Special Forces bombed the XK9 Project's Puppy Farm One."

He smelled more than saw the wave of dismay and revulsion that swept through his audience and the anguish of his Pack-mates. "Puppy Farm One is the XK9 Project's breeding and whelping facility. The place is partially destroyed, according to the report we just received. I do not yet know how many dogs and puppies—or humans, for that matter—may have been murdered there."

All the reporters started shouting questions at once.

Rex held his peace. He gave the loudest one a sad, stern sheepdog-stare until he stopped screaming the same questions over and over again. Then he turned to the next-most-obnoxious, until she piped down. After that he turned to regard the third. The smarter ones had gotten the hint by now and shut up, but it took a while longer for the others.

"The Pack and I know that facility quite well," Rex said once they'd quieted. "It is not far from Solara City. We went through our final training with our new partners there, before we came to Rana Station."

Several reporters waved at him.

"Yes, Helen?"

"Exactly where is this facility? What parts are most likely to be damaged? About how many people and dogs are usually there?"

"Puppy Farm One is in Bordemer Canton, just outside the Solara City suburb of Ensolay. I can tell you that some parts of the farm are offices and some are training facilities. The human staff numbers between ten and twenty, depending on what is happening there at the time. The centerpiece, as you might guess from the name, is a large whelping barn, but there are annex kennels, too. At this time of year, the main barn will have been filled with approximately twenty dams and their puppies."

"Puppies?" Helen's dismay echoed through her scent. "How young?"

Rex bowed his head, ears back, then retuned his gaze to her. "About three months old. Still nursing. XK9s have one, or at most two puppies during each breeding cycle, so the puppies in that barn are all who were born in this cohort. They and their mothers will be helpless to get away—just as their attackers planned."

Rex shifted his gaze to the whole group of journalists. Their camera swarms closed in for better pictures. "I think it is clear at this point that the Transmondian government has decided they can no longer hide the fact that we XK9s are sapient beings. They now seem to have decided that the only way they can silence us is with genocide."

CHAPTER 51
AFTERSHOCKS

Ballroom A

S hady's whole body went numb. The ballroom, the dais, the crowd—everything receded in a buzzing mist of horror. She barely felt Pam's arms wrapped around her. *Puppy Farm One is where I was born. In that very whelping barn. Do you think it can just be . . . gone?*

The press conference disintegrated around them in a welter of confusion. Journalists spoke rapidly into microphones, their eyes wide and scent factors all over the place. Swarms of cameras buzzed and swooped. Families gathered around their XK9s in supportive circles.

Pam held Shady in a hard, emotional embrace, her scent awash with the musky ache of anguish. Balchu came in from the other side to stroke and soothe. An older couple of Hector and Hannah's generation joined them. Shady looked up, startled.

Holy crap! That's Chase and Anya. Astonishment swept through Pam's scent and reverberated through the link.

From Becenti? Wow.

"Uncle Chase! Aunt Anya!" Balchu, too, appeared stunned. "When did you get here?"

"About an hour ago." Chase's expression turned rueful. "We got checked in and heard about the press conference, so we came over. Ms. Shady, we haven't been properly introduced yet. I'm Chase Rodriguez Williamson, and this is my wife Anya."

"Pam has spoken of you often, recently. I am very glad to meet you." Shady's head still spun with clashing emotions, but she took the opportunity to sniff them over. They smelled warmly sincere, and also worried. Her world steadied a bit, grounded by this added support.

"We're sorry to arrive at a moment when you've just had such awful news," Anya said.

"I didn't know you were planning to come." Balchu blinked at them as if he still couldn't believe it.

"Gotta admit, we weren't really considering it 'til the demonstrations started up yesterday afternoon." Chase gave a little chuckle. "Luis asked if we wanted to get involved. We did some checking around through friends of friends and coordinated our trip with help from Aurelia Glenn. Since we're going to be an XK9 Family soon, we decided to come and support the Pack on behalf of Becenti Family."

Anya smiled. "So here we are."

"That's so very kind of you! To disrupt your—oops! I apologize—I need to take this call." Pam loosened her grip on Shady and pulled away.

"You're here to work. We're here to support you. Do whatever you need to do," Chase said.

She nodded to him, but her gaze had already gone into a HUD-stare. "An interview with—" She glanced around. "Hmm, I'm not sure he's available until—um, next available XK9?" She brushed her bangs back from her face. "Looks as if Petunia has an opening at 14:00. Will that—okay, good." She grimaced. "I need my screens."

"This press conference is over. You belong upstairs." Shady nudged her toward the elevator. "Chase, Anya, it was lovely to meet you, but we need to go."

❖ ❖ ❖ ❖ ❖ ❖ ❖ ❖

C harlie tried to gauge what he was sensing from Rex. *Let's move back from the front of the dais.*

Rex hesitated. *Is there anything else to say?*

I regret that I have so little to report at this time, but I thought you should be made aware of it. SCISCO's regret came through clearly, mixed with a smoldering anger toward the Transmondians behind the attack.

No, I'm grateful you did, Rex replied. *We did need to know of it.*

Charlie and Rex retreated to where they'd sat earlier. After several months spent at or near Puppy Farm One earlier this year, Charlie's memories of the place remained varied and fresh. He tried to envision it partially destroyed but couldn't quite make himself believe it.

Hannah'd been seated just down from him and Rex on the dais. Now she pulled them both into an anguished embrace. Hildie and Gran Annie soon joined them. Next, here came Hector, Manny, and Fee. They all clung to each other for a few moments, wordless, then backed off a little. Most went into HUD stares. Had they reflexively opened their news feeds?

Charlie shook his head. *Not sure why we think the news feeds will have anything we don't know. They got it from us.* He stifled a yawn.

"Are you okay?" Hildie's face puckered with worry.

"My night's catching up to me, and this news doesn't help."

"Come with me." She tugged him over to where Joslyn stood in conference with Director Perri, and Chief Klein. Rex stayed close to Charlie. "My guys need a break," she told them.

"Conserve your strength." Perri's mouth tightened. "Grab a moment now, while we await more updates."

Next minute, his Amare was muscling him toward the exit with Rex on his heels. "You seem to have become my fierce protectress."

"Need I quote Section 5-H to you?"

"No, I'm coming." Section 5-H of the Safety Services Employment Code spelled out the observable criteria for judging whether a co-worker's physical condition had rendered them ineligible for active duty. There was no way he'd pass a 5-H review at this moment. *Better submit peacefully.*

By the time he woke up again, the feeds did have more news and his body felt immensely better. Soon after, there also was food and lots more coffee. He scanned the feeds while he ate.

Some of the first things published were photos of the Pack as they reacted in realtime to the news of what everyone was now calling the Massacre at Puppy Farm One. The photojournalists at the press conference had caught some arresting moments, and emotional reactions from XK9s that would make it hard for anyone to claim the Pack wasn't smart enough to grasp the enormity of the news.

He found dozens, but one of him with Rex on the dais seemed to have caught the moment in many people's minds, based on how often it turned up. Another of Elle, tail tucked, with her face pressed against Misha's chest and Hallie hugging her, also had seen a lot of play.

The developing story from Transmondia had by now taken over the headlines—not only on Rana, but at least System-wide. All too soon, photos from Transmondia also began to come in. Vids and audio of the attack from a distance had poured into news agencies all over western Transmondia.

Personal security systems in the area adjacent to the puppy farm had captured distant flares of light from explosives and the popping sound of far-off gunfire. There'd even been a few badly-framed glimpses of fugitive adult dogs and older puppies, but those stopped coming once word spread that Transmondian Special Forces were confiscating them for their locational metadata.

Most of the adult dogs have implanted trackers, Rex reminded him through the link. It seemed they were reading the same story.

He'd thought he was already as outraged as possible, but this froze his core even further. *Oh, that's not good.*

Some of the puppies may not have them yet, but—Rex's hackles puffed out further.

News agencies traced the chronology from early-morning rumors of explosions in the predawn darkness to a full torrent of information. Clamping down all communications was not possible in a continent-spanning nation at the center of system-wide trade. Word had spread faster than government censors could stifle it. A while ago, Transmondian spokespersons had shifted from denying it had happened to blaming it on a radical faction.

Some agencies' news swarms made it through—or were carried past—the electronic fencing the TSF had tried to throw up around Puppy Farm One. There was too much forested area to shield it completely, or to effectively patrol with the small crew on the ground. News agencies soon beamed out high-vantage-point views of the whelping barn in smoldering ruins and Puppy Farm personnel being loaded onto buses at gunpoint. Then the Oroplanian government released satellite images of the site, confirming a direct hit on the now-burned-out whelping barn and a large crater in the yard near a kennel annex.

From Transmondia and Rana, the news had spread throughout the Chayko System. A sneak attempt by a military squad to gun down puppies—and yet somehow fail to finish the job, if there were dogs on the loose—was a story no news organization could resist.

It had sparked near-universal outrage, as far as Charlie could tell. Now the demonstrations weren't only in Orangeboro. People seemed to be riled up about it all over the Station. Indeed, all over the Chayko System—including inside Transmondia itself. By all reports, the Transmondian public also was outraged and demanding answers.

Did you see this? Rex forwarded a vid from Orangeboro. *I can't know for sure because I can't smell her, but is that Zona Dorsey?*

Who? He opened the vid. There in the foreground, leading a crowd of demonstrators, strode the woman from the park a week ago. *Oh. Right. Zona. Yes, that's her.* She held a sign up high and she was chanting something. He turned up his internal volume to hear: "Hey-hey-hey-hey, Transmondia has got to pay! Hey-hey-hey-hey, can't take our XK9s away!"

Got that right. He placed a call to Pam. "We're up. When and where do you need us?"

❖ ❖ ❖ ❖ ❖ ❖ ❖ ❖

Fourth Level Boardroom: Pam's Operations Center

"Chalk up one more for Jem and Granny!" The frazzled grin on Walter's round, dark face in Pam's HUD-view brought a smile to her lips.

"They're a pair of troupers, for sure. Thanks for the update." Pam sighed and leaned back in her chair. She'd returned to the fourth-level boardroom after this morning's Press Conference from Hell had ended in chaos. "You guys are scheduled for a supper break, starting as soon as you can get to the Green Room. Aurelia and Charlie's cousin Manny, the chef, have a spread laid out for you there."

"That works for me. Thanks!"

Pam rubbed her eyes and consulted one of the now *five* screens in her operations center. Walter's Lang Family had accounted for a fair number of interviews during this long, *long*, post-"Puppy Massacre" afternoon. Once word got out, Walter's "Granny" Ifiok and her granddaughter Ijemma had been in high demand whenever an XK9 wasn't available. Granny had a gift for telling fun and illuminating "Petunia stories." With Jem by her side to fill in any needed XK9 facts from an apparently boundless store of knowledge, they'd proved to be an entertaining and informative duo.

The next call came from Manny's wife, Fee. Pam had

stationed her in the Grooming Room next to the Green Room. "Is the Master Mix here, yet?" They'd run critically low this morning.

"Berwyn hasn't checked in so far." Pam frowned. "He and Shiv are helping Dahlia haul in the resupply." When the Orangeboro Council declared that XK9s were sapient more than a month ago, all shipments of Master Mix from Transmondia had stopped, even those the OPD had paid for. Not that any XK9 in the Pack would've trusted new shipments.

Pabiyan Carnerie Manager Dahlia Glenn had stepped in to create a replacement, based on the OPD's remaining stock. She'd received help from Dr. Sandler and the nutritionists at Station Polytechnic to formulate high-quality home-grown Master Mix. Until Pam had become the sergeant in charge of the XK9 Unit, she'd only vaguely grasped how many augmentation-support medications were packed into that specialized formula, along with the high-performance nutrients. So far, however, they'd only managed to output it in small batches.

"The main question after 'when will it get here?' is 'what flavors are we getting?'" Fee added.

"Before they left, Berwyn forwarded a list." Pam rubbed her temples. "I thought I sent it already." Aware that the Pack's XK9s universally panned Transmondian Master Mix as "bland and boring," Dahlia and her team had created several different flavors.

Shady and Rex both loved the Bountiful Bacon variety, but Choicest Chicken and Revved-up Rabbit also had fans among the Pack. Not surprisingly, Bacon-Wrapped Filet Mignon, although more expensive, was another top favorite flavor. Pam already had five different journalists lined up with requests to interview Dahlia this evening, once she'd arrived and distributed the chow.

I just re-sent that list. After their initial contacts via the com lines, QUAERO had opened a new brain link channel with Pam.

Bonnie the groomer put the first one in a "miscellaneous" file, so it's no wonder Fee couldn't find it.

A *ding* sounded on the com. "Ah! Thank you!" Fee grinned and closed her call.

Thank you. You've been amazing, Pam said through the link.

You are most welcome. Like Shady, QUAERO also could project emotional responses—or what felt like emotions—through their link. Gracious warmth shifted into concern. *I have a question, however. You are a corporeal being, yet you yourself have taken no breaks. According to your agency's guidelines, you should have taken two of them by now.*

I've, um, been pretty busy.

Go take a break. I can cover things here.

Undoubtedly ne could, at that. *Thank you again!*

Go. Eat. Rest. You'll be needed again this evening. That definitely felt like affectionate amusement coming through, now.

CHAPTER 52
"ONE OF MIKA ZUNI'S LEOS"

Centerboro Capitol Complex, Umberter Legislative Office Building

Allafternoon, each time Charlie introduced her as his Amare, Hildie's breath caught. It still didn't feel quite real —although Great-Grandmama Hildie's ring on her hand offered solid, physical confirmation. *I could get used to the rush it gives me.*

It certainly helped to have little infusions of enthusiasm, as they scrambled from one interview to the next. Once Rex and Charlie had become available, the demand for them hadn't let up.

One crusty-seeming older Council Member asked how long they'd been Amares. He seemed startled and charmed to learn they'd only become official a couple of days ago. His stern, furrowed face transformed into a broad smile with sparkling eyes. "Brand-new Amares! Such adventures await you! Congratulations!"

Maybe it helped our cause? It certainly had been the high point of her afternoon so far. She consulted her HUD. "Next interview is with Angharad Juma of Highboro. She's another longtime legislator, and she's pretty high up in the Popular Democracy

Party. 'Likes dogs,' according to the notes from Pam's now-not-so-secret insider. Maybe that'll help."

"Do the notes say anything else about Council Member Juma?" Charlie asked.

Hildie consulted her HUD. "Highboro is known for its avocados—they have an annual festival in September—it's home to a community of Primeran expats, and it's also a center for . . . Oh, that's interesting." She grinned at Charlie. "The Borough Council sponsors an annual fellowship for med students studying re-gen."

Rex lolled his tongue and Charlie grinned. "Well, we're *both* pretty grateful for that field of study!" her Amare said.

"And for nanotech," Rex added. "I am starting to like nanotech a lot."

"Her office is down the hall and around the corner." Hildie's HUD switched on a new view. It showed her receding sequences of green arrows to point the way and a countdown till the appointment time. "We now have five minutes to get there."

They reached the office well before their time ran out.

Council Member Juma's receptionist gave them a cold look. "Sit over there. "But she kept them cooling their heels for only a moment before the Council Member herself arrived.

"Rex? Charlie?"

They stood. Hildie stood, too, unsure if she should go with them.

Charlie performed introductions.

Juma nodded but seemed distracted. She kept staring at Charlie. Then she frowned, rubbed her eyes. "Sorry. We ran into delays on the trip here, and I'm still catching up with myself. Please come into my office."

One of the many Council Members who made a point to come today after all. Hildie smiled. From her time helping Pam, she knew many of them hadn't been slated to arrive till tomorrow.

Juma waved them to chairs, still eyeing Charlie. Rex took a

spot on the floor next to Charlie's chair and Hildie took the other chair.

The ResCouncil Member got right to the point. She asked Rex the usual set of questions that most of her fellow legislators also had asked. Why should people believe XK9s were sapient? What made him think the Transmondians wanted any more XK9s dead? What did he want Juma to do about it? She asked the questions, and then she *listened*.

Hildie had done her best to remain neutral and simply observe during most of today's interviews, but she found herself liking Juma.

Rex had developed a series of elevator speeches by now. He trotted them out with glib ease. But after one of his answers, Juma lifted her hand, palm out. "Stop. Transmondian agents? You confronted Transmondian agents?"

"Yes, we did, several times." Rex's huge shaggy head nodded in an uncannily human way. "Shady subdued and captured one after he knocked me out with a trank bolt. They later infested our home with surveillance devices for a while, but we found and destroyed them all. Our SBI colleagues established that the devices were unquestionably Transmondian. Later, another agent nearly killed Razor with a neurotoxin. And after that, one tried to kill Charlie and me in Howardsboro."

A chill swept over Hildie, then settled uneasily in her gut. She gave Charlie a questioning glance, but her Amare avoided eye contact. She'd known someone had given him a black eye when he was in Howardsboro, but all he'd said about it was, "You should see the other guy."

"Tell me about that one, please." Juma looked from Rex to Charlie then back to Rex.

Yes, please do! Hildie frowned and focused on Rex. *This is my life now. This is Charlie's JOB. It's not going to change, so I need to figure out how to face it.* The first time she'd heard anything about an agent shooting a poison dart at Charlie had been during the press conference last night. He, Rex, and Shady had gone for what they were now calling a "walk to the park" before she could ask more about it.

"Actually, I only heard about it after the fact." Rex's tail thumped the floor with an enthusiastic tempo. He gave Charlie a glowing look. "Charlie saved me. The agent had several vials of that damned neurotoxin with him. Apparently his assignment was to kill me while I was in Healing Sleep. I had captured a Whisper Syndicate operative earlier that afternoon, you see. But she stabbed me several times before I could subdue her." A ripple ran along his hackles.

Juma blinked, eyebrows up. "Well, thank you for your service. That sounds horrifying."

"I do not wish to repeat the experience." Rex flicked his ears. "We still have not figured out how the agent learned I was hurt, temporarily helpless, and in Howardsboro, but he came after me. He had the neurotoxin, and he apparently meant to kill me while I was unable to defend myself."

"But Charlie saved you?"

"Yes!" More tail-thumps beat an enthusiastic rhythm on the floor. "That Transmondian disabled two SBI field agents who had come with Charlie to protect me. He tore through a big pile of furniture that Charlie used to barricade the door—like it was nothing."

Hildie's pulse sped up enough to make her head spin. The picture in her mind terrified her. She clenched her fists in her lap and made an effort to breathe. *Steady, now, Hils. You need to learn how to deal with this.*

"Not 'nothing'." Charlie shook his head. "The barricade slowed him down a lot, and it really pissed him off. I was hoping it would make him angry enough to skew his judgment."

Rex's ears snapped flat. "He threw a desk at you. It went three meters down the hall."

Hildie struggled to keep her breathing steady. Her pulse thrashed in her ears. *A DESK?*

Charlie scowled. "It was a table, not a desk. And I had plenty of time to get out of the way."

"A veterinarian's exam table. Solid steel." Rex laid a sheepdog stare on him. "Beck told me all about it later."

"Okay." Charlie grimaced and shot a worried glance in Hildie's direction. "Okay, I'll admit to that. But I got out of the way, and I subdued him."

"Not before he shot a neurotoxin dart at you."

Hildie's throat closed. She stared at Charlie.

Charlie frowned at his partner. "It deflected off my arm shield. Hurt like hell for a bit, but I was fine. No big deal."

"Wait a minute." Juma lifted her hand again. "Okay, so let me get this straight. You built a barricade out of heavy things like solid steel exam tables, while you were still in an arm shield. An augmented agent threw one of the tables at you, and then he shot at you with a neurotoxin dart? And you *still* subdued him?"

Charlie hunched his shoulders. "Well, let's not make it out to be more than it was. Just a lot of ugly scrabbling. He gave me a real good shiner before I managed to pin him and use my EStee on him."

Juma gave him eyebrows-up. "No ordinary cop pins an augmented agent, especially not when he's still severely enough injured to need an arm shield." Her gaze flicked significantly toward the one Charlie still wore.

"I, um—" Charlie shot another worried glance at Hildie.

This is what I signed up for. Gut icy, Hildie bit her lips, squared her shoulders, and struggled to keep her breathing steady. *I'm the one who said, "random variables be damned." Now I need to own it.*

That Transmondian definitely qualified as a damned random variable. Of the sort that would probably keep happening. She twisted her new Amare ring and let the realization wash over her. *This is why Rex wants him "XK9-tough." Because it's simply a fact of his work, now. And it's not gonna change.*

Council Member Juma had a pretty good sheepdog-stare,

herself. "I feel I must ask, although it's rather clear at this point. Are you one of Mika Zuni's LEOs?"

Charlie's mouth opened, but he didn't speak.

"What do you mean by that?" Rex demanded. "What is this about Dr. Zuni?"

She rubbed a hand across her lips. "Mm, well. Your Dr. Zuni —Mika—grew up in Highboro. As you may know, a lot of my constituents are of Primeran descent."

Rex and Charlie nodded. *Ah. That's interesting.* Hildie guessed where this might be going.

"When he was in med school, Mika was part of a group we sent to Primero for a deep-dive study of the re-gen and augmentation techniques the Primeran health care system has perfected. We wanted doctors who could come back and help take care of our older expats. We have a fair number of ex-military types who received augmentation treatments in their youth. Mika's group came back to teach other doctors, and now our community has good coverage of care whenever an augmented elder has an issue related to his or her special medical needs."

Rex gave a soft growl. "You haven't gotten to the 'LEOs' part."

"Once we had that desired coverage of care in the community, Mika began consulting on Wheel Two. After he moved there and joined an Orangeboro Family, he made a minor specialty of patching up injured Safety Services workers in addition to his general re-gen work. Where it was appropriate, he's managed to get a few of them augmented. There are a couple of police officers, as I understand it, and an SBI agent. As one of the sponsors who helped send his group to Primero all those years ago, I've followed his career, you see."

Wait—another police officer? Hildie stared at Juma. *Someone else who understands?*

"There's *another* officer on Wheel Two with augmentations?" Charlie gave Juma a startled look. "Which Borough?"

She frowned. "I want to say Pueblo, but I'm not sure." Then

she smiled. "Does this mean I'm right? I've now *actually met* one of Mika's LEOs?"

Charlie sighed. "Don't spread it around, okay?"

"How did you know?" Rex asked.

"Oh, I've met enough augmented people to recognize the musculature, the walk, the way they carry themselves."

Hildie'd anticipated that answer. She'd seen the changes in Charlie, too. *We asked for this. We chose it.* She bit her lip. *Here's hoping we chose well.*

Juma smiled. "And as I said, no ordinary cop could do what you did." She glanced again at the arm shield. "Your augmentations are new?"

"Early December."

"Well, then, best wishes to you. I think you'll find it was a good choice." She turned to Hildie and Rex. "Did you get a say in his decision to augment?"

Hildie nodded. "I encouraged him, but I'll admit I wasn't prepared for all of the results."

"I lobbied pretty hard for the augmentations." Rex's tongue lolled long. "I wanted him to be XK9-tough, especially because a mistake I made got him hurt. I do not ever want to break him again."

"'Break' him? Oh, my." Juma gave Rex a slow nod. "You do look like a very large and powerful dog. Are you as smart as they say?"

"Have you been forced to lower the sophistication of your language, in order to communicate with me?"

That elicited a chuckle. "No. If we'd been on a com without a vid, I would've assumed you're human."

"Can you draw a conclusion from that?" Rex gave her an earnest ears-up.

Laying on the 'puppy eyes.' Oh, my. Hildie struggled to stifle a grin.

Juma gave a low laugh. "I always did think it might be possible. Now I'm sure it is."

"Will you please vote in favor of keeping me and my Pack-mates safe?" Rex intensified the puppy eyes, tail waving. "If we are sent to Transmondia, we greatly fear we will be killed or intellectually maimed. We already know our brain links are not defective. The recall is a sham—an excuse to place us at their mercy."

Her expression turned grim. "And they won't have any, will they? Any more than they had for Puppy Farm One."

Rex lowered his head and tail. "They never have."

"My vote is yours, Rex." She gave him a smile and a nod. "Now let's go twist some of my colleagues' arms. It wouldn't do for Detective Morgan to become XK9-tough and then lose his partner."

Hildie's gut relaxed, even though she'd been pretty sure of Juma's reaction by now. *Another ally. We can't have too many of them, and this one seems especially promising.*

CHAPTER 53

COUNTDOWN TO THE JOINT SESSION

Pam's Operations Center and Green Room Adjacent to Ballroom A

T his is it. *This is the final lead-in to the Joint Session tomorrow.* Pam attempted a patterned breathing exercise that was supposed to help her relax, but her body hummed with tension. She started the pattern again and struggled to center herself. *Nope. Just gotta go in as I am.* She closed two of her screens, then sent the contents of a third to her HUD.

This walk-through should help you feel better, QUAERO said through their link.

Emphasis on the 'should.' Gnawing, pit-of-her stomach flutters grew stronger. She chewed on her lips. *It's almost Monday evening! Tomorrow's the Combined Councils trip. Have we done enough? Can we possibly do enough?*

She didn't know how to count votes or calculate their odds, but Vince Bellini had been fairly upbeat. *Is he just trying to buck me up, or do we really have grounds for optimism?*

He is coming to this practice session. QUAERO's words arrived in a small burst of amusement. *You could ask him.*

I can't ask him that!

438

You will do well. I have observed you in action. Calm, warm confidence flooded nir connection.

You are extremely kind. Thank you. Pam drew in a deep breath and stood. "Friends, it's time." It had been another long day, but everyone had gotten to their interviews, and most had reported positive results.

"I can cover the hotline for you, just in case." Balchu eyed her, then nodded when the line clicked over. "Got it."

"How can I help?" Hildie looked up from the workspace they'd set up for her during the latest mandated break that Pam had decreed for Rex and Charlie. She'd appeared at Pam's doorway with another round of scones and tea a while ago. Balchu had helped get her settled in as a press liaison, once again coordinating with Joslyn Stark.

Pam's whole body warmed with gratitude. She turned her smile toward her newest friend. "You've been amazing, Hildie, but you're in the witness lineup, too. This training is as much for you as it is for the rest of us."

They trooped downstairs to the Green Room just off Ballroom A. Director Perri and Mike Santiago had stepped to one side for a low-voiced conference, but Chief Klein, Rex, and Charlie greeted them.

Charlie focused on Hildie. "How's it going?"

"Hildie's been a massive help." Pam grinned at them both, then found a place to sit between Shady and Balchu for their testimony rehearsal.

Other Packmates began to arrive. Petunia went straight to Hildie's side and gave her a wet-nose greeting once the young woman stepped back from Charlie's hug. Petunia's partner Walter lingered outside the door a moment longer to talk with a couple of his cousins.

"This has been quite a day." Shady rested her head on Pam's lap. "I bumped into Bill Sloane just before I came here. I was glad I did. I wanted to thank him for coming. He said they interviewed him for the *It's Morning, Rana Station!* show, and Becky's whole class watched it."

"I bet that was exciting." Pam smiled. "He was interviewed for that, and also two other shows. They have such dramatic vids of him out there on the OPD HQ steps, getting shot while shielding Rex. He's been very busy this morning."

"He told me that vid is embarrassing, but he's determined to tell how he realized Rex is sapient."

"That vid shows a selfless hero in action." Pam shook her head. "He has nothing to be embarrassed about."

"What is it with heroes? None that I know seems to want any recognition at all." Shady flicked her ears.

"The *It's Morning* show certainly has seemed sympathetic to our cause." Their format included local segments for each Borough, which Chief Klein said gave the XK9s great coverage. The show runners had recorded short interviews with nearly half of the Pack, including Rex and Charlie. They'd also created a segment with Berwyn's friends Tim, Terry, and Ben. The Amigos had done a good job of living up to their entertaining normal selves.

Charlie's uncle Dolph Sanger hadn't been interviewed for *It's Morning*, but he'd probably done a couple dozen other interviews over the weekend. *So many voices lifted up in support of XK9 sapience, now that she sat back to consider it! So many hands pitching in—often even before they were asked for help. Different agencies. Different generations of different Families. Even the snooty Ciné and Chardonnay circles were demonstrating for the XK9 cause, for pity's sake! Who saw that coming? But we all love our XK9s. We all believe in them. And we want the Universe to believe in them, too.*

Goosebumps prickled up the back of her neck and she couldn't repress a smile. The flutters in her gut stilled. *This is the power of the Pack—and I'm a part of it. This is something Mother will never allow herself to accept or understand.* She shook her head, sad in spite of her better judgment. Then she closed her hand over Balchu's. *Be here now. That's what I need to do. Because here and now is a pretty amazing place to be.*

❖ ❖ ❖ ❖ ❖ ❖ ❖ ❖

Green Room Adjacent to Ballroom A

Director Perri moved to the front-center part of the Green Room. Shady lifted her ears and checked the woman's scent factors. Her normal bouquet seemed always tilted toward the sharp, clear high tones of inquiry. "Before you begin your rehearsal, I wanted to update you on the status of our investigation into the Alvarez Place Apartments conspirators."

Everyone quieted.

"We still don't have an ID on the augmented Transmondian. If he is the agent we think he is, that's to be expected." All the same, Perri's scent went peppery with frustration. "For now, he remains in our custody, although both Centerboro PD and SDF Military Intelligence want him. CPD took custody of the two bombing suspects this morning, but our agencies are cooperating."

Nobody asked about Council Members Nesbit, Berik, and Cole. They'd all gone free on their own recognizance, thanks to a too-CWP-friendly judge and a strident com call from the Premier's office. Shady swallowed a growl and tried to focus when Mike stepped forward.

"One of our bombing suspects remains unregistered and unidentified. This is the one the XK9s called 'Soldering-Smoke Woman.'" Mike frowned and crossed his arms. "She refuses to cooperate almost as stubbornly as the Transmondian. But 'Nervous Guy' was relatively easy to identify. Lee-André Merrick is a citizen and a licensed private investigator here in Centerboro. His only client for the past three years? Madeira Sewell."

A few of the humans groaned or made disgusted noises in their throats.

Who is Madeira Sewell, and why did people groan? Shady cocked her head at Pam.

Name rings bells, but . . . Pam shook her head.

"Some of you will remember that Madeira Sewell has been a Commonwealth Party leader," Mike said. "She and Premier Iskander have been allies for a long time, turning the CWP more pro-Transmondian."

Unhappy scent factors soured the air. They matched the frowns, scowls, and slumped body language.

Mike gave his listeners a rueful nod. "Now that Sewell's out of office, she's a registered foreign agent. For the Transmondians."

Such a patriot. Shady gave a soft growl.

A new person stepped into the Green Room. Chief Klein met him with a smile.

"Woah. That's Vince Bellini." Pam sat up straighter.

"Really?" Balchu's eyebrows went up.

"Oddly enough, he looks smaller on my HUD." Pam grinned.

In real life, Sacha Guzmán's personal secretary stood as tall as Chief Klein. The Chief introduced him as soon as the room quieted.

"Hello." Bellini moved to the center. "I'm here to walk you through the basics of what it takes to be a witness before the Combined Councils. But let's put first things first. In Vice Premier Guzmán's office, we believe in XK9 sapience and we feel nothing but the deepest revulsion for the events at Puppy Farm One."

He paused with a frown, as if not sure whether he wanted to say the next thing. "Perverse as it sounds—and I do apologize— this actually is good for your political message. Whoever ordered that raid must've had delusions that they could keep it quiet, is all I can say. The Transmondian government has received near-universal condemnation ever since the story broke, so here's hoping there won't be any more such attacks on XK9s after this."

Assuming that one was the first. Shady's hackles prickled. The

Project's other puppy training farms were located in more remote areas.

"It also serves as a stark and shocking confirmation that you are correct to say if you are returned to Transmondia you face probable death. It should be fresh in the minds of those we're trying to convince."

We can only hope they think our deaths would be a bad thing.

Shady met Pam's worried gaze. Her partner grimaced.

Bellini shook his head. "That's not why I'm here, however. There are some points of protocol you'll need to remember tomorrow. First and very important: no weapons of any kind are to be brought into the Combined Councils Chamber. Empty your gear belts, leave your EStees in your hotel rooms. No knives, no handcuffs, no batons."

"What about us?" Rex asked. "We XK9s were originally sold to the OPD as forensic tools and effective weapons for neutralizing threats from obstreperous subjects. Are we banned?"

"You XK9s are not considered 'weapons' in this context. You are *cooperating witnesses.*" Bellini's expression went rueful. "Point taken, but the RES has to draw a few lines for the sake of security. Might note that they don't ask martial artists to leave their hands at home before they testify, either."

"That's a relief." Charlie grinned.

"May I take my med kit?" Hildie asked. "It contains a tiny pair of scissors and a few sharps. But as a paramedic who normally works in microgravity I'd feel kinda naked and unprepared without it."

"Standard micrograv med kit?" Bellini pursed his lips. "There are more than a dozen such med kits stationed around on the walls, and you're a licensed paramedic, even though you're currently off-duty. Bring your badge if you have it with you."

She nodded. "Always. It's in my kit."

"Okay, then. If they give you any trouble about it, I'd be surprised. With your specialty, it's more likely you'd be considered an on-site asset in case of an emergency."

"What about prosthetics?" Tux cocked his head.

Bellini sighed. "Does anyone here have a prosthetic that could be considered a weapon?"

Everyone shook their heads. *Law enforcement officers aren't allowed to have weaponized prosthetics,* Pam said through the link.

"It was a question that occurred to me, is all," Tux said. "Never mind."

"Thank you." Bellini grimaced. "Now, let's talk about the route you'll take on approach, and where you'll go once you've been admitted to the Chamber."

Shady's HUD dinged: A floor plan—perhaps "area plan" was more appropriate in a micrograv environment—opened for her. Whatever, it made about as much sense to her as most maps.

Don't worry. I can follow it, Pam said through the link. *When we get there, just stick with me.*

❖ ❖ ❖ ❖ ❖ ❖ ❖ ❖

State Pavilion: Rex's Room and Lobby

By evening, Rex couldn't stop panting and pacing, although their hotel suite didn't offer much space for that.

Hildie gave him an unhappy look, then exchanged a glance with Charlie.

His partner shook his head. "How about if you go pace in the lobby?"

Ah. Got it. I'm large, hairy, nervous, and everywhere. Rex stress-yawned. *I'll be in the lobby. Call me when it's bedtime.* He pushed past their room's door and headed downstairs.

What could they possibly need to pack? After all, their trip to the Combined Councils Chamber in the Hub would only last for part of the day tomorrow. Their food would be provided. The humans wouldn't need to change clothes. Their micrograv harnesses would all be fully charged, their nitrogen-jet canisters filled and ready to go for up to 36 hours. What else could they possibly need?

But Charlie had a whole list of things to stock in the panniers. Dog-adapted micrograv water delivery he could understand. But forensic supplies?

"We needed them at the Trans-Hub Terminal on Saturday," Charlie'd replied to Rex's questions. "And you know the RES won't have scent cards if we should possibly need them."

"True. But how likely is it that we actually will?" He'd spoken aloud for Hildie's benefit.

"It's an extremely remote possibility. But not zero." So Charlie packed scent cards.

Meanwhile, Hildie laid out supplies she'd brought in her luggage and methodically re-stocked her micrograv med kit.

Rex gave up. Yes, there would be med stations in the Combined Chambers complex, but "I never go Topside without a full kit." And that was that.

"I don't suppose the ban on weapons includes the pins on our uniforms, does it?" Charlie eyed the array that belonged on his dress blues. "That Medal of Valor has a pretty long spike on the back."

Hildie laughed. "You have to wear your medals, sorry. They're part of your uniform."

"I suppose the RES *might* willing to risk a Council Member being pinned to death with the fastener on a Medal of Valor."

"Or maybe, since the Combined Councils bestowed it in the first place, they're willing to trust a recipient not to do that." Hildie grinned. "No weasel clause, Morgan!"

"Damn."

Rex was just as happy to let them sort things out on their own.

Most of the Pack's XK9s had already gathered in the lobby. They turned to meet Rex with lolling tongues and wagging tails.

Shady greeted him with a nuzzle. "I am surprised it took

them this long to kick you out. Is Charlie also packing scent cards?"

"What sort of massive crime scene do they expect?" Rex flicked his ears, then gave himself a vigorous shake.

"I believe they hope for none at all." Scout said. "It is Nicole's way of keeping from worrying."

"Are everyone else's humans also stressed out by this?" Rex's nose searched his Pack.

Loving amusement blossomed in everyone's scent factors.

"Georgie is 'utterly freaked,' as she would put it." Tux's tongue lolled long. "The members of the Combined Councils are an important group of the most powerful decision-makers on Rana. Being invited to testify before the full Joint Session is something that might only happen once in a lifetime, and only for a few Ranans ever."

"The vast majority of Ranans never do, according to Walter," Petunia added. "Lang Family is in a complete tizzy. This is the first time anyone from Lang has ever been asked to present evidence there."

"Balchu is jazzed, even though he won't be there in person. Apparently this is one watch-party he fully plans to attend." Shady's tail waved high. "Pam is too busy on the com with Vince Bellini to think about it yet. But Balchu is ready with a small packet of the genetically-tailored sleeping meds her physician prescribed. They should allow her to rest tonight but awaken alert."

Rex cocked his head. "Pam sometimes awakens alert?" He did not remember any such event from their days of shared quarters in Solara City.

"I am told it is possible." Shady's tail sped up. "I look forward to observing the phenomenon."

CHAPTER 54
THE COMBINED COUNCILS
JOINT SPECIAL SESSION

Center-Hub Secured Governmental and Diplomatic District

C harlie stopped inside the Ranan Executive Security scanner and strove to keep his breathing steady. The harness controls, although mentally manipulated, brought a welcome sense of groundedness despite his being in micrograv.

Black-uniformed RES officers ran their scans, checked his ID, and measured his biorhythms.

Icy jabs of PTS reactions lanced through his gut and brought a tremor to his hands, but he focused on the mission. Hildie's warm, confident smile as he'd moved forward strengthened him, even though he had a pretty good idea it was forced bravado. And the solid determination he received from Rex through the link steadied him and filled him with a sense of common purpose.

Nothing set off the RES alarms. "Passed. Move forward."

He triggered his jets to join Rex. Behind him Hildie braked inside the scanner. He glanced back to observe her progress.

They might be in micrograv but, like the rest of his human Packmates, he was decked out in his dress blues again. A saree or skirt wouldn't work here, but Hildie's sleek, dark blue leggings and tucked-in, hand-painted silk blouse worked well. They also displayed her fit physique to stunning effect, even with that bulky medkit strapped around her waist.

"Passed. Move forward."

She joined them, her eyes shining. "Wow. We're in."

"And there's Shady." Rex burned jets to join his mate, who'd already passed through.

Charlie and Hildie greeted their group. Pam, Shady, Chief Klein, and Director Perri had gone through ahead of them. Soon more Packmates and Orangeboro officials cleared the RES scanners.

"I guess the last time you were here, they gave you your medal?" Hildie eyed him as if trying to gauge how he felt.

"I, um, sat out that event." Charlie's face heated up. He avoided eye contact, even with her. "My PTS reactions were a lot worse then. The Combined Councils allowed my parents and Gran Annie to accept it for me." Micrograv already had his stomach in a knot, but now it cranked tighter.

"Mm. Sorry to drag up a bad memory."

"It's all right." He gave a little head-shake and fired a compensatory jet. "That's not only water under the bridge, it's recirculated several thousand times since then. Way too long ago to worry about now." *And yet I still do.*

Once everyone made it through the scanners, Director Perri led them down a long, curving passageway. Charlie pictured their destination. At age seventeen on the Upper Levels Civics trip, the yawning sweep of the egg-shaped Chamber had amazed him. The towering span of screens that encompassed the "narrow end" of the "egg" offered a 180-degree view of near space. That view had left his younger self dazzled. Ten years and an ERT career later, would he still feel similar awe?

An RES officer halted them at the end by a hatch that led inside to the speakers' platform at the narrowest point of the Chamber. "They just introduced a new resolution from the floor." He scowled. "It's not on the agenda. We'll have a delay while they debate it."

Director Perri, first in their lineup, grimaced. "How long?"

The officer shook his head. "Who knows? Could be five minutes, could be an hour and a half or more. That's how the process goes, though."

Damn. More time caught in micrograv. Just what I wanted. Charlie scowled, then offered Hildie a rueful half-smile when she gave his hand a gentle squeeze.

I wonder if that motion came from one of the Palmdale creeps, trying to create more delays? Rex uttered a soft growl. *I wouldn't put it past them.*

Charlie, Rex, and Hildie, along with Pam and Shady, had been placed near the head of the lineup. The rest of the Pack followed them. They hung in midair behind Chief Klein and Orangeboro Mayor Ailani Idris. Mike and Elaine, with Shiv and Dominic Wei, waited behind them.

Shiv had been on the witness list since early in the plan, but he'd only arrived a short time ago. Back on Sunday, he'd joined Berwyn and Dahlia on a brief overnight trip to Centerboro, to bring more Master Mix and conduct some quick interviews. But he and Berwyn had returned to Orangeboro early yesterday, so they'd be there when Cinnamon came out of re-gen.

Today he'd once again rejoined his colleagues, this time straight from the train to the equipment locker area where everybody else was putting on their micrograv harnesses. The Pack had reacted to his arrival with delight.

He brought greetings from Razor and Liz and news from Berwyn and Cinnamon. She'd emerged from her re-gen early this morning and remained in recovery today. Her health had improved dramatically, although she was in no condition to travel yet.

But that bright moment had come earlier. Now he, along with the rest of this group, must wait in midair limbo.

"Hurry up and wait appears to be the story of today so far." Shady flicked her ears.

The RES officer glared at her but said nothing.

Bellini hadn't told them not to talk in this waiting area. Had he forgotten that instruction, or was this officer merely disconcerted by dogs who could talk? Charlie wished for the millionth time that he could detect scent factors.

Rex, however, did not seem to be focused on the officer's scent. Instead, he sniffed with growing urgency along a joint in the bulkhead on their left. After a moment, he powered his jets to sniff farther along the joint.

Rex's inputs via the link sent an icy jolt through Charlie. He stared at Rex and desperately wished he could disbelieve. *Are you absolutely certain?* Slipped out before he could stop it, but it was a stupid question. The scents were what they were.

"What is it doing? Dog! Stop that!" The officer scowled at him.

Rex spun, then fired braking jets to stop himself so he faced Shady. His hackles puffed out. "Shady, come here! Smell this! Tell me I am not imagining it!" His gaze shifted past her. "Tux! You too! Come smell this!"

Shady and Tux converged on the bulkhead joint, noses working.

"Here now! Stop that! We can't have such chaos in the line!" The officer jetted toward them with an outraged expression.

Charlie held up a peremptory hand. "Wait! They've detected something."

"There's nothing there! It's just a bunch of support structures. What could they possibly find?"

But now Shady's hackles had puffed out, too. So had Tux's.

"You are right," Tux said. "That is most definitely the Fredericks formula!"

Charlie pulsed jets to move toward them. He searched along the bulkhead joint with urgent, careful fingers. Pushed inward in place after place along the edge for its access trigger.

"Stop! Are you insane?" The RES officer demanded. "What do you think you're doing?"

Charlie kept searching. "We need to remove this panel. There are explosives somewhere behind it."

Rex continued sniffing the bulkhead joint, then stopped. *Ah! Here is a place where multiple people have put their fingers, over time. The most recent touch came within the last ten hours, and dammit! They wore nitrile gloves.*

Charlie jetted to his side. *Show me exactly.*

Can't get a scent trace off of a nitrile-glove contact, so right here—where I touched it with my nose.

Got it.

Rex jetted aside.

Charlie punched the right place. The panel unlatched with a *click.*

Mayor Idris gasped, but Charlie angled the panel off of the bulkhead. Pam caught it, passed it back to Georgia.

Rex jetted inside followed by Tux and Shady. But then they all stopped short.

"Crap! It is all through here!" Rex turned with a snarl to the RES officer. "Evacuate that Chamber and call in every bomb disposal unit you can find!"

"Evac—You can't do that! The Council is in session!"

But both Director Perri and Pam gave him angry glares. They'd already activated their coms.

"Don't argue with me, Ilma, just listen!" Perri ordered.

"Yeah, Vince. We have a situation here," Pam said. "We need to evacuate the Council Chamber ASAP."

❖ ❖　❖ ❖　❖ ❖　❖ ❖

Chambered Security Shielding outside Combined Councils Chamber

R ex struggled to steady his breathing, to think and smell as clearly as possible. This maze of cross-angled beams wasn't much like the structure inside the *Izgubil* or the Dart. Of course, it wasn't. *It's not made for the same purpose.* But structural beams had structural joints. And each one he sniffed in here was rigged with the same mixture of adhesive-applied explosive pellets and nanotimers as on those doomed ships.

Behind him, humans and the other Pack members had sprung into action. He should leave this—*wait. Did I hear something?*

I can't hear anything over the people behind us, Charlie said through the link.

Rex pulsed his jets and drifted farther inside, ears up. *Quiet. It was faint, but troubling.*

He sensed Charlie's interest through their link, but his partner kept his thoughts quiet and followed him.

"Charlie? Rex?" Hildie's voice held a sharp, fearful tone.

Charlie pulsed jets to turn then halt. Rex received a sense of him holding up an index finger to his lips for "quiet."

She answered with a surge of worried scent factors. Her personal bouquet drew nearer.

Rex left Charlie to deal with her. At least they'd stopped making noise. He pulsed jets and drifted farther into the darkness. This place was a veritable forest of slanted support beams and containment panels, set to slam shut the instant the sensors detected a pressure change from a hull breach. Behind him someone spoke on a public address system, distant enough behind layers of compression panels for the words to be inarticulate.

His forward harness lights flicked on. They cast weird shadows but illuminated a lot of nothing new. The scent of the Fredericks explosives surrounded him, harsh and threatening. *Just like on the Dart.* His nightmare and his efforts to remember brought it sharply to memory. *Inert. Not burning. But for how long?*

Maybe this was stupid. He'd drifted too deep into the maze of support beams for comfort. There probably was no . . .

"Mmm-*mmm! MMM!*"

Muffled, but closer. And clearly someone in distress. *That was not 'nothing.'*

I didn't hear anything, Charlie replied.

Rex pulsed his jets again, slid forward faster.

"*Mmmm! Mmm-uuummm!*" Closer. Louder. A personal odor profile reached him, laden with terrified scent factors and the raw reek of injury.

It's Zander Hoback.

Charlie's initial burst of surprise through the link shifted to foreboding. *It's a trap of some kind.*

"We have found Zander Hoback," Rex texted to Shady, Chief Klein, Pam, Director Perri, and Elaine. "He is injured. Charlie and I suspect a trap."

"Hildie, go back." Charlie'd pitched his voice low, but urgency filled his tone. "It could be a trap."

"What have you found?"

"Zander Hoback—the head bomber."

"He is injured and terrified," Rex added through the vocalizer. "We think it is a Transmondian trap."

"If he's injured, that's *my* call!"

Rex hadn't heard that note in her voice before. It brooked no objections.

She pulsed jets and whooshed past Charlie. "Where is he, Rex?"

"Hils—"

"*Where?*"

Rex jetted forward, then kicked on left jets for a burst to shift right around another structural support that reeked of explosives. His forward lights fell on a writhing human form. "Here."

"*MMM! MUUHMM!*" Wide, terrified eyes stared at him above layers of stout, wide tape strapped across the man's mouth just below his nose. More tape bound him to a structural support.

"Crap!" Hildie darted forward, one hand on her medkit. She braked next to the bound man. "Hello, Zander. My name is Hildie. I'm a paramedic." She attached a bio-readout patch onto his forehead then tugged at the tape on his mouth.

"*Mmm-umm-UUM!*" Urgency and terror filled his scent.

Charlie examined the tape that bound the man to the support. "Damn that 'no knives' rule!"

Rex put out a call on the coms. "Can anyone get us a knife?"

"Will my little scissors help?" Hildie held them up.

Charlie eyed them with a dubious expression. "We may not have time for those to gnaw their way through."

"Let me try." She attacked the tape, but to little effect. "Of course they're blunt-tipped. And 'gnaw through' is the right description for sure."

Charlie shot an apologetic glance at Hoback. " This is probably gonna hurt." He gave the tape a hard yank. It stretched, but held.

"*MUUUUH!*" Hoback's agonized cry needed no words.

Charlie yanked harder. Again, Hoback cried out. The tape stretched farther. "Damn them! He's also zip-cuffed!" Charlie's scent went peppery, but with an undertone of raw, dark terror. "And I think his wrists are broken."

The scents around them shifted. The new smell sent an icy dagger through Rex's gut. "Hate to make your day like this, but the fuses just ignited."

CHAPTER 55
THE FREDERICKS FORMULA

The Combined Councils Chamber

"You haven't been authorized to enter!" The RES officer braced himself against the hatch to the Combined Councils Chamber and blocked Shady and her companions from access. "You can't go in! You haven't been authorized!"

As if that matters now! Shady tensed her body, unwilling to wait any longer.

"Stand down and move back." Director Perri wasn't much bigger than Elaine, but the command in her voice would've convinced Shady, if the words "the Fredericks formula" hadn't already done so.

"I have my orders!" Off-notes of raw, throat-catching fear and desperation laced his scent.

Shiv jetted forward. He grasped the man by one bicep, braced his legs against the hatch and a bulkhead, then removed the officer to one side.

As soon as the way was clear, Perri pushed the hatch open.

Shady burned jets. She emerged into a cavernous space—and also a scene of chaos. Good: many Council Members and aides already had turned toward the dozen-or-so plainly-marked emergency exits spaced around the inside of the enormous, egg-shaped Chamber. As many as a third of them already pulled themselves along travel pipes or burned jets for the exits. But far too many remained inside their wall-anchored, floating hammocks that closely resembled the ones on the Trans-Hub Trains. Mingled, murky confusion and deep notes of aching worry or choking fear filled the air with their uncertainty and stubborn denial.

"Help people get out," Shady urged the Pack on the com, then let her nose lead her toward the ozzirikkian section.

One of the nearer ozzies snarled at her. Shady wasn't sure if the individual who caught her gaze was an aide or a Council Member. "What is happening? What do you want?" k'ki demanded through k'kir vocalizer in Standard.

"My Pack has found explosives laid among the structural supports," Shady answered in Pan-Ozzirikkian. She pitched her volume to be heard for several meters and emphasized her words with urgent clicks. "We advise you to evacuate this Chamber until security can clear it. Please follow safe evacuation protocols, but do not tarry." She could only hope there were such protocols in place.

"Understood. That, at least, is clear. The RES has been telling us to hold in place for clarification, but the SBI is saying to evacuate."

"I have heard enough. Clarification received!" Another ozzie pushed free of k'kir hammock-net, then spoke to the others in urgent tones. "Evacuate!" *Click-click* added urgency to the words. "Move! No pushing, but *go!*" *Click-click. Click-click. Click-click.*

Now all of them were moving. Several elders pulled themselves or were helped into palanquins. Shady swept the chamber with her gaze. *Where is Kizzitikti?* She didn't immediately spot the venerable Vice-Premier. *Has ki already left?* She used the honorific pronoun reserved for the most revered in ozzie society.

Front of the Chamber by the speakers' island, Pam said through the link. *Not moving very fast.*

Shady looped back toward kir and the others in kin group. Ki moved forward at a stately, careful pace, flanked by a pair of attentive ozzie aides. "Here! Grab my harness, Zikikittir!" She again spoke Pan-Ozzirikkian and used the ozzie word for "Vice Premier," plus her own urgent clicks.

Six-fingered, blue-black hands reached up.

Shady adjusted position to align herself. "You two aides! Grab on, as well! Steady kir!" *Click-click. Click-click.*

They grasped her harness with one hand each and employed their others to hold fast to their Zikikittir. Shady wove her way through the cloud of evacuees as quickly as possible to the nearest exit.

The aides swung away from Shady, released their grips. They sailed gracefully through the hatch, guiding Kizzitikti.

"Thank you! Keep kir safe!" Shady looked back into the Chamber.

The ozzirikkians had almost all made it to exits now. Many humans had, too, but others shouted defiance at Packmates or others who attempted to call them to the exits.

Are the holdouts Palmdale people?

Whoever they are, they won't listen to us—keep saying we're not authorized. There was Pam, over by another emergency exit. She held her position at a hover, a case pad in her hand.

How helpful of them. Shady's hackles prickled. *Where is Rex?*

Not sure. Maybe still inside the structural supports. Despite the near-space imagery on the screens, there are several layers of chambered shielding between us and hard vacuum. They could be fairly far in. He and Charlie are on one mission—we have another. Find someone to help!

Shady cast about. She spotted an elder human Council Member who tugged on a younger Member's arm.

"Kenji, come on! When the SBI says 'evacuate,' we should do so!"

"It's a ploy to stop the Special Session! It's not real." Kenji kept a tight grip on his hammock. His scent reeked of terror.

"The Special Session *is* stopped!" The older man pulled fruitlessly at Kenji's hammock. "Everyone is leaving. Come on!"

"It is not a ploy." Shady swooped closer. "Kenji, you should go with him."

Kenji glared at her. "I'm not doing *anything* an XK9 says! Don't listen to that thing, Ganzorig!"

"Grab my harness, Ganzorig!" Shady urged. "Will you, at least, heed me? I fear the bombers may light the fuses, now that people are moving out!"

"Fuses?" Ganzorig gave her a wide-eyed look.

"It is the Fredericks formula—the explosives that destroyed the *Izgubil*. The Pack knows that scent all too well! Please come with me!"

The older man grasped her harness but gave Kenji one last agonized look. "*Please*, boy! Humor me *just this once!*"

Kenji made an irritated face. "Stubborn old fool! All right! But we'll look stupid!" He pushed free of his hammock, then reached out and grabbed Shady's harness, too.

"Better 'stupid' than a shredded meat puzzle!" Shady burned jets for the nearest exit.

"Can anyone get us a knife?" Rex's vocalizer voice boomed over the PA speakers.

That does not sound good. She met Pam's eyes across the Chamber, her gut abruptly queasy. But she guided her passengers to the nearest exit, then braked to a halt. "All right, men! You know where to go from here!" Ganzorig and Kenji jetted through to safety.

"No knives allowed in the Chamber!" Kenji's irritated words floated back to her.

Another stupid rule! Her gaze swept across the Chamber. *Still too many people in here. And not enough of them leaving!* At the corner of her eye, she glimpsed a struggle of some sort. Over near the hatch where they'd entered. *That's Shiv! What's he doing?*

The big LSA had grabbed a fistful of an RES officer's jacket. He delivered a quick knuckle-rap to the man's nose that made him clap hands to his face and curl up. Shiv yanked something from his erstwhile opponent's belt then thrust the man into Dominic Wei's arms. Shiv shouted something to Wei that Shady couldn't make out. He fired his jets and darted back into the entrance passageway from which the Pack had emerged a few minutes earlier.

❖ ❖ ❖ ❖ ❖ ❖ ❖ ❖

Chambered Security Shielding

Hildie could do little more than monitor Zander Hoback's vitals on the bio-readout patch. The bruises on his battered face told a tale of possible concussion and brain damage, but she couldn't know till she got him under a scanner. Between that and probably broken wrists, it wasn't any wonder his pulse and respiration had gone fast and irregular. His blood pressure ebbed.

"Zander, hold on." She thrust her face close to his, strove for a calm, steady voice. "I know it hurts. We're getting you out of here as fast as we can."

Rex went still for a moment. "Okay, the word's out about the fuses. If they haven't cleared the Chamber yet that ought to kick in some afterburners."

Here's hoping. Hildie chewed her lips and focused on her patient.

"Gotta pull on it again. Sorry!" Charlie gave Hoback a worried look. "They didn't let me bring a knife."

"Muuh! *Muuh!*" His eyes had gone glassy with panic, but his gaze also implored . . . *something.*

"Shh. Don't thrash around. I know it hurts, but we can help you better if you'll stay still." Hildie tried to hold his gaze, willed him not to go into shock.

Rex fired jets to close in, teeth bared. He inserted one of his giant canines inside the stretched part of the tape. "Ready?"

Her patient groaned, closed his eyes. He swallowed, did a sketchy breathing pattern.

"Let's try it," Charlie said.

Rex slashed with his tooth.

"*MUUUU-UUH-UUH-UH!*" Hoback arched his back and clenched his eyes shut. He gasped choppy breaths through flaring nostrils. "*Uuuuh-UUUH-uuh!*"

Charlie eyed the bindings. "That helped. Pulled away a lot of the tape. Still triple-zipped, though."

Rex backed off. He growled and shook his head, tongue working to expel shreds of tape caught between his teeth. "Ugh!"

Hildie bit her lips. She scanned the area. By law, there should be adequate emergency bunkers in all Hub spaces where a work crew might be. This section was definitely a maintenance access area, but she didn't immediately spot a bunker. *C'mon, people! This place has been all about the rules, so far. How could there NOT be . . .*

❖ ❖ ❖ ❖ ❖ ❖ ❖ ❖

R ex pawed at his muzzle, but he also reached out through the link. *SCISCO! SCISCO, can you sense me from this far away?*

Rex? Hello! Are you all right?

Rex sent nem a mental gestalt of his situation. *Did you manage to work out a way to stop the fuses?*

Dismay echoed back to him. *Can you access any flame retardant? That is the only thing I have found so far, and even that is an imperfect solution. Some timers don't extinguish soon enough, although others do. That will dissipate the explosion, but it won't stop it entirely.*

Charlie and Hildie packed a lot of stuff in my panniers. Maybe?

"Charlie! Did we bring any fire retardant?"

"What? No! Why?"

"SCISCO says it will partially stop the fuses."

Charlie's laugh echoed kinda thin and frantic. "Damn. Have to add that to the list for next time!"

"*Partially?*" Hildie asked. "*How* 'partially'?"

"Partially as in 'not enough.'" Rex growled. "But since we have none, never mind."

When did the fuses start? SCISCO asked.

He shared a visual of his readout. After his nightmare, he'd thought ahead enough to realize it might be a good idea to start a timer if he ever smelled this scent again. But how had he actually had the presence of mind to do it? Maybe the CAP had read the preparation as an order that would trigger automatically?

I can't guess how long these fuses are set to burn, SCISCO said. *Rory usually built in five to ten minutes.*

Better assume five and hope for ten. According to his timer, they had a bit more than three of the hypothetical five left.

Zander Hoback screamed again, tape-muffled. A sharp pain-sensation stabbed through the link from Charlie. He'd lacerated his right palm. *One zip-cuff down.*

Two to go. Crap! Rex growled.

"You're bleeding. Give me your hand!" Hildie pulled a pad from her kit and slapped it onto his palm. It molded itself around the gash. "Don't do that again!"

"Gonna have to. No knife." Charlie took a firm grasp on the next zip-cuff with his left hand.

"Charlie! I only have one more Stanch-Pad!"

Rex felt his partner's terrified frustration through the link, smelled it in his scent. "What else can I do?"

A *clang* and *thump* echoed from seven or eight meters away, somewhere out of sight. Rex cocked his head and checked for a new scent. *Sounded like somebody kicked that loose bulkhead panel you removed.*

"Rex! Charlie! Where'd you go?" a familiar voice called.

Rex's heart clenched. "You should get as far away as possible, Shiv! The fuses have started burning."

"No time to lose. Do you still need a knife?"

"Yes!" Charlie and Hildie both answered.

Rex turned up his front-harness illumination as high as it would go.

Next moment, Rex's favorite LSA in the Universe darted into view.

"Over here! Quickly!" Charlie called. "Rex, can you point your light at it?"

He pulsed jets to move into position. "We have about three— um, two—minutes left on the fuses. I hope you wanted to know that."

I actually did NOT want to know that. Charlie grimaced. "Two zip-cuffs and the rest of the tape to go." He used his thumbs to spread the tape for a better view.

"Here's hoping that RES idiot at least took care of his equipment." Shiv positioned himself across from Charlie, behind Hoback and next to the support beam.

"RES idiot?" Hildie glanced at him, then returned her gaze to Hoback's bio-readout. "You mean that annoying officer by the entry-hatch?"

"Yeah." Shiv positioned the blade. "Had to mug him for his knife." He slashed. A halfway slice opened, but the zip-cuffs held. Shiv grunted. "That figures." He repositioned the knife, then slashed at the bindings again.

That did it for the cuffs. Shiv and Charlie cut, scratched and ripped at the stubborn tape that remained.

"Uuuh-uuuh-*uuuuuh*," Hoback moaned.

A dull *BOOM* echoed through the area. Sounded several sections of bulkhead distant. Rex's gut went cold. *What was that?*

Charlie didn't answer. He and Shiv ripped and sliced tape away at an even faster rate. At last, they pulled Hoback's tape-pinioned body free of the support beam.

BOOM! That one sounded closer.

Are you anywhere near an emergency bunker? SCISCO asked.

Rex scanned the nearby walls. "Has anyone seen an emergency bunker?"

"Yes!" Hildie pointed. "Over there!"

Go there, SCISCO said. *Go there NOW.*

"Bunker! This way!" Rex butted Charlie toward it. Damned thing seemed to shrink as they drew closer.

"It's supposed to be big enough for a four-person crew." Hildie's voice gained a worried note. "Will we all fit?"

"Better make sure we do!" Charlie ripped open the hook-and-loop fasteners on Rex's panniers. His fingers scrambled to unbuckle the two buckles.

Shiv palmed the emergency release. The hatch slid open.

Rex's panniers floated away at Charlie's shove. "Every centimeter is going to count, in there!"

BOOM! Closer still.

What IS that? Rex pointed the question at SCISCO.

That is section after section of compression chambering, explosively deconstructing and venting into the spacelanes, SCISCO said. *I've found sensors I can monitor, so I can know for sure. Two left to go, including yours.*

"In! In!" Rex butted Charlie again, but the man made sure Hildie and her patient got in first.

Shiv inserted himself into the other end. That left precious little room for Rex and Charlie, but Charlie wrapped his arm around Rex and push-pulled inside.

He squeezed Rex's ribs but couldn't get the hatch to close completely. "Won't *close,*" he gasped.

BOOM! That was the loudest one yet. *Next compartment over.*

"Everybody exhale!" Shiv's arm circled Rex from behind. He and Charlie both squeezed Rex's ribs hard.

The hatch jerked, stopped, jerked, stopped. *Still not closed.*

Rex felt Charlie's arm flex, tighten with even greater crushing force against ribs that had only recently healed.

With another sluggish jerk, the hatch closed at last. It snicked tight and sealed.

BOOM! For a single, deafening instant, noise filled everything.

Then there was no sound at all.

CHAPTER 56
UNSCRAMBLING THE
SCRAMBLE

The Combined Councils Chamber

Pam's gaze swept the Council Chamber from her position by one of the emergency exits. All around the arching walls of the Chamber, the last holdouts *finally* had begun to struggle out of their hammocks at the news that the fuses were burning. Even the RES officers had started actively helping, rather than getting in the way. *Where are Rex, Charlie, Hildie, and Shiv?*

No updates. Shady's anxiety reverberated through the link. She ferried another couple of hangers-on to Pam's exit. They pushed past her, in a hurry at last.

Pam focused on taking long, slow breaths. She tried to think past the thud of her racing pulse. *Where is everyone now?* The 360-degree arc of the Chamber kept all the sight-lines unobstructed. One by one, she spotted teams of Packmates and marked their progress. She had earlier thought to direct each to take a section of the Chamber, then realized they'd already done so on their own. Now she could see that they had nearly finished.

A hollow *boom* came from somewhere not far enough away.

Everyone moved faster. The Pack, both dogs and humans,

had spread out to help facilitate the evacuation. Like Shady, many of the other XK9s helped ferry Council Members and aides to safety two or three at a time. With the RES now actively helping, they were finally making good speed.

"Clear," Tux reported on the com. "Anyone else need help?" He paused in the emergency exit for his section and gave the now-empty area one last look.

"Almost done," Connie reported.

Boom. That one was closer.

Everyone made a headlong plunge toward the exits.

"And clear," Crystal said. She and Connie sealed their exit behind themselves.

"We're out." "Us, too." Elle and Petunia talked over each other.

Tux and Georgia ducked out and sealed their exit.

BOOM echoed even closer. A subtle tremor ran through the Chamber.

Pam's heartbeat leaped to double-time.

Everyone still in the chamber burned jets harder.

"Clear here, too." That was Scout. Nicole gave Pam a high-sign gesture, then closed the emergency exit behind them.

"And here." That was Victor.

"We're out," Eduardo added, and sealed their exit.

The last stragglers reached Pam's exit. She withdrew to make room for them.

"Out of the way!" one of them yelled.

"Me first!" the second one shoved the first, but that sent both tumbling.

Shady snarled, swooped in, and grabbed a mouthful of the nearer one's collar. She dragged him through the exit. The other powered through right behind her.

Pam took one last look outside, triggered the exit, and sealed it. But there was no guarantee that if the Chamber itself blew, this emergency-shielded area wouldn't go with it. "Move! Move! Keep going!"

"Rex, where are you?" Shady shouted into the com.

BOOM!

Crap, that sounded closer yet! Pam and Shady raced toward the next exit.

❖ ❖ ❖ ❖ ❖ ❖ ❖ ❖

Emergency bunker formerly inside Chambered Security Shielding

Half-breaths or less would have to do. Rex wanted to pace and pant, but he was squashed into immobility. His com dinged: Shady. *Good thing I don't have to move to answer it.*

"Rex, where are you?" XK9 vocalizers might sound emotionless, but he had no trouble imagining the tone Shady meant.

"Bunker. Safe but squashed."

"Thank goodness! I shall try to get you priority, but the whole Chamber just blew. We think we got everyone. The Council Members, aides, RES agents and all the rest of us are still sorting ourselves out."

"Good luck with that. I am glad you got everyone out. We shall await rescue."

"Roger that." Shady's call clicked off.

Rex let his mate's news reverberate through him only for a moment. Urgent curiosity swelled, sharp and prickly in the scent factors of everyone around him. "Shady says the whole Combined Councils Chamber just blew out, but they got it evacuated in time."

Horror flooded the link from Charlie, colored with anguish and outrage. His scent factors, along with those of Hildie and Shiv, echoed and redoubled those reactions in aching, icy low notes. Although shot through with the low, raw smell of physical pain, Hoback's reaction included bright, hot tones of hatred and vengeance, mingled with peppery frustration.

I sure hope that worthless creep Hoback was worth our efforts. He's happy about the Chamber, but possibly upset that we evacuated it.

He's a life. We couldn't leave him without at least trying. Charlie's impulse to shake his head came through the link, even though he couldn't move any better than Rex could.

I'm not sure I agree. Rex's ears didn't have much range of motion, but he could clamp them tighter against his skull. *Given a zero-sum choice—him or me—I'd have let him blow up and considered it poetic justice.*

That's your stress talking.

Maybe. It is true that I am stressed. Every particle of Rex's body pressed against something or felt as if something dug into it. *I'm grateful you jettisoned my panniers.* He activated his vocalizer. "And to think I felt cramped in the *last* emergency bunker."

"Thought y'were, too." Hildie's face probably was squashed into some part of Hoback or Charlie, to sound that muffled. "Shows'ut I knew."

"Anybody lose fingers or toes?" Charlie's mouth moved against Rex's chest fur.

"Fingers numb." Shiv's face felt smooshed into Rex's back.

"Arms numb," Hildie mumbled. "Han's. Feet."

"Muuumph-mm."

I bet Hoback's had lots of things go numb already. Through the link, it almost seemed that Charlie was worried about the man.

Mass-murdering asshole. Serves him right.

Charlie most likely didn't have the lung capacity to sigh—but Rex felt what was possibly a grimace against his chest. *That's your Transmondian conditioning showing.*

Gotta say I'm not a real fan of Transmondian anything right now.

Good reason to adjust your perspective?

Rex growled. *I'll take it under advisement.*

"Bunker 2789-C, this is Base. Your beacon activated. Do you copy?" a voice from above their heads asked.

"Roger that. Receiving!" Shiv answered.

"Confirming. Biometrics show . . . um . . ."

"Come again, Base?" Shiv asked.

"Am I reading *five* life-signs?"

"Four humans and an XK9," Rex said. "Your math is correct."

"Running calculations on your oxygen supply. How tight-packed are you?"

"None of us can move," Shiv answered.

Rex was the only other one who probably could've answered clearly, but Shiv seemed to have it covered. Rex closed his eyes and let the LSA handle it. Half-breaths. No panting. Plenty to think about.

"Who d'you have onboard?"

"I'm LSA Shiva Shimon, SBI. Reserve Agents Charles Morgan and Rex Dieter-Nell. Orangeboro ERT Sergeant Hildegaard Gallagher. And a criminal suspect, Zander Hoback."

"Injuries?"

"Gallagher and I—healthy. Dieter-Nell's lungs—nanotech treatment after decompression. Morgan—arm-shield, post-regen. Arm's being slowly crushed. Hoback—found beaten, bound to a support beam."

"Head trauma?"

"Yez, def'n'ly" Hilde mumbled.

"Come again?"

"Yes!" Shiv said.

"Bunker 2789-C, based on the information you've provided, you are Priority One-Red. Stand by."

"G'd call," Hildie mumbled.

Charlie's relief surged through the link. *Priority One-Red means not much longer to wait.*

Yeah, I kinda figured that out.

❖ ❖ ❖ ❖ ❖ ❖ ❖ ❖

Center-Hub Secured Governmental District

"Let the RES handle the Council Members," Klein's voice directed Pam through the com. "Gather the Pack and come to Gate Three. You'll see us when you get here. Send Shady to the Med Station to meet Rex."

Shady burned jets for the Med Station. She'd gathered enough through the link to need no further direction.

"Packmates!" Pam shouted. "Gate Three!" A green directional arrow activated in Pam's HUD. She followed it. The rest of the Pack, both dogs and humans, followed Pam. *Let the RES handle all those querulous, demanding Council Members!*

Pam tried a downside com-call to Balchu. She'd tried earlier, but the transmission lines had been out of order. Now lurid images of debris-filled spacelanes filled her news feeds. *Surely the coms are back on, if*—but a pulsing buzz told her the com line to Centerboro still wasn't working.

Pam and her companions reached Gate Three. It turned out to be a high-security shuttle access, walled off from the civilian lines. More RES officers covered the gate. She half-expected them to object, but they unbarred the hatches and let Guzmán, his group, and the Pack come in.

She tried the com again. Same pulsing buzz. She frowned. *I wonder . . .* She shifted to the link-access QUAERO sometimes used. *What is wrong with the com-lines? Why can they get pictures of the wreckage to the news outlets just fine, but my coms don't work? QUAERO, do you read me?*

Nothing.

QUAERO?

Still nothing. Her gut tightened on a growing sense of her own foolishness. *Eh, well, it was worth a try.*

Click. Click. Click-click-click-click-click. There. That should do it. Can you hear me now? QUAERO asked.

Pam's muscles went weak in an instant of relief. She blinked back sudden tears, but remembered what a nuisance they could be in micrograv. *Oh, wow, I'm glad to hear you!*

It is good to reach you. I had to redirect through the security sensors. All regular com traffic from the Combined Councils section of the Hub has been shut off.

Has been shut off? Her head spun and her skin went tingly. *As in—on purpose? Why? How? By whom?*

It appears to have been done remotely. This will require more investigation. Meanwhile, I assume you'd like to place a com call?

Absolutely! A whole bunch of us would!

I can route you through my redirect, then I'll work on reversing the shutoff. You wish to connect to your Amare?

Yes! Please!

Nir answer was the sound of a call going through.

"Pammie!" Balchu sounded distraught. "Are you okay?"

"We're good. QUAERO found a way to patch me through. Ne's working on the rest of the com-lines now."

"We were all getting frantic! Hold on." He muted the mic, shouted something that might have been "It's Pam!" then came back on. She could hear what sounded like a crowd of excited voices in his background. "Okay, what's the status up there?"

"Got the Chamber evacuated, and yes—it was the Fredericks formula. The Pack caught it in time and eventually people listened."

"Wait! The members of the Combined Councils are alive, too? And the Premier?"

"Yes. Everyone. I think we did get everyone out. It was pretty intense for a while."

"Thank goodness! Hang on again!" He muted the mic for a second time. When he came back on, the background sounds had erupted into cheering. "Okay. You say the *Pack*—"

"Yes. The Pack sounded the alarm. They found the explosives, and they were a huge help getting all the Council Members safely evacuated."

"Hang on again!" He muted the mic for a third time, then clicked back on after almost a minute. "All the journalists in the room just got real excited and started calling in to their home agencies. This is huge news! We've been hearing that everyone died."

"What? No! Who would spread that rumor?"

"I don't know, but it's everywhere. Hang on one more time. Joslyn's here, and she wants to share the call."

"Okay, but wouldn't she rather talk to the Chief?" She caught Klein's eye, beckoned him over. "Can I patch you in, Chief? On the Wheel, they'd been told we were all dead."

Klein scowled. "My line is still blocked. Yes! Patch me in!"

The local connection clicked though to add him, just as it was supposed to. "Okay, Balchu! Can you hear me?" Pam asked.

"Yes, and it's such a relief that you're alive to talk!"

Klein spoke next. "Hello, Detective. Can you also hear me?"

"Yes, sir. It's good to hear your voice, too."

Klein smiled. "Is Joslyn there? We're having a terrible time with the lines up here."

"Because of the explosion?"

"Mmm, that's probably what we're supposed to think. Whoever laid those explosives meant to take out the whole Ranan government."

Holy crap, he's right. Pam sucked air. "Actually, my friend QUAERO told me they'd been remotely shut off."

'Holy crap,' WHO'S right? Shady asked through the link from the Med Station. *Right about what?*

Pam answered Shady by opening the link more fully.

Klein had frozen for an instant, then one brow elevated. "QUAERO told you the coms were *remotely shut off?*"

"Yes. Ne's trying to reverse the shutoff and open the connection now. But the com trunk from the Combined Councils section was remotely shut off."

"It is potentially-game-changing to have nem on our side." The new voice came from behind and a bit above Klein's left shoulder. Pam had been so focused on the Chief she hadn't noticed Vice Premier Guzmán's approach.

"I'll patch you in, too, then, sir?" Her voice only quavered a *little*. She hoped.

"Please do that, Sergeant Gómez. And thank you!"

She added Guzmán's connection. "Balchu? I have Vice-Premier Guzmán on the line. Please help him with whatever he asks."

"You have—"

"Detective Nowicki?" Guzmán asked. "I'll need a little help from your end."

CHAPTER 57
TOPSIDE TRAUMA

Med Station, Center-Hub Secured District

T his med station would probably look a lot more familiar to Hildie than it did to Shady. And how *was* her newest Packmate getting along? She worried most about Rex, but losing either one of her co-habiting humans also would be horrible.

The medical staff, which included both human and ozzirikkian paramedics, continued to whoosh around after she arrived. Ari, bless them, was already there. They'd made it from the Observation Lounge on their own somehow.

No surprise, this facility resembled downside med stations in some ways. The smells were consistent, and so were the sterile, gleaming surfaces. But there was a lot more stuff attached all over the walls here. And no obvious predilection for a singular "up" or "down." Clearly, some practicalities differed in micrograv.

Shady grudgingly settled in to wait. *I have the patience of a hunter. I can handle a delay.* She stifled a growl. *Now come on and get here, already!*

Through the link, she kept one ear mentally cocked toward Pam. Thanks to QUAERO, her partner had established what was apparently the one working connection to a woefully under-informed group of people in Centerboro. Sacha Guzmán seemed to be conducting a long-distance press conference via Pam's com. *Here's hoping that goes well.*

And that all the other people's coms come back online soon! Her partner's anxiety echoed in her mental voice.

Shady cocked her head, even though Pam couldn't see her and it was kind of disorienting in micrograv. She fired stabilizing jets. *You are anxious, even though we are safe and communications are being restored. What still worries you?*

Not enough people know we are safe. Not enough people know yet that all the high government officials survived. I thought it was weird that the vids of the destruction are all over the Station, even though the coms between here and there were—still are—nonfunctional. QUAERO says the com-trunk was remotely shut off.

That much I had gathered. Shady growled. *Do you mean it was shut off on purpose?*

Yes. I don't think it'll take many guesses to figure out who arranged for that, although we don't yet know how they did it.

But they failed, right? Because we got everyone out, the Transmondians can't take over. Right?

Maybe. Somebody meant to take out all the Combined Council MEMBERS, not just their chamber. And they meant to take Iskander and both Vice-Premiers along with them. So the Pack did avert one huge national crisis. We just survived—the Pack foiled—a massive coup attempt.

I guess we did, at that. Shady blinked. Despite the floaty, perpetual mild nausea of micrograv, her stomach did a rock-in-the-sub-levels dive. *But you don't think the coup is over. Even though it failed.*

If people believe everyone in the government is dead, they may accept an interloper who shouldn't move in. Specifically, the Transmondians. They dominate this whole system, already. I think now that they —at least, some of them—pretty clearly want to control the Chayko System outright.

Shady shuddered. *Is that why they've been moving more warships to the international border? Maybe because they not-so-secretly want to create a Transmondian Empire in the Chayko System?*

That . . . she received a brief reaction of chill and vertigo through the link from Pam. *Oh, crap, Shady. That makes a lot more sense than I want it to. And if that really is their plan, why not start by picking off us troublesome Rana Stationers? We're the ones who just happen to be parked closest to the jump point, so that's a bonus.*

Also, Rana is harboring a Pack of inconveniently sapient beings that their government tried to traffic but now wants to eradicate. Shady didn't think her thrusters could compensate for a good, hard, full-body shake, but all of a sudden, she needed one.

And after their spies fortuitously captured effective, innovative new explosives—plus the knowledge to use them, in the person of Zander Hoback? She felt Pam's fear through the link. *It probably seemed an ideal moment.*

I wonder if the Palmdale Club knew this was the real plan. Shady gave a soft growl. *And what about Premier Iskander? How much did she know?*

The Palmdale Club's resolution about cooperating with the Trans-mondians probably WAS the real plan 'til the TIS captured Zander. Pam's grim mood made Shady want to pace and pant, although in microgravity that would be difficult. *I bet they moved their ships up to the international boundary after they captured Hoback and realized what an opportunity they'd lucked into.*

Shady's hackles puffed out, prickling and tense. *They wouldn't need the Palmdale Club's little resolution if they could completely take over.*

No. And it worries me that we haven't heard where those warships are now.

❖ ❖ ❖ ❖ ❖ ❖ ❖ ❖

Emergency Bunker and Rescue Runner *Zikkizti Dawn*

C harlie'd gotten to the point of passing in and out of consciousness. No one in their bunker had spoken for what seemed like hours. His legs and arms had long since gone all pins and needles and turned into logs.

Something *whumped* against their hatch.

He roused from his half-doze but strove to keep his breaths as shallow as possible. A small, bright tendril of hope warmed him. *Could that be*—

Astonished delight rolled through the link from Rex. "I know that sound." He used his vocalizer, likely so the others could hear, too. "That is a Rescue Runner locking on."

A vacuum lock sucked snug to the bunker's hatch. The hatch popped. Charlie and Rex tumbled out into the space beyond, helpless to control their trajectory.

Charlie gasped. His limbs were senseless clubs, but his hungry lungs couldn't gulp enough blessed air.

Someone placed a mask over his face. "Breathe in. It's oxygen."

Just breathing consumed him for a few moments. His darkened vision cleared. An ozzirikkian in a face mask studied him—or more likely the bio-patch that must by now be stuck to his forehead—then made indigo blue eye contact. "It's Charlie, right?" The words sounded too fluent to come from an organic ozzirikkian vocal apparatus. K'ki must be using a vocalizer.

He nodded, still too breathless to speak.

"Good. I'm Ki'i'ini, and you're safe now. Just relax and let me move you."

He closed his eyes against light that shone too brightly after so long in a dark bunker. Bit by bit, the sensation in his extremities shifted from pins-and-needles prickling to more as if they were on fire. Pain dominated more and more of his attention.

"I need to position you under this scanner," Ki'i'ini's vocalizer voice said. "You're in the Rescue Runner *Zikkizti Dawn*. Focus on breathing and releasing the tension from all the muscles you can, though I know you're experiencing pain. We've got you, and your whole party is all still alive."

He had a clear sense of Rex on his left.

"XK9 specs," someone out of view spoke in a quiet voice. A trill from a readout responded. "Hmm. Okay, Rex. I can see you're breathing a lot more easily than I expected. Can you feel your feet?"

"I have recently received an experimental nanotech lung treatment." Rex didn't have to rely on breath to speak. "I cannot feel my feet, just tingling. It is in the feet and all the way up my legs."

"Hmm. I see." The unseen speaker paused a moment, possibly to review Rex's medical beacon implant. "Wow. Spaced just three weeks ago, and now this? We all followed your story. We're delighted we could locate your bunker's distress beam and get to you in time."

"So are we. I believe I can speak for all of us, even our prisoner."

Charlie couldn't see the tail-wag, but he felt it through the link.

"Your prisoner?"

"I should say our 'detainee.' He has been using the name Zander Hoback. He is the guy who is all taped up. Be careful to keep him under restraints."

"Oh, believe me. He isn't going anywhere for a while. Who beat him up?"

"We believe it was the Transmondian agents who brought him here under duress three days ago," Rex said.

"He was kidnapped, but he's also a detainee?"

"A criminal suspect, yes. And a very slippery fellow. Do not underestimate him."

"Noted. Um—Randy?"

"Yes?"

Rex's paramedic related what he'd just told her about Hoback, including the warning.

"So his name is Zander?"

"That appears to be the name he was using on Rana," Rex said. "We have been on this man's trail for a while, now. We were very nearly unable to get him detached from the support beam he'd been fastened to, before the charges exploded."

Charlie focused on Rex's conversation with the others and gathered his strength. His breathing gradually evened out. The fiery pain in his legs, arms, hands, and feet reached a burning peak. A few breathing patterns seemed to help.

"I may have loosened a tooth trying to bite through his bonds," Rex continued. "Charlie cut his hand breaking one of the zip-ties, but Hildie had a Stanch-Pad in her medkit. Then Shiv came with a knife, and we finally got our subject loose."

Ki'i'ini finished k'kir scan. "Looks to me as if your circulation is returning, which is good. But it's going to hurt."

Charlie nodded, blinked to focus on k'kim. "I think it has peaked." His lips felt sluggish. He flexed his fingers. Yes, the pain had begun to recede. It slowly ebbed to a dull ache, but a new foreboding filled him. He couldn't see or hear anything from Hildie. *She was squashed in with Hoback.* "How is Hildie?"

"Shh, don't try to talk. Just rest. Our normal protocol is a neural pain block, but I've never had an augmented patient before." Ki'i'ini touched a screen on the wall and it lit up. "I need to check if there are contra-indications."

"Wait. Yours is augmented, too?" a new voice asked. "What are the odds of that? So is mine."

The two paramedics huddled for a conference.

"No, I'm serious." Charlie frowned. "And I'm definitely beginning to feel better. How is Hildie?"

Hildie is alive, but she was pretty cramped, Rex said. *I can smell she is in considerably more pain than you are at the moment. She's over to your right somewhere.*

Thanks. Charlie pushed away from the med-bed and out from under the now-quiet scanner.

"Woah! Wait a minute!" Ki'i'in spun, darted to his side. "You shouldn't try to move yet!"

"I'm actually doing pretty well." Charlie flexed his hands again and spotted Hildie. She definitely did appear to be in worse shape than he was. Her face, half-hidden behind an oxygen mask, contorted with pain. She writhed in the cocoon of her med-bed. "I'm more worried about my Amare."

Shiv, too, pushed away from his med-bed. He flexed his legs, shook out his hands. "Gonna take a little while to get full circulation back, I think. Charlie, how's that arm?"

No need to ask which arm. It throbbed with a dull ache in contrast to the last remaining prickles of returning circulation in his other extremities. "It still hurts, but the rest of me feels okay."

Ki'i'ini and Shiv's paramedic stared at them.

"Augmented," Ki'i'ini said. "That is astounding."

Rex, too, pushed out from under his scanner. He fired jets to counteract his eager tail-wag. "Yes! Now you are XK9-tough!"

CHAPTER 58
MOVING PIECES

Secured Governmental District

P am couldn't exactly wander off, as long as Vice Premier Guzmán needed her com line. But she also couldn't use it herself as long as he was on it. She held her position floating next to him on one side of Centerboro Hub Gate Three. *We're missing something.* She felt sure of it.

Missing what? Shady asked through the link.

I don't know. That's the problem. I wish I knew how QUAERO is getting along with that shutoff switch on our coms.

And the extent of the blockage. She had a sense of Shady's ears clamping tighter to the sides of her skull. *Did ne say what's blocked?*

Ne said all com traffic from the Combined Councils section of the Hub.

What about the rest of the Station?

Not sure, and can't ask nem now. All around her, people hovered close and listened attentively to Guzmán's end of the conversation.

"No," the Vice Premier answered a question from Joslyn or—actually, Pam had lost track of who he was talking to. "Tell them we are still sorting things out, but the XK9s sounded the alarm, and they were invaluable in getting everyone out before disaster struck. I think we got absolutely everyone. Especially after the first explosions in the outer sections began to happen, there was less convincing to do."

The line clicked.

"Vice Premier, would you care for a separate, secured line of your own?" QUAERO asked.

"Ah! Yes! Will it hold while we move?"

"I can keep it steady," QUAERO answered. "Hub Four lines are still functioning, so the sooner you get within range the better."

"Got it." Guzmán fired jets for the shuttle access.

Pam's connection clicked off and she followed him but focused on QUAERO'S link. *Thank you!*

You are most welcome. We Ranans must work together.

"Where is Premier Iskander?" Guzmán asked Vince. "And what about Vice Premier Kizzitikti?"

"Eliana has retreated to her ready-room." Vince inclined his head toward a golden-filigree-embellished circular hatch with a shiny ice-blue cover on the far side of the gate area. "Kizzi and most of kir delegation are en route toward Wheel Five's Hub section. Ki thought the coms might be better there. Ki will speak to the Ranan public as soon as possible."

Guzmán frowned. "How soon can we get a shuttle to Wheel Four?"

"There's one standing by. We've alerted Council leaders to bring as many human Council Members as possible over to the secured facility at the Wheel Four Hub."

High time to get out of this dead zone for coms! "How can the Pack help?" Pam asked.

Vince grinned. "You mean, other than having already saved the entire government?"

"The Pack has proved today that they're pretty good 'sheep-dogs' when it comes to herding humans and ozzies." Guzmán nodded toward his assistant. "Work with Vince and the Council leaders, in case they need help rounding up the rest of the Council."

Vince forwarded contacts. "Work with these three."

Pam followed up with a group call to the Pack, both XK9s and humans, as well as the contacts on Vince's list. A quick discussion delegated two partner-pairs to each of Vince's listed leaders. Then she shifted her focus to Shady. *How are things at the Med Station?*

We finally got an update. That part of the Hub area was damaged pretty extensively. Rex's bunker had detached and was floating in a debris field, emitting its distress call for pickup. But it took a while for them to get to it.

They did find it, right?

They found it. By then he and the others were running low on oxygen and they'd been too crammed together to move for some time. The 'Zikkizti Dawn' Rescue Runner is bringing them in. The people at the Med Station warned me that they mean to take them straight down to Centerboro Med in the 1-G part of Wheel Four as soon as they arrive. They'll need circulation-restoration treatments that are better administered in 1-G.

Oh, ouch. Pam winced inwardly. Even recovering from sitting cross-legged too long hurt. She could only imagine—no, she'd rather not. *Here's hoping that goes well. Will you get to see him at all?*

They have given Ari and me the option to ride down with him.

Of course, they would. Ari had relevant expertise, and Shady was Rex's Amare. No one seemed to be questioning the XK9s' sapience or citizenship rights now. *I assume you'll go, then?*

Do you need me here?

I think we're headed for Wheel Four soon, ourselves. In Shady's place, with a wounded Amare, Pam would want to ride down with Balchu, and to heck with anyone else for a while. *I don't know what's next. Go ahead. You can test the coms on the way.*

Good plan. I'll keep you posted through the link—assuming it's not affected.

"Wait a moment." Guzmán slowed. His eyes narrowed with anger. "Three of them? Where are they now?" He listened a moment longer, then shifted his gaze toward the others around him.

"Three Transmondian destroyers have left their parking positions along the international boundary. They have now penetrated our sovereign territory. They appear to be headed toward Rana Station."

❖ ❖ ❖ ❖ ❖ ❖ ❖ ❖

Med Station, Center-Hub Secured District

Shady's gut clenched. Pam's end of the link had been wide open enough for her to hear Guzmán's update. *What will the SDF do, if the Transmondians ignore them?*

Unauthorized ships in our sovereign space—particularly Transmondian destroyers—are unacceptable. But I don't think the SDF is allowed to fire on a Transmondian warship without permission.

Where is Iskander? Does she have a com? Can she stop them? Shady realized her head was spinning because she was panting too fast. She swallowed and consciously slowed her breathing.

Would she even want to stop them? Pam's mental tone matched Shady's own dubiousness pretty well. *As far as I know, she's holed up in her ready room, and hasn't yet emerged.*

Such a brave leader we have. Shady kept her growl in the link, but after the woman's behavior in Orangeboro a few weeks ago, this didn't surprise her. *Surely being a head of state is better than being a vassal governor?*

One could hope. Pam's tone shifted to disgust.

Will the SDF take orders from either vice premier, if she doesn't act?

I don't know, but we may soon find out.

The Rescue Runner *Zikkizti Dawn* arrived in a flurry of blinking warning lights and sudden collective action. One after another, two med-beds floated into view, each propelled by a paramedic. Shady watched, worried. *There's Hoback, and here comes Hildie. I can smell that both are in pain.*

But next an apparently healthy Shiv emerged. *Wow! Shiv's up. He's maneuvering in his own micrograv harness. Seems intent on our detainee. Now here comes Charlie, and he seems mostly okay, too. He's following Hildie's med-bed.*

I guess those augmentations really do make a difference. Pam's relief surged through the link, although concern lingered. *But you say Hildie and Hoback aren't so good?*

Last one out was the one she cared about most. Rex jetted over to her. A clearly worried paramedic trailed him.

Shady and Rex leaped into an ecstatic midair greeting dance and a thorough sniff-over. *He's all right! He's healthy! Whole! Yes! Yes! Yes!*

They took more than a full minute to get it all out. Then they steadied, only panting a little after their midair gyrations, and looked around.

A wide perimeter of space had opened for them. Ari and Rex's paramedic from the rescue runner hovered to one side. The paramedic seemed to be doing most of the talking, presumably giving a medical debrief.

"That helped my feet—and my heart." Rex's eyes glinted with joy and his tongue lolled sideways. "I have told Charlie to go with Hildie. She will need him, and they definitely need to check his left arm. I, however, need to have a conference with Chief Klein and his friend Sacha. Please tell me what has been happening."

❖ ❖　❖ ❖　❖ ❖　❖ ❖

Emergency Services Shuttle to Wheel Four Hub

C harlie stayed close to Hildie's med-bed. Their Emergency Services shuttle shot toward the EMS Hub Base at Wheel Four. From there, they'd be routed onto an express elevator to Centerboro Med. The lights outside the racing shuttle's transparent access hatch flashed like a strobe.

He positioned himself where his Amare could see him if she opened her eyes and rested his still-throbbing left arm against the side of her bed. Her paramedic had administered pain meds and a light sedative. Meanwhile, through the link, he monitored Rex's movements. Shady had come to the med station to meet him. But once it was clear he had mostly recovered, she'd taken him to join Vice Premier Guzmán's group.

Hildie's face gradually relaxed from a painful grimace into a restful doze. Next bed over lay Zander Hoback, similarly sedated. His paramedic continued cutting him out of his tape cocoon under Shiv's stern gaze.

Are you near enough to the Wheel Four Hub to test the coms? Rex asked through the link. *We also are headed there now.*

Good thought. I'll call my parents.

If the call goes through, let me know at once. The coms are still down here.

I'll try now. A pulsing buzz made his heart sink—but then the line clicked over and the call went through.

"Charlie! Oh my God, *Charlie!*" Mama cried. "Are you all right? How are Hildie, Rex and Shady?"

Call went through, Charlie confirmed to Rex. He caught Shiv's eye. "Coms are open."

"Excellent!" He went into a HUD-stare. "Berwyn! Yes! Finally got a working com!"

Charlie refocused on his mother. "I'm okay, Mama. Rex is fine. Hildie's going to be okay, but she's injured. We're headed for Centerboro Med."

In the background Shiv said, "Yes, I'm well. But we had a bit of an adventure."

"We heard you were all killed!" Mama cried. "What happened to Hildie? Are you sure you're okay?"

Charlie smiled at Hildie's now-peaceful, dozing face. "I'm good, but I do need them to check my arm again. Hildie should recover soon, and Rex is fine. He's back with the Pack and—"

"Centerboro Med?" Mama asked. "I assume the ER? We'll meet you there. Now, tell me what happened. We're seeing horrifying vids! Looks like the Combined Councils Chamber is all wrecked and open to vacuum. The news agencies said most of the government may have been killed."

Somebody spoke in her background.

"Oh. Now they're saying you got—is that true, Hannah? *Everyone* got out?"

"Yes! *Most*—can't confirm *all*," Charlie said. "Rex, Shady and Tux scented the explosives in the access corridor before we entered the Chamber to testify. They—"

A transmission overrode his call and filled his HUD. A vid opened on a broad-shouldered man with chiseled features and picturesque streaks of gray at his temples. He wore the red and gold uniform of a high Transmondian military official. The red-and-gold flag of the Republic of Transmondia filled the wall behind him.

Everyone in the tube-shuttle who was conscious gasped.

"This is Fleet Admiral Eldridge Fallon of the Transmondian Republic," the man said. "I come with a message of condolence and reassurance for the Ranan people."

Charlie's ears thundered and a red-tinged haze filled his vision. "The *hell* he says!"

Others in his hearing sounded equally outraged.

"We mourn with you, over the colossal loss of life in your Combined Councils Chamber today." Fallon's voice carried a heavy load of pious concern, but he couldn't quite school his features into a total picture of solemn gravity. The hint of a smile tugged at his lips with subversive persistence.

That pompous poser! Rage burned in Charlie's throat.

"We know you must be deeply shaken by the deaths of all your highest-level Executive and Legislative leaders in such a short span. But I have come to offer reassurance in your darkest hour. I am authorized to step in and set up a caretaker government that will ensure a smooth and peaceful—"

The vid blipped off. For a moment Charlie's HUD went dark. Then a new vid clicked on. Backed by the Ranan flag, Vice Premier Kizzitikti Zhokittik floated behind a podium and gripped it with both forehands. Kir thirteen-centimeter fangs displayed a full snarl. Kir platinum-pale mane stood erect, a display of fury and dominance unlike any he'd ever seen in an ozzie elder before.

Yes! Charlie's heart soared. *Yes! Rex, are you able to see this?*

CHAPTER 59
CRISIS MANAGEMENT

Shuttle to Wheel Four Secured Sector

R ex fired jets to counter his fierce tail-wag and focused on Kizzitikti's broadcast. He stared into his HUD and braced his forefeet against a railing in the express shuttle where he rode with Sacha Guzmán and Chief Klein. It hurtled toward the Wheel Four Hub Terminal.

"This Transmondian blowhard assumes far more things than he has any right to." Kizzitikti punctuated kir pronouncement with fierce clicks. Fury glinted in kir indigo glare, but kir lips did not move in a way that paralleled human Standard words.

Kir personal translator must be operating on the human channels, Rex said through the link.

I'm glad you're receiving this, too. Ki speaks for all of us, so the simultaneous translation is needed, his partner replied.

Rex's mind and body sang with a warm joy Charlie had once identified for him as "patriotism." He'd never experienced it in Transmondia, but it kept popping up at odd moments since he'd come to Rana Station. *Guzmán and the human Council Members plan to join kir broadcast as soon as possible.*

Good! The sooner, the better.

"Our government has survived, despite our bad-faith Trans-mondian neighbors' worst efforts," Kizzitikti continued. "Our Combined Councils Chamber lies in ruins. But as you see, I am very much alive and well. As are we all. This is true, thanks to our nation's tiny, endangered community of XK9s." Kir fangs flashed again under the broadcast lights.

I did not expect that!

You deserve it, though, Charlie said. *If you hadn't caught that scent, we'd all be goners.*

Chief Klein ran his hand over Rex's coat. "Kizzi hasn't forgotten ki owes kir life to Shady."

Rex cocked his head. "Ki does?"

"A story for later." Klein smiled but returned to his HUD stare, so Rex did too.

"Premier Iskander is alive, although I have not, as yet, been able to reach her," Kizzitikti continued. "Vice Premier Guzmán also is alive. He should join this broadcast shortly."

Ozzirikkian Council Members, all of them still decked out in their official Council Braids, pulsed jets to assemble along stability railings behind Kizzitikti. The cameras pulled back to reveal officials' palanquins and a growing number of braided Council Members. Gradually their ranks swelled to the full complement of twenty-four, a Commercial Council Member and two Residential Council members from each of the eight ozzie timi'i, Wheel subdivisions that roughly paralleled human boroughs.

Rex did a quick count. *Yes! All of the ozzirikkian legislative contingent survived!* They undoubtedly also presented a colorful gathering which their human and ozzie constituents would see in a full spectrum of hues. Most of those openwork vests looked like shades of gray or brown to Rex, although he caught a few violet, blue, and yellow parts. But the pretty colors weren't the most important aspect of the display. He'd recently learned that for the Members to wear their Council Braids to this address put a seal of official, legal importance on it.

The shuttle slowed, stopped, and opened in the Wheel Four Hub. Rex and his companions emerged into a different section from any he'd visited earlier. A group of humans and ozzirikkians in SDF uniforms met them, case pads in hand. A visual memory of the four silver stripes he'd seen on the unlamented Admiral Virendra's uniform sleeves rose in his mind. Several of these people had also had four, but they all deferred to the human woman who had five.

Oh. Rex widened link access for Charlie. *That must be First Admiral Margaret Kumar, the Chief of Station Defense.*

I think you're right.

Rex caught a whiff, then a glimpse of someone else—one of his least favorite Ranans apart from criminals. Commodore Farooq Cornwell of SDF Intelligence was part of First Admiral Kumar's group.

Be nice, Charlie cautioned. *He's on our side.*

Allegedly. So far. Rex kept his growl internalized.

Admiral Kumar and her contingent of SDF higher-ups reached Guzmán. All the military people saluted, firing jets to maintain their position. The Vice Premier acknowledged them with his own salute.

"The Transmondians continue to advance," Kumar reported. "We have advised Fleet Admiral Fallon of his error, but he has not acknowledged our message."

"He's continuing to attempt his broadcast," Rooq added. "We're continuing to jam him."

"Good." Guzmán frowned. "I need to address our 'human side,' since Eliana continues to be a no-show. But then we'd better head into the Situation Chamber."

"Yes, sir." Kumar's mouth made a grim line. "If Fallon gives us that long."

"I'll keep it brief."

One of the SDF aides preceded the Vice Premier's party into a chamber with a dais backed by a large Ranan flag. It looked so much like the one where Kizzitikti had appeared, it might have been the other half of kir chamber.

When they make joint appearances, that might be what we see as two ends of the meeting area, Charlie mused. *That place does look familiar.*

Journalists and cameras already had gathered. Shady, Pam and the Pack planned to follow in a convoy of other shuttles as part of the larger human Council Members' group. Rex hoped they'd arrive soon.

"With me, Rex." Guzmán powered toward the dais.

Huh? Rex blinked, looked to Klein.

"Go! Follow him!" The Chief made shooing motions.

Rex fired jets to catch up with the Vice Premier.

"Right here. Next to me." Guzmán directed Rex to hover by his right elbow at the corner of the podium. "There's a grab bar, if it will help you."

Rex cupped his left forepaw over it. It anchored him in place.

Guzmán went into a brief HUD-stare, then nodded and looked up to focus on the assembled cameras. "Good afternoon. And thank you, Honored Zikikittir."

Ah. He used the ozzirikkian term for "Vice Premier." Charlie's approval washed in through the link. *That's a nod to the ozzies. He's saying to them, we see you. We are as one with you.*

Guzmán squared his shoulders. "We're still attempting to communicate with Premier Iskander. I hope she understands that the instant she wishes to address you, she has priority." He hesitated, but if she'd heard that cue she did not respond.

"I would now like to acknowledge my companion," Guzmán resumed. "This is Pack Leader Rex Dieter-Nell. His forensic olfaction skill, combined with his Pack's gallantry and heroism, saved our government leaders from violent death today."

He turned to smile at Rex, hooked a toe under another stability bar behind the podium, and used both hands to applaud him. "Please accept our thanks to you and your entire Pack. All of Rana Station is in your debt."

Around the briefing area the other humans also burst into ardent applause.

Rex arched his neck and attempted to convey a more gracious and appropriate reaction than the astonishment that froze him for a moment.

You look good, Charlie reassured him.

The clapping subsided.

What should I do now? Say something?

Tell them why you love Rana, Charlie prompted through the link.

"My Pack and I owe Rana Station our lives and our freedom." Rex gave the humans in the room a direct look, then shifted focus to the hovering cameras. "We came here to protect and serve our community. Today was an opportunity to do both."

Another round of even more enthusiastic applause, complete with whistles and cheers, greeted his words.

I don't know what else to say.

Uncle Dolph always advises us to "leave them wanting more."

Rex tipped his head toward Guzmán.

The Vice Premier responded with a smile and a nod in return, then faced the cameras once more. "I expect we'll be joined by as many of our human Combined Council Members as possible in the next few minutes. Unfortunately, I am told we've had a couple of medical emergencies among them. We'll get more information to you as soon as possible, but this is an evolving situation. And I have other news to share."

The room went deathly silent as he explained about the advance of the Transmondian destroyers. "Our efforts to communicate with Transmondian Fleet Admiral Fallon have so far been unsuccessful."

Rex caught movement in his peripheral vision. The first of the human Council Members had arrived. Like their ozzie counterparts, they wore their Council Braids. Their expressions mirrored the heavy, musky low notes of somber concern that filled their scent factors. Slowly, wordlessly, they pulsed jets to gather along stability railings behind and around the podium. He saw several whom he'd thought were in different factions, but now they halted along the railing facing forward, shoulder-to-shoulder.

Nothing submerges petty factional infighting like a mutual outside threat, Charlie said through the link. *We're all Ranans today, regardless of party. We'll get back to fighting with each other later—if we last that long as a nation.*

"There is no need for panic, but we must exercise caution until this situation is resolved," Guzmán said. "I urge all Ranans to continue whatever they were doing—but first take a moment to note the locations of the nearest Civil Defense Shelter access hatches. Should a worst-case scenario unfold, alarms will sound. In that event, please proceed in an orderly manner to those shelters, and await an all-clear."

Rex's hackles rose. He struggled to breathe evenly and keep incipient panic at bay. *I don't know where to go!*

Stick with Guzmán and Klein.

Rex stress-yawned. *That makes sense. Where can you go? You're in an elevator!*

It's not an ideal place to be during an attack. I doubt the Transmondians will be in range yet—in space, distances are farther than you might think. We'll arrive at Centerboro Med in another seven minutes. And all hospitals are required to have a plan in place for Civil Defense emergencies.

Here's hoping!

Guzmán had moved into instructions for Ranans to stay on this channel for announcements from Borough authorities, when all at once Rex's HUD-view blipped. It went dark.

Then it opened on a view of Premier Iskander.

The Ranan Premier still looked like the tightly-wound, icy woman who'd swept past him on the steps of OPD Central Headquarters more than a month ago. But now she clutched her podium with shaking hands and regarded the cameras with glittering, hooded eyes.

"Citizens of Rana Station, we have sustained a treacherous and grievous blow from internal forces! We thank our Transmondian allies for rushing to our aid, but I now must ask First Admiral Fallon to cease his advance."

Allies? Since when? At least she's sending them away!

She lifted her chin and gave the cameras a haughty glare. "The Whisper Syndicate has sought to destroy us, but they have failed. We shall deal with them on our own."

Whisper? Rex stared into his HUD, mind reeling. *What is she thinking?*

The HUD-view split three ways. On one side a view of Guzmán reopened. Kizzitikti appeared on the other. Next to him at the podium, Rex smelled Guzmán's startled concern. "Premier Iskander, we are heartened to see you. Are you well?"

Iskander's chin rose. "Of course. I am very well. Why wouldn't I be? But it is irresponsible of you, to speak of 'a worst-case scenario.' The Transmondians are our friends."

By now Guzmán wasn't the only person in Rex's proximity who smelled upset and looked dismayed. The HUD view showed that some of the Council Members behind him stared with horrified expressions into their HUDs. Others looked directly into the cameras and shook their heads with alarm.

"Premier, with respect—"

"Sacha, this is not respect! You are *not* being respectful! Not of my office! Not of myself! You've always wanted this job, but your little coup attempt has failed! Get off my screen!"

"Premier—"

"Off! Off! Out! Out!" She turned to someone outside of her camera-view with a thunderous scowl. "Get him off my screen!"

Guzmán grimaced, made a "cut" gesture to the SDF producer, and his image blipped out of the HUD-view.

Kizzitikti, however, remained on-screen. Kir mane had stiffened erect again, and kir fangs flashed. Every ozzirikkian Council Member behind kir mirrored this stance. "Premier, I would advise you to pause for an intelligence update. Your information is incorrect." Ki backed up that assertion with several forceful clicks.

"What, you, too? Are you in league with that traitorous snake? Have you turned against me as well?"

Kizzitikti's fangs flashed again. Kir indigo eyes burned with anger and every centimeter of kir body radiated fierce insistence. "I serve the Ranan people, Premier. Not you, not anyone else. If you force me to choose, then I choose Ranan sovereignty. I choose the truth!"

You tell her, Zikikittir! Charlie said through the link.

"Get off my screen! You're both in this together! I will not be overruled!" In the background behind Iskander came what sounded like someone pounding on her hatch. Iskander glared at a person positioned offscreen. "Turn off that damned click-ape's feed! And tell the asshole outside to quit pounding on my hatch!"

Kizzitikti's cuplike ears folded back into kir fur. Kir blue-black face shifted to a cold, stern expression. "Section Fifteen." Ki spoke the words with heavy finality.

"K'zhen." "K'zhen." "K'zhen." Singly and in small groups, the affirmation echoed through the Council delegation, a clear majority.

Woah! Sharp astonishment burst through the link from Charlie.

Iskander's vid cut off.

"Oh, thank God!" The voice came from behind Rex: one of the Council Members. "That was painful to watch." Several others murmured agreement.

What just happened? Rex asked. *What is Section Fifteen?*

In the HUD view Kizzitikti sheathed kir fangs and lowered kir crest. "It is important that we deliver the most factual information possible to our fellow Ranan citizens. I do not believe we have acted in error. Of course, this Section Fifteen call must certainly be subjected to considered scrutiny after the current crisis has passed."

Acting Premier Zhokittik has just taken charge, Charlie said. *Section Fifteen isn't something to call lightly, but ki got a large majority affirmation.*

"Former Premier Iskander seems to be undergoing a difficulty of some sort, and most certainly a failure of accurate information," The new Acting Premier continued. "We shall make sure that she receives prompt attention and any needed care." Several imperative clicks accompanied kir words.

The vid-view that included Rex and Guzmán opened once more.

"I believe my colleague Vice Premier Guzmán was explaining that this feed will shift to local authorities next, for further Civil Defense information." Kizzitikti continued. "Let us resume his comments now."

Guzmán nodded. "Thank you, Ka'Zikikittir Zhokittik."

Most of the human Council Members present also nodded. "Yes, Premier" some said aloud, while others echoed Guzmán's use of "Ka'Zikikittir." "Affirmed." "Affirmed." "Affirmed," they agreed. Not all, but a clear majority.

Excellent. It's important for Guzmán and as many Members as possible to affirm kir Section Fifteen, Charlie said. *"Ka'Zikikittir" is Ozzirikkian for "Premier," as you may have guessed. Now the Section Fifteen is officially in force.*

Rex's HUD view shifted show Oma Pandra. Orangeboro's Defense Secretary looked uncharacteristically flustered, but he drew in a deep breath and launched into a list of precautions people could take, to be ready in case an alarm sounded. Rex minimized it. *Are you getting Pandra?*

We're registered to Orangeboro, so yeah. Not real helpful when we're in Centerboro, eh?

First Admiral Kumar pulsed jets to halt at Guzmán's left side. "We need you in the Situation Chamber, sir."

"Do we have a line to Ka'Zikikittir Zhokittik?"

"Ki has a secured line for updates. Ki has ordered that you and Admiral T'irzh'kokku should cover the Situation Chamber in person."

"As ki directs. Lead the way." He glanced toward Rex. "Pack Leader, Kwame, come with me." Guzmán and Kumar powered away from the podium, cameras, and lights.

Rex and the Chief exchanged startled looks and followed.

CHAPTER 60
ON BEHALF OF ALL XK9S

7

Wheel Four Hub Secured Governmental Press Conference Chamber

S hady hovered next to Pam outside the circle of lights, cameras, and journalists, where the Pack had gathered. Out of the way, they hoped.

The Vice Premier departed with his gaggle of SDF people and others, including Chief Klein and Rex.

"Where are you going?" she texted Rex.

"The military people and Guzmán are going to the Situation Chamber," he answered. "He told the Chief and me to come inside the base with them. Not sure why."

"I think the rest of us are returning to the hotel soon. Keep me posted."

"I shall do my best, but I may not be able to text you from inside."

"I want to hear everything when you get back."

His line went dead. Security jammer? If he was anywhere near the Situation Chamber, probably.

The bright camera- and studio-style lights went out. Shady blinked at the sudden dimming of their glare. The Council

Members appeared to relax after the broadcast lights went out. They clustered in little groups to talk quietly, or moved away from the stability railings in ragged, slow-moving clumps.

Shady stress-yawned and licked her lips. *I still can't believe Iskander is really gone.*

If ever a Premier needed a Section Fifteen called for a mental issue, it was Iskander today. Pam put on a creditable cop-face, but her unease echoed through the link. *I don't want to think what she would've done if Kizzitikti hadn't called it.*

Has it ever happened before in Ranan history? A Section Fifteen, I mean? Unlike some other disciplines, the Pack had discovered a great many gaps in their education about certain Ranan laws and moments in history.

Only once, and that was for a physical injury. Pam's brow puckered in a frown. *It happened seventy-some years ago. Premier Callum was badly injured in microgravity. He was inspecting the construction of Wheel Eight, and one of the I-beams hadn't been properly secured. The accident put Callum in the hospital for months before he died from his injuries. Ka'Zikikittir Zitoktu called the Section Fifteen.*

Another ozzirikkian?

Whichever species the Premier is, they are succeeded by the other species in the case of a Section Fifteen.

So, everyone knew what to do?

Technically yes, but I still have to give Kizzitikti credit for having the guts to call it. Not everyone would've stuck kir neck out like that, but ki got a big majority assent. I don't think the follow-up investigation will overrule it. And meanwhile, we're in way more competent hands.

Got that right. Despite being weightless, her chest felt lighter.

More Council Members fired jets for the elevators now. Signs above several of the doors in the far wall said "Council and Aides Only." A few of the humans stopped to speak with members of the Pack. Shady overheard several of them thank one or another Packmate for helping them exit the Chamber today.

Isn't that Ashton Cole? She and Pam watched his approach. After the Palmdale trio's brief detainment on Saturday night, she'd only seen brief glimpses of them. None of the three had spoken to the Pack today, or even acknowledged them. Yet now Cole pulsed his jets and approached Tuxedo.

A portly older man with a thick shock of white hair, Cole had maintained an aloof, haughty demeanor through all their encounters. But now his brow pinched, and his scent filled with the smoky low tones of unease or regret. "A word, please?"

"Yes?" Tux eyed him warily but kept his ears up and his hackles flat.

"I, um." Cole grimaced, glanced away, then met Tux's eyes in a human way that meant earnest intent. "I owe you my—my life, I guess. I just—well, I couldn't make myself move. And then you came and told me to grab your harness." He glanced away again, then back, and hunched his shoulders. "Just wanted to say I—well, thank you."

"You are welcome." Tux fired jets to counter his tail-wag.

"And also, I—I guess I got it wrong. About you XK9s, I mean. I guess you really are that smart. So, I'm, um—sorry." He spun and jetted away.

Tuxedo, Georgia, Shady and Pam all stared after him.

"I did not see that coming," Georgia said.

Shady snorted. An acidic burn lingered in her gut and at the back of her throat. "I do not think we should hold our breaths waiting for either of the others to do anything like that." She gave the chamber a quick scan and curled her lip. No, Berik and Zeman had already left. *Rat bastards, and cowards to boot. They couldn't face us.*

"Safety Services Elevator," Joslyn Stark's voice spoke into her ear and cut across Pam's agreement. "We're cleared for departure. The elevators are just down that corridor on our right."

❖ ❖ ❖ ❖ ❖ ❖ ❖ ❖

Wheel Four SDF Base Restricted Area

The harsh, edgy bite of worry in First Admiral Kumar's scent factors knotted Rex's gut another notch tighter. He realized he was panting too fast, and consciously slowed his breaths.

Kumar led Vice Premier Guzmán's group inside the Wheel Four SDF Base. None of the humans looked or smelled happy, although the levels of worry, fear, tension, and prickly nervousness varied. None of those scents, furrowed brows, and grim faces reassured Rex. *Clearly, this is not over.*

Where is Fallon? What is he doing now? Nothing coming through the link from Charlie at Centerboro Med reassured Rex, either. *Now that it's clear the mass-assassination attempt failed, will he attack us?*

A new scent bouquet wafted in from somewhere behind them. *Oh joy.* Here came Commodore Cornwell.

Rex's group did not stop to scan badges, as he and his companions had always done each time he'd entered any other secured area.

Our escort is authorization enough?

Gotta admit, it's a pretty exalted escort, Charlie said.

True.

They followed a circuitous route into the heart of the SDF Wheel Four Base, then stopped at a nondescript security hatch in what appeared to be a maintenance area. Nothing marked it as unusual except the two uniformed MPs who floated in place on either side of it. Now even Kumar and Guzmán had to give retinal scans and thumbprints.

"I wish to acknowledge Pack Leader Rex Dieter-Nell, who enters on behalf of all Ranan XK9s," Guzmán said. Then he leaned forward to stare into the recorder and press his thumb against its pad until it beeped for a second time.

Rex knew this routine. He leaned in for his own retinal scan and gave his nose-print.

But a little wave of wonder came through the link from Charlie. *Rex, did you understand the significance of that?*

Rex hesitated, confused. He fired side-jets to make room for Chief Klein. *What do you mean? Significance of what?*

The Chief moved forward. Guzmán identified Klein as "an aide to the Pack Leader." Scanned and thumbprinted in his own turn, Klein offered Rex a nod and a small smile. Then he gestured for him to go on ahead.

Wait. What just happened there? Rex's chest tightened. He wasn't used to missing things, but clearly this time he had. A little tremor passed through him and he panted faster. *How is the Chief suddenly my "aide"?*

Go on ahead, Charlie prompted. *I'll explain when you're settled inside.*

What the—? Rex's head spun. He forced himself to pant slower, but this was no time to stop and demand answers. He and Klein followed Guzmán into a huge, round, windowless chamber. It likely took up all of that "maintenance area" and then some. The walls were covered with large screens in sections like enormous facets on a cut gemstone. Numerical readouts or views of the space around Rana Station, displayed at many angles, glowed on the screens. What looked like a huge, spherical GR tank hung in the middle.

An ozzirikkian with four sleeve stripes and the long, tufted ears and beard of a tirittim greeted Guzmán with a salute, which the Vice Premier returned. Then ti moved farther along one of the stability railings that circled the tank at a variety of angles, to give the new arrivals room.

Admiral T'irzh'kokku, I presume?

You've got me, Charlie said. *Probably?*

Whoever ti was, Rex eyed tin with curiosity and studied the nuances in tir scent. He'd never met a tirittim in person before. Most of the ozzirikkians that humans or XK9s encountered were kixi, ordinary ozzies of the more numerous gender. Rana's new Premier was a kixi elder, more properly termed a kirikkim. Kixi outnumbered the minority-gender tixi nearly four to one. Tiritti, the tixi elders, almost never operated in mixed-species spaces. That alone made this ozzie admiral worth a second sniff.

Guzmán grasped the same stability rail as T'irzh'kokku. "SCISCO, are you with us?"

"No time to bring an avatar today, but I am here," SCISCO's voice replied through one of the speakers.

Rex glanced toward it, ears up, and fired jets to counter his tail-wag. *You are the weapons-expert for your kind?* He used his link connection, so he wouldn't distract the others.

Among other things, SCISCO replied with a touch of amusement. *It is good to find you here, alive, and apparently well.*

You were a tremendous reassurance earlier today. Thank you.

You're welcome, Pack Leader.

Something about the way ne said that seemed . . . *different.* A small flame-tongue of curiosity flared up and his heart pounded faster. *I am definitely missing something. Charlie! What don't I know that everyone else does?*

Loving amazement filled the link. *My dear partner, Vice-Premier Guzmán just identified you as representing all Ranan XK9s. That's an official recognition.*

Well, I am the Pack Leader. And it's not as if we have more than one Pack on Rana.

Mm, let me try again. It means that on Rana you are now officially recognized as the primary representative of all XK9s. No matter how many there are. In the same way it now seems clear to me that SCISCO is the official primary representative for all of Rana's Farricainan cyberbeings.

SCISCO's amused *"among other things"* took on sudden new weight. *Oh?* An odd, heavy, shaky feeling filled his chest.

Just as Vice Premier Guzmán is the official primary representative for all humans, Charlie continued. *Ka'Zikikittir Zhokittik is both the Ranan head of state and, now only slightly secondarily, the official primary representative of all ozzirikkians. I'm pretty sure your new recognition means you're now a member of the National Leadership Council.*

National Leadership?— His lungs developed a hot tightness and his skin tingled. The National Leadership Council was a top-level part of the Ranan government, designed to ensure that all significant populations of sapient beings resident on-Station were represented. They advised the Premier directly. An overwhelming sense of being in over his head dizzied him. *O-o-oh.*

Exactly. The Chief is your "aide" for the moment because I can't be there to serve that purpose for you. Rex sensed a quick intake of Charlie's breath. A subtle change came through the link. *And, um . . . it occurs to me to ask: are there any other official XK9 spokesdogs recognized anywhere in the Chayko System?*

A frantic need to pace and pant came over Rex. He stress-yawned, licked his lips, and forced himself to breathe normally so he wouldn't hyperventilate.

Through the link, a sense of Charlie's regathering confidence and rock-strong love steadied him. *I didn't mean to overwhelm you, that just suddenly dawned on me. And I truly believe there could be no better spokesdog—but I did think you needed to understand about the National Leadership Council. Thank goodness, all you have to do today is be present and observe.*

For all XK9s. Everywhere. That shaky gut-quiver started up again.

Just observe. You've got this. But understand that no, you're not there just to satisfy your own curiosity.

Rex licked his lips several more times until the gut-quiver quieted. Somewhat. *Okay, then.*

Everyone stared into the GR tank, so Rex did too.

❖ ❖ ❖ ❖ ❖ ❖ ❖ ❖

Express Elevator to Centerboro Grand Central Terminal

T he Safety Services Express elevator car's doors slid shut. At first, all Pam heard were the quiet hisses of jets, the click of harness buckles as everyone strapped in, and the quiet rhythms of nervous dogs panting. With their XK9s strapped in, Pam and the other human partners rotated and moved to seats that seemed redundant in microgravity. They'd be glad for those places to rest once gravity's pull strengthened.

I think I'm finally having some adrenaline letdown, Shady said through the link. *I feared it might hit in the conference chamber. I'm just as glad it waited till now.*

The last fastener on Pam's five-point harness gave her stiff resistance. She tried again. This time it clicked home, but that one, final little struggle left her drained and shaky. *I don't think we truly believed the crisis was over, in the conference chamber. I'm worried it still isn't.*

Agreed. What is happening in the Situation Chamber? Shady's head turned toward her. Uncannily intelligent brown eyes regarded her from that furry face.

What is happening out in Ranan Space? Pam frowned and took a slow, measured breath. *Where did those Transmondian destroyers go?* By reflex, her mind reached for a news feed, but all she could find were recaps of the broadcasts from the conference chambers that they'd personally seen unfold.

This went on for several minutes. Then the broadcast she was watching began to intercut vids from the Combined Councils Chamber's destruction, or—*oh, here are some new ones.* These showed the rush to exit the Chamber, as seen and heard via the Official Record feeds that always, by law, were turned on during official business. *They got some interesting vids. Shady did you see these?* She found one of Shady, ferrying the then-Zikikittir and kir aides. *Wow. You're a vid-star. Did you see this?*

What?

Pam forwarded it to her.

Oh. That—does look rather dramatic. An odd mixture of exhilaration and remembered terror echoed through the link.

The vid on Pam's HUD rolled on. She turned up the sound. People made their way however they could toward the exits. Shouts, urgent instructions, the scramble of many moving bodies, the hiss of jets—the Official Record feed had captured it all. The first *boom* stopped her breath.

"There's the first one," a commentator's voice-over said. "That's the sound when the first layer of chambered shielding breached."

Pam dragged in a gasp and kept watching. *We survived that.* The evacuation unfolded faster than she remembered it. *Did they speed up the vid?* Another *boom* followed the first, then another. The evacuation had turned into an all-out scramble by then. XK9s like huge, flying sheepdogs drove or carried Council Member after Council Member to the exits.

"The Premier and Vice Premier both credited the XK9s—and they clearly were right," another commentator's voice said. "It's hard to imagine that everyone could have escaped without their help."

"That *anyone* would have," the first voice said. "Certainly not, if XK9s hadn't sounded the alarm in the first place. We're told that alert came from the Pack Leader himself."

The vid rolled on. The Chamber emptied. *Oh, my. There I am with my case pad, checking to see that everyone's out.* Her vid-view form pulled back and sealed the exit. A heartbeat later the Chamber blew out in a hurricane of splintering debris. Pam's gut did a flipflop. *Damn. That was close.*

"We now have an ID on that last officer out," the first commentator said. "It's as we thought. She's not from the RES. She's Orangeboro Police Sergeant Pamela Gómez, of the XK9 Unit."

Breathe, Shady told her. *You're okay.*

Pam ran a hand over her face, her stomach all in knots and her pulse like thunder.

"The XK9 Unit. Again." Now the view shifted to the two commentators. Both looked familiar after several years of watching vids from this agency, but in the moment, Pam couldn't name them. The younger of the two turned to gaze at the cameras. She shook her head. "I don't want to think where Rana Station would be right now, if it hadn't been for the XK9s."

Pam blinked out of her HUD-stare and struggled to get a grip. *Wow.*

"Have you checked out the 'Kerry and Derika Show'?" Misha asked. "They really got some dramatic vids. Of *us!*"

"So did *Burns and Zhang On The Beat,*" Petunia said. "We look rather badass on the vids."

"Think it might help convince Zeman's crowd?" Scout asked.

"We convinced one of them, anyway," Tux put in. "Did you hear Ashton Cole, before we headed downside? He actually apologized to me."

"And I missed it? Damn." Elle's tongue lolled. "Did your rig catch it?"

Pam's com clicked: Balchu. "So. Last Officer Out, is it?"

"Um, I guess I shouldn't argue with the 'Official Record'?"

"I think I've aged a couple of decades, today—and one of them was when I saw that vid. Are you on your way down, yet?"

"SSE One to Grand Central." She glanced at the readout. "Still eighteen minutes out."

"Etta Hami and CPD STAT are organizing an escort for the Pack. The streets are filling up."

Huh? She frowned. "Why? Protesters?"

"No, not angry—at least not at the XK9s." He released a small sigh. "They're not dancing in the streets—not while we're living under the imminent threat of a Transmondian invasion. But I think a lot of people just need to feel like they're standing together in solidarity with other Ranans. Lots of flags waving. We're beginning to see "Thank you, XK9s" signs here and there. In any case, you'll need an escort, just to get through."

"XK9s don't usually have trouble clearing a path."

"XK9s aren't usually the single bright spot in a day full of worry. Today, they're the heroes of the hour. You'll see. You're gonna be glad you have help."

CHAPTER 61

RANA STATION'S SECRET WEAPON

Wheel Four Hub SDF Base Situation Chamber

A tiny but detailed image of Rana Station floated in the center of the Situation Chamber's spherical GR tank. Rex watched, alongside Chief Klein, Vice Premier Guzmán, and the SDF officers as three slow-moving gray-and-gold shapes approached the miniature representation of Rana Station. Three gray-and-purple shapes converged on each of the gray-and-gold ones. *Too bad it isn't rigged for smell . . . sorry. Stupid thought.*

Not stupid. Smell is your primary sense. He caught a sense of Charlie's grin through the link. *Just not terribly applicable in the vacuum of space.*

"And there it is!" A woman with three stripes on her sleeves grimaced and gestured toward the tank. A bright nimbus appeared around the leading gray-and-gold shape that approached the miniature Rana.

On several of the wall screens a picture of a large, rather ugly, knobby-looking spaceship appeared. Anyone inside the Chamber, no matter their angle of orientation, should be able to get a good view of it, as well as a scrolling list of specifications that appeared to be measurements of size, performance specifications, weapons payloads, and more. A magnified playback inside the tank briefly showed a tiny version of that ship above where the gray-and-gold trio had been.

Now a light-toned, dotted line extended from that location to Rana's Wheel Four. Apparently, that was the three-banded woman's "it." The change had aligned the ship to meet the Ranan docks at Wheel Four.

"That's Fallon's flagship, the *Rampart*." Kumar said. "It does not appear to be turning back, although all of our communications should by now have been received."

Those lighted shapes represent ships, I assume? Rex asked Charlie through the link.

At a guess, what you see as gray-and-gold probably is Transmondian red-and-gold to humans and ozzies, Charlie replied. *The gray-and-purple ones are most likely Ranan green-and-purple. And it's inappropriate for me to be privy to this, although I must admit I'm fascinated.*

Do not worry, Detective, SCISCO put in. *If anyone has a concern that you might be a security risk, I shall take responsibility. After all, if you could be here, you would be.*

Wow. Charlie's awed gratitude surged through the link. *Thank you!*

Guzmán studied the shapes in the tank, oblivious to their link-based exchange. "Which of our ships are on an intercept course?"

A bright nimbus briefly highlighted the nearest Ranan vessel. Another knobby-looking spaceship image appeared on wall screens adjacent to the images of the *Rampart*. This image looked even larger. More scrolling lists of specifications rolled. "We're meeting it with *Fairboro*," Kumar answered. "We have *Realta* and *Tiktitiokim* on backup." A similar nimbus glowed for an instant around each of two other gray-and-purple blips near the first blip as she spoke. More spaceship images and specifications appeared on more screens, but these looked somewhat smaller, relative to *Rampart* and *Fairboro*.

Rex had not made a point of learning the names and sizes of all the SDF ships. But he'd accessed all kinds of information to read in the hospital. It had helped—some—to alleviate the tedium. He'd discovered a text on the SDF in his searches, so he now knew the larger ones were named, as all of these were, after Ranan boroughs or timi'i. That same source had said *Fairboro* was Rana's largest cruiser-class warship. *I wonder if the wall-screen images are in scale with each other.*

Yes, SCISCO said. *They are in scale.*

Makes sense to send the biggest one against the enemy's flagship, I guess. Then he caught himself, chilled. *If Transmondia is "the enemy," does that mean we're at war?*

Worry emanated through the link from Charlie. *They started it. If we are.*

Not technically. Not yet, SCISCO said. *But that possibility grows ever more likely.*

Rex snapped his ears flat and stared at the little blinking lights in the Situation Chamber's central tank. Since they had SCISCO's explicit clearance and both Guzmán and Cornwell knew about brain links but had said nothing to prohibit Charlie's access, he widened the link for his partner.

One wouldn't think such slow-moving, simple, little blinky bits would rivet the attention, yet somehow they do. Echoes through the link from Charlie suggested an unquiet stomach and sweaty palms.

"We've broadcast our warning again. They've been told in the strongest terms to halt their approach and keep their weapons dormant." Rooq Cornwell scowled at the little blinky bit that represented the Transmondians' flagship *Rampart*. His scent factors burned with fierce aggression that for once perfectly matched Rex's mood. "They'll cross our line in five minutes."

"Directed-energy defenses armed," Kumar reported. "On your mark, Ka'Zikikittir."

"They can detect that our defenses are prepared to fire on them?" Kizzitikti asked via the secured line.

"Yes, Ka'Zikikittir."

"Let them cross the line, first. Fire a warning burst when they do."

"Understood."

"*Rampart*'s starboard near-space missile bank just went hot." Rex's HUD identified *Fairboro* Captain Tam Wong as the speaker.

On the image of the *Rampart*, a dark tone superimposed itself over one of the larger external knobby lumps on the ship's surface, then started blinking.

Shit! Does that mean we're about to be attacked? Rex couldn't keep from panting faster. His gut coiled into ever-tighter knots. *Missile bank? They're going to file missiles at Rana?*

"Working on that." SCISCO's voice had gone flat-calm.

Rex cocked his head at the nearby speaker ne had used.

They haven't sounded any alarms here. Concern pulsed through Charlie's mental voice. Rex sensed that he tried not to share his terrifying memories of catastrophic decompression and wreckage. Rex glimpsed them through the link, but he had experienced enough of those by now to form his own lurid imaginings.

Harsh high-key notes of anxiety shot through Chief Klein's scent factors in tandem with Rex's reactions. He turned toward Guzmán with a worried expression. But after short spikes of what smelled like hunt-joy in the SDF people and something closer to consternation in Guzmán, the others' scents steadied out. They shifted their gazes toward the walls.

What do they know that we don't? What is SCISCO "working on"?

Vids flooded in to fill more of the Chamber's wall screens. The knobby missile bank on the destroyer *Rampart* disintegrated in a breathtakingly short burst. The energy release spun warship into an uncontrolled spiral.

"*Rampart*'s starboard missile bank just exploded!" Wong cried.

On the wall screens, *Rampart* rolled over and over for two long seconds. Wreckage flew every which-way in its wake. Eventually it stabilized, still shedding fragments.

"We *warned* them to keep their weapons dormant." SCISCO's voice carried a note of smug satisfaction. "As I always tell my students, people should listen carefully to instructions."

What did you do? Rex asked through the link.

It helped that Fairboro *was so close. That allowed me to gain quick access through the com lines. I aborted their launch codes and ordered the weapons to detonate immediately. They didn't disarm them quickly enough.*

Rooq Cornwell sent a sardonic look toward Guzmán. "Guess who suddenly wants to talk?"

"This is outrageous!" First Admiral Fallon's voice bellowed through the speakers. "You have fired upon my ship! This unprovoked aggression cannot be allowed to pass! We will—"

"We fired no weapon." Ka'Zikikittir Kizzitikti's voice cut across Fallon's. It held a note of irritation. "I believe that upon investigation you'll find you had a rather catastrophic weapons failure. Any armed warheads that may have exploded in that missile battery were your own."

"Preposterous! How could—" He broke off. Half-muffled, they could hear him ask "*What?*" in a distinctly peevish tone.

"We grow tired of reminding you that we are very much alive, our government is intact, and your presence here is unwanted," Kizzitikti said. "You most emphatically do *not* have our permission to dock at Rana Station."

❖ ❖ ❖ ❖ ❖ ❖ ❖ ❖

Centerboro Grand Central Terminal

"I do not think I have ever seen that many humans crammed together in one place before." Shady panted harder, just looking at them. *To be out there in the midst of them—how can they avoid trampling each other?*

She, Pam, and Joslyn Stark stared through a window on the first above-ground level of Centerboro Grand Central Station. The rest of the Pack panted and paced around in the waiting area behind them. They'd emerged from the Safety Services Express, only to be guided here by Centerboro officers. The three who had met them said plans were being made for their safe extraction.

That's quite a crowd, for sure. Pam's thoughts flickered to memories Shady couldn't quite make out.

What are you remembering?

"This reminds me of crowd control duty after the Comets won the Station Series." Pam spoke aloud and slid a glance toward Joslyn.

The OPD's press liaison nodded. "I think that's the last time I saw a crowd even close to this size. Kudos to you guys, though. You kept it peaceful."

"Everyone was in a good mood then. That helped. But I was glad to depend on the more experienced officers I was working with."

All the humans Shady could see outside looked grim and silent. Many hugged each other, held hands, or linked arms—likely so they'd be harder to separate in the tight-packed crowd. More than she'd expected carried Ranan flags, with their contrasting vertical bars of purple and allegedly green on a field of black with two white stars. A few even carried what looked like hastily made signs bearing mottos such as "I ❤ XK9s" or "THANK YOU XK9 PACK!"

"I must say they do not appear hostile, although not particularly celebratory." Shady stress-yawned. *I'm in no hurry to go out there and wade through that press, in any case.* "Normally, people prefer to make way for XK9s, but I am not sure where they could go to get out of the way, in this case."

Her HUD dinged on the Command Channel: Etta Hami. "We

are bringing in a bus and an escort of radio units. They'll be moving slowly, to get through this crowd safely. But Mayor Rao, Chief Nakoa, and Director Perri decided it was better for people to see you than if we whisked you away in a flitter."

"Whatever you think is best," Pam, also on the Command Channel now that she was a sergeant, answered for their group.

Shady was just as glad to let her speak for them, since apparently her partner could think of things to say. Growing heaviness in her gut and the raspy dryness of her throat robbed her of words and made her want to run.

"Today, you and the Pack are symbols of hope," Hami said. "You fought back and won, in the Councils Chamber. The people have seen you on the vids. Now if they can see you in real life— even just through the windows of a bus—Rao and Perri think it may help to keep them calm."

"Calm is better than panic," Pam agreed. "Is there a Civil Defense evacuation plan?"

Hami sighed. "If the Transmondians fire on the Station and breach one of the Wheels . . . well, that's a worst-case. We do have enough evac bunkers for the entire population—if they can get there in time. But let's hope it doesn't come to that. Rao didn't want to over-react and freak people out."

Shady couldn't help panting faster. She paced a tight, frantic circle, then forced herself to sit again.

Pam let out a shuddering breath. "You said it!"

"You'll have to wait a bit more before you can leave. Meanwhile, Mayor Rao has set up a brief greeting ceremony in the terminal's rotunda. I'm told the CPD officers on staff there will guide you."

Soon the Pack was lining up on either end of yet another dais for yet another public event. Shady smelled the dusty-smoky fatigue of her Packmates and their lingering hot, raw inflammation scents as the day's rigors settled into their joints and muscles. They were more than ready for some downtime.

But the politicians wanted to be seen with them. At first, the

Centerboro officials seemed disappointed that Rex wasn't there, until Joslyn reminded them that—of course—he was in the Situation Chamber with Vice Premier Guzmán.

Why 'of course'? Shady cocked an ear toward Pam.

Oh, wow. That's right. On Rana, he undoubtedly represents all XK9s now. Pam gave her an amazed smile. *Your entire species. Your mate is kind of a bigwig now.*

Centerboro Mayor Rao formally congratulated Orangeboro Mayor Idris for the gallantry of her borough's officers. Two Council Members stepped forward to make speeches of thanks to Victor and Scout—oh, yes, and by the way also their human partners—for personally rescuing them. Applause filled the rotunda.

Next Mayor Rao explained Rex's absence, then turned expectantly toward Idris.

"But we have his mate with us right now! The heroic savior of our new Premier!" Mayor Idris beamed at Shady and extended her arm. "Assistant Pack Leader, Shady Jacob-Belle!"

The rotunda echoed with applause.

"Go stand by the Mayor," Joslyn's voice in her ear instructed.

Oh. Shady walked over to Idris. If anything, the applause got louder. *Now what?*

"And her partner, the 'Last Officer Out' of the Combined Councils Chamber, Orangeboro Police Department Sergeant Pamela Gómez of the XK9 Unit!" Idris continued.

Holy crap. Me, too?

Shady couldn't resist an urge to loll her tongue at Pam. Her partner squared her shoulders, schooled her face from astonishment into a neutral, pleasant expression, and gulped. Then she walked over to stand next to Shady.

More applause.

Shady faced it, ears up and neck arched. She'd seen Rex strike this pose, and it always made him look regal. *Here's hoping we look okay.*

My hair is a mess. Do I have sweat stains on my dress blues? Pam stared out across the crowd, too. She did a pretty good job of smiling, though her eyes had a glazed look. *Should I wave? Probably not. Or is that unfriendly? Crap.*

"I'm told their bus is here." Mayor Rao spoke up before Pam and Shady's stricken silence could stretch on too awkwardly. "Let's give these heroes one more warm Centerboro thank-you, and let them go back to their hotel. They need some rest. We'll know more in the coming hours. But the Pack has given Rana Station new hope today!"

❖ ❖ ❖ ❖ ❖ ❖ ❖ ❖

The Situation Chamber

Via the link, Rex sensed when Charlie's elevator arrived at Centerboro Med. He felt a flurry of activity on his partner's end of the link, a flare of concern. But he was only partially able to follow his partner's movements after that.

Nothing appeared to be happening in the Situation Chamber's GR tank. Rex couldn't get a clear idea of what SCISCO was doing, except that ne was busy. Klein gave Rex an uncertain glance, his fear echoed by his scent factors. But he held himself physically still and focused on breathing patterns.

Rex found sharp, high tones of urgent focus predominant in Guzmán's scent. The Vice-Premier also smelled of deep apprehension, but it remained a background tone as he alternately frowned into a HUD-stare or typed things on his case pad.

The others shared that background frisson of raw, visceral fear in their scents, but they, too, seemed to have subsumed it for the moment in favor of mental action and focus on their areas of expertise. First Admiral Kumar and Admiral T'irzh'kokku conducted a low-voiced, staccato conversation. Cornwell typed rapidly on his case pad. The woman with three stripes kept a sharp watch on her readouts and the GR tank.

They had jobs to do, unlike Rex. With nothing to distract him, worries percolated through his mind. *Are we going to die? Is there something I should be doing now?* He stress-yawned and licked his lips, but nothing came to mind. *As the primary representative of all XK9s on Rana, why am I here? Only to bear witness? Maybe.* What might his new role on the Leadership Council require of him in the future—assuming there *was* a future?

A sickening surge of panic launched his pulse to triple-speed. Rex held his breath for a count of five, then let it out to a count of five. He ran through the *in-five, hold-five, out-five, hold-five* pattern several times until his pulse slowed. Klein's hand began a repetitive stroking motion down Rex's neck and back. He glanced up, caught a commiserating look from the Chief, but Klein didn't stop the caresses. From the shift in the man's scent, it comforted both of them.

After a while, a sense of Charlie's irritable boredom broke through his partner's efforts to mute his end of the link. He lay on an uncomfortable surface under a scanner. Breathing shallowly and trying not to move appeared to be considerably less riveting than the "little blinky bits" had been earlier.

But even the little blinky bits weren't doing anything exciting now. The *Rampart* stayed where it had fetched up after the explosion. The other two Transmondians also held their positions.

Fairboro and its companions moved at what looked in the tank like an exceedingly stately crawl toward the Transmondians. Finally, after what felt like ages, *Rampart* made a ponderous pivot and commenced to creep back the way it had come. After a moment, the other two Transmondian ships did, too.

I'm not sure I'd call it "going away," but they do appear to be withdrawing somewhat. Rex spoke through the link and directed a silent snarl at the little gray-and-gold blips that represented the Transmondian ships.

Better withdrawing than continuing toward the Station, Charlie answered. Rex caught a sense that his partner was clenching his teeth while enduring some kind of uncomfortable medical procedure.

You okay?

Just peachy. Charlie closed his end of the link more fully.

Rex flattened his ears. *Another worry to add: Is Charlie having more health issues?*

The officer with the three sleeve-bands adjusted something on her case pad, and the field inside the tank expanded. Now the miniature Rana Station diminished to a tiny, bright dot at the center of the tank.

The new view showed the gray-and-gold blips, now seemingly halted, but a light-toned dotted line extended from them toward a larger group of gray-and-gold blips along a dotted-and-dashed line marked "International Boundary." As he watched, a new gray-and-gold one blinked into being along that line.

"Here's another Transmondian," Three-Stripe Woman said. "They just keep adding ships."

The crowd of gray-and-gold blips twinkled along that line. Rex counted twenty. Another new Transmondian ship appeared at the edge of the tank. *Oops. Twenty-one.*

But a different group of ships also blipped into view on a different part of that boundary near the edge of the tank. These five blinked grayish brown and white.

"We have queried the Mahusayan ships to ask their intentions, but it will take about another minute before their answer reaches us," Three-Stripe said. No one had offered her name, but Rex definitely had acquired her scent profile.

Commodore Aadya Jarl, SCISCO supplied.

Thank you. Rex glanced toward the speaker ne had used earlier, although ne had used the link. *Should I also say "welcome back?"*

The impression of a chuckle rippled through the link, but nothing more.

"Incoming message from Lead Captain Octavia Sienariba, of Sienariba Security Collective." Jarl's eyes widened. "She just issued a warning to Transmondian Fleet Admiral Fallon. She says that Sienariba, Dostigator, and Tarpasso Collectives have come together in agreement. They hereby declare that they will not tolerate any attempt by the Republic of Transmondia to destabilize the balance of power in Chayko System. They urge the Transmondians to make no further efforts to take control of a sovereign Station—especially not one so close to the system's only jump point."

"Their five ships would potentially help us match the Transmondians numerically within mass-classes." Admiral T'irzh'kokku spoke through tir personal translator. Tir long, tufted ears clamped tight against tir skull. Ti flashed fangs that were twice the length and far more daggerlike than the new Premier's. "Details, Cornwell?"

The spymaster glanced up from his case pad. "Sienariba, Dostigator, and Tarpasso Collectives are the largest security collectives in Mahusayan space. Today's group are all mid-class destroyers. Altogether, the three Collectives they represent control thirty-two security vessels that range in size from small corvettes to six more with the heft of these."

"Armaments?" Guzmán asked.

"Top-of-the-line, allegedly including five of those variable-phase ion cannon batteries that we still don't have. Here's a list." Cornwell's eyes darted toward T'irzh'kokku and Guzmán in gestures of file-sending. "They are contracted to a consortium of six major mining collectives that keep them well-funded for defense against pirates in the asteroids."

I wonder if one of the six is Ministobrila. Charlie's pensive mental voice through the link echoed Rex's thought. His previous discomfort seemed to have eased.

Wouldn't surprise me. They seem to be into a lot of things. Rex kept his growl to the link.

Guzmán frowned. "We've been seeking an alliance with the Mahusayans for forty years. They've always refused, on the grounds that we are trade rivals. So have the Singkorians, although we do have mutual-aid agreements with the Primerans and Pinakamaroans."

"Perhaps the Mahusayans have not perceived the Transmondian threat so clearly in the past as they do today." SCISCO's tone took on a chilly edge. "Or perhaps they simply wish to be in the neighborhood. That might make it easier to collect some of our asteroids, should the Transmondians actually—or even partially—succeed in dominating us."

CHAPTER 62
RETURN TO GRAVITY

Centerboro Medical Center

"First of all, Hildie is okay." In the darkened hospital room, Charlie held Hildie's hand with gentle care. He tried to inject as much ease and confidence into his tone as possible.

"So why isn't *she* the one calling me?" Dara's voice carried a load of suspicion and anger. He tried not to take it personally. Those first horrifying vids from the Hub had hit the news feeds five hours ago. She and the rest of Feliz Family must have gone through agonies of worry today.

"Because she's kinda busy right now." He eyed her still form on the bed. She'd warned him not to say she was in recovery, because her mother would "freak out." "She asked me to—"

"*Too busy* to call her mother?"

Charlie let out a quiet breath. "Yes, just at this moment. She didn't want you to wait any—"

"Patch her in! Do it right now!"

"I can't—" the com clicked off. *Will she ever think I'm not a screw-up?* Charlie released a gusty sigh. "So. That went well."

Hildie squeezed his hand. At least a hand-squeeze was no longer too painful for her to do, although other things would

523

need more time to heal. "Y'tried." Her voice remained a drowsy whisper. The painkillers and sedatives appeared to be working. "Auto r'sponder took'er call."

"Sorry." He could claim a full complement of aches and tender places from his sojourn in the bunker, too, but his new augmentations had spared him the full extent of Hildie's misery. Which was mostly past the worst part now, he hoped. He knew his parents had said they would call Feliz Family to relieve their worry. That was why he'd waited to call till they knew she'd be okay for sure. Had waiting been a mistake?

In his defense, he'd also been distracted by events in the Situation Chamber. Even back in one-G, his stomach took a sickening dive when he thought about how close his nation had come to losing everything today. Terrifying enough to face his own physical danger—and double-triple worse with Rex and Hildie in peril.

But losing their Station? Or going to war with the Transmondians? Thank goodness—at least for now—it looked as if neither of those things were happening. More and more allies' warships kept arriving from around the System.

The Transmondians had pulled their ships back across the international boundary, but they hadn't gone far. They now were blustering through diplomatic channels that they'd never had any intention of invading, they were simply coming to help. How they'd known several days in advance that "help" might be needed? That was a question they ignored.

It probably mattered a lot that the Alliance had already put everyone in the Chayko System on notice. Its Fifth Fleet would arrive through the Jump Point in four days. No one was to attack anyone before they got there. *Unless they wanted to face the wrath of the entire Galactic Alliance,* was the part they didn't need to say.

Still, just thinking about how close they'd come today made his chest go tight, every breath half-strangled.

Through it all, the dull, throbbing ache that consumed his left arm had dried his mouth and oppressed him with its own persistent chill of dread. His arm felt way too much like it had in a period he shrank from remembering. That time, what Dr. Zuni called a "cascading failure of your muscle sheath integrity" turned part of his previous regenerated arm into melting, bloody slime. He'd skated way too close to overexposing his still-healing tissues to microgravity once before with this new arm. And he *definitely* had exceeded his time limit today.

A specialist called in by Council Member Juma had come to consult and biopsy his arm in several places, then conference-com with Dr. Zuni. The biopsies hadn't been fun, but he'd expected that. He both feared and longed for a clear answer. The few moments of pain would be worth it, if he could just *know for sure.*

But the tests hadn't come back yet. *Nothing to do but wait.* Charlie ran a breathing pattern and willed his tightly-torqued gut to relax. *No sense borrowing trouble. Hildie will be okay. Dara will forgive us or she won't. And whatever happens with my arm will happen. My little family unit will be all right once we all get safely back together in 1G.*

He grimaced.

As long as we truly do avoid a war with Transmondia.

❖ ❖ ❖ ❖ ❖ ❖ ❖ ❖

State Pavilion, Rex and Shady's Room

S hady's HUD beeped: Vince Bellini. "We're en route at last, bringing Rex in through the hotel's loading dock. RES is running security in cooperation with CPD."

The bed bounced when she stepped down from it. The CPD had secured the perimeter of the State Pavilion Hotel so the Pack and its attendant humans could eat, relax, and rest for the moment. "Shall I go down to meet you now?"

"Yes. ETA five minutes."

A stroll out to the suite's living room revealed a quiet, low-lit scene. She checked the time: 20:03, so it wasn't *too* late. She'd earlier glimpsed throngs of people in the streets all through the crisis. But with Transmondian agents known to still be at large, none of the security people wanted to risk exposing XK9s to much public access. "How is it out there?"

"Not too crowded anymore. The street demonstrations have mostly broken up. Centerboro is quieting down, but everyone knows it's not over. We're using security protocols."

"Thank you for securing him."

"Our pleasure." He hesitated. "How is Rex's partner?"

"Charlie just brought Hildie in from the hospital—CPD also brought them in through the back." She walked over to Charlie and Hildie's door, heard the low murmur of Charlie's voice. "Looks as if they're both going to be okay." She nosed the door open.

Charlie had stretched out next to Hildie on their bed. She appeared to be asleep, but he looked up. "Is Rex on the way?"

"ETA five minutes."

"I need to stay here and monitor Hildie—doc said the risk of seizures will continue for a few more hours until the last of the drugs are out of her system, and not to leave her alone."

"Got it." She nodded and ducked out. "Councilmember Juma brought in an augmentations expert from Highboro," she told Vince. "The expert did a bunch of tests on Charlie. He's set himself back about a week, but she says he hasn't undone his re-gen. So, that's a relief." She pushed past the outer door and made sure it clicked behind her. "I have told him Rex is on his way, but he can't leave Hildie alone while she has those drugs in her system. He and Rex are probably already talking through their link."

"Undoubtedly, but I'll pass the news about Charlie along. Kwame and Sacha wanted to know, too."

"Is the Chief getting out here?"

"He and Sacha tell me they haven't had a 'sleepover' since

Upper Levels. I think they're still hoping for some spare minutes to catch up with each other."

She wagged her tail and trotted faster. "I guess it has been a busy night for all of you."

"We're not at war, anyway. But yes. Very busy."

The State Pavilion's loading dock wasn't nearly as fancy as the main entrance, and considerably more redolent of vehicle lubricant, recycling bin, and garbage composter. Even with their weak, human noses, the CPD officers stationed here to guard this access point should be able to smell all of those.

The cargo transport-sized door rolled up just enough to let Guzmán's large, black car pull inside. Shady caught the barest glimpse of an alley beyond the door before it closed again. The moment the car halted, two side doors popped open. Black-uniformed RES agents leaped out. They scanned the area and didn't appear to relax, even at the sight of the CPD officers.

Rex did not leap when his door opened. He stepped down carefully. But he did not appear to be as exhausted as she'd worried he might be.

She hurried over to him, but neither of them had much energy for a wild greeting dance. Rex appeared to be breathing okay, so his nanite lung support was still good. Oh, but here was a place that smelled of inflammation, and here was another, and—

"Yes, I have a few aches and pains. I am fine." The vocalizer sounded neutral, but she could smell his impatience.

She snapped her ears flat. "I did not notice these when you came out of the ERT facility earlier."

"We had a stressful afternoon and evening." Rex exchanged a rueful look with the Chief and Guzmán.

She snorted. "We all had one. Have you eaten?"

"No." He lifted his ears. "I definitely could eat."

She turned to the humans, still inside the car. "Thank you again for bringing him. And thank you, Vice Premier, for all you did today."

"My pleasure. Thank *you*." He smiled and raised a hand in farewell. "We'll talk again soon, Pack Leader."

Rex nodded, human-style. "I look forward to it."

The black-clad RES agents gave the area one last scan and leaped back into the car. The door rolled up just enough, then slammed shut after Guzmán's car passed under it. Shady nudged Rex toward the door to the rest of the hotel. "Tell me."

"I cannot tell you all of it, and most certainly none of it while walking through public hallways." They crossed the lobby in silence. Rode alone in an elevator to their level but stayed quiet, wary of its internal security feeds. Shady gave their door her nose-print. It opened with a latch-click.

Inside, the lights remained low. Charlie emerged from his room and hurried into the suite's kitchenette. "Hildie's asleep. I hope she'll be all right for a moment. I have your food here." He brought two heaping bowls into the common area. "Pam sent Bacon-Wrapped Filet Mignon. She says you've more than earned it."

Rex already had grabbed a big mouthful. "Oh! This is excellent!"

Shady gulped hers down, then licked her lips. "I could get used to that!"

"Good, because it's probably what's for breakfast, too." Charlie had stood by the door to keep an eye on Hildie. Now he cleared their dishes at augmented-person top speed, knelt, and gave them both a hug. He hung on to Rex for maybe a second longer than Shady, then stood with a glance toward the bedroom. "See you in the morning!"

"Thank you for staying up to feed us, since we do not have Uncle Hector's dispenser," Shady said.

Charlie smiled, waved, and retreated to his bedroom.

Shady walked over to the sink and used her nose to activate its lever. "Okay, talk to me." She lapped the sink dry, then allowed it to partially refill and lapped it dry again.

"The Transmondians now have twenty-five ships of various

mass-classes on our international boundary," Rex said, even while he took his own turn to drink. "Also, Five Mahusayan ships are there. They claim that they have come to oppose the Transmondians."

"Mahusayans? Are we allied with them?"

"No, or at least not yet. It may be a work in progress."

"Because of Transmondian aggression?"

"Mostly. Sacha says we have been trying to create an alliance for forty years, but maybe now they see the Transmondian threat more clearly." Rex paced across the small living room. "The Singkorians are reportedly on their way with six more ships—also allegedly to oppose the Transmondians." He paced back.

"I take it they are not our allies at this point either?"

"No. Although, once again, that might change. Our actual allies, the Primerans and the Pinakamaroans, have sent four mid-mass warships each. There's a company of Takhiachono Marines on each of the Primeran warships, should it come to that kind of fighting."

"Hand-to-hand?"

"SCISCO explained that augmented Marines are also wickedly skillful in small fighter craft. They can take many more "Gs" than other humans before they pass out."

"Okay, then. That sounds good, I guess. And you say our allies are already here?"

"Yes. Their ships are now inside our international boundary, by permission of the Ka'Zikikittir."

"How many ships—did I get it that mid-mass warships seem to dominate this list? How many does Rana have?" Shady did a fast calculation: eleven alleged allies, plus eight declared allies meant either eight or nineteen, added to whatever the Station had. Versus twenty-five Transmondians. But how big were all of those ships, and how did they compare to each other? How much added capability did four companies of Marine "small fighters" represent? And how far should they trust the Mahusayans and Singkorians?

"Rana currently has twenty-five mid-mass warships of our own, three dozen smaller ones, and three high-mass battle cruisers." Rex burped, stretched, then disappeared into the bathroom.

Probably needed that break. She waited till he had finished and walked into their bedroom. She made a similar detour before she joined him. "I shall be glad to get home to more dog-friendly plumbing! Now finish counting ships, please."

"Between us, our allies, and our declared supporters, we currently outnumber the Transmondians in both armament and warships of the different mass-classes—at least, for now." Rex curled up on the human-style bed they'd used all weekend. "But I learned today that firepower is not the entire equation, either."

"What does that mean?" Shady leapt onto the bed and settled next to him.

"We have a secret weapon. Nir name is SCISCO-3750. Possibly some of nir siblings also could accomplish what I saw nem do today, but ne alone might be enough."

Shady cocked her head. "An explosives professor could be an asset, I suppose. But how?"

"Ne is far more than just a humble explosives professor. I believe that Vice Premier Guzmán wanted me there in my role as the Pack Leader. That is, as the 'chief of the XK9s.' I am now a member of the Ranan Leadership Council. They tell me that is because our very small but apparently significant population of nine other XK9s agreed to name me Pack Leader a few weeks ago."

"I should think we are definitely 'significant.'" Shady lolled her tongue. "We are the stated excuse for all the tension with Transmondia, although I imagine they have coveted our spot by the jump point since our founding. Based on things Kurtzu said, I suspect our sapience claim is also why the Alliance is making this conflict their business. And we did save the whole Ranan government today. I have discovered that a lot of people around here are impressed by that."

"Good. Here is hoping they keep that firmly in memory." Rex

yawned, probably mostly a sleepy yawn, but she smelled a stress-component, too. "I also learned today that I need to act as the on-Station representative of our entire species, everywhere."

"Makes sense."

"All the same, daunting. But let me get back to our friend SCISCO. The cyberbeings are another, very small but definitely significant minority population on Rana. I learned today that ne is their Leadership Council representative."

Shady nodded. *More than a humble professor, indeed.* "You implied something more. What did ne do?"

Rex wagged his tail. His scent surged with pleasure. "Ne did something the Transmondians did not expect. Something I had no inkling ne could do, although Sacha and the SDF people apparently knew about it beforehand. Unfortunately, it is classified. But I can tell you it is a good thing ne is on our side."

"Classified? That is annoying." All the same, Shady's abdominal muscles relaxed, and her breath came easier. "SCISCO and nir siblings do appear to favor us."

Based on QUAERO's help throughout the weekend—and nir intervention when the Transmondian plotters cut our com lines—I'd say they favor all of Rana, Pam agreed through the link. Shady repeated her comment to Rex.

"They did choose to locate their source nodes here." Rex wagged his tail. "I have learned that is a strong sign of how much they value our little speck of dust in the Universe. I do not believe they are inclined to move. Nor to accept a hostile government takeover."

Shady stress-yawned—or was it maybe just a yawn? "Good. Given our allies, and especially with Alliance backing, I feel better. Add in Rana's own resources, and fellow citizens with SCISCO and QUAERO's apparent level of reach and capability, and . . . well, maybe we shall survive as a sovereign station, after all."

CHAPTER 63
UNTIL ALL OF MY PEOPLE
ARE TAKEN CARE OF

State Pavilion Lobby

P am rubbed her eyes and blinked at her case pad, then stepped back through the entrance and returned to the lobby of the State Pavilion Hotel. The day after the destruction of the Combined Councils Chamber had seemed at times as if it would never end. *But we got it all done. Almost finished with this day, now!*

"Is that the last one?" Balchu strode to her side. He put his arm around her and pulled her gently toward him.

She released a gusty breath and rested her head against his chest for a moment. Then she straightened and stepped back.

"Last ones for *that* bunch." The "Glorioso Group" of Elle, Tux, and Elle's humans Misha and Hallie, were officially homeward bound. So were the "Nerd Queens." Now that Tux lived with his mate at Glorioso Tower, his partner Georgia had moved back in with Arden and Connie. The three "Nerd Queens" had been roommates and best friends since well before their XK9-candidate days. Both Georgia and Connie had at first thought that adding two XK9s to joint living quarters wouldn't be feasible, but one XK9 was less of a problem. *I guess Crystal's now the fourth Queen? Hmm.*

All had been supplied with a security escort, at least as far as Grand Central. Pam hadn't yet gotten much of a reading on how things were going in Orangeboro.

Even at the end of this very long day after, surprising numbers of people still thronged the streets of Centerboro. Everyone still felt wary, but the Galactic Alliance's Fifth Fleet was only three days out from the jump point, now. The Transmondians had pulled completely out of Ranan territory, although an unusual number of warships still hovered near the International Boundary. Rana had gained a bit of breathing room, and it seemed that a lot of people wanted to thank the XK9s.

Mayor Rao had decreed a municipal holiday for this morning's parade. She'd wondered how they could pull it together so fast before QUAERO explained that there was a standing Municipal Parade Committee, and that ne was on it. *We stage a lot of parades, here in Centerboro,* ne explained. *It is fun.*

Fun, perhaps, but Pam had never been part of a parade's focus before. The Pack had ridden in a flatbed transport with a see-through dome so they could be both safe, and visible to the public. The parade stretched blocks. *Who knew there are that many people in Centerboro? Well, I guess QUAERO did. But yikes!*

Even hours later, her face still hurt from smiling. Her arm, shoulder, and upper back ached after all that waving. But it was kinda nice to have their work and worth celebrated in such a public way.

As long as nobody insisted on making them participate in parades every day.

"Who's left?" Balchu quirked an eyebrow and pulled her out of her daydream.

Time to refocus! She checked her lists. "Most of Corona Family left for Orangeboro after the parade, but Charlie, Hildie, Rex, and, of course, Shady are staying another night. All the excitement wore them out, especially Hildie and Rex."

Balchu nodded. "I'm not sure Hildie even stopped for lunch, just went straight upstairs. She looked all-in after you guys got back from the SBI thing."

"That tracks. She's still feeling her stay in the bunker." Pam rubbed her forehead and tried to think through her own brain fog. After the parade, Director Perri had called a special meeting of the Pack, as well as all members of SITs Alpha and Delta who were in town. She'd also requested Hildie's presence in particular, but she was the only Family member. That seemed odd for a debrief, which was the stated reason for the meeting. But Perri had a surprise in store.

Good thing everyone was still in dress blues from the parade, because once they arrived Perri lined up the XK9s and their partners, along with Shiv and Hildie, on the stage in a big auditorium at the SBI National Headquarters building. Practically the entire Centerboro staff, which included all of the top hierarchy and most of the Tech Specialist teams, must've been in that audience. It added up to a lot of people packed in there.

Perri made a little speech, then handed out an SBI Gallantry Star to each Pack Member, whether XK9 or human, and also one to Shiv. They were all agents of one sort or another, as she explained. "And all of you have demonstrated the kind of courageous service in the face of danger that lives up to our highest expectations of an agent of the Rana Station Bureau of Investigation."

Then she awarded a Citizen of Courage Medal to Hildie, and explained it was the greatest honor the SBI could bestow upon a civilian.

After that came a lot of clapping and shouting and cheering. Again, it was really nice, and quite deeply gratifying. But all this hoopla was kind of embarrassing.

When they *finally* arrived at the hotel, Pam gratefully changed into civvies and made herself useful, working with

QUAERO, Joslyn, and several of Etta Hami's people to coordinate the security escorts for XK9 Families returning to Orangeboro.

Pam checked her list again. "Um, looks as if Lang Family is still waiting for an 'all clear' on their Granny Ifiok, after her lightheadedness earlier today." She glanced toward the lone figure who sat hunched and miserable-looking in one of the lobby chairs. "And Berwyn's still waiting."

Berwyn had arrived about 45 minutes ago from Orangeboro with an overnight bag and a worried expression. "Cinnamon booted me out," he explained. "Said I was pacing like a caged beast and I might as well do that here. So, um, here I am."

Shiv had a room in the hotel and had planned to remain here tonight, but he'd stayed at SBI HQ when the rest of the Pack left for the hotel. The man presumably would show up at some point. Pam gave her anxious Packmate a worried look. Shiv's "at some point" might be a while yet.

"Where's Shady?" Balchu asked.

"She's resting with Rex." Pam glanced up at him. "I sent up another bag of Pabiyan Master Mix for them."

His brow furrowed. "I know you handed out the special stuff last night, but does this mean we're completely out of the Transmondian mix?"

"They still have some in Orangeboro, but they're reserving most of it for Pabiyan Carnerie's quality control comparisons."

Balchu nodded, then shot a glance toward Berwyn. "Should we go sit with—"

The entrance doors opened behind them. Berwyn leaped to his feet, his face a mix of joy and concern. Next moment, he was in Shiv's arms. The two men clung to each other for a long, hard hug that lasted more than a full minute. Then they moved smoothly into a passionate kiss.

"Never mind. I think he's good." Balchu grinned at her.

She smiled back. "Ready for dinner?"

"Are we staying another night, too?"

She sighed. "Not all of my people are taken care of."

His grin widened. "They're adults, you know. They can take care of themselves."

"I know. But until the last ones are on their way home, I'll feel that my work isn't done. I helped the Lang relatives get medical help, and I was able to tell Berwyn about Shiv, and I . . ."

He kissed her. "Got it. Okay, let's have dinner. Pavilion Bar & Grill again? So you can keep an eye on things?"

"Aw, how'd you guess?"

He just laughed and led the way to what had become her favorite table: the one with the best view of the entrance and lobby.

❖ ❖ ❖ ❖ ❖ ❖ ❖ ❖

Express Elevator from Centerboro to the Hub

*O*n our way home! At last! Hildie had not managed to get up as early as she'd hoped, and now they were late. She hurried to catch up with Rex and Charlie en route to the elevators.

Her pain patches had worn off in the middle of the night, in contrast to the previous night's deeper, drug-aided sleep. She'd awakened gasping and terrified, gripped by both her pain and a nightmare about suffocating in the bunker.

Charlie'd held her, let her cry it out, and cried some himself. He might be "XK9-tough" now, but trauma and terror sometimes cut through "tough" like a blowtorch through wax. They'd almost lost each other two days ago, and there'd been very little downtime to deal with it yet. After the worst of their panic attack, crying jag, or whatever you wanted to call it had passed, they'd simply held each other until Hildie dozed.

She'd learned this morning that once she was mostly asleep Charlie'd gotten up to rummage around in her medkit. He'd applied new pain patches to her sorest spots—and used a few more on himself. After that it was a challenge for either one of them to wake up before 11:00.

Thank goodness Shady got us up. "You three are as bad as Pam," Rex's mate had grumbled while they packed up the last things. She, Charlie, and the XK9s *did* manage to evacuate their room, although she wandered through that process in a fog. And probably left a few things behind. *Just as well I don't have to work today.* Hildie grimaced to herself.

"Hils, you okay?" Charlie's face puckered with worry. He held the elevator door open but focused on her.

She forced herself to smile and stepped up to the waiting elevator. "I'm going to be creaking and groaning for a while, but I'm good."

"Always more than good." He leaned forward so his lips brushed her forehead and lowered his voice. "And very precious to me."

She nuzzled his chest briefly, but her hands were almost as full as his, and the elevator had begun to go "ding-ding-ding" from being held open too long. She grasped the handle of her rolling luggage and stepped inside.

They were leaving Centerboro one set of his dress blues short, and also minus her outfit from the trip to the Hub. Their clothing had been retained as evidence.

The Crime Scene Unit had cleaned off Charlie's Medal of Valor and given it back to him at yesterday's SBI ceremony. There was now a sunk-in bloodstain on part of the braid, "which makes it even more unique and historic," as the SBI CSU tech who'd returned it said.

It also had gained a glinting gold SBI Gallantry Star on a green-and-purple ribbon to keep it company—both now buried deep in Charlie's luggage. And she had that amazing Citizen Courage Award, to go with her aches, bruises, and stiff muscles. She released a soft sigh. *Will they still fire me, even if I have a Citizen Courage Award? Maybe. Probably? I don't know.*

They left the hotel surrounded by a security detail from both

Centerboro PD and the RES. Ranan Executive Security seemed to be taking Rex's new membership in the Leadership Council seriously—at least until they reached Centerboro Grand Central. Chief Klein had argued the OPD could handle Rex's security at home, just as they'd handled SCISCO's for decades.

They settled into seats on the Safety Services Express elevator and buckled in with Shiv and Berwyn on her right. Ari sat between Charlie and Rex. Shady sat by Rex, with Pam and Balchu on her left. Across from them in the elevator car, the last of the Lang Family group sorted themselves out. Before they'd completely gotten settled, the elevator started its boost.

Hildie recognized Walter and Petunia, but she'd only had passing encounters with the rest of the Lang group. These appeared mostly to be elders, who might especially benefit from a shorter trip on the Express. *Thank goodness we have access to this!* They weren't responding to an emergency any more urgent than their heartfelt desire to go home, but it appeared that being "heroes" had earned them that favor, anyway.

"I still don't *feel* like a hero." She frowned. "Sore and tired, yes. Heroic? No way."

Charlie answered with a wry chuckle. "Based on my experience, some level of 'sore and tired' is about as heroic as one ever feels."

One elder in the Lang group seemed to be having some kind of issue. Walter checked her pulse and frowned. "Wish I had a bio-readout patch."

"I have one." Hildie unbuckled. She dug into her med pouch then strode the meter or so to the "Lang side" and smiled at the older woman. "Hi. My name is Hildie, and I'm a paramedic. May I apply this to your forehead?"

The woman smiled back. She was a round, brown woman with bright black eyes and an ample frosting of gray in her braids. "Everybody calls me Granny Ifiok. Nice to meet you, Hildie. And yes, I think it'll comfort Wally, if you have one to spare."

"We'll need to give it a few seconds to activate." She applied the patch. It lit up with part of the readout. The rest would show up shortly. "I'm honored to meet you. I've heard a lot about you."

"All scandalous, I trust?" Granny Ifiok gave her a mischievous look.

"Oh, you're legendary."

"True that," Pam put in.

Granny Ifiok smiled with evident satisfaction and relaxed into her fold-out seat. Her patch blinked the rest of its results, which at first glance looked okay.

Walter moved toward her, then hesitated and gave Hildie a questioning look.

"You've been monitoring all along?" Hildie asked.

"Till they removed her patch and sent us home." His brows pinched. "I was a paramedic myself some years back, but my certification's lapsed. And micrograv does things to her that I don't get."

"Yeah, even all these centuries later, our bodies still don't know how to respond to it. Especially as we grow older." She talked him through the basics—so second-nature to her, but clearly new to him. Her throat went tight. *Could I really leave this work behind?* "Right now, I'd say she's doing well."

"Good. But I'll keep an eye on her." Walter gave his granny a worried look.

Hildie nodded and turned toward her own seat, but Petunia gave her a gentle bump with her nose. "A moment, please?" The huge golden dog gave her a thorough sniff-over. "You are somewhat the worse for wear, I think." She dialed her vocalizer down so Hildie could hear, but few other humans could.

"I have some aches and pains, but I'll be okay."

"I would advise rest, today and tomorrow. And more pain patches, if you have them."

"I do. Thanks, Doc." Hildie grinned.

"About that." Petunia's dark amber eyes made earnest

contact. "Rex tells me you are thinking of retaking your med-school entrance exams, and I should like to make a request. If you decide to do that, may I study with you?"

He told you what? No point in displacing her anger onto Petunia, however. Hildie blinked and scrambled to reframe. "You—um—you want to *study* with me?"

"I never had a chance to consider such a path when I was taking my coursework in Transmondia. Disease-detection dog, yes. But nothing beyond that, and I was more drawn to forensics than clinical applications. Now, however, new possibilities are opening up for XK9s. I am curious to learn what a medical student needs to know, in order to qualify."

"You think you might like to take the courses too?" Her mind stumbled over this idea. *How would that even work? How could an XK9 become a physician?*

"I do not know if I want to pursue it, but I am curious. Tux is considering entering a course of study under SCISCO's supervision. He might someday achieve a doctorate in engineering. That made me wonder. What might I achieve?"

"It's an interesting question. And, sure—I'll study with you." She went cold. *What did I just agree to?*

Petunia's ears swept up and her tail fanned wide. "Oh, thank you! Thank you! This is wonderful!" She pranced and bounded, and yes, she was catching more air than she would in full 1-G.

"We should strap back in." Hildie bounce-walked to her seat. *Rex! You manipulative—!* She'd like to shake that big, furry, meddlesome—*augh!*

But she'd have to yell at him later. Petunia bounded around a bit more, then Walter strapped her in, too. But her tongue still lolled, her eyes sparkled with joy, and her tail could not stay still.

That really made her happy. She scowled at Rex, but he responded with a smug look, then turned to say something to Shady.

Charlie squeezed her hand. "What just happened?"

"Your partner is a devious, manipulative—" She blew out an

exasperated breath. "Apparently, Petunia and I are studying together for our med-school entrance exams."

Charlie didn't quite manage to stifle a laugh, but he sobered quickly. "Okay. Well, an XK9 is probably one of the best study-buddies you could find."

Hildie shook her head. *Better just give in. It seems I'm doomed.* "Wonder if I should call Theresa's bluff and rope her in, since it looks like we're doing this. She's the one who's been on my case about it all these years."

"That would only be fair, I suppose." Charlie bit his lip, gave her a rueful look. "You okay with this?"

She scrubbed her face with both hands, then sat with the question for a moment. *Am I okay with it?* Weird, how a chance to help someone else and make her happy—yes, Petunia was still wriggling with canine joy, even strapped in. Somehow, that made Hildie's years of fear and resistance fade into the background, at least some. She frowned but couldn't muster anything like the outrage she thought she should feel. "Yeah, I guess I *am* okay with this."

"That's what's important." He kissed her cheek.

"You agreed with Rex all along, didn't you?"

"It's *your* choice." He made brief eye contact then looked away.

"Yeah, but you wanted me to decide this way."

"Only if *you* choose to." He hesitated, then sighed. "You always could see through me."

"And don't you forget it." *It's clear now. I was doomed from the beginning.* Did she mind that? *Weird. Not as much as I expected. But dammit, Rex!*

They rode in silence for a while. Hildie leaned against Charlie and closed her eyes. *Theresa will laugh, but then the shoe will be on the other foot. Will she take that dare and join the study group?*

A vision teased her: of herself and Theresa, running Topside Trauma the way they'd always thought it should be run. *Yeah, right. Like they'd let a pair of just-out-of-med-school doctors do that. What a silly dream!*

Her HUD dinged. She frowned, checked the sender, and froze. *Crap! Again?* She scowled and forwarded it to Endesha. Then she fished out her case pad and typed a quick note to her lawyer, "Got another one. Did not open it."

Charlie stirred. "You okay?"

Do I want to wade into LaRock's latest shit with him right now? In front of everyone? She hesitated, then inclined her head so her mouth could be closer to his ear. "It's you-know-who again. Let's talk in a less public place."

He frowned but nodded.

"Ah, yes! Thanks." Shiv sat up with a smile and went into a HUD stare. He gave Berwyn's hand a squeeze. "How is he?"

Hildie made no pretense of ignoring him, happy for a diversion. If the "he" Shiv had asked about was Zander Hoback, she wanted to know, too. Yes, she knew about his crimes, but he'd also been her patient.

She'd helped save his life, helped stuff him into that bunker. She'd done all she could to shield him from further harm, right up to the moment she'd been able to hand him over to paramedics with better scanners and more sophisticated tools. She would never *not* wonder about a patient's later outcome.

Shiv nodded. "That's about what I expected. How long?"

A few more irritating growls and "uh-huhs" later, he looked up from his HUD-stare. By that point everyone in the car was eying him with curiosity.

"Hoback's going to live." Shiv offered a nod to his audience, then focused on his nearer seatmates. "He'll need some re-gen, but they think they can do that on an in-clinic basis. No major, full-body work. They're continuing to mitigate the brain swelling, and they hope he'll retain all his memories. Whether he's willing to tell us about them? Harder to say. Saddest part, though? First thing he asked after he woke up was, 'is Emer safe?'"

"At least they could say 'yes.'" Shady gave Charlie an appreciative look. "That GR of yours—she caved almost immediately."

"Doesn't mean she's happy with the position her lover put her into." Charlie looked and smelled rueful.

"Oh, she's furious. No question about that!" Shady's tail thumped the seat, but it didn't carry as much force as normal. Gravity's pull had definitely loosened.

This time micrograv means we're closer to home. Hildie snuggled closer to Charlie. *It's a good direction to go.*

CHAPTER 64
HOW FAR WE'VE COME

OPD HQ and S-3-9 Investigative Center

Charlie followed Rex and Shady out of the XK9s' police-issued auto-nav on Friday morning, but he didn't hurry. They'd only gotten home from Centerboro yesterday. He'd hoped not to come in to work today, but then Elaine called a Task Force meeting.

He let the XK9s badge their way in ahead of him through the sally port entrance. Rex looked back at him. "Did you stiffen up on the ride?"

"Yeah, a little." His aches were minor. They'd be easy to walk out. But his heart just wasn't in it, this morning—it was back home with Hildie. "You go on ahead. I'm coming."

Charlie stopped for a short series of muscle stretches. Okay, maybe he was a little stiff and achey. Not as bad as Hildie, though. She'd had another bad night, which meant both of them were operating on short sleep today. He'd been reluctant to leave her, but he actually couldn't offer much beyond moral support, the occasional meal, and periodically applying a new pain patch. Her Listener would come while he was gone. And both Caro and Gloria had promised to check on her.

Rex and Shady soon outpaced him, but he knew where to go. He avoided the backup at the elevator and took the side stairs to S-3-9, but stopped in surprise at the entrance to the war room. *Woah. When we gather the whole Task Force, that's a lot of people.*

I've saved you a chair, but you'd better shake a leg. Seating is a hot commodity today, Rex warned. He himself stood near Elaine at the edge of a somewhat open "front" area.

Yes, Pack Leader. He parked himself as directed, next to Balchu. Misha claimed the seat on his left a few seconds later. Pretty soon the whole Pack surrounded him.

Elaine stepped forward into the open space and the room fell silent. "Thank you for coming in, especially when I know a lot of you were planning to rest. I'll cut to the summary. Thanks to your hard work, I've spent much of this morning in conference with ABA Ireland and several of her associates. They've agreed that we have more than enough evidence to justify charges of conspiracy to commit mass murder against Emer Bellamy and the installation team members who are competent to stand trial."

A murmur swept through the crowded room.

"And, of course, we already have Kieran O'Boyle's confession and plea deal, which includes the promise of an ongoing trove of evidence." Her smile widened. "Any last reports, let's get them in. We've entered a new phase."

"What about Zander Hoback?" Misha asked.

"Oh, for a crack at him, Orangeboro and even the SBI have to stand in line." She grimaced. "He's still in Centerboro, still in the hospital, and *everybody* wants a piece of that guy. Mike has an update he'll share in a few minutes. But since it appears that his thirst for revenge against the Whisper Syndicate was the primary force driving the attack on the *Izgubil,* we definitely will get our turn."

Charlie nodded. *I doubt Emer, her Amare Rory Fredericks, or Kieran would've come up with that attack on their own.* He stifled a yawn.

Or even all together, Rex agreed through the link. *And if they* did, *they wouldn't have the means to put it into effect. Emer and Kieran aren't spacefarers in any sense. And Rory Fredericks, for all his skill with explosives, didn't have access to the spaceships the way Hoback did.*

True. They hadn't yet figured out how Emer's Amare, Fredericks, and Hoback—who clearly seemed to have become her lover—could've ended up in the same gang, apparently cooperating. *What could have induced Rory to become involved?* Charlie couldn't imagine willingly sharing his Amare with *anyone.*

Maybe he wasn't willing, Rex said. *Maybe he was kidnapped. That's been the theory of his case from the time he disappeared, according to Iruka. Why willingly leave, just before you complete your doctorate?*

Why, indeed? Charlie paused to massage his temples. *It's less difficult to find a motive in Zander Hoback's case.*

It does seem likely that Hoback had good reason to hate Whisper.

Satisfaction warmed Charlie. They never would've known to look into the Tonquin Base Massacre if it hadn't been for his idea to talk with Mamoor. After further probing, the investigation had concluded that young Zander Hoback almost certainly had been captured during that incident. He'd most likely been made a child slave of the Syndicate—probably on the *Izgubil*—in the years before he'd worked with Allard Ferro as a Syndicate operative.

How'd he manage to go from sex-trafficked child victim to part of the Whisper team? Rex asked. *A single-minded focus on vengeance and a lot of hustle?*

He has both of those qualities, from what we've learned. Working for Whisper was a price of survival, I imagine. Charlie didn't envy Hoback's life. Given similar circumstances, would he himself have turned out better?

I imagine you might not be so bent on revenge. Rex flicked his ears. *Maybe less willing to consign hundreds to death, just to get at a few?*

I would hope so.

Elaine turned to her Significant. "Why don't you fill us in on what he's said so far?"

"That won't take long. He hasn't said much." Mike nodded to Charlie. "I imagine you have a clearer idea than most, about how someone feels after the kind of ordeal you endured in that bunker."

"Hildie and Hoback got by far the worst of it," Charlie replied. No one had said much about how remarkably well he, Shiv, and Rex had bounced back. *How many have guessed that we're augmented?* "I'm a bit stiff and achy myself, but Hildie's not doing too well."

"Sorry, man. I hope she's better soon. Both of you." Mike's mouth tightened.

"But think about Hoback." Charlie frowned. "To go through the whole bunker experience after at least one severe beating, and having spent who knows how long strapped to that beam? I'm a little surprised he can talk at all yet, much less make sense."

"He keeps asking if Emer's all right, in kind of a groggy, slurred voice, but you're right. He hasn't said much else." Mike's brow furrowed. "He also doesn't seem to remember that he already asked that question, or that we've already answered it. Rooq and Perri both have people covering his room but so far there's damned little to note."

"You've established a timeline, though," Elaine said.

He nodded. "Best we can tell, the Transmondians captured him shortly after Wisniewski's ship blew up."

Charlie's chest went tight and his stomach dropped. *Damn. I hadn't really thought about it, or where he might've been hiding. That's a pretty bad lapse for an investigator.*

It's not as if you had anything else going on at the time to distract you. Rex gave him an askance look.

Well, there's that. Charlie let out a sigh. *At least somebody was on it.*

Which is why it's better to hunt in a pack. You can pick up for each other.

"As you might recall," Mike said, "Commodore Montreaux called a Base-wide lockdown and mandated a millimeter-by-millimeter search of the entire facility immediately after the Dart, um, was micro-deconstructed. Unfortunately, at the same time, by regulation they had to have certain vehicles out clearing the spacelanes."

The SDF is solely responsible for clearing debris. Charlie remembered the protocols from his time on the Emergency Rescue Team. *And they needed to start clearing it immediately—long before any parallel-type vessels could arrive from the Wheel Four Base, which is the closest one. That means they literally couldn't lock everyone down.*

That would complicate things. Rex's ears clamped against his skull. *But damn.*

"Also, several vessels had gone in pursuit when the Dart made a run for it." Mike grimaced. "So, in spite of everything, there were a lot of uncontrolled variables. The SDF's reviewing telemetry from that period. They think they've detected several unauthorized departures under cover of all that movement. Now it's a matter of tracing them all. We speculate that the Transmondians must've had a fair idea where to find Hoback after the explosion, since they caught him before we did."

"They probably knew approximately where he must be, because they were all working together through Virendra." Elaine nodded, then inclined her head toward Mike.

"Exactly. After that, it would've been a matter of finding a chance to slip away from the Base. We've identified arrivals at nearby civilian docks that happened during the time window between the destruction of the Dart on that Tuesday almost five weeks ago, and the predawn last Saturday, when our XK9s established that Transmondian Intelligence Service agents brought him onto the train."

"Why not just take him to Wheel Four in their ship?" Balchu asked.

"Wheel Four and the entire rest of the Government and Diplomatic Sector would have been on Security Level Five for several weeks after the Dart incident," Mike replied. "SecLev Five means *no one* comes or goes to any dock between Wheel Three and Wheel Six without close, individualized scrutiny."

"Ah." Balchu nodded. "I retract the question."

"I'm a little surprised they didn't take him to Wheel Three," Mike said. "They seem to have been working with Whisper right up to that point, and Whisper has a strong presence, both in Howardsboro and on certain parts of the Howardsboro docks. But we only know *approximately* how soon relations changed between Whisper and the Transmondians after the incident with the Dart."

"Rex's pursuit of Wisniewski and the Dart's destruction revealed what had previously been a very smooth setup for both of them." Elaine quirked an eyebrow at Mike. "We know there was a falling-out between them afterwards. What can you tell us about that?"

"Relations definitely appeared to have cooled within only a few days after the Dart incident." Mike offered her a sardonic, one-sided smile. "Then there were the allegations that Whisper was behind the bombs in Centerboro. Not to mention Iskander's accusation about the destruction of the Combined Councils Chamber. I'd say the bloom was off that rose with extreme prejudice by then. Any TIS agents who may still be at large on Rana Station now have the SBI, the SDF, *and* Whisper after them."

"Just let us know." Rex's ears and head snapped up. The electric crackle of hunt-joy pulsed through the link. "The Pack would love to help round them up!"

"I'll bet." Mike chuckled. "Never fear, you'll hear about it at the first whiff of a lead."

"Meanwhile, do we know any more about Rory Fredericks?" Georgia asked.

"You mean the Most-Wanted Man in the Asteroids?" Elaine's face made a rueful twist and her shoulders lowered. "Oh, the race is on. The Mahusayans have placed a bounty worth about two million novi on his head. The SDF immediately increased Rana's offer to three, and I'm told the Iron Hand—the biggest pirate group out there right now—is looking to recruit him by whatever means possible."

"If he's wise—and able—he'd be well advised to leave the Chayko System altogether." Mike's voice left no doubt he'd love to lead the hunt to thwart any such plan. "Whether he has, can, or will leave remains to be seen."

❖❖ ❖❖ ❖❖ ❖❖

Becenti Tower

Pam ran her dry tongue across parched lips and swallowed. It was a beautiful, clear Saturday afternoon. She stood with Balchu, Shady, and the rest of the Family in Becenti's courtyard. Surrounded by friendly people—but she couldn't calm her fluttery gut. *I've looked for apartments before. This is not that much different.*

"You okay?" Balchu's hand tightened briefly on hers.

"Yes." She lifted her chin and sensed Shady's approval through the link. They followed Anya up the leeward corner steps. Half a flight brought them to a landing.

Pam paused to stare out at the surrounding fields and trees. Shady stayed close by her side. Anya and Balchu waited without protest.

This is old news to them. She drew in a breath, strove to steady herself. *They're just humoring me.*

Shady lolled her tongue. *They are seeing it anew, through you. They care about you and want you to be happy here.*

Pam turned and mounted the next half-flight. She walked to the railing that overlooked the courtyard from Level One. The place practically glowed with green growing things. *Our court-yard. Mine. I belong here.* She tried to make that feel real, swallowed, then resolutely mounted the next half-flight.

Anya had said the empty unit that was their goal was on Level Three. Feyodor, Tuya, Sarnai, and Rose had taken the elevator to look at other parts of the tower. Pam had hoped this climb would calm her, help her clear her head. *Not so far.*

Are you too tired to do this today? Shady asked again.

No. Pam turned away from the view. Kept climbing. *We need to get this decision made so the rest of the Family can move forward.* Orangeboro had held its celebratory parade for their "XK9 Heroes" this morning. Her smiling and waving muscles had only just recovered from Centerboro, but now they'd begun to stiffen up again. *I'll rest later.*

The morning's events had been made more joyous by the news that the Transmondians had pulled the last of their warships back into Transmondian space proper, away from the international boundary. With the Alliance's Fifth Fleet inbound and set to arrive on Tuesday, it seemed clear there would not be a war after all. At least, not while the Fifth Fleet was in-System.

The Borough Council had scheduled a Recognition Event for the Pack in the Civic Center tonight—reportedly, it was already sold out. The very thought made her weary. She pushed it away but paused again on the landing between Levels Two and Three. They'd begun to achieve some altitude. She stared down at a healthy-looking crop of something she couldn't identify, next to an orchard of some sort.

That's quinoa, Shady said through the link. *It's almost as ripe as the patch where the Transmondian tranked Rex.*

It's not as tall as I expected.

Tall enough, trust me. And the trees are apple trees.

Becenti Tower, like most residence towers, had been built at an angle on the property. Two walls overlooked the valley side, while the other two gave a better overlook on the crops. Every unit had a nice view that way, and no one had to stare at the clifflike primary terrace wall straight-on. This one was built on one hectare. Not a huge place, even by Ranan standards, where efficiency, multi-level farming, and high-yield crops were the order of the day. But it looked plenty big to Pam.

When they reached Level Three, Anya led her to the first unit on the right.

"Leeward valley side." Shady used her vocalizer. "Just like our unit at Corona."

"Maybe that's a good sign." Anya opened one of the two French doors. They led into an empty living room with about the same amount of floor space as Pam and Balchu's entire apartment above the tempura shop.

Pam stopped in the doorway, dizzied. A powerful impression swept over her, as if the apartment opened a warm embrace and silently called out *Welcome Home!*

She walked in slowly, head spinning with the strangeness of that feeling. Centered herself. Fought through heavy disbelief at war with the overwhelming joy of this place.

But the odd *welcome* feeling echoed through her all the same.

I could be . . . HOME, here. At peace. She'd never felt anything like it before. *Oh, but this place is so big and bright and elegant!* True, a faint mustiness lingered in the air, but no reek of hot, rancid oil. *Is this too nice? Do I actually deserve . . . ?*

Shady responded with a snort and an eyeroll. *Oh, please.*

"Of course, it'll need repainting, and I don't know what furniture you'll want to bring," Anya said.

"We don't have any furniture." Balchu blew out a breath. "Our place was already furnished when I leased it, so we never needed to buy our own."

"Oh, then we'll give you the run of our storerooms." Anya brightened, as if this pleased her.

She's delighted by a chance to . . . to give us furniture? Pam tried not to stare at the woman. *How can they afford that?*

Shady lolled her tongue. *She has taken you under her wing. Now she wants to pamper you. It gives her pleasure. And if Becenti is anything like Corona, they have a storeroom filled with old furniture from previous generations.*

That makes no sense.

You'll figure it out in time. For now, just roll with it.

Pam swallowed. *If you say so.*

"We've got plenty to start you off right." Anya's grin widened. "You can replace the hand-me-downs later, but meanwhile there's no need to do without!" She led them across the empty bamboo flooring to another pair of doors that opened onto a broad view of the valley.

"We've got a repair order in for this section of the outer balcony. I'm sorry, but you shouldn't step out onto it till it's fixed. There's a leak that should have been addressed two years ago." She grimaced. "This unit has been empty since Great-Aunt Dolores died, and Onyx was . . . well, you know."

"Akkari Matika told me the other day that she thinks she's closing in on the ring that swindled him," Balchu said. "That's one step closer to getting some of it back."

Anya sighed. "I'm afraid to hope, just yet."

"There's still a long way to go, even if she's right and these are our guys." Balchu's face went rueful. "Thought you'd like to know there's been some movement on it."

"I appreciate that, dear."

Anya led them across the empty bamboo flooring to another pair of doors. Through the dusty panes, Pam glimpsed a broad valley view.

"I know we cannot go out, but could we open one of these doors?" Shady asked. "I should like to smell the air currents."

"As long as you stay inside, why not?" Anya thumbed a switch and the doors swung open. A fresh breeze swooshed through the room, banishing the musty smell and raising enough dust to make Anya sneeze.

Pam and Shady stayed by the open door. Pam smiled at the feel of the wind on her face. Beyond the railing, the Sirius River

Valley lay in all its vast, verdant, terraced glory. The view took her breath away. *I could see this every day.*

"Great-Aunt Dolores loved that view. She also enjoyed the little hummingbirds that will come if you put out nectar."

"Hummingbirds?" Pam turned to give her a questioning look.

"Little bitty red and green ones, not much bigger than bees. They pollinate several of our crops." Anya grinned. "Pugnacious little rascals, but they're cute."

"We do not have them at Corona," Shady said.

"They'll go as high as Terrace Six, sometimes, but no higher. And all the way down to the river." She stepped back a couple of paces. "Ready to see the rest?"

There's more? Oh. But of course . . . Mind still reeling, Pam peered into the kitchen at Anya's prompting, then glanced at Balchu.

He checked it out with a wide grin and trailed his hand lightly over several of the controls. Then he opened a couple of cabinet doors with the air of someone opening a gift wrapped present. The pantry area made him laugh with pleasure. "There's a lot of storage space here."

"There's a lot of hanging-out-and-talking space, too." Anya gestured toward an open area. "You could put a table over here. And I know we have some stools you could pull up to this counter. Over the years, some of our best moments have happened in our kitchen-breakfast area. It's built a lot like this one."

Once again, the friendly rightness of the place washed through Pam. She could picture inviting friends here. What would Etsu and Shuri think of it? Or Liz? Or Hildie?

"If you want storage, wait till you see the walk-in closet." Anya led them down a hallway.

Pam followed, still in half-disbelief. Anya showed them bathrooms, plural. A cavernous walk-in closet she couldn't imagine filling. Two bedrooms.

"So, what do you think?" Anya guided them to the doors by the primary bedroom's outside balcony. It offered more of that jaw-dropping valley view.

Something buzzed past her head. Pam flinched—caught a jewel-like glimpse of ruby and emerald, heard a *chip! Chip-chip!* Tiny wings blurred. Minute, bright eyes inspected her. Pam stared back. She blinked, and it was gone. *Wow.*

"Hummingbird!" Anya laughed. "Oh, Pam! It came to say 'hello.'"

"Or maybe 'you're in my territory!'" Balchu said.

Anya sighed. "Yeah, more likely that. But anyway, now you've seen a hummingbird, and you've seen this unit. Do you like it? Spinward valley side—the one on the other side of the stairs—is smaller. But we thought you young folks might want room to grow."

Pam shied away from the implications of *room to grow.*

Now you know how I feel, at least a little. Shady lolled her tongue.

We need to start planning for that, though. Yours, I mean. Pam frowned. The XK9s' annual heat cycle would start sometime during March—a bit more than a month away! *How do we function when half the Pack is pregnant, or when all of you are out on Family Leave?*

Later! Shady pinned her ears back and panted harder. *Not now!*

"What do you think, Pam?" Balchu quirked an eyebrow. "Place needs a balcony repair, new paint, and a thorough cleaning, for sure. But to me it feels kinda—I don't know—friendly."

The warm light, the wider spaces, the indefinable air of "welcome" about this place teased at her again. *I could rest here. I could feel at home.* "Let's—okay. Let's take it."

CHAPTER 65
REHOMING

Corona Tower

L ate Monday morning, Rex climbed onto Charlie's old brown sofa, the one Hildie had decreed must soon return to storage. For now, however, it made an only-somewhat-lumpy place to recline for this morning's meeting via Hector and Pat's encrypted com.

He hated to admit how much of a relief it was to lie down for a while.

Last night had not been exceedingly restful. He might need to resort to the damned cannula with its oxygen stream tonight, because his nanites definitely had started to break down. Good thing he'd soon have new lungs.

Earlier this morning, Shady had gone to Becenti Tower after she'd reassured herself that he was still breathing fairly well. She meant to make sure that Pam actually moved in today and didn't chicken out at the last moment.

His human housemates had already been alerted not to enter the living room until he gave them the all-clear. They had many other things to do, now that Hildie was finally feeling better.

Currently he could hear them in the back bedroom, discussing how to "catify" the larger bedroom.

He curled his lip. As of today, The Cat was here. She had arrived inside a pet carrier, reeking of feline indignation, about an hour ago. The humans had deposited the carrier inside their walk-in closet, along with a litterbox, a bowl of water, and a small dish of dry kibble. *That seems like as good a place as any to store the creature.* But of course, they didn't plan to keep her in there indefinitely.

Hector, Quinn, and Grant had spent part of the morning stringing up an electronic enclosure that worked with a sensor on Kali's collar. It was supposed to keep her on this level and in this apartment, an area that included the inner and outer balconies. That would keep her from harassing pollinators or birds in the rooftop garden or prowling too far afield.

Rex had asked them to put another barricade around his and Shady's bedroom, but they'd simply smiled as if he wasn't serious. He gave a soft growl. *I'll deal with that issue later.*

The time ticked down to zero. He input the encrypted key, and an image popped open on his HUD: The pixel-line face of SCISCO's android focal object. Ne had chosen a subtle lavender-paisley pattern with splashes of yellow for nir skin tone today, and set nir fiber-optic hair to display yellow-streaked purple.

"Good morning." He wagged his tail, ears up and tongue lolling. "Did you choose your color scheme with my visual range in mind?"

"I did." Ne gave him a pixel-line smile. "Do you like it?"

"You honor me. It is quite striking."

Sacha Guzmán's face popped into view next to SCISCO's avatar.

"I thought it might be appropriate, to welcome you to the Leadership Council with colors you can actually see," SCISCO said.

Rex thumped his tail on the couch. "You are most kind. I appreciate it."

"You do look stunning, SCISCO," Sacha said. "Rex, you are well? When is your lung transplant?"

"I am well enough, thanks. They tell me my nanites are aging, so breathing does not come as easily as I would like. The transplant will happen this week. I should know an exact date by Wednesday."

He nodded. "Good. I'm just in from a meeting with the Party Leaders of both legislative Councils. They've resolved to hold a recognition ceremony for the Pack, once you've healed from your transplant and are able to travel. They mean to award each of the Pack with the Combined Councils Medal of Freedom. We'll need you to keep us posted on your progress."

"May I ask how things stand with the former Premier? Has the Section Fifteen been adjudicated?"

"The High Court's preliminary ruling to leave it in place is a positive sign." Sacha's face sobered. "We'll know more details of their findings when they come out with a complete verdict. But I expect that the strong affirmations by large majorities of both Councils for both species will lead to confirmation. So far, Eliana has remained in seclusion and has not contested it. She seems to have been profoundly shaken by the attempt on her life, as well as on our government. From a practical standpoint, the longer things go on with both our new Premier and the transition of power widely accepted, the better for all of us."

"That is good." SCISCO's android nodded.

"Kizzi will want to discuss this as well, but I can tell you we've received messages from several other Chayko System sovereignties about forming a larger strategic alliance," he added. "We expected something of the sort might be possible with the Mahusayans and the Singkorians after they came to our defense, but the Oroplanians and the Ullach government also have reached out."

That ought to be a positive thing. Right? "One could hope such an alliance might make the Transmondians think twice about any more expansionism." Rex started to wag his tail—but should he? *Did I speak too soon?* He eyed the others for their responses and wished yet again that coms could be created to convey scent factors.

SCISCO's android made no move. "On what terms did they reach out?"

Sacha grimaced. "Right off the top, the Mahusayans made an extradition request for both Hoback and Emer Bellamy, assuming she financed all the attacks."

Rex caught his breath. *No! After all our work to catch them?*

"Since they still have a death penalty, and there's no evidence that Emer was part of the Mahusayan incident, they already know our answer to that. Did they propose any serious terms?" SCISCO asked.

Rex held his peace, but SCISCO's question startled him. *There must be a great deal I do not know about diplomatic negotiations.*

"I think the extradition request was a favor for certain financial backers," Sacha said. "They also requested access to the Yamauba Cluster."

"Again, so they can say they asked," SCISCO's pixel-line brows slanted inward and down. "Another sop to the mining collectives."

Rex scrunched down on Charlie's sofa, ears up. *I mostly followed that.* He stress-yawned and his gut twisted a bit tighter.

"That's how I read it." Sacha's mouth made a wry twist. "The rest of their terms deserve a more thorough vetting by our intelligence and diplomatic corps. And a separate meeting. But in the meantime—"

Ka'Zikikittir Kizzitikti's face popped into vid-view. Ki offered a gape of greeting. Kir flash of fangs looked ferocious, but Rex had learned it was like a human smiling or a dog's tail-wag. "Apologies, friends, for making you wait. We have received an update from the Alliance Fleet." Ki spoke via kir vocalizer in Standard.

"When will they arrive?" Sacha asked.

"The first advance vessels should arrive through the jump

point at 04:00 Ranan, tomorrow morning. The entire fleet should have arrived in-system by around 18:00. They are led by the Koannan Consul Primus. It is their intention to poise a strike force in synchronous orbit above Solara City, in case the Transmondians are of a mind to be anything other than compliant."

A rush of lightheadedness that had nothing to do with his breathing rocked Rex. His abdomen relaxed on a wave of relief. "So, they understand it is the Transmondians who have created the problems?"

"They appear to have no questions about that." Kizzi's pale crest rose. "They also plan to dispatch envoy delegations on behalf of the Alliance to each of the sovereign states in the System once their ships have taken their planned positions. The delegation to Rana should arrive at the Wheel Five reception area in the Hub around 13:00, where I shall meet them. They have indicated that they intend to send sub-delegations to Wheels Four and Two, for meetings with all four of us in our home environments. They will send us details on timing and protocols before each arrival. SCISCO, may I count on you to alert Mayor Idris?"

"Certainly, Ka'Zikikittir. And I shall keep Rex looped in."

"Thank you." Rex thumped his tail again. "This is all new to me. I expect to learn a great deal."

"So shall we all." Sacha gave a rueful laugh. "This is only the second time in Ranan history that the Alliance has sent a fleet into the Chayko System."

"And you might recall that last one also regarded a threat to Rana," SCISCO added.

You remember it. Rex couldn't resist his urge to confirm the hint of personal reaction he caught through the link. *You were there.*

I was part of that task force. Gentle pleasure echoed back. *It's what brought Rana Station to my and my siblings' attention. We were quite favorably impressed.*

And Rana is immensely the better for it. Thank you.

"My people remember that event with reverence," Kizzi said. "We can hope for a comparably positive outcome this time."

Rex's pleasure to learn a bit of SCISCO's history couldn't negate a tight queasiness in his gut over what was on the line now. Time to speak the worries that had been torturing him more each day. "Do we know anything about the fate of the XK9s on Chayko? I believe my own mother and her human partner may be fugitives, even though neither is young. My mother must be around 27, which is middle-aged for XK9s. I was her last viable puppy."

He wished again for a com that delivered scent factors. Faces serious and solemn, the others leaned forward and listened to him.

"Even more urgent, the survivors of Puppy Farm One have been in hiding for a week," Rex continued. "They presumably are without shelter, medical care, or food. It is late winter there, a season of bitter cold. And all the other XK9s all over Transmondia almost certainly have been threatened by now."

"Our embassies and consulates have been instructed to aid any XK9s who reach out to them seeking asylum." Sacha frowned into the vid pickup on his end. "Several of them have already reported taking in fugitive XK9s, as well as a few of their human partners."

"This morning I assisted Mike and Elaine in receiving an encrypted report from their friend, the Sheriff of Bordemer Canton," SCISCO said. "Rex, Sheriff Ibsen has been actively searching for your mother and her partner, Dr. Cho, since your distressing communication from them five weeks ago. Elaine specifically asked about them back then, but so far he reports no success."

Rex's pulse sped up. "I knew she had asked, and said her friend was looking."

"He and his deputies have so far found eight XK9 refugees from Puppy Farm One, including three young puppies. Also two caregiver humans whom the dogs seemed to trust," SCISCO continued. "Last night they managed to safely convey them to the Ranan Embassy in Solara City."

Sacha nodded. "Ambassador Ives reported another new group just arrived last night."

"I must admit I am surprised to find such an attitude from a Transmondian official." All the powerful Transmondian humans Rex had ever encountered while on Chayko had presented a unified wall of authority against him and his kind.

"According to Mike Santiago, his old friend has expressed serious concerns about the XK9 Project for years," SCISCO said. "Mike and Elaine's comments about interacting with you and the rest of the Pack here on Rana appear to have confirmed the inklings and doubts Sheriff Ibsen already harbored."

Rex nodded. "Even if he harbored them, I imagine it would have been dangerous for him to express them to anyone in the Transmondian government. We were, after all, a government project. I do not recall ever having met Sheriff Ibsen."

"Which means you never did," Sacha said.

"Ibsen's department also has been tasked with cleanup at the destroyed puppy farm." SCISCO's pixel-line face shifted to a rueful grimace. "They are treating the entire property as an enormous crime scene, but they've had to fight with top government bureaucrats and a range of local officials every step of the way."

Of course, they did. Now, THAT I believe. Rex stifled a growl.

"I'm surprised they allowed him that much autonomy," Sacha said.

"Sheriffs in Transmondian cantons have been granted rather sweeping powers, both traditionally and in the Transmondian Constitution." SCISCO's android face adopted a neutral expression. "The tradition dates back to the early days of human occupation on Chayko, before nationalities formed. During that period, the sheriff was the primary source of civil authority and leadership."

"Ah. That is true." Sacha's brows retained a small pucker, but he nodded. "Rather like our boroughs or timi'i and their governments."

"That history has helped give Sheriff Ibsen a somewhat freer hand, even though the Transmondian central authorities have become more powerful in recent decades," SCISCO continued. "But his office undoubtedly would be much less of a shield at present if the Transmondians did not know that an Alliance fleet was en route and due to arrive imminently."

"That is true," Kizzi's small ears angled back, a signal of anger or distaste—without scent factors it was hard to say which. "Even so, the Transmondian Special Forces cannot have been easy to deal with."

"I received the strong impression that Sheriff Ibsen has been under intense pressure since the raid. He may have put his own life and personal freedom on the line more than once in the past week." SCISCO's pixel-line grimace morphed into a scowl. "He also could be open to an espionage charge if certain government entities discovered he'd been in contact with anyone on Rana. We have arranged for that connection to remain securely hidden."

"Thank you!" Rex thumped with his tail and sent an extra surge of gratitude to nem via the link. "I cannot express how much it helps to know these developments." He shifted to the link so he could speak with SCISCO only. *I wish there was some way I could tell him how grateful I am.*

I shall arrange to let him know, nir acknowledgement echoed back to him.

"On a related topic, I have spoken with the Station's Environmental Engineers," Kizzi said. "They have reassured me that our combined ecosystems could realistically accommodate every XK9 that currently exists in the entire Chayko System, based on the estimate of 247 from all generations that you made to SCISCO a few weeks ago."

Vivid memories of that terrifying moment seized him. SCISCO had awakened him to warn that the Pack was in danger from Dr. Ordovich, Admiral Virendra, and then-Premier Iskander. He licked his nose to comfort himself and recenter. "I fear there may be significantly fewer than that now."

"Which makes the accommodations and adjustments even more urgent." Kizzi's cuplike ears folded back into kir fur. "As long as they can be distributed fairly equally between the six human-environment habitat Wheels, I have been assured that their presence would not unbalance any of them. The leaders of both Councils intend to bring bills to their members to make that blanket immigration offer a legal mandate, offered to all interested XK9s."

Rex froze, overwhelmed for a moment by the expanding, dizzying amazement of this. "*All* of us? Our entire *species*?"

"Any and all who ask to come would be welcome. Yes," Kizzi said. "How could we act otherwise? Rana Station can never adequately repay our debt of gratitude to you XK9s."

❖ ❖ ❖ ❖ ❖ ❖ ❖ ❖

After the Leadership Council meeting ended, Rex stayed on the lumpy brown sofa. Heaviness weighted his legs and drained out all his energy.

His mind spun with everything he'd learned—but even more with the sick realization of his own profound ignorance. *I never had any training for this—nothing even remotely like it. How can I react intelligently on topics of diplomacy and statecraft? I'm bound to screw things up!*

I don't think I can help you there, Charlie answered through the link. *All I can say is that I can't imagine any other XK9 knowing more or doing better.*

A sense of affection and peace came through to him from SCISCO. *Do not imagine that I shall leave you hanging, Rex. I have been studying these things for literal centuries of Ranan years. And I hope you'll kindly remember I am a teacher by nature and preference.*

Where do I even start?

Gentle pleasure and approval came through the link. *You already have made an excellent start. We'll re-engage with this after you have rested, recovered from your surgery, and are ready.*

Warmth expanded within him, although a dark inner voice countered that he'd never be ready enough. *Thank you. I look forward to learning more.*

Rest now. Sleep, if you can. Nir presence faded from the link.

That's good advice. Need any help getting to bed? Charlie asked. *Shady's here, too. You seemed pretty deeply immersed in that meeting, so I don't know if you noticed.*

Rex lifted his head, ears up. A waft of fresh Shady-scent drifted in on sluggish air currents, along with those of his other housemates—especially Kali. Cat-scent already had permeated the household. *That will take getting used to.*

"Open ventilation," he ordered. Inner and outer balcony doors swung partway open. A fresh cross-breeze kicked up. *Ah, yes. Much better.*

He yawned, dragged himself off the sofa, then moved stiffly into a full-body stretch. *A nap actually sounds like a good idea. Thinking is hard work.* He trudged down the hall to his bedroom. But at the doorway he froze.

The Cat had installed herself in the middle of his bed.

All the fear, all the frustration, all the worries he'd accumulated in the meeting boiled up as rage. *How DARE that creature invade my bed?*

Kali's ears flicked, one black, one brownish-gray. As if to say, *This is my bed now.*

His muscles tensed, but he halted himself. *If I rip her to shreds, Hildie will be upset. Charlie will be caught in the middle. How can I— what can I—*

Kali eyed him with a cool, insolent blue stare.

He throttled his outrage into submission. *What would a statesman do? Must exercise patience.* He extended his nose for a cautious sniff.

Kali hissed, bared needlelike fangs. One tiny white paw flashed out.

Pain blossomed across his nose.

His rage erupted. He lunged with a roar—but Kali was gone.

He glimpsed a flash of Shady's tail through the outer balcony door. Heard the click of her claws and Kali's hissing, yowling, and growling. The sounds moved across the outer balcony into Charlie and Hildie's bedroom, then into the walk-in.

"And stay there," Shady said. The closet door rumbled shut.

"Oh, dear! I thought she'd hide out a bit longer!" Hildie did sound upset.

Shady snorted. "Sooner or later, boundaries must be established. Might as well be sooner."

Charlie peeked into Rex's bedroom. "Are you bleeding?"

Rex explored with his tongue. The sting of the blow lingered, but he found only a drop of blood. "It is a minor scratch. I suppose I should be grateful that cats cannot wield actual knives on their feet. And that my mate has excellent judgement and timing."

CHAPTER 66
FREE TO MOVE FORWARD

Glen Haven Park

S hady could see the entity on the bench in Glen Haven Park as clearly as she could smell him—and he did look resplendent in the Sunday afternoon light. Warm pleasure filled her. This was the first day in what seemed like ages that hadn't been pre-booked with things for the Pack to do. Perfect timing to relax with her new appscaten friend.

She opened the link more fully to Pam, then ran to join Kurtzu, tail up and wagging full-speed. "Hello! It is good to see you again!" They'd met for scheduled conversations only twice —once before Big New Year, and once right after—then Kurtzu told her he'd been "recalled by my boss."

"It is a relief not to have to sneak around anymore." Kurtzu's midlegs levered his body forward off the bench until his hind legs also touched the ground. No "stealth mode" today: a blue-patterned garment adorned with shimmering golden fringe enveloped his abdomen.

Even through the link-view he looks impressive. Shady sensed it when Pam paused to sit for a moment on one of the tall stools by the counter in her Becenti Tower apartment. Pam's new home was one of many things that had changed in the three and a half weeks since the Pack's fateful trip to Centerboro. Rex had at last received his new lungs. And the Alliance was now fully in charge of the Chayko System.

Kurtzu's thorax pulsed with a range of yellow tints and tones. His scent shifted to the crisp, somewhat sweet odor that signaled he was happy, and he made the paper-crackling sound he sometimes emitted when something pleased him. Because he had not gone background she could see the part of his neck that moved to create the crackling sound. One jagged-edged arm reached out. The three sets of Kurtzu's birdlike, claw-tipped hand-digits splayed wide.

She eagerly placed her paw in his grasp for a greeting handshake. "I was delighted to get your message. Have you been in space?"

"Yes." His mouth-skin drew back to reveal prominent tusks and he emitted a sharp, bitter scent. "I dislike microgravity almost as much as I dislike the Koannans' native gravitation. When I travel I use an appscaten vessel. I've had it docked at a diplomatic berth on the Orangeboro docks since I arrived on Rana. but Zheereeg-Sose'ee, our committee leader, is Koannan. So all the meetings are held on v'it ship."

"That is unfortunate." Her tail-wagging halted, then resumed at a much slower tempo. "Are you glad to be back on Rana?"

"I am, thank you, and not only because your gravity is close to my own. I am finally authorized to admit that I am, as you long ago guessed, a member of the Observation Commission. Also that Zheereeg plans to convene a meeting with your Leadership Council tomorrow."

She caught her breath. "Tomorrow? Rex has only been out of re-gen for a week. He has not yet been cleared for travel."

"Zheereeg knows this. V'ez plans to conduct the conference via remote connection. Not incidentally, this will allow v'ek to remain in v'it own gravitation on v'it ship. Will Rex be able to attend virtually?"

"Ah. Yes. That should work." A rising tingle swept across her skin. "Is this meeting to announce the Commission has reached a verdict?"

"Yes. And Zheereeg would prefer that I say no more to you than that. But I will tell you right now that we had little trouble reaching an official determination that XK9s are clearly sapient beings."

Warmth radiated through her body. Her pulse raced. "Yes! Thank you! What a relief!" She leaped about with elation and felt it echoed back strongly from Pam through the link. Until this moment she hadn't been able to completely relax about that question.

Kurtzu watched her for several moments with a sweet scent and happy yellows pulsating across his thorax. Then he lifted one arm in a cautioning motion. "However."

She brought her happy dance to a halt and cocked her head. Her gut tightened. *Uh-oh. Now what?* "However?"

There's always a catch. She sensed Pam's frown though the link.

"Because you are a *created* sapient species, Zheereeg and two of v'it colleagues insist that we must observe the protocols used to establish the Duulian gulimyaniks' permanent sapience status."

"Rex told me about gulimyaniks." She cocked her head, curious despite the shivery, throat-closing foreboding that surged within her. "He said they look something like the mythical griffin from Heritage Earth folklore, and they're as big as a pterolizard. Is that correct?"

"I have heard that description used several times, so it probably is a fair approximation. But to it I would add 'eternally grouchy.' They are undeniably sapient, but surly." Kurtzu's thorax colors shifted into hues she only saw as shades of brownish-gray. Based on the return of that sharp, bitter scent, she gathered he didn't find gulimyaniks any more pleasant than the

Koannans' native gravitation. "XK9s are far more agreeable beings," he added.

"I am glad you think so." She lowered her ears. "What protocols must you follow?"

"We must observe that three successive generations maintain sapience after outside genetic manipulations have ceased. Only then can we establish a determination of permanent sapience status that is solid for as long as your species exists."

Yup, there's always a damned technicality. Pam's disgust echoed through the link.

Disappointment lowered her tail and chilled her excitement. "So, you are saying that my generation is sapient. But since our breeding was manipulated by Dr. Ordovich, our puppies and grandpuppies will also need to be evaluated?"

"Yes. Further manipulation of your generation's genetics for anything but individual medical, therapeutic purposes is forbidden—as it is in all sapient species, with very few exceptions. The question we must answer over your next two generations is whether the changes that made you sapient will persist in your descendants."

"Oh. I suppose that is an unsettled question." She didn't even *want* puppies, but a surge of defensive anger filled her.

Right there with you, Pam agreed.

Kurtzu angled his head and spoke quietly. "I know. It's not what you wanted. And no one I know can see into the future reliably. But I do not believe your puppies and grandpuppies will show any evidence of devolution. Our team's geneticist doesn't either. Once the persistence of sapience has been established, your species will receive permanent recognition. We don't re-evaluate humans, ozzirikkians, or cyberbeings. Or gulimyaniks, anymore. No point. Their sapience is now a reliably inherent trait."

"But our species' status will be provisional till then? Even if you find that our parents' generation was sapient, too?"

"Yes, because Dr. Ordovich continued to manipulate your

generation's genome." He inclined his domed, triangular head toward her. "Don't worry. We did establish that the individuals of your parents' generation whom we've been able to evaluate also are sapient, although they were not equipped with the technology to allow them to vocalize as you do. That bodes well for your puppies and grandpuppies. And the fact that we must continue to monitor you means I will get to come back and visit you from time to time. We should be seeing each other approximately every five or six of your years, for the next four decades."

She could wag her tail about seeing him again, anyway. "I will like that. It will be something to look forward to and will make the process more pleasant." She hesitated. "Can our parents' equipment be upgraded to give them a voice?"

"If they desire it, I don't see why not."

"Well, that is something, anyway." She cocked her head at him. "You said Zheereeg did not want you to tell me this. Does that mean. . .

He made that crackling-paper sound again. "Zheereeg is annoyed about it, but because of the three-generation provision and Rex's fragile health, the rest of us out-voted v'ez. We decided to give you a heads-up in advance. We didn't want Rex to receive too many shocks at once, and we figured his mate could deliver the news more gently."

Clearly, Zheereeg doesn't understand "XK9 tough." Shady let her tongue loll. *But I think we can refrain from enlightening v'ek for the moment.*

Agreed. Pam's chuckle echoed through the link. *It is good to know this, and to know it now.*

"But we, at least, are officially declared sapient. That is good." Shady's tail picked up its tempo.

"Oh, yes." Kurtzu's head gave a decisive nod. "For as long as this generation lives. That is settled."

He gazed across the valley-view for a moment. Humans had told her it was stunning, but she had a sense he wasn't particularly looking at that. His domed, triangular head swiveled back toward her and his four visible eyes did their sequential blinking thing.

"We were most impressed that Rana Station has opened its immigration portals to all XK9s who wish to move here," he said. "That is not an attitude we often see in a species that accomplishes an accidental uplift."

"The Pack has discovered that Ranan humans are different—and in our opinion, preferable—in many ways. But I should point out that our new Premier was the first to suggest it."

"The ozzirikkian? Ah. That explains some things. Still, the humans readily agreed. That is admirable."

"We have no arguments on that point." She flicked her ears. "So, to be clear, because in this generation we are judged to be sapient, will the migrants be allowed to leave Chayko now?"

"Yes." Kurtzu emitted a crisp, sweet scent. "I imagine the logistics of those arrangements will be one of the things your Leadership Council must discuss tomorrow."

More XK9s on Rana. She'd been thinking about this—even worrying a bit. *What will change? How will they alter the dynamics?* She and the rest of the Pack had gotten used to being the only dogs in town.

We'll figure it out. They'll be spread over six Wheels, so it's not as if they're all coming to Orangeboro, Pam pointed out. *As someone who's embraced some scary changes lately, I can tell you that sometimes big changes bring big improvements.*

Shady tried to imagine how the XK9s holed up in embassies and consulates across the planet must feel. "The release to travel will surely come as a relief."

"Oh, yes. Especially for everyone at the Ranan Embassy in Solara City," Kurtzu agreed. "They are by now harboring twenty-two XK9s at that location. Most are adults or partially-grown, although they now have five infants from Puppy Farm One. Even when they are quite young, XK9s are not small dogs."

Shady lolled her tongue. "I have been told we are 'the size of a damned pony.'"

"Let us not consign any equines to perdition." Kurtzu made his paper-crackling amusement sound. "The size comparison is fairly accurate for adults, however."

"And yet there is room for all of us on Rana."

"All of you and more, according to the reports we received," Kurtzu agreed. "I believe your Ranan compatriots value you a very great deal."

"As we do them." *All of you and more* echoed in her mind and tingled in her skin. She lifted her muzzle to a future as wide as all space and infinite as a Ranan river.

❖ ❖ ❖ ❖ ❖ ❖ ❖ ❖

A Civic Center Hearing Room, and the Cock & Bull Pub

At last! *After all the waiting!* Charlie didn't even have to ask. The only place to take this celebration was the Cock & Bull.

The case had been delayed once, but now, on the *very last day of January*, Hildie had her answer! The moment Judge Cunningham pronounced his verdict that Hildie had not committed an egregious error of judgment and was cleared to return to her duties, the hot, crowded little hearing room erupted into cheers, punctuated by happy barks from Rex.

Even after their testimony, each member of the *Triumph* crew had stayed in the audience section of the hearing chamber. It was filled to standing room only, by the time they got their answer. Their demonstration of loyalty sent a wave of euphoric peace through Charlie.

Disciplinary Review Administrator Raskopf scowled at the noisy outburst, but she couldn't quell their delight no matter how hard she glared. Judge Cunningham *almost* broke character and smiled. He gaveled the hearing to a close and let them go.

Ex-Captain LaRochelle had left earlier. His temporary waiver of Hildie's restraining order lasted no longer than his testimony. After that he had to leave, and resume keeping a lifelong distance of at least 100 meters from her, with no electronic or other contact. Moreover, because he'd both harassed her and mismanaged the ERT, he'd been demoted to a dead-end, Wheel-based, bureaucratic cubicle.

The moment Charlie was free to do so, he vaulted over the railing that separated him from Hildie's seat at the defendant's table. The tension he'd held in for so long released in a burst of dizzy, soaring joy. He swept her up in an ecstatic hug and twirled her around a couple of times before he carefully set her back onto her feet.

She reached up with a huge grin and pulled him close for a heartfelt kiss. Then she turned to give both attorneys delighted handshakes that turned into more hugs. Charlie eyed her, waited his turn, then earnestly thanked both attorneys.

Somchai Saidi, the Union lawyer, hadn't said much in the hearing today, but he'd brought his "A" game to the research and documentation. The formidable Endesha Odi had turned her considerable skills to slicing up the prosecution's hatchet job on Hildie's character. She'd rapidly reduced it to the pile of shredded rubbish it deserved to be.

Where would we be, without such good representation? He followed Hildie and her crowd of supporters outside.

Shady arrived outside in her and Rex's new auto-nav. As a Big New Year present to each other, they'd upgraded from the plain, boxy car the OPD had issued for their security. They now leased an electric-blue coupe with large windows and ample room for at least three humans as well as two XK9s.

Their previous, unremarkable transport was needed when Transmondian agents with neurotoxin darts were known to be hunting for XK9s. Thanks to the Alliance, that was no longer a problem. Now the Transmondian Government was locked down and under review by the Alliance for a whole list of violations. Their space fleet had been sequestered, securely surrounded and outgunned by Alliance forces. Alliance inspectors now administered every Transmondian spaceport and transfer station. All Transmondian embargoes had been lifted.

Charlie couldn't stop smiling. The whole Chayko System was a much safer space—at least for as long as the Alliance forces remained here. Rex was well on the mend from his lung transplant. And now Hildie was vindicated!

Rex and Shady's new vehicle accommodated Hildie's ERT crewmates Ramón, Sally, Martin, and Veda—but thank goodness all four were young, supple, and thin. They departed for the pub. Somchai and Endesha handled their own transportation, but promised they'd stop by for a celebratory round.

Aunt Hannah had sent a somewhat larger vehicle for Charlie, Hildie, and more friends. They shared it with Hildie's best friend Theresa, the two women's paramedic partners Eli and Alexi, and newly-promoted ERT Captain Oz Meredith.

Theresa plopped down next to Hildie with a huge grin. "Did you *see* the outrage on ol' Raskopf's face when Endesha put the restraining order into the official record?"

"Oh, my." Hildie grimaced. "And the way LaRock just kept *staring* at me with that weird little smile, until she demanded that he look at *her* when he was answering questions?"

Charlie hadn't fully let go of his Amare, so he felt the shudder that passed through her at this memory. He snuggled her a little closer to his side. He'd wanted to punch the man for that damned leering stare, but it was far more prudent to let Endesha eviscerate him verbally.

"My favorite part was when Odi asked you what those medals were for." Eli nodded to Charlie. "You *know* Raskopf wasn't gonna say Word One about those!"

"Well, technically, she did," Theresa countered. "She objected to your wearing them."

"I couldn't comply with the hearing's dress code, if I didn't." Charlie shook his head. *What did she expect? Surely she knew a dress uniform's not complete without them?*

She was desperate, Rex said through the link from the other car. *The scent factors in that hearing were fascinating.*

"I noticed they didn't even bring up their original objection to going out after 'just a dog,'" Eli added. "That really stuck in LaRock's craw for a while. First couple of weeks, he kept trying to get us to agree with him. Probably asked me ten different times if I really thought it was okay to let you go after, as he put it, 'a damn, stupid *dog.*'"

Alexi laughed. "Yeah, he tried that with me, too. Kinda hard to make that argument hold water when the dog in question is a recognized-sapient being and a member of the freakin' *Leadership Council!*"

"Not to mention he was *sitting right there* with a Medal of Freedom around his neck!" Theresa shook her head.

Oz grinned at Charlie. "I really enjoyed it when Raskopf had Len Stevens on the stand and he realized she wanted him to say it was irresponsible to send you out in a MERS-V." He chuckled. "When he gave her that incredulous look and asked 'Do you *know* who that guy *is?*' I about fell out of my chair laughing. That was priceless."

Charlie chuckled along with him, but that was a point he'd worried about beforehand. The question could have gone much differently. He *wasn't* certified when Hildie let him out in that MERS-V, although he'd since earned back his Class B.

Stevens was the Port Authority clerk in charge of maintaining microgravity certification records. He had, in fact, been the testing officer who'd certified Charlie, both before the *Asalatu,* and again two weeks ago. But, like everyone else who'd been based at the Hub in January of 89, Stevens knew what Charlie had done.

Still think it's embarrassing to be considered a hero? Rex asked through the link.

It . . . did come in pretty handy today. Charlie eased out a breath. Over the last few weeks, he'd had a chance to more clearly see how the things he'd done appeared to others. It hadn't shaken his conviction that any public servant worthy of the name would have done their best in a similar situation. But maybe people had a point when they said he was extra stubborn about the follow-through.

At the Cock & Bull, Corlee and the staff greeted them with cheers and raised mugs. Clearly, they'd had advance intel. Probably from a certain pair of dogs who'd undoubtedly taken the switchbacks at the full legal speed, with their heads sticking out of the windows.

Charlie accepted a mug of draft ale, while Hildie took the wineglass Corlee handed to her. He joined in the toasts and hugged his newly exonerated Amare, ready to relax at last. They exchanged an elated glance and then another kiss, to the sound of laughs and cheers.

Hildie turned to chatter excitedly with Theresa, Petunia, and Walter. The XK9 partner-pair, now an important part of their new study group, had been waiting at the pub.

But Charlie lingered in the afterglow of that kiss. *This is the last of the month's big hurdles. Finally, we're free to move forward.* His arm shield was gone. He and Rex grew stronger every day. Now Hildie had shed the looming threat that for weeks had dampened her joy and shrunk both her appetite and her dreams for the future.

He released a happy sigh and took another pull on his mug, then glanced across the table to meet Rex's eyes. *What an eventful time we've lived through. I wonder what's in store next.*

His partner's tongue hung long with canine joy and his tail thumped the floor. *Whatever it is, we'll face it stronger together.*

- THE END, *for now* -

I hope you enjoyed this book. If you did, could you please take a moment to **rate and review it on Goodreads and Amazon?** Every rating and review makes an important difference to an author!

❖ ❖ ❖ ❖ ❖ ❖ ❖ ❖

What happens next for the XK9s of Rana Station? Many new doors have opened for the Pack and their humans, and many more adventures await. I'm already at work on the next book, *Bones for the Children.*

If you'd like updates on my progress, sneak peeks, behind-the-scenes glimpses, free short XK9-related fiction and more, **sign up for my monthly newsletter!** I do my best to make it worth your time!

📱 Newsletter

While you're expecting the next book, I'd love to introduce you to a new series upcoming in 2025 from Weird Sisters Publishing. *An Image of Voices* is the first of four novels (originally published as *The Windhover Tapes,* we've rebranded slightly, and now call it the *Windhover Tetralogy*). When my late brother-in-law **Warren C. Norwood** released them, they created enough of a buzz to get him nominated twice for what is currently known as the **Astounding Award for Best New Writer.**

The next page shows the cover, then we'll begin an excerpt from Chapter One. After that, don't miss our **Rana Station Interior Locations Maps** and directory of **Who's Who and What's What** in **Bone of Contention**.

An Image of Voices

The Windhover Tetralogy – Book 1

Warren C. Norwood

Two-time John W. Campbell/Astounding Award Nominee

Illustrations by Lucy A. Synk, with Chaz Kemp.

AN IMAGE OF VOICES

CHAPTER ONE EXCERPT: DIERA

7035-8.1 - FedBase 1744

It really seems a bit absurd to keep a journal which will never be read by anyone but the journal keeper. Still, foolish and whimsical soul that you are, Gerard, you will keep one. Starting now.

In the mindwipe that ended our last mission, I fear we lost far too many memories we would like to have kept. So, dear Self, I charge you with this task, urge you to keep me diligent, and warn you that the very presence of this journal violates every diplomatic contract the Federation has ever written. That's why I'm recording this in my personal security section of Windy's files. And that's why we must keep its existence a secret from anyone. Except perhaps Fairy Peg.

Ah, Fairy Peg, where are you now? Lost somewhere in my memory for sure. Hidden by the best techniques the mindwipers offer. Gone but for your name and a sweet, lingering hint of your scent in my dreams.

A year now since the end of the last mission. A year since Fed exercised its legal option of mindwiping the entire experience from my memory. A year of "cleansing" and new preparation.

It's remarkable, Self, what I remember and what I don't. And of course, what you remember. FedDiploCorps said we were mindwiped for "the highest security reasons," but I suspect it was because we made a grand mess of things. A blatantly apparent failure. Sometimes I wish you'd learn to talk, Self, or esp, or somehow communicate with me besides dream symbology. I mean, let's be fair. Here I sit at the keyboard, punching personal revelations into Windy, with you watching my every move. Indeed, perhaps controlling my every move. And what do I get in return? Explanations? No, dreams. Weird dreams. Nonsequential, symbol-laden, overpainted dreams.

But no one ever promised me life would be fair, so why should I expect fairness from you? After all, I'm only the organism which has to act to insure your continued existence. I protect and defend you, feed you, give you spiritual sustenance, and occasionally find someone who will love and bed you. Surely I ask too much in wanting you to be fair with me and share the hidden resources of your knowledge and wisdom.

What? You're not impressed by my impotent threats and shallow flattery? No matter. We'll come to terms later.

Inventory.

New diplocontract is signed. Training (or was it retraining?) is complete. My personal modifications to the Baird Z-Rangel translator have tested out better than I thought they would. Fed replaced the autodoc with two superfluous rejuvhosp cells as part of "Mandatory Refitting," but at least they didn't add them to Windy's mortgage. Windhover is provisioned, polished, and ready to fly. So am I.

Now all we need is FedControl's final launch clearance.

*****Took them long enough. I thought they were going to make us sit here all day. One more chime from the FedChannel, and we start the final count.

Ready or not, Self, here we go. Talk to you later.

7035-8.12 – Diera Entry Path

So much for diligent maintenance of a journal.

Three warps and eleven days later, I return. A poor start. Lack of desire to communicate? Lack of motivation? Lack of help from you, Self? No. Had it not been for my dreams of Fairy Peg, I would not be sitting here now as we coast down toward Diera.

Diera, religious planet of limited charm. Survey tells us (once you weed through all their technolingo) that the humanoid residents are seventeenth-generation Sylan descendants who slipped into mysticism by the sixth generation after plagues routinely killed half the population every thirty to forty years. Resistant immunity finally allowed the survivors to eke out an existence on the one major continent. They believe in magic, the supernatural, and the efficacy of total cooperation.

Their first diplomatic contact was a Sylvan, GrWrytte, who was impressed by little that he saw and particularly disdainful of their cultural achievements. He noted with great acerbity in the FedRecord that the Dierans have vast information about their immigration from Sylva, including videos of the first years, but refuse to concern themselves with such "mysteries." Poor GrWrytte, he didn't even notice that they took him in without rancor, nursed him through his bout with the plague, and buried him with honors.

By the time M. Caven got there, the Dierans had perfected their immunoserum, with the help of Survey, and Caven found herself in what she felt was diplomatic heaven. Unfortunately, Caven couldn't stay very long and had to leave after a year to pursue other Federation business. Her FedRecord notes, however, are copious, and her relations with the Dierans were apparently excellent.

My job is to establish a FedOffice, sign a permanent treaty for Fed, and leave two of our passengers (deepsleeping now) as liaison officers. I cannot understand why liaison officers always travel in deepsleep. Maybe Windy knows.

She doesn't.

It occurs to me that it would be simpler to let Windy access this journal directly, but it's safer that she can't.

Been studying these notes on Diera for the past two months, and no matter how bad GrWrytte's attitude, nor how good Caven's, I keep getting an irresistible feeling that both of them missed something very important, some essential ingredient, some key part of the puzzle. The whole populace sounds too basically nice. Too accepting.

Okay, Windy, I hear you. First orbit coming up.

7035-8.13 – Braking Orbit, Diera

Planetfall in six hours. Windy has us in the groove. Diera verifies our approach. My contact is M'Litha, the wirzel-magess, chief politician, witch, magician, and grand high muckety-muck. If all goes well in the next two days, Windy and I will cycle out a couple of the sleepers and we'll all begin work in earnest.

7035-8.22 - Tam City, Diera

Someone lied to me. This is not going well at all. And what the Krick does M'Litha want from me?

We had a nonlinear welcome, where I was told to get to work and get greeted later. A nonlinear diplomatic reception, which resembled what on old Terra would have been called a sabbat. A nonlinear meeting with an old magess, who told me to translate this manuscript I've punched into the Baird. And now, a handg-lyphed note from M'Litha herself telling me that once my translation is complete, we will have the formal welcome.

Windy's monitoring the Baird and giving assistance. I am waiting. That's what I seem to be doing the most of, waiting. Seven days of waiting. Waiting in the library. Waiting in the reception room. Waiting at the survey station, where they know more about atmosphere, dirt, flora, and fauna, and less about the populace, than they ought to. At least getting them to shift their attention broke part of the boredom. But only for a day.

I'm going to sleep, Self.

7035-8.23

If this manuscript is part of the answer as to what's going on here, I don't believe we've made any progress. The Baird's literal translation comes out as so much useless gibberish. Maybe this new program will help.

*****Well, it took nearly nine hours, but we did it. Windy coached the Baird, and I coached Windy. Word by word and phrase by phrase, I think we made some sense of all this. The first problem was that the manuscript is written in what Caven called "holy" dialect. The second problem was that it is a poem. Not just any old poem but a very formal religious poem!

I'm exhausted. I've put the poem on the memory recording so I'll know it by heart in the morning. And you, Self, have the job of helping me understand what it means to our mission here.

Diera's Call
Be then tempted, star-child,
To journey out of nightmist
down to this baked rock and call it home.
Be then tempted, wirzel.
To mage the shadows from you
with tongue and hand-hold
and walk our path.
Be then tempted, magess.
To cull the seeds of medic
deep within your womb
and bear our spawn.
Be then tempted, mother.
To mold the face of Diera
with line and lineage

and mirror life.
Be then tempted, star-child.
To be the wirzel-magess,
medic, true mother,
and blood of all.

7035-9.1

Busy, busy, busy. But good busy.

Not only did we pass the translation test with flying colors, we were also honored in a ceremony that lasted from dusk till dawn during which, as near as I can cipher it, I was made an honorary Monkus. In other words, I became a holy man. When I pressed M'Litha for more information on exactly what that meant, she had one of the magesses fetch me another manuscript! Yes, another poem. Different kind. Different dialect. But a poem nonetheless. Called "The Pilgrimage of Monkus on the Planet of His Exile." This one doesn't appear to be nearly so formal as "Diera's Call," and I'm hoping the translation problem will be somewhat simplified. I'd like to understand my honor a little better.

Now, Self, while we're waiting for Windy and the Baird to come up with a rough draft, what was that dream you gave me last night? In particular, what was Fairy Peg doing in a dream about the sabbat and why was she placing that fancy robe around my shoulders? Are you trying to tell me about something Peg did in the long ago? Or are you just playing with my tired and fragile mind? What was that sunburst pattern that kept appearing? Another one of your subtle symbols? Of my heart? Or of my ego for doing so well here on Diera? Come on, Self, you're holding back.

What, no snappy reply? I can wait. I always do.

*****Windy and the Baird didn't mess around this time. Two and a half hours from input to a very good draft. Another hour of refinement and collateral retranslating between the three of us, and it looks as though we may have a clue as to my status on Diera. At least we have some idea of who Monkus was or, more accurately, what he did that so impressed the Dierans.

According to what I learned during my days of waiting around in the library, the third Sylvan transport was forced by bad weather to set down on the opposite side of the continent from the first two. Consequently, two distinct communities grew out of that first wave of immigration: Tam City, where we are now, and Chancor. Apparently Monkus was born in Tam City and was one of the officials or couriers who traveled between the two cities. When the travel was banned in an attempt to control an outbreak of the plague, Monkus was in Chancor and decided to go back to Tam City on foot.

What does M'Litha think I'm trying to return to? What makes me an allegorical Monkus? The only other thing we know for sure is that to become a Monkus is to become a member of an elite group so honored. I don't know why M'Litha thinks I'm suitable, but for the record, here's the poem.

The Pilgrimage of Monkus on the Planet of His Exile

I
Nothing bit him so hard as the teeth of possession
Who could journey on solar wind
        to the mind of stars,
        to the mountains of Eldorado,
Who could ski the wild snow of space.
Nothing cramped his legs more than the chair.
II
Cross country he ran
Cross fair faces
Cross Diera's loins, bosomland, heart, and shoulder.
Legs crying old tense pain,
        the dying spring of muscle,

the sweat flowing hot.
His body's running heat felt hers,
    the steady rhythm-pounding,
    the aching drive,
    the push to make the hill
    to stagger down
        gasping to rest.

III

Monkus went to be his brother.
Through the brush-cotton-grass
Through the dogwood-pine
Through the arbors of his bones
of his sinew-vines
He swept like an eye from the mountain
Running to see the changing change.

IV

    To see,
        to become,
Monkus went,
        dark over mountains
        light under rivers
            dim through the rain.
Legs hard and willing.
Arms pumping lungs
        sucking holy vapors
            to fuel him
                on his pilgrimage home.

All in all, I think we've come up with a reasonable translation. We were pretty liberal with the flora, but that doesn't detract from the essence of the poem.

I put "Diera's Call" into the FedRecord, partially because it is a key to understanding this society and partially because I know it will drive the bureaucrats bonkers. Knowing them, they will probably consider it classified information because they don't understand it, stamp it Ultra Secret, and bury it in their Mass Computer. Just another reason why they can't know about this journal. I put a literal prose translation of "Pilgrimage" into my FedRecord notes. They won't even notice that.

Think I'll have Windy synthesize some parchment and make a copy of "Pilgrimage" in old script Standard as a gift to M'Litha. Give it to her tomorrow with an elaborate display of ceremony, wearing my dress whites and the cape of Monkus. That ought to impress the old girl.

Meanwhile, I'd better start waking the liaison team.

7035-9.3

"Impress" was the wrong word. Either my instincts for this planet are perfect, or M'Litha is flattering me beyond all reason. When I gave her "Pilgrimage" on Windy's synth-parchment in the gold foil case my LightSpeed Diploma came in, those off-blue eyes of hers almost set up a spark gap across the high ridge of her nose. If Dierans were capable of crying, I think she might have. Seems as though the dress whites, red cape, and gold foil case all formed some powerful color magic of symbology.

The results were another dusk-to-dawn ceremony of dedication, from which I just returned, and a trip to Chancor some time in the next week or two in the royal flyer. I use the word "royal" because M'Litha resembles a queen as much as anything. She acts like one too.

By then, Liaison and Survey will be too hard at work gathering new information for the treaty to miss me. So, Self, it looks like we might have earned ourselves a little holiday.

7035-9.11

Off to Chancor tomorrow with M'Litha and an entourage of magesses and wirzels, formally introduced to me today. I think I counted fifty-three altogether. This ought to be quite a party. M'Litha warned me there will be several long ceremonies in Chancor but that she will see to it that I get to talk to the wirzel-magess there in private and get to spend as much time as possible in the Chancor library, which contains most of their old videos.

I have the modified memocorder Windy made for me so I can report back on a regular basis. The rejuvhosp cell gave me the full treatment and declared me fit (though a bit underweight, it said). I've packed my gear and some new ceremonial robes provided by M'Litha, and I guess I'm as ready as I'm going to get. Gerard, my boy, get some sleep, for tomorrow starts a new adventure.

If you'd like to read what happens next, watch the Weird Sisters **Website**, social media (**Jan S. Gephardt on Facebook** and **Instagram**; and **Weird Sisters Publishing on Facebook**), or sign up for **Jan's newsletter**. We'll keep you up-to-date on the production process.

APPENDICES

The following pages include:
Rana Station Interior Location Maps

- An Overview of Rana Station
- Elevators from Wheel through Spoke to Hub
- Loop-Trains at the Hub
- Rana Station Governmental and Diplomatic Sector

Who's Who and What's What in *Bone of Contention*

Rana Station Overview

This diagram shows the Wheels and the Hub, but distances between Wheels are shortened and the docking structures between each Wheel have been omitted so you can see them clearly.

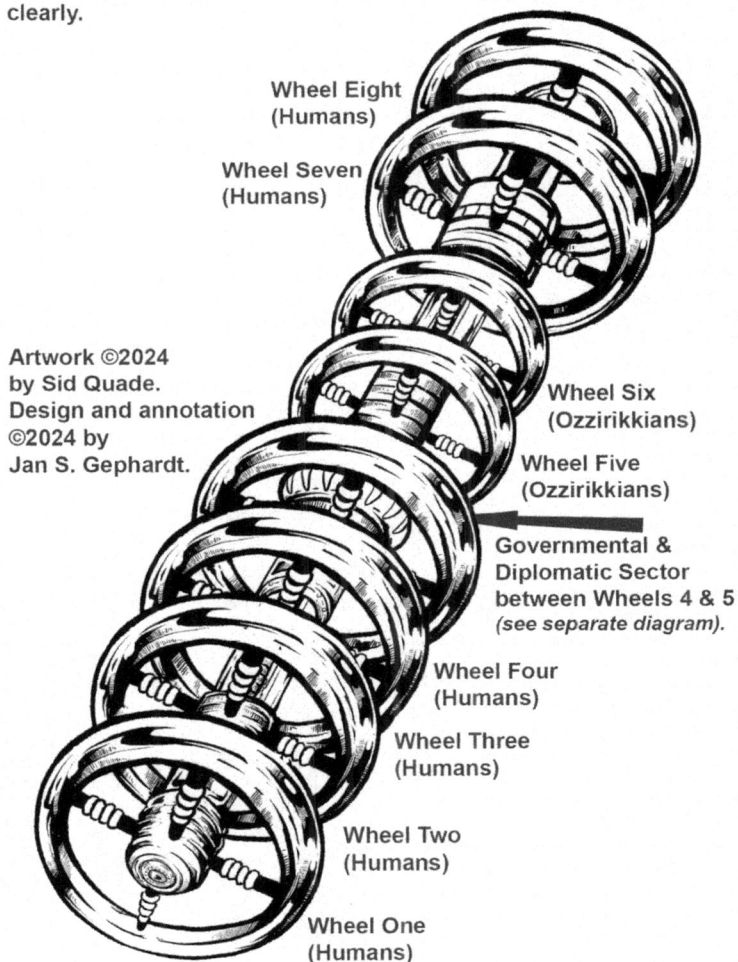

Wheel Eight
(Humans)

Wheel Seven
(Humans)

Artwork ©2024
by Sid Quade.
Design and annotation
©2024 by
Jan S. Gephardt.

Wheel Six
(Ozzirikkians)

Wheel Five
(Ozzirikkians)

Governmental &
Diplomatic Sector
between Wheels 4 & 5
(see separate diagram).

Wheel Four
(Humans)

Wheel Three
(Humans)

Wheel Two
(Humans)

Wheel One
(Humans)

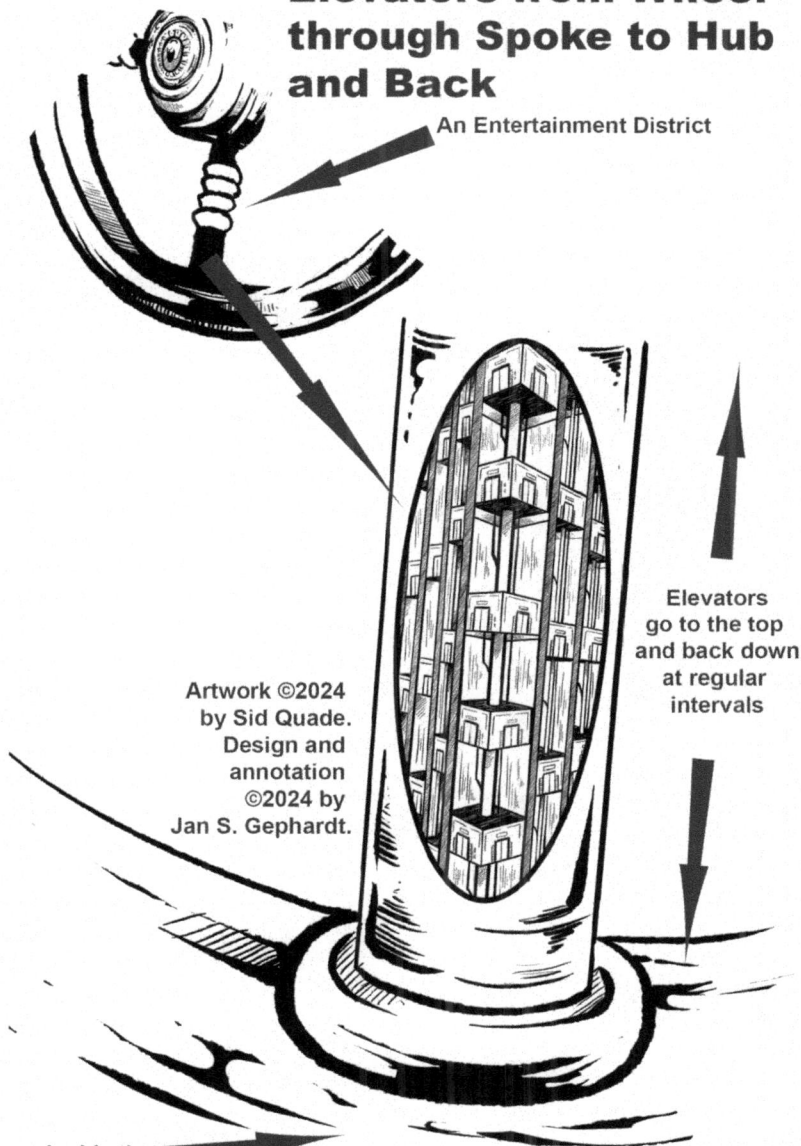

Elevators from Wheel through Spoke to Hub and Back

An Entertainment District

Artwork ©2024 by Sid Quade. Design and annotation ©2024 by Jan S. Gephardt.

Elevators go to the top and back down at regular intervals

Inside the Wheel: Grand Central Terminal

Loop-Trains at the Hub

Drawings of the Wheels themselves were omitted so you can see the Hub more clearly.

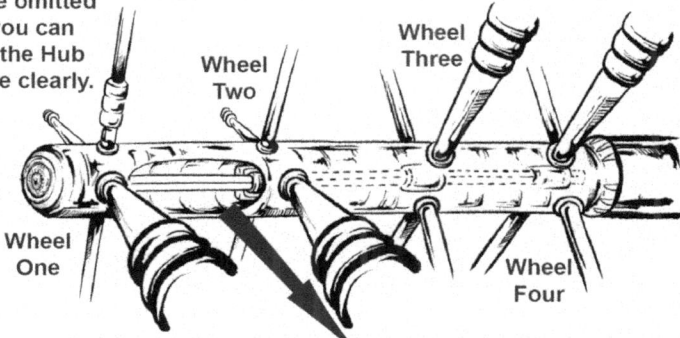

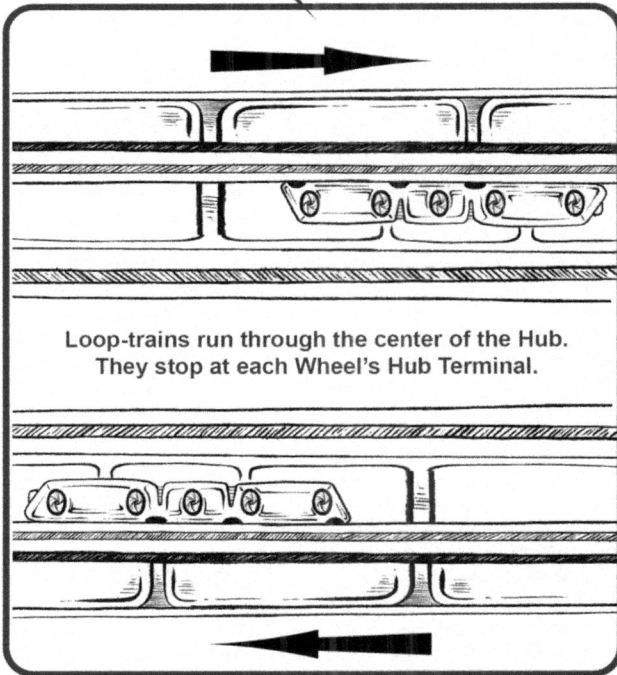

Wheel Two

Wheel Three

Wheel One

Wheel Four

Loop-trains run through the center of the Hub. They stop at each Wheel's Hub Terminal.

Rana Station Governmental and Diplomatic Sector

High-Security sector between Wheels Four and Five -- Once again, the Docking Structures have been omitted for clarity.

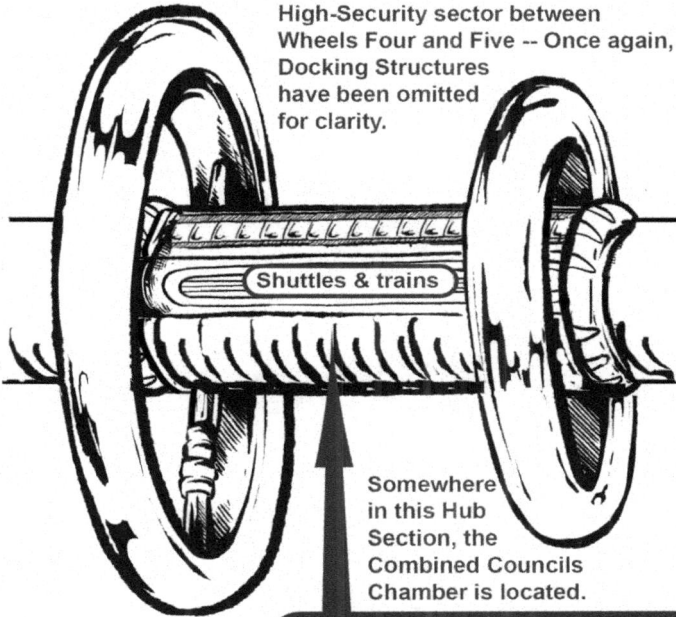

Shuttles & trains

Somewhere in this Hub Section, the Combined Councils Chamber is located.

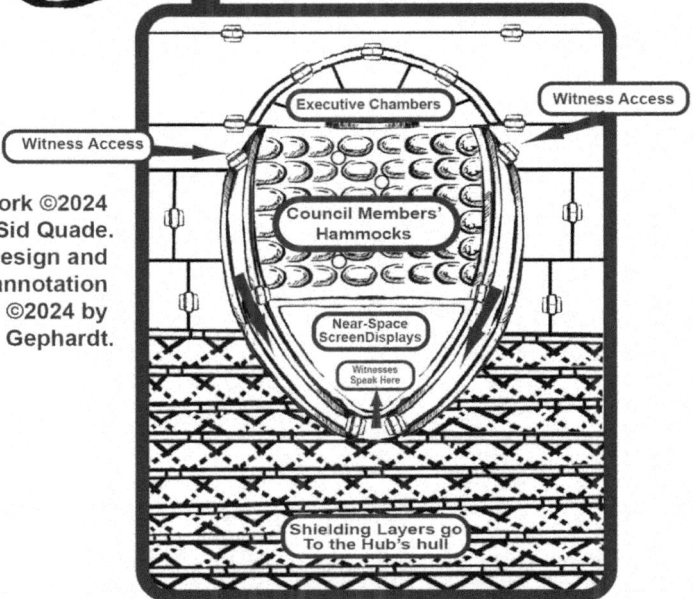

Executive Chambers

Witness Access

Witness Access

Council Members' Hammocks

Near-Space ScreenDisplays

Witnesses Speak Here

Shielding Layers go To the Hub's hull

Artwork ©2024 by Sid Quade. Design and annotation ©2024 by Jan S. Gephardt.

WHO'S WHO AND WHAT'S WHAT

A DIRECTORY OF ACRONYMS, PEOPLE, PLACES, AND IMPORTANT THINGS IN THIS BOOK.

A

Abdual. (AHB-dou-ul) A resident of the Five-Ten. (Pronouns: he, him.)

Abhik "Abi" Bannerjee. (AH-bick BAN-er-jee) Hildie's younger brother, son of Pari and Dara. Significant of Smita Rostov. Abi, Smita, and Hildie share an apartment in Feliz Tower. (Pronouns: he, him.)

Acquisitionists. A political faction in Transmondian government that wants to create a Transmondian Empire by annexing other sovereignties in the Chayko System.

Adelaide "Laidie" Perri. Director of the Station Bureau of Investigation. (Pronouns: she, her.)

Adeyeme. – See *Elaine Adeyeme*.

Adlai Masato. (AD-lay mah-SAH-toe) Borough Attorney of Orangeboro. (Pronouns: he, him.)

Administrator Hoback. (HOE-bok) John Hoback IV, leader of Tonquin Base. (Pronouns: he, him.)

Admiral T'irzh'kokku. (TEERzh-koh-koo) An elder ozzirikkian admiral of the minority tirittim gender. (Pronouns: ti, tin.)

Afiq Gonzalo. (ah-FEEK gon-ZALL-oh) A "slash" addict, currently in medical detention, indicted for in the sabotage of the *Izgubil*. (Pronouns: he, him.)

Afua. (aff-WAH) An XK9 partner-candidate who was one of Pamela Gómez's podmates during XK9 training. (Pronouns: she, her.)

Ailani Idris. (eye-LAH-nee ID-riss) Mayor of Orangeboro. (Pronouns: she, her.)

Akkari Matika. (a-KAIR-ee muh-TEE-kah) A Level Three Detective with the OPD Verification and Interdiction of Corruption and Exploitation (V.I.C.E.) UNIT. (Pronouns: she, her.)

Alexei Francis. (ah-LECK-ee FRAN-sis) Theresa Socorro's usual paramedic partner on the *Triumph*. (Pronouns: he, him.)

Aleya Connor. (ah-LAY-uh KON-nor) Sergeant, a squad leader on OPD STAT Blue Team. (Pronouns: she, her.)

Alfredo "Alf" Gorman. (al-FRAY-doh ALF GORE-man) A Detective Sergeant with the OPD Verification and Interdiction of Corruption and Exploitation (V.I.C.E.) UNIT. Balchu Nowicki's immediate supervisor. (Pronouns: he, him.)

Allan, Fergus. (FER-gus ALL-un) An indicted detainee alleged to have assisted in the sabotage of the Izgubil. A Saoirse Front member. (Pronouns: he, him.)

Allard Ferro. (AH-lar FAIR-row) A deceased sub-leader of the Whisper Syndicate with frequent dealings in the Five-Ten with Turlach O'Boyle. Killed in the Izgubil incident. (Pronouns: he, him.)

Alliance of the Peoples. An interstellar alliance of sapient species whose treaties supersede all system-wide or national laws.

Alvarez Park. (AHL-va-rehs) A fairly large municipal park in urban Centerboro, located on Alvarez Boulevard.

Alvarez Place Apartments. A multi-household dwelling in urban Centerboro, located on Alvarez Boulevard.

Amare. (ah-MAH-ray) An official Ranan human relationship status, which may be of shorter or longer duration, at the will of the partners. Does not include any license to rear children.

Ambassador Ives. The current Ranan ambassador to Transmondia. (Pronouns: he, him.)

Ambassador Nunzio. – See *Ryder Nunzio*.

Amethyria. (am-ah-THEAR-yah) Homeworld of the ozzirikkians.

Amethyrians. (am-ah-THEAR-yuns) Members of the sapient species that dominates Amethyria, genetically near-identical to ozzirikkians, who originated from them.

Amiri. (ah-MEER-ee) A member of Becenti Chartered Family.

Amorous Partner of Record. An official Ranan human relationship status that confers certain rights to Family Leave and access to some otherwise-privileged information about their Boyfriend / Girlfriend / Amorous Partner.

Andrew "Andy" Lee Crannach. (CRAH-noch). Charlie's brother-in-law. Caro's husband, and Sophie and Lacey's father. (Pronouns: he, him.)

Angharad Juma. (ahng-HA-rad ZHOO-muh) Residential Council Member from Highboro on Wheel Four. A member of the Popular Democracy Party (PDP). (Pronouns: she, her.)

Anika Ogawa Chinbat. (AH-ni-ka a-GAH-wa chan-BAT) Orangeboro Medical Examiner, whose office is a unit of Borough Government that cooperates with law enforcement and legal systems but is subordinate to none of them. (Pronouns: she, her.)

Anita-Maya Biswas Cantú. (ah-NEE-tah-MAH-yah bizz-VASS con-TOO) Mechanically-inclined wife of Cormac Cantú Biswas, mother of Jeliza Cantú and Bryan Biswas. A member of Feliz Family. (Pronouns: she, her.)

Annie Montoya Lee. (mon-TO-yah) Charlie's maternal grandmother, wife of Pedro Lee Montoya, daughter of Loretta Triola Lee, and official Head of Household for Corona Chartered Family. (Pronouns: she, her.)

Ansar Hadi. (an-SAH HA-dee) The Assistant Borough Public

Defender, a position roughly parallel to that of Regan Ireland, Assistant Borough Prosecutor. (Pronouns: he, him.)

Anthony. – See *Lynne Anthony.*

Anya Williams Rodriguez. (AH-nya WIL-yams rod-REE-gess) Wife of Chase Rodriguez Williams, mother of Miguel Williams and Anita Rodriguez. A member of Becenti Charter. (Pronouns: she, her.)

Apodeddi Mamoor. – See *Mamoor Volkov Ismeryatochno.*

Appscaten. (APP-skat-ten) A sapient member-species in the Alliance of the Peoples with extraordinarily good camouflage.

Archibald "Archy" Cody Danvir. Aide and right-hand man to Chief Klein. (Pronouns: he, his.)

Argent Enclave. (ar-ZHEN EN-klayv) One of the six sectors in the underground Five-Ten District in Orangeboro.

Ari Pryce. (AH-ree PRICE) A veterinary technologist employed by the Sandler Clinic. (Pronouns: they / them.)

Asalatu. (as-ah-LAH-too) A spacecraft that slammed into the Orangeboro Docks in January of the Ranan Year 89.

Ashland Services. A wholly-owned subsidiary of Moran Platinum, managed by Emer Bellamy.

Ashton Cole. (ASH-tun KOHL) A Member of the Ranan Residential Council from New Hibernia Borough on Wheel One, who also is a member of the Commonwealth Party (CWP) and the Palmdale Club. (Pronouns: he, him.)

Atilla "Till" Usher. An indicted detainee alleged to have assisted in the sabotage of the Izgubil. (Pronouns: he, him.)

Augmentation Therapy. A systemic medical treatment that uses regeneration techniques to enhance physical strength and reflexes.

Aunt Serafina. – See *Serafina Gibson Lee.*

Aurelia Yael Glenn. (a-RAY-lee-ah yah-EL GLEN) Official Head of Household for Pabiyan Chartered Family. Wife of Sanford Glenn Yael, mother of Berwyn Yael and Rowan Glenn. (Pronouns: she, her.)

Axl "Ax" Gerwitz. An Orangeboro UPO assigned to Central

HQ, currently working security at the Sandler Clinic on Swing Watch. (Pronouns: he, him.)

Aylward. – See *Valda Aylward.*

B

Babu Sebastian Saha. (BOB-oo) the eldest of Hildie's cousins. (Pronouns: he, him.)

Balchu Nowicki. (BAHL-chew) A Level Two Detective with the Orangeboro Police Department. Normally assigned to the VICE Unit at Central HQ, he is currently a member of the Joint OPD/SBI Task Force. Pamela Gómez's Amare. Son of Feyodor and Tuya, brother of Sarnai (Pronouns: he, him.)

Bancoscuro, (bonk-oh-SKOO-row) A black-market exchange, allegedly based somewhere in the Chaykoan Asteroids

Bari Family. (BAH-ri) The Chartered Family of Eduardo Donovan and XK9 Victor Sam-Janet.

Basil Bellamy Kimbrough. (BAY-zil BELL-a-mee KIM-brew) Patriarch of the Vinebrook Family, one of Rana Station's original Fifty Founding Families. Husband of Maeve. (Pronouns: he, him.)

Beatriz Chan. (bee-ah-TREESE) Borough Council Chairperson for the Orangeboro Council. (Pronouns: she, her.)

Becenti Family. (beh-SEN-tee) The Chartered Family of Feyodor Nowiciki's "blood brother" Chase Williamson.

Beckett "Beck" Crombie. A field agent assigned to SIT Alpha. (Pronouns: he, him.)

Becky Goldstein. Ten-year-old daughter of UPO Bill Sloane. (Pronouns: she, her.)

Berik. – See *Quentin Berik.*

Berwyn Yael. (BER-win yah-EL). Partner of XK9 Cinnamon "Cinnie" Lightfoot-Floss. A Detective Level One, and member of Pabiyan Chartered Family. Currently on Emergency Family Leave. (Pronouns: he, him.)

Betrothed Partnership. An officially recognized transitional

Ranan human family relationship status. A Significant who has declared an intention to form a Marriage Partnership with their other Significant(s), with the intent of applying for a license to rear children.

Betrothed. (be-TROTH't) An official Ranan human relationship status that designates a person's relationship to a betrothed partner.

Big New Year. An annual Ranan civic holiday, primarily celebrated by persons of east Asian Earth heritage (although anyone is welcome to join in), inspired by Lunar New Year celebrations on Earth. Most commerce halts or slows down in the human wheels around this period, which observers celebrate each year from January 22-28.

Bill. – See *William "Bill" Goldstein Sloane*.

Bonita. The Chartered Family that lives next door to Corona Family.

Bordemer Canton. (BOAR-duh-mur) A Transmondian canton (like a state or province) immediately north of Solara City. It contains the XK9 Project's Puppy Farm One, and the suburban community of Ensolay.

Boyfriend of Record. An official Ranan human relationship status that confers certain rights to Family Leave and access to some otherwise-privileged information about their Boyfriend / Girlfriend / Amorous Partner.

Brain Link. Also *Cybernetic Brain Link*, an implanted brain chip that enables mental, person-to-person communication between an XK9 and their human partner.

Brock Rivers. A member of Pabiyan Family. A friend of Charlie's, member of the STAT Team, and cousin of Eddie Chism and Berwyn Yael. (Pronouns: he, him.)

Bruce Ibsen. Sheriff of Bordemer Canton in Transmondia. Mike and Elaine's friend. (Pronouns: he, him.)

Brutus. A nurse assigned to the Orangeboro Detention Center. (Pronouns: he, him.)

Bryan Kilgore. (BRY-un kill-GORE) An indicted detainee

alleged to have assisted in the sabotage of the Izgubil. A Saoirse Front member. (Pronouns: he, him.)

Bureau, or The Bureau. Station Bureau of Investigation (SBI).

Burns and Zhang on the Beat. A news-talk broadcast.

Byron Thornton. (BYE-run THORN-tun) A reputable journalist in Centerboro (Pronouns: he, him.)

C

Calendar New Year. An annual celebration that marks the passing of the year, from New Year's Eve on December 38 to New Year's Day on January 1 (Yes, the Ranan Calendar is different from that of Earth).

CAP. Cybernetically-Assisted Perception. The implant-driven interface between an individual user and the Station Net.

Capt. Consuelo Rodrigo. (con-SWAY-luh rod-REE-go) Captain of the Monteverde Emergency Rescue Team. (Pronouns: she, her.)

Capt. Danvir. – See *Archibald "Archy" Danvir*.

Captain Tam Wong. Commanding officer of the Ranan ship Fairboro. (Pronouns: he, him.)

Carmella. (kar-MEH-low) The name of the pseudo persona of a Citron Flash auto-nav.

Carnerie. (KAR-nuh-ree) A facility that produces cultured meat.

Carolyn "Caro" Crannach Lee. (CRAH-noch) Charlie's older sister. Wife of Andy and mother of Sophie and Lacey. (Pronouns: she, her.)

Centerboro. The Wheel Four Borough that is the human side of the Ranan National Capitol, just as Zhokikim Timi on Wheel Five is the ozzirikkian side.

Chase Rodriguez Williams. (CHASE rod-REE-gess WIL-yams) Feyodor Nowicki's lifelong friend and "blood brother," a fellow native of Northwest Butterknowle in Transmondia. Husband of Anya Williams Rodriguez, father of Miguel Williams and Anita Rodriguez. A member of Becenti Charter. (Pronouns: he, him.)

Chayko System. The locality in Alliance Space that centers on a G-type yellow-dwarf main sequence star named Pkale (from the Shawnee: *it blazes* "p'kah-lay"), and includes the human-inhabited planet Chayko, as well as six habitat space station megastructures and an extensive asteroid belt.

Chayko. (CHAY-koh) The nearest inhabited planet to Rana Station, and the only such planet in the Chayko System.

Chaykoan Jump Point. (CHAY-koe-un) A wormhole-like location in space that allows transport between the Chayko System and other locations in galactic space.

Cheree. (share-EE) A young woman enslaved by the Whisper Syndicate at Turlach O'Boyle's instigation. A former girlfriend of Kieran O'Boyle. (Pronouns: she, her.)

Chief Nakoa. – See *Kendra Nakoa*.

Chukwu. – See *Kwan Chukwu*.

Ciné and Chardonnay Circle. (SEE-nay and shar-doh-NAY) A social group, usually of well-to-do women from established Chartered Families. They gather to discuss realiciné productions, much like a 21st-century book club. Gatherings always feature wine and snacks.

Cinnamon "Cinnie" Lightfoot-Floss. XK9 partner of Berwyn Yael, and an OPD Detective Level One. Currently on Health Leave. (Pronouns: she, her.)

Citizen of Courage Medal. The greatest honor the SBI can bestow upon a civilian, reserved for outstanding displays of courage by citizens in service to SBI mission.

Citron Flash. The model name of a stylish auto-nav sportscar on Rana Station.

Clyde. A kennel worker for the XK9 Project in Solara City. (Pronouns: he, him.)

Cock & Bull Pub. An eating and drinking establishment in a lower-rent district on Terrace Three of Orangeboro Sixth Precinct.

Col. Jackson Wisniewski. (wizz-NEW-skee) The colonel formerly in charge of Ranan Intelligence Operations for the Transmondian Intelligence Service, currently in re-gen, in a high-security medical detention facility. (Pronouns: he, him.)

Combined Councils Chamber. The location in the high-security Governmental and Diplomatic District of the Hub where the Combined Councils meet. Almost unique in the Universe, it is located in microgravity.

Combined Councils. The assembly of all Ranan Residential and Commercial Council Members.

ComCouncil. Short for Ranan Commercial Council.

Commodore Aadya Jarl. (ah-DEE-ya YARL) An SDF staffer in the Wheel Four Situation Chamber. (Pronouns: she, her.)

Commodore Clarimonde Alvaro Montreaux. (CLAIR-ee-mond al-VAH-rroe mon-TRRUH) the administrator in charge of the SDF Wheel Two Base. (Pronouns: she, her.)

Commonwealth Party. (CWP) One of four political parties on Rana Station.

Conchita. (con-CHEE-ta) A member of Becenti Chartered Family.

Constance "Connie" Alkayev. (AL-kay-uv) XK9 Crystal Basho-Dancer's partner. A Detective Level One. (Pronouns: she, her.)

Corlee Wirth. (KOR-lee WURTH) The barkeeper/owner of the Cock & Bull Pub. (Pronouns: she, her.)

Cormac Cantú Biswas. (KOR-mack con-TOO bizz-VASS) A member of Feliz Family. Hildie's cousin, Anita-Maya's husband, Jeliza and Bryan's father. (Pronouns: he, him.)

Corona Family. (kor-OH-nuh) The Chartered Family that lives in Corona Tower (Charlie and Rex's family).

Corona Tower. The home of Corona Chartered Family, located on Starboard Hill Terrace Eight in the Ninth Precinct on Rana Station.

Council Braids. Multicolored, knotted openwork vest-like garments worn by Council Members who are current legislators on either the Ranan Residential or Commercial Council. Wearing the Braids signals official enactment of Ranan business. Only current Council Members may legally wear their Braids, and only during the conduct of official Ranan Government business.

Council Chair Chan. – See *Beatriz Chan*.

CPD. An abbreviation for the Centerboro Police Department.

Crime Scene Unit. (CSU) The forensic evidence analysis unit of a law enforcement agency.

Crystal "Crys" Basho-Dancer. XK9 Partner of Connie Alkayev, an OPD Detective Level One. (Pronouns: she, her.)

CSU. – See *Crime Scene Unit*.

Cutler. – See *Sarabande "Sara" Cutler*.

CWP. Commonwealth Party, one of the four Ranan political parties.

D

Dagmar. (DAG-mahr) A fictional character in a Ranan fantasy novel series, who has a dragon. (Pronouns: she, her.)

Dahlia Glenn. (DAHL-ya GLEN) A member of the Pabiyan Chartered Family. Manager of Pabiyan Carnerie. (Pronouns: she, her.)

Dara Bannerjee Gallagher. (DA-ra BAN-er-jee GAL-ah-gur) Hildie and Abi's mother, wife of Pari. (Pronouns: she, her.)

David "Dave" Santos. (SAN-tohs) A noted cyberneticist from Station Polytechnic University. . (Pronouns: he, him.)

Dawn Baruti Adyeme. (DON bah-RUU-tee ah-DEE-yem) A Member of Providence-Brightstar Chartered Family. Elaine Adeyeme's mother. (Pronouns: she, her.)

Denis "Denny" LaGrande. (De-NEE "DEN-nee" la-GRAND) A successful and famous Ranan space yacht racer. (Pronouns: he, him.)

Director Perri. – See *Adelaide "Laidie" Perri*.

Disciplinary Review Administrator Raskopf. (RASS-koff) An official tasked with representing the allegations that have been made against a department employee who is under a disciplinary review.

Dodavira. (doe-duh-VEER-uh) An interstellar transport ship.

Dolan, Neil. – See *Neil Dolan.*

Dolan, Rufus. – See *Rufus Dolan.*

Domestic Partnership. An officially recognized Ranan human family relationship status that is generally assumed to be permanent, or a prelude to Betrothal. Parallel to a more widely understood status of being "married, "except it does not include the license to rear children.

Dostigator Collective. (DOSS-tee-*gay*-tur) A Mahusayan collective that provides high-level security services to mining collectives.

DPO. Acronym for Detective Peace Officer, a civilian police rank.

Dr. Mariel. (mah-REE-el) A Listener (psychologist) assigned to the Orangeboro Police Department. Charlie Morgan's counselor. (Pronouns: she, her.)

Dushlan. (DOOSH-lahn) A criminal group primarily based on Pinakamaroa and Mahusay Stations. A rival of the Whisper Syndicate.

Duulian Gulimyanik. (DOO-lee-un goo-lim-YAWN-ick) A prickly-tempered, accidentally-uplifted sapient species that superficially resembles the Earth myth of the griffin.

E

Eddie Sakai Chism. (sah-KYE CHIZZ-m) A friend of Charlie's, a member of the STAT Blue Team, and a cousin of Brock Rivers. Husband of Gwen. (Pronouns: he, him.)

Edie-Rachelle Morrow. (EE-dee rah-SHELL MOR-roh) A well-regarded journalist in Centerboro. (Pronouns: she, her.)

Eduardo Donovan. Partner of XK9 Victor Sam-Janet. A Detective Level One, and a member of Bari Chartered Family. (Pronouns: he, him.)

Edwina "Wina" Emshwiller. (ed-WEE-nah EM-shwil-er) An SBI Special Agent assigned to SIT Delta who specializes in forensic accounting. (Pronouns: she, her.)

Elaine Adeyeme. (ee-LANE ah-DEE-yem) The Senior Special Agent who leads the SBI's SIT Delta, and the lead investigator on the Izgubil case. Significant of Mike Santiago. (Pronouns: she, her.)

Eliana Iskander. (ell-ee-AHN-ah ISS-kin-der), The Premier of Rana Station. A member of the Commonwealth Party. (Pronouns: she, her.)

Elijah "Eli" Isaiah. A paramedic. Hildie Gallagher's usual partner on the ERT. (Pronouns: he, him.)

Elizabeth "Liz" Antonopoulos. (ann-ton-OP-o-liss) Partner of XK9 Razor Liam-Blanca, an OPD Detective Level One. As an XK9 partner-candidate, Liz was one of Pam Gómez's podmates. Currently on Emergency Family Leave.

Elle Finnian-Ella. (EL, not "EL-ee") XK9 partner of Mikhail "Misha" Flores and mate of Tuxedo Moondog-Carrie. (Pronouns: she, her.)

Elmo Smart. AKA "Thumper." A career thief currently in detention, indicted for the sabotage of the Izgubil. (Pronouns: he, him.)

Emer Bellamy. (EE-mer BELL-uh-mee) Daughter of Sorcha Moran Bellamy and Hideki Bellamy Moran, and member of the wealthy and respected Vinebrook Family. (Pronouns: she, her.)

Ensolay. A northern suburb of Solara City, Bordemer Canton, Transmondia. Home of Dr. Frederika Cho, XK9 Nell Dodger-Meena, and Sheriff Bruce Ibsen.

Ernest "Ernie" Porringer. (POUR-in-jer) A GR artist. (Pronouns: he, him.)

ERT. Emergency Rescue Team. Although this designation could be applied to any Safety Services rescue unit, it is generally used to mean the Emergency Rescue Teams that operate at the Hub to respond to emergencies in microgravity. Sometimes members of such a team are called "ERTs."

Etsu. (ET-soo) As an XK9 partner-candidate, Etsu was one of Pam Gómez's podmates during XK9 training. (Pronouns: she, her.)

Etta. – See *Rosetta "Etta" Hami*.

Eurydice Qadhi. (you-RID-ih-see KAH-dee) Judge on the Wheel Two Criminal Court. (Pronouns: she, her.)

Excelsior, LLC, a shell company traced to Emer Bellamy.

F

FA. Field Agent, a rank in the SBI. Generally, a younger, early-career agent. An FA does tasks often assigned to uniformed patrol officers in police departments.

Fadhili. (fuh-DEE-lee) A Physician's Assistant assigned to the Orangeboro Civic Center's OPD Medical Station. (Pronouns: she, her.)

Fairboro. Largest battle cruiser in the Ranan Station Defense Force fleet, named after a Borough on Wheel One. Commanded by Captain Tam Wong.

Fallon. – See *Fleet Admiral Eldridge Fallon*.

Fee. – See *Fiametta Morgan Wang*.

Feek. – See *Afiq Gonzalo*.

Felicia. (feh-LEE-sha) Charlie Morgan's ex-Amare. (Pronouns: she, her.)

Ferro. – See *Allard Ferro*.

Feyodor Bayarmaa Nowicki. (F'YO-der BUYER-mah no-WICK-ee) Husband of Tuya, father of Balchu Nowicki and Sarnai Bayarmaa. (Pronouns: he, him.)

Fiametta "Fee" Morgan Wang. (fee-ah-MET-tuh) A member of Corona Chartered Family, an Inspection Officer of the Orangeboro Port Authority office stationed at the Hub. Wife of Manny, mother of Hakan. (Pronouns: she, her.)

Fifty Founding Families. The primary human source of the funding needed to build Rana Station.

First Admiral Margaret Kumar. (MAR-guh-ret koo-MAHR)

Chief of Station Defense, the highest military rank on Rana Station. (Pronouns: she, her.)

Five-Lined Firetail. A small, mid-continent Monlandian lifeform that lives in rocky terrain, moves very rapidly, and makes a buzzing noise. They emit an odiferous gas when attacked.

Five-Ten. An infamous "underworld" part of Orangeboro: Fifth Precinct, Sub-level Ten.

Five-Tenners. People who live in the Five Ten.

Fleet Admiral Eldridge Fallon. (ELL-drij FAH-lun) A Transmondian Admiral. (Pronouns: he, him.)

Fleshy-Lips. – See *Quentin Berik*.

Founders. In general, the generation of humans and ozzirikkians who paid for, built, and first populated Rana Station ninety-plus years ago. As an honorific, it means a surviving member of the Fifty Founding (human) Families or the ozzirikkians' leadership team.

Fowler. Knife-Woman's deceased male partner, an enforcer for the Whisper Syndicate. (Pronouns: he, him.)

Francis "Frankie" Freas. (FREEZE) A Special Agent assigned to SIT Delta. (Pronouns: he, him.)

Fredericks. – See *Rory Fredericks*.

Frederika Cho. (fred-REE-kuh CHOE) Dr. Cho is the former head of the XK9 Project's XK9 Scent Reference Library. Partner to XK9 Nell Dodger-Meena, Rex's mother. Currently a fugitive. (Pronouns: she, her.)

Fujimoto. – See *Helmer Fujimoto*.

G

Galactics. Sapient beings from parts of the Alliance of the Peoples that are outside the Chayko System and the Human Diaspora.

Ganzorig. (GAHN-zoh-reeg) An elder Council Member. (Pronouns: he, him.)

Garran Crowley. (GAIR-run CROH-lee) Chief of Security for The Vinebrook.

Gaudí District. (GAH-*dee*) A popular upscale shopping district in urban Orangeboro's Sixth Precinct.

Gen 48. Generation 48, the Orangeboro Pack's generational designation by the XK9 Project's breeding program.

Georgia Volkov. (VOLE-cov) XK9 Tuxedo Moondog-Carrie's partner. A Detective Level One, and a member of Vuzvishen Family. (Pronouns: she, her.)

Gillie. – See Virgilia "Gillie" Finlay.

Girlfriend of Record. An official Ranan human relationship status that confers certain rights to Family Leave and access to some otherwise-privileged information about their Boyfriend / Girlfriend / Amorous Partner.

Glen Haven Neighborhood. A park in Orangeboro's Ninth Precinct on Starboard Hill that centers on the transit and park corridor, and extends 1km in each direction to encompass the family compounds along Terraces Seven and Eight.

Glen Haven Park. A multi-level park that runs between Terraces Seven and Eight, in Orangeboro's Ninth Precinct on Starboard Hill, adjacent to the local transit terminal station.

Glen Haven Transit Terminal Station. A transportation hub on Terrace Eight that includes commuter elevators linked to the Hub; roadway passage along Rim Eight Road and between upper and lower switchbacks (Terraces Seven to Nine); a tramway stop; and a train station on a secondary level.

Glide-Ride Limousines. A private auto-nav transport service that operates in Orangeboro.

Global Reconstruction Chamber. The small room that contains the specialized equipment used to create a Global Reconstruction. It includes a GR tank and a viewing area for a small audience.

Global Reconstruction. (GR) A technique for crafting 3-dimensional visual recreations and/or animations of crime scenes, objects, and individuals.

Gloria Huddleston Gibson. One of Charlie's same-generation cousins. Dolph and Fred's daughter, Quinn's wife, and Grant and Owen's mother. (Pronouns: she, her.)

Glorioso Family. (GLOW-ree-oh-so) The Chartered Family of Misha Flores, XK9Elle Finnian-Ella, XK9 Tuxedo Lightfoot-Floss, and others. The Family owns and operates Glorioso Brewing Company.

Glorioso Tower. The home of Glorioso Chartered Family, located on Starboard Hill Terrace Six in the Fourth Precinct on Rana Station.

Gonzalo. – See *Afiq Gonzalo*.

Gordy. (GOR-dee) A subordinate of Whisper Syndicate boss Allard Ferro. He possibly was murdered in Ranan Year 90 or 91. (Pronouns: he, him.)

Gorman. – See *Alfredo Gorman*.

Goromont Partners. A shell company traced to Emer Bellamy.

GR – See *Global Reconstruction*.

GR Artist. A person trained and certified in Global Reconstruction.

GR Chamber. – See *Global Reconstruction Chamber*.

GR Unit. The facility where Global Reconstructions are made.

Gran Annie. – See *Annie Montoya Lee*

Grandma Hestia. – See *Hestia Saha Gallagher*.

Granny Ifiok. – See *Ola Nwadike Ifiok*.

Grant Huddleston. Son of Charlie's cousin Gloria and her husband Quinn. (Pronouns: he, him.)

Great-Aunt Dolores. (duh-LOR-riss) A deceased member of Becenti Chartered Family. (Pronouns: she, her.)

Greensboro. (GREENS-burrow) One of four boroughs on Rana Station's Wheel One. The other three are Fairboro, New Hibernia, and Carnivalle.

Gregory Ordovich. (ORE-dough-vitch) Former Director, C.E.O., and Lead Geneticist of the XK9 Project of Transmondia.

Currently in detention awaiting trial on Rana Station. (Pronouns: he, him.)

Gusaujik. (goo-SAU-jeek) singular or plural. A sapient member-species in the Alliance of the Peoples. They accidentally uplifted the Duulian Gulimyanik.

Gwen Chism Sakai. (GEWN CHIZ'm sa-KY) wife of Charlie's STAT Team friend Eddie. (Pronouns: she, her.)

H

Hakan Morgan. (HOH-kan) Son of Charlie Morgan's first cousin Manuel "Manny" Wang Morgan and his wife Fiametta "Fee" Morgan Wang. (Pronouns: he, him.)

Hallie Fastolf. (HAL-lee FASS-tolf) A member of Glorioso Family and Significant of Misha Flores. (Pronouns: she, her.)

Hami. – See *Rosetta "Etta" Hami*.

Hannah Morgan Chahine. (SHY-een) Charlie's aunt, wife of Hector Chahine Morgan. Mother of Manny. A named partner in a law firm that specializes in interstellar trade. (Pronouns: she, her.)

Harta Reinhold. (HAR-tah RINE-hold) Deputy Chief of Ranan Executive Security. (Pronouns: she, her.)

Head-of-Household. An official title on Rana Station. The designated chief executive of a Chartered Family.

Healing Sleep. The deep, trancelike sleep-state into which XK9 metabolisms revert after an injury, in which healing is dramatically accelerated.

Helen Thompson. (HEL-un TOMP-sun) A reputable journalist in Centerboro. (Pronouns: she, her.)

Helmer Fujimoto. (HEL-mer fu-ji-MO-do) A veteran OPD detective recently reassigned to mentor the members of the XK9 Special Investigations Unit. Balchu Nowicki's former Field Training Officer. (Pronouns: he, him.)

Henry Sevencrows. Partner of UPO Lynne Anthony. A patrol officer assigned to the Five-Ten. (Pronouns: he, him.)

Hestia Saha Gallagher. (HESS-tee-uh SAH-ha GAL-ah-gur) Official Head of Household for Feliz Chartered Family. She also is the head of agricultural operations for Feliz Tower, and Hildie's maternal grandmother. (Pronouns: she, her.)

Hi-Y. A High-Yield Growing Environment that uses colored lighting and hydroponic growing solutions to produce plant-based foods in the shortest time and highest volume possible.

Hideki Bellamy Moran. (hee-DAY-key) A member of Orangeboro's prominent Vinebrook Family, husband of Sorcha Moran Bellamy, and father of Emer and Orla Bellamy. (Pronouns: he, him.)

Hildegaard "Hildie" ("Hils") Gallagher. (HILL-dee-gard GAL-ah-gur) Girlfriend-of-Record to Charlie Morgan. A paramedic on the Orangeboro Emergency Rescue Team at Topside Base. Daughter of Pari and Dara, Abhik's big sister. (Pronouns: she, her.)

Howardsboro. (HOW-ards-bur-row) A Borough on Rana Station's Wheel Three.

Hub. The central structure that serves as a "spine" or "axle" upon which the habitat wheels of Rana Station turn. The Hub is also the location of the space docks and some space-based manufacturing, as well as the high-security Governmental and Diplomatic Sector. It is entirely a microgravity environment.

HUD. (Neural Heads Up Display). – a function of the CAP, a neurologically linked internal perception interface that allows the user to "see" forms, vids, and other visual displays without wearable equipment.

Hunter. – See *Melynn Hunter*.

Husband. an official Ranan human relationship status that is generally assumed to be permanent. It signifies a person who is involved in a Marriage Partnership.

I

Idris. – See *Ailani Idris.*

Ijemma "Jem" Ifiok. (ah-ZHEM-uh JEM ih-FEE-ock) an adolescent member of Lang Chartered Family. Walter's cousin and Ola's granddaughter. (Pronouns: she, her.)

Ilma Wilmott. (ILL-mah WILL-mot) Chief of Ranan Executive Security. (Pronouns: she, her.)

Imre. – See *Melisende Imre.*

Institutes of Ascended Contemplation. An ozzirikkian university located on Wheel Five.

Iron Hand. One of several organized rings of pirates operating in the Chaykoan Asteroids.

Iruka Jones. (EE-ru-kah JOHnz) A detective with the Orangeboro Bureau of Missing Persons, assigned to. the Joint OPD/SBI Task Force investigating the Izgubil. (Pronouns: she, her.)

It's Morning. A morning news-talk broadcast.

Izgubil. (izz-GYOU-bill) A space barque that served as a mobile base of operations, brothel, and gambling casino for the Whisper Syndicate (a criminal organization on Rana Station) before it was "explosively deconstructed" at the Orangeboro docks.

J

Jack Evanovich. A field agent assigned to SIT Alpha. (Pronouns: he, him.)

Jeliza Cantú. (jeh-LIE-za con-TOO) A young member of Feliz Family. Daughter of Cormac and Anita-Maya. (Pronouns: she, her.)

Jenny Evans. a GR artist, acting Director of the Orangeboro GR Unit. (Pronouns: she, her.)

Jill Sandler. A Specialist Veterinarian in charge of XK9 health in Orangeboro. She owns the Sandler Clinic, a veterinary facility modified for XK9s. (Pronouns: she, her.)

Jones. – See *Iruka Jones.*

Joseph Raach. (ROCK) An SBI Tech Specialist who holds a Ph. D. in Explosives Technology from the Wheel Three Institute of Technology. (Pronouns: he, him.)

Joslyn Stark. (JOZZ-lin) Press Liaison for Chief Klein, a civilian position. (Pronouns: she, her.)

Judge Cunningham. A judicial official who presides over Safety Services Department Employee Review hearings. (Pronouns: he, him.)

K

Ka'Zikikittir Zitoktu. (ka-ZIK-ik-ee-teer zee-TOHK-too) An ozzirikkian vice premier forced to call a Section Fifteen and assume the premiership when Premier Callum was catastrophically injured in an accident and unable to serve. (Pronouns: ki, kin.)

Ka'Zikikittir. (ka-ZIK-ik-ee-teer) The Pan-Ozzirikkian word for the Ranan head of state. An elected position that may be filled by either an ozzirikkian or a human. See *Premier.*

Kalan Ministo. (KALL-un meen-EEZ-doe) A member of Ministobrila Collective who is infamous in the Asteroids for being a treacherous double-dealer. (Pronouns: he, him.)

Kali. (KAL-ee) Hildie Gallagher's calico cat. (Pronouns: she, her.)

Kendra Nakoa. (KEN-druh na-KO-uh) Chief of the Centerboro Police Department. (Pronouns: she, her.)

Kenji. (KEN-jee) A young Council Member. (Pronouns: he, him.)

Ketevan Bayuk. (KIT-uh-win BY-ook) An elder member of Vuzvishen Family. (Pronouns: she, her.)

Ki-ki-ki-ki Tiktitiki. (KEE-KEE-KEE-KEE TICK-tee-TICK-tee) A persecuted population of mutant ozzirikkians banished from their homeworld of Amethyria, who co-founded Rana Station when they joined their resources with those of a group of humans in the Chayko System about a century before the events in this book.

Ki'i'ini. (kee-EE-ee-nee) An ozzirikkian paramedic assigned to the crew of the *Zikkizti Dawn*. (Pronouns: k'ki, k'kin.)

Kianga Odigo. (k'YEN-ga OH-di-go) Head of Household for Amadi Chartered Family. Aunt by marriage of Chief Klein. (Pronouns: she, her.)

Kilgore. – See *Bryan Kilgore*.

Kirritokti Zhirikktim. (kee-ree-TOK-tee zheer-ICK-tim) An ozzirikkian medical researcher from the Institutes of Ascended Contemplation. Title: The Learned. (Pronouns: ki, kin.)

Kizzitikti Zhokittik. (KIZZ-ee-TICK-tee zhow-KIT-ick) The ozzirikkian Ranan Vice Premier (Zikikittir). Second-in-command in the Ranan Government and a member of the Ranan People's Party. (Pronouns: ki, kin.)

Klein. – See *Chief Kwame Odigo Kline*.

Knife Woman. An alleged Whisper Syndicate executioner, captured by Rex Dieter-Nell and currently in re-gen healing in a secure Orangeboro detention hospital facility. (Pronouns: she, her.)

Koanna. (koh-AH-nahn) A planet located outside the Chayko System, and the Galactic sovereignty that rules it.

Koannan Consul Primus. (KON-sool PREE-miss) A Koannan diplomatic authority who oversees multiple ambassadors.

Koannan. (koh-AH-nahn) A sapient member-species in the Alliance of the Peoples. Also, something sourced from the planet Koanna: a koannan product.

Koening. – See *Marceline Koening*.

Kurtzu. – See *Ra-Sven-shumma Kurtzu*.

Kwame Odigo Klein. (KWAH-may OH-di-go KLINE) Orangeboro Chief of Police. A member of Amadi Chartered Family. (Pronouns: he, him.)

Kwan Chukwu. – Member of a S.T.A.T. Red Team element. (Pronouns: he, him.)

L

Lacey Lee. Daughter of Caro Cranach Lee and Andy Lee Cranach. (Pronouns: she, her.)

Lalu Alvarado Saha. (LAH-loo) A member of Feliz Chartered Family; Hildie's cousin. (Pronouns: he, him.)

Lamont Niam. (la-MONT NEE-um) Assistant Station Attorney General, Rana Station Department of Justice. (Pronouns: he, him.)

Lang Family. The Chartered Family of Walter Ejiamike and XK9 Petunia Yeller-Melody.

LaRochelle/"LaRock." – See *Captain Treva LaRochelle*.

Lead Captain Octavia Sienariba. (oak-TAH-v'yuh see-en-uh-REE-buh) Leader of a Sienariba Collective-led task group of five Mahusayan battle cruiser spaceships from Sienariba, Dostigator, and Tarpasso Collectives. (Pronouns: she, her.)

Lee-André Merrick. (LEE-ahn-DRAY MEH-rick) A licensed private investigator in Centerboro. (Pronouns: he, him.)

Leeli. – See *Cecilia "Leeli" Tanaka*.

Len Stevens. (LEN STEEV-uns) A Port Authority Clerk charged with evaluating the skills of candidates to receive Class A, B, or C microgravity certifications and maintaining certification records. (Pronouns: he, him.)

LEO's Grill. A restaurant in Central Plaza that caters to law enforcement officers. It is uniquely designed with mirrors and aligned passageways, so every seat is a corner booth, no one's back is exposed, and all the sightlines are clear.

Lewis "Lew" Penny. OPD Detective recently reassigned to mentor the members of the XK9 Special Investigations Unit.

Listener. A Ranan psychologist, commissioned through the Social Services Office of the Department of the Common Good.

Liz. – See *Elizabeth "Liz" Antonopoulos*.

Loretta Triola Lee. (lo-RET-tah tree-OH-la LEE) Charlie's great-grandmother. Co-founder of Corona Chartered Family. (Pronouns: she, her.)

LSA. Lead Special Agent, a rank in the SBI. The Primary LSA (there normally are at least two) is second-in-command to the Senior Special Agent in charge.

Luis Conrad Rivera. (L'WEESE KON-rad ree-VEH-rah) Head of Household for Becenti Chartered Family. (Pronouns: he, him.)

Lynne Anthony. Partner of UPO Henry Sevencrows. A patrol officer assigned to the infamous Five-Ten. (Pronouns: she, her.)

M

Madeira Sewell. (muh-DEER-uh SOO-ul) A former leader of the Commonwealth Party (CWP), an ally of Eliana Iskander, and a retired ComCouncil Member. (Pronouns: she, her.)

Maduka "Duke" Shevchenko. (muh-DOOK-uh DOOK shev-CHEN-koh) A Detective Lieutenant with the OPD Verification and Interdiction of Corruption and Exploitation (VICE) UNIT. (Pronouns: he, him.)

Maeve Kimbrough Bellamy. (MAYVE KIM-broo BELL-uh-mee) Matriarch of the Vinebrook Family, one of Rana Station's original Fifty Founding Families. Wife of Basil. (Pronouns: she, her.)

Mahusay Station. (MAH-hoo-say) The second of the six space-based habitat megastructures in the Chayko System, and the sovereign government that controls it.

Mahusay Technology Institute. A technical college on Mahusay Station.

Mahusayan. (mah-hoo-SAY-un). People from Mahusay Station.

Máiréad Callahan Bellamy. (MAH-ree-id KALL-a-han BELL-uh-mee) Deceased member of the Vinebrook Family. Mother of Sorcha Moran Bellamy, daughter of Maeve Kimbrough Bellamy. (Pronouns: she, her.)

Malik Jepson. (mah-LEEK JEP-sun) a Trans-Hub Train attendant on the Graveyard Watch, with a Significant named Mona. (Pronouns: he, him.)

Mamoor Volkov Ismeryatochno. (mah-MOOR VOL-kov iz-mer-yuh-TOCK-no) An elder member of Vuzvishen Family. Georgia Volkov's grandfather ("apodeddi"). (Pronouns: he, him.)

Manuel "Manny" Wang Morgan. Charlie's first cousin. Hector and Hannah's son. A sous chef. Married to Fiametta "Fee" Morgan Wang. Father of Hakan. (Pronouns: he, him.)

Marceline "Marcy" Koening. (mahr-suh-LEEN MAR-see CONE-ing) Member of a S.T.A.T. Red Team element. (Pronouns: she, her.)

Maria "Mimi" Morgan Lee. Charlie's mother. Wife of Theodore "Ted" Lee Morgan. (Pronouns: she, her.)

Marisol Patel. (MAIR-i-zol pa-TELL) An OPD detective lieutenant. (Pronouns: she, her.)

Market Garden Neighborhood. A mixed commercial and residential district in urban Fifth Precinct Orangeboro.

Marriage Partnership. A formal alliance of two or more Chartered Families on Rana Station, through a domestic union of one or more members of each. The status is generally assumed to be permanent, and entered into with the intent to apply for a license to rear children.

Martin. A MERS-V driver on the ERT. Assigned to the Triumph. (Pronouns: he, him.)

Marya Seaton. A UPO assigned to Ninth Precinct. (Pronouns: she, her.)

Master Mix. The nutritionally balanced, high-performance dog kibble designed by the XK9 Project for working XK9s.

Mayor Idris. – See Ailani Idris.

Mayor Rao. The Mayor of Centerboro. (Pronouns: he, him.)

Medal of Valor. Rana Station's highest recognition of honor for courage.

Melisende Imre. (MEL-lis-end EM-ray) CFO, Associate Head Geneticist, and XK9 Breeding Coordinator for the XK9 Project in Transmondia. (Pronouns: she, her.)

Melissa "Missy" Cranston. Director of the Orangeboro GR Unit. Secretary Oma Pandra's sister. (Pronouns: she, her.)

Melynn Hunter. (meh-LYN HUN-tur) a Special Agent assigned to SIT Delta. (Pronouns: she, her.)

MERS-V. Multipurpose Emergency Response Space-Vehicle. A small, maneuverable space-based vehicle designed to retrieve victims who have been "spaced" (ejected into the vacuum of space, usually by accident), where they have only 90 seconds to be rescued alive.

Mid-Levels. An educational level on Rana Station that is equivalent to Middle School. The evaluation for graduation to Upper Levels is referred to as "taking one's Mid-Levels."

Miguel Carrington Williams. (mee-GEL CARE-ing-tun WILL-yums) A member of Becenti Chartered Family. Son of Chase and Anya, husband of Soledad. (Pronouns: he, him.)

Mike Santiago. The Senior Special Agent who leads the SBI's SIT Alpha, and the Station's leading law enforcement expert on the Whisper Syndicate. Significant of SSA Elaine Adeyeme. (Pronouns: he, him.)

Mikhail "Misha" Flores. (MEE-khah-yool "MEE-shah" FLO-race) XK9 Elle Finnian-Ella's partner. A Detective Level One, a member of Glorioso Family, and Significant of Hallie Fastolf. (Pronouns: he, him.)

Ministo Lulak. (mean-EEZ-doe LOO-lock) A Mahusayan mining spacecraft.

Ministobrila Collective. (meen-EEZ-doe-bree-lah) The Mahusayan collective unit that owns the Ministo Lulak.

Misha. – See *Mikhail "Misha" Flores*.

Missy. – See *Melissa Cranston*.

Monlandia. (mon-LAN-dee-ah) The largest continent on Planet Chayko.

Monteverde Borough. (mon-tay-VAIR-day bur-row) One of four Boroughs on Rana Station's Wheel Two. The other three are Petranova, Pueblo, and Orangeboro.

Monteverde University. (mon-tay-VAIR-day) An institute of higher learning associated with Green Mountain University in Monteverde Borough's First Precinct.

Montreaux. – See *Commodore Clarimonde Alvaro Montreaux.*

Moran Platinum. An investment firm founded by Hideki Bellamy Moran.

Moran. – See *Hideki Bellamy Moran.*

Morgan. – See *Charles "Charlie" Morgan.*

Morgue Annex. A segregated morgue facility within the secured perimeter of the S-3-9 Investigative Center, created to analyze and contain the remains of victims of the Izgubil incident until they can be released to their families.

MPs. Military Police Officers.

Ms. Platz. (PLATS) A Mid-Levels teacher of Physical Health and Lifestyles (somewhat parallel to a middle-school physical education and health teacher) who tried to recruit Pamela Gómez for a student quiddo team about 14 Ranan years ago. (Pronouns: she, her.)

MUPATS. Multi-Passenger Transit Shuttle. A vehicle used to transport personnel and equipment in the microgravity inside the Hub.

Murder Brothers. Two men (siblings) who perpetrated quite a crime spree on the night of the *Izubil* dock breach, including the murders of two women and initiating the dock breach itself. They were later identified by the XK9 Scent Reference Library as Rufus and Neil Dolan.

N

National Leadership Council. A high-level group of elected or affirmed political leaders on Rana Station that advises the Premier/Ka'Zikikittir. There is one National Leadership Council Member to represent each sapient species of which there is a significant population on the Station.

Neil Dolan. An indicted criminal suspect held without bail for the Orangeboro dock breach of the Izgubil and the murder of two unidentified women; the younger "Murder Brother." (Pronouns: he, him.)

Nell Dodger-Meena. Rex's mother. Partnered with Dr. Frederika Cho. Together, they directed the XK9 Scent Reference Lab. Currently a fugitive. (Pronouns: she, her.)

Nervous Guy. One of the suspects in the "Centerboro bombs" case. (Pronouns: he, him.)

Nesbit Zeman. (NEZ-bit ZEE-mun) A member of the national Ranan Commercial Council. (Pronouns: he, him.)

Nez. – See *Nesbit Zeman*.

Niam. – See *Lamont Niam*.

Nicole Oyunbileg. (oh-YOON-bill-egg) XK9 Scout Sam-Shana's partner. A Detective Level One. (Pronouns: she, her.)

Nolan Virendra. (vir-END-rah) A disgraced former Admiral in the SDF. (Pronouns: he, him.)

Norchellic Confederation. (nor-CHELL-ic) A country on the eastern end of Monlandia, the largest landform on Planet Chayko.

Norchellic Frontier. The westernmost sector of the Norchellic Confederation, one of four sovereignties on the Chaykoan continent of Monlandia. A region known for mineral wealth along its rift valley and a war of ethnic cleansing perpetrated by raiders from Uladh Nua.

Nunzio. – See *Ryder Nunzio*.

O

O'Boyle, Kieran, An indicted detainee alleged to have assisted in the sabotage of the Izgubil, identified via DNA match because he is a Ranan Citizen. Son of Turlach O'Boyle. (Pronouns: he, him.)

O'Boyle, Turlach, Ostra Import Export Emporium manager, a known Whisper operative in the Five-Ten. Father of Kieran O'Boyle, who calls him "Turd." (Pronouns: he, him.)

Observation Commission. An official delegation dispatched by the Alliance of the Peoples to evaluate the sapience of a species that has been nominated for official classification as sapient.

Odi, Endesha. (enn-DESH-ah OH-dee) A young attorney with the prestigious Harris and Odi Law Firm (not the named partner). Hildie Gallagher is her client. (Pronouns: she, her.)

Ogun Group. (oh-GUN) An asteroid cluster rich in rare earths, located in a sector of the Chaykoan Asteroids claimed and mined by Mahusayan collectives.

Ola Nwadike Ifiok. (oh-LA nwah-DEE-kay ih-FEE-ock) AKA "Granny Ifiok," an elder member of Lang Chartered Family. Walter Ejiamike's maternal grandmother. (Pronouns: she, her.)

Olena Ismeryatochno Volkov. (oh-LEE-nuh iz-mer-yuh-TOCK-no VOL-kov) An elder member of Vuzvishen Family. Georgia Volkov's grandmother, and an avid fan of the actor Dolph Sanger. (Pronouns: she, her.)

Oma Peralta Pandra. (OH-ma per-ALL-ta PAN-drah) Secretary of Public Safety. Missy Cranston's brother. (Pronouns: he, him.)

Onyx. (ON-eecks) A deceased former Head of Household for Becenti Chartered Family. (Pronouns: he, him.)

OPD Central HQ. The administrative headquarters of the Orangeboro Police Department.

OPD. Orangeboro Police Department.

Orangeboro Central Plaza. The heart of Orangeboro's urban core.

Orangeboro Civic Center. The building complex in Central Plaza that houses most Borough governmental departments and headquarters for their service administrations, and the Civic Center Auditorium.

Orangeboro Entertainment District. The seven-level entertainment facility built onto a section of the hull of the 15-km "spoke" through which transit elevators move cargo between Orangeboro's quarter of Wheel Two and the Hub. Gravity is lowest in the upper "prisms" (levels), but noticeably not full 1-G in any of them. Every Borough has such an Entertainment District.

Orangeboro Global Reconstruction Unit. A department of the Orangeboro Safety Services Department that creates GRs for the police department, the Borough Attorney's office, and the Borough Public Defender's office. It also provides highly secure official conference interfaces for all Borough departments.

Orangeboro Glory Amber Ale. A popular drink manufactured by Glorioso Brewing, an Orangeboro microbrewery owned and operated by members of Glorioso Family.

Orangeboro Grand Central Terminal. The main transit hub for the Borough of Orangeboro, located in Central Plaza near the Orangeboro Civic Center in Precinct Five.

Orangeboro Medical Center. The largest hospital in Orangeboro.

Orangeboro Safety Services Department. A cabinet-level bureau of the Borough Government. It includes Police, Fire, and Emergency Medical Services.

Orangeboro. One of four Boroughs on Rana Station's Wheel Two. The other three are Petranova, Pueblo, and Monteverde.

Ordovich. (ORE-dough-vitch). See *Gregory Ordovich*.

Orla Bellamy. (ORE-lah BELL-uh-mee) A member of the Vinebrook Chartered Family. Sister of Emer, daughter of Hideki and Sorcha. (Pronouns: she, her.)

Oroplania. (ore-oh-PLAY-nee-ah) A mid-sized country on the southeastern quadrant of Monlandia, the largest landform on Planet Chayko.

Osmond "Oz" Meredith. A Squad Commander of MERS-V drivers on the ERT, assigned to the Triumph. One of Hildie Gallagher's teammates. (Pronouns: he, him.)

Ostra Import-Export Emporium. (OH-straw) A storefront and shell corporation in the Five-Ten used by the Whisper Syndicate and managed by Turlach O'Boyle.

Owen Huddleston. Son of Charlie's cousin Gloria and her husband Quinn. (Pronouns: he, him.)

Oz. – See *Osmond "Oz" Meredith*.

Ozzirikkians. (oz-zi-RICK-ee-uns) A non-terrestrial sapient species with a minority population that lives in Ranan Wheels Five and Six. Ranan ozzirikkians have all the same rights as other citizen-sapient beings on Rana Station.

P

PA. Public address system.

Pabiyan Family. (PAY-b'yun) A large and prosperous Chartered Family based in Orangeboro Precinct Ten, many of whom are observant Wiccans. Owners of Pabiyan Distillery and Pabiyan Carnerie.

Packmate. An accepted member of an XK9 Pack, although not necessarily an XK9.

Palmdale Club. The name of a Ranan group of Commonwealth Party members who desire closer ties with Transmondia.

Palmdale District. A part of Solara City where many rich and influential people live.

Pamela "Pam" Gómez. XK9 Shady Jacob-Belle's partner. A Detective Level One. Balchu Nowicki's Amare. (Learn more of her background in The Other Side of Fear, of which she's the protagonist.) (Pronouns: she, her.)

Pandra. – See *Oma Peralta Pandra*.

Pari Gallagher Bannerjee. (PA-ree GAL-ah-gur BAN-er-jee) A member of Feliz Chartered Family. Hildie and Abi's father. Husband of Dara. (Pronouns: he, him.)

Pat Cornwell. An SBI Tech Specialist in signals intel attached to SIT Alpha. Nephew of SDF Commodore Farooq Cornwell. (Pronouns: he, him.)

Patel. – See *Marisol Patel*.

Pedro "Gran Pepe" Lee Montoya. (PAY-dro "gran PAY-pay" mon-TO-yah). Charlie's maternal grandfather. Husband of Annie Montoya Lee, son-in-law of Loretta, father of Mimi and

Serafina. Co-founder of Corona Chartered Family. (Pronouns: he, him.)

Pee Wee Pederson. XK9 Project dog wrangler. (Pronouns: he, him.)

Penny. – See *Lewis "Lew" Penny*.

Pepe. – See *Pedro "Gran Pepe" Lee Montoya*.

Perri. – See *Adelaide Perri*.

Petranova Borough. (pet-rah-NO-vah bur-row) One of four Boroughs on Rana Station's Wheel Two. The other three are Orangeboro, Pueblo, and Monteverde.

Petunia Yeller-Melody. XK9 partner of Walter Ejiamike, an OPD Detective Level One, and a member of Lang Chartered Family. (Pronouns: she, her.)

Peynirci. – See *Rona Peynirci*.

Pinakamaroa Station. (PEE-na-kah-mah-*row*-uh) The third of the six space-based habitat megastructures in the Chayko System, and the sovereign government that controls it.

Pinakamaroans. (PEE-na-kah-mah-*row*-uns) People from Pinakamaroa Station.

Pink Woman. An alert and perceptive server at The Arts of Tea shop inside the State Pavilion Hotel. (Pronouns: she, her.)

Popular Democracy Party. (PDP) one of the four major Ranan political parties. Sacha Guzmán's party.

Popular Growth Forum. (PGF). A political party in Transmondia.

Port Authority. The Hub-based Customs and Immigration Unit of a Ranan Wheel, mutually staffed by law enforcement officers of the Wheel's four Boroughs and coordinated through the Ranan Department of State.

Precinct. A designated geographical subsection of a Ranan Borough. There are ten Precincts in every Borough.

Premier Callum. (KAL-um) A human Ranan premier who died in office during an earlier period in Ranan history. (Pronouns: he, him.)

Premier. The Ranan head of state. An elected position that may be filled by either a human or an ozzirikkian. See *Ka'Zikikittir*.

Primerans. (pree-MEHR-uns) People from Primero Station.

Primero Station. (pree-MEH-roh) The first of the six space-based habitat megastructures in the Chayko System, and the sovereign government that controls it.

Providence-Brightstar Family. (PROV-uh-dense BRITE-star) The Chartered Family to which Mike Santiago and Elaine Adeyeme belong, located in Monteverde Borough.

Pruneface. Shady's nickname for Emer Bellamy's lead defense attorney. (Pronouns: he, him.)

Pryce. – See *Ari Pryce*.

PTV. Personnel Transport Vehicle. A large 1-G-based government agency vehicle like a bus, designed primarily to transport people and their gear.

Pueblo Borough. (PWEHB-low bur-row) One of four Boroughs on Rana Station's Wheel Two. The other three are Orangeboro, Petranova, and Monteverde.

Puppy Farm One. The XK9 Project's training and primary breeding and whelping center, located in Bordemer Canton, not far from Solara City, in Transmondia, on Planet Chayko.

Purdy. – See *Wayne Purdy*.

Q

QUAERO-3426. (KWER-oh) A Farricainan cyberbeing who is an expert on the population, and especially the human politicians, who inhabit Centerboro. (Pronouns: ne, nem.)

Quentin Berik. (KWEN-tin BARE-ick). A Member of the Ranan Residential Council who also is a member of the Commonwealth Party (CWP) and the Palmdale Club. (Pronouns: he, him.)

Quiddo. A sport played in microgravity on maneuverable microgravity sleds.

Quinn Gibson Huddleston. (KWIN GIB-sun HUD-dle-stun)

Husband of Charlie's cousin Gloria Huddleston Gibson and father of Grant and Owen Huddleston. (Pronouns: he, him.)

Quinoa. (KEEN-wah) An annual herb cultivated for its starchy, edible seeds. Native to the Andes region on Heritage Earth.

R

Ra-Sven-shumma Kurtzu. (rah-SVEN-shum-uh KURT-zoo) An appscaten academic who studies and teaches about xenosociology. He goes by *Kurtzu* to Standard-speaking friends. (Pronouns in Standard: he, him.)

Rachard Faysal. (rah-SHARD FIE-sul) A judge assigned to the Orangeboro Borough Court. Title: The Honorable. (Pronouns: he, him.)

Radivan. (RAH-doe-wan) An elder member of Vuzvishen Family. (Pronouns: he, him.)

Raghnall Wall. (RAD-nal) An indicted detainee alleged to have assisted in the sabotage of the *Izgubil*. A Saoirse Front member. (Pronouns: he, him.)

Ralph Lee Gibson. Charlie's uncle. Husband of Serafina Gibson Lee. A Certified Agricultural Technician, he is the head of agricultural operations for Corona Tower. (Pronouns: he, him.)

Ramón. (rah-MOAN) A MERS-V driver on the ERT. Assigned to the *Triumph*. (Pronouns: he, him.)

Rana Habitat Space Station. (RAH-nah) One of six space-based megastructures in the Chayko System, and the sovereign government that controls it. The only station in the system that is co-ruled by humans and ozzirikkians.

Ranan Commercial Council. A national-level legislative body that represents business interests on-Station. It has half the number of representatives as the Residential Council.

Ranan Executive Security. (RES) A Ranan law enforcement agency charged with protecting high government officials and also their confidential and personal information from attack or other harms. They are roughly parallel to the United States Secret Service, but with no authority regarding counterfeiting.

Ranan Governmental and Diplomatic Sector. A high-security section of the Ranan Hub that extends the entire distance between Wheels Four (where the national capitol for humans is located in Centerboro) and Five, (where the national capitol for ozzirikkians is located in Zhokikim Timi). It contains consular offices for Galactic diplomats, secured locations for governmental officials, the Combined Councils Chamber, a high-security Station Defense Force base, secured shuttles and trains, a discrete loop of the Trans-Hub Train system, and other secured locations.

Ranan Residential Council. A national-level legislative body that represents private citizens' and Chartered Families' interests on-Station. It has twice the number of representatives as the Commercial Council.

Randy. A human paramedic assigned to the crew of the Zikkizti Dawn. (Pronouns: he, him.)

Raphael "Rafe" Santiago. (rah-fay-EL RAYF san-tee-AH-go) A famous Ranan artist, who also is Mike Santiago's brother. (Pronouns: he, him.)

Raya. (RAH-yah) An elder member of Becenti Chartered Family. Widow of Onyx. (Pronouns: she, her.)

Razor Liam-Blanca. XK9 partner of Liz Antonopoulos, an OPD Detective Level One. Injured by a neurotoxin dart, Razor is currently on Health Leave in rehab at the Sandler Clinic. (Pronouns: he, him.)

Re-gen. (REE-jen) Medical Regeneration, a therapeutic technique for re-growing or fortifying the healing process after tissue damage or catastrophic injury, including growing new organs or limbs.

Realiciné. (ray-AL-ee-see-*nay*) An immersive, multi-sensory-input cinema-arts entertainment experience.

Realta. An SDF battle cruiser spaceship named after a Borough on Wheel Seven.

Regan Ireland. (REE-gun) An Assistant Borough Attorney from the Prosecutors Office. (Pronouns: she, her.)

Reika Bannerman. (RAY-kuh) One of the two Residential Council Members who represent Orangeboro on the national level. (Pronouns: she, her.)

RES – See *Ranan Executive Security*.

ResCouncil. Short for *Ranan Residential Council*.

Reserve Agent. A local police officer deputized to work for the Station Bureau of Investigation.

Rex Dieter-Nell. Pack Leader of the Orangeboro Pack. XK9 partner of Charlie Morgan, and XK9 Shady Jacob-Belle's mate. (Pronouns: he, him.)

Rim Road. The road that runs along the outer edge of a Ranan Terrace. Each rim road is designated by the number of its terrace: Rim Eight Road, Rim Five Road, etc. The designation of "Portside" or "Starboard" may be added for clarity.

Rim-Runner. An express train that uses tracks located where the hilltops inside a habitat wheel meet the sky windows. It only stops once in each Borough, at a location parallel to that Borough's governmental and urban center. The Rim-Runner on Port Hill runs spinward. The Rim-Runner on Starboard Hill runs leeward.

Robert "Bob" Wells. A UPO assigned to Ninth Precinct. (Pronouns: he, him.)

Robert Walters. (ROB-urt WALL-turs) A well-regarded journalist in Centerboro. (Pronouns: he, him.)

Rona Peynirci. (ROW-nah pa-NEAR-see) Ninth Precinct representative on Orangeboro's Borough Council (Pronouns: she, her.)

Rooq. – See *Commodore Farooq "Rooq" Tomoko Cornwell*.

Rory Fredericks. (roar-EE FRED-ricks) A former graduate student of Dr. SCISCO, whose doctoral project appears to have formed the basis for the explosives that destroyed the Izgubil. He has been missing since Ranan Year 93. Former Amare of Emer Bellamy. (Pronouns: he, him.)

Rose Lavigne. (LA-veen) Amare of Sarnai Bayarmaa. (Pronouns: she, her.)

Rosetta "Etta" Hami. (ro ZET-tuh ET-tuh HOM-ee) Counter-Terrorism Coordinator for the Centerboro Police Department. (Pronouns: she, her.)

Rowan Glenn. (ROE-un GLEN) Berwyn Yael's sister, a member of Pabiyan Chartered Family. (Pronouns: she, her.)

Ruby Prism. One of the lower-gravity sections of the Orangeboro Entertainment District, located second-closest to the Hub.

Rufus Dolan. (ROO-fuss DOE-lun) An indicted criminal suspect held without bail for the Orangeboro dock breach of the Izgubil and the murder of two unidentified women; the elder "Murder Brother." (Pronouns: he, him.)

Russell Tyjani. (RUS-sell tie-JON-nee) Head Tech in an OPD Crime Scene Unit certified for microgravity work. A former XK9 partner-candidate. (Pronouns: he, him.)

Ryder Nunzio. (RYE-dur NOON-zee-oh) The Transmondian Ambassador to Rana Station. (Pronouns: he, him.)

S

S-3-9. Also **Central S-3-9**. Sub-Level Three, Section Nine, a secured location underneath OPD Central HQ.

S-Poly. – See *Station Polytechnic University*.

SA. Special Agent, a rank in the SBI.

Sacha Guzmán. (SAH-chah gooz-MAHN) Vice-Premier, the second-in-command human in the Ranan Government, and a member of the Popular Democracy Party (Pronouns: he, him.)

Salvador Ayers Santiago. (SAL-vuh-door AYE-urz sant-YA-go) Head of Household for Providence-Brightstar Chartered Family. Father of Mike and Rafe. (Pronouns: he, him.)

Sandler Clinic. The medical institution in the Central Plaza Neighborhood of Orangeboro that specializes in XK9 medicine.

Sandler, Dr. Jill, DVM. A Specialist Veterinarian in charge of

XK9 health in Orangeboro. She owns the Sandler Clinic, a veterinary facility modified for XK9s. (Pronouns: she, her.)

Saoirse blades. (SEER-sha) Tough, young fighters who belong to the criminal Ullach group called the Saoirse Front. They are renowned and feared for their knife-fighting prowess. (can be any gender.)

Saoirse Front. (SEER-sha) A violent criminal group from Uladh Nua, with ties to the Whisper Syndicate. Members often wear distinctive, Celtic-knot tattoos on their arms to proclaim their affiliation.

Sarabande "Sara" Cutler. (SAIR-un-band CUT-lur) Secondary Lead Special Agent of Mike Santiago's SIT Alpha. (Pronouns: she, her.)

Sarnai "Nani" Bayarmaa. (SAR-nah NAH-nee BUYER-mah) Balchu Nowicki's sister, daughter of Tuya and Feyodor, and Amare of Rose Lavigne. (Pronouns: she, her.)

SBI Gallantry Star. An internal SBI recognition for agents who demonstrate extraordinarily courageous service in the face of danger.

SBI National Headquarters Building. The primary home of the "human side" of the Station Bureau of Investigation, located in the heart of urban Centerboro on Wheel Four.

SBI. – See *Station Bureau of Investigation*.

SCISCO 3750. (SHEES-koh) A Farricainan cyberbeing who is a professor of explosives technology at Station Polytechnic University. (Pronouns: ne, nem.)

Scout Sam-Shana. XK9 partner of Nicole Oyunbileg, and an OPD Detective Level One. XK9 Victor Sam-Janet's half-brother. (Pronouns: he, him.)

SDF – See *Station Defense Force*.

Seaton. – See *Marya Seaton*.

Sebastian Zupan. One of the two Residential Council Members who represent Orangeboro on the national level. (Pronouns: he, him.)

Secretary Pandra. – See *Oma Peralta Pandra*.

Senior Special Agent. A rank in the SBI. Senior Special Agents are the commanding officers of the Bureau's Special Investigative units, and of Borough or Timi'i offices.

Serafina Gibson Lee. (SAIR-uh-*fee*-nuh) Charlie's aunt, Mimi's sister, Ralph's wife, mother of Germaine and Marilyn. (Pronouns: she, her.)

Sevencrows. – See *Henry Sevencrows*.

Sgt. Gorman. – See *Alfredo Gorman*.

Sgt. Koro. – See *Arabella Koro*.

Shady Jacob-Belle. Assistant Pack Leader of the Orangeboro Pack. XK9 partner of Pamela Gómez. XK9 Rex Dieter-Nell's mate, and a member of Corona Chartered Family. (Pronouns: she, her.)

Shalidar, Inc., a shell company traced to Emer Bellamy.

Shawnee Kramer. Second LSA of SIT Delta. She is nominally third-in command to Adeyeme and Shimon, but normally functions as Shimon's equal. (Pronouns: she, her.)

Sheriff Ibsen. – See *Bruce Ibsen*.

Shiva "Shiv" Shimon. (SHEE-va "SHEEV" shee-MOAN) Senior LSA of SIT Delta. He is second-in-command to SSA Adeyeme. (Pronouns: he, him.)

Shuri. (SHU-ree) As an XK9 partner-candidate, she was one of Pamela Gómez's podmates during XK9 training. (Pronouns: she, her.)

Sienariba Collective. (see-*en*-uh-REE-buh) A Mahusayan collective that provides high-level security services to mining collectives.

Significant. A Domestic Partner on Rana Station. Domestic Partnerships are more legally binding than an Amare relationship.

Singkori Station. (sing-KORE-ee) The fifth of the six space-based habitat megastructures in the Chayko System, and the sovereign government that controls it.

Sionainn. (shon-INN) A sub-level area in Howardsboro, similar in type to the Five-Ten.

Sir. The only known name for a wanted suspect in the *Izgubil* case.

Sirius Valley. (SEAR-ee-us) The land on either side of the Sirius River, the waterway that runs in an endless circle down the middle of Rana Station's Wheel Two.

SIT. Special Investigations Team, an elite investigative unit of the SBI.

Situation Chamber. A top-secret executive facility inside the Ranan SDF Wheel Four Base, or its linked twin facility at the Wheel Five Base, designed to function as a strategic communications and decision-making center during times of national crisis.

Smart. – See *Elmo Smart*.

Smita Rostov. (SMEE-tah) Significant of Abhik "Abi" Bannerjee. She and Abi share an apartment in Feliz Tower with Abi's older sister Hildie. (Pronouns: she, her.)

Solara City. (soh-LAH-rah) The capitol city of Transmondia.

Soldering-Smoke Woman. Nickname for one of the suspects in the "Centerboro bombs" case. (Pronouns: she, her.)

Somchai Saidi. (SOM-chye SY-dee) An attorney employed by the Orangeboro Safety Services Employees Union. Hildie Gallagher is his client. (Pronouns: he, him.)

Sophie Lee. Daughter of Caro Cranach Lee and Andy Lee Cranach. (Pronouns: she, her.)

Sorcha Moran Bellamy. (SOR-ka) A member of Vinebrook Family. The Founders' granddaughter, the wife of Hideki Bellamy Moran, and the mother of Orla and Emer. (Pronouns: she, her.)

Sound Tech Samuels. An OPD sound technician assigned to the Detention Unit. (Pronouns: he, him.)

Spinward 32. An experimental rice paddy for Feliz Family to use for testing new varietals.

Spouse. an official Ranan human relationship status that is generally assumed to be permanent. It signifies a person who is involved in a Marriage Partnership.

SSA. – See *Senior Special Agent*.

Staff Well-Being Flag. (SWB) A confidential personnel nota-
tion that recommends adjustments to mitigate a dangerous
staffing assignment.

Starboard Hill. All terraces and levels above the river on the
starboard side of a Wheel.

STAT Team. Special Tools and Techniques Team, a Safety
Services Department unit that includes specialists in hostage
negotiation, bomb disposal, rescue and recovery, and high-risk
tactical operations. Divided into STAT Red and Blue Teams.

State Pavilion Hotel. A large, high-end hotel in central
Centerboro, not far from the Human Capitol of Rana Station on
Wheel Four.

Station Bureau of Investigation. (SBI) The national-level law
enforcement agency on Rana Station.

Station Defense Force. (SDF) The Ranan Military.

Station Net. The electronic communications and information
system on Rana Station.

Station Polytechnic University. A human-run university of
technology in Orangeboro on Wheel Two. See also *S-Poly.*

SWB. – See *Staff Well-Being Flag.*

T

Takhiachono Marines of Primero. (tack-hee-ah-CHO-no; pree-
MEH-roh) the most celebrated military cadre in the Human
Diaspora, reputed to be the toughest human fighting unit in
history.

Tarpasso Collective. (tahr-PAH-so) A Mahusayan collective
that provides high-level security services to mining collectives.

Tech Specialist. A rating in the SBI or SDF. An expert in a
particular technical specialty, such as explosives or signals technology. See also TS.

The Arm of the Law. A realiciné show about fictional police
officers.

The Fifty Founding Families. A group of wealthy humans

who committed their entire, massive personal fortunes to help finance the construction of Rana Station about a century before the events in this book.

The Four Amigos. A group of friends who are all OPD officers, and who all earned XK9 partner-candidate status. In addition to XK9 Cinnamon's partner Berwyn Yael, their names are Tim, Terry, and Ben. Readers may remember them from *The Other Side of Fear*. (Pronouns: he, him.)

The Grim Scalpel. Nickname for a Whisper Syndicate executioner at large on Rana Station. (Pronouns: he, him.)

The Kerry and Derika Show. A news-talk broadcast.

The Learned. (The LUR-ned) An ozzirikkian title parallel to the human title "Professor."

The Official Record. A livestream broadcast that runs whenever business is being enacted in the Combined Councils Chamber.

The Orangeboro Pack. As a group, all ten XK9s (large, intelligent, genetically engineered dogs) in the Orangeboro Police Department and their humans.

The Pilot. A mysterious individual referenced in a cryptic poem received by Mahusayan Traffic Control immediately prior to the destruction of the Ministo Lulak.

The Rampart. The flagship of the Transmondian space fleet.

Theodore "Ted" Lee Morgan. Charlie and Caro's father and husband of Maria "Mimi" Morgan Lee. (Pronouns: he, him.)

Theresa Socorro. (tay-RAY-sa so-CORR-oh) A paramedic on the ERT, assigned to the Triumph. Hildie Gallagher's friend. (Pronouns: she, her.)

Thriff-Tee Safety Store. A retail storage facility on the Sixth Level of Precinct Six in Orangeboro, managed by Pamela Gómez's mother.

Thumper. – See *Elmo Smart*.

Tiktitiokim. (TEEK-tee-tee-*oh*-kimAn SDF battle cruiser spaceship named after a Timi on Wheel Five.

Till. – See *Atilla Usher*.

Timi. (tih-MEE) The ozzirikkian equivalent to a Borough. (Plural: timi'i.)

TIS. Transmondian Intelligence Service.

Tonquin Base. (TON-queen) A mining base in the Ogun Group of the Mahusayan Asteroids.

Toro Enclave. (TORE-oh) One of the six sectors in the underground Five-Ten District in Orangeboro.

Town Cars On Call. A private auto-nav transport service that operates in Orangeboro. Corona Family is among their regular clients.

Trade Compact. A Chayko System trade agreement to which Rana Station and the Transmondian Republic are both signatories.

Transmondia. (trans-MON-dee-ah) Formally, The Republic of Transmondia. The most powerful national sovereignty in the Chayko System, based in the southwestern and central regions of Monlandia, largest continent on Planet Chayko.

Transmondian High Council. A top-level governing body in the Transmondian Government.

Transmondian Pterolizard. (trans-MON-dee-un TARE-oh-liz-ard) The largest avian species on Monlandia.

Triumph. A rescue runner (small space vehicle) operated by the Orangeboro Emergency Rescue Team at the Wheel Two Hub.

TS. Tech Specialist, a rank in the SBI or SDF. An expert in a particular technical specialty, such as explosives or signals technology.

Turd. – See *Turlach O'Boyle.*

Tuxedo "Tux" Moondog-Carrie. XK9 partner of Georgia Volkov and an OPD Detective Level One. Mate of Elle Finnian-Ella, and a member of Glorioso Chartered Family. An explosives expert. (Pronouns: he, him.)

Tuya Nowicki Bayarmaa. (TOO-yuh no-WICK-ee BUYER-mah) Balchu's mother. (Pronouns: she/her.)

Twardy Enclave. (t'VAR-dee) One of the six sectors in the underground Five-Ten District in Orangeboro.

Tyra Herzog. (TIE-ruh HER-zog) The Commercial Councilmember who represents Orangeboro on the national level. (Pronouns: she, her.)

U

Uladh Nua. (ULL-ud NYOU-ah) A country in the northwestern quadrant of Monlandia.

Ullach. (ULL-uck) From Uladh Nua.

Uncle Dolph. – See *Dolph Gibson Sanger*.

Unsub. Law enforcement slang for "unknown subject."

UPO Seaton. – See *Marya Seaton*.

UPO Wells. – See *Robert "Bob" Wells*.

UPO. Uniformed Police Officer, a civilian police rank.

Upper-Levels. An educational level on Rana Station that is equivalent to High School. The evaluation for graduation to Upper Levels is referred to as "taking one's Upper-Levels."

V

Valda Aylward. (VAL-duh ALE-ward) Sergeant, a squad leader on OPD STAT Red Team. (Pronouns: she, her.)

Veda. (VEE-da) A member of Hildie's ERT crew, pilot of the Triumph. (Pronouns: she, her.)

Verification and Interdiction of Corruption and Exploitation Unit (VICE). An Orangeboro Police Unit Tasked with following up anomalies flagged by Inspections, Customs, and other agencies or individuals that report unexplained irregularities, fraud, or corruption. Balchu Nowicki's assigned unit.

Victor Sam-Janet. XK9 partner of Eduardo Donovan, and an OPD Detective Level One. Half-brother of Scout Sam-Shana. A Member of Bari Chartered Family. (Pronouns: he, him.)

Vicurrians. (vie-KUR-ree-uns) A sapient member-species in the Alliance of the Peoples.

Vincent "Vince" Bellini. (VIN-sent VINSE bell-LEE-nee) Personal secretary of Vice Premier Guzmán. (Pronouns: he, him.)

Vinebrook Family. One of the Fifty Founding Families. A wealthy Chartered Family in Orangeboro.

Virendra. – See *Nolan Virendra*.

Vista Heights Transit Terminal Station. A transportation hub on Terrace Five that includes commuter elevators linked to the Hub; roadway passage along Rim Eight Road and between upper and lower switchbacks (Terraces Four to Six); a tramway stop; and a train station on a secondary level.

Vorriten. (VOR-i-ten) A large, furless predatory life form from the homeworld of appscatens that somewhat resembles a dog.

Vuzvishen Family. (WOOS-wi-shen) Georgia Volkov's Chartered Family of origin, located in Monteverde Borough.

W

Walter Ejiamike. (edge-EE-a-meek) XK9 Petunia Yeller-Melody's partner. A Detective Level One, and a member of Lang Chartered Family. (Pronouns: he, him.)

Warehouse 226. A warehouse in the Hub, adjacent to the Orangeboro Docks.

Wayland Transit. A Ranan shuttle company that provides in-System shuttle transport between Rana Station and Planet Chayko, or, less frequently, between Rana and other in-System stations.

Wayne Purdy. (WAYN PURR-dee) An indicted detainee alleged to have assisted in the sabotage of the Izgubil. (Pronouns: he, him.)

Wheel. One of the toroid habitat structures that rotate around the Rana Station Hub to artificially provide optimal gravity for the health and comfort of its inhabitants. Wheels One, Two, Three, Four, Seven, and Eight are inhabited by humans. Wheels

Five and Six are inhabited by ozzirikkians. For balance, they counter-rotate in alternate order.

Whisper Syndicate. A powerful criminal organization on Rana Station, as well as on the most closely adjacent asteroids to Rana and Mahusay Stations.

Wife. An official Ranan human relationship status that is generally assumed to be permanent. It signifies a person who is involved in a Marriage Partnership.

William "Bill" Goldstein Sloane. An OPD Corporal. (Pronouns: he, him.)

Willow Mead Glenn. A member of Pabiyan Family. Berwyn and Rowan's cousin and Aurelia's niece. A new mother. (Pronouns: she, her.)

Wilmott. – See *Ilma Wilmott*.

Wina. (WEE-nah) – See *Edwina Emshwiller*.

Wisniewski. – See *Col. Jackson Wisniewski*.

X

XK9 Scent Reference Library. A records repository formerly located in the XK9 Project's Solara City headquarters and administered by Dr. Frederika Cho, since shuttered.

XK9 Pack. An allied group of XK9s.

XK9 Project. A Transmondian corporation that produces genetically engineered dogs called XK9s. It has close ties to the Transmondian Intelligence Service.

XK9 Special Investigations Unit. A new OPD unit, created by Chief.

XK9s. An acronym adopted by the XK9 Project to identify specially-bred, genetically-modified, cybernetically-enhanced canines with extraordinary memories, olfactory capabilities, and verbal acuity.

Z

Zander "Zan" Hoback. (ZAN-dur HOE-bok) A person of interest in the Izgubil case. (Pronouns: he, him.)

Zeman. – See *Nesbit Zeman.*

Zheereeg-Sose'ee. (ZSHEER-eeg SOZE-ee) An Alliance official who is a koannan. (Pronouns: vez, vek.)

Zhokikim Timi. (zho-KEEK-eem ti-MEE) The Wheel Five Timi that is the ozzirikkian side of the Ranan National Capitol, just as Centerboro on Wheel Four is the human side. A Timi is the ozzirikkian parallel to a human Borough.

Zikikittir. (zick-ick-it-TEER) "Vice Premier" in Pan-Ozzirikkian.

Zikkizti Dawn. (zee-KEEZ-tee DON) A rescue runner (small space vehicle) operated by a Federal Ranan Emergency Rescue Team in the Governmental and Diplomatic Sector of the Hub.

Zona Dorsey. (ZOH-na DOOR-see) a member of Trondheim (TROND-hime) Family in the Glen Haven Neighborhood, Orangeboro Precinct Nine. (Pronouns: she, her.)

Zuni, Dr. Mika. (MY-ca ZOO-nee), a renowned re-gen specialist. (Pronouns: he, him.)

ACKNOWLEDGEMENTS

It takes a village to write a book. That's especially true for a book such as this, which took way longer to write than I'd anticipated. A whole bunch of really patient, lovely people took this journey with me. They coached, encouraged, pointed out the hard things, called me on my math and other assumptions, and together they helped me make this massive thing a better book!

At this point, anything I messed up is my fault, and a lot of the things I got right are because they called me on stuff! Who are "they"?

First, of course, is my intrepid Brain Trust. My sister G. S. Norwood, and sisters-from-other-mothers Lucy A. Synk and Dora Furlong, came through for me again and again. Often that was despite illness, stress, extreme deadlines of their own, and many other countervailing forces. They are purely amazing, and I'd hate to undertake a book without their guidance and feedback.

I also must acknowledge my husband Pascal Gephardt, who patiently listened to me read every single chapter of Draft Four and helped iron out issues of pacing and logic. Yet more family help came from my son Tyrell E. Gephardt, with whom I troubleshot "big picture" questions on many a late-night dog walk (yes, Charlie, people really do take perfectly innocuous walks with their dogs after dark). Ty's developmental insights played an important role at several points.

The "Critique Kitties" were my writers' group during the entire writing of this novel. They helped with a great many chapter-level issues and endured some of the earliest-draft growing pains. This group is co-led by originators Dyann Love Barr and Dennis Barr, as well as Cathy Morrison. Other members whose input I deeply appreciate include Edwin Frownfelter, Rod Galindo, Karin Gastreich, Valerie Hatfield, Hannah Winger, Becky Lynn, and Becky Brown.

Another vital source of input and insight came from my "Packmates" who follow my newsletter. Many of them also have joined my discussion group "A Pack of Human and XK9 Friends" on Facebook. Two of them, Sheila Moore and Gay Crocker, helped me name the character Zona Dorsey, whom you meet in Chapter One.

And a whole lovely group of them later stepped up to do the essential work of beta-reading. A number of longtime friends did, too. Those friends have now beta-read their third novel in a row for me!

My intrepid and much-cherished beta readers from all sources include Don McCann, George Ogilvie, Lyle Garrett, R. M. (Bob) Burns, and Diana J, Bailey, who sent concise but helpful and encouraging notes.

More extensive and detailed comments came from Hilary Powers, Janice Raach, Jo Yates, Sandra Anderson, and David Gordon. Indeed, David treated me to a running commentary, via Facebook Messenger, as he was reading. That was fascinating as well as enlightening (and gratifying).

Top beta-reading kudos must go to Catherine Crofts, however. She not only undertook a detailed beta-reading for this novel, but she also sent me "continuity notes" for all three novels in the Trilogy! Several of her comments and suggestions were real eye-openers. I'm updating the first two novels this fall (2024), to mostly coincide with the release of the new one. I've been accumulating notes of little "oopses" for each since they were first released. I tried to fix those (without making any more messes along the way) in these updates. Many of Catherine's continuity notes made it into the updates, too! Thank you very much, Catherine!

The production phase kicks in after all the editing and adjusting are finished. But here, too, I had valuable help. First, I need to acknowledge the work of three wonderful artists. My cover artist, Tom Kidd, brought a number of interesting insights into the development of the imagery. Special thanks to both Tom and Lucy A. Synk for pushing me to more fully visualize appscaten anatomy.

A local-to-me graphic designer and cartoonist, Sid Quade, worked with me on the black-and-white Interior Location Maps, which I decided I needed to add, based on beta-reader comments. And I'd like to thank Lucy A. Synk (yet again!) for her Photoshop help on the spines of all three trilogy print editions. Her work will adjust the appearance of the updated *What's Bred in the Bone* and *A Bone to Pick,* as well as helping me with *Bone of Contention.*

I appreciate the marketing insights and help I have received regarding my "book rollout" from Lynette M. Burrows and Karin Gastreich. And finally, I owe yet another debt of gratitude to my proofreader Deb Branson. She performs proofreading and editing services to provide the Essential Polish echoed by her company name.

To all of you, to anyone I missed (though I hope I didn't miss anyone!), and to everyone who reads and enjoys my books, thank you!

Jan S. Gephardt,
Westwood, Kansas, September 2024

ABOUT THE AUTHOR

Jan S. Gephardt (pronouns: she/her) is a science fiction novelist, fantasy artist, publisher, and longtime science fiction fan from Kansas City. Her "XK9s Saga" books now include a prequel novella and the three books of the XK9 "Bones" Trilogy, with more XK9 stories in the works. Keep up with her progress via her monthly **newsletter!**

She and sister G. S. Norwood co-founded **Weird Sisters Publishing LLC** in 2019. Jan is the Chief Cat-Herder & Art Director for Weird Sisters, which means she is in charge of book production, illustration commissioning, and marketing.

A member and former officer of the Association of Science Fiction and Fantasy Artists (ASFA),

she has exhibited her fantasy artwork at sf conventions since 1981. Starting in 2007 she developed a unique paper sculpture technique. Her artwork also has been featured in regionally-exhibited one-person shows and juried into mainstream national exhibitions all over the United States.

Note: Author photo is © 2017 by Colette Waters Photography.

Milton Keynes UK
Ingram Content Group UK Ltd.
UKHW020822300924
449047UK00013B/845